GOL

J.W. Webb

Acknowledgement and thanks to:
Catherine Romano, for editing
Julia Gibbs, @ProofreadJulia, for proofreading
Roger Garland, www.lakeside-gallery.com, for illustration
Debbi Stocco, MyBookDesigner.com, for book design
Ravven, ravven.kitsune@gmail.com, for cover art.

ISBN 13: 978-0-9905157-9-1 (Paperback)
ISBN 13: 978-0-9863507-0-2 (Digital)

Druthan Crags

Scaffa's Isle

IRON WASH

KHANDOL

Xandoria

Northtown

RODRUTHA

Longships

ENDLESS OCEAN

GULF OF RAKEEL

Lake of Clouds

Garron Fields

Dreckhall

The Ridings

Rakeel

GALANIA

TREGGAR

Dog Island

Galanais

Far Look Island

Irulan's Cave

BAROLA

DOVESS

Torvosa

Castle Barola

Barola Town

SHIMMERING SEA

Reveal

SARGANIA

Port Dovess

Castle Of The Winds

SEA of STORMS

A map of GYL

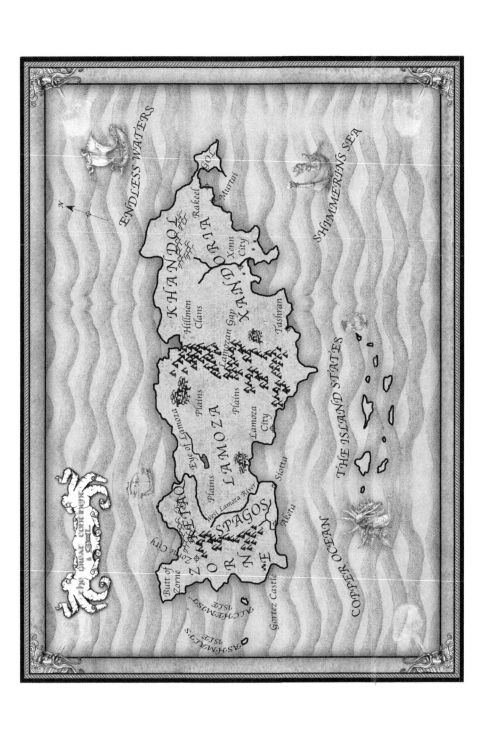

For Joanne

Your love, warmth, and laughter guided me
back into the light

Table of Contents

Book One
Barola And Beyond

Book Two
Quickening And Fall

Quickening

Fall

When Ashmali's flame is freed to burn

The Sea God will awaken

Then shall come Gol's final hour

When Demon's fire meets Ocean Power.

Book One

Barola And Beyond

Chapter 1

The Baron's Daughter

"Cut him, damn you!" Eon Barola leaned out from the battlements of the high keep where he held power to vent his frustration down on his encumbered son.

"Kill the bastard before he makes a eunuch of you!" The Baron wiped sweat from his face and cursed his son's incompetence.

This show was becoming a farce. A sorry joke. The lord of Barola Province watched with growing anger as his second son failed to get passed the prisoner's guard. Aldo was proficient but he lacked Rosco's aggression or Paolo's finesse. His other boys would have skewered the Treggaran by now. Paolo particularly would have made a fine show of the spectacle—a swift disembowelment or else an intricate display of thrust and parry culminating in the enemy's ritual beheading. Aldo was making hard work of this.

Eon's soldiers had captured the Treggarans last week in a raid across the border. There had been nine of them, dragged, chained and beaten, beneath the gatehouse of his castle. Only three remained living. Rosco had butchered two with an axe whilst Paolo had worked his skill on four in the dungeons below, just to ease his boredom. That had left three, and Paolo had done for two in as many minutes.

Eon winced as the prisoner ducked beneath a clumsy sweep from Aldo's sword. He lunged low, getting a clean slice at his son; opening his forearm from wrist to elbow. "Idiot boy...! Finish him before you disgrace us all," the Baron yelled down from the keep's high parapet. He could see Paolo and Rosco grinning and making lewd gestures at their brother.

Aldo, red faced and angry, launched himself at his opponent in a savage series of hack and slice, but each blow was countered by calm disdain from the Treggaran. The man was a fine swordsman and Eon Barola was getting increasingly vexed by his middle son's growing clumsiness. Finally he lost all patience and signalled Paolo, bidding him finish this fiasco. His youngest grinned, shrugged and preened, before sauntering down the steps leading to the fighting pit below. From there Paolo watched with arms folded, awaiting his chance.

The Treggaran was on the attack again, short sword stabbing—cobra swift—feinting left and right; probing, waiting for that fatal opening. It wouldn't be long. Aldo dwarfed the Treggaran, all Eon Barola's sons were big men, but Aldo was sweating and coughing, defending himself with desperation rather than skill.

Paolo, bored now, snapped his fingers, and a man-at-arms tossed him down a crossbow, cranked with bolt ready. Paolo levelled the weapon. He watched, waited, then squeezed—just as Aldo slipped on a loose stone and sprawled akimbo.

The Treggaran closed for the kill, but Paolo's bolt seared through his right thigh making him lose balance and pitch forward over the prone and sweating Aldo. Together the two rolled and bit chunks off each other in the bloody, dusty ground. Paolo, laughing at the spectacle, retrieved another bolt from the guard, and quickly reloaded the crossbow. This one thudded into the Treggaran's left buttock, pinning him to the ground as he yelled out at the lancing pain.

Aldo rolled free, regained his feet, and still puffing, reclaimed his sword. The Treggaran was a brave man. He waited with sword held ready as the red-faced Aldo lumbered close. But Paolo robbed his brother of his chance. A third bolt entered the prisoner's mouth, passing through the base of his skull—killing him instantly. Paolo sighed as the Treggaran crumpled and stilled, his lifeblood pooling crimson around him.

"Shadowman take you, Paolo... I was about to finish him. He was *my* kill!" Aldo launched a meaty fist at his laughing brother. Paolo caught it mid swing. He twisted Aldo's arm, locking it behind his brother's back before sending him sprawling again.

"That's where you should stay, brother." Paolo dusted his embroidered doublet with customary fastidiousness. "Down in the pit all covered in—"

"Enough...!" the Baron boomed down from the keep's parapet above. "Paolo, I would speak with you. Bring your idiot brother and Rosco too, if he's at hand." The eldest son had left the arena before the fight was over, to quench his varied appetites.

"I have matters to discuss with you three," continued the Baron, his canine bark reaching them easily despite the distance. "Oh, and feed that dead Treggaran to the fishes." Paolo signalled two men-at-arms to carry the prisoner's corpse down to the postern—a gift to the Sea God.

Paolo awarded his scowling brother a mocking grin, before entering the doorway opening into the keep. He then began winding his way up the long stairwell to join his brooding father on the high parapet above. Aldo followed, still cursing and sulking, and moments later the shaven-headed Rosco bulked through the doorway, emerging into the afternoon sun like a child's nightmare.

It was late summer in Barola Province, a rich lush corner of the continent called Gol. The land visible across the bay looked verdant and lush, and the sea breeze lifted the golden hawk on its scarlet field—the high emblem of Barola, fluttering on its pole thirty feet above the roof of the keep.

The Baron's Keep dominated Castle Barola. Its southernmost wall fell sheer to the sea-washed rocks far below, and its lofty elevation awarded far reaching views of both causeway and town.

Eon rubbed his close-cropped beard and watched with cold

dispassion as his boys approached. He ignored them for a time. Instead he let his dark gaze survey the bay, as was so often his habit; taking in the tall palms, the long sandy beaches and gentle wooded slopes framing the town at the causeway's far end.

Eon studied Barola Town for a time as his sons coughed and muttered close by. It was half a mile away across the water, a mish-mash of huts and smoky crofts, where dogs barked and fowl squawked as naked children chased them through the dusty lanes with sticks; and where women chored and men hauled in the day's catch.

They were his people: the Barolans. His to rule and his to tax. And tax he did—heavily. Eon's keen gaze took in the causeway's length. Cobbled and sloping, it bridged castle to town when the waves allowed.

The tide was out now and the embankment showed high above the weed-strewn rocks, running arrow straight to the gate-house and outer barbican. Eon could see tiny figures far out on the causeway, it was market day tomorrow and traders would be arriving soon in preparation—all would be bustle and excitement. At last content with his perusal, the Baron turned to his sons.

"Your sister is to marry." It was a statement leaving no room for response. "A month hence she will be betrothed to Varentin Gallante. I have written House Gallante—all is arranged." *Gallante: a ridiculous name for a baron that poisoned his own father, and then smothered his mother while she slept. Still, the alliance should prove convenient and aid our struggle with Treggara.*

"Varentin's a pompous turd." That was Rosco. Eon's eldest and biggest was broad in face and body. Heavily muscled and square of jaw, with flat broken nose and narrow set, squinty-brown eyes glaring out beneath heavy beetlebrows. "Liss'l run rings round him." He leaned forward and spat out over the battlements. "Those Galanians are two-faced dogs, Father."

Eon awarded his first-born a withering stare. "Thank you for your input, Rosco, but if you intend to keep your wits in your groin refrain from opening your mouth again." Rosco made to respond but his father's glare stopped him. "I will need you boys to put on some kind of show for the wedding—not your usual dog and cock fights—something more elaborate. Are there any other prisoners left in the dungeons?"

"Pitiful things, Father," responded Paolo as he studied a manicured nail. "I've worked on a few so I doubt they'll live much longer. The rats have been at them too—and they smell... Should we send out another raiding party? I'll be happy to lead."

"The Treggarans won't be fooled so easily next time," answered the Baron. "Leave it for now, Paolo. I shall think on this. In the meanwhile, you three keep a watch over your little sister; she's bound to be petulant when she hears she's to be wed. I don't want her doing anything stupid like her mother."

"Lissane deserves better than Varentin Gallante," blurted Rosco, who harboured an unsavoury fondness for his sister, ever since he had happened into her chambers whilst she was disrobing. She'd fought off his advances like a she-wolf but Rosco owned to optimism. Until now...all the Galanians were fit for was buggering each other. *Damn you, Father...*

"Lissane will do as she is bidden," snapped the Baron. He needed this alliance to work. With Galania on side they could put paid to Treggara's ambitions and then turn toward Dovesi Province, capturing Torvosa City by stealth. Duke Toreno was far too trusting: his patrician-head lost in the stars, and his son, big honest Clarde, much too noble of heart—fools, the pair of them. With House Dovess undone, its lapdog Sarfania would soon collapse, leaving only Rodrutha in the far north—and they were all mad anyway and thus of small account.

Rosco was right about Varentin: the boy was a spoilt turd—but that would work to Barola's advantage too. Eon would steer House Gallante's heir through Lissane; the girl had his wit and her mother's lost charms.

Discounting bleak Rodrutha, (which was easy) Eon Barola would be overlord of Gol inside three years. It was something he had yearned for since the Rebellion saw off the last of the Kings. The Baron's eyes misted over as he visualised his final triumph at Torvosa Castle. It was simply a matter of planning: the odd poisonous letter, an occasional discreet knife in the night.

Gol shall be mine...

Eon dismissed his sons without further word and turned to peruse his view again. The Baron's shrewd black eyes studied the numerous figures down on the causeway, much nearer now, fast approaching the bailey and outer keep. There were creaking wains and carts, farmers guiding stock, and traders with their variable wares. He saw beggars, merchants, even brightly garbed astrologers, and one or two foreigners— Dovesian by their look, with stiff proud gait and sullen faces. All were arriving for market day tomorrow.

Eon was about to turn away when he saw *her.* She was walking beside a tall gangly youth who was laughing and grinning like a fool. *Lissane...daughter...*she had disobeyed him again, strolling into town like a common fishwife after getting her idiot maid Belshareze to cover for her. *I'll have that servant beaten...* Eon's mood blackened further as he saw her laugh at something the boy said. He turned.

"Wait!" the Baron's curt bark stopped his sons before they vanished below. "Who is that stripling accompanying your sister down there?" He pointed across to where the two figures could be seen strolling along the causeway. Eon Barola was livid. He had bid Lissane stay away from Barola Town on pain of incarceration, yet she'd dared thwart his wishes—again. He'd spared the rod too often with that girl, he decided. It was Aldo that answered him. The middle son finally having recovered from his sulk.

"Erun Cade, he's called," said Aldo, nursing his bloodied arm and wincing. "He's a by-blow of Garret the smith; you know the smithy in the wood at the edge of town." The Baron nodded impatiently. *Of course he knew it, and Garret Cade had fought for him during the Rebellion...why was his son so obtuse?*

"The boy's a useless mooncalf," continued Aldo, oblivious to his father's thunderous brow, "and I hear his father's got no time for him... the mother died some while back during the winter blights."

Aldo was pleased with himself now. It had long been a habit of his to study the doings and goings of the townsfolk. He liked to bully them whenever possible, it made him feel important. Aldo liked feeling important and he was in his element at present.

"He claims to be a poet," he continued, "or so they say...a dreamer, certainly. I've seen him with our sister before." This last statement was a lie but one that worked, the Baron's face was darkening by the minute.

"Paolo, you will address that youth some place quiet," said Eon Barola. Paolo smiled his cat-cream smile. "Go now," he motioned them take their leave, "bid the guard inform your sister I would speak with her soonest."

The Baron showed them his back and resumed his study of the afternoon. But the beauty had fled the bay. Instead Eon saw his dead wife's face awarding him that baleful stare. *She is too like you, Leanna...it might prove her undoing yet...*

Eon turned from his repose and made swift short strides toward the door leading to the stairwell below. His eyes black as betrayal and mind laden with guilt, Eon would seek accustomed solace in drink. He'd turn his sharp mind to other matters while he awaited his troublesome daughter in his study.

***

Lissane was worried as could be. They were too close to the castle. If they were spotted her father would be livid. But Erun wouldn't listen to her fretting. He had told her not to fuss with that big sunny smile of his and she (idiot that she was) had believed him. And now her father's castle loomed above—a grim statement of everything she loathed and wanted to escape from (though not in the way that her mother had.)

Mother took the easy way out.

But her mother was as different to Lissane as the seas were to land. Leanna Barola had sported long plaits of wheat-golden hair. Lissane's locks were glossy raven-black, tumbling from her shoulders in a wild cascade, halting inches above her waist. She was taller than her mother too, with large violet eyes that could see through fools in an instant, and a pale completion and patrician nose that bespoke good breeding.

Leanna had tanned easily, her skin olive and her eyes a softer blue than her daughter's. Lissane shunned the summer sun lest she burn as she had in the past. Her mother had been kindly to servants and fond of animals and birds. Lissane cared little for either, saving Belshareze, her maid and only confidante. She wasn't cruel though—not like her brothers—just proud and remote, except when sharing smiles with Erun Cade.

Castle Barola dominated the bay surrounding it. The stone claws of the outer walls clung tenaciously to sheer rocks beneath. A fortress build to withstand storm and siege. From a distance Castle Barola resembled a great dragon, coiled and wary, waiting to take flight.

The outer walls were eighty foot in height and twelve foot thick. Beyond these a maze of buildings: barracks, stables, taverns, armouries and stock enclosures, led to an inner ring of curtain wall rising another fifty feet. Within this second wall were contained the fighting pits and training ground, together with the dank grill-covered hole that led down, via torch lit stairs to the oubliette below.

At the southern end of the castle reared the High Keep: a square bluff of crenulated granite, its parapet brooding sixty foot above the inner wall, dominating both bay and countryside around. The Baron's Roost, the town's folk called it, and steered well away.

It was Lissane's father's habit to gaze out from that high place every morning, surveying all that he owned while his lips supped on the fruit of his vineyards. There were few times when Eon Barola wasn't in his cups these days.

Even now Lissane could feel his weighty presence frowning down at her, (although at this hour he was usually in his study) sense those obsidian-hard eyes boring inside her skull: probing, questioning, demanding and coercing. No wonder her sweet mother had thrown herself from the keep that stormy winter's night. Baron Barola was a monster and his sons were worse, particularly one of them. Lissane, resilient and resourceful, had learnt to survive...but to protect her lover from their claws? That was a task beyond even her skills. The only solution was to escape. Lissane and Erun Cade were working on that.

"We had best part company," Lissane told her lover. *If Father knew what you did last night, my darling, he'd have you gelded, disembowelled, and flayed dry from the castle walls. And I would be flogged like a common whore by Grudge, or worse, Paolo himself.* She looked up and frowned, knowing how stupid this was. "We're too near the castle, someone might see us," she urged him.

Erun Cade grinned at her. He was too cocksure—the only fault she saw in him saving perhaps his naivety. "Let them look," Erun said, squeezing her arm. He was seventeen, a year younger than she, and handsome in a gap-toothed freckled way. Long limbed and agile though spare of frame, his hair a tangled tumble of reddish brown, with eyes a mischievous sparkle of blue-grey—the colour of winter seas, she had often thought.

They had met during market day inside the castle walls just a few weeks past. He'd been with his father, the dour farrier, Garret Cade. Their eyes had danced back and forth in the crowd, and later that night she'd sent Bel to flush Erun Cade out from one of the taverns.

This was all her fault, Lissane had known the risk she was taking, but the thought of defying her father (though terrifying) was exciting and cause enough. Lissane had none of Erun's brash youthful confidence. She knew what her family were like.

"I'll fight any of them or all at once," he told her, grinning. "I'm not scared, Liss, and I want to scream out your name so all know how much I love you."

"You're a fool, Erun Cade," she muttered, shaking free of his grasp as they approached the outer gatehouse from where the bailey loomed squat and baleful. Lissane was angry with herself now, and worried. "And you're making me a fool too. You haven't a clue what you are saying, my love. I'm the Baron's daughter."

"I don't care. I love you, Liss." That was that. Simple. If only it were so, but he just couldn't see it. To Erun Cade, nothing was impossible.

Lissane reached out and squeezed his hand briefly and then turned away. "I love you too, you lump-head... but it's too risky going inside together: If he finds out...?"

"I'm not frightened of him."

"Well then you really are stupid, my love," she responded, before covering her face in a vain attempt to hide her presence before the gate guards. "*Everyone* is frightened of Father, and for good reason."

"We'll journey west," he was ignoring her, "cross the mountains and make for Torvosa City. They say Duke Toreno is a fair man."

"And my father will uproot those mountains one by one until he finds us. I told you, Erun, there is only one way to escape. The sea...the City States, or else Rakeel and the Great Continent. We can lose ourselves in its vastness."

"Then we will do it tomorrow," he insisted.

"No," Lissane shook her head. "It has to be planned... thought out—Father has spies everywhere. We'll have to steal a boat—and one seaworthy at that."

"I've got a boat hidden outside the village."

Lissane froze, hearing a shout from the gatehouse and, looking ahead, saw two burly men-at-arms carrying halberds, their steel glinting in the sun. They were approaching at speed. Lissane's heart skipped a beat. She knew *he'd* seen them. They were idiots, she and her lover... stupid bloody idiots.

"You had best turn back, my love," she told him, waving him away, "and quickly before you come within crossbow range of the bailey walls," she urged him. "Flee while you still can, Erun. I think my father has seen us; those guards are coming our way. Go!"

Lissane pushed her lover away and then turned to await the two pike-men, now hastening along the causeway with purpose in their strides. Lissane set her jaw and strutted arrogantly toward them, awarding the pair a wintry look as their crossed halberds blocked her way forward.

A distance behind her, Erun Cade clenched his fists in frustration and rage. He hesitated a moment and then, defeated and glum, turned and trudged moodily back toward Barola Town. If he had a sword he would have faced those guards like a man.

Erun Cade's face reddened with anger at both himself and her family; at his sides, his fists were clenching and unclenching with violent frustration.

You had better not hurt her, Baron...

Everyone knew how Baroness Leanna had been driven to madness by the cruelty of her husband. Erun Cade vowed he'd kill Eon Barola and his sons should they hurt Lissane too. He would do for them all...*somehow.*

Lissane Barola felt the familiar dread as she faced down the guards with her best imperial stare. "Well?" she glared at the bigger of the two, the one whose broad yellow sash cutting diagonal across his hauberk marked him as the leader. "What is this nonsense?"

"My lady, your lord father has requested your presence at his study at once," answered the man, sweating profusely, weighed down by heavy kettle-helm and hauberk. The Baron insisted that his men-at-arms wore full mail and helm whilst on duty at all times: even though the Treggarans would never dare a raid on the castle itself.

"Is it customary to accost the Baron's daughter as though she were a common wench?" Lissane snapped at him. "Stand aside! I'll make my own way to the keep. I am well aware of the placement of my father's study." The guard took a step backward, his eyes uncertain beneath the helm.

Lissane brushed passed the two soldiers as though they were invisible. Despite that they insisted in flanking her until she arrived, red-faced and jittery at the Barbican's gates. She turned once; there was no sign of Erun Cade lingering on the causeway, or else loitering with those traders at the far side. Lissane felt a wash of relief dampen her eyelids.

Flee, my love...get out of Barola while you can. It's too late for us but you can still escape them.

There were fresh crowds filing the causeway now as afternoon waned and rising waves began reclaiming the weed-strewn rocks. High tide was approaching fast. Very soon Castle Barola would be an island again, until the following morning. Time enough for her lover to escape. She prayed to Zansuat, God of the Oceans, that Erun Cade made good use of it.

The gatehouse swallowed her in. It stood on an outcrop, fifty foot short of the larger island where bulked the castle main. The wave-tossed gap was bridged by a long drawbridge: a huge construction of oak and iron, weathered and bleached by wind and sea—wide enough for ten men to march abreast or four horses to trot.

Lissane hurried across it, the guards following noisily behind and the white foam of crashing water eddying thirty feet below her feet. The men at arms saluted and then let Lissane be when she reached the main gates. She ignored them as she stepped beneath the massive portcullis, entering the dank, mouldy tunnel that bored gloomy through the outer wall.

In seconds she was through it and back in the sunshine again. Lissane squinted at the glare as she ventured inside Castle Barola for the first time that day. She emerged from the shadow of the walls to weave her way through the various buildings: the castle smithy, stables; the latrines and barracks and such, ignoring discreet stares and polite nods from any passing, and making brief and brisk for the second gate.

Here another tunnel, lit by murder holes and firelight from above, opened into sunlight and the inner castle with its fighting pits and training grounds. Edgy and nervous, Lissane walked on up toward the southern end.

The Keep loomed ahead—a cold, grey finger swallowing the evening's light. Sheep-cropped grass led up to its circular granite base. The oak door yawned ajar as she clonked the latch free. Lissane entered within, her violet eyes adjusting to the torch-lit smoky corridor ahead.

Lissane passed by the feasting hall with its sconces, benches and roaring hearth. She reached the stairwell and, with heart heavy as lead, the Baron's daughter commenced the long, spiralling climb way up to her father's study.

Despite her own chamber being within it, Lissane hated the keep with its twisting stairwell and dimly lit latrines and draughty guardrooms. It was dark here. Always cold—even in summer. The arrow slits were the only windows allowing light before reaching her bower and the Baron's airy quarters high above.

And above those sumptuous rooms stood the lofty parapet from where her mother had jumped on that storm-cursed winter's night, twelve years earlier. Lissane had despised her mother since then. Leanna had escaped, leaving her five year old daughter to grow up with the monsters that were her remaining family.

She passed her rooms, there was no sign of Bel her maid, but that wasn't surprising. At last, Lissane reached the top level where her father resided. She approached his iron- studded door, nodding to the huge bearded guard standing so silently there. He bowed stiffly to her in return and motioned her inside.

Lissane liked Grale. He was still Barola's champion, despite being over sixty years of age. He'd fought in the King's army as a lad and had many a tale to tell. Lissane knew Grale for one of the few honest men her father employed. She could trust him, which was a rarity in Castle Barola these days.

Grale's back was arrow-straight; he was still as strong as Rosco, her eldest brother, despite the latter being nearly thirty years his junior. The champion's greying hair and beard melded into one shaggy, bear-like fuzz, almost occluding his grizzled face. Despite his fierce appearance, Grale's smile was one of the few kindnesses she had ever known. Particularly after Leanna had died and she had so needed a friend. Lissane took a deep breath, awarded Grale a valiant smile and then rapped once loudly on the door.

"Enter," said a dark voice within. Lissane steeled her nerves and pushed the door open. Inside the Baron waited, an uncorked bottle in one hand while the other fondled the golden hilt of his jewelled dagger. Lissane shut the door behind her and took a step forward to confront her father once again.

***

Ten thousand miles away a mountain spewed fire on its sur- rounding island and the cool blue waters of a nameless sea. The earth shook and quivered. Thunder rolled as rocks crashed through valleys and trees sizzled as flames ate them whole.

Within hours the entire island was nothing more than a

scorched grey pile of ash. No bird sang and no beast clambered below. All was smoking death and ruin. The sea surrounding the island's forgotten coves hissed and bubbled, sending steamy vapours high up into the atmosphere. Way up there the skies were choked with bitter dust.

A huge rent had opened inside the mountain. Formerly it had been a cave. A vast cavern containing the essence of the fire Elemental, Ashmali. A Demon so terrible the gods themselves had entombed him lest his wanton flames consume the world.

For many millennia island and mountain kept their prisoner secret. Occasionally Ashmali's breath would seep out, scorching slopes and blazing through heather. But the invisible bonds restricting the Demon stopped him causing any further ruin. And so things stayed until that dark hour the sorcerer arrived and broke the age old spell.

Chapter 2

Concerning Erun Cade

Erun Cade, petulant and nasty with mood, wound his way back into Barola Town, ignoring everyone and everything as his bitterness grew like a poisonous worm inside him. She would be with the Baron by now. He, Erun, should be with her, not skulking here among the huts and hovels like a scolded pup. Why had he just stood there gaping and let her go?

What is the matter with me..?

He would see Lissane tomorrow during the market. He'd slip in quiet and smuggle her out...somehow. But Erun knew the chances of achieving such a bold action were slim and would probably only get his obtuse head on a spike above the barbican gates. That would not help his beloved.

It was all too much; the world was a stinking filthy place. Erun Cade hated Barola Province and its savage ruler, despite having never travelled, and he despised his own father for letting his mother die of an ague three winters back. Erun had loved his mother. Savana had been a kindly soul, doting on her husband and boy. But she was gone, leaving his father bitter and Erun Cade confused.

Mother never harmed anyone, yet the gods took her amid pain. Why take so gentle a soul? Especially when those deserving early death seemed so often to thrive into dotage—such was Erun's opinion on the matter. Now the only thing he had to live for was Lissane. That and the vague dream he could make it as a poet in some distant province. And now he'd let Lissane go too. It stank.

Erun kept walking, his expression thunderous and tread heavy. He left the buildings behind and commenced crunching down the pot-holed lane, on toward the knot of pine trees fencing the back of Barola Town.

No thick castle walls to protect the townsfolk from Treggaran attack. They didn't matter—only Eon bloody Barola and his sons were of account. Everyone else in Barola Province was expendable. Even Lissane the Baron's only daughter—he'd sell her too for a price, the bastard.

The whole thing reeked of bile. Barola was corrupt—a worm-rotten apple—and the other provinces rumoured to be worse. The only exception being Dovesi, the old stronghold of Flaminius the king back before the Rebellion. Aside from that province the whole of this continent called Gol was a wretched squabbling nest of mistrustful rulers, and subjected hungry tenants.

Dovesi was different, they said. The former home of the Kings, whose current ruler, Duke Toreno Dovess (one of a few remaining loyalists,) was a man said to be both honourable and wise. They could have gone there tomorrow or at least started out. *Perhaps we still can?*

After two miles of sticky incline through sweltering summer woodland, and with flies buzzing loudly in his ears, Erun Cade reached the clearing where his family had made their home after the Rebellion.

The forge had been constructed by his father, after the uprising and murder of the last King, Flaminius, had changed everything. Garret Cade had been a soldier at that time as had most, fighting for the Baron. But Garret had always been skilled with his hands and took to smithy work with comparative ease, in time making a name for himself throughout Barola Province.

Erun Cade was different. He hated manual work—rather he would while away his hours comprising poems and witty songs. He was arrogant, his father told him, but Erun knew that he was gifted also. One fine day Erun Cade would prove them all wrong, these barons and petty lords, and as a travelling songsmith would court all the rulers of Gol, and the Great Continent beyond. All well and good. First he had to rescue Lissane from her father's clutches so the pair of them could make good their escape.

Erun shared the thatched house with his father. Theirs was a frosty relationship. Garret viewed his boy as a useless dreamer and Erun irrationally blamed his father for letting Savana die. He had to blame someone, and the Baron was excused this time.

Erun had small love for the forge's master these days. Garret Cade was mind-weak and boring—so his fiery-hearted son believed. He was a soak, was Garret, all his free time spent in the nearest tavern at the edge of town.

The smith had no friends as such, being solitary and blunt in nature, and often took to brooding in his cups. But because of his skill at his craft, Garret had the respect of the townsfolk, which was more than could be said for Erun Cade. If Garret viewed his only son as a dreamer then most the townsfolk saw him as a fool, and an indulged one too.

Erun had no friends as such. He'd never wanted any, being too immersed in his dreams and schemes. Erun had lain with the odd girl several times, he was comely enough and charming when he wanted to be. But most had tired of him quickly when they realised how he shunned honest work. Poor women need strong hardworking husbands, not aspiring poets.

Erun had let them return to their boring lives. He had never shown interest in any trade, instead he focussed on his poetry and songs and other frivolities. Garret, despairing, had all but given up on him. Father and son spoke little these days.

Now Garret Cade stood in the entrance to their cottage, his bulk filling the doorway. Garret still wore his smith's apron and his bare sooty arms were folded, the great muscles corded and veined from years of toil. Garret was shorter in height than his son, but he was barrel-chested and extremely strong.

Garret Cade's face was a permanent black-bearded frown, the eyes pale blue and resentful. His lips set hard and sucking at the pipe he always carried between his teeth. Erun nodded across to his father in curt fashion as he made for the door; hopefully the smith would have seen to supper by now, however Erun couldn't smell anything—which wasn't a good sign.

"What's about, Father?" Erun asked. He tensed when he saw Garret's quizzical expression and waited for the inevitable confrontation.

"You tell me," responded his father, after removing the pipe from his mouth and spitting on the floor. "You're the one everyone's talking about. Right little character, you are."

"I don't know what *you're* talking about. Is there anything to eat?" Erun made to go into the cottage but his father still barred his way.

"Did you honestly think that people wouldn't notice that you were spending time with the Baron's daughter?" Garret Cade shook his head in disbelief. "You're a damn fool, boy, and you may well prove the death of both of us."

"I love her and she me... the pox on anyone else!" Erun, although shocked that his father knew of their dalliance (they had been so careful—or so he'd thought), could feel the easy anger rising up inside him. He was ready to fight anyone now, even his father.

"She's Barola's bloody daughter, boy! If he finds out he'll skin you alive. Cannot you see how stupid you've been?"

"I love her," replied Erun lamely. "I always will, and besides the Baron knows already." Garret's broad face blanched at that last comment.

"I need a drink," the smith said eventually, his voice laden with resignation. "You can get your own supper, Shadowman take you. I'm away to town and I won't be back till late. If I were you, boy, I'd get praying and packing. You're no bloody use to me and now Eon Barola will be after your hide. You had best take to the hills, laddie, and soonest."

Garret shook his head. He didn't understand how he could have spawned such a fool boy. Erun was in real danger now. They would probably both have to slip away—at least until the girl was wed and this unfortunate incident forgotten. One thought chilled him to the bone.

"Have you been with her?"

"What...?" Erun's face had reddened.

"You know what I mean," Garret pressed him. "Is she a bloody virgin or not?"

"I...yes...no. We spent last night together, down on the dunes south of the castle. There was no one about. We weren't seen, Father."

"I'm going to the inn," growled the elder Cade. "I need to think and drink a way out of this. I suggest you gather food and clothing for a long trek into the mountains. We'll leave at midnight. Be ready or else I'll skin your bloody hide myself and save Barola the trouble." Garret's mind was racing now.

At least the causeway will be covered until dawn. So no need to rush and plenty of time for a few ales. But where to go when we reach the mountains?

"I'm not going anywhere, Father," Erun's jaw was set firm. Garret ignored him as he shoved past, and stony-faced began the long trek into town. "I am not leaving Barola," Erun yelled after him. "Not without Lissane!"

No reply. Erun's shout was swallowed by the trees and his father was soon out of sight. Red faced and hot, the younger Cade entered the low-beamed murky cottage and started rummaging the pantry for some kind of supper.

Part of his anger was he knew his father was right. Erun was well aware that he was behaving like a petulant fool. But when was love ever rational? To love is to rage. To soar high beyond the mundane thought and deeds of this turgid life. Lissane Barola was *his* girl. Somehow they would find a way through, and Shadowman take anyone who got in their way.

Erun reached down and retrieved a crumpled note he'd dropped earlier. It contained words from his latest poem. An ode to

Lissane's eyes. He'd thrown it away after considering it unworthy but now awarded the note a second glance.

Liss

Your heart is my heart; your soul mine too
Your eyes live in my eyes, our arms entwined as one
To love you is my meaning, my purpose and my
mission
Your scent fills my morning, afternoon and night.
With you there is no darkness-
Only golden, wondrous light.

Erun pulled a face. Total crap. He could do so much better than that. But his love for Lissane had clouded his vision. The words just hadn't come lately. There were too many random factors scattering thoughts inside his troubled head.

When Lissane had summoned him from the tavern that afternoon it had seemed like a game. A fun tryst—the wealthy Baron's daughter wanted to dabble on the dark side. Erun most happily would oblige her.

But Lissane had been caught and Erun too. His easy tongue had hooked her with smiling words, whilst Lissane's purple gaze had stolen Erun's vision. Since that afternoon he'd seen or thought of little else.

They'd lain together three times now. Reckless with love. Never for a moment believing they'd be caught. A most dangerous stupid game—how it had excited them. The lovers had believed they were clever enough, careful and sly, but like bugs in amber they'd been caught. Trapped and exposed to the cruel world around them.

Erun bunched his fists and on impulse slammed the left one into the door frame, causing his soft knuckles to bleed. He didn't care. It was time for action—no point loitering here.

But as time passed like judgement, Erun did nothing. Just stared and moped and fretted.

A noise outside shocked him into movement. Something in the woods. A beast, perhaps? Erun glared moody across at the darkening trees, but their eerie stillness mocked him and so he went back inside the cottage and took to loitering and rummaging again. Outside evening fell to night. Shadows lengthened and birds perched silent.

***

Lissane studied her father's features as he sat behind his ornate ebony table and scrutinised her in the heavy silence. His was a deeply tanned face, handsome once but fleshy now, the skin loose beneath jowl and eyes. Those eyes were granite hard—the same black stone of his castle's walls (although often bloodshot of late.)

They were eyes that broke hard men long before rack and noose took hold. The nose was blunt, the face surrounding heavy-browed and square of jaw, with dark thinning hair and neatly trimmed goat-beard. Be—ringed, fleshy fingers stroked his chin while with the other hand the Baron pawed at the stiletto he always kept close by.

Lissane took a step toward him. She had learnt to mask her fear. "Father, I—"

"Be silent, bitch," the Baron growled like a nasty dog. "You were told not to go to the town. You have no business there. And yet you disobeyed me in this like some wanton tavern slut, and not for the first time, and doubtless using that stupid Belshareze to double for you."

"Bel played no part in this, I—"

"Silence, slut! Were you anyone else you would be whipped bloody, my girl. Your mother was never such trouble."

My mother was a coward...

"Father, please..."

"The boy you were with on the causeway. Who...?"

"He's just a friend—nothing more. He was reciting poems to lighten my mood." Lissane prayed that her lover was far from the town by now.

"Poems...? How nice..." Suddenly the Baron smiled in his mercurial way. His quicksilver moods were part of the reason why he was so feared by everyone in castle and town. There were few could read Eon Barola, and Lissane had never achieved it although she came much closer than most.

"We won't dwell on the matter," the Baron said, placing the dagger aside and rubbing his big hands together. "Take a seat, my beloved... I have news concerning your future." Lissane felt the sudden stab of ice lancing into her bowels...*my future.* He motioned for her to sit over in the corner chair beneath the flickering sconce.

"You are to wed, my dearest."

"No...Father, please...I—"

The Baron raised a jewelled hand to dismiss her. "In three weeks at the midsummer festival."

"Who?" The icicle was growing within her.

"Prince Varentin Gallante, heir to Galanais and all its wealth." Lissane felt her stomach heave; she had met the so called 'Prince' Varentin on two occasions. He was four years her senior and an arrogant pig. He was cruel and twisted and effeminate and she had loathed the sight of him. Varentin hadn't even noticed her.

Most Galanian nobles were interbred, overfed, greasy-palmed gold traders who had the audacity to name their realm a principality instead of a province. Even Dovesi, by far the noblest of the six regions comprising Gol and ancestral home of the kings, was still only a Duchy.

Galanais was a city of whores and murderers. Alone of the six provinces, Galania openly practised slavery following the traditions of the Great Continent across the Shimmering Sea. Such practice was repulsive to Lissane. Barola's people might be poor but at least they owned stock and garth. Slaves didn't even own their bodies.

The Baron watched her shocked expression with a small smile.

"I will not be gainsaid in this, daughter," he told her.

"Varentin Gallante is a monster." Lissane's gaze was on the door. She felt like a trapped, stunned bird seeking a tiny window in a very dark room.

But then so you are, and my brothers also.

"The Galanians have never been our friends, Father," Lissane said eventually. "They are deceitful and the Chatelaine Soph—"

"All the more reason," the Baron cut her short with a dismissive hand. "The boy is somewhat indulged—I'll grant you... but that should enable you to play him wisely. You will be my eyes and ears across the mountains, Lissane."

"Father, I don't—"

"Enough!" Eon Barola's meaty fist bludgeoned the table as a hint of frustration darkened his stare. "The matter is closed, Liss. You are dismissed," he waved her away. "Oh, and if you see any of your brothers lurking send them up to me. I've a task for them tonight. You may leave."

Lissane left before the tears welled up in her eyes. She would not be weak in front of him: that had been Mother's way. All she could think about was her lover—how and when and if she would see him again. Lissane determined there would still be a way, impossible as that now seemed to her.

Lissane tried to visualize Erun Cade's lovely face with his long shaggy locks and winning smile; those cobalt-slatey laughing eyes. Instead all she could picture was the greasy smirk of Varentin Gallante, as he pulled the legs off a spider he had shown her when they were children during one of House Barola's rare visits to that western land. Lissane set her quick mind to working. By the time she caught up with Rosco at the stables, the Baron's daughter had already planned a way out.

***

Eon Barola gnawed at the thighbone and watched his sons file idle into his study. Paolo's sharp green eyes were curious; Aldo's brown and blurred by wine, and Rosco's blue and belligerent, annoyed by this sudden summons.

My boys... my brutal, vicious, nasty boys...

"I have a task for you three after nightfall," he told them between crunches and wiping the grease on his sleeve. "One suited to your particular... skills." Paolo raised an eyebrow to that.

"What task, my lord?" Rosco was still wary, though his expression was less hostile.

"You'll take Grudge and Hacker, man the smaller skiff and

slip ashore under cover of dark. Beach the skiff a mile or so beyond the town and steal away. Do not be seen or heard by anyone."

Eon knew it was a gamble letting his boys loose but Grudge would keep an eye on the three of them, ensuring things didn't get out of hand. "Make your way to the smithy just outside town," he told them.

"Aldo knows where it is, on the Dovess road at the edge of the wood leading up to the mountain passes." They nodded eagerly, sensing a night's dark enjoyment ahead. And so the Baron informed his sons of what he required of them and afterwards even Rosco grinned. Paolo's smile was radiant, his father was right. This was exactly the sort of task he was born for...

***

A world away a lone figure sat hunched at the stern of his ketch. He was weary but triumphant. Almost giddy with joy. His name was Ozmandeus and he had just achieved the impossible. He had captured the essence of the Demon, Ashmali.

The fire Elemental was now safely contained in an amulet the size of a gull's egg Ozmandeus wore around his neck, his well-crafted spells having ensured none of the demon's fire slip out. Despite his soothing spells the amulet burnt whenever it touched his chest. Ozmandeus wasn't worried. Pain was a small price to pay for so lethal a weapon.

Miles behind, the tormented island belched filth into the ocean. Ozmandeus didn't care. His spell craft ensured the boat's uncanny speed kept his body safe from debris and scorching ash.

The sorcerer paid no heed to the darkening skies overhead. Instead his gaze was focussed on a speck of land in the distance. His destination. A second island forty miles east of the volcano. Alchemists Isle, they called it—his former home. Ozmandeus's witch-spell would ensure he reach its harbour inside an hour. Once ashore he would claim his reward. The souls of his brethren.

Chapter 3

Dealers in Dusk

The hour was late and the night deathly still. Above their heads the moonless sky, dark and silent as judgment. Grudge and Hacker manned the oars, dipping them noiselessly into the glassy water surrounding Barola Castle, as the three brothers brooded and drank.

Paolo was seated at the prow, his keen eyes scanning for the dark smudge that would reveal the sandy shoreline ahead. He'd spy it soon. They were approaching at speed. Rosco and Aldo were sharing the skin of wine aft—both quite drunk now. Long minutes passed, oars dipped and rose without a sound as the brooding bulk of the castle slipped astern, swallowed up by night and gloom. They all wore dark, heavy cloaks concealing their weapons within. The shore emerged; wide sleepy palms fanned shadows above the pale line of beach.

They hid the skiff in mangrove a mile north of Barola Town as was discussed. Hacker leaped ashore to tie-off to a vacant stump, whilst Grudge and Rosco shoved hard from behind, both waist-deep in cool summer water. Paolo and Aldo were already striding up the adjacent beach and making for the cover of the nearby trees.

They reached the road in minutes and stopped there, listening to the silence. Paolo grabbed the wineskin from his brother and drained it while they waited for the others to join them. Moments later the five were stealing silent toward the distant lamps of the sleeping town.

***

Garret Cade wiped his mouth and ordered another from the youth manning the kegs. It was approaching midnight—time he was on his way.

That fool boy better have things ready.

Garret drained his fourth flagon, belched and lumbered outside without a glance at the few silent drinkers still remaining. Garret had formed the start of a plan. His instinct told him he should have grabbed the boy and made for the hills at once, but he had needed time to think, and Garret Cade could only think clearly was when he had a tankard clutched in his meaty palm.

Ale was his only comfort these days. Crutch and courage, it steadied his nerves and reminded him of the man he used to be. His mind was tuned now, clear and sharp. Garret knew what had to be done and it was past time he started doing it.

No need to panic, though. That would serve no purpose, and they would need to keep their heads during their journey. It would be alright, the two of them had more than enough time to slip away unseen and unheard. It was market day tomorrow, so with luck no one would miss them until late that evening at the earliest.

They would make for Galania, west of the mountains—a hard long trip even in summer. He'd find work in the border region, and the Baron's men were unlikely to range that way. Most of Barola's attention was on Dovesi or Treggara these days. The old King's Road to Torvosa was well used and they would be apprehended in days, and the way north through Treggara would prove far too perilous.

The Treggarans were their enemies, they daren't fare that way. Baron Garron and his spawn were the Shadowman's children, and Dreekhall, their manse, a very grim place—or so it was said.

That left the hardest route across the spine of Gol. The high passes through the mountains were arduous and rarely used these days, thus their safest bet.

The Galanians were a queer lot, Garret allowed, but they generally kept to themselves; the stiff necked rulers habitually preoccupied with their perennial loathing of neighbouring Sarfania, the humid swampy country south of their borders.

Galania's relationship with that land mirrored Barola's with Treggara, although their animosity was of a more subtle kind. That lot preferred poison to the sword. Baron Sarfe was friends with Duke Toreno of Dovess, a friendship that the vain 'Prince' Gallante resented.

As long as they kept away from Galanais City they would be fine. There was always work for a smith and his boy, whether shoeing horses or mending tools. They would claim to be refugees fleeing from Treggaran raiders, many such had fled from the borderlands during recent years.

As he walked, Garret recalled the day he'd first arrived in Barola Town after the Rebellion. He had fought proudly for Eon Barola back then, and had cheered along with everyone else when the barons finally caught up with the hated king and cut Flaminius the Third down from his high horse. Such an ignoble end to so vain a monarch.

Like many on that day, Garret had fervently believed that a new age of fairness and decency had arrived in Gol. The kings had held the six provinces in tyranny for many centuries and now, at last, a new order had been spawned.

But instead things had only got worse. Much worse. The barons had quarrelled over boundaries and spoils, leading to further petty wars and conflicts. The common folk were forgotten—worse, they were bled dry by taxes and forced to work as serfs for their greedy masters. Only the Galanians used slaves openly in Gol —a factor of their trade with the Xandorian Empire across the sea where 'slaves were more numerous than the leaves in a forest'.

The peasant's life was little better than slavery, in Garret's opinion. The common folk might be free of chains, but they were weighed down by poverty and hunger and mostly ignored by their betters.

For fifteen years the barons had squabbled, plotted and schemed against each other while their people were taxed brutally: all to pay for their extravagancies, their frequent feasts and tourneys—and these so often concluding with death in the dark.

An endless cycle of raid and counter raid. Barola plundered Treggara; the Treggarans torched a Barolan village in return. It made no sense. The Galanians and Sarfanians tried new ways to poison each other; whilst in the far north, the wild-haired Brude, psychotic baby eater and self-styled 'King of Rodrutha' hung the flayed hide of any foreigner from Druthan Crags for decoration.

Only Dovesi maintained a peaceful stance. The premier province and home of the former kings was confident in its strength, showing little interest in the robber barons' scheming and plotting across its borders. Noble and serene, Duke Toreno Dovess held himself aloof from his neighbours' constant altercations. But Dovesi could afford to be complacent. That land was rich and besides, they had the Games. The Games were the lifeblood of Gol, held annually outside Torvosa Castle in a vast open arena built millennia before by the ancients for sacrificial worship.

For one glorious month in high summer all provincial bickering was put aside. Instead the barons and their nobles took part in a festival of strength, speed, and honourable conflict. The common folk could take part also, should they be skilled with bow or spear. No commoners were allowed to carry swords as these were considered the chosen weapons of the nobly born.

Deals were made and broken annually during the festivities, alliances formed and assassinations planned. At the Games any man could become a hero, or else fall short and lie broken and defeated on the bloodied turf. The barons loved the Games, and House Dovess had grown wealthy from their annual revenue. Before, the kings had squandered the monies. Now they were managed by Clarde, Toreno's son. A great champion at the Games, none questioned Clarde Dovess's integrity.

Garret had been once, saw how his *betters* behaved and

vowed never to return. He'd banned Erun from going also, much to the lad's chagrin. The Games, he told his boy, were not what they were but rather had sunk to a debauched debacle of slaughter and mayhem. The barons, like the kings they replaced, rode roughshod over their people. Just like Flaminius, they were obsessed with wealth and power. Nothing had changed; Garret doubted that it ever would. The barons played while the people paid, such was the order of things here in Gol.

Eon Barola was the worst of them, or so Garret believed now. That one was clever and highly ambitious. Not for him the constant petty squabbling of his peers. Barola's lord dreamed of domination. The Baron was of an age with Garret Cade, both had been young men during the Rebellion, and at that time Garret had admired Eon Barola above any other man.

He well recalled the fire in his lord's eyes and the savage joy he'd exuded in that final battle on the hill outside Torvosa Castle. The king had fallen, Flaminius the Depraved, the barons each hewing a piece from his broken corpse. Barola got the head; he'd pickled it and hung it from the Keep that summer—a feast for fly and raven. Funny, it just seemed like yesterday to Garret Cade.

Since that time Eon Barola had plotted and schemed, while his sons won year after year at the Games. All three were more than proficient in horse-craft, weaponry and single combat. Paolo, the youngest, was particularly gifted. He never lost at tournaments, unless matched against Clarde Dovess or Estorien Sarfe—both legends of recent years. Men held that the only match for Paolo's swordplay was his arrogance, though none would dare utter such a notion out loud.

Shadowman take the Baron and his sons, and his bloody daughter too. Especially her...

Garret rubbed his tired eyes and stifled a yawn. Perhaps it was for the best, this enforced exile he planned. There was nothing for them in Barola Town. Garret Cade and his son would start a new life west of the mountains. That indolent boy would learn what it was to do an honest day's work instead of moon-calving after barons' daughters and reciting stupid poems.

The time was long passed for Erun Cade to wake up to what he was, the low born son of a common soldier turned blacksmith. The boy had delusions of nobility. An ailment that could very easily shorten him by a head—especially now he'd deflowered Barola's daughter (and Garret's head too just for having seeded him.)

Garret Cade glanced skyward: the hour was late. He strode past the last house, pushed through the opening in the hedge wall, and took the steady climb up toward the shadow of woods where waited cottage and forge. Ahead the lane dusked and cornered into gloom.

***

Lissane Barola woke just before midnight. In her dream she heard her brothers laughing as they tore the wings from a giant butterfly, a thing of rare beauty and innocence. She looked closer and noticed the creature had Erun Cade's sea-stormy eyes.

Lissane screamed and her brothers turned toward her, Paolo's mouth was dripping blood and Rosco was reaching for her silken shift, his fat face flushed with drink and lust. She woke then, her sheets sodden and her brow glistening with sweat.

Outside the night hung still, the only sound the soft billowing of curtains at her nearest window. Lissane knew something was out there. She wrapped a shawl around her nakedness, and shivering crept to the window, taking her seat on the broad ledge as was her custom at eventide.

For a time Lissane gazed out from her lofty view, letting her sleepy eyes adjust to the gloom. Her chambers were the second highest in the Keep, only her father's rooms and the flagged parapet lay above. Unlike her father's, Lissane's windows all faced out to sea which suited her well. She had always been drawn to the ocean and its moods. Watching now, Lissane saw a distant star piercing the cloud-wracked gloom.

But what was that movement in the distance? Smoke? No... this was tangible and strange to behold. Lissane looked closer; something...or rather someone was stirring out there. A huge shape lumbering at the edge of her vision, hard to define at first but becoming clearer as she watched, her violet eyes now adjusted to the gloom.

A cloud or a mist perhaps? No. Lissane felt certain this was a living being. It resembled a man moving slowly, crouched and bent as though in pain, his massive bulk darker than both sea and night sky surrounding him. Lissane watched entranced as the smoky figure waded closer until it dominated the horizon.

Then she recognised the Sea God. Surely this was mighty Zansuat limping toward her through his waves, with weed-strewn beard unkempt, and naked, corded torso; shouldering a mile-wide net that trailed like an enormous wave behind him.

Lissane watched spellbound as the Sea God's head turned toward the rocky outcrop where her father's castle stood. She felt that sweeping dreadful gaze scanning the walls... searching and seeking—for her. Then she felt the hypnotic power of that fathomless stare fall upon her at her window, and Lissane, afraid, covered her face with her pale hands.

But those mystical, shifting eyes bored inside her head until, unable to resist, Lissane opened her lids and gaped wide at he who had had come out of the night. The god's eyes pinned her as a fish hooked dry and gasping—within their depth lay hidden every secret of the ocean. They were calm and tumultuous: turbulent yet serene. There was sorrow there too and Lissane wanted to cry out, call to him, asking...pleading... but her mouth could only frame the words.

Why have you come to me? What dire chance waits upon the rising sun?

There was no answer save the surge of wave greeting rock far below, and the faint drumming as sea breeze salted the glass on her windows. The god's face was hard to define, shifting in and out of the night: impossibly close yet immeasurably distant. Lissane became aware of another noise—her heartbeat, fast and thudding as she watched, trembling; her hands frozen and clutching her arms, and her sharp nails digging into the soft white skin. Her night eyes mirrored a moon-gazey hare, caught between fear and fascination. For what seemed an age he gazed upon her from far out to sea, that silent giant, dwarfing both castle and shore.

Then the spell broke. He turned his back on her and, hauling his nets around in a wide sweeping arc, slowly retreated to the place where sky merged with ocean, eventually fading from view. Lissane watched from her high window seat until the Sea God's shadow was swallowed by the night.

She couldn't move. For long minutes she sat there in silence shivering, oblivious to the moist track of tears welling at the corner of her eyes, and then beading down her cheeks. The fisher folk said it boded ill to see the Sea God alone at night. Foreboding or not, it *was* significant, she knew, and her intuition whispered to Lissane that after today her life would never be the same.

She started when the keen sound of a harp-string plucked clear chords just outside her room. Lissane felt an icy shiver run the length of her back. Castle Barola had no such harper, and her father bore no love for musicians. The music was eerie; it turned her head toward the door. The music faded off into the distance.

Silence.

Lissane sighed. Weary of mystery she returned to her bed, tucking her pale limbs beneath the sheets. In the next chamber, Belshareze her maidservant cried out in her dreams. Lissane closed her eyes and tried to relax.

The phantom harper no longer played his melancholy tune in the passageway outside. Perhaps he never had and mayhap the Sea God too had been a dream. But dreams were important and Lissane, try though she did, could snatch no more sleep from that uncanny night. She was worried so, for her lover mostly. Something was wrong.

Oh, Great Zansuat of the Waves... protect my Erun Cade.

***

The night dragged on. Alone in the smith's cottage Erun still fretted. He knew he was being stupid hesitating, but just couldn't decide what to do. And the more time he wasted worrying about it the worse he felt. Garret would be back soon and another argument would follow. Erun had to make a decision in the next few minutes or else give up on ever seeing Lissane again.

Trouble was, Erun knew his father was right but that knowledge helped him not at all. Damn and blast it. Let the smith go to Galania and good luck go with him. Erun couldn't leave without Lissane. They were meant to be together.

At last his mind was made up. Erun Cade would wait for his love, hide out somewhere in the woods. Then at the right moment he'd cross the Causeway and find Liss. Yes, it would be tricky and dangerous. That didn't matter. Somehow they'd slip past the Baron's clutches and reach the boat he'd stolen the other evening, taking to sea and escape.

They would wend south along the coast. Within a week or two they would reach Dovesi Province, follow one of the rivers up to Torvosa City, or else another safe haven—if anywhere was safe at this time of distrust and uncertainty.

Duke Toreno was no friend of Barola and was rumoured an honourable man—which was more than could be said for Eon Barola. Erun paced about and muttered, wasting another half hour before finally deciding when he should cross to the castle. Sooner rather than later, he thought, whilst dithering some more.

He'd creep into town in the early hours, steal across the causeway as soon as it showed above the water and then spin some yarn to the guards. He was good with words—it was part of the reason why Lissane had fallen for him. Part of the reason...

He'd steal a cloak and hood, mix with the crowd. He'd find Lissane somehow, or else her maid, Bel. Erun trusted Belshareze. The maid had proved both discreet and helpful during the last weeks. On second thoughts he might be better off finding Bel and asking for her help. But then if Bel was implicated the Baron would skin her alive. No. He had best do this alone.

It didn't matter. Together he and Lissane would plan the hour when they could meet secretly at the stolen boat—hidden in the high reeds three miles north along the shore. Erun knew that his chances of success were slim, but he had to do something. Leaving Barola without his love was not an option.

Mind set at last, Erun grabbed some food and a few extra garments for warmth and then closed the door of the cottage behind him.

Outside the night had closed in. The woods hedged close out of the dark, almost smothering the little glade containing cottage, forge and stream, his only home for seventeen years. Erun knew he shouldn't have moped for so long. It must be nearly midnight and Garret would be back any minute, and another row was the very last thing he needed.

He turned toward the lane then stopped.

What's that?

A noise behind him. Shuffling feet? Erun froze. Then someone laughed and he turned, saw a shadow watching him beneath the trees. A man stood there, his face shrouded by the night but Erun could tell he was grinning.

"Who?" There was a sudden muffled noise behind him, a rustling and the sound of heavy footfalls. "What?" Erun tried to run but something hard struck him on the back of his skull. He fell forward onto the track, his head reeling and his vision blurred.

"Carry him across to the forge, we can work on him there," a voice purred close to his ear. Erun felt strong arms lifting him up from behind, and someone cursing in his ear as they dragged him painfully toward the forge. He must have lost consciousness for a time...

***

Far away Ashmali's Mountain belched its last flame before crumbling and crashing into the sea. The sky blazed crimson. Had the occupants of the Citadel cared to look they would have seen the vivid colours and trail of smoke clogging the western horizon. Were that so they might have stood the slimmest chance. Though even that was unlikely.

Proud fools. The Order had posted no guards. So confident were they none dare land on their island domain without prior permission from the High Lord Sorcerer himself. But they had forgotten about Ozmandeus.

The one the Order had branded the Renegade smiled wryly. His fellow warlocks would never expect *his* return. Ozmandeus had been expelled after the bitter quarrel last year, banished on pain of hideous death by authority of the Order. Idiots. They should have killed him while they had the chance.

Ozmandeus steadied his ketch as it approached the harbour arm. He worded the closing spell and the craft's sails drooped limp and lifeless, allowing the vessel to slow and glide silently towards the nearest dock. Ozmandeus allowed himself a few moments gratification, turning on the bench, letting his keen gaze casually follow the wake's shrinking path to where sea sparkled distant before melding into blood-red cloud.

The murdered sky. All that remained of Ashmali's Island. It felt so good to survey the result of this hot afternoon's work: the column of smoke still darkening the horizon, and distant crusts of ash floating down like grey snowflakes to settle in brief, blazing sparks on the summer water below.

The volcano's wake left an explosion of light and ruin, flashes and bangs and distant rumbles, trailing off into slow rhythmic thuds. Its final spurts would be visible from the coast of Zorne— maybe even further. The tidal surge would follow, wrecking coast and village. Folk would be watching and listening everywhere, fearing the worst. They were wise to do so.

The one exception was the Citadel. His former associates and masters up there had higher purposes, or so they deemed. The Renegade eased the tiller a touch, steering the skiff alongside the main dock serving Alchemists Isle, avoiding chop, and smiling as he took in the chaotic walls of the sorcerers' manse, high above.

Ozmandeus's former home was a huge ugly building, intimidating and captivating. The Citadel, they called it—though no single word served to describe such a weird and awful place. It confused the eye: a hypnotic collection of twisted towers and crooked, wind-scoured turrets, snaring the gaze of any naïve enough to venture near.

The sorcerers' dwelling dominated the island surrounding it; both surreal architecture and garish hue were fashioned to inspire terror. That worked usually. But not on this occasion. They would suspect nothing. The order believed itself untouchable and even Ozmandeus was beneath their concerns. That indifference was crime enough, but there were more pressing reasons why they deserved to die.

And die they would. Soon. But first the Order would know his triumph. That was the point. The key factor. Those fools up there had to know *why* they had failed. Let them despair as they witness the full horror of the Demon unleashed. It all felt so good—the culmination of months of careful planning finally reaching fruition.

Alchemist's Isle had been Ozmandeus's home for many years. He'd come late to study but his quick mind and cunning tongue soon surpassed his fellow students. He'd been happy up there, contributing much, but those pompous fools had driven him away.

Jealous and vain, they had cast him from the Order. Just because he was free thinking and bold. They all hated him. Those bastards always had. At first that had hurt, but Ozmandeus soon came to realise his powers were unique, and he had talent and will beyond any of them.

The witchmasters and trained sorcerers didn't trust him either. Ozmandeus wasn't like their other students. He was a maverick. An outcast from Zorne that had stolen upon their narrow lives. Upsetting the balance. Introducing radical new ideas, daring to question the wisdom of his betters. How the other warlocks had mocked him and laughed at his 'wild' ambitions. Then came the quarrel and his branding as the Renegade.

"Return and you will suffer the Death of Nine Knives." (An archaic and ghastly punishment involving heated daggers inserted inch slowly into orifice, nerve and organ, all while the miscreant hangs spell-suspended over glowing coals.)

The High Lord Sorcerer had struck him then, as though he were a wayward child.

"Those who question our wisdom are beyond contempt. I name you Renegade. May the gods curse your upstart bones."

And so Ozmandeus departed the island in disgrace before completing his training. Six months passed and no word of him reached the Order. Another six months, Ozmandeus's fellow students and masters forgot about him. So with that in mind the Renegade decided he'd write them a note. A short message:

I have returned and I've brought you all a present.
It was time for payback.

Vengeance and pride. Both were factors behind this latest action. They had cast him out as though he were nothing. Another motive was ambition. But the real reason was 'just because he could'. With his unique skills Ozmandeus had achieved something only the gods would dare.

Even the High Lord Sorcerer—were he to have the courage (and he didn't)—couldn't pull off this stunt. A deed so terrible it would unlatch the door to a new era in which he, Ozmandeus of Zorne, the despised Renegade, would take control.

Ashmali the Fire Demon, so long incarcerated, was free again to feed on mortal flesh, thanks to Ozmandeus's bold actions alone. It was time to reveal his deadly secret. The Renegade fingered the amulet containing the demon's essence as he vaulted onto the dock. It was time. At his word the ketch's ropes lashed themselves to mooring posts. The Renegade glanced up at the monstrosity of stone high above and smiled like a wolf. It felt good to be home again.

"I'm back!" Ozmandeus yelled up. "I hope you are ready!"

***

Chapter 4

Midnight at the Forge

"Strip him and bring him here." Paolo's gloved hands caressed the poker. Behind him Aldo had the fire well stoked and Rosco was casually emptying one of the Garret Cade's ale barrels into three flagons. Paolo stood dreamily smiling, the blazing poker held lightly (almost lovingly) in his left palm.

At his word, Grudge the servant grabbed Erun's rough garments and tugged them from his body.

"Not much flesh on that," Rosco grinned. "Little shit's skinny as a rake."

"Maybe we should start with an eye," Paolo flicked the poker a little so that its glowing tip hovered a foot above the Erun's head.

"Shove it up his arse," suggested Rosco. "That should make him squeal." He belched loudly and reached for more ale. Aldo said nothing, just stared down at the prone and naked youth with cold dispassion, as if he were watching the castle butcher preparing to slaughter a goat.

Erun Cade was stirring now, groaning, so Grudge struck him hard across the face, silencing him again. Grudge then shouldered Erun over to a central wooden beam supporting the roof above.

Aldo pushed a stool beneath him, while Rosco lashed the captive's arms around the pillar and stool, tying his feet as well. Paolo watched on, his emerald eyes hot with anticipation.

"Such a pretty boy," he purred. "I can see why our sister took a shine to you...poet. Almost you tempt me too. A quick buggering wouldn't go amiss. But alas, we've not the time...not if we're to do this *properly.*

"Oh by the by, peasant, my little sis's pledged to that dry stick Varentin Gallante." Paolo traced a long finger down the length of Erun's cheek, his manicured nails drawing a fine ribbon of blood as they scraped the skin.

"I'd expect he'll have to beat her bloody for a time before she opens to him willingly. Lissane's like that—very proud. Bit of a shame really how things have turned out. Are you listening to me, boy?"

"He's out cold," muttered Rosco, losing interest.

Paolo grinned. "Time to wake him then."

He turned to Grudge, his eyes now flints of jade. "Hold his head up." Grudge obeyed, tugging Erun Cade's tawny tangle back sharply as his master lowered the glowing poker.

"Wakey wakey, Erun Cade. I've been talking to you and you haven't been listening. That's very rude. You should answer when your betters address you. Perhaps this will get your attention."

Almost affectionately Paolo rested the red hot iron against Erun's left cheek, searing through skin and muscle, roasting and puckering the flesh. "Smells like roasted hog," Paolo said, and the other brothers laughed at that.

***

Erun woke to searing agony as the poker burnt deep into his face. He screamed and screamed before losing consciousness again. A slap brought him round, his vision was blurred by tears and his left cheek burned horribly. He could smell his own flesh smouldering where the poker had seared it, cutting deep from just below the eye, nearly blinding him and curving down to the corner of his swollen, bloody mouth. Erun's mind was wandering, he felt feverish and somehow removed from the abomination that was happening to him.

His watery eyes opened: his vision, although blurred, was still intact. A face loomed above and he recognised Paolo Barola. The real fear came then, accompanied by shame as Erun felt his bladder loosen below.

"Look he's fucking pissed himself." That was Rosco Barola's grating voice Erun registered in a corner of his mind.

"They generally do when they see me. That or worse." Paolo loomed close again, smiling as always. "Methinks we'll employ this rod somewhere else. Somewhere... appropriate."

Paolo lowered the glowing poker toward Erun's groin. Grinning, he stopped inches short of the boy's shrunken sex and rested the flat edge of the poker head against the inside of his left thigh.

Searing agony exploded inside Erun. He tried to cry out but no words would come. The flesh blistered and smouldered as Paolo slowly traced a red brand the length of Erun's sweating thigh. The pain was intolerable, the fear red and ragged, crushing him... breaking him.

Just before he passed out Erun heard a roar followed by the clash of angry steel. It seemed to come from someplace else—beyond the pain that was his prison. Then the darkness closed in and Erun Cade knew no more...

***

Hacker glowered into the trees. It always happened to him; Grudge got to play with the big boys whilst he, Hacker, was left out in the cold. He could hear them laughing inside. No doubt Rosco had found some more liquor by now and the bastards were getting oiled—not that they weren't half wasted already.

Grudge would have had a few too; Master Paolo was fond of his little squinty servant, Shadowman take him. Hacker was sober, bored, and sick to his bones of the Baron's indulged sons and their *entertainments*. But Hacker was a soldier and a good one too. His lot was to serve without question and do as he was bidden.

It didn't mean he liked it though. He heard a scream coming from the forge and felt sorry for the poor boy they were playing with. Hacker had seen what Paolo had done to the Treggarans they captured in the last raid. Though he was a hardened veteran of the Rebellion, the sight had left him without appetite that whole day.

The Baron's other sons were cruel men, like their father. Paolo Barola was something else. The youngest brother radiated fear, wielding it as other men would swords and axes. The whole castle dreaded him and Hacker was no exception.

He was well paid though and well fed, thus better off than many. There were perks too, at times. Hacker had had his share of women and spoils over the years. He couldn't really complain—and if he did who would listen? So in the main he kept his lips together and got on with the job he was tasked with. There were times like this, however, when he'd sooner not be around, but such was his lot, he just wished he could close his ears.

Hacker yawned and stretched his back, thinking of the warm bed back at the barracks and the town girl he'd laid last night. A new sound reached him, coming from back down the track. Footsteps!

The smith returning to his forge!

Hacker reached for his axe and then froze. The sound of approaching feet had vanished. Instead silence. Then a shadow loomed over him.

***

Garret Cade had felt the tension grow with every step. He knew something was amiss and his soldier's instinct bade him be wary on approaching his home. He left the track and silently took to the trees a short distance from the glade.

Garret, approaching with stealth, could see the bulk of what looked to be Hacker, Rosco Barola's henchman, moping idle beneath the shadow of a large elm. Garret felt the cold stab of dread clutch his loins. He heard a shrill terrified scream coming from inside the forge.

What are they doing to my boy?

Garret's feet took him toward Hacker before he realised it and, as the big man turned toward him, Garret's huge palm snapped up hard under the other's nose, crunching the small bone and killing Hacker instantly. Garret knelt to quickly relieve the dead man of his axe and, the fury now rising within him like bubbling lava, roared hatred as he smashed through the door, entering the forge from without.

***

The poker stopped inches from Erun's flaccid member. Paolo Barola glanced up in surprise, seeing the thick door swing open and the heaving bulk of the smith shoulder in on them.

Damn you, Hacker, you were meant to watch for this bastard.

Rosco's sword was out in a nonce, but he was fuddled with ale and slower than normal. The axe blade turned aside his clumsy lunge and the handle's broad tip butted into his face, sending him sprawling on his back across the rushed floor. Grudge dived low to trap the smith's legs, but was rewarded by a raised knee in the face that sent him crashing after Rosco.

Aldo, bleary eyed and cursing, waded in with sword ready, but he too was drunk and arrogant in his fury. One thrust went too far: the blacksmith leaped aside, and stepping back swung down hard with the weapon.

Hacker's axe bit into Aldo's flesh and bone with a meaty thud, severing his left hand at the wrist and sending it spinning toward the flame. There it hissed and crackled like a monstrous spider, the fingers clawing toward the fire. Aldo bellowed as he clutched the spurting stump, then he fainted and slumped over a chair.

Garret grinned, he took a step forward to finish the job, but Paolo's twisted dagger took him between the shoulder blades and sliced upwards, deep and red, cutting into his heart from behind. Garret Cade fell into the darkness—down and down...nothing...

Paolo grimaced as he took stock.

A bit of a mess—Father won't be pleased.

He glanced across at Aldo and winced and then turned and kicked Grudge into motion. "Bind that idiot's wrist before he bleeds to death," he told the servant. Grudge stooped to obey, tearing a cloth from a sheet nearby and then kneeling to attend to the now groaning Aldo.

"Wait one minute." Paolo leant across and brought the poker down on Aldo's oozing stump, staunching the flow and sealing the wound. Aldo screamed and fainted dead away again. Paolo grinned, "Very theatrical, brother, I must commend you to the mummers' guild."

Behind him, Rosco took to his feet in a fit of rage and, seizing Hacker's axe swung hard down, striking the smith's head from his shoulders and sending it spinning out of the doorway into the night. "Enough," said Paolo, shaking his big brother's shoulder. "We had better be going, Rosco. We need to be back in the castle before dawn, and if any of the village spot us Father will have our hides. He's going to be furious enough as things stand."

"What about that?" demanded Rosco, pointing the axe toward the unconscious scarred body of the younger Cade. "I'd better do for him as well."

"Grudge can see to him after he tidies up. Let's get moving!" Paolo motioned his brother to carry the prone Aldo out the door. He turned back and spoke briefly to his servant.

"Take the smith's body into the woods where the wolves will see to his bones and no one need be any wiser. Once that's done come back for the boy—he's not going anywhere in a hurry. If he wakes, slit his bloody throat. Slit it anyway. But don't make any more mess; we don't want any of these stupid peasants getting vengeful notions."

Grudge gaped at him so Paolo kicked him hard in the right shin. "Get on with it, man!" Paolo Barola snarled. Grudge, nursing his bruised leg, grunted and began struggling with the bloody bulk of Garret's headless corpse.

The brothers left him without another word. The game was over and things hadn't exactly gone to plan. They needed to be elsewhere and fast. Without words, the two conscious brothers slunk back toward Barola Town, keeping close to the hedge's dark perimeter and making sure they weren't seen. Rosco sweated noisily as he laboured with his prone brother, until Paolo kicked him to silence.

He wondered how they were going to break this to the Baron. They were only meant to scare the boy and bully him a bit—score a few well placed marks, not butcher his father and murder him as well.

Bugger that idle bastard Hacker.

They'd glimpsed Hacker's corpse on the way out. Paolo wished that he could bring the soldier back to life so that he could kill him again, more slowly. They reached the skiff and Rosco slung Aldo onto the planking as if he were a sack of grain. They took an oar each and rounded the castle just as the first ribbon of morning's promise pinkened the sky ahead.

***

The glade felt creepy after the brothers had fled. Grudge acted swiftly, seeing to the blacksmith's corpse well before dawn woke the birds in the woods above, and then returning to the forge to drag off the boy.

The sight that greeted him there (or rather didn't greet him) wasn't good for Grudge's future prospects. Erun Cade had vanished. Gone—disappeared into thick air and the ropes that had tethered him lay neatly severed and curled on the bloodstained floor.

Shit.

Grudge heard a sound outside. He turned. There it was again, only this time clearer. Music. Grudge felt the tiny hairs stiffen on the back of his neck as the clear clean notes of a harp broke the glade's silence. He shivered.

What in Shadowman's name is that..?

Grudge's squinty eyes scanned the glade, following the long shadows from tree to tree. There was no one there—just the harp's weird song drifting in an out of earshot. There was something both beautiful and disturbing about that music, and Grudge, feeling his knees trembling, was suddenly hit by an urge to be elsewhere. He had the nasty feeling that someone uncanny was watching him from beneath those trees. But who and why? It made no sense.

He turned about and turned again. Nothing: he was alone in the glade. *Stupid bloody imagination—that's all.* There was no one about—all was empty and still. Grudge questioned his senses. Had he drank that much? He didn't think so. The brothers had done for the barrel, and he'd just assisted in its draining. The harp notes rose and fell, tormenting Grudge's ears with their melancholy beauty. Something was very wrong here, he decided. Time to go.

Grudge fled as morning's golden kiss banished the shadows and the music fell suddenly silent around cottage and glade. The birds started then, daring to speak now the strangeness had gone.

Hours later a sheepish Grudge slunk quietly back into Castle Barola via the postern. He asked Grale—who barred his way at the Keep's gate—for Paolo's whereabouts. The grizzly old champion dourly informed him that both Paolo and Rosco were in with the Baron who, Grale cautioned, was in a rare red rage. Grudge entered the Keep and clambered worriedly up to the Baron's chambers. He hovered for a time outside the door of Eon Barola's study, biting his lip at the raised voices within.

On reflection Grudge now considered discretion a more sensible course. With that in mind he took his weary, worried bones to the nearest alehouse and got well and truly soused.

The fate of Erun Cade, decided Grudge, was out of his hands. Far better he stay quiet for a time. But during that night and for many after, Grudge's dreams were filled with ghostly harps and the sight of Garret Cade's severed head grinning at him from the dark. Grudge frequented the taverns a lot in the following weeks.

***

The select members of the Order always convened around the high table on appropriate occasions. That had been the way of things since its founding three score years ago. Forty alchemists were seated there now. Men and women gathered from all corners of Ansu. For sixty years they had held council on this their island, weaving their witchy threads and plotting away the hours in self-gratification.

Amongst those gathered today were alchemists pure and

astrologers garbed in ritual robes reflecting the light. There were students of ancient thaumaturgy, graduates in witch-lore and even necromancers clad in their customary black.

Some there could levitate inanimate objects, hurling them miles through space; others bend lesser men's wills to their own with cruel coercion. All were hated by the little people. Hated and feared.

Throughout those years Alchemists Isle had become a place of dread to be avoided at all costs. Merchants, fishers, and even war-galleys from distant Xandoria, all gave the rocky isle with its weird crooked citadel the widest berth possible.

It was most unusual for all forty sorcerers to be present at one time. They had so many diversions and often were away—busy in this place or that. But this was no normal situation. What confronted them now was a matter of highest import. Or so the High Lord Sorcerer had announced.

The High Lord had summoned this 'most urgent meeting', bidding all attend or risk expulsion from the Order. Thus they were seated, watching him now like bored children awaiting their lesson. All were edgy and peeved; each one had better things to do. But, fearing him, they waited in wary silence.

Among those gathered were the pale and swarthy, the skinny and rotund; the virile young and frail ancient—all studying the inscrutable gaze of their venerable patron. He spoke at last; his words quiet yet authoritative and easily reaching the far corners of that sweeping, roomy, hall.

"Chosen, this morning I received a spell-note carried on the night breeze and signed by the apostate, Ozmandeus. The content was obscure but its purpose evident. A challenge. The Renegade is up to something. We have been lax—we need to silence him before he can stir up trouble again." Several nodded at their master's words whilst others gazed whimsically out at the evening sky, wishing they were elsewhere on this bright late-summer day's wane.

"What do you propose, Lord?" The question came from a corpulent, balding Wizard, with an accent that marked him as Xandorian.

"We must link minds...seek out Ozmandeus and destroy him utterly," the High Lord responded. "Now, Chosen. We have delayed long enough in this matter. Foolish was I to let that one go, I should have guessed he'd be unhinged enough to return here. Come, help me put an end to this pest. Link arms and fuse—let me reach you with my power."

The forty obeyed: felt the surge of joyful energy rush through their veins as their master's thought entered their minds. With arms entwined and minds channelling outwards, the sorcerers waited for his next command.

But it never came.

Instead someone else tore inside their heads, making them cry out in pain at the sudden violence of his assault.

An impostor? A rival wizard?

As one their concentration broke and the link failed. The Chosen fell forward, broken as are icicles slipping from a thawing bridge at winter's end. Then *he* spoke and their ears stung with his mocking tones.

"It's too late." The voice was clear and strong and *familiar*. It clove clean through that tense atmosphere like a headman's axe severing the neck of one condemned. Only they were the condemned on this occasion.

All faces turned toward the double doors now suddenly swung wide open. A tall figure stood between them, cloaked and hooded yet easily recognisable. He awarded those gathered a mercurial smile.

"I said I would return one day," Ozmandeus told them. I have something to show you."

Chapter 5

Moods and Shadows

Eon Barola said nothing at first, just stared into his wine-glass, gloved forefinger and thumb turning the crystal around and around; the scraping, whining sound putting the brothers' teeth on edge, and rattling their already frayed nerves. Then with sudden violence their father's hand closed hard over the vessel, shattering glass and spilling wine between suede-clad fingers.

"You were not seen?" Eon Barola demanded. "Are you certain of this?" The Baron's voice seethed menace—a kettle approaching the point of boil. But Eon Barola was nothing if not controlled. Even his violence was measured, inch by inch—gauged to perfection for maximum affect. Fear was his province.

"Aye, Father." Paolo's face was pale and Rosco stood sweating beside him. They hadn't wasted much time, deeming it wise to wake the Baron at once, informing him of their mishap at the forge; and now as he watched, Paolo could see the fury building within his father's eyes. "We were careful," he ventured tentatively.

"You were... *careful*..." the sarcasm stung like a wasp. "I expected better from you, Paolo. You at least, I thought, could be trusted with this minor task. You were told to hurt the boy—scare him witless. Not butcher him and his father besides.

"Garret Cade was useful, good smiths are hard to come by these days. Besides, he fought with me at Torvosa when we slew the King. I do not forget such things." He reached for another goblet and filled it with his favourite vintage. "And now Garret Cade is dead meat, thanks to your inane incompetence."

"I know, Father...we—"

"It was Hacker's fault!" Rosco blurted, and the Baron turned on him with baleful eye.

"You sodden turd—did I ask your opinion?" Rosco blanched and bit back an angry retort. "What use are you to me, Rosco?" Eon Barola pressed. "Supping ale and tupping a whore... that's all you're fit for, my lad. At least Hacker had his uses—and now he's dead as well. And where is Aldo hiding?"

Rosco paled at that last question. His bloodshot eyes flicked nervously across to his younger brother. "Well?" demanded his father.

"He was hurt," Paolo said lamely.

"Hurt...? *How* hurt?" Eon's dark gaze narrowed dangerously.

"He was careless," replied Paolo, forcing confidence into his words. "He...he's lost his left hand, Father. Garret Cade cut it off with Hacker's axe, and then I killed the smith. I'm... sorry."

Paolo was extremely aware of how close his father's right arm was to his ornate dagger, resting as it often did at the right corner of the Baron's table.

Eon saw where his youngest was looking and smiled grimly. "You might be good, boy," he whispered. "But you're not *that* good." Paolo shrugged and feigned innocence. "Neither are you sorry, I'll warrant."

Eon Barola sighed, drained his goblet, and then reached for another bottle, uncorking it and downing a sizeable gulp from its neck, before replenishing his goblet again. "How is Aldo faring?" he demanded.

"Oh, he'll be alright," responded Paolo, relaxing again. Rosco was still looming beside him, oozing sweaty scowls. "I cleaned the wound then sealed it with a hot iron. It will trouble him for a time and doubtless he'll have a fever—but he'll survive, I reckon."

"Shame it wasn't his fucking head," snapped the Baron. "Aldo's never used that so he wouldn't miss it." Eon Barola rubbed his tired eyes with a gloved palm.

Treggarans: we'll blame it on the Treggarans.

"Your sister will prove difficult for a time," he told them, his thoughts turning to Lissane and the approaching visit by 'Prince' Gallante and his flatulent son. "She was fond of that wastrel."

"I could comfort her," ventured Rosco, whose piggy eyes had brightened at the notion.

"You'll leave her be," growled the Baron. "I'll see to the girl when this mess has been sorted out. Leave me now, the pair of you, I need to think clearly. That's impossible with you idiots leaning over me." The Baron waved an imperious arm, dismissing the pair. "Go!"

Rosco took no further prompting and hastily retreated to the door, but Paolo stood his ground for a moment longer, his green cat's eyes still on his father's dagger. "I will make it up to you, Father," he vowed.

Eon studied his youngest son, the pride of his jaded litter. He rubbed his close-cropped goatee and managed a shallow smile. "You have talent, Paolo, and you're bright. But you are no match for me, boy. You never will be. To rule a province takes a cunning hand. You are too rash...too hasty."

Barola leaned back in his chair, his left hand lightly brushing the gilt handle of the dagger. Paolo raised an eyebrow but said nothing. "Come share a glass with me, lad," urged the Baron in a softer voice. He signalled his favourite offspring forward and Paolo, eyes wary now, straddled a stool joining his father at the table, though still keeping his distance.

"You shouldn't challenge me, son," Eon Barola said. He casually slid the bottle along the table and Paolo snatched it up, taking a long hard pull then wiping his mouth on his black velvet sleeve. "Your brothers have few uses beyond killing Treggarans. I can't say that I'd mourn the loss of either much. But you are no fool, Paolo. I expected more from you than this...*disappointment.*"

"We *were* unlucky." Paolo held his father's gaze, his feral green sparring with the bloodshot menace of his sire. "As Rosco said, Hacker let us down. He must have been taking a piss or something to let the smith get the better of him. I've seen Hacker kill three men in as many minutes before now."

"Garret Cade was a good fighter in his day," responded the Baron. "And cunning with a blade. I doubt Hacker got much warning." Eon Barola placed both palms flat on the table. "Well, what's done cannot be undone," he added. "We'll spread word there was a raid late last night."

"Makes sense," Paolo nodded.

"A small party of Treggarans: young bloods—not wanting to risk the town but after an easy kill. We'll say we buried Garret and his son in the forest after giving them full rites. That should appease enquiring minds. Go now, boy," he waved Paolo away. "I need to think this through."

Paolo took a last gulp before taking to his feet. He hesitated for a moment longer. "What is it?" Eon's irritation was growing again. He was tired and the hour had passed from late to early. Dawn had been and gone. "What do you want from me, boy?"

"Let me in on your council, father," Paolo urged him. "I could aid your ambitions better were I aware of your notions."

"But can you be discreet, son of mine? Politics is a subtler game than butchering men—however intricately—and I am a political animal unlike you, boy." The Baron studied his son's handsome face: those cat green eyes never blinked, and an easy, impertinent smile tilted the right corner of his lip.

You're a confident bastard, Paolo. I'm going to have to watch you.

The Baron turned away addressed the door. "Can I rely on your discretion and...loyalty?"

"Yes, Father."

"Good. We will speak more of this later. Go now." The Baron dismissed Paolo a second time and then reached across the table to reclaim his bottle, his quick mind focussing on future events as he studied the contents of his goblet.

That boy could prove useful; he's as sharp as I am. But I dare not tell him everything.

.In the next room the girl awaited Eon's attentions. He'd acquired her from a village some years ago when Leanna had frosted toward him. Cora was half his age but Barola was still an energetic man. He finished his wine with a final gulp and made swiftly to his chamber. Tomorrow he would deal with Lissane—or maybe the day after.

***

At first the news of Erun's death was like a blade of ice twisting jagged in her belly. It had been Grale that had told her. Lissane had seen no sign of her father or brothers for three days. Grale had mumbled something about a raid by Treggarans—a night attack culminating in foulest murder at the forge, with both her lover and his father dead.

Lissane had denied it initially, refusing to let it in and locking herself up in her bower for hour upon hour. Belshareze had brought food but she'd hardly touched it. Bel's pretty face was awash with tears but Lissane couldn't weep. Not yet. It all seemed so odd. So *wrong*—a nightmare come true.

Belshareze left her amid tears. Her maid and confidante fared to the town to discover what she could and keep her worried mind busy. Lissane hardly noticed her departure. Her world had faded to grey. Summer devoured by deepest winter. Inside her mind Lissane's random thoughts wandered between dreams and waking. She drank little, ate nothing. Bel came and went, whispering soothing words and asking what she should do. Lissane ignored her.

It was on the fourth day that her father's insistent rapping and heavy voice woke her from beyond the door. Belshareze was elsewhere and Lissane sitting all alone at her ledge by the window. She wore a pale white dress that matched her wan expression. She turned her tired head toward the door.

"Lissane...daughter...we need to talk." Her father's voice was unmistakable. "Come on, girl, let me in," he insisted. Lissane turned her head again and let her forlorn gaze fall on the water, so far below her window seat.

*Just go away...*She knew he wouldn't, though. He'd just keep growling and knocking the door until she could stand it no longer. So Lissane wiped her salty eyes on her kerchief, straightened her cotton dress, and then, heavy hearted, let her stiff legs carry her to the door. Lissane threw back the bolt and let the Baron in. Her violet gaze met his wolf stare for a moment, and then she turned her back on him and returned to her ocean perusal—her tired gaze lost and faraway.

Eon Barola stood watching his daughter for a time, dark flinty eyes calculating, gauging her reaction and disapproving of her sad demeanour. Her father looked immaculate this morning, with scarlet doublet laced by gold at collar and cuff—not that she'd noticed. His black leather riding trousers were studded with silver discs over an inch in diameter and tucked neatly into his soft doe-skin boots. Eon's broad face was ruddy and fresh, the dark eyes demanding her attentions.

"We need to talk," the Baron told her again, his voice blunt and his manner impatient. "Your betrothal... Varentin Gallante and his lord father will be arriving in three weeks' time." She ignored him. *Go away.*

"I can't have you moping like this, girl," Eon added. "House Gallante would take that ill. You're a Baron's daughter—not some dreamy-eyed fisher's get. Are you listening to me, girl?" When she still didn't respond he changed tactic, his grating voice softening, feigning empathy; trying to reach her pain, or pretending to try.

"I'm sorry for your loss, girl, really I am," he told her. "Those young Treggaran louts have got out of hand lately, and now I'm down a good smith. An unfortunate incident, but one of small consequence to House Barola."

Lissane turned and for the first time let her violet gaze survey her father. She didn't like what she saw. The Baron looked weary, there were dark rings under his eyes and a stale odour that hinted at old wine and recently spent semen. He took a step toward her; another, his fists clenching and unclenching and his demanding gaze darkening like winter cloud. She turned away again. She didn't fear him—not today.

I'm not my mother...

"I know you were fond of that boy," Eon Barola said, "but it was very foolish of you to let your heart stray to one so baseborn, Liss." She could feel those hard eyes probing her defences, chipping away at her fragile walls; stone by stone, piece by piece.

This must have been how Mother felt...

"Damn your insolence, girl—you will respond to me!" The Baron, his patience exhausted, took four more steps to reach her. "Look at me!" Lissane's walls crumpled when she felt his callused hand lifting her chin up sharply so that she had to look up at him. The tears came then, but she wouldn't let him in—just stared at the bare wall behind him, her mind wandering and lost.

The slap sent her sprawling. Lissane was dimly aware of his heavy ring breaking the skin on her cheek, and she felt her shins scrape on the stone flags as she fell. She could hear his heavy breathing as he leaned over her, staring and scowling—eyes black as murder. Then she heard the Baron's heavy footsteps retreat and her door thud shut as he slammed it hard behind him.

*He is gone...*Lissane closed her eyes, letting the warm freedom of sleep release her again. Her body hurt and the touch of the slate flags was cold against her skin, but Lissane Barola was oblivious to both. She must have slept for a time—her mind journeying back through the years.

Mother—I will join you soon.

***

It is dark in the passage. So dark. Her pale gown shimmers as she makes for the winding stairwell. The sconces gutter as night's stormy wind pierces the Keep's inner skin and freezes her bones. She feels nothing—hasn't for years. Her face is a mask. Those once warm, honey eyes now glazed with sorrow, and the famous long braids dishevelled wild and free.

Free as her soul at last.

She gains the stairs, taking them two at a time, her bare white feet silent on that cold black stone. She passes his room quickly, hears his heavy night voice and the leman stirring at his side. Had she the courage she would enter his chamber, pick up his jewelled knife and open his throat. It would be over in seconds... so silent so easy. She shudders—what if he awakens..? She walks on, determined, reaches that final door.

Beyond waits winter and her escape.

She pushes open the iron-studded door leading out to the lofty, rain drenched parapet above. Her hair is whipped wild by the icy blast of winter's worst. Her eyes are dark pools. She looks up, ignoring the rain that has already soaked her thin gown; she smells the clean night air, sees the clouds scurry fast and high overhead, their weird shapes shifting from dragon to giant and from griffin to demon.

The gods are angry tonight. They need a sacrifice and she is coming. The storm threatens to topple her as she struggles toward the battlements. She slips, bruises her body but hardly notices. Regaining her feet, she climbs upon the parapet wall to stand, arms out wide at either side, the wind buffeting her frail starved body. Her toes grip the glistening stone and somehow she keeps her balance in the tumult.

She looks down.

Far beneath her feet, the surging boom of midnight water rages at the castle walls. She feels the Sea God stir from his long sleep beneath the waves. He is waiting for her, beckoning, promising escape from both sorrow and pain.

She is ready: hears her thudding heart beat slowing, feeling calmer now that the time is almost upon her. She looks down again, seeing the storm surge whitening where water battles rock far below. Icy rain batters her face numb, and the shrieking wind shreds her hair like a torn banner.

She doesn't care. It is time. She smiles and closes her eyes, taking that first step out into the night. She falls. The cold sharp air rushing passed her ears. Down...down...and down again, into the noisy darkness and beyond. Leanna Barola is free at last. And the waves reach up to carry her home.

***

Lissane woke with a jolt. The dream had rushed through her like a storm in the night. She lay in her bed now, the covers wrapped around her—heard Bel's soft breathing in the other room. They both were warm and safe. But the dream of her mother had been so vivid Lissane could still see Leanna's haunted expression and ravaged face.

And to think that I blamed you all those years ago, when it was his cruelty drove you to it...Mother, I'm so sorry—I understand now.

Ghosts. Everywhere in her life now were ghosts. Lissane would that she could join them. She felt cheated and abandoned. Part of her wished that she also lay broken and lost in those eddying waters below, instead of safe and warm beneath her linen sheets.

It was late—how late, Lissane couldn't guess—the castle was silent and her widow cloaked by cloud-wracked night. Her body ached from her earlier fall, and she could smell the salve that Bel must have rubbed on her leg. At some point the girl must have dragged her into the bed while she slept. Lissane had no recollection of that.

This night felt so strange. Almost unreal. Lissane felt an odd calm, as though she were watched by one who would protect her. She opened her eyes, allowing her violet gaze to rest on her window, its pale panes framing the night outside. A solitary star winked back at her, and for a fleeting moment Lissane thought that she heard a hint of music, the faintest strumming of a harp. But she couldn't be sure. She felt at peace though and watched for a time, letting her eyes adjust to the gloom of her bower.

It was then that she saw her.

The woman was hard to define; she seemed to shimmer like water as she sat motionless, watching Lissane from the seat at the window ledge. Woman or girl, it was impossible to tell, Lissane guessed she was both and more. The woman's eyes reflected the stars' silvery light, and her long hair glistened like the waves parading the bay outside.

Those eyes were huge pools of light, sometimes green, then grey and blue, then back to silver—shifting in hue like the many moods of the oceans. Hypnotic and compelling was that gaze, reaching deep inside Lissane and soothing her questioning thoughts as a lover's kiss.

When she spoke the stranger's voice was a whisper, hardly audible and yet it filled the room, penetrating Lissane's defences where her father's grainy growl could not.

"You will see him again, in time." The voice was soothing but cold—like clean fresh water on tired grimy skin.

"He is dead—they are all dead," Lissane heard herself respond—her own voice rasping and hoarse.

"Your mother, yes, she came to us long ago. But the one you have loved lives yet...and in time you will be together again."

"No! He is dead and you are just another dream." Lissane couldn't allow herself to hope. She *was* still dreaming and would wake soon to cold daylight and a brutal future. But not yet. Let this sweet dream carry her where it would.

"Aye, you dream, daughter..." Had the woman read her thoughts? Certainly she was smiling, and though Lissane could only just make out the curve of her face, she could feel those uncanny eyes soften toward her.

"Erun Cade's fate will carry him far from these shores for a number of years, but you will meet again before the fall—before fire and flood takes final hold in this land. Lissane shook her head: she made to reply but the woman raised an arm and Lissane's challenging words froze on her lips.

"Rest easy, girl. I would warn you of perils to come. Gol is on the brink of ruin for the Demon is unleashed, as was foretold. Your sons, Lissane, shall be kings of men, but their kingdom will be far from here. Gol's time is almost over. It shall fall upon you and yours to save what can be saved in that final hour."

Lissane, her eyes adjusting to the night, could see the woman clearer now. She was outlandish, near naked, her skin pale green and translucent, and the veins showing like gossamer threads. Her hair was a tangle of silver coils, unkempt and wild with weed, it covered her bone-skinny frame.

"*War is coming and torment also.*" The woman's voice was everywhere, resonating through the room," *When Ashmali comes you must be ready, daughter.*"

"What must I do...?"

"*When the time comes you will know. Another will visit you then. Until that time you must be strong, Lissane—sister. A period of trial awaits you, and a journey into darkness. Hold to hope and courage, and you will emerge victorious and your seed rule wisely for a thousand years...*"

"Who are you?" Lissane challenged, this dream was even more real than that of her mother. She studied the woman but still couldn't define her face that clearly. Was she old or scarce more than a child? It was impossible to tell. They locked eyes for what seemed an age; finally the woman turned away.

"*I am Rani, a daughter to Zansuat, Lord of the Waves. Below and beyond lies his domain—the endless oceans. Every day my father's kingdom grows—for your lands are sinking. Gol was His once and He will claim it back soon.*

This was old news to Lissane, even the peasants knew that Gol was sinking and one day would disappear entirely. But that day was decades away, not soon. Every year the sea claimed more ground and many places she could remember as a child were now lost forever—but still the process was slow and would take many years.

"*My father would save you and your future seed from the ruin that is coming, Lissane. For you too are of his blood on your dead mother's side. This land is benighted by evil, year by year the Shadowman's hold strengthens—for men are weak.*

"*Only clean water can purge the rot. But your heart is good, Lissane, and you are strong—the task will fall to you and others to save those worth saving. Fear not! We shall guide you in the hour of need.*"

Lissane steered away from that. If this was a dream she would challenge it. "You say that my lover still lives," Lissane heard herself say. "Where can I find him then? What must I do?"

The women didn't reply. It was as if she hadn't heard and was thinking of something else—something sad and still to come.

"I must leave—dawn's light approaches."

Even as she spoke, Rani's features were engulfed by a sudden mist seeping in through cracks in the window panes. It congealed with uncanny speed, filling Lissane's bower with damp, creepy silence, until she shivered, feeling sudden chill. The fret's icy fingers clawed toward her where she lay. Lissane could no longer see the woman, Rani.

She called out but her voice was muffled by the fog. There was no answer...nothing. Long moments passed in troubled gloom. Then a sudden violent wind shook her shutters and the sea fret lifted dispersing as swiftly and silently as it had come.

Outside her window Lissane could now see the sky lightening with dawn's bright promise. The sea woman had gone. Perhaps she had never been there. Nothing appeared as should be. Lissane closed her eyes again. At least in her dreams she could walk with her lover once more.

She pulled the bed covers over her tired body again; whatever this day would bring Lissane Barola wanted little part of it. She slept late. On waking, Lissane saw Bel's kind hazel eyes smiling down on her. She rose and broke her fast, steeling her heart for what was coming. Varentin Gallante.

The strangeness of that night dwindled from her memory in the busy days that followed. But even so Lissane allowed a tiny part of her to hope. If Erun Cade yet lived, then so would she.

***

"Renegade!"

The Witch-Lord's pale eyes were guarded as they locked on Ozmandeus grinning by the doors. "You signed your death warrant returning here. I—"

The words froze on the old man's lips as his body shook with sudden fear. Pressure like hidden steely fingers squeezed his head until he cried out in pain.

"Stop...please stop!"

The hall crackled with sudden fusion, the windows bulged impossibly until their glass imploded inwards, spraying those watching aghast with shards like daggers.

Ozmandeus alone was unaffected by the flying shards. He just laughed, seeing their fear, and then took a step toward the Witch-Lord who now cringed like a broken thing in front of him.

"A fine gathering of fools I see here before me," he scoffed. "Relax. I come in peace." The words had the opposite effect on those gaping at Ozmandeus, though the Witch-Lord no longer gripped his head in pain, the awful pressure having released at a wave from the Renegade's hand.

"Despite your obtuse prejudice and animosity, I hold no grudge," smiled Ozmandeus. "You see, I'm bigger than you are. Stronger. To prove it I have brought you a gift, my former brethren."

Ozmandeus reached deep inside his cloak, exposing the blazing amulet containing the Demon's essence to those watching in horror. Some gasped out loud as that fiery light tore into the hall, while others took to their feet in sudden alarm.

The Witch-Lord's eyes were frosty with loathing. He was afraid—a new emotion for one such as he. That fear made the master of the Citadel hate his former student more than ever. Ozmandeus infused that hatred with relish and challenged it with a triumphant smile.

"Yes, Witchmaster," he laughed, "you were right to call me your most twisted student. See now, what I have achieved whilst you all were sleeping." He lifted the amulet over his head, freeing the heavy gold chain from his thick oily curls. The Renegade's erudite face was hard and his eyes shone with a blazing passion.

"This is Ashmali. An Elemental: last of the great Fire Demons that so long ago purged these countries. He is my captive now. A willing prisoner, I have promised him your souls this very day."

On hearing that the Witch-Lord straightened. Summoning his reserves the grey beard lowered his staff, wording a sharp command. He stopped short when the rod blazed with sudden searing flame. The Witch-Lord yelled, cast it down as though it were a serpent.

But his reactions were much too slow.

The flame was already hunting. Questing, flickering through the hall with fiery stabbing tongues. Ashmali's Breath. It was suddenly everywhere at once, licking and biting—a terrible white-yellow flame.

Fire devoured the golden drapes filtering the sunlight. Flame scoured the walls and floor, greedily eating the rushes that popped and crackled before disappearing in the blaze. The blaze waxed in fury: a living thing, leaping up in sudden joy, licking the emerald robes of the Witch-Lord as he stood, trapped and screaming—unable to move. Those robes melted like liquid jade as the fire delved deeper, hungrily seeking the warm terrified flesh of its first victim.

And then Ashmali fed. The Witch-Lord screamed horribly as his face was burnt away by the flame's scorching claws. Ozmandeus laughed out loud as his former mentor perished. The amulet swelled in size until his hands could hardly contain it. The amber lump blurred and congealed, changing from formless shape into something almost human. Hinting at solidity yet like quicksilver unsubstantial and hard to fathom. Only Ozmandeus could look directly at the Demon. Only he could witness the hunger in those alien amber eyes. And only he could endure the cruel talons and eager flicking tongues.

From those tongues now surged sudden forks of fire, each one claiming a screaming, fleeing sorcerer and reducing them to ashes. The hall was now a frenzied madness. Men and women trampled over each other in their desperate panic to escape. Some made for the far doors, others sought to cast their bodies from the windows—eager to be broken on the rocks below. None succeeded. All were consumed. Ashmali fed and fed and fed. It seemed to last forever, but could only have been a matter of minutes before the flames abated and quiet re-entered the ruined hall.

The sorcerers were consumed and the feared Order no more. The entire Citadel stank of roasted meat and ash. Ozmandeus, his eyes smarting, put forth his iron will to summon the famished Demon back within his curtain of power. He was the Firelord now. He had to be in control all the time—couldn't let Ashmali rule him. Were he to slip for just a second then the Demon would render him to ashes and smoke. He dare not let Ashmali become too powerful else it prove his ruin.

So Ozmandeus chanted the potent words he'd learned over and over, until his throat was red-raw and his voice barely a whisper. At last Ashmali's amber form wavered and withdrew, and his smoky essence shrank back in sullen defeat to the size of a gull's egg—easily contained by the amulet that was his prison. And the walls of the pendant closed hard and unflawed over his flame. And so he became quiet.

But even after he had the Demon safely confined, Ozmandeus could feel Ashmali's angry spirit resisting him and trying to scorch him too. But Ozmandeus was well prepared. Although it was only the first time he had unleashed his Demon, the Firelord had spent long hard months creating his spell-wall. As long as it held strong the Elemental could not harm him. Ashmali was his slave and he the Firelord. The Demon's master who all shall come to fear.

Free us...so we can feed.

The Elemental's voice was almost inaudible—a crackling, hissing whisper. Ozmandeus ignored its protestations and slipped the amulet back over his head. He then held his palm closed over the talisman for long minutes, his dark features taut with concentration and his forehead beaded with sweat. The Renegade winced as the heat of his prisoner's wrath burnt holes into the calluses on his palm. He shut out the pain and instead willed the fiery spirit back to deepest slumber again. It was all about control. He must never drop his guard.

"Sleep, Demon."

Finally Ashmali subsided and withdrew within his prison, defeated, but yet angry and resentful. Ozmandeus could feel Ashmali's hatred glowering as hot coals beneath his cloak.

"I will free you soon, my friend," Ozmandeus told the Demon, as he rubbed his scorched hand and worded a healing spell to moisten the dry broken skin. "But first you must help me conquer my enemies. They are many. We will start with Zorne. After that— who knows?"

In the following months rumours spread east like invisible

fire across the Great Continent, reaching as far as Lamozan City. Men spoke of a new terror ravaging the western lands. Zorne was no more, they said, Spagos all but destroyed by flames. Over time the rumour spread and spread, at last crossing the Lamozan Gap and entering the eastern outposts of the Xandorian Empire. And so in time the Emperor himself was made aware.

Chapter 6

Irulan

Erun Cade woke to pain. Searing, burning agony. His legs felt like molten lead and his face stung as though angry wasps had swarmed over him in his sleep. He groaned and blinked, his eyes eventually opening on a strange place. There was a cool wind on his face and a familiar sound, a soft and constant surge and sigh.

Was he by the sea? Erun turned his head and winced as the hot pain lanced up his legs again. Then his watery eyes caught movement to his left. Erun blinked again.

A stranger watched him from several yards away. An old man, sitting calmly on a hollow sun-bleached log, his wretched thin legs crossed and twiggy-fingers interlaced. A queer creature he appeared to Erun—all bones and tan. The lean face leathery and lined, half hidden beneath peppery grey-white hair and thin wispy beard; the nose hooked blade sharp, and his lips curled thin with a wry almost smug expression.

The stranger's left eye was blue as a blackbird's egg. His right was missing—in its place a hollow pool of scarred, puckered flesh. The grey mass of hair was both shabby and unkempt, like old twisted wire. Matted and filthy, it tangled down well below his knees. The stranger wore only a shabby dirty tunic around his narrow waist made of some bleached cracked animal skin. He stank of weed and rotting fishes.

Erun shuddered. Where was he and who was this ghastly creature? Had the Shadowman taken him? He didn't think so. The Shadowman's realm was said to be dark and cold, here was light aplenty, and a keen salty smell that reassured him again of the sea's closeness. What had happened to him? Erun cursed the pain shooting up his leg as he turned on his side to study the stranger again. The old man said nothing—just watched him in silence from his driftwood perch.

"Who are you?" Erun Cade croaked, finding his voice at last. His mouth was dry and sore and the words felt raw on his blistered lips. "Why are you watching me like that?" Erun didn't know what to make of this ungainly creature. Perhaps he was feverish? Something bad had happened to him—that much was obvious.

"So much for the gratitude of youth." The stranger's voice was sharper than a butcher's knife—it belied his frailty. "I fix him up, feed him on honey and milk, while he fevers and sweats like a hog on heat. What get I in return—heh? Ingratitude and stupid bloody questions: who am I, indeed?"

Erun Cade didn't know what to say. This stranger (though decidedly odd) didn't appear overly dangerous. "Sorry," he muttered through clenched teeth as the pain shot up his legs again. His face wasn't quite so bad now. He could feel something slimy clinging to it. He reached up with a grubby hand.

"Leave it alone!" snapped the stranger as though addressing a tiny child. "Don't fiddle! It's bound to be sore for a time. How are those legs feeling?"

"They hurt," replied Erun.

"Well, of course they hurt. They're going to hurt for some days yet. Most likely get worse before they improve much. They're nasty burns, boy, and you are lucky I got to them in time. But are the wounds healing inside? Do they feel... cooler?"

"I think so," Erun glanced down at his right leg. He winced when he saw the angry scarlet welt, the broken crust of blister and blackening yellow bruise. He surveyed the left leg. That one was even worse. A long scabby scar scored a scarlet, jagged line from just above the knee up toward his groin. Erun was horrified when he noticed just how close to that region the wound traversed, and then blushed when he realised him was naked.

"What happened to my clothes?" Erun demanded of the stranger with an outraged expression.

"How should I know?" his healer snapped. "You were starkers when I found you, laddie."

"What happened to me?" Erun vaguely remembered walking back along the causeway away from the Baron's castle. He'd been with Lissane. They were going to elope that very evening. He had had it all planned. But something must have gone wrong. Horribly wrong—he couldn't recall what. Then he saw Paolo Barola's leering face as he lowered the poker, and the memory of that horror flooded in on him like a tidal wave of despair. Erun screamed and then fainted. Mercifully the blackness claimed him again...

He woke some time later and noticed that the stranger still watched him from his woody perch. This time the dishevelled wretch clutched a wooden harp between his bony fingers, holding onto it guardedly as if someone were about to steal it from him.

It was a shabby instrument of rude design, with odd runic symbols carved all along its arching sides. The strings, though, were taut and toggled at either end.

"You were fortunate, boy," the strange old man told him as he peeled off a perfect note with the harp. The chord hung in the air for several seconds before dwindling and fading off. It sounded oddly familiar to Erun. "Few escape the attentions of Paolo Barola."

"I'm going kill that bastard," replied Erun with sudden violence. He remembered everything now. It were though somehow that clear sharp note had brought back his memory—driven hence into his inner cave by the horror of what had happened that night.

The forge...*they murdered Father.*

His father had tried to save him but the Barola brothers had butchered Garret Cade. Erun felt an icy worm of hate chisel into his heart "I'm going to kill him. And the others—all of them," he told the stranger. He was sitting up now, the brand on his head blazing angry.

"I don't know what she saw in you, boyo." The stranger plucked his harp again, sending another chord out into the atmosphere. Again the sound was familiar. Where had he heard that before?

"What do you mean?" Erun glared at the old man, annoyed by his abrasive manner. The stranger had set aside his harp, and instead, was enthusiastically scratching his vagrant rump with a bony finger, and all the time watching Erun with that weirdly unfathomable, one-eyed stare.

"What are you talking about, old man?" Erun was angry now, and if he could move he would have reached across and hit this obnoxious creature.

"The Baron's blue-eyed daughter, boyo." The stranger curled a thin lip upwards in what might have been a smile, but it was hard to know for sure. On that sour face the expression mirrored a grizzled hound. The vagabond's teeth showed little sign of decay though, which for some reason surprised Erun Cade. "Whatever does she see in you, lanky-lump that you are?"

"You leave her out of this!" Erun Cade bit back. Despite the searing pain up both legs he willed his stiff body into motion and, after a brief struggle, shifted over and then flopped down again, resting his aching back against a log.

The stranger watched his every move with interest, the canine smile still loitering on his lips. Erun glared back at him with fierce defiant eyes. "Who are you, old man?" Erun demanded again. "What do you know about me and Lissane?"

"Scarce more than everyone else in Barola Province, I should think," replied the stranger as though he were addressing a lackwit. "Words spread faster than bush fires. You should have known that, Erun Cade."

"We never told anyone... always took care not to be seen." Erun was on the defensive now; he still couldn't understand how people had found out about him and Lissane. The two of them had been *so* careful. He was suddenly struck by a terrible feeling of guilt. "What about Lissane? What's happened to her? If those bastards have hurt her!"

"You had best forget the Baron's daughter, laddie." The stranger's eye had narrowed to a shrewd glint of sapphire. Erun didn't respond to that. Instead he studied the stranger's face once more, trying to glean what this bizarre creature was all about, and why he would risk the wrath of House Barola by saving a foolish wretch from the gallows, or worse. Erun knew he should be grateful to this peculiar old man, but for some reason he wasn't. Instead, Erun felt both resentful and stroppy.

The stranger's eye had shifted to the clear blue of northern ice. There was knowledge in that gaze, and something else...power. Who was he? Erun, disconcerted, feigned indifference. But he could still feel that icy orb probing him from beneath wintry beetle-brows. Erun suspected there was something unnatural about this old man, something disturbing and not quite right. But he owed him his life and should show some gratitude. Trouble was he didn't feel grateful at this moment. Instead he wanted to strike something and this peculiar old man was the only visible target.

"What have they done to her?" Erun pressed again. He'd made his mind up now. Once his body was healed—and that wouldn't be long—he'd get a sword from somewhere, or an axe, pike, spear; anything sharp and nasty. The sharper and nastier the better. Once armed, Erun would steal into that stinking castle and kill the Baron's three sons; they'd murdered his father—Erun Cade was bound by honour to avenge Garret.

Lissane would understand. She hated her brothers, he'd be doing her a favour too. A strange noise like a bubbly sneeze issued from the direction of his companion. Startled, Erun turned his head; was both surprised and annoyed to see the old man laughing at him. A weird laugh that—a sort of hiccupy wheezy snort.

"You've got some balls, boy—I'll allow you that much," the stranger grinned. "Though, I daresay you would have lost those precious sweetmeats had master Paolo had his way." The stranger wrinkled his nose, which was very long and bent like a twisted dagger. "Do you honestly think you stand a gnat's chance against those three, laddie?" Once again the stranger had read his thoughts. It was disconcerting but Erun held firm.

"I have to try," he replied stiffly. "They killed Father at the forge, and Shadowman knows what they might do to Lissane—be they her brothers or not. Besides," he continued, "they're only two and a half. Garret cut Aldo's hand off before they murdered him."

Erun now recalled how he'd seen that out of the corner of his eye, and remembered grinning despite his agony and fear. But Erun's smile had fled when he saw Paolo cut his father down, and the sweating giant, Rosco, strike the smith's head from his shoulders.

Garret Cade had died like a warrior; Erun Cade owed it to his memory to do the same. He boldly held the stranger's gaze for a moment then turned away, flush-faced. That single eye was so hard to read. Impenetrable and oddly disturbing. Within its depths Erun saw many things: contempt and admiration, mocking humour, silent rage, patience and ageless cruel wisdom—were just a few.

The stranger yawned as one suddenly bored. He scratched his shoulder with a stick he'd retrieved from the stony ground beneath his feet. There was no sign of his harp. Erun had no idea where it had gone. It wasn't like this scruff had copious pockets.

"Don't be daft, laddie," he told Erun, his abrasive voice mellowing slightly. "Aldo Barola one-handed is more than a match for you, and he was always the least dangerous of the trio.

"Young Paolo is the deadliest fighter west of the mountains, only Estorien Sarfe and Clarde Dovess are rumoured greater skilled with blade and bow. You, stripling, wouldn't last five seconds. Besides," he continued, still prodding the stick into the sandy soil at his feet. "You'll need time to heal those lanky legs and build some muscle, you're way too skinny for a warrior. And you need to curb that sulking. What happened was no one else's fault. You tempted fate, boy and she obligingly stung your arse."

Erun's sulk deepened hearing that. "I've never been that interested in fighting, until now." Erun had seen what good fighting did common folk in Barola. Any altercations were dealt with by swift floggings or worse, a prompt termination by rope or axe. Baron Barola did not tolerate insurrection on any level.

"No indeed, but you will be when *she's* finished with you."

"What are you talking about?" Erun was irritated again—in no mood for another mystery. "Who is *she*?" he demanded, lifting a hand to scratch his sore face.

"Leave it alone!" Erun's hand froze. "And enough questions for now." The oldster poked his stick into the earth three times and scraped a weird squiggle that looked like it meant something, although Erun couldn't begin to guess what. After a minute he looked up, appraising the boy with that icy disturbing one-eyed gaze.

"You're hurting, boyo, I know that—who wouldn't be? Don't worry about the baron's daughter; she is made of sterner stuff than you think. Besides, she'll soon be wed to Varentin Gallante. You had best forget Lissane Barola."

Erun was about to challenge that latest statement but the old man waggled a bony hand, dismissing his words before they left his mouth. "Enough, I said. Know when to speak and when to listen."

"Just tell me your name, stranger, and I'll ask no more," promised Erun. In his mind he was already devising a way into Barola Castle without being seen. He had to try something, couldn't let them drag Lissane off to distant Galanais where he'd never set eyes on her again.

"I doubt it," the old man smiled one of his weird crooked smiles. "But I suppose you deserve that much at least." He fiddled with his stick for a moment more, and then cast it aside, glancing slyly across at Erun Cade, who shrugged indifference.

"I've had many names over the years—I'm much older than I appear, laddie. Yes, really..." he scowled, seeing the quizzical expression on Erun's face. "Some call me Irulan. Irulan the Hermit," the stranger told him.

"Though Irulan the Wanderer would probably be more appropriate. I've never been a hermit, antisocial filthy creatures. I spend little time in one place, you see, and like to move around at will.

"But to simplify matters, Irulan the Hermit will suffice. Yes, that will do for now." The self-titled anti-hermit rubbed his hands together and yawned. "Rest for a time now, laddie, else you'll exhaust both of us with your daft questions. Tomorrow we've a journey to make."

"A journey? Where?" Erun didn't feel up to much walking at present.

"Oh, not that far," came the reply. "It's only a brisk walk to my cave up there in the hills. Every pretend hermit has to have a cave, boy. You should know that—bright spark that you are. Make the most of this rest period and you will feel stronger, Master Cade. Tomorrow we commence your training. Now get some sleep."

It was as though the last four words were heavy coins placed on Erun's eyelids. All his pains, questions and concerns fled like wind-blown leaves, leaving instead a deep weariness and contentment. Within seconds he was lost to dreamless sleep.

***

The watchtowers blazed and smoke coiled black over the last ruined village. Six hamlets had now fallen to his fury, and only two days passed since his return to the mainland. The few guards and villagers left breathing were now chained and collared—he would have a use for them later. They knelt cowed and weeping, slaves awaiting that dark purpose. The rest were broken, ruined bodies.

Those had dared challenge his arrival. Some he'd impaled on stakes, whilst others were hanging from creaking gibbets, where crow and vulture gathered greedily to feed. Their souls he would claim with his necromantic arts, when time allowed.

Man, woman, and child: their life forces would fuel his power, serving him in death as they couldn't in life. Ozmandeus would come back for them in due course, but now he had another task.

If Zorne City was to crumble it would take more than just his cunning and spell craft. Ozmandeus would need aid. His sorcery was strong but those walls had never fallen to wizard or army, and he dare not unleash Ashmali until the chosen time. If he peaked too early it would end in disaster.

There was another way. He still had useful contacts from earlier days before his self-imposed exile. At that time Ozmandeus had been just another power hungry noble, not fully skilled as a warlock: he'd often needed the help of armed men to acquire what he needed for his swift ascension. His hunger for knowledge had driven him to attend witch-school at the Citadel. Despite his new knowledge he needed an army to achieve the ground work. The answer was easy.

Mercenaries. There were many in Zorne, hard fighting men who would willingly rally to his raven banner. Ozmandeus had always paid well in the past, and Zorne's proud denizens were hated by many in the hinterlands. The rewards would be great for any fighting man stout enough of heart to follow where Ozmandeus led them.

There had been one particular captain. A killer black of heart, resourceful and ruthless and...useful. The Renegade had employed his skills before. He now recalled the brigand's stronghold lay quite close to this village, away off in the hills—perhaps ten miles or so. That captain would do anything for gold, and his men had been a scourge upon Zorne's peasant folk for years.

In time Ozmandeus would not need such carrion-fighters in his employ. But that time was still some way off. He must be wary in these early days. The warlocks of the Citadel were no more but there were others in Zorne, and beyond. He dare not arouse their suspicions until he was ready to destroy them utterly.

First he had to master Ashmali completely, so that he could channel the Demon without any risk to himself. That would take time and patience. In the meantime he would need soldiers—a trained disciplined army fit to conquer.

East beyond the mountains sprawled the Xandorian Empire: powerful, brutal and commanding ten times the military strength he could hope to raise—even after Zorne's destruction and his resurrecting those earlier slain. Ozmandeus must needs tread carefully, lest the Emperor hear of his movements and send an army or two through the Lamozan Gap.

The Xandorian Elite were feared by all—and wisely too. In time Ozmandeus would be strong enough to face down the Empire—they would learn to fear him. In time. First things first. He must deal with his enemies in Zorne City—the lords and petty nobles that had laughed him out of court when he had chosen to pursue the necromantic arts, scoffing and deriding his wide ambitions. That would take careful planning.

Ozmandeus grinned as he hoisted his lean frame up into the high saddle of the black courser he had stolen from the captain at the last watchtower. Destroying the Citadel had been joyous, but Zorne City's annihilation would put paid to the last of his enemies. Then would his vengeance would be complete.

With Ashmali tamed and slave to his will, Ozmandeus would gain further lands. How the war-crows would flock to his calling! All would fear him—even the Emperor in his jade palace would quake at the mention of the new Firelord of Zorne.

Ozmandeus winced in sudden pain, feeling the amulet burn into his chest as the Demon stirred.

"Soon," he told his creature. "Soon, I'll let you feed again, Ashmali." The Renegade ignored the scorching pain and blinding headache brought on by his willing the creature to quiet. Soon he would be master. He need only hold his nerve, and steer with cunning.

Ozmandeus forced a tight smile, channelled his pain into anger and dug in his heels, letting the courser's hoof-beats take him far from the choking stench of corpse and village. Behind him, a cloud of carrion clustered in his wake, cawing and swooping hungrily—sensing that the blood-fest had only just began.

Chapter 7

The Cave

When Erun woke it was under the bright scrutiny of late summer morning. He did feel better, much stronger and his legs less sore than they had been, although they still stung mercilessly. He had some kind of shabby yellowish shawl covering his body—quite where the hermit had acquired that from was yet another mystery.

Erun shoved all such questions aside. He was hungry. Adding to that the morning was already warm and he desired to feel the sun on his aching limbs. He hoisted up the moth-eaten shawl and winced.

Looking down at his scarred legs, Erun noticed that the hermit had put some more slimy stuff on them. It looked revolting—a yellowy-green congealed ooze that smelt of decaying meat, or worse. But whatever it was—it worked. The blisters had shrunk and the scar tissue almost healed together, though here and there a bead of puss still wept through.

Whatever else he may be, this Irulan was a healer of remarkable skill. Erun should have felt grateful but he didn't. He just sat moping under the morning sun.

Irritable and itchy, Erun decided it was time to attempt movement. He placed his hands on a large rock behind him and pushed. Using his arms as levers Erun hoisted his body erect, wincing as the sharp tearing pain lanced up his legs. He stood leaning, wobbling, fighting the pain for a time and grimacing; and then ready at last, Erun let go of the rock, allowing his feet to take his full body weight.

Erun felt dizzy for a moment or two and swayed a bit, but despite that managed to stay on his feet. He was grinning like a vacant loon when Irulan appeared with a large bundle of garments, which he tossed at Erun's feet. Added to these was a dry hunk of crusty loaf, this the boy caught one-handed when the hermit launched it his way. As with the shawl, Erun was at a total loss to know how Irulan had acquired food and garb in this barren place. He glanced down at the clothes as though they were adders coiling toward him.

"You're up I see," Irulan grunted. "That's good and not before time. And what are you gawping at?" The hermit awarded his charge a withering glance. "Eat that bread and put those clothes on, laddie," he said. "You'll need your strength today, and it won't help getting your arse burnt by the sun, either, let alone those healing bean-sticks supporting it."

Erun gnawed at the bread and pulled a face when he saw the quality of the garments lying at his feet. The brown tunic was leather and faded and full of holes. The woollen grey-green leggings looked like they'd been gnawed at by rats. How was he supposed to pull those wretched things on anyway?

Erun munched and swallowed his breakfast, ignoring the beady gaze that clocked his every movement. The pretend hermit scratched his left ear and muttered obscenities, until Erun, realising that there was no point arguing, shrugged and reached down for the clothes.

He dressed slowly, taking great care not to catch his wounds on the baggy cloth—Irulan watching over him like a disapproving crow. When Erun finally strapped the things to his waist (and that only after an endless struggle of cursing and wincing, and with Irulan tutting and muttering) he discovered that the leggings stopped full six inches above his ankles and looked beyond ridiculous. But it was better than being naked at least—a small kind of progress.

Aside from these awful clothes were two shabby knee-length boots and a floppy leather hat. It didn't make for a pretty sight. Irulan caught his look and glared at him.

"Well, what's the problem now?" he enquired. Erun said nothing but his face looked longer than his trousers. "Why are you standing there gaping like a sun-dried toad?" demanded his healer. "Come on! We've a journey to make—and quickly."

"I...my legs...you said I would need time to heal," complained Erun. Irulan awarded him that cold eye and then shook his head in disgust. He mumbled something about gratitude and then without further fuss, briskly turned his back on the youth and commenced the long trek up from the stony beach and wooded valley that had been their home for the last week.

Erun's legs were sore and aching but he was surprised to discover that he could walk without too much difficulty and, as the warm summer's day dwindled towards afternoon, he felt stronger than he had that morning. Whatever that foul stuff was that Irulan had spread on his legs it certainly worked miracles. For the first time since his ordeal at the forge, Erun Cade felt a glimmer of hope.

The beach was far behind them now, though Erun could still see its sandy ribbon framing the vast expanse of blue beyond whenever he glanced back. They cleared the rooky woods and skirted the Baron's vineyards covering the fertile fields south of the castle.

Irulan set a merciless pace, never once turning to check if his charge was keeping up. By evening their road led up into brown dusky hills, and before long the way became steep and Erun, puffing and sore, was pushed to keep apace with his wiry, whip-lean companion. Despite the incline, his legs were still holding out well and he felt remarkably good considering his trauma.

Throughout the walk Erun had been planning and plotting in silence. He'd made his mind up to stay a few days, learn what he could from this uncanny old pseudo hermit. Then he would slip away at a given moment and be about his vengeance. Quite how to achieve that Erun wasn't sure—not having fathomed that bit out yet. It would come to him when he needed it—you have to be confident about these things.

Erun studied the stick twig-thin, tanned back of the old hermit, as he hopped goat-like between thorn, bramble and briar. Irulan had barely uttered three words all day; he seemed edgy and impatient as if many things were on his mind. Erun was determined to find out more about his odd companion when they reached their destination—if they ever did.

It was getting dark when they finally arrived at Irulan's hidden cave. Erun had stumbled into its yawning mouth before he realised it, so well disguised was the cavern's entrance. There was just enough light to see that they had passed beneath a great fissure in the hillside; here, two rocks leant against each other like drunken sleeping giants.

Clutches of thorn covered the entrance, disguising it from the straying eye. Inside the cave opened to a wide basin of smooth limestone. Here and there were pots and things and general clutter. A worn rug covered a large part of the stone floor. High above them a smoke hole chimeyed up through the rock, allowing the dim evening light to filter down and cast dancing dust motes awhirl. Glancing up, Erun caught the bright glint of a distant star.

Irulan signalled Erun take his seat on the rug and wait, resting his limbs. The hermit ventured off to gather a few dry sticks he'd prepared before. He returned within minutes and soon had a hearty blaze underway. Erun said nothing, he rubbed his legs which were itching now that he'd stopped walking. Irulan glanced his way and pinned him with that steely stare.

"You hungry, boyo?"

"Yes." Erun had completely forgotten about food. Saving the stale bread this morning, they hadn't eaten anything all day, and for that matter the day before. Now all of sudden food was all he could think about.

"Good," grunted the hermit. "That's good—you heal fast. That healing jelly usually stays a man's appetite for several days." He reached down and retrieved a sizeable pebble from the floor, before turning quick as a snake, and hurling it at Erun's startled face. The boy barely caught it before it impacted with his nose. "Your training starts now," the almost-hermit told him. "There are coneys out there gawping at the stars. Go brain a couple."

Erun gaped for a minute in disbelief. He hadn't expected to be the one providing supper. He was a poet, not a bloody cook.

"You still there?" snapped Irulan. Erun swore under his breath and then, wearily taking to his feet again, stormed out on the quest for dinner. Half hour later he returned with a brace of rabbits slung limp over his shoulder. He felt very pleased with himself.

"What you grinning at?" Irulan snatched the rabbits from him, and set about skinning them with a sharp knife he'd got from somewhere in the cluttered cave. Within minutes he had the meat well underway, spitting and turning over the bright crackle of flame.

Erun was ravenous by the time the rabbits were cooked. Neither of them spoke until their meal was nothing more than a collection of crunched bones. It was some time later that Irulan turned to him, his single gaze reflecting the firelight's glow.

"You had some questions, I recall?"

Erun was caught off guard. "I...I never thanked you for saving me," he said. "I mean back at the forge...you must have just walked in. How did you come to rescue me from *them*?"

Irulan leaned back against the wall of the cave and sighed as though suddenly weary. The firelight crackled and hissed, casting flicking shadows across his features awarding him a wild demonic look.

"I was close by when I heard raised voices and the sound of a struggle," Irulan told him. "Curious, I took a look in at the forge. I took stock quickly. It was apparent I could do nothing while the brothers were still there, but when they left you in the hands of their servant I acted swiftly, squirreling you away while he was off seeing to your father's stiffening corpse. He was going to slit your throat wide open, boyo. I managed to dissuade him."

"You killed Grudge?" Erun found that impossible to believe. Grudge was feared by everyone in Barola Town. Only Paolo and the Baron were held in more dread by the townsfolk. Master Grudge had a nasty reputation. Were half of it true, he was not a man to accost.

"I didn't need to." Irulan was smiling that lopsided smile again. "I put it in his head to see to your father first, and when he returned we were well away, and this Grudge in no mind to linger. I left my music in the trees, you see, he was well spooked when he left the glade."

Put it in his head...music..?

Erun had no idea what to make of any of this but he decided to let it go. "You say that you are a traveller, Irulan, but you appear to know a lot about Barola and its citizens. How did you find out about Lissane and me?"

"I've been frequenting these parts for a while now," Irulan responded matter of factly. "I find that it pays to know what your neighbours are about—lest they catch you off guard. You know... do something unpredictable. It's why I avoid people on the whole. They can be quite peculiar and sometimes do the oddest things.

Yes and you're a fine one to notice. Erun pulled a splinter of bone out from a gap in his teeth. He yawned, feeling suddenly sleepy. Irulan's gaze was on the fire.

"As for you and the Baron's girl," Irulan snorted derision. "A young love so bright shines out for all to see. There were many watching you pair, I'd warrant. Most kept their teeth together, fearing Barola's wrath turn on them too, were he to discover your indiscretions. You were both stupid on that causeway. Lissane particularly should have known better. It was obvious someone from the castle would see you looning over her and dribbling."

Erun, flushed and angry though he was, couldn't challenge that. He was curious though as to how this oddball pretend hermit knew about it. The old sod must have been on one of his rare trips to town. Looking back, Erun felt an utter fool for his reckless behaviour in front of Eon Barola's walls.

He felt guilt too. His father would still be alive were it not for his idiotic actions that day. "It was just that I loved her...love her," he responded lamely. "I could think of nothing else but spending my life with her, and bugger everyone else and what they thought."

"Instead you were the one that was buggered," scoffed Irulan.

"Well, almost anyway. Those scratches on your legs are nothing, boyo; Master Paolo had only just got started. They branded your face—do you remember that?"

"Aye, and it still burns—though not as badly as my legs did." Erun gently ran a finger along the lumpy swelling that blistered up from his left eye to the greasy hairline above. The skin felt puckered and swollen but there was little pain. Irulan's alchemy had worked wonders here too. Still, he could have so easily lost an eye. Erun glanced at the old man's missing orb and shuddered.

"That mark will be your constant companion," Irulan told him. "Let it serve as a reminder that folly is not affordable in these tempestuous times."

"You speak of lessons," Erun said. "What is it you would have me learn, and why bother...I mean, you don't appear the sociable, kindly type. Why spend time on a lovesick fool?"

"It is the duty of the old to guide the young—whether they are foolhardy and vain, or else completely idiotic as in your own case," Irulan responded with a slight smile, whilst Erun pulled a face.

"Suffice to say I was looking for an apprentice—someone to pass on my copious knowledge of lore and wisdom, and while I still have my wits about me, and still just enough flesh sticking to my bones to keep me alive."

Erun couldn't stifle the smirk. "An apprentice hermit—*how wonderful*," he added, gingerly scratching the scabs on his forehead.

"Leave that!" Erun stopped in mid itch. "And you can wipe that gormless grin off your face too. I'm not a sodding hermit, it's just a disguise—I told you as much. You stand to learn much from me, boy. If you keep your head together."

Erun didn't respond, just glared daggers into the fire. Irulan continued in a softer voice. "I was a soldier once, laddie." Irulan sighed as if he too were suddenly weary. "And other things. I've seen a lot, you'd be surprised." He scratched his ear and farted enthusiastically.

"But then, who are you really? And why chose me when you know my heart is on other matters?"

"I don't give a toss where your heart is," Irulan croaked like a soggy crow. "Who am I and why choose you? That's for me to know and you to find out—if you're smart enough. You've a deal to learn about this world and how to stay alive in it. I will do my best, although it pains me."

"We'll start your training here in this cave," Irulan informed him, "and then, when you can take a piss without soaking your leg, and maybe know a thing or two about staying alive. Then, boy, when I deem you ready, you will journey north to *her* island. She will teach you the finer details. She is good at the finer details and she owes me a favour or two."

"If I go anywhere it will be back to Castle Barola to take my revenge on the Baron's sons," challenged Erun. "I must avenge my father, Irulan, so that his shade can rest. You must understand that, being an old soldier."

"I understand that you are a lump-head and a mother's tit, boy," responded Irulan with a snort. "It may happen that one day you do cross blades with House Barola's charming sons. But that time is far from now. There are legion skills you must learn in battle craft: survival, tenacity; endurance and cunning are just a few. Then you will need experience. Are you listening, boyo?"

Erun was feeling very sleepy now. He didn't want to keep challenging this strange old man that had saved him, and who still apparently wanted to help him—the gods alone knew why. Besides there was something unnerving about his new acquaintance. Erun sensed that Irulan the (not really a) hermit was not one to cross. He'd have to pay back the debt he owed the old man for his life, but that could wait. Vengeance could not.

I'll just pick my time and slip away in a few days when the old boy's nodded off.

"Aye, get some sleep," grunted Irulan, his glinting eye had narrowed to a probing slit of cobalt. "We'll be up before dawn breaks." The words had barely passed from Irulan's lips before Erun sank into a warm welcome sleep. He woke once, heard the old man muttering something in the dark.

"Scaffa, you bitch, you're going to love this one. Keep your legs closed though, I know what you're like with the young ones."

were the only words Erun made out before sleep claimed him like a tidal wave again.

***

Maelchor watched as horse and rider crested the rise leading up and across to his gates. His heart missed a beat. He knew that horseman. Ozmandeus, a former noble who had left the mainland to pursue a career on that dreadful island where the witch-lords prowled.

A clever twisted man, Ozmandeus was hated by those ruling Zorne City. Fearing his many plots against them they had sent soldiers to raid his castle in the south. They'd found nothing, Ozmandeus having fled to the island. Rumour was he'd been banished from there too. Maelchor wasn't overly surprised, he'd done a few jobs for this Ozmandeus back when the ambitious lord was conducting raids against Spagos for funds and spoil, his black heart ever on undermining those that mocked him up in Zorne City. He'd been a good payer but it was never easy work. Ozmandeus was a wasp in a room. You could never relax when he was around.

Maelchor was a hard man but even he could not quell a shiver when he felt the raw power radiating across to him from the swiftly approaching rider.

What's this you have brought upon us, warlock?

The captain told off two guards, bidding them unlatch the heavy steel-studded gates, and allow their visitor into the bailey. Ozmandeus ignored the guards as he urged his horse beneath the iron portcullis, and up and across to where the captain now stood waiting. Ozmandeus vaulted from his saddle and Maelchor, watching on, motioned an attendant see to the sweating horse.

He studied the lean features of his former employer as Ozmandeus strode purposeful toward him. The Renegade looked much older, but then ten years had passed since he'd left Zorne to pursue his cursed sorcerer's arts. The eyes were the same though, coaly black, avaricious and predatory.

The close-cropped beard was frosted with recent grey, and dark shadows sunk beneath those hungry scary eyes. Maelchor was a big man but Ozmandeus towered over him. The captain folded his arms and rested a light palm on the carved vulture head that served as his sword pommel. His sharp mind was a jumble of emotions: excitement, anticipation and fear being foremost.

"Maelchor, we meet again." The Renegade thrust out a gloved hand and Maelchor clasped it in his own. He motioned his steward to prepare food and wine, and then asked politely that his guest follow him inside the bailey. There was a strange heat radiating from Ozmandeus and the sorcerer looked as though he were in pain. Maelchor thought to enquire after his health, but something stopped him—best leave that be. Inside, a hot meal and cool wine awaited. They talked long into the night.

"How many..?" Ozmandeus demanded of Maelchor after their discussion reached a satisfactory end. Outside dawn gilded the fields, banishing shadows to the deep woods covering the valley below.

"Two thousand—perhaps three," replied the captain. "But I will need time, Lord."

"Time you shall have—but don't tarry," responded Ozmandeus. "Three thousand mercenaries should prove sufficient," he added.

"Where is this fortress you so yearn to break? It must be rich indeed to fill the coffers of three thousand, gold-hungry fighting men."

"It is rich beyond your dreams, Maelchor." The Renegade sipped the last of his wine, a slight smile lifting the right corner of his upper lip.

"It is called Zorne City."

Maelchor's eyes widened in alarm. *Is he insane?* "It would take a force of twenty thousand men to take Zorne City—and even then? It has never fallen, Lord."

The Renegade pinned him with that relentless stare. "Do you doubt me, captain?"

"No...I just—"

Ozmandeus stood; stretched his lean body. "I must be away, I've many things to attend." As he moved, Maelchor caught a glimpse of the amber amulet hanging from Ozmandeus's chest. He felt suddenly afraid—an emotion he'd not known for many years. That amulet contained something unnatural, Maelchor felt certain of it. Something evil. He pulled his gaze away, annoyed by the stab of irrational fear gripping his loins and urging him to run for the privy.

The captain struggled to his feet; dusted off his breeches, trying vainly to disguise his discomfort. "I'll get them to bring your horse across," Maelchor said, relieved that his guest was departing.

Ozmandeus turned to study him with those coaly chilling eyes. "I trust that I can rely on your loyalty, captain—for old time's sake?

Maelchor nodded, feeling increasingly uncomfortable beneath that stare. "Oh, and fret not, my doubting friend, three thousand freebooters shall prove sufficient for the task ahead—you will see."

Maelchor wanted to challenge that but his mouth felt tinder dry. He kept it shut, and instead, glanced again at the amulet which Ozmandeus was now caressing with his right hand, as though it were a woman's breast. The mercenary captain shuddered and quickly turned his gaze away. What evil had this warlock brought upon them? Maelchor stood to get rich—that he didn't doubt. But at what cost to his soul?

He was glad when Ozmandeus departed the bailey—as were his men. They too had felt the awful power emanating from the sorcerer's person, and though all were tough veterans of many campaigns, it had unsettled them to a man.

Once finished with the privy, Maelchor banished the disquiet from his mind. There was much to be done. Time to gather a fighting force from old confederates and allies. But what could he tell them? That a crazed insecure warlock proposed they sack Zorne City? No, he'd find another way.

The funny thing was he no longer doubted they would succeed in this rash venture. The Renegade's confident smile had convinced him. That and the Demon sleeping on his chest. For surely only a Demon from the ancient world could radiate such malevolent power.

Maelchor watched from his high tower, saw Ozmandeus's

courser canter briskly toward the rising sun, He stared on until horse and rider were both lost beneath its golden glare, his gaze lingering until only the white dust kicked up by the beast's hooves showed in the brightness of morning. Ozmandeus had gone—for now.

In the following weeks steel clashed on steel, as men practised hard in the training fields below the bailey. As days followed nights, more men arrived to pitch tents outside his walls. Autumn beckoned, the host surrounding Maelchor's bailey waxed two thousand strong. And still they came: the gold-hungry—murderers, rapists and killers every one.

Chapter 8

The Galanians

Prince Varentin Gallante reined in his horse as his father's entourage crested the rise, stopping for a moment to survey the terrain unravelling ahead of them. Below and beyond, the foothills of the mountains forked down into steep wooded valleys, eventually reaching the wide, sweeping curve of blue-green water that must surely be Barola Bay.

Varentin was a stranger to this eastern region of Gol, although his father had visited the Barola clan often in the years following the Rebellion. He and Eon had been fast friends during that earlier time. That friendship had waned recently, due to the political pressures and widening mistrust that had evolved as each ruler sought gain from his neighbour.

It was only to be expected: Galania traded with Treggara, and the Barolans had been quarrelling with that province for a half score years. His father and Eon Barola had steered clear of each other in recent times, their old friendship declining into mistrust and frosty resentment. At last year's Games outside Torvosa Castle, Baron Barola had shunned the Prince, and instead favoured his arch foe, Baron Sarfe and his son Estorien, (who Varentin particularly despised) with polite discussion. Varentin had commented on that to his father, but the serene Hal Gallante had just shrugged in reply.

But that was last year—dead and gone. Politics was always changing in Gol, and this proposed betrothal (Prince Gallante had told his only son during their journey) would be more than useful for Galania. Baron Barola was a shifty ambitious snake, better kept close and on side—so his father had said.

Varentin hadn't really listened though. This recent proposal of wedlock to the Barolan girl held little interest to him; almost it could be happening to someone else. He would do his duty, of course. Tupping the wench now and then wouldn't be a bother. He'd get her broody and swelling, then return to his usual diversions. And Varentin had lots of those.

This trip was irksome, however. Varentin hadn't wanted to make the long arduous journey across the mountains, had rather suggested that the girl be brought to Galanais, amid regal pomp for a betrothal worthy of his high state. It seemed wrong to Varentin that his noble father had to reach out to these Barolans, who, compared to his own people, were rustic and crude—to say the least.

The whole business reeked of the kind of bland diplomacy that Varentin abhorred. He wiped the sweat from his brow with a gloved finger and then cast a dispassionate eye on the landscape below. He could see the Baron's castle away off in the distance—scarce more than a square, ugly rock, jutting out of the water at the southern end of the bay. It looked forlorn and unimpressive compared to the ornate towers and sparkling marble walls of Galanais City, his home.

And we are to be received in such a place...

Straining his eyes, Varentin Gallante, could just make out the breaking line of water where it met with the causeway, foaming and crashing onto the stone. The tide was still out, but they would need to hurry; the Gallantes had no wish to overnight in Barola Town. Not for Prince Varentin and his sire the idle chatter of the small folk. He turned to his father, who sat on his mare in arrogant silence beside him.

Hal Gallante looked as dignified and poised as ever. His fine silver hair spilled out from beneath the burnished, horsehair crested helm; and his polished steel hauberk, and plate mail glittered with sapphires and emeralds. The viridian cloak Hal Gallante wore covered both the prince and his silver bridled-steed below, and the long, curved sword at his waist was crusted with jewels from Rakeel.

As always, Varentin felt a pale shadow beside his father. Though his own attire was hardly less magnificent, with matching cloak and tunic of soft saffron wool, and striped baggy leggings of blue kidskin, swallowed by long, black riding boots engraved with filigree of golden lace.

Varentin didn't cut such a magnificent figure. He lacked his father's aquiline features and clear green eyes. Varentin's eyes were dark brown—like his mother's—and his hair was long and glossy black; with sharp widow's peak, and already thinning dome. His almost handsome, petulant face showed pale beneath the heavy ornate helm, and Varentin wore his silver hauberk with determined discomfort. This younger Gallante felt more at ease with the silk and velvets he favoured, when at court in far off Galanais.

Oh, to be back there...

Varentin glanced back at the column of soldiers filing behind, some two hundred strong. They looked disciplined and smart in their green cloaks, and highly polished steel helms and breastplates, the long spears slanted over their left shoulders and oval shields slung across their burnished backs.

Those shields all bore the emblem of his father—a white ship crossing green ocean. Theirs was a party strong enough to impress Baron Barola and his clan, but not so many as to harbour his suspicions. Eon Barola was renowned for his mistrustfulness, and Prince Hal Gallante had instructed his retinue to be polite and civil at all times.

That caused rancour in Varentin also, the heir to Galanais saw no reason to court friendship with this uncouth robber-baron and his shoddy, rustic household. This latest fractious alliance had only been achieved over the last few months. Hal Gallante still traded with Treggara, but that troublesome stone had been laid to rest for the time.

The betrothal of Varentin and Lissane Barola had been arranged in secret by the two rulers, without any word getting out to the other barons. Varentin had shown little interest in it. They said that the girl was blessed with beauty. So what? He had his other diversions. They had pretty slaves aplenty of either sex in Galanais, each one highly skilled in carnal practice. If they failed to please him, Varentin did away with them, and the methods he employed brought some satisfaction. There were so many ways to end a life. That kept them keen to please and...*imaginative*. This Barola girl would have to work hard to satisfy his many appetites.

Mother will school her well...

Prince Hal Gallante raised a gauntleted arm to his men and then heeled his grey mare down the steep slope, leading to the nearest cleft of woodland. Prince Varentin waited a moment longer as if unwilling to continue. He scowled, then urged his mount forward, signalling haughtily to their escort to follow on behind, although they were doing so already.

They filed down the nearest valley—a gleaming snake of steel and gold—and after a time emerged resplendent in the evening sun. The woods had now given way to ordered fields of tilled grain, and rows of olive and orange trees—their boughs weighed down with late summer fruit.

Small folk watched them pass, their peasant eyes wide and excitable, as they gaped in awe at the stunningly clad riders wending their way down toward the Baron's town and castle on the shoreline. Varentin spared them not a glance, though many a maiden fluttered long lashes at him and dared to smile.

By the time the Galanians reached Barola Town the water was spilling over the causeway. Hal Gallante never hesitated for a moment: he spurred his beast forward and the party from Galania splashed and trotted across the breakwater, making in orderly fashion toward the distant castle perched gloomily on its blunt square rock—a half mile or so ahead.

As he cantered behind his father, Varentin Gallante felt the cold seawater soak into his boots and drench his thighs, as the eager waves reclaimed the causeway. He shivered and glanced ahead at the lofty castle walls, feeling little warmth emanating from that direction. A few lights winked from the high keep dominating the castle's southern flank, but all else loomed silent and grey.

Barola Castle—perched on its rock like a beached leviathan, a squat pile of unimagined granite, its flanks patrolled and hemmed on all sides by crashing wave and spume. Varentin thought of far off Galanais, a place of intricate beauty, dazzling wealth and sophistication. At Galanais, the palace, citadel and castle main all melded into stone perfection. This place... if the Baron's daughter was as ugly as his castle she'd get scant service from him.

They reached the outer bailey as the sea swallowed the last weed-strewn ribbon of the causeway's crown. Barolan guards flanked their approach on both sides of the entrance, garbed in garish tabards of scarlet and black—Barola's colours. The long drawbridge spanning the gap between bailey and main castle was lowered swiftly for them to continue forward.

Despite its grim countenance Castle Barola boasted strength with its lofty walls and towering Keep. Washed by waves on all sides, such a stark stronghold would withstand months of siege craft—Varentin allowed it that much. But then who would want to take such a dung heap anyway?

The castle was barbed by inner and outer portcullis; murder holes shed light from above, and the walls were thick and damp. A grim place to attack, yes, Varentin conceded moodily as he guided his steed beneath the inner portcullis, and then on through the dank tunnel emerging inside the main castle at last.

Barola was waiting for them in the courtyard, two of his sons by his side. The baron wore a patient, measured smile, with scarlet-clad arms folded, and stout legs braced even. His garb was of plain wool and leather, red and black, with longsword at his hip—a complete contrast to the richly clad retinue from Galania. The Baron oozed confidence though. This Barola was a tough bastard, Varentin had heard.

The younger prince reined in his horse alongside his father.

He studied their host's household. Here stood men at arms, country nobles, servants and womenfolk also. There was no sign of
anyone fitting Lissane Barola's description. Was the girl not present to welcome her intended? Such an insult was not to be borne.
Varentin Gallante steadied his horse and glared at the Barolans
with deep mislike. Behind him the last of the riders filed in, and
Barola whistled across to the stablemen to see to their horses.
Varentin dismounted and tossed the reins to a boy. His father was
already speaking to Barola.

***

Eon Barola had watched with calm dispassion as the peacock
procession of riders clattered out of the tunnel, entering into his
castle as though it were their own. He disliked Prince Gallante and
trusted him not at all—despite their closeness in the heady years
following the King's fall.

The Galanians were all show; there was no real substance to
any of them. Their ruler, the only self-styled 'prince' in Gol, opined
himself above all other men. Toreno Dovess was generally held to
be the noblest born ruler in Gol, and he was only a duke. After the
Rebellion, Hal Gallante had bestowed himself with a new title to
match his swelling ego.

This Gallante was anything but gallant. The Galanian ruler
was both proud and aloof, and his lady, the Chatelaine Sophistra,
known mostly for her skill in subtle poisons.

Sophistra was feared by all at court in Galanais—and rightly
so. She was far more cunning than her husband and those that
crossed her soon disappeared. Sophistra was a conniver who
played her husband well. She fawned on Varentin, but her daughter she ignored. But then no one took much note of Morwella. The
girl child was rumoured half mad and spitefully capricious. Such
was House Gallante.

None of this concerned Eon Barola. What did interest him were
power and control, and a profitable trade access with the affluent
west. Galania had gained much from her closeness to Rakeel and the
Xandorian Empire. That relationship was something Eon coveted.

Xandoria across the Shimmering Sea, ruling an empire so vast and wealthy it was hard to imagine. The Xandorians had invaded Gol back in the old days when Flaminius's grandsire ruled strong in Torvosa. Three times his knights had sent them packing. But back then the kings were strong. Now there were no knights anymore, their class being banned when the barons took control, among them Eon Barola. But they didn't need knights these days. They needed poison and cunning and sharp silent steel.

And Barola needed allies across the sea.

With Lissane settled comfortably in Galanais, and acting as his eyes and ears, Eon could play the Galanians at will. In time he'd cement a deal with the Xandorians that would eventually bypass Galania Province. He'd undercut their prices and make the long voyage around Gol's southern coast a viable option.

Xandoria had no shortage of mercenaries and Eon had a growing need for fighting men. Hal Gallante was too obtuse to see through the Barolan's schemes, Sophistra too wrapped up in her intrigues at court. That said, Lissane would have to keep her guard up while she was around. The Galanians' weakness was that they thought they were strong. They were rich certainly, but overconfident and proud.

Eon Barola knew his own strength. Hal Gallante was a richly-clad bag of wind. One *well placed needle...* Lissane would get over her current obtuseness when she realised her potential as spouse to Galania's heir. She was sharp enough to succeed with his tasks, having both discretion and cunning.

In time, through Lissane's gathered knowledge and subtle dispatches, Barola would open direct discussion with Rakeel, and begin undercutting the Galanians, thus neutering their hold on trade with the Empire.

Eon needed weaponry and fighting men aplenty if he were to win this war with Treggara. But there were other reasons too. Across the sea lay the answer to his ambitions. There was wealth and power to be gained from good relations with Xandoria. Once Treggara was dealt with, and with Hal Gallante in tow, he could turn his attentions toward Torvosa. Within five years all Gol would be his. Of course the Xandorians would want something in return. Simple. He'd give them Galanais.

The Baron studied the younger Gallante. He had never met Varentin, though his boys had come to know him during their feasting and wenching at the Games. Varentin was a year or so older than Lissane, and looked both indolent and ill at ease—which suited Eon Barola well.

A mere shadow of his father, Lissane would play this one without too much trouble. She would have to watch the mother, though. Sophistra would prove her biggest challenge, that bitch would be watching her every move. But Lissane had her father's tenacity. Next to Paolo she was his brightest child. Lissane would survive in Galanais, he felt sure of it. And if she failed there were other ways.

She was only a daughter. No great loss to House Barola, though he was fond of her despite her insubordinate nature. Moreover, should his daughter come to harm it would give Eon an excuse to seek aid from Dovesi Province in taking his revenge.

Toreno was too much of a nobleman to refuse him. It didn't matter which city fell first: Torvosa or Galanais. Either way, Barola would be the winner. Once settled, he'd remarry and sire more children. He was still young enough. In a short while Eon would influence power both sides of the mountains. The south would crumble. The north? Only Rodrutha would remain hostile and no one gave a toss about Rodrutha these days.

The Baron smiled his warmest welcome as he waited for the Galanian lords to dismount and settle. The soldiers looked good in their sparkling white and green, their discipline having improved since the old days, but Eon reckoned his men would cut through them like so much chaff in harvest time.

They were noisy and haphazard compared to his fighters. Soft too in their appearance, like their ruler, grown fat on trade and spoil—with every comfort made available to them. Every Barolan man-at-arms was worth three of these handsome jays. It was good to see. Eon cast an eye at his people who waited in respectful silence for these exotic guests to organise and preen themselves into a formal greeting (a process that seemed to take forever.) He turned to Paolo, who stood behind him with arms folded in leisurely manner. Paolo was grinning openly at the clatter and chatter of this visiting party.

"Where is your sister?" Eon Barola demanded of his son in sharp whispered tones. "She should be here."

"I've no idea, Father," replied Paolo. "Perhaps she is overcome with delight at her forthcoming nuptial to this paragon from Galanais." His cat-green eyes hid none of the contempt he felt for Varentin Gallante and his father.

"Go, get her and be quick about it—lest they take umbrage," the Baron growled. Eon could feel his irritation growing every second. *How dare she thwart my will in this, these Galanians won't take kindly to her absence. Damn the girl...*

At last Gallante's troop was ready and the ritual greetings could be carried out in the proper fashion. Eon Barola cared little for this protocol—a legacy of the kings. Nonetheless he exchanged cold kisses with Hal Gallante, and then opened his arms to greet the Prince's son in welcoming fashion.

The Baron wrinkled his nose when he caught the spicy reek of the boy's perfumed sweat. He swallowed his revulsion and smiled at Varentin.

"Welcome, Princes Hal and Varentin, and all your people also." Barola's smile was expansive, but his eyes couldn't hide the anger he felt that his daughter hadn't deemed it necessary to appear.

"This castle is yours for as long as you wish it," he informed them. "Every comfort shall be yours, my lords, and your soldiers can feel free to practice at sword and archery whenever they wish it." *They need all the practice they can get by the look of them...* "Also, the taverns of town and castle will stay open during these celebrations. Ale and mead shall only be matched by fine Barolan fare."

Prince Hal Gallante nodded, clearly unimpressed. "Where is the girl—Lissane?" he enquired, looking around, seeing no females present save serving maids and such like, hurrying to and fro in the distance.

"My son wishes to embrace his future bride," he said. "Come, Eon, you old fox. Where have you hidden her?"

"She is overcome with excitement," replied the Baron, waving a dismissive arm and shrugging off the prince's question. "You know how these young girls are, Hal. Paolo has gone to see to her in her chambers. I promise you will not be disappointed." This last was addressed to Varentin. The younger Gallante just looked bored and turned away; Eon's dark eyes glittered dangerously as he studied the boy.

He even smells like a perfumed turd.

He forced a smile. "Come, most noble guests. A feast awaits us in the main hall of my Keep." *If that girl doesn't appear within minutes I'll flay the skin off her back.*

Eon Barola bade his men-at-arms escort his honoured quests through the castle grounds and up into the Great Hall that made up the entire bottom level of the Keep. It was a feasting hall fit for kings—though Eon doubted it would impress these pompous Galanians overmuch.

The vaulted ceilings were airy and high, and the wide stone pillars ornate, each one intricately carved. Huge beams trussed above, whilst ahead a fire hearth twenty foot across, roared and fizzed with orange flame. Hounds lounged and yawned on the polished flags and busy retainers hurried to and fro.

Three heavy oak tables straddled the hall with long benches flanking them. The tables creaked beneath the weight of food and drink that covered their entirety. Beyond these and nearest the fire, stood a smaller table of carved mahogany, traced with gold leaf and set high on a plinth, so those seated there could look down on the rest.

The guards led Hal Gallante and his son to this high table. Eon and a sweating Rosco joined them, leaving two vacant seats. The inner circle of ranked castle guard and men-at-arms took to the benches alongside the Galanian officers. The lower ranks were already underway in the taverns below. There would be no fighting—both rulers were feared here.

And in the hall both sides feigned cordiality. That said, every man present kept a firm hand on his feasting knife. You never know how drink affects a foreigner. Weapons were now banned from the great hall due to the many violent incidents that had occurred over the years—most having involved the Baron's sons whilst in their cups.

Eon Barola, though inwardly seething, skillfully guided the conversation away from Lissane. He questioned his guests concerning events in western Gol, though his spies had informed him of the answers already.

Hal Gallante complied readily enough; he had apparently forgotten about Lissane Barola, and now began discussing latest happenings with something approaching enthusiasm. From him Eon learnt that a Treggaran raiding party had crossed north into Rodrutha and captured one of Brude's nieces. When they demanded tribute, 'King' Brude had bid them kill the bitch because he never liked her anyhow. This they did promptly, by cutting her throat and tossing her naked body in the moat at Dreekhall. Brude was beside himself, saying that he had spoken in jest and she had been his favourite—that he'd bedded her a dozen times himself.

One of his wilder sons (and they were all wild), Red Torrig, had vowed to storm Dreekhall and cut the hearts out of Baron Garron and his vile spawn. This Torrig purposed to slay ten Treggarans every day for the rest of his life. Eon Barola had heard of Red Torrig—as mad as his father by all accounts, but despite that rumoured to be a skilled mariner and war-chief.

Story went Red Torrig had sailed down from Longships Strand and beached on the Treggaran coast, with a host of screaming face-painted Rodruthans. What had happened next was not known. Eon suspected that they hadn't got far. The brutally efficient Treggarans would cut this Torrig and his brigands to ribbons before they came within sight of Dreekhall.

Doubtless by now Red Torrig hung skinned and dripping over the battlements of that fortress. Still, it was diverting news and would keep the Garrons busy for a time. Eon managed a smile at that thought, whilst to his right Rosco roared with laughter when he heard this news, and even Hal Gallante smirked a little. It was good to know the Treggarans would be elsewhere occupied for a time. It all helped Eon Barola's ambitions.

A draught lifted the fine hairs on the back of Baron Barola's head. He turned; saw the doors creak open as a sudden hush entered the hall. Then he saw her at the doorway—his daughter. Lissane had come at last.

She wore a long velvet gown of deepest emerald: it hugged Lissane's slender curves from the graceful arch of her neck to the ivory hint of her ankles. The sleeves were fluted; laced with golden trims, and her black silky hair crowned by a slim coronet of filigreed silver. Her small pale hands were steady at her side; each long finger sported a jewel-encrusted ring.

Eon smiled, forgetting his anger as he watched Lissane approaching their table with a serene confidence he'd seldom seen in her before. Paolo attended her left side—all smiles and smug satisfaction. Lissane looked magnificent this evening.

Out of the corner of his eye, Eon saw the admiration light up Hal Gallante's face, though Varentin hardly spared her a glance. Still grinning, Paolo stood by as she took her place beside her future betrothed.

No one there (not even her father) noticed the dark rings under Lissane's heavily kohled, violet eyes. None present marked the tightness of her bloodless lips as she took her seat at their table. The Baron introduced her and then hoisted his glass, toasting their guests. And so the feast began in earnest. There were two present that didn't enjoy it.

***

The Magister glanced up from his papers. "What is it?"

"News from the south, sire. Ozmandeus is back."

"Are you certain?" The Magister folded his parchment and placed it into a drawer. He wiped his sweating face on a kerchief and fussed his small hands together. The soldier, one of his personal guard, looked uncomfortable. It was dangerous bringing bad news to the Magister of Zorne.

"Well?"

"Yes, sire, he's been spotted leading a host this way."

"A...host?" The Magister leant back in his high arched chair and awarded the soldier a cold gaze. "How large is this host?"

"The witness reported three thousand horseman, sire—led by the rebel lord himself."

"Three thousand? Who was the witness?"

"A farmer, sire."

"A...farmer." The Magister wiped his round face again. It was very hot in his study. Despite his discomfort he started to chuckle. The soldier looked even more uncomfortable so the Magister bade him leave. As he sped below, the officer heard his ruler's chuckle rise to harsh laughter. Strangely, the soldier didn't see the funny side.

Chapter 9

The Feast at Castle Barola

Lissane felt the rapacious gaze of the Great Hall's occupants undress her as she entered within, gliding calmly toward her father's table and taking her place at his side. She smiled demurely at the guests, attending Prince Hal and his sulky son with polite disposition. She even laughed at Rosco's jokes—cruel and obscene though they were. But it was all a mummer's farce. Lissane felt numb from the neck down and cared about nothing.

The Great Hall was all noise and laughter this evening: crackling fire, rich smell of sizzling pork and beef; clanking feasting knives and goblets, belching, stinking warriors, and farting, jittery hounds that lurched about getting under the retainers' feet in their relentless quest for scraps and bones. To Lissane this feast was just another nasty dream, and she had had her fill of those of late.

When Paolo had sauntered into her bower he'd found her waiting, sitting at her window and watching the distant dance of wave and sky. Belshareze had been to Barola Town to seek more news concerning Erun Cade. She'd returned with nothing new and Lissane had sent her away again.

Bel's pretty hazel eyes had been rimmed by tears, the maid

had liked Erun too. Belshareze was kindly in nature and well liked in castle and town, with her blonde wavy locks and easy smile. She was Lissane's only real friend but the Baron's daughter had little time for her at present. That too was upsetting the younger girl, who had always been a party to her lady's inner thoughts.

Lissane, on hearing Paolo's soft approach, had opened her door to him, calmly announcing she was ready. That had surprised him. So had her dress—bought by her father last year in distant Torvosa. She had never worn it until this evening.

Paolo had never seen his little sister look as beautiful as she did then. Lissane hadn't even glanced at her brother as she walked from the room, taking the stairway two steps at a time and gliding down to the Great Hall below.

Lissane was ready for this charade—saw no way of averting it. During the last few days she had eaten little and spoken to few, saving Bel—and then only in terse brief whispers. But her mind had focussed as the cruel hours wore on. Gone were the useless dreams of her lost love.

Lissane had to be practical. Above all, else she was a survivor. Gone too, was the echo of the dream-woman Rani's words and what she had foretold. Dreams were for lovers and she was alone. To Lissane it seemed apparent she had only the one choice. Live or die. Survive what comes, or else drown in a sea of sorrow.

Leanna had chosen the second option. Lissane no longer blamed her mother for that, but deep in her heart she hoped to one day avenge her lover—even take the lives of her own siblings, if she could prove them culpable for Erun's passing.

Lissane would be cursed by the gods for a kinslaying, but she cared little about that. Whenever she saw Paolo's creepy servant Grudge, his narrow eyes had shifted awkwardly away from her. *That one knows something for sure.*

Of her brothers she'd seen very little until today. Bel had told her how Aldo had lost a hand in the same raid by Treggarans that had left her lover and his father dead. Lissane couldn't care less about Aldo. He was weak. It was Rosco and Paolo she suspected most.

It had taken strength of will, but Lissane knew there was only one way through this, and that was to comply with her father's wishes. These Galanians couldn't be any worse than her own family. And there were few at the castle she would miss—though one or two of the townsfolk had been her friends when she was a child. Lissane *would* miss them but only for a short while.

Lissane had watched from the Keep, seen the colourful Galanians cantering resplendent through town, and then crossing the causeway as the hurrying waves frothed at their horse's legs. They had made for a brave sight, that much she would allow. But once they were inside the castle walls, Lissane had soon lost interest and returned quietly to her chamber. Let them come to her; Lissane had been in no great hurry to meet her intended. But she was ready now.

She would wed this pinch-faced Varentin and do her duty as was expected of her. What did it matter now that Erun was dead and gone? Besides, she'd always wanted to travel to the opulent west (though not in this manner) and being so far away from Barola might breathe new life into her hollow heart. At least she hoped that might prove the case—eventually.

After their initial brief appraisal of her beauty, the Galanian princes paid Lissane small heed. Instead, Hal bantered with her father and brothers about politics and such, as his dour son watched on—all present deeming her feminine ears unworthy of such intricacy. Lissane fed one of the lean hounds a bone as she listened in to the raucous talk flowing back and forth across the high table. Lissane prodded her food and sipped the cool wine—watching and listening.

Her father was deep into his cups, his florid face looking relaxed and amiable—a well fed shark, he could turn in a second. Paolo, to his left and across from her, exchanged jibes with Varentin—the latter replying in terse irritated tones. And Rosco's moony troll-face reddened by the minute. Lissane's eldest sibling gulped horn after horn of mead and mulled wine. He was well under way. She ignored the pig and instead focussed on Varentin Gallante and his father.

Prince Hal Gallante was still a handsome man, despite being well past his fiftieth year. He was erudite and serene with strong aquiline nose and long silvery mane, both polite in manner and cold as windblown ice. Beside Hal Gallante's elegant dialogue her father's nasal bark sounded harsh and uncouth. The senior prince's attire was magnificent. He held his head high, taking only small sips from the heavy goblet resting in his palm.

His son was different. Lissane's first impressions of her intended were of a half starved ferret. He looked a resentful creature—all petulance and bile. This Varentin had hardly spared her a glance, and on the few occasions that he had (and this only after Lissane had politely tried to make conversation) he'd fended her off with a look of disdainful annoyance.

So this vile creature was to be her husband. Lissane fingered her eating knife, wondered whether she should slash her throat now and spoil their bloody alliance. But no, she would weather this façade and survive, whatever this popinjay and his stern family threw her way. Lissane would flourish in Galanais, she decided. She would have to. She'd learn new skills, gather allies, listen and watch. Then when the time was right and she knew the truth, Lissane Barola would take her revenge.

Then the troubled shade of Erun Cade could rest in peace. Only then would Lissane release her soul from the prison that was her weak girl's body. If only she were a man, or else a fighting maid like Slinsi Garron of House Treggara. She could challenge them all in the arena below. Would that she could... Lissane didn't have Slinsi's legendary fighting skills, but she was strong willed and determined. She would find a way in time.

Drink flowed and the talk switched to baser matters. The men at the benches below were rowdy at their cups. One or two fights broke out between the guardsmen and their guests, but nothing serious. A cold bucket of water or else a sharp kick from Paolo Barola put paid to these minor quarrels promptly.

Most of the soldiers were getting on famously, though at least half dozen lay sprawled in drunken slumber on the floor, blissfully oblivious of the Baron's hounds that lurched and drooled, and even pissed over them in their ceaseless quest for cast off bone and brawn.

Servants came and went in ignored silence, food was devoured and yet more drink consumed with zeal. Her father's growling laughter battered Lissane's left her ear as he guffawed at something humorous Hal Gallante had said. Her brothers were in their element tonight. Paolo preened and Rosco swilled and belched, both revelling in what they did best. Varentin's nut brown eyes looked glazed with boredom. His gaze was anywhere but on her.

At last Hal Gallante stood up, straightened his expensive tunic and thanked his host, before announcing his retirement to bed and leaving them to their continuing recreations. The Galanians had chosen their own sleeping quarters in the castle grounds, not wishing to be that close to these Barolans in the lonely quiet of night. A field of tents creaked and sagged down there.

Lissane watched him go, and moments later Varentin followed, leaving the hall without word or glance in her direction. That left her lot. The Baron was in jovial spirits, but he too was weary and before long he had retired aloft for slumber, or maybe some idle play with the young maid who warmed his sheets at night. Lissane followed him, leaving her two brothers and the now mostly snoring soldiery to the remaining night. Rosco's drunken brown eyes watched her departure, whilst Paolo smirked deep into his wineglass at some cleverness only he perceived.

***

It was sometime later when Lissane heard the queer scraping at her door. Someone was without. She'd been sitting deep in thought at her window again, just dreaming and watching the new moon steer a path through racing cloud. Belshareze lay sleeping in the second chamber. She'd been to the tavern and had taken some drink. Her gentle snores were distant yet constant. Lissane had no wish to sleep tonight, she had slept too much of late and her dreams had awarded little solace.

The scraping came again, this time followed by a muffled cough and awkward shuffle.

"Who is there..?" Lissane felt an icy shiver creeping up her spine.

"Liss, it's me...Rosco...I..." The scraping came again.

Rosco...

Curious but wary, Lissane glided to the entrance of her chamber. She turned the key, allowing the night air to rush in as the oak door creaked ajar with her eldest brother's bulk showing behind it. Rosco's looming shadow filled the space vacated by the door. He lurched toward her, stinking of drink and stale sweat. Looking down, Lissane could see he'd soaked his breeches with either wine or something worse.

Her brother took another step toward her, his great moon-face smiling inanely, and the piggy dull brown eyes hungry in a most unhealthy manner. "I would speak with you, sister," he managed to say.

Lissane stepped back, allowing new space to fill the gap between them again. He made to fill it but her accusing finger jabbed hard into his ribs, making him belch and curse in surprise.

"I've nothing to say to you, murderer. The only reason I'm wedding that foul Galanian is to get away from you."

"Liss... I...you don't mean that." His eyes reminded her of a rutting boar. "I'm sorry about your lover but shit happens. Those Treggarans are cunts. I just want to...comfort you." He reached down and lifted her hand to his full fat lips, placing the softest kiss on her rings. It seemed a bizarrely gentle action for so big and clumsy a man.

Lissane snatched her hand away and spat at his grinning face. "Get out, troll breath, else I call the guard and have you flogged like a common thief in the night!"

Rosco's huge face darkened dangerously. "Bitch...ungrateful bitch," he slurred. "I was only trying to comfort you... tell you that you don't have to wed that Galanian bastard. I could—"

Rosco's right hand shot forward with sudden violence, grabbing out for the warm place between her thighs. Lissane leapt back in alarm, her left leg kicking out hard at her brother, trying to catch the swelling bulge between his legs. He blocked her kick with his calf and pushed her to the ground. He stood over her then, and grinning, began unlacing his breeches.

"This is what you need, you spoilt bitch...I—" Rosco froze when the cold kiss of steel pressed hard into the soft tissue under his chin. Lissane twisted the knife she'd slid from the sheath, hanging by the belt at his waist. A fat bead of blood teared down the steel and reddened her hand. She prodded the blade again, forcing her brother's head back. Rosco's ale-sodden eyes bulged in surprise and sudden fear. Lissane smiled.

I can do for this one at least...that's a start.

"Stop...!"

Lissane's hand froze as the Baron's throaty growl filled the room. Over in the next room Belshareze woke with a start and cried out. No one noticed her pale face watching on in horror as she sat up rigid in her bed. Lissane glanced sideways, saw her father enter with his captain of guard—the silent, grim faced Harrow.

"What occurs here?" The Baron tore into the room, saw the wild look on Lissane's face and the knife's reddened blade glinting in the moonlight trapped by the window. Then his bloodshot glance dropped to the damp patch beside his son's unlaced breeches, and then in a sudden nasty violence his fist shot out, striking Rosco hard across his right ear and knocking him to the floor.

Captain Harrow grabbed Lissane's wrist and gently eased the knife from her arm, she didn't resist—her eyes were glazed and her mind cold as death. Together they witnessed the fury of the Baron unleashed.

"You fucking slime..!" Eon Barola's strong hands hoisted his son up and rammed him hard against the wall as though he were a child. Rosco held up a hand to ward off his father's fury. The Baron's be-ringed fist knocked it aside and cannoned into his son's upper lip, splitting it open like an over ripe plum.

Rosco begged for mercy and yelped like a punished puppy, but to no avail, the rage was on his father. The Baron struck again and again, continuing for several minutes, until Rosco groaned and slunk to the floor.

"That's where you belong you filthy, incestuous bastard," Eon kicked hard at his son's ribs and back, bruising him badly. On and on he went until Rosco sprawled in an unconscious heap of congealed blood and salty tears. Finally, exhausted by his rage and the violence of his assault, the Baron withdrew and stared down for a moment at the crumpled wreck that was his eldest child.

Eon Barola regained his composure slowly. He hawked and spat on the floor before lurching over to the window ledge where he sat for a time, seething like a cornered beast in the dark. Lissane watched him in frozen silence and in the other room, Belshareze's eyes were wide and her white hands covered her mouth.

Lissane released her arm from Harrow's grip and turned to confront her father. She mouthed a word but the Baron's growl stopped her. "You will sleep in your maid's bed for the rest of the night," he told her. "This room is...tainted. On the morrow you will prepare for the long voyage west. Prince Gallante's wish is to leave soonest. I would have preferred the Galanians stay for a while yet, but now I'd sooner you were gone from here. You are blight on this house just like your mother before you, Lissane."

She glared at him but he didn't notice, just motioned her away. "We will speak via pigeon henceforth, daughter mine." He turned to brood out at the darkness framed by the glass. His voice had grown distant—cold.

"I wish you well with your future betrothed, Liss. Now join your maid in the other room and leave me to the ghosts and shadows that are my only comrades." The Baron lurched to his feet and turned toward the door. "I said go!"

Lissane moved not a muscle. Her violet orbs raged at her father and the accusing words came slowly at first. "You... killed her, didn't you, Father—"

"What?"

"Leanna...oh, not with fist or knife no, but with years of relentless, measured cruelty. You wore her down as though she were a cornered hind and you the huntsman—and her so gentle of heart." Lissane's pale hands gripped the crimpled folds of her nightgown as though she meant to rip them apart.

Her father turned his heavy gaze upon her. "What's this nonsense...?" His dark eyes narrowed dangerously, and his right hand lowered to finger the ruby covering the pommel of his dagger.

"Yes, go on, Father!" Lissane raged at him. "Stab me with your hunting dagger—kill me too and put an end to this charade!" Lissane stepped toward him, her eyes deep pools of cobalt wrath. "I don't fear you, Father. I'm not Leanna Barola for you to crush in your hand. I hate you...all of you! And I hate this fucking house. So go on, plunge your knife in my throat, silence my words and have done with it all!" Lissane took another step forward until she stood scarce two feet in front of the Baron, her heeled height allowing her to pin him eye to eye.

Eon Barola, uncertain for once and taken aback by his daughter's defiance, mouthed a word and fingered his dagger. To his right, Captain Harrow looked askance and worried, clearly wishing to be anywhere else. Forgotten in the other room, Belshareze sat weeping, her hands still covering her mouth, and her naked breasts showing stark in the light cast from the patrolling moon outside.

Silence.

Eon Barola and his daughter stood glaring at each other for what seemed an age. Then the Baron sighed and something inside him gave. "I'm done with you, Lissane," he said in a weary voice. "Go with your intended and prosper in Galanais. I want nothing more to do with you."

She didn't reply so he shrugged and shouldered past as though indifferent. But his black eyes carried the haunt of a guilt that had never left him and he looked shaken to the bone.

The Baron left the room, pausing only to address his captain. "Take that offal below and sling it in our darkest hole." Her father's head jerked back in the direction of Rosco's motionless shadow. "Let him fester in his own filth for a while."

Harrow, hastening to comply, reached down and dragged Rosco's bruised body up from the floor. With a grunt the dour captain heaved the Baron's biggest son over his left shoulder like a sack of grain and swiftly strode from the room. The Baron watched from the door, gave Lissane a final baleful glare before following without further word, and pausing only to retrieve the guttering candle he'd left in its sconce outside her door.

Lissane watched his departure from her chambers: the Baron looked ailing and tired. She wished him dead by sunrise. Lissane hardly noticed when the (still weeping) Bel threw her brown arms around her and fussed in her ear. Lissane smiled at her maid and bid the girl return to her bed, and Bel obeyed reluctantly.

Lissane returned to her window seat. Outside the waxing moon rode high over rain cloud. The air was metallic—charged by the tension. Weariness claimed her at last and returning to bed, she slept for a time. When morning came Lissane Barola was more than ready to leave. And she wouldn't have long to wait.

***

The storm raged high overhead and rain slanted icy daggers into their eyes, making them squint and blink beneath their helms. They rode in silence. A grim column of sodden, hard-faced riders; clad in glinting black armour and long sable cloaks, filing in orderly fashion behind their captain and the sorcerer.

Zorne was scarce twenty leagues ahead. At times some of the horsemen had spotted the city's scouts watching their progress and turning away before coming within bowshot. They would already know in Zorne. Word had spread fast of Ozmandeus's return. Soon the citizens would be lining the city walls, awaiting the first glimpse of the Renegade and his band of brigands.

At the van, Ozmandeus smiled cruelly as he rode beside his captain, Maelchor. The Magister in Zorne and his elite would be laughing when they got word that such a tiny force of desperate men dared threaten his unconquerable city.

How they would laugh. Zorne had never fallen and it never would, they'd say. Not even to an army of a hundred thousand men—and those with the aid of siege towers, trebuchets, scorpions and battering rams. Ozmandeus's mercenaries—the scouts would have already informed them—had only their weapons and savage cunning, a rag-tag force of less than four thousand fighters.

It was risible—they'd say. And yes, of course Ozmandeus would employ sorcery. But the Magister had a dozen sorcerers, each one easily a match for this Renegade. But then they didn't know about his secret weapon, those pompous fools. Ozmandeus fingered the hot amulet dangling from his neck. It still burnt at times as the spirit writhed angrily within its bonds, but Ozmandeus had become accustomed to the pain by now, and besides, his protecting charm kept the worst of it at bay.

That afternoon they sighted the walls. The men pitched tents whilst Ozmandeus approached the city alone on his horse. Tiny figures watched his approach from the high crenulations. He paid them no heed. They were nothing and very soon would be reduced to smouldering ash.

The Renegade stopped a short distance before the gate. He slipped the amulet from around his neck, holding it aloft so all could espy its amber glow and feel the hungry menace of what it contained. He laughed up at the walls, feeling the denizens' hearts quaking at this new evil he had brought to cause their undoing.

"Behold Ashmali!" Ozmandeus shouted, his deep commanding voice easily carrying up to those watching above. "Your doom is upon you—fools!"

Silence followed. Ozmandeus laughed—mocked that silence. And then without further word, the Renegade turned his courser about and returned promptly to the camp where his men were already preparing for battle. It was just a charade—they wouldn't have to fight. Tomorrow he would unleash the Demon and then everything would change.

Chapter 10

The First Lesson

Three months had passed since Erun Cade's narrow escape from the Barola brothers. Autumn's gold and russet hues now crusted the canopy of growth below and surrounding the cave's secluded entrance. Summer had gone and now this autumn was fading fast.

Erun Cade had still done nothing to avenge his father's ghost, or save Lissane. But at least he was healing fast. Truth was he had never felt so good in his body, though his mind was still a tumbled mish-mash of anguish and venom.

He had tried to slip Irulan's net twice now but the cunning old weasel always seemed to anticipate his moves. The first time he'd stumbled blindly into Irulan at the cave entrance while he'd been stealing out into the dark. Erun had troubled to make certain that the old man had been asleep before venturing out. He'd heard him snoring only moments earlier and yet here he was blocking the way out and grinning like a loon.

Erun's second attempt at escape was just two weeks ago. He'd almost made it back to the road one rainy night, when his foot caught in a rabbit snare. And there he remained, trapped, helpless and soaked, for the rest of that night until the pretend hermit found him crouched and sheepish in the morning.

Since then Erun Cade had put his vengeance on hold for a time. It was frustrating, but if he was honest with himself Erun had grown rather fond of his captor/healer. And besides, he was learning many useful things that would stand him in good stead come the time for his revenge. Irulan was irascible and enigmatic and bloody-minded to boot, but he was the most knowledgeable creature Erun Cade had ever encountered.

The youth's training had started with an endless stream of monotonous tasks. Fetching water from streams, building cairns on the high hills above, for the gods only knew what purpose. Certainly Irulan never explained. Under duress Erun learnt to mend his shabby clothes when he tore them and, with the hermit's weird array of tools, managed to make new ones. He was taught to forage and learnt how to survive in wilderness as the season fell towards winter. He'd mastered fire craft and wood skills: could stalk a deer in silence taking note of the wind's direction, and catch a shiny brown trout with his quick young hands in the hurrying, icy streams below.

All this was well and good to know, Erun decided. But the only thing he really wanted to learn now was how to fight. He knew Irulan could teach him that also, if he only would. But his mentor didn't make it easy for Erun to ask, and some of the tasks the hermit gave his protégé were bizarre in the least, rendering Erun both bewildered and annoyed by their alleged necessity—and he never achieved them quickly enough in Irulan's opinion. Though why the need to hurry?

Another month slipped by. Last summer's joy had faded to a dream long past. Erun now questioned that he would see Lissane again. But his love, though cooled, was still strong. He wouldn't abandon hope, he would try find a way yet.

As the leaves browned, dried and fell, and the woods sparkled with diamond hoarfrost; and far off to the east the distant glimmer of the ocean paled from steely blue to silvery grey, Erun Cade decided it was time he made a stand.

It was on another rainy day that he finally dared challenge the old man. Erun had been digging trenches all morning and was soaked to the skin, whilst the pretend hermit remained warm and dry in the cave smoking fish above the fire. Erun's patience—never long—was worn thin and his mood had worsened by the hour. Come afternoon, he decided he'd had enough.

Erun noisily abandoned his thankless task, took to the woods above; there he found two rods of ash and hastily cut them into makeshift spears. These would do for a mock battle, he was going to brain that old hermit.

Both staves were thick as Erun's wrist, each one solid and good to grasp. Erun wielded each in turn, whirling them over his head as though he were fending off a host of foes. At last satisfied with the staves and his ability to use either one, Erun returned to the cave and tossed one of his weapons at the old man. Irulan, crouching by the fire, looked at the stick as though it were a serpent. Erun motioned the hermit to retrieve it and join him outside.

"I'm sick of all this digging and rolling rocks," he moaned at his mentor. "Why don't you teach me how to fight? You say that you were a soldier, Irulan. Well I'm strong now, old man. Strong enough to be on my way, though I'd be grateful for any sword tricks you could learn me."

"Sword tricks?" Irulan's chuckle was laden with contempt. "Think yourself worthy of a sword, Master Cade? Swords are for the noble classes, boyo, not hot-headed lack-wits and peasant brats." His eye narrowed as he saw the boy's knuckles whiten on his stave.

"My father wasn't a peasant," snarled Erun. He felt the red brand twitch on his forehead as his anger took hold. The scar had healed nicely as had his legs, but those he could hide. The mark on Erun's face would accompany him to his death.

"What do you intent to do with that?" Irulan raised a quizzical brow. Erun now gripped his stave in threatening fashion and was advancing on the hermit in slow, measured steps.

"If you don't pick up your weapon," Erun hissed, "I swear I'll swat you where you stand. Defend yourself you grumpy old sod!"

Irulan didn't move. Instead he watched Erun's heated, noisy

advance with dubious interest. "Mind you don't trip over that tree root," the hermit said. "You haven't a clue what you are doing with that stick, boyo." His scornful tones stopped Erun in his tracks. "Your posture is entirely wrong, see," Irulan pointed, hinting at the youth's wide stance, "and you are holding that stick like a confused shepherd at market whose sheep have all gone stomping off. I think Garret Cade was right about you, laddie, you're just a useless mooncalf—a dreamer. All wind and no motion."

You old bastard—I'm going to floor you for that!

Erun had heard more than enough. He felt the rage inside him reaching boiling point at the mention of his dead father. His tenuous tolerance was now suddenly blown apart like splinters in a gale. Those long months of stewing and scheming, finally torn asunder by a sudden violent hatred for everything and anything— including (and at this moment especially) this irascible old pseudo-hermit, Irulan.

Erun swung hard and fast, launching the thicker end of his stave at the old man's head. Irulan ducked quickly and grinned at him, the stave sailing over his head. Erun stopped mid swing and turned on his heels, ramming the butt of his stave down hard toward Irulan's scrawny midriff.

Irulan twisted to his left and the stick struck air instead. Erun cursed and panted, his face now scarlet with furious exertion. He tried cunning: levelled his weapon, and with both hands parallel leaped at the hermit. He thrust hard at Irulan's face, trying to knock him from his feet, but the old man stepped back out of reach and grinned at him again.

"You don't appear to be hitting anything, boy," Irulan told him, helpfully.

"I'll clout you yet—so I will." Erun slid his hands down the length of his staff until he gripped the rod two thirds of the way down. He swung hard and low at his tormentor's legs, seeking to knock the hermit off his feet.

Irulan leaped aside with astonishing speed and agility, especially for one who appeared so old and decrepit. Again the blow went wide.

Erun gaped at the space where Irulan had been standing half a second ago. How had the old sod managed that? Then something hard knocked the ash rod from his grasp and he yelped with pain as a sudden jolt shot up his arm.

Next thing he was sailing through the air, his head colliding painfully with the stump of an old dead oak. Erun groaned on impact and then winced as he rubbed his spinning head. He heard croaky laughter, opened a watery eye and blinked at the rain.

Irulan stood above him; Erun's stave clutched between his old knobbly fingers, the broad tip resting lightly under the boy's chin, forcing his head back ever so slightly.

Erun's aching body slumped in defeat and all the rage slipped from him like useless steam venting from a forgotten kettle. He *was* useless. If he couldn't floor an ancient bag of bones like Irulan, what chance had he against the Barola brothers? No chance. He might as well go drown himself in the sea.

Irulan tossed the stick aside. He reached down, gripped his miserable apprentice by the collar with both leathery hands, hoisting him up to his feet.

"The first lesson," Irulan said, "is not to lose your temper, laddie. Keep cool. Any fool can lash out blindly like a cornered animal. The warrior's sharpest weapons are patience and cunning, not brute strength and bestial rage. Patience and cunning—remember that."

Erun shook his head, sending a wave of giddiness through his body, causing him to lose his balance again. Irulan caught him before he fell. The hermit's grip was deceptively strong. Erun muttered a reluctant thank-you between tight lips. He felt depressed and crestfallen, but now held a new respect for his companion.

"That trick with the stick," he enquired when he'd gotten over his giddiness and regained his composure a little. "How did you do that?"

"Trick? That was no trick, boy," replied the old man. "I read your body language, is all. Used your own strength against you, disarming you in the process. A rather basic manoeuvre actually, a bright lad like you could learn it in an afternoon."

"Well, will you teach me then?" Erun's gloominess was driven away by the sudden urge to learn all that this beguiling old crotchet knew. "Will you teach me how to fight, Irulan? You said you would."

"That depends on your commitment, boy." Irulan's single, icy orb pinned Erun as a hawk clocks its prey. "I mean, why I should bother if you keep running off like a thief in the night...and after all I've done for you, patching you up and all?"

"I'm sorry...I...want to learn now, and...I *am* grateful."

"That is good," nodded the hermit. "There is much that you could learn in time, lad, you're not slow witted and Scaffa will perfect your skills...providing you're tough enough to impress her, of course.

"She is not soft like me, boyo. That one has no tolerance of weakness in any form...I should know. But before you journey to her distant island you will need a certain level of proficiency, else you end up gutted and gored and left for the crows on some lonely highway."

"I'll stay...I swear it," insisted Erun, wondering again who this Scaffa was and what she would teach him. At least he was willing to learn now. More than willing he was hungry. "I want to master all that you can teach me, Irulan."

"All...?" Irulan chuckled. "That would take you a lifetime and more, boyo. Still, if you are keen and alert you'll discover enough to keep you alive in the arduous months ahead." He retrieved the rods and tossed one across to Erun. "Keep hold of that one," he told Erun. "We'll continue tomorrow. Be prepared for more bruises."

"Why not now..?" Erun saw no reason to delay.

"You have a trench to dig, I believe."

"But—"

"The honing of Erun Cade starts tomorrow, laddie." Irulan's raised hand left no room for challenge, and besides, Erun's new-found respect for him had silenced any forthcoming complaints. "The training will commence only after the daily chores are finished. The quicker they're completed, the more time we'll have for fighting. May I suggest that you go get digging?" Irulan's single eye studied the clouds above his head. "Best get to, laddie. Looks like more rain on the way."

That evening the hermit bade the tired Erun Cade follow him deep into the recesses of his cave. After a while the way opened to a wide space, and Irulan's spluttering candle allowed just enough light to spill on the many curious objects strewn about this hidden recess. Erun was speechless, he'd suspected his host had a stash of gubbins stowed away someplace but here was all manner of equipment. It must have taken years for the old crow to acquire this lot. Erun glanced askance at his mentor.

"How came you by all this, clutter and stuff?" Erun asked him and Irulan just shrugged in return.

"I've collected many things over the years," he responded. "There are bits and pieces scattered across this entire continent and beyond that only I know about, laddie. All have their uses from time to time. Here, take this." He reached over, retrieved a short hunting bow and bag of freshly fletched arrows. "You will need these shortly."

Erun's eye rested on a long curved sword glinting in the candlelight. "What about that?" he asked, wondering how Irulan had got hold of such a fine looking weapon. "Surely I could use that too."

Bow and arrows was well and good, but a sword like that one...

"You need to walk before running, boy. Here, take these too." The hermit handed Erun a large bundle of clothing for him to carry back. It was heavy and along with the bow and arrows he was fully laden. "Make your way back...I'll be along soon. Don't get lost, follow the firelight's glow," Irulan told him before disappearing in the gloom. Erun, obeying reluctantly, stumbled back with his burdens, his mind both curious and questioning.

When Irulan returned some while later he found Erun fully garbed in his new attire. A long grey woollen tunic, warm and thick, pulled down tight over a blue leather shirt, with close fitting dark brown breeches, and a plain broad leather belt.

Over these rather gloomy garments, he had draped a long battered cloak of dun coloured wool, trimmed with fox fur at collar and hood. At least the clothes were warm. Erun had become accustomed to wearing so little and was now sweating like a hog on heat. Irulan grunted approval when he saw the youth decked out in his new attire. He motioned Erun go sit by the fire, but not so close as to singe his cloak. Here the old man produced yet another bundle which he began unravelling for the sweltering Erun's perusal. It was small and oddly shaped. Erun baffled, couldn't begin to guess what was contained within.

His curiosity got the better of him. "What is that..?" Erun asked.

"This, my lad, is a harp. Not just any harp, I'll add. This is how you will feed yourself on the long road north. You say you've a love of poetry and stories, and indeed all men must have a trade. Fableweavers, songsmiths and harpers are welcome in most provinces for the pleasure they bring, especially during the raw winter months.

"If you are careful you'll journey through Treggara and Rodrutha without coming to any harm. Once you've learned to pluck chords from this to a reasonable standard. It will take time to perfect your skills, but time you have got and will have. Besides, those rustic northerners lack the refined tastes of the twitchy nobles who so often frequent gilded Galanais or proud Torvosa City."

Erun's eyes widened as the cloth slipped from the bundle revealing the small wooden harp, stringed and ready to play.

"I cannot play that." Erun's chagrin showed clearly on his face. He had been hoping for another weapon not a bloody harp. Yes, he'd been a poet of sorts but now he yearned to be a fighting man. The thought of crossing vast snowy Treggara, armed with a wood harp and a few arrows left him feeling woefully inadequate. Besides, poetry and song was the old Erun Cade. That boy had died at the forge alongside his father.

"I will instruct you in its use," said Irulan, ignoring the face his charge was pulling, and speaking with a finality that brooked no room for argument. Erun rolled his eyes in disgust. Despite his long face the young man took to his feet and began preparing supper without a word said. Irulan watched him, his single eye glinting with wry humour. The lad was learning at last.

***

The high born of Zorne watched in fascinated silence as the distant host pitched their tents below. Such affront was beyond belief. Their leader, the arrogant outcast Ozmandeus, was clearly insane. Three thousand men had dared set themselves against the towering walls of Zorne. Those walls, two hundred feet in height, had cast back armies of twenty times that number.

Zorne was impregnable. A city only rivalled by Xandoria in the distant east. For a thousand years it had stood, its rulers aloof and confident in their autocracy. And now this renegade sorcerer dared threaten them with a paltry three thousand men.

The nobles watched the colourful palanquin arrive on the twenty foot wide platform that was the high battlements, the dozen half-naked slaves straining and sweating beneath it. It was most unusual for the Magister to trouble himself up here. But he too was curious. He even honoured those watching by stepping out of his carriage and waving the now prostrate slaves away so he could see what sport the walls had brought today. A great occasion, this would prove. A fascinating diversion for so many spoiled monotonous lives.

There they stood waiting: Magister, lords, noblemen and women; their slaves servicing their every need beneath the sunshine, ensuring they lacked no comfort.

There were musicians everywhere playing lute and lyre, and clowns capering behind obscene masks. Fire swallowers and naked wrestlers there were also, and stalls providing every manner of fare and drink. Most popular were the oiled slave dancers performing sexual acts, their lithe young bodies entwined and writhing.

Despite these many distractions most of those gathered chose rather to gaze down with cool contempt on the rustic host below. Soldiers lined the walls also: pikemen, archers and artillery—the trebuchets and scorpions were now in place. As one they watched the single rider approach. The outcast Ozmandeus. Madman or fool? Probably both.

The Magister laughed as the black rider yelled up to them

before turning his steed and trotting back to his camp. Such arrogance and to what gain?

Curious, the Magister allowed his slaves to set the palanquin down to shield him from the sun's bright glare. He was about to announce something to those gathered when a violent shudder shook the walls.

A boom and thud followed then a weird crackle and rush of blinding light. The Magister had no time to turn and see what had happened. Ashmali's flame tore his face off before he could even voice a scream.

And so fell Zorne City. First domino in the line.

Chapter 11

The Honing of Erun Cade

Throughout that long winter Erun Cade learnt much from the canny old wanderer, Irulan. He became highly proficient at his chores, allowing more and more time for weapon play. His young body waxed supple, muscles hardened and stamina grew.

Erun learnt how to defend himself using only his arms and legs, incorporating a series of blocks, twists, and counterstrokes. Irulan taught him the correct use of a quarterstaff—the peasant's own weapon—and he learnt to shoot the hunting bow with both accuracy and speed, until his fingers bled and his arms ached mercilessly.

He learnt to fletch and glue the shafts when one was lost or broken, and to fashion bowstrings out of animal gut. Erun loved it all, but still he yearned for the sword he'd glimpsed in the cavern that evening and determined to ask Irulan for it at some time—although he suspected what reply he'd receive.

But these new fighting skills were only part of his training, or what his instructor had come to call honing. Irulan saw his young protégé as a knife: blunt and dull, but forged from good quality steel. In time it would sharpen far keener than common metal. In time it would be deadly.

"You grow stronger, boy," he told Erun one afternoon after they had sparred with the staves for well over an hour. The pseudo-hermit's endurance was another thing that baffled Erun Cade. Irulan never seemed to get tired. He didn't eat much and seldom slept passed a few winks. Erun, who slept like a butcher's dog and ate everything available, couldn't keep up with the old fart. It irked him sometimes.

"Body strength is well and good," the Irulan told him, "but without a disciplined mind it is less than nothing. There are other weapons besides the bow and the sword. Knowledge, cunning and wisdom will often carry through where a sword will fall short. Courage alone will often win the day." Irulan changed tack then. It was another of his quirks.

"What do you know of the history of this land of ours—this Gol?" When Erun began answering, Irulan cut him short. "Ignore what the barons have rewritten, boy. Tonight and for many to come, while you study at that harp, I will reveal to you the true histories of Gol."

Thus, during those long cold nights, Irulan would school his apprentice in the use of the harp and watch him play until his fingers seized. Erun learnt to tune and care for the instrument, and over time began putting music to the many tales he was hearing from Irulan.

The harp, though plain and ugly in fashion, gave out an uncanny sound—both weird and ethereal. Erun came to love it. Some of the tales he knew already from the taverns of Barola Town, but most were new to him. There were weird fables of foreign lands, of sea beasts and strange peoples long since vanished.

He heard of the voyage of Rogan One-Hand who had sailed so far east he'd spied alien shores on some mist-bound continent. However most of the stories concerned the old kings that had preceded the Rebellion. Erun was strumming notes to a verse concerning the last king, Flaminius the Third, and getting on rather well, when Irulan stopped him.

"What do you know of the time before the Rebellion?" Irulan asked him.

Erun shrugged. "That it was a cruel, dark time. The king was mad, they say, and the barons were left with no choice but to usurp his throne."

"Flaminius wasn't evil," responded Irulan quietly. "But he was surrounded by evil men. These courtiers were both ambitious and hungry for power. They were clever too. They preyed on the weakness of their monarch, manipulating his mind and feeding him with paranoia. Each conniving baron warned the king against his neighbour, when all along most of them sought his ruin and dreamed of overthrowing him.

"Eon Barola was one such player—though not the worst at that time. It was Hal Galiant of Galania—now styling himself Gallante—who orchestrated the final masterstroke that toppled Flaminius.

"Galania had much to gain from independence, you see. That western province had become very rich what with its trading with powerful Xandoria beyond our shores. Galiant bought mercenaries from that land. He held secret councils with the young Eon Barola, and Volt Garron of Treggara, and occasionally Brude from distant Rodrutha—though that one was usually caught up with stopping his own family trying to usurp him. They're a wild lot, those Rodruthans—always have been. The war that followed was swift and brutal. Toreno Dovess stayed loyal to the crown as did the Sarfanians, though both were persuaded to capitulate at the end."

Erun placed the harp aside and Irulan continued with his tale. "Still listening, boyo?" Irulan pulled a face and emptied a nostril into some dubious looking cloth. He snorted, emptied the other one. "That's better—can't speak properly with snot up my nose." Erun refrained from comment.

"Flaminius's paranoia destroyed him, you see," Irulan explained. "If he had been a stronger, or braver king then he could have turned the tide against the barons. Even at that late hour there were many lesser nobles in Gol who mistrusted them, and rightly so as it turned out. But in despair Flaminius slew his wife and children with his own golden dagger, and then cast his body from the high walls of Torvosa City. The barons gave out that he had fallen in battle. Both Eon and Garron boasted of killing him. They hung the king's head over the gates of Torvosa until sun and raven did its work. Eon Barola, still not satisfied, had the skull pickled and sent back to his own castle to parade from his Keep.

"Sounds like something he would do," muttered Erun before spitting into the fire.

Irulan grinned wryly. "Oh, how the barons feasted those nights in Torvosa City. The iron grip of the kings was no more, they said, and a new 'sensible order' brought to Gol. Better days had come—they gave out. And for a while the people believed them. It had been the folly of Flaminius and his fathers that they had ignored their small-folk."

"You were involved with the Rebellion then?" Erun was fascinated but Irulan ignored the question.

"As I said," continued his narrator. "Those 'better days' were short-lived. The barons soon grew distrustful of each other, each believing (and rightly) that his neighbour was plotting his downfall to aid their own ascension. They tenuously forged alliances and broke them overnight. Assassins thrived in those early days; bodies were found wormy and rat-gnawed in backstreets, their throats slashed and their purses gone. In the end all trust was lost and a new dark descended on Gol."

Irulan scowled with disapproval. He stood, grumbled something inaudible, tossed another faggot on the fire, then stretched his scrawny rump and sat down again. All the while Erun watched him in silence.

"Even the gods were forgotten—at least the kings had always been devout. These barons shunned worship, claiming that only the weak need fear the old gods. Their people they subjugated and overtaxed; the gods were ignored and their temples abandoned by these new rulers, who worshipped only power and greed." Irulan paused again, this time reaching across the fire to drink from the jug he kept close by.

"So has it been for many years," he added, after gulping back a swig. "But at last things are about to change. You see, boyo...the gods have had enough and decided to intervene with all this malar-key—well, one or two of them, anyway."

Gods? Erun yawned. He didn't know much about the gods. Of course he'd heard the stories and all that creation stuff. That didn't mean he swallowed it.

"What change? Will there be another war?" Erun asked him, hoping it were so. His new confidence had left him chafing at the bit, and though he had discovered patience and a modicum of wisdom, he was still young and determined to have his revenge. Besides, in the chaos of conflict he had more chance of seeing Lissane again.

Wars changed things. But the bit about the gods he didn't comprehend. The gods were remote distant figures of myth and fable. His father had never really believed in them and Erun was of similar mind, particularly after losing his mother.

And since Barola had banned the ancient rituals, most folk had kept what piety they had well locked away. Besides, it seemed irrelevant and he doubted the gods (if they did exist at all) would show any interest in him. Why should they? Erun let that thought be and listened on.

"Oh yes war. And worse—much worse." Irulan wiped his mouth and stoppered his flask placing it back by the fire. "Gol is falling into ruin, my boy."

"Falling...ruin?" How so? Surely things aren't that bad?"

Irulan belched into the fire. "Inch by inch, year by year, Gol is sinking—that's a fact. Zansuat's watery hold grows stronger on this continent. Gol was his domain once. He would have it back, and now his anger grows at the pride of these upstart barons.

"At the time of Flaminius and his fathers the Sea God was re-vered by all, as were the Sky God, Talcan and Lanione of the Trees. Even old Oroonin was revered by some—though most failed to ap-preciate his multiple talents and instead feared him as a trickster."

"So?"

"Yes so. Now it is only the small-folk who carry on with the time honoured traditions. Zansuat is slow to anger, boyo, but when aroused he becomes terrible as only the ocean can be. A time comes close, mark my words, when Zansuat shall rise in wrath and Gol shall be no more. There. That's it, I've said my bit. Don't say you've never been warned."

"But what has all this got to do with a war?" Erun hadn't a clue what the old git was waffling about. The conversation was boring him now. "So what if the Sea God is going to drown Gol, there isn't much I can do about it."

"Shut up and listen. The Sea God is not the only doom facing Gol." Irulan waved his twiggy arms about with wild expansion. "Another, more pressing danger threatens from afar." Erun Cade scratched an ear. He couldn't begin to grasp how Irulan came by all this stored wisdom (if that's what it was). He must have spent years loitering outside taverns and eavesdropping, or else begging for soup and stuff.

"What other danger?" Erun ventured, just to humour the old boy.

"Far from here lies a country called Zorne. A distance barely imaginable, and yet, much too close. A man of hate has used forbidden sorcery to release an ancient menace from its island prison. He plans to use this 'demon' as his conduit to destroy his enemies and thus gain power. What he cannot realise is that this creature is ultimately uncontrollable and may well destroy him instead in the end."

"Right." Erun made sure he had one eye open.

"Should the demon destroy his captor and win free, then carnage and destruction will ensue," Irulan's eye gleamed evilly in the firelight. "Zorne will crumple and many other lands too. This creature has a hunger that only the gods can contain. I fear that the vast continent flanking Gol's western seaboard will be destroyed in time."

Erun scratched his head. "If this all happened so far away then how do you know about it? I mean—do you speak to crows and whatnot?"

"I listen to the voices carried in the wind. And, yes, birds can be useful too—you'd be surprised. News travels fast, boy," Irulan stated airily. "A shrewd man can learn much via his ears should he but choose to listen. Most don't, of course, it's the same dismal spiral of cock up piled on cock up. But then, that's the human race for you."

Erun let that one go. Odd though this conversation was, he decided to give Irulan the benefit of the doubt. Though he wasn't sure about the talking birds bit.

"But surely there have always been such despots and demons and such?" Important though this might be to someone a very long way away, Erun failed to see its significance to him sitting in this cave. Didn't he have enough to concern him without worrying about problems on another continent? Besides all this waffle was making him sleepy. He wished Irulan would change the subject, talk about swords or something useful. No chance.

"Not like this one." Irulan picked a morsel from his left nostril, examined it then flicked it in the fire. "Ozmandeus, this sorcerer is called. He is ambitious and worse...vengeful. The creature will feed on his hate, aiding him at first, but eventually...well. No mortal can long control an Elemental without intervention from the gods. Especially a Fire Elemental as powerful as Ashmali."

"A what? And who is Smali?"

"Ashmali. Remember the name." Irulan awarded him a sharp glance before continuing. "Long ago: long before the first kings broke loose from the Xandorian Empire and came to Gol and settled—indeed before any man bred and bled amidst these wind-blown shores, this place we call Gol was frequented by very different peoples. Some were mortal and some not.

"Amongst these various colourful folk were the creatures the gods called Elementals. These ancient beings were small in form, almost gelatinous and liquid in appearance. They were essentially spirits and took shape when needed in the nature of their element. There were four kinds, of course: Water, Air, Earth and Fire.

"The Fire Elementals were the most feared for they were destructive and reckless. Immortal and petulant, these beings were nevertheless favoured by some of the gods. Talcan lorded over the Elementals of Air, Elanion/Lanione those of Earth. Zansuat's darlings were the Water Elementals—many such still dwell in his deeps.

"But the Fire spirits served the one you call the Shadowman,

whose true name is never used—though it is known to some." It
was obvious to Erun that 'some' included Irulan but he didn't press
the point. "They were all capricious, these creatures, and many
were filled with spite and cunning. But only the Fire Elementals
were truly wicked. Destruction was the gift bestowed on them by
their vengeful master."

Erun yawned and blinked at the fire.

"You listening?"

"Yes..."

"Hmm. This is for your sake not mine, boyo. Pay attention."
Erun blinked again.

Irulan continued under duress. "When man the rude intruder
arrived, the Elementals fled. Though gifted and mercurial they
were few in number, and these clumsy newcomers were both numerous and unstoppable in their rapacious noisy hunger for land
and power.

"Most Elementals disappeared during that time, but some
remained hidden in the darker corners of Ansu, harbouring resent
and vengeful notions. These were the most powerful spirits and
many were cruel and malicious besides.

"I have heard tell of one such creature residing in the far
south of Sarfania: another is rumoured to dwell beneath the Lake
of the Clouds—somewhere way up in Treggara. Doubtless there are
others lurking in Xandoria and in the wild lands beyond.

"This Ashmali is unique, however." Irulan's silver eye seemed
distant. "The most powerful of all, his earlier destruction caused
the gods to imprison him on an island off the coast of Zorne. Know
where that is?"

"Haven't a clue."

"In the west. Great Continent—way beyond Xandoria."

"Oh."

Irulan scratched his rump and pulled a face. "That was then.
The gods are not what they were, their power has faded in these
lands, and now this maverick warlock has freed the Demon. None
can guess what may follow." Erun yawned, this was all very worrying but he needed sleep and soonest.

Irulan continued as though his charge was invisible. "You see, boy, this petty necromancer won't be able to stop the creature. Ozmandeus is as much a prisoner of Ashmali as it is of him, though he is unaware of that, and in arrogance believes himself strong enough to control the spirit. The fool probably won't realise his peril until Ashmali cooks his ears and fries his brain."

Erun yawned again: his left eye kept closing. Irulan stopped to pick at his nose again and toss the excavation into the fire. The hour was late and the cave deathly still. Erun studied the pseudo hermit's ravaged face in the glow.

"Where was I?" Irulan glanced around as though someone or something had stolen his train of thought. He looked edgy all of a sudden, as if he had said more than he should.

Erun yawned once more and covered his mouth. All this was fascinating but he was becoming more than a bit lost and the hour was getting late. Sleep was pulling at him hard now. He ventured a question, if only to hold off sleep.

"If this Zorne is so far away why should we worry here in Gol?" Erun asked. "I mean, won't this fire thing...this Asalli burn itself up long before it reaches our shores?"

"Ashmali! It is possible, yes," responded Irulan. "But unlikely. You see, the Fire Elementals hate mankind and Ashmali is no exception. They believed that the gods lost interest in them when the newcomers, these short lived creatures called man first appeared.

"Ashmali is a very vengeful spirit, boy. Methinks he will turn his captor's mind, driving him on to destroy all that man has built before burning him to ash and breaking free to trouble the world once more. That huge continent could be reduced to ashen ruin in a matter of years. After that comes Gol, for the Demon's strength will grow and his hunger for destruction drive him onwards. I see a time coming soon when Gol is caught between fire and water and lost to the world forever."

"Is there nothing that can be done?" Erun was barely managing to keep his eyes open. He still couldn't grasp what relevance this had for him. Nor did he fully trust Irulan's words. He questioned again why this wily old bag of bones had chosen to help him.

What does he really want from me?

Irulan awarded him a bleak stare. "Perhaps there is," he said, "though all things must fade in time...even the gods." Erun was surprised to see his mentor's eye glistening with moisture. He looked frail and sad and old for a moment. Strange, that. Erun was filled with a sudden urge to suggest something, anything, to set matters right in the world.

"What can I do...?" he asked the hermit. *Why do you need me?*

"Sleep for now, young Erun Cade." replied his host with a wry smile. "I have said more than enough and you will learn more in time, so don't fret."

Irulan curled up by the fire and rubbed his weeping eye. Erun's eyes were closed. For a while Irulan watched the flames dwindle and fade to ash. "Your honing is complete, my boy," he whispered. "In the morning you'll commence your long journey north to Laras Lassladden." Erun never heard him, though. He was already sound asleep.

***

Ash and smoke and so many burning corpses—word of Zorne's ruin spread like wildfire from the west. The Firelords of old had returned to claim back their lands, so men said. In sultry Spagos farmers heard tell of marauding dragons bringing flame and death to that exotic city beyond their borders.

Amongst the ice yurts of northern Ketaq, shamans shuddered words of doom and prophesised an imminent end to all mankind. In Lamoza City, canny merchants sold their wares and hastily took to eastern seas as rumour of the flames reached them. South over sparkling waters, in the teeming Island States, gossip and nervous chatter filled the sweaty taverns. Invincible Zorne had fallen to sorcery and fire.

But to vast Xandoria came no word yet of Zorne's demise. In Xenn City, the Emperor lounged within his palace in decadent splendour while his edgy generals planned their widening campaigns beyond the Lamozan Gap.

But along the coast in Rakeel, a lone astrologer trawled through his star charts and fretted long into the night. The omens were bleak: the stars spoke of ruin, destruction and fire in the months ahead. The Demon had arisen as was foretold, and the days of the Empire were growing short. He would write his friend Toreno across the sea in Gol. Together they would watch and wait for that appointed hour. And when the time came he would leave these soon to be forsaken shores, and make for distant Torvosa.

Chapter 12

Galanais

Lissane sat on her mare impatiently as the Galanian visitors waited for the portcullis to winch open, allowing their departure from her father's draughty castle. The morning was cold and bright with winter's promise. She'd not spoken to the Baron since the savage unleashing of his fury the night before.

Instead Paolo had stolen into her bower earlier that morning. Her brother informed her with his silkiest smile that the finer details for her betrothal would be concluded this very morning, with all the usual blessings and such from those in attendance.

The wedding proper would take place in Galanais, he'd informed her, although she already knew. None from House Barola would attend. It was an insult both to Lissane and her future spouse that amused Paolo, who had no liking for the vain Gallantes.

Not that that mattered in the least to Lissane either. It was a joy to be rid of her family. But for her honour's sake and Barola's too, she had to ask him who would be accompanying her on their venture west. Surely she was not to undergo such a journey alone and in winter?

"You'll ride out in full pomp with our departing guests," Paolo had grinned. "Father has no great wish to hold you back from your doting intended. He wants the best for you, sister, as do we all. Oh, you'll have your maid of course and Grale is going too, though he will be coming home as soon as you are safely contained within the gates of Galanais," her brother had told her. "House Barola cannot be long without so worthy a blademaster as Grale."

Lissane had said nothing. Instead she'd glared at Paolo as he'd stood framed in her doorway, her violet gaze challenging his cat-green mocking sparkle. "You had best hurry, sister," Paolo told her then. "Father's humour's is of the foulest this morning. One is given to wonder what you have done to upset the old boy so."

Ask your brother…

He'd grinned at her then. "I'll not be attending your departure, Liss; I've a tavern to frequent and then those ailing guests to attend down in the oubliette. I like it down there with the mould and cold and enduring stink of shit and fear. Farewell, sister, I wish you joy in Galanais."

Paolo had turned with a flourish of hem and heel and sauntered out of her room, his costly attire matched only by his arrogance. Lissane had watched him leave with cold dispassion.

I'll glean the truth out of you one day, brother. And when I do I will make you pay for Erun's death—just you wait and see.

Once gathered and ready and the portcullis winched high, the Galanian party left Castle Barola behind and urged their mounts to trot across the causeway, Lissane among them. They were underway at last. For Lissane it wasn't soon enough.

***

That wintry journey over the mountains took long weeks and snow proved a constant trial, blocking the high passes and barring their way. Despite that, Lissane and Bel loved it. Neither Gallante senior nor junior spoke much to Lissane during the voyage and that suited her well too.

She rode alongside Belshareze whose constant excitable chatter, although annoying at times, was all the company she required. Grale, wary and taciturn, steered ahead of the ladies, keeping his eyes alert and the sword loose in his scabbard. Grale didn't like these Galanians but then Grale didn't like anyone overmuch.

Lissane felt a freedom she hadn't encountered before. The freezing air pinked her cheeks to rose and the mountain vista infused her senses. If she had exchanged one family of monsters for another, then so be it. Lissane would deal with that later. For the present she took pleasure from their arduous ride and the cold, whistling wind whipping at her cloak and hair. All around the panorama of the mountains dwarfed her worries and postponed her anxieties. This was what freedom felt like.

A day came when they reached a high ridge and cresting it eagerly, saw the vast unfolding expanse of Galania reaching out and down to a distant glassy bead on the horizon that could only be the Shimmering Sea. Lissane spied rivers and forests and the odd smoke trail from farms and homesteads in the wide green valleys below. It was very beautiful, this Galania, her new home.

Soon they were descending out of the mountains and the weather had mellowed to mild again. It was deep winter by now, but Galania's verdant fields were blessed by a climate even kinder than Barola's. Her own province, temperate most of the year and hot during high summer, was prone to sudden sea storms and high winds. Galania was sheltered by the distant mountainous arm of the closest shore of the Great Continent across the bay of Rakeel. The spires of that Xandorian city were said to be visible to the keen-sighted on a clear day. Lissane hoped that she would get her chance to see them soon.

Hal Gallante's realm was bathed in golden sunlight for most of the year, raining just enough to water crops and green the fertile terrain dominating this western province. It was special here, Lissane decided that bright morning, and took to hoping that she could at least recover some lost joy in such a lovely land as this one looked to be.

Two days later she spied the gleaming towers of Galanais. Belshareze whooped at the sight and Lissane smiled alongside. Tall and golden they appeared those towers, lancing up to the heavens like slender spears. As they drew close Lissane and Bel chattered excitedly, Galanais's glory stunning them both for a time, though Lissane kept her own emotions more guarded than did Bel, who gawped and giggled openly at the splendour of the city filling their horizons ahead.

Galanais was beyond impressive. It was huge, certainly, but also beautiful, with those tall towers of whitest marble and domed minarets studded with jade and lapis lazuli, their spiky crowns blazing in the winter sun. A chain of wall linked by crenulated forts at every hundred feet or so, and seven miles in length, curtained the city from north to south, blocking the road ahead; this too sparkled with the colours of semi-precious stone and flints rendered to the surface of bastion and buttress.

Beyond the wall, the myriad buildings of the city framed the sky toward the distant ocean. Here were all shapes and sizes, none dull on the eyes. It seemed to Lissane that everything in this city was a sight to behold. She felt suddenly ashamed of her father's drab walls left far behind.

At the city's centre, Lissane could see the great curve of the citadel itself, its gilded flanks blazing with sunlight and rising high above the rest of the buildings, as her own castle dwarfed Barola Town. But to compare this place with Barola was absurd. Lissane now understood why these Galanian nobles were so proud, Castle Barola must have appeared more than rustic to Hal Gallante and his disapproving son.

Lissane's enthralled eyes were drawn to the distant citadel, home of the 'prince' and his household, and soon to be hers too. She wondered what life would be like living in so grand a place. There was a brief moment in that afternoon that Lissane Barola felt almost happy. But it was only a moment. It didn't last.

Belshareze yelled in her ear when she spied the gates of the city a mile ahead, swallowing their road and opening into the city beyond. Taller than the keep of her father's castle they were, perhaps over two hundred feet high, and fair to gaze upon. Even from this distance Lissane saw scores of ornate carvings of beasts and birds, and stranger things, etched on the surface of both gate and wall. These creatures seemed to come to life in the sunlight. They rode on, the gates looming close and the lofty walls parading off at either side, before fading into the hazy distance.

A fanfare of trumpets somewhere above the gates announced their arrival amid shouts. Lissane and Belshareze, looking up, saw the tiny figures of guards lining the high crenulations above like so many motionless ants. The gates were thrown back and wide as the trumpets blared, within moments they had passed beneath the high walls and entered into the tangled maze of lower Galanais.

Lissane's tactical eyes marked the lack of defences. Barring the walls there was nothing: no ditches lined with stakes, no killing ground or barbican with murder hole and spiked portcullis, or any drawbridge bridging staked pits or pike-filled water. It were as though this place disdained such crude barbarity. Galanais, Lissane decided was a very confident city. And why shouldn't it be?

Crowds teemed and bustled as they threaded their way through the colourful maze of twisted street and cobbled square. Lissane smelt spices, some familiar and many alien to her senses, roasting flesh, animal dung, sweat, piss, and all the other usual odours and stinks surrounding city folk.

She'd been to Torvosa as a child and thought she knew how cities were. But Galanais was different; though not nearly as stern and antiquated as Torvosa, this was a place richer and larger by far. She saw all manner of people thronging the streets. The Galanians themselves were not dissimilar to her own folk, but there were dark skinned Sarfanians from the swampy province below, and freckled-faced tattooed giants that must surely be traders from wild Rodrutha.

She recognised Treggarans, warlike and dour, their long fair hair tied in plaits, and proud Dovesians garbed in their native blue—the old colour of the kings. But there were other outlandish folk dressed in peculiar fashions that could only be from Xandoria and other exotic lands across the Shimmering Sea.

But the one thing that surprised her and clouded that bright winter's afternoon for Lissane were the slaves. In her eagerness to depart House Barola she'd forgotten about slaves. Galania, alone of the six provinces of Gol, traded in slavery. It was another factor they shared with the lands across the sea, indeed most of these slaves were prisoners of wars waged in those foreign lands.

They were everywhere, dressed in drab greys and browns, their tunics and shifts short sleeved and cut high above the knee. Their faces were downcast as they hurried to and fro about their many tasks. Now and then Lissane and Bel jumped, hearing the sharp crack of a whip as scowling overseers drove their sweating charges out of the city to work on the fields beyond.

There were pretty girls too—many younger than Belshareze— and perfumed boys, all wearing the same neutral tired expression. Lissane saw shaven headed eunuchs and older men who must be scribes and suchlike. She wondered what it would be like to be a slave. *Someone's property.*

Lissane shuddered at the thought and instead set her mind on guiding her horse through the teeming streets. It was no good though; Lissane felt her previous joy vanish like morning mist as she witnessed the abundance of suffering all around. Galanais's gilded sparkle faded to rust as she watched the shackled and col- lared run by.

Beside her, Bel cried out as a half naked boy was cruelly whipped for tripping across their path. Lissane tore her gaze away. Were she ever given the chance she would change this cruelty, she vowed.

The road widened as it corkscrewed round before climbing up and out of the lower city. They passed shops and vacant temples, stables and slaughter houses. She saw markets aplenty, each a far more colourful affair than Barola's weekly event.

Off to her left—a mile or so distant—she could see the masts of tall ships moored up alongside the quays. Galanais was flanked by the broad sluggish River Gal to the north and the Shimmering Sea to west and south.

As they gained height the air became cleaner. Soon Lissane could smell the ocean and hear the cry of gulls and terns above the clamour of shipwright and stevedore. The road, now tree-lined, spiralled up for over a mile, leading them high above the tiled roofs of the lower city.

Up here the houses were a grander affair, with lawns and

fountains and wide palisades fanned with lazily swaying palms; they had reached the homes of the well to do. Rich merchants, courtiers and advisors to House Gallante lived in these privileged places. Even the slaves looked smarter up here, though they didn't appear any better fed, nor were their expressions any different than those in the city main below. They turned a corner, and the glimmering majesty of the Citadel rose before them.

Belshareze gaped as she reined in at Lissane's side. The home of Prince Gallante and his family outshone the rest of Galanais like a diamond among zircons. The perimeter walls were like a miniature copy of the city walls below, but more ornate even than those, and cunningly wrought to capture the light from both sky and sea. White marble and jet onyx, they were crowned by statues, and alcoves hid lanterns that shone above the city main like moonlit gossamer during night time.

The only entrance visible was a wide gate of golden bars opening into expansive gardens of trailing vines and scented roses, with chiming fountains and ornate statues frequenting every corner with motionless serenity.

Through this maze of scent and colour (despite the lateness of the year) a cobbled road of polished white marble led toward more golden gates, these opening into a wide, polished piazza, itself leading across to the huge central building which was the main palace and central hub of the citadel.

The palace was huge, its entire surface gleaming white marble traced by gold and jet onyx, and the vast dome above golden as the noonday sun itself. The sight of it almost took Lissane's breath away. Even Belshareze was lost for words.

At each corner of the palace a tall minaret stood guard, the coruscating crests were of a height with the main dome, their tips rose-pink in hue. These four spikes were crowned with burnished gold and fluted outwards at their tips, showing broad pennants sporting the White Ship of Galania on its emerald backdrop, fluttering high above their heads.

As their party approached the palace doors, Lissane saw that a line of people awaited their arrival. She saw slaves and soldiers and others too. Most dropped to their knees as Hal Gallante and his son rode through the inner gates. A score of slaves hurried forward, grabbing the reins as prince and retinue dismounted and made their way towards a small group of people that stood slightly removed from the rest. A young man approached Lissane and bowed, holding the reins of her mare as she dismounted. She thanked him with a kindly smile and was rewarded by a look of abject terror.

"You don't smile at the slaves, my lady," Grale whispered behind her as he vaulted from his horse. "They'll be whipped bloody if they respond. Just ignore them's best," he urged her. "It's the way things are here." Lissane didn't respond. She felt angry and wanted to shout but kept her own counsel and said nothing. To her right Belshareze looked worried. What would these proud folk make of her doe-eyed servant? Lissane squeezed her arm in reassurance and Bel managed a nervous smile.

A short, confident looking woman glided over from the knot of richly clad people to Lissane's right. She approached the prince, who leaned down to kiss her gloved hand. This lady was garbed in a silk gown of scarlet and gold, trimmed with pearls at neckline and hem, around this she'd pinned a long cloak of deepest green wool—the ship of Galania embroidered on the back with semi precious stones.

A crowd of well dressed women flocked behind her, awaiting her commands like flustered hens. Surely this must be the Chatelaine Sophistra, of whom Lissane had heard so much. She was a handsome, waspish looking woman in her middle years; there was grey in her hair, and her eyes were flinty jets, shrewd and clever, the oval face surrounding them tanned like fading leather, with slightly upturned nose and haughty manner. She radiated authority with upright gait and imperial stare, and on first glance Lissane knew that this woman was not to be crossed.

Her hair was dark in the main and piled high on her head, with fine silver filigree keeping it in place. The Chatelaine's perfume arrived before her: it hinted at jasmine and rosewater. Her eyes were kohled dark; the thin lips the red of crushed ripe cherries. Her smile was both economical and tepid. When she spoke her words were clipped and functional, though her voice was a tone deeper than Lissane would have expected.

"Welcome home, Lord and Son, and to you, my sweet daughter to be." The Chatelaine's barbed gaze rested on Lissane for the first time. There was small friendship in that appraisal. Lissane held her stare for a time, muttered polite thanks and then turned away, red-faced. She wasn't often flummoxed but there was something unnerving about this woman. Lissane didn't like her and she knew that the Chatelaine could tell, and had already logged that in her clever mind.

Tread carefully.

Lissane felt the alarm bells tolling deep inside her; she would have to be on her guard around Sophistra Gallante. This uncanny woman would read her like a book if she wasn't careful to hide her feelings. The Chatelaine gazed at her for a moment longer as though she were surveying a prize heifer at market. She curled her upper lip and let her gaze slip past Lissane, a slight superior smile showing on her face.

"She is comely enough, Varentin," the Chatelaine announced to her son who had just joined them, and now stood fussing and chiding at a retainer struggling to help him free himself from his riding attire. "A touch thin and pale of complexion methinks, but you will soon put that to rights when you have ploughed her a few times."

Sophistra laughed at Lissane's shocked expression. "Oh, she's a coy one it seems; we will have to watch our manners—won't we." Her laugh resembled a crone's cackle and sent a shiver up Lissane's spine. "Those hips look strong enough for issuing fine sons. She will do, Varentin." The Chatelaine turned away to address the milling group behind her.

"Prepare the main hall for a welcome feast. My lords and their soldiers will be hungry after their long ride, and show our proud lady of Barola to her quarters. See that she is bathed and coiffed, and every comfort offered her. Morwella, child, go with your new sister now... and be pleasant to her, dearest."

Lissane's eyes rested on a young girl who had emerged from the crowd, and now stood staring at her from behind her mother's cloak. Morwella Gallante was twelve years old: an odd looking creature, with black hair a-straggle, and thin pale features dominated by huge dark hypnotic eyes. There was mischief in those eyes and malice too, and the look she awarded Lissane compounded disdain and irritation.

"Must I, Mother...?" Morwella's voice was a whiney sulk. She had a slight lisp caused by the hair lip; her teeth when bared were uneven and off white. Lissane, despite trying not to, disliked her at once. *Another enemy.*

"Go, child, and mind you're polite." Princess Sophistra ushered them both away and turned to once again dictate to the people gathered around her. Her husband and Varentin had already vanished inside the main doors, and their men taken to the barracks to scrub up ready for the feast. Grale loomed awkwardly behind Lissane whilst Belshareze hovered nervously at his heels.

"I'll be alright," she told her guard as he bulked and fretted. "Go enjoy the sights of the city, Grale, Bel and I will be just fine." Belshareze's blonde bob waggled agreement but her honey eyes were filled with doubt. Grale mumbled something inaudible and nodded reluctantly.

He wasn't happy here, that much was evident, and Lissane couldn't blame him either. But they were to make the best of it. Grale gave her a last look before shouldering his saddlebag and trumping off toward the barracks at the far end of the building, where he would take his lodging during his short stay at the palace.

"I'll be close by should you need me, my lady," he called back to Lissane but she waved him away with a dismissive hand. Lissane turned on her heels and, accompanied by Belshareze, followed the po-faced Morwella inside the gates and into the citadel proper.

***

It was the light that impressed Lissane most. Castle Barola had been so dark and gloomy, especially in wintertime. The gilded Citadel of Galanais was a world of difference, the entire palace radiated light. The rooms Lissane and Bel glimpsed at as they walked on by were both expansive and airy, with ornate tapestries and paintings on the white, gold veined, marble walls.

Flanking wide corridors were blank faced statues of silent alabaster, whose dead eyes watched her pass in silent judgement. There were spiral metallic stairways leading up and away and tiered balustrades awarding sweeping vistas of the central halls.

Behind these were curtained alcoves offering discreet hides for casual dalliance and misadventure. The Citadel of Galanais seemed even bigger, once within its walls. The inner palace lay at the very centre where Gallante and Sophistra had their chambers. None were allowed there without prior invitation and an armed attendant watched silently around the clock.

Lissane glimpsed its jewel-studded doors and the green cloaked guard outside leaning on his spear, but had little time to register more as Morwella was not for tarrying. Lissane and her wide eyed maid were soon lost in the maze of white stone and high arched ceilings—even these were covered in intricate mouldings and ornate paintings of what nature neither girl could guess at.

But Morwella left them no room for gawping: setting a cracking pace, she skipped briskly around corners and weaved through the many rooms without so much as a glance behind to see if Lissane was keeping up. Whenever anyone blocked her way Sophistra's diminutive daughter just shoved at them and they moved aside swiftly, as though stung by a bee.

Lissane couldn't help noting how servant, slave, and retainer all seemed to dread this little girl. Like her mother, Morwella seemed to have the ability to unnerve people just by staring at them with those baleful moons.

She now led Lissane and Bel up a wide stairway of mottled marble. The colour of northern ice, with polished treads tapering up to an ornate arch revealing an entrance to one of the lofty minarets flanking the four corners of the palace. The arch opened in on another stair—this one a spiral that twisted and wound, up and up, corkscrew-tight and giddy.

This stair was lit by flickering sconces, but they weren't

needed at this hour, for the light reached here too. Lissane's bower was at the very top, both she and Bel were breathless when they reached it—Morwella having allowed no respite during their hurried ascent.

The door to the chamber was ajar: Morwella strolled in with Lissane and Bel following goggle-eyed behind. The bower comprised the whole top of the minaret with only roof and sky above. A perfect circle: lit by mirrors that cast back the sun's golden glow, filling the rooms with light and sparkle.

The atmosphere up here was both airy and fresh, the rooms all furnished with comforts beyond anything Lissane had imagined. She stood gaping for a moment while Morwella's scary eyes appraised her critically. Belshareze hovered at the doorway, feeling out of sorts in these opulent surroundings.

"These shall be your quarters even after your nuptials," she squeaked, grinning annoyingly up at Lissane. "My big brother prefers his own company after dark...you'll have plenty of peace to sit and watch the stars, I daresay."

Lissane ignored Morwella; instead she let her eyes take in the room. There were eight windows placed at intervals of symmetrical perfection and spanning the entire circumference of the bower. They were gilded around the rims and shaped like doves with wings outstretched. The glass was of a fine quality Lissane had never encountered before. It made her wonder how she had seen anything from her old salt-stained window back in Barola.

The windows here opened out on city and sea far below and beyond. This was nothing like her room at home in Barola. It was triple the size. There were heavy rugs of myriad hue and stitch criss-crossing the floor, and cushions and drapes of every size, colour and shape. Sculptures of bronze warriors lined the walls and ornate statuettes of handsome ladies paraded tables, whilst jewelled lanterns hung by golden chains from the pearl-encrusted ceiling, so high above her head.

The bed dominated the main room. It was large enough to sleep ten, in Lissane's opinion, and the high wooden pillars parading its corners were intricately carved and dark with antiquity.

Lissane couldn't help smiling. This was a room fit for a queen—never mind a baron's daughter.

Morwella awarded her a withering glance. "Mother insists you're to have every comfort," the girl told her. Lissane noticed for the first time that Morwella's huge eyes were slightly crossed and the left a touch larger than the right. This girl was an ugly creature, Lissane decided. That said, it was hard to feel sorry for this child. There was something disturbing about Morwella. Something not right—as though not all was as should be inside her head. She radiated a kind of malevolence that tingled the spine.

Lissane couldn't help but note how quiet Belshareze had been since Morwella first appeared. Bel seemed terrified by the menacing girl and kept her distance whilst still hovering over by the doorway.

"They'll call you when you're needed," added Morwella, as though that was obvious and she'd been over-kind saying it. "You won't need your *servant*." The last word was delivered with icy contempt as the girl's flinty moons flickered in Belshareze's direction. "You had best send her back to Barola...I doubt she'll fare well here. She looks to be a frail sort of thing."

Bel shrank back against the door, a pale hand clutched against her breast. She was lost for words and appeared on the edge of tears. "You've two female slaves to see to your needs, sister to-be," Morwella informed Lissane, whilst her twisted grin fed on Belshareze's discomfort.

"Handpicked by my mother. Oh, and a male one will fetch and carry should you require him—you only need holler. If you get horny he'll fuck you too." Morwella giggled at Lissane's horrified expression. "Varentin won't mind, he'll prefer you well oiled."

"I will be chaste and loyal to my future husband—of course." Lissane wished Morwella would leave. She questioned the girl's sanity and was now even more worried for Bel.

"Loyal?" Morwella shrieked the word. "Pale stupid stick, are all easterners so dense?" Lissane ignored her.

"When you are abroad in the city," Morwella continued, waving her thin arms about with an imperial arrogance parodying her mother's, "a fine silk palanquin will keep you protected from sunlight and the plebeian filth." Lissane glanced over at Bel, saw her expression and signalled her to relax. Bel managed a strained smile in her direction but her eyes were moist.

"Your mother is most kind." Lissane offered a stiff smile in Morwella's direction.

"My mother is a bitch-slut," replied Morwella with sudden vicious venom. "A filthy rutting dirty whore. One day I'm going to slit her throat wide open—like this."

Morwella made a sudden jerky movement with her right hand, horizontally sliding it across her own throat and then laughing out loud at their stunned, horrified expressions.

"Be seeing you, sweet sister to be...enjoy your solace." She blew Lissane a kiss, spat in Bel's direction and then skipped joyfully out of the room, leaving both Barolan girls to wonder how they would fare in the weeks to come. Compared to acid-eyed Sophistra and her horrible daughter, Lissane's own family appeared almost normal.

The girl Morwella was disturbing in every sense. The child was clearly deranged and the girls (particularly Bel) would have to watch their backs when that one was around. Somehow Lissane would have to protect Belshareze from Sophistra's spiteful daughter. But it wasn't just Morwella. Lissane had noted the cold disdain these foreigners had for their servants—let alone the poor slaves.

But they would get used to Galanian ways, Lissane decided. She would not be fazed by these people, however unpleasant they appeared. And Belshareze needed to wise up, the girl was far too naïve. Sink or swim—it applied to both of them.

Lissane was her father's daughter and though he was a drunken bully, Eon Barola was no coward. Survival was all that mattered, Lissane told herself as she patrolled the rooms, fingering objects and marvelling at their design and hue. *Survive and thrive. Learn everything whilst playing their games. Then return home and find out what really happened to my Erun.* It was simple really.

***

The column of riders filed south. Behind them the flames of Zorne City's demise reddened the skyline over a hundred miles away. Ozmandeus rode beside Maelchor. Both men were silent and deep in thought. Ozmandeus's mind wandered, he wasn't feeling well. Unleashing the demon's destruction had been easy, but re-containing Ashmali had been harder than before. The demon lived to burn and it had taken extreme effort on Ozmandeus's part to force the Elemental back inside his amulet.

As for Maelchor and his men, they were shocked. Hard men they were but none had witnessed such reckless carnage. There wasn't one among them as didn't wonder how this would end. But they kept their mouths together and silently begged the gods that the creature the sorcerer controlled never level its rage on them.

They entered the sharp fold of a valley. Ahead reared a castle. A craggy mound of rock and iron. Castle Gortez, home of Ozmandeus's family for countless years. They would be stationed here for a time, perhaps most of winter while the sorcerer got his strength back. But then what?

Maelchor drank heavily that night, as did his captains. They were rich from the spoils of Zorne. But they weren't overly happy. As for Ozmandeus—no one except his old retainer saw him in days.

Chapter 13

An Alliance Achieved

A month passed in Galanais and the planned nuptial loomed nigh. Lissane hardly saw anything of her intended, (which was no disappointment) and what brief encounters they had were both curt and businesslike.

Varentin Gallante seemed totally devoid of interest concerning her, which to Lissane was continuing good news. She would endure Varentin for as long as she had to. Besides, if what Morwella said were true then she would be left to herself most of the time. Life at Galanais shouldn't prove that bad. She hoped.

Her days were exciting enough, though. Life for the Galanian nobility was both indolent and exotic. Lissane's three personal slaves attended to her every need with silent swift efficiency—something which the self-reliant baron's daughter found difficult to adjust to. She was as kind to them as she dared be, and kept her Belshareze close at most times. The poor girl's nose was still out of joint after their encounter with the obnoxious Morwella. Bel was normally such a cheerful giggly soul, but House Gallante clearly overawed her, and Belshareze wasn't sure of her status here—though she knew that it was low.

The girl put on a brave face most the time and Lissane was grateful to her for that. Bel would be alright, she just needed time to adjust. Grale, the old champion, stayed close as he promised, though Lissane insisted that she was more than capable of fending on her own. She had always liked the blunt speaking soldier and she would miss him when he returned to Barola late next month.

Lissane Barola used the time given her well, gaining as much knowledge as she could about Galanais City and its myriad occupants. There were days spent exploring the upper city, albeit under the cover of her ornate palanquin. That was another thing that took some getting used to, but Lissane was determined to adapt to this new life, and anyway there was nothing back in Barola Province now that Erun Cade was gone.

Apart from vengeance...

During those early weeks, Lissane and her maid got to know their way around the Citadel. They swiftly learnt who was who and more important who to avoid. In the main that tended to be Morwella and her frosty mother. Fortunately neither of these showed much interest in Lissane after their initial encounters.

Sophistra was too involved at steering courtly matters of state, and her daughter habitually stalked the kitchens like a spiteful kitten, preying on the cooks and scullions and fussing the cats that lurked thereabouts—it served as her main entertainment at that time.

Hal Gallante, she saw but twice. On both occasion he sat his fine courser out in the piazza. The first time the prince was back from hunting, his gaudy armour spattered with mud, and milling yapping hounds spilling and drooling about his horse's hoofs.

On the second occasion Hal Gallante had just returned from a survey up north in the Ridings—a wild strip of country flanking the sea and close to the Treggaran border. Lissane had been present in the piazza as he noisily dismounted and she had tried to speak to her future father in law.

Hal Gallante had hardly noticed her however, even though she had smiled up at him as he paraded the square in his gleaming plate.

This time another nobleman accompanied the prince and sat his horse in brooding silence whilst refusing to dismount. The stable hands steered well clear of this one as they attended the other soldiers and such. Lissane studied the newcomer. Her eyes were drawn to him as a moth is to fire.

This stranger had a granite face with slate grey eyes and heavy jowl. He was handsome in a brutish way, with beetle-brows, blunt nose and shaggy dusky mane. He sat his horse with arrogant confidence as his shrewd, slatey eyes raked the crowd as though he were sniffing out potential assassins.

Those light eyes caught Lissane's violet gaze for the briefest instant and the stranger smiled ever so slightly. Lissane blushed as she felt the weight of that wilful gaze drift down to her bodice, undressing her with a silent hunger. Lissane tolerated his bold surveillance of her assets and rewarded his gaze with cold indifference, but deep inside she couldn't quite quell a shiver.

This silent rider—unlike the splendidly garbed attendants and laughing, shouting soldiers surrounding their prince—was garbed entirely in sable. His cloak and tunic were of blackest cloth, and his ring mail painted pitch on steel with no adornment of design showing.

A black helm hung from his saddle and long midnight gauntlets covered his hands, whilst his black leather trousers vanished inside thigh length black boots. The rider's weapons were sable too: a long hafted battleaxe hung from the right side of his broad belt, and a-hand-and-a-half sword swung from the left, its steely length hidden by a scabbard of worn black leather. Both weapons appeared to be fashioned from some dull durable metal. They looked heavy and nasty and like their owner radiated a brutish competence. He wore his shaggy hair long and loose, the sooty tangles covered his broad back in ragged coils.

Torlock, this black rider was called, Lissane learnt later. It was a name she would come to hate. He it was that was now Champion of Galanais and Galania. A fighter noted for skill at arms and brutal efficiency, but foremost for his total lack of compassion. Torlock was a killer and an ambitious one too. He made Lissane's skin crawl. To her relief, Hal Gallante's champion was seldom seen at Galanais. Torlock spent his time down at the Sarfanian border, monitoring their neighbours' movements across the Sarfe River, and engineering the odd discreet raid. The Galanians weren't officially at war with Sarfania—not like Barola and Treggara. But there was little love lost between the two western provinces of Gol, and this Torlock stirred up what trouble he could, for such was his nature.

As for the Sarfanians. Lissane had heard a deal of talk in the Citadel concerning them. They were a dark-skinned folk, their province low lying and hot, and much of it overrun with marshy swampland. The Sarfe River marked the boundary many leagues south of Galanais. The Sarfanians had often been openly hostile to Galania in the past though they traded with her when the need suited both provinces, and there were always southerners here at court.

Reveal was where Razeas Sarfe, baron and ruler of that land held power. It was rumoured to lie amidst a swamp. An impenetrable maze of mangrove, reed and rush, very difficult to access without scouts, let alone attack—hence its name.

Baron Razeas was said to be a cool headed ruler and a mild mannered man; he alone had stayed loyal to Torvosa during the Rebellion—at least until the final days when no choice was left to him but to rally to the other barons, or else face execution.

Eon Barola had always had a quiet respect for House Sarfe and its ruler, deeming them shrewder than most. Razeas had three sons: Estorien, Carlo and Kael. Kael was a boy of fifteen winters, hot headed and energetic, but yet to prove his mettle—and Carlo away at sea and feared lost.

But Estorien Sarfe was tried and tested. He was a skilled horseman and superb swordfighter, and had often been the darling of the Torvosan Games. Only Clarde Dovess (heir to Torvosa) and Slinsi Garron, wildcat of House Treggara, had bested him at tourney over the last three years. Even her brother Paolo respected him. This Estorien had unhorsed Rosco Barola three times—something which had made Lissane smile when she heard it.

All this and much more besides, Lissane gleaned from various people residing in the palace. The Galanians loved gossip and their favourite topic was always Sarfania. This all became suddenly relevant when one day, amid excited whispers; her slaves informed Lissane that the aforementioned Estorien Sarfe would be attending her wedding.

"He is very handsome, my lady," Claris, the elder of her slave girls told her. She was from the southern borderlands and had spied this Estorien on numerous occasions. She clearly had a crush on him.

Weeks passed in a rushed flurry of activity. Messengers came and went and strangers filled the palace—all guests for the coming wedding. There were notables from every province, saving her own and far off bleak Rodrutha. Toreno's heir, Clarde, had come from Dovesi Province with his young family, and two of Baron Garron's younger daughters from distant Treggara, but not Slinsi—which was a disappointment to Lissane, who had so wanted to meet the legendary female warrior. These Treggaran lasses were about Morwella's age, both pale-eyed maids with blonde braids and fair freckly skin. They seemed shy and ill at ease and Lissane felt for them.

There were oddly garbed courtiers from Rakeel and Murkai, the two closest Xandorian cities, lying just across the Shimmering Sea. Adding to these were countless merchants and well-heeled folk from the many country estates outside Galanais. But the most excitement came with the arrival of Estorien Sarfe and his party from the south.

The Sarfanians were in the main short of build and dusky skinned. They dressed in saffron and amber loose-fitting tunics and trousers, both women and men wearing their dark oily hair long in ordered plaits and ringed with gold.

Estorien Sarfe stood out from the rest like a jewel among pebbles. Belshareze had become acquainted with a few of the gossips. She had heard the hubbub announcing Estorien's imminence and had run off to inform Lissane.

Curious, Lissane had followed Bel into the main citadel. There were people everywhere. Lissane had been calmly gliding down the central stairway alongside Belshareze when she first saw him.

Estorien Sarfe glanced up as though feeling her presence, despite the crowd all around him. Their eyes locked and she felt her heart missing a beat. Something inside her surged. He *was* handsome, yes...but there was so much more. Lissane sensed a rare kindness in his intelligent eyes.

The Sarfanian smiled up at her as she watched on from her vantage point, high on the stairs. Estorien was shorter than her, though not small like many of his attendants were. His smooth skin was dark mocha, and his eyes a smiling nut brown. He wore a close-cropped beard trimmed neatly and scented with oil. He ignored the fussing, clucking servants and courtiers crowding close—his eyes were only for Lissane.

She felt frozen in time. She heard Bel giggle and whisper something inaudible, but took no notice. His almond eyes still on Lissane, the heir to House Sarfe strolled across to her, letting a servant take his heavy travel cloak from his shoulders. He waited smiling as Lissane and Belshareze descended amid excitement in the hall.

Lissane's eyes studied him as she approached. Estorien's garments were a match for any of the Galanian nobility. He wore a loose tunic of dyed cotton in brightest saffron yellow, laced with purple, and buckled at the front with sapphire studs. His long silky hair was neatly combed, held in place by a silver filigree clasp at the nape of his neck. It displayed the twin rearing snakes emblem of his province and house.

On his tunic was pinned a heavy golden brooch, also displaying the symbol. Estorien's hose was of pale blue linen tucked neatly into long black boots of softest leather, their tops turned over and trimmed with gold lace.

Above this he wore a cloak of sea blue and at his waist hung a slender curved sword. Lissane's eyes drank him in. His hadn't left her.

To Lissane it seemed that there was no one else present. It

was as though that crowded, bustling place hung both silent and empty. Such was the hypnotic charm radiating from those almond eyes of this beguiling stranger. Estorien's grin widened as Lissane presented him a pale hand. He kneeled down to place a kiss on her scented fingers. She noted how he moved with the fluid grace of a warrior born. He shared that much with Paolo but aside that they were poles apart—opposite sides of a coin.

He spoke then. "I had heard tell of the beauty of Eon Barola's only daughter," Estorien said, his voice soft and cultured, with a slight lilt marking him as a southerner. "But you surpass expectation, my lady, as the Jewel of Rakeel is rumoured to outshine common rubies a thousand fold. Estorien of House Sarfania—at your service," he told her and turned to wink at Belshareze, who replied by glowing scarlet.

"This must be Belshareze...are all Barolan girls so beautiful?" Bel purred but Lissane kept her head.

"I see you've done your homework, sir," she smiled, and he bowed slightly in return. Lissane was suddenly aware of how silent the hall had become. All eyes were on the spot at the foot of the central stairway. Few of those eyes were friendly. Only the Sarfanians appeared relaxed and at ease.

Lissane, aware that she was flirting, didn't care a jot, but prudence beckoned. *This is unbecoming, word will reach them...* With discipline she reined in her emotions. "I am honoured to meet you, sir," she announced coolly, whilst sweeping the onlookers an imperial glance, "I was Lissane of House Barola but now I'm a lady of Galanais. I bid you warm welcome here, my lord, both you and yours, to this fair city."

Lissane knew that it should have been Prince Gallante, or else his consort Sophistra that officially welcomed the Sarfanians, but she didn't care. Let them gossip and bitch about her in the palace. This Sarfanian outshone her intended and his kin as a hawk does sparrows. She kept her head. "We must speak later," she told him in a voice that only he could here. "I would learn more of your country. I've heard little but gossip to date."

"Your father...?" Estorien's head turned as he scanned the

crowd below, as if noticing them for the first time. Most had now lost interest and were chattering amongst each other in conspiratory tones, though one or two still stared balefully at the two figures talking by the stairs. "I haven't seen him yet. Have you any word on his arrival? I would congratulate him on his daughter's sharp wit and radiant beauty."

"Baron Barola has more important matters to attend than the marriage of his only daughter," answered Lissane, with more irony than she had intended. Estorien's almond gaze widened hearing that. He was clearly shocked by her sardonic tone. He made to reply but Lissane stopped him by lightly placing her left hand on his arm.

"My father and brothers are kept busy conducting their war with Treggara, my lord," she told him, while Bel strained to listen. The girl had recovered from her excitement and now looked worried again, aware of the many faces. "Besides," continued Lissane, "Barolan nobles lack the sophistication of you western lords. My family's manners are rough and more suited to the battlefield."

"Even so...One of them should be here," replied Estorien, clearly unimpressed by her answer. "It's a dishonour to you, my lady. Why, who will present you to your husband if not your father the Baron or else the oldest brother?"

"Grale, Barola's old champion, has stayed in the city to perform that task," responded Lissane. "He is an honourable man and one I trust. Besides I'm content with things as they are and it's better this way," she added this last sentence in a whisper. "The less I have to do with House Barola, the happier I'll be. I'm Galanian now, Lord Estorien, and pleased to be." He didn't reply to that but his face looked deeply troubled by her words.

"I will speak with you later then, my lady," Estorien said, and then in an almost inaudible whisper added. "You're wasted on this Varentin." She made to reply but he had already turned away to rejoin his party across the hall.

The moment passed. They were soon parted by the crowd, and Lissane was forced to make polite conversation with all manner of stupid people until Prince Gallante and his household finally deigned to arrive from their chambers, amid barking hounds and trumpets blazing. Lissane never got the chance to speak to Estorien Sarfe again until the night of the wedding, but she never ceased thinking about him and those last whispered words he'd left her with.

The special day finally came and went with a wealth of colour, splendour and music. There were crystal flagons of wine and brandy, huge trenchers of piping hot meats and fowls. Whole swans and hogs heads adorned the furnished tables of the main hall of Prince Gallante's inner Citadel.

There were platters of fish and sweetmeats aplenty, huge quantities of beef and pork and rare viands from across the Shimmering Sea. Slaves and servants rushed to and fro in dutiful silence as the worthy guests toasted and roared.

Grale did his duty stalwartly giving the Barolan lady away to the heir of Galanais, amid cheers and clapping.

Lissane looked radiant that day, in a long gown of shimmering silver and a diadem crowning her head of sea pearls mounted on silver filigree. Her eyes were kohled, and her lips rouged to oval perfection. It was a handsome affair, this wedding; the only sour face present was Varentin's. Even Hal Gallante was merry at his cups. But as ever her new husband looked bored and made no effort to conceal it—least of all to her. Sophistra was smiling today, though that smirk would have best suited a hyena. The girl Morwella was nowhere to be seen. Not that she was missed by anyone present.

Prince Gallante, now splendid in emerald and silver, the white ship of Galanais emblazoned on his breast, ushered in the priest of Talcan the Sky God, who rather hurriedly (or so Lissane thought) uttered the sacred words of union. And then it was done. Lissane was married: no longer a maid. But her real trial had only just begun.

***

She drank too much wine that evening, which was probably just as well considering what happened later and in the days to follow. The feast lasted throughout the night and well into the following morning. Lissane was congratulated and toasted by many a noble and his lady wife. She smiled at each politely and asked the relevant questions.

Then it was Estorien's turn. He slid into a chair next to Belshareze whilst Varentin was away to the privy—his fifth time that night. It was more than apparent to Lissane that her husband had other diversions. She couldn't care less. Bel swapped places and Estorien leaned, close making certain that no one was observing them.

Most were drunk by now and the chatelaine's eyes were elsewhere at this moment. Hence the Sarfanian had chosen his time well. When Estorien spoke his voice was clear and his words grave. He too had drank a lot of wine but it didn't show, saving that the pupils of his eyes were dilated and his brown face flushed with sudden passion.

"Lissane, I need to speak with you. I...this wedding isn't right...Varentin; he's a stuck up prick. You deserve better. I—"

Lissane cut in with whisper and smile. "It's too late...besides I doubt he'll trouble me often. He and his family have shown me and mine nothing but contempt since we arrived here, but then we are used to that—aren't we, Bel?" Belshareze hadn't heard. Her blonde mop covered her eyes and she looked about ready to nod off.

"Then they are all dogs." The Sarfanian's expression had darkened, and there was a dangerous violence accompanying the growly timbre of his loudly whispered words.

"It's not important." She touched his arm, urging him ease from his dark expression. "I can look after myself, Lord Estorien. Please...do not be concerned over me."

"Estorien...I'm no lord," he insisted, and was about to add something else when her husband re-emerged.

Varentin slumped into his chair, ignoring the both of them before rudely reaching passed the Sarfanian to shove a haunch of honeyed ham into his gaping mouth. "I'm going to bed," he muttered amid dribbles. "You may join me there, wife." He stole an acid glance at Estorien, who gave him look for look. Lissane felt a sudden stab of cold enter her heart.

Without further word Varentin took to his feet, kicked the chair aside and left the feasting hall. She followed him in dutiful silence, and everyone watching (or sober enough to do so) cheered as they departed from the feast. Everyone that is, except Belshareze and Grale and Estorien Sarfe—her only friends in that place at that time. Grale's brow was lined with worry, and Bel looked upset. Estorien Sarfe's almond gaze burnt deep into Varentin's back as though he could set him ablaze by sheer malice.

Varentin's quarters were three times the size of her own. Lissane considered them not nearly as nice. The furnishings here were dark and the statues and figurines, baroque and rather disturbing. Many depicted violent or carnal scenes of blatant depravity. They filled Lissane with revulsion. She shuddered, wondering what he would make her do.

Her husband ushered her in without comment, snapped his fingers at the waiting slaves; most ,Lissane now noted, were nubile girls of tender age whose tiny shifts left little to the imagination. There were boys too all had heavily kohled eyes and sad lonely faces. Within moments they were gone, leaving husband and wife together at last.

How I have dreaded this moment.

Varentin ignored her for a time as if relishing her ill-disguised discomfort. He took his seat at a couch and reached down to light the opium pipe he kept handy. Since she had arrived in Galanais, Lissane had discovered that this ugly smoking habit was commonplace among the sophisticates of western Gol. She liked it not and in her own province it was seen as an indulged weakness, and its use despised. Though there were some that partook.

At last Varentin deigned to look at her. "Well, come here then," He motioned her toward him with an impatient wave of his hand. Lissane hesitated, her heart suddenly fearful and girlish, dreading these next moments. "Look at you...you're too thin, Mother's right." His brown eyes had none of Estorien's sparkle. They were stoned, dreamy sluggish pools of lust. They tore at her like blunt scissors on cloth.

"Mother is right, I suppose, she usually is. I'll need to fuck you a few times...get you fat with child, and then I can leave you to rot in your bower with your silly maid. I'm sure that you'd prefer that—wouldn't you, wife?"

"This wasn't my idea," Lissane stuck her chin out and clenched her fists at her side. He laughed at that. "What is funny?" Lissane demanded.

"You're so rustic, you Barolans: so prim and fucking proper," he responded, waving his pipe at her and spilling scented smoke into the room, "but that's not surprising, considering."

Varentin's face looked distorted in the gloom of the room, and the flickering lamplight caught the lazy malice in his eyes. "Best get to the task, I s'pose," Varentin said. He laid aside his pipe and stood in front of her. "Take of your clothes." Varentin ordered Lissane. "I would survey my property."

Lissane shuddered and, silently screaming rebellion, unclasped her gown, letting it pool silently in the darkness below her feet. She wore nothing beneath it and her pale nakedness was covered with goose bumps for this room now seemed colder than any other in the palace.

Varentin smiled, both at her nakedness and discomfort, and then unlaced his silken hose, letting his manhood leap free. Then he was upon her with a savagery she hadn't prepared for. He shoved her face first onto a divan, taking her from behind—fast and hard—ramming into her and hurting her inside, and all the time grunting like hog on sow.

Lissane endured the assault in miserable silence despite the pain, and thankfully in moments it was over. He left her sore and sprawling on the bed and returned to his opium in the gloom. "You may return to your bower if you wish," he told her. "I've no further use for you tonight."

"It's our wedding night...we're meant to stay together," Lissane managed. Had she a knife, she would have put out his eyes "It won't look good when people see me leaving." She wouldn't let her hatred show.

"Oh, and I'm supposed to care a fig about that—am I?" He

dismissed her with a brisk wave of the hand. "Don your gown and leave me be, bitch. You may return tomorrow at a similar hour. I'm to get you with child soonest so that dear old Galanais has an heir after me. Go!"

Lissane offered no further argument. She slid from the bed, slipped into her now crumpled garment, and took her leave from her betrothed. He never gave her a second glance.

The palace was eerily deserted at this late hour, although raucous laughter still reached her from the feasting hall, where the stalwarts still quaffed and scoffed at the remaining fare. Lissane weaved through the silent passages of the palace: a pale shadow passing as a ghost that drifted lost through deserted palisades and empty stairs. She reached the minaret stairs and stole up to her room in shattered silence. She stopped in surprise, noticing her door was open, and a single lantern spilled light on the seated figure within.

It was Estorien Sarfe.

"I suspected you'd return here," he told her. "I've sent the slaves and your girl to bed, they were all exhausted anyway."

It was then that the tears came; Lissane couldn't hold them back any longer. Estorien took her in his arms, just holding her with a gentleness she had forgotten since Erun Cade had left her. Neither of them spoke much, and long before dawn he slipped away—lest anyone catch sight of him. But before he left her, Estorien promised one thing. "I will kill him," he said. It was enough.

**

And so it was that for many nights Lissane Barola, newlywed bride of Varentin Gallante, and Estorien Sarfe the visiting noble played a very dangerous game. They were careful and they were discreet. Estorien would listen as she raved at him about Varentin's cruelty.

"Soon," he would tell her then, and ease her anguish. A day came when Varentin didn't want her. She returned early, waited up. Estorien arrived and for the first time they made love. The die was cast. There was no way back now. But Lissane didn't care, she had found love again and love would prevail. Winter warmed to spring and Estorien departed for his home. She held to his promise. One day soon...

***

Eon Barola was seated at his table, a flagon of red wine in his left hand while the right gripped the crusty parchment of the letter—the first correspondence from his troublesome daughter since her wedding to Prince Varentin. It was short and succinct but then he had expected that.

The Baron now regretted his outburst of temper the night before Lissane's departure. It was the drink that had spoken. He shouldn't have blamed the girl as he had, but it was too late now, and besides, what really mattered was the link now finally accomplished between the two houses. Liss was bright, she might not love him (probably still hated him) but she would stay loyal to House Barola, of that much he was sure. He read the letter again before casting it aside. It read thus...

Father, Greeting,
A month has passed since the wedding, all is well enough.
I am attending the Prince's councils twice a week and learning
much concerning the ways of this province. That knowledge I will
impart to you as and when the time presents itself.
I will send further word soon.
Your daughter,
Lissane.

Eon rubbed his tired eyes and drained his flagon. The hour was late and he was weary and sodden with drink. Outside, causeway, town, and hills beyond were coated with fresh snow, and the castle gates glittered with sparkling rime in the moonlight.

A lone candle guttered in the far corner, and the fire in the hearth was now long past its best. It was time he made for his chamber. At least the girl would have warmed the bed for him, but he had no other need for her tonight. In the months ahead he would plan, make the most of the information his daughter sent him when it came. A fresh trade link via Galanais could only enrich Barola. He needed gold. Gold that would pay for the mercenaries he would use to topple Toreno Dovess, after he'd dealt with Treggara. There was much to attend to but at least he had made a start.

Eon shifted the covers and gazed down at the sleeping girl's naked body for a moment before sliding in beside her. He allowed himself a grunt of satisfaction before closing his tired eyes. His schemes were well under way and the long planned alliance achieved.

***

The fever had lasted for weeks now. It wasn't the usual mind-wasting, sap sucking sweats that common men had. It was a Sorcerer's Fever and Ozmandeus had it bad. His days were hazy and wandering. But his nights... He saw them burning, over and over again—so many corpses, so many screams. Zorne City's fall had had a profound effect on the surrounding regions. The entire country was now his to rule and every day more freebooters enlisted in his army.

But for what purpose? The Renegade had achieved all his objectives. His vengeance was complete and there were no enemies left to mock him. The old order had been obliterated by Ashmali's fires. Everything Ozmandeus had set out to achieve he had accomplished with remarkable ease.

But it wasn't enough. Deep inside his raving, churning mind, Ozmandeus knew that it wasn't nearly enough. The Demon still hungered, his fiery breath burning deep inside the Renegade's skull, causing him to cry out loud at night, as though he were a hungry swaddling babe.

Ashmali spoke to him in his dreams too, the voice rasping and relentless. *Feed me...I need to feed...I hunger for flesh...*it hissed at him. Every night the voice grew stronger and the Renegade's pain worsened, until at last he could take no more.

"I will feed you—I promise," he cried out," and soon...but free me from this pain."

"I hunger for souls," the voice had become tangible, and it seemed to Ozmandeus that a shimmering shape now leaned over him where he lay, fretting and sweating between the sheets. On his chest, the amulet's heat had scorched dark marks and burnt away all the black hairs that had once grown there.

"I MUST FEED!" The Demon's voice erupted both inside and outside his head and searing pain lanced deep between Ozmandeus's eyes. He screamed out loud and covered his face with his sweaty hands.

"I will give you Xandoria!" the Renegade yelled at the room. "I will give you the entire Great Continent! Just free me from this pain!" Ozmandeus's wild shouts had the servants running in from the corridors outside, where they had held vigil for these past many nights.

The sight they saw stopped them dead in their tracks. The Master was sitting up in his bed naked and untouched by flame: but his sheets and blankets, and the drapes, the carpets, the wall tapestries, and even the rushes on the floor were black and smouldering from a fire now spent. All was cinders and ash: but the sorcerer was himself again.

"I need food and fresh clean garments," he told the terrified retainers, his eyes were hollow and his voice rasping. As one they rushed to obey.

That very evening Ozmandeus stood on the high parapet of his castle. Gortez had been the family home for generations. They had driven him away, his enemies, but now he was back. And with Zorne City no more—even the ruins were shrivelled to dust, and the Renegade had ordered the survivors sow salt into the fields around—his castle of Gortez was the new seat of power in the land.

It was now deepest winter, and white covered the distant hills and valleys. Ozmandeus studied the fields below his castle, unlike everywhere else these were yellowy green—for no snow settled within a mile of Ashmali's breath.

The Renegade allowed himself a slight smile that evening—the first for many days. The searing agony had vanished completely that morning as Ashmali relinquished his hold. Now the Demon slumbered at peace deep inside his amulet, seeming content with the sorcerer's promise.

Let him slumber unawares, Ozmandeus would strengthen the binding spells, the Demon mustn't break through again. It would prove his ruin.

I must become stronger...need to keep him contained. I cannot let him rule me. I...am the master...

During the rest of that winter slaves and soldiers made ready for the planned invasion. It would start with Spagos and Ketaq. Both these countries would topple easily. Lamoza would prove harder, and Xandoria? Time would tell. The Empire was strong.

But then who can hold out long against Ashmali? Let the Emperor tremble—his days are running short. The Firelord is coming! Ozmandeus smiled again. His was the right decision, a man cannot stand still and it was his destiny to conquer wide realms. By spring they were ready to march.

Chapter 14

Enemy Country

Erun Cade watched the shrinking shore as the ferryman poled his barge across the eddying current of the Stonewash—the broad brown sluggish river marking the troubled boundary between Barola and Treggara.

As he watched, Erun felt a string of emotions wash through him: sadness, anger, excitement and fear, were but a few. A week had passed since Erun had mumbled farewell to Irulan and his gloomy cave, commencing his long trek north. He'd been in no hurry and had spent nights in taverns along the way, practicing his newfound skill with the harp and spinning yarns to the country folk, his new confidence growing daily. North Barola was pleasant country and the weather was mild for the time of year, hence his early journeying was easy enough.

But what awaited him in enemy country? He would steel his heart and focus on the many things that he had learnt. If it didn't kill him it would make him stronger.

The ferry thudded to a halt as it reached the north shore. The grizzled ferryman snatched his tossed coin from mid air and grunted terse thanks. He was Treggaran and not over friendly, but then that was to be expected. Erun left boatman and river without a word and followed the track leading out to the wild hill country ahead.

Treggara. Enemy country—a land of murderers and marauders…or so he had always been told. "You're from Torvosa," Irulan had told him, "But have stayed in Barola for a time: that will explain your accent. Keep to the main roads and you will be safe enough. Songsmiths and fableweavers are protected under the old king's law, and all six provinces still adhere to that—even Rodrutha. Keep your wits about you and you'll be fine."

During those first days Erun noticed little change, this country was not dissimilar from the lands south of the Stonewash, but it was becoming much colder. He now wore the fur cloak that Irulan had given him as a parting gift, wrapped tight around his shivering torso. Erun had the bow slung across his back with shafts alongside in their quiver. Aside these he wore a knife at his belt and clutched his ash stave in his gloved right hand. Both weapons and staff would fend off wild beasts and robbers—he hoped. The wooden harp he kept hidden and dry, buried beneath the folds of his heavy wool cloak.

The way grew steeper on his fifth day in Treggara: the road now wound up through high hills, their crowns covered with frosted firs. Until now he hadn't seen a soul, Treggara appeared vast and empty and the lands about desolate—untouched by plough or axe. When Erun topped the hills the weather worsened, the wind blasted his ears and icy knives of sleet stabbed at his face and hands. This Erun endured for several hours, but then just when he was considering another cold wet night beneath the leaden skies, a light showed through the trees ahead. At last, a sign of habitation.

Erun trudged toward the distant glow. He was soaked to the skin and frozen stiff by now, despite his heavy cloak. Icicles hung from his nose and his breath rasped as he hoisted his tired legs forward. Erun now wished that he had bought a pony with the limited coin Irulan had given him, but the pseudo hermit had insisted he walk because songsmiths *always* walked.

Another hour of miserable trudging awarded him a clearer

view of the light. It revealed a low thatched house, smoke clinging to the squat grey chimney and dim light spilling out from the few narrow windows. Not very welcoming, but Erun no longer cared.

When at last he reached the door he was relieved to discover that by some miracle, he had come across an inn out here in the bleakest wilderness. He neglected his harp for his fingers were stiff with cold and his throat dry. Instead Erun paid good coin for food and ale and took to his bed early with few words uttered.

The inn was mostly empty, just the odd farmer loitering in a smoky corner and the lone innkeep and his daughter, all indifferent to Erun's presence. Before dawn greyed the sky, he was on his way again.

Two weeks passed with little to tell. Two weeks of trudging through hills caked with snow, icy hours spent bordering frozen lakes and tramping through grim silent forests. He spent most nights alone in the dark with a solitary fire for warmth, though he did encounter the odd homestead where he played and was allowed bed and food and occasionally ale.

Winter deepened fast and the snow kept falling until the world was white. A day arrived when Erun Cade saw a line of slate grey hills topping the horizon in an unbroken wall, ranging out from east to west. He had reached central Treggara now and would need to be careful.

The Bloody Garrons—the cruel rulers of this land—kept their estates hereabouts, so Irulan had informed him. They were rumoured to be a nasty lot and best avoided on all counts. An hour before nightfall Erun reached the wall of hills and saw that the road cut a sharp right, almost tunnelling into a sheer cleft in the rock that he hadn't noticed until now.

Ahead reared a castle of sorts: a bleak, rain-washed rectangle of black stone, its four blunt towers fading into the murky whiteness above. The dreary walls were shouldered by the sheer stone flanks of the slaty hills, and pale light crept from the tiny slits in the stone—the only windows evident.

Erun could see no way past, for the road ran straight up to the castle gates. He had no wish to get any nearer to the place but nonetheless needed to find a way past. He dreaded to think what manner of folk dwelt in such a bleak place as this. He hesitated and then, shrugging off his defeat, turned to make his way back down the track, a slumped shiver of misery in that forlorn place. He would have to battle his way over the hills, but the thought of climbing those sheer heights awarded him little solace.

Too late. Erun froze when the strengthening wind carried the sound of clattering hoofs approaching fast from behind. He tried to hide but soon realised it was hopeless; the riders had already emerged from the bends below and they had spotted him at one. There were six of them, clad in grey cloaks and mail and each was armed with long spears, and swords and axes hung swinging from their belts.

Erun braced himself for confrontation as the riders sped towards him. Their faces were occluded by dark helms, each one crowned by a spike over six inches in length. The leader halted his horse scarce feet away from where Erun squatted in misery. There was foam on the creature's bit and it stamped and bucked its head.

The lead rider's helm bore the golden double headed axe—the symbol of House Garron. Hard grey eyes showed through the slits of his otherwise black enamelled helm. He levelled the spear at Erun's throat, forcing the youth back against the shoulder of the hill and pinning him there. The leader's men filed in close behind him, hedging Erun on all sides, their own long spears adding to his.

"And who might you be, vagabond or spy?" The leader's voice was raw and emotionless. He leaned forward in his saddle and glared down at Erun, who still stood frozen to the spot. "Speak now else I'll slice your throat."

Somehow Erun kept his nerve, remembering his training from Irulan. *Never let them know you're afraid. Be calm...confident...and mostly you will get by. Mostly...*

"I'm a songsmith," he answered, keeping his gaze steady as he watched the leader's horse snort and toss its head again. "A skilled teller of yarns from distant Dovesi Province. I've heard tell of the generosity of Treggara and hence am seeking new employment in the northlands."

The riders glanced at each other and laughed. The leader eased his spear forward so that it pierced Erun's neck and he felt an icy stab of fear as a bead of red stained his cloak.

"I think you are a Barolan spy," the leader said. "But we'll soon find out, eh lads?" The riders nodded and one or two grinned. "His lordship's away but two of his sons and a daughter are present; Slinsi in particular enjoys a good singsong, though her patience is short, and as I recall the last songsmith to visit our hall was fed to the hounds after he broke a harp string. The hounds are always hungry. Shame really, he had rather a good voice. But... 'tis only right we let you have a go, soggy tosspot or not."

He turned to his men. "This idiot can play at the feast to-night...we'll soon discover his qualities one way or another." He signalled the nearest rider. "Arden, dismount. The wretch can take your steed."

The rider slid from his horse and presented the reins to Erun without a word. After that the leader withdrew his spear so that Erun could mount the beast. This he did awkwardly, for he was both frozen and terrified to boot.

They took his bow, arrows and knife, and slung his stave aside in the ditch as though it were worthless. As one the riders then escorted him into the castle, the lone horseless warrior following on behind. Erun glanced up gloomily at the towering stone walls as they approached the stronghold.

An outer wall opened to iron gates: beyond these creaking rusty monsters was a muddy moat, its surface part crusted in brown dirty ice. A wooden planked drawbridge, perhaps six foot wide, spanned the gap. Beyond this Erun saw another gate and heavy portcullis cranked high. This second gate was swung wide open, its mouth yawning into the murk of the castle grounds beyond.

Hunched in the saddle, Erun took note of the construction; compared to this place Castle Barola was like a palace. Everywhere Erun looked; iron, stone and timber were stained with pitch, or else painted black, awarding the castle a macabre appearance. There were no adornments in view, just slabs of faceless stone, pierced now and then by pale slits for archers to shoot out from. Looking up, Erun saw bleak battlements holding up the snow-laden sky.

"Welcome to the Dreekhall," said the leader with a harsh laugh, before spurring his iron-shod beast across the drawbridge and on into the castle with Erun's borrowed steed hard on his heels. They passed through a square bailey and entered into a filthy courtyard; here they dismounted and the other riders led their horses away to the stable yards, somewhere off to the right.

Erun glanced about nervously in the gloom. The ground beneath his feet was squelched mud stained with cattle dung and other unmentionable filth. It stank even in this temperature. There were pens of sheep and cows, and close by a boar rutted away at a sow, whilst chicken and cocks scampered and squawked and got under feet.

Wooden balustrades paraded the inner walls, awarding passage between the rooms above, and narrow rickety wooden stairs let up to them from the central courtyard. Erun shivered; *what a horrible place.*

Dreekhall. Shitehall would be more appropriate.

The leader shoved Erun toward a heavy wooden door showing through the gloom. "This way," he muttered, struggling with his chinstrap before eventually freeing the heavy helm from his head. A shaggy mop of fair hair spilled free, the face beneath it slab hard, with cynical steel-grey eyes and badly broken nose. The brows were heavy, his lips and chin hidden by greying beard and a curved scar angled down from the outer corner of his right eye. Erun wondered whether all Treggarans were this ugly.

The door opened to a huge, lofty hall, framed by firelight, and with shadows dancing on the featureless walls. At the far end a fire threw some welcoming heat in their direction as a servant stoked the flames assiduously. Two shaggy figures were seated at a table, idly watching the retainer bellow and agitate the fire. Erun's captor coughed politely as he approached but they refused to turn their heads.

"That you, Dorrel?" asked the nearest after an uncomfortable few seconds' silence. His voice was harsh and blunt.

"My lords, I found this intruder on the road...claims to be a singer from Dovesi, but has the stench of Barola all over him." The leader prodded Erun in the back and motioned him on toward the fire. The two slouching figures watched in lazy silence as Dorrel and his charge filed before them and awaited their word.

Erun was grimly reminded of Eon Barola's sons as he nervously studied the hard faces of the two young men, now observing him as a man studies a stray mangy dog that has happened into his yard. They were almost identical in appearance—though one had dark straggly hair, the other's being snowy white and fine as gossamer. He remembered now that Volt Garron had many children but by far the most feared were the twin eldest brothers, called Slye and Rante, and the girl they called Slinsi Garron.

Slye and Rante were aptly named. They were huge men, mid twenties in years and both nearly seven foot in height. The one who had spoken (Rante, Erun soon discovered) was the dark haired twin. Slye was an albino, his face skull-like and his eyes a pinky red. Both had huge hands, veined and scarred and clearly well used. Each twin wore wool and leather of faded brown cloth, and there were gold coils and bangles glittering on their sinewy arms. Rante ran a dirty finger through his greasy beard.

"A songsmith..? Is he any good?"

"So he claims, my lord," responded Dorrel without much conviction.

"Well, good, he can serenade us this evening at the feast... it will serve as a little diversion before we butcher that bastard, Torrig." He turned to his pale brother, who just sat glaring balefully at Erun. Erun forced his shivering body to remain calm, though every instinct urged him to bolt outside. Rante and Dorrel were bad enough for sure, but just looking at the monster that was Slye Garron gave Erun Cade the willies.

"Have we decided how we're going to kill that Rodruthan bastard yet?" Rante asked his brother matter of factly.

"Slinsi's had a few ideas," Slye responded, his voice a mirror of his twin's. His pink eyes were still on Erun as he reached over for a jug of small beer resting idle on the table. Slye poured a liberal amount into a heavy metal goblet and took a long pull. He wiped his mouth on his sleeve and belched with vocal enthusiasm.

"I think we should boil him alive, personally. We haven't tried that on anyone yet...could be quite a laugh." He looked around as if there might be someone close they could try out first. Erun felt a worrying development occurring in his bowls. He squeezed his buttocks and preyed nothing slip out. He noticed that the retainer had discreetly departed minutes earlier.

"I think we should flay Torrig alive then send his cured hide away up to his father, as a warning of what happens to those who mess with House Garron," suggested Rante, taking a long pull at his own goblet. Mercifully now ignored, Erun and his escort watched on in fidgety silence.

Slye barked a short laugh. "He already knows that, Rante, after you gutted his niece last month. Oh, by the by, is her body still floating in the moat?"

Rante shook his head slowly. "Methinks the pike will have reduced it to bones by now...that or the eels." Rante took another slurp. "I don't know why you had to do away with her, brother. She was comely enough—for a Rodruthan bitch."

"She pissed me off," replied Slye, wiping his beery beard on the grubby tablecloth that had once resembled silk. "She started crying when I was pumping her arse."

"So you slit her throat and tossed her naked body in the moat, and now the whole of Rodrutha is screaming for vengeance," laughed Rante. "Father's not too happy about that. He wanted to finish our business with Barola this spring, but now he's got these Rodruthan twats raiding our northern borders—he'll have to deal with them first."

"Rodruthans have always raided our borders," shrugged Slye, "they raid us then we plunder them...much like Barola. Besides, Father's not ready to tackle Eon Barola yet. That one's a sleekit, conniving weasel; it will take some good planning to finish him and his brats, though I dare say Slins would fancy another crack at that Paolo."

Erun remembered hearing somewhere that the female warrior Slinsi Garron had battled with Paolo Barola during a Games held two years past in Torvosa. The outcome had been inconclusive, though Paolo had always claimed to have had the upper hand. "You still here..?" This last was directed at Dorrel.

"My lords, I wondered what you wanted done with this... pris...this songsmith...?" Dorrel was clearly uncomfortable in the presence of Volt Garron's burly sons. He was a tough man but these twins were enough to turn most men's blood to water. They were vicious and nasty predators of the worst kind, violent and savage like their father, Volt Garron, but said to lack both his control and cunning. Slye in particular was prone to sudden rage and savagery. Watching the pair now, Erun didn't think either a match for Paolo Barola. They were savage and cruel certainly, but they lacked Paolo's feline lethalness—or so he thought.

Rante awarded Erun a cold glance with his heavy blue gaze. "Feed him something and then toss him in one of the dungeons," he said with a shrug. Slye looked bored now. He yawned and then filched a chicken leg from an adjacent table and commenced ripping at it with his yellow brown teeth.

"Not the one Torrig's polluting," added Rante. "This fellow can idle the hours away down there until this evening—get his strength back. Poor tosser looks half dead. Besides, if he's any good we'll let him live...for now. If not we can feed him to the pike, or else Slins might want him. Both she and the pike are always hungry." Dorrel nodded briskly and made to leave, shoving Erun in front of him, but before they had taken two steps Rante Garron called out in mocking tones.

"You had best watch yourself, Dorrel," he said. "When Father learns that that Rodruthan wolfshead carved a way through seven of your best men, he'll have your scabby hide too." Dorrel departed the hall at haste, his face bleak and his eyes filled with angry loathing. He told a guard to drag Erun Cade to the kitchens, fill his stomach and then escort him down to the dungeons, and then left them to it.

***

Erun Cade's body ached with cold and damp. The four walls enclosing him stank of fear and shit. He cursed himself for a damned fool. He should never have come near this place, Irulan had warned him to stay well away from Dreekhall...and here he was trapped like a bug in a jar, and awaiting an uncertain and most likely, very unpleasant fate. He now felt more miserable than at any time saving the day after the murder of his father, and the loss of his beloved Lissane.

At least his stomach was full, though. Erun would focus on that and escape. There had to be a way out of this shithole. His mind drifted to and fro as that awful day wore on. Erun wondered how Lissane fared back at Barola, and whether she had finally wed Varentin Gallante. He hoped not. Six hard months had gone since last he'd seen her face. He missed her still, though not as much as he thought he would, and that made him feel guilty.

Erun had learnt much in the last six months, he now considered himself a stupid dreamer. He saw the idiotic naivety of his belief that he and Eon Barola's daughter could ever elope safely in this cruel world. He had been so confident—then. Everything had been possible—then. He would make it work. Erun Cade and Lissane Barola would win through and live. Where and how?

I'm an idiot...

And now Lissane was lost to him forever and his father's ghost still unavenged. Instead on a weird old pretend hermit's advice, Erun was embarking on some stupid journey to seek out the battle skills of a legendary warrior queen. Well, he would be if he wasn't stuck fast in this horrible place. It was ridiculous. He would laugh out loud if he wasn't so bloody miserable.

Introducing Erun Cade the warrior. It was risible. These Treggarans were warriors, as were Barola's sons. Even old Irulan was more of a fighter than Erun Cade would ever be. *Father was right...I'm a damned fool and soon I'll be a dead fool.* He wept for a time then.

Tears run out, Erun fumbled for the harp still held in place in a pouch inside his cloak. Drawing it out he began to play, tentatively at first and then with more confidence. The longer he played more positive he became, until he cast aside his earlier despair and focussed instead on his hatching plans for escape.

He would survive this night, Erun determined. He had a fine singing voice and Irulan had taught him enough tales to stand him in good stead, even in this shite company. Erun had only to hold his nerve and not break any strings like that poor other fellow had. Erun was not for pike or cauldron. He would survive—he had to.

Erun continued to play for over an hour, stopping only once when he heard a distant raspy voice accompanying him. Erun couldn't begin to guess the identity of that voice. The melancholy strain of the harp drifted up and out from the dungeons, causing the guards to shake their heads in bewilderment. It was a strangely beautiful sound in that dreary, awful place.

At last exhausted, Erun laid his harp aside and stretched out on the filthy rushed floor. He smiled then; despite his dire predicament, Erun Cade had discovered something new. His fighting spirit. He must have slept for a time.

***

Fires scorching the horizons, the skies dull brown and hazy. For days it had been thus. Spagos was burning. The six witch-riders watched in fearful silence from the borderlands. Their native Ketaq spread flat and brown behind them. Those flames were coming, Ketaq would be burning soon—their country was domino number three.

For days the witch-riders had watched, grim-faced and resolved. Each was a trained shaman and leader of this or that tribe. They were feared among the people, savage and wild as Ketaqis were. But these six knew when they were beaten. Ozmandeus. A madman from Zorne had awoken some ancient horror and now the west lands were burning. They could wait no longer—in days the fires would be here.

As one they reached their decision. The tribes would ride north. For the first time in over a thousand years the Ketaqi would return to the ice regions that spawned them. Life would be hard up there, many of the people would perish. But what choice did they have? The demon was coming. So began the exodus of the Ketaqi folk. A people on the move: behind them fire ahead the frozen wastes.

Chapter 15

Red Torrig

Erun woke cold and damp when the door creaked open, spilling wan torchlight into his pit, and then grunted when a heavy boot collided with his shin.

"Get up, singer," croaked a deep voice. Looking up, bleary eyed, Erun saw the same guard that had dragged him here looming over him—all bushy beard and missing teeth. "The feast's underway and you're expected. I hope you're good, boy, for your sake; the lads are well into drink already. There'll be murder at some point tonight."

He reached down and yanked Erun to his feet and with flaming brand in hand, led him back up to the now dusky, silent courtyard above. Outside, black rain glistened the walls and lightning speared down from the bitter void above. The earlier snow had been washed away by this freezing icy rain.

"A rare night," muttered the guard gloomily as he ushered Erun Cade toward the feasting hall from where raucous shouting could now be heard. "And me on duty too," he grumbled. "Make your way to the far end with your harp, lad....they're expecting you. Good luck." The grizzled soldier left him standing gormlessly outside the huge double doors that opened in on the feasting hall. Dreekhall—aptly named.

Erun pushed at the nearest door allowing him just enough room to enter. He stood gaping stupidly for a minute, taking in the sights and many sounds of House Garron at play. The hall that had seemed massive when last he had been here now appeared snug, an unruly raucous crowd now filled the long benches, and paraded at the high table ahead. The foggy atmosphere reeked of cooked flesh, candle wax, wet dog and farts.

It was apparent that the feast had been going at full pace for a time. Erun kept his cool despite the fear stabbing into his bowels. He'd voided them three times in the cell but they were still queasy.

A quiet shadow in that noisy place, Erun wended his way down the long sides of the benches, toward the roaring hearth where the brooding sons of Baron Garron and their ghastly cronies quaffed at wine and ale, and pawed playfully at the half naked maids that served them ale and mead.

Men whooped and prodded Erun as he squeezed passed, tenaciously forcing his way through the tight throng. Hounds showed him their teeth and cockroaches crunched under his feet. He heard a whoosh and ducked instinctively when something heavy flew passed his right ear. He heard a chunky thud followed by a groan and, looking across, realised that he hadn't been the target of this missile.

A man hung there by his wrists. He'd been stripped to the waist and his back whipped bloody. The hanging man's wiry torso was snaked blue with intricate tattoos, and splattered with fresh blood and purple bruising, the combination giving him a demonic appearance.

The prisoner's face was occluded by long shaggy hair, flame red in colour and unruly, hanging down well below his belt. His sinewy body swung from the highest cross beam to the left of the fire some six foot above the floor. Both the prisoner's naked chest and back showed beads of sweat from his close proximity to the hungry flames.

It was this wretch who had been the target of the missile—a

huge thigh bone that had collided with his shoulder and sent him swinging back and forth again. More came as the revellers roared in glee at their new game. The prisoner swung about like a stringed puppet. He must have been in agony, though he made no sound as the various projectiles thudded into his flesh, adding fresh welts and more broken skin.

Erun, ignored now, gained the high table and produced his harp with a practiced flourish. "I'm the songsmith Flavion," he announced in bold tones to the nobles at that table. Erun hated the pompous title that Irulan had given him. It seemed to work, though. They all glanced his way.

"Songsmiths all have poncey names," the pretend hermit had told him when he had complained about it. "It adds to their mystique and separates them from the commoner." Besides, one such Flavion had been a king or so he'd heard someplace. "I'm here to perform for your pleasure," he continued "My lords. I—"

"Get on with it—lest you want to feel this kiss your belly!" Rante Garron's hard eyes filleted Erun as he fingered his dirk with sweating paws, the twin's face was flushed and he'd obviously been drinking for several hours. To his left, Slye sat with one of the maids on his lap. He'd unlaced her jerkin so that her ample breasts swung free. He now squeezed one with his left hand while his right kept a firm grip on his goblet. Slye had just finished arm-wrestling a huge one-eyed warrior; they had lit candles either side of their elbows as they heaved to and fro, scorching the hairs on their forearms and grunting with exertion. Slye had won, naturally.

It was at that instant when Erun felt the gaze of another on him, and his eyes were drawn to the figure seated to the right of Rante Garron. A woman sat there. She was looking at him—this woman—staring at him in a suggestive way that made Erun's manhood swell inside his trousers and his face blaze scarlet. This had to be Slinsi Garron. *The pike woman...*

Slinsi Garron was not much shorter than her brothers. But the twins were brutal ugly men, whereas this Slinsi was comely, be it in a feral, hungry kind of way. She had snake eyes of the strangest yellowy brown. They seemed to notice and approve of what was occurring inside Erun Cade's trousers.

Her lips were pouty and full: her face tanned and handsome—though certainly not pretty. Her nose was too big and her eyes too weird. The hair was honey hued, long and wavy. But it was Slinsi Garron's smile that was the most wickedly entrancing thing about her. She was smiling at him now and Erun Cade almost forgot what he was about to do. Almost.

"I'm Slinsi. Are you going to play for me, singer?" Her voice was husky and deep. She was still smiling at him. Then Slinsi leant forward, resting her bangled brown arms on the table and sliding her tongue along her lower lip. "Play for me, singer. Just for me..." Rante mumbled something in her ear and Slinsi snorted a chuckle.

Erun tore his eyes away and set about his task. He shouldered his harp and somehow summoned calm, shutting out the fear—quelling his farty arse and the scary pounding in his pants. Instead focusing on the words that Irulan had schooled him so many times, to get to that sacred place where the true songsmith kept his soul.

Then Erun sang:

I am the river, the stream and the ocean,
I am the fountain, ever constant- yet liquid in motion,
I am stronger than stone - more mighty than the
mountain,
I am the Songsmith the weaver of fables,
I am the beacon...the voice of the gods,
I am beginning...now here my voice.

"It's a bit dreary," complained Rante, slurping at his beer.

"Oh, piss off," snapped Slinsi irritably, her snake eyes watching Erun's fingers dance along the harp strings. Erun ignored them, continuing, his voice now clear and strong, and his fingers working the harp with perfection.

That noisy hall grew silent at last as the young songsmith weaved his tales, his voice clear as mountain water, and the peals of his harp strings eerily beautiful. It seemed to those there that they had never heard stories like these told by this young harper called Flavion.

An hour passed—two, maybe three. Still Erun sang and, despite this place, and regardless of the danger, he began to enjoy himself. The music was inside him and the fables he wove painted colour in that grim, grey hall. When at last he stopped, the feasters hooted approval, and Slinsi, grinning broadly, tossed him a golden arm ring that had until now garlanded her own wrist.

"He lives...!" roared Rante, banging his goblet on the table, spilling wine over its already stained surface. Even Slye was smiling—though it was a smile you would expect from a wolf. The wench on his lap was now completely naked, and sat giggling as Slye's free hand walked two fingers up her left thigh. "Come, singer," the albino shouted, "take some food and ale, and then you can continue."

That night Erun sang until his voice was hoarse and the fingers of his hands bled. He wove tales of the kings and the Rebellion, together with ancient fables of distant lands and wild creatures that frequented them. Well had Irulan taught him. It was almost dawn when finally he was allowed to rest. They cheered and toasted Erun Cade amid roars and banging of knives on tables, and Slinsi blew him a kiss.

At last morning beckoned. Several warriors took their leave with this or that girl out into the rain-soaked gloom. Most remained in the hall, being far too drunk to venture beyond their benches. Within minutes they were asleep with the dogs, amid snores and farts, their prone shaggy shapes strewn across the rushes.

The twins had departed to their quarters, Slye (having noisily humped the girl on the table) had been in almost jovial spirits, and (the by now furiously drunk,) Rante had absconded with another beauty.

Before leaving the hall, Rante had taken to giving the prisoner a hard time. He'd retrieved a whip from the wall and had cracked it on the wretch's back furiously, adding fresh welts. Erun could see the blood pooling at the prisoner's feet, and he wondered how it was that this fellow was still alive. He was some tough bastard, that was for sure.

At last Rante had tired of his game and withdrawn from the hall with his wench. That left dogs and sleeping warriors. The servants and mead-maids had long since departed, saving those sharing the rushes with their drunken masters.

And then there was Slinsi. The alarm bells sounded off inside Erun's head.

Shit...

Slinsi Garron looked both alert and playful. She approached on all fours as he sprawled exhausted on one of the vacated benches, she'd been supping at a flagon of honey mead—the colour of her hair. Erun looked up as she lounged over him. He could smell her musky breath, and saw that the pupils of her big weird eyes were dilated. She kneeled before him, reached for his trousers and deftly unlaced the cord.

Oh shit and double shit...

Slinsi took his length in her mouth, working back and forth with her lips, while he took hold of her large breasts and fumbled enthusiastically until they tumbled free of their linen cage. Erun tried thinking about Lissane, tried feeling bad or embarrassed... anything. It was no good—the scary woman was all over him. Slinsi teased him down below for a time and then, just before he reached that crucial moment, cruelly curtailed her actions, and instead rose up to kiss him wetly on the lips. Erun sucked at her lips noisily for several moments and then tore urgently at her leggings, until Slinsi Garron lay naked and laughing on the table.

Erun gazed down at her long brown body, taking in the strong, muscular arms and thighs, the wicked yellow eyes, the erect nipples, and especially the thick, honey-coloured thatch between her legs. He wondered if he were in love again. Certainly he was excited. But no, this was just honest lust—raw and rampant.

It had been ages, after all, since last he'd done it. And he'd been doing it every day back then—despite what he had told his father. Besides Lissane was married now so why should he feel guilty? Erun couldn't stand it any longer. He lurched forward, straddling the table, and spilling what was left of the mead as Slinsi pulled him down onto her, amid raucous drunken laughter. He took her three times in three different ways, until at last sated and exhausted, the two of them slept like trolls.

***

The voice woke him like a warning bell tolling in his head. Slinsi lay sprawled on top of him, her snores battering his ears. Erun slid out from underneath her. She stirred, blinked and then commenced snoring again. He draped a redundant cloak over her nakedness and went and sat down close to the fire.

What to do now? Erun's mind drifted. The earlier plans of escape had been driven away by first his euphoria of song and tale, and then his turgid lust. Now he was on edge again. What to do? Somehow he had to escape. Erun glanced at the sleeping Slinsi and wondered if he really wanted to.

Then someone spoke, jolting him out of his dreamlike state as though a hammer had struck him between the eyes. Erun, startled and spooked, turned to see that the battered prisoner had raised his shaggy head, and now regarded him with fiercely defiant eyes— the colour of summer skies. There was intelligence in that gaze and a glint of irony.

"Morning, Singer, now that you've finished recovering from shagging that bitch, kindly untie these bonds. I need a piss."

Erun was too startled to respond so he just gaped stupid at the swinging, bloodied wild-eyed apparition. The prisoner's freckled face was dominated by those huge blue eyes, and the fine spirals of faint tattooing that covered his cheeks and brow. He sported scars as others did jewellery, and in each ear hung three large golden hoops. His hair was the most striking thing: very long and red as morning's embers.

Erun couldn't recall seeing such a wild looking character. Of course he had noticed him last night but had had other things on his mind. The prisoner looked slightly amused by Erun's shocked expression, if a bloodied, whipped; hanging man awaiting a hor-rible death could look amused. *Rodruthans are all mad...Where did I hear that?*

"What's the matter—never seen a Rodruthan before?" The hanging man's shrewd blue eyes were measuring Erun, as though gauging his courage.

"No..." Erun managed, feeling decidedly uncomfortable beneath that sardonic stare. Rodruthans were also rumoured to be cannibals among other things. And this prisoner looked hungry...

"Come on free me, boy, before that bastard Rante Garron comes back, and starts poking sharp things up at my arse because he cannot sleep."

Erun shook his head. He felt groggy this morning from lack of sleep and overexertion. "If I free you I'm a dead man," he told the Rodruthan. "All I want is to get out of this place in one piece. I'm sorry, but you are not part of my plans. If I keep entertaining this lot for a few more nights they might let me go. Besides, Slinsi's taken a shine to me."

"Yes, and they might slit your throat and bugger your arse too, if I know Treggarans. And as for Slinsi Bitch-cow...old snake eyes will tire of you soon, boy. She don't keep lovers for long, and those still living tend to be broken, useless things when our Slins has done with them."

The prisoner made a rough sound in his throat that could have been an attempt at laughter, and spat a large gobbet of red phlegm on the floor. "Free me, Singer, and I'll get us both out of here...you can trust me, I'm Rodruthan. We always keep our words."

Erun would sooner put trust in an angry adder. "Some chance," he responded, taking a backwards step. "You're half dead by the look of you—not fit to go anywhere. And I'm unarmed and ... maybe you haven't noticed but we're surrounded by snoring, overfed warriors of House Garron."

"These bruises are nothing, Singer, I've received worse beatings from my sisters. Besides," the Rodruthan jerked his shaggy head toward the snoring sprawl of Treggarans, "that lot won't stir until well after lunchtime. Treggarans never could take their grog."

Erun sighed and, harshly questioning his judgement again, grabbed an abandoned knife from the closest table and walked across to the Rodruthan, reaching up above his head to sever the rope. "What of the soldiers outside? The night watch and castle guard?" he enquired as he sliced.

"Oh, bugger them too," answered the Rodruthan. "They're

only Treggaran offal... no match for Red Torrig of Rodrutha." Erun slid the blade between the prisoner's fingers and the Rodruthan slumped to the ground with a deep appreciative sigh.

"Oh—that's nice," he said after a moment's respite. "Thanks, Singer, I was getting a bit of cramp in my left leg. Torrig's the name, by the way, in case you're hard of hearing."

'Red Torrig'... some throat slitting highwayman most likes...

"So I gather," replied Erun, before introducing himself to the Rodruthan.

"I didn't think that you were from Torvosa," chuckled Torrig, as he rubbed his chafed wrists and flexed his sinewy arms. "Those Dovesians are all so stuck up and proud." He scratched an ear and regarded his new companion with an open, frank expression.

"So you're a Barolan called Erun Cade, and not Flavion the poncey Singer of Dovess. Slinsi will be disappointed. Best not tell her, hey." Torrig slapped Erun's back, nearly knocking him over. "You must be bonkers as I am boy, wandering in on this fine hostelry like some vagrant sheep on slaughter day."

Torrig's eyes rested on the food still left at the tables. "I'm rather peckish," he announced, and then reached across to a table and rammed a wedge of pork in one corner of his mouth. The other corner he reserved for a large gulp of wine. "That's better," he munched and slurped, "tis thirsty hot work all that hanging about listening to bonking Barolans. You've got some energy lad—I'll give you that."

*You were watching...*Erun pulled a face.

"Hadn't we better be leaving?" Erun suggested, stoically ignoring the gibes in his direction. He glanced round the hall, fearing that at any moment one of the sleepers would awaken, or else a guard or (far worse) Rante or Slye Garron would enter the hall and find them standing there like gormless idiots.

"I suppose so," replied Torrig with a shrug. "I had hoped to skewer Rante Garron with his own eating knife, but I'll make do with a few guards instead. Come on, Singer! What are you waiting for? We've an escape to enable."

Torrig, beaming broadly at Erun, thrust a prone reveller's

knife into his belt and tossed another across to his new associate. Erun snatched it with his right hand and nodded terse thanks. "My vengeance can wait awhile yet," the Rodruthan added before stepping carefully around the prone sleepers, with Erun Cade stealing close behind.

A dog opened a bloodshot eye and showed his teeth, but Torrig lobbed the hound a redundant sausage, and they reached the doors without any trouble. Erun turned back and awarded the prone, still snoring shape of Slinsi Garron, a final mournful glance. She might be a violent madwoman, but he had rather liked her.

***

The Lamozan Gap. A missing tooth in the long mountain range separating Lamoza from Xandoria. A narrow plain framed by firs, for years contested by both countries. A place of ambush, treachery and deceitful eye. A dangerous place where traders traded with stolen coin whilst their armed guards watched on, stony-eyed. Those honest folk wishing to pass must needs pay high toll to the mountain bandits frequenting either side. The Lamozan Gap—the only gateway into the west.

Through it now tore a single rider. At full pelt, his roan lathered and his apparel torn and shabby. This Darl the messenger had ridden for days now, his news couldn't wait. Darl's master, the Chancellor in Xenn, needed to know first-hand about what was really happening out west.

The rumours were true. Spagos fallen and now Ketaq. Aketa burned and Siotta ablaze. Both those ancient cities brought low by the horror from distant Zorne.

And there was panic in Lamoza City. They were next in line. Riots and craziness were breaking out in the streets, so the messenger was told by the many refugees he'd met. The Demon is coming—that was what people were saying there. The priests alone arguing it was the gods themselves, tired of mankind and his foolish ways. Apocalypse and ruin.

Darl hadn't believed the rumours so he had ventured west until he witnessed the smoke for real. And the fear. The sheer terror had almost unmanned him.

. Stout of heart, he'd ridden into the storm, heeding not the warnings of those fleeing across his path. He'd ridden hard, passing close to the southern edge of the Eye of Lamoza, that great lake renowned for its wild birds and water fowl. There were no birds there now. Days later he reached the forests of southern Ketaq where the River Spagos marked Lamoza's western boundary. But the Spagos was dry and the forests ablaze.

Then Darl saw it—the shape in the fire. An alien, flickering face towering a hundred feet above the trees. The face of a demon fashioned by flame. The messenger had his proof. Time to leave. Within minutes he'd overtaken the last fleeing stragglers from the borderlands, hearing their screams as the questing flame devoured them.

Darl the messenger rode harder and harder until his exhausted horse fell dead beneath him. Then he walked, half ran; stole another horse from a party of sleeping merchants in a wood. Then, mounted again, Darl the messenger pressed on hard into the east lest the heat and crackle of flame consume him too.

Exhausted, Darl reached the Gap. Mercifully it was clear. Once through, Xandorian guards checked him at the border until he showed them the seal. He was the Chancellor's chosen man so of course they let him through without a word, though they were puzzled by his grim state and battered attire. Darl was well known as a hard character—a fighting man and a lone wolf. He was also admired for his immaculate garb and fastidious manners in court. What had happened to reduce such a man to this gibbering worn-out wreck? Darl ignored their worried questions, instead he traded horses and pressed on. A week later he reached Xenn City. It was two days after that the Chancellor deigned to hear him.

Chapter 16

Escape from Dreekhall

Torrig and Erun Cade vacated the feasting hall in silence and stole warily into the courtyard, two pale shadows, flitting from wall to wall. It was fully light now and still raining heavily, the grey-black castle walls hung heavy with mist.

"This way, Singer," Torrig grabbed Erun's arm and hoisted him about. "We need to get to the north gate, it's all right—I think I remember the way. Keep close and don't trip over anything." Erun rolled his eyes.

Another door loomed out of the murk, as dripping; they reached the far end of the courtyard. Torrig winced as the door creaked when he pushed at it. "Needs oiling," he muttered, and then shouldered his way through the gap. Erun followed his heart in his mouth, and his head continually questioning his sanity. A dim passage led past more doors before opening out to another yard of sorts. Erun froze, he could see a figure leaning on a spear and watching the rain.

"Wait here," whispered Torrig, slipping the knife from his belt. He took the guard at a run. The Treggaran glanced around, hearing hurried footfalls, his jaw dropping in surprise. Torrig's pilfered knife tore into his neck, severing his jugular and spraying crimson gore up the wall.

The guard slumped forward, his helmet slipping from his head. Torrig snatched it before it clattered on the stone cobbles of the passage floor. The Rodruthan knelt to retrieve the guard's sword: he grinned stupidly as he tossed it from hand to hand.

"That's better," Torrig said, winking back at Erun. Erun gaped at the blood now pooling slowing over the stone, and then jumped as his companion shoved him hard. "Wake up, Singer; we've a way to go yet! No time for sleepies." Erun nodded, gingerly stepped across the dead Treggaran's corpse, and then followed his annoyingly cheerful companion out into the rain again.

They cleared the open space and reached a wide gate leading beneath the inner curtain walls. "The dungeons are down there." Torrig motioned a side door, and Erun vaguely recalled being led out of here by the grizzled guard last eve. Was that really only yesterday? He wished that he had his bow or even the stave; though both were now lost, and he felt ashamed that he had so easily misplaced Irulan's gifts.

He still had the harp at least, although that wouldn't prove much of a weapon, more of a hindrance probably. Nevertheless, Erun fumbled at it fondly beneath his cloak just to make sure he still had it. After last night's performance, he now considered himself to be a proper songsmith.

They now crept stealthily along the wide tunnel that opened on another bailey with a view of the north gates ahead. They passed a guardroom where another soldier sat dicing at table, some yards off to their right. He wore no helmet or mail and yawned, taking a long pull at the tankard he clutched in his left palm.

Torrig hurled the knife: the guard lurched forward, his head slamming onto the table, and the knife's bone hilt showing from the base of his skull. The Rodruthan retrieved the blade swiftly, pulling the guard's head back, and Erun recognised the bearded old soldier that had shown kindness to him the evening before. Those dead eyes now accused him in the half light.

Erun felt suddenly sick. He hated all this killing, but was determined not to vomit in front of the Rodruthan. "You're a rare one, Singer," said Torrig, looking askance at Erun's shocked expression and greenish hue. He shook his head. "Never seen a dead man before?"

"Once..." Erun stopped short when felt something hard slapped into his palm and, looking down, saw that Torrig had shoved the Treggaran's sword into his grasp. "I...I'm not familiar with swords," he said, wishing that Irulan had let him practice with the sword he'd discovered in the cave.

"Just hang on to that bit and poke the pointy end at anyone who gets in bloody the way," Torrig told him. "We'll be fine. Come on—it's just the outer bailey, and then we're free." Erun winced, *oh, is that all*...The sword's leather grip did feel good in his hand, however.

Ahead, twenty yards or so over a mound of grazed grass, reared the Dreekhall's outer walls. They loomed grim and stark out of the rain: not a comforting sight. The only way through was via the north bailey, under a wide arch that showed like a ghastly mouth in the wan, grey light ahead. On Torrig's word they made a rush for it. To either side of the arch were stone stairs—Erun noticed as he sped—leading up to the high crenulations above. Erun didn't want to think about the guards up there. The thought of a crossbow bolt in his back was not comforting in the least.

Torrig grabbed his shoulder and motioned him stop, placing a grubby finger on Erun's lips. "I'll go see," he told him with another of his manic grins. Seconds later he was back, still grinning, and leaning close to whisper in Erun's ear. "There are six of them," Torrig said as though that were excellent news. "If we rush them now—we can skewer the lot, and then win free before those lazy turds on the walls notice anything. You ready, Singer?"

Erun was anything but ready, but managed to nod weakly all the same.

"You sure?" Torrig was staring at him.

"Very happy."

"Cheer up, Barola; you're with Red Torrig of Rodrutha!" Erun rolled his eyes for the third time, and then followed on with heart in mouth, and sword clutched hard and sweaty between his fingers.

They entered the northern bailey and Erun took quick stock of the guards. Three diced at a table, and two others leaned on heavy spears. These were gazing out from the gatehouse, their expressions sombre and their spiked-helmeted heads dripping, as they watched the rain descend in torrents outside. That left the captain, who was perched on a bench to their left, working on the edge of his huge battleaxe with stone and oil.

Torrig took him first. Before Erun had a chance to raise his sword, the Rodruthan had launched his wiry, agile body like a missile into the room.

A wildcat starved and snarling, Torrig pounced on a table, he twisted, kicking the captain full in the face with both feet parallel, and sending him sprawling across the floor. The gamers cursed in alarm and leapt from their tables with swords held ready. Torrig weaved past one questing blade, ducked under another, before thrusting his sword hard into the ribs of the third man. He twisted the blade and kicked the body free; then his lightning-swift back thrust sliced open the neck of the second dicer, while the third circled him wide eyed caution.

The Treggaran lunged, Torrig danced aside with an acrobat's grace, and sliced down hard, severing the man's sword arm just below his elbow. The guard screamed and slunk to the floor, trying to quell the scarlet jet spurting out from his stump. Torrig despatched the wounded guard with cool precision. "You still awake, Singer?" Torrig turned and yelled back at Erun, who stood motionless and gawping inanely behind him.

The two guards manning the door now rushed back into the bailey, the first launching a spear at Torrig's exposed back.

Erun watched the spear arc and fly towards his companion. Suddenly all those intense weeks of training kicked in. His fear gone at last, Erun leaped forward, his right arm whirling across the hurled spear's path, knocking it aside. He landed lightly on the balls of his feet, and then dived low beneath the second spearman's probing thrust, slamming his body into the mail vest, pitching the guard backwards, and then colliding on top of him as he fell, his arms flailing at his sides. This Treggaran was stronger than Erun though. He rolled free and rammed his steel covered head hard up into Erun's face. Erun heard the horrible crunch of bone as searing pain exploded between his eyes. He saw stars and spewed as the bailey did three-sixty.

The guard grinned at him and fumbled for his dagger, but then his eyes glazed and his helmeted head rolled free from his body, the new wash of blood soaking Erun's face and shoulders and occluding his still spinning vision. Torrig hoisted the spewing Barolan to his feet with a grin. He now carried the captain's axe in one hand. The fool had seized Torrig's leg, pulling at him while he finished off the second spearman. A swift downward stamp had crushed the guard captain's windpipe, allowing Torrig to reach down for the axe. "Nice weapon, this!" Torrig grinned at Erun, who managed a grunt in reply. "Nose hurt, Singer? Never mind...could have been your head, hey."

"Thanks," Erun muttered without meaning it. It had all happened so fast. All six Treggarans were now dead, but Erun's head was still spinning, and his nose was screaming at him.

He buckled forward and spewed again on the corpse of the headless guard. Torrig shoved his sword through his belt and shouldered the axe. He grabbed Erun's collar, pulling him erect, and dragging his newfound friend as though he were a grain sack, beneath the rusty iron portcullis and out of the gatehouse.

Somehow Erun found his legs. They sped along the drawbridge, Erun's eyes were streaming with water, and he was only dimly aware of the filthy rime-covered moat below. He heard shouts, and panicked when a spear struck the timber a yard to his right. Another broke the ice on the moat. But within moments they were out of range of spears and the crossbowmen were nowhere in evidence. Erun thanked the gods for that. He sped after Torrig, on down the sharp slope that led away from the castle walls, to the wide stretching fields beyond and below.

One sharp eyed fellow did take aim from the parapet, his crossbow quickly cranked and ready. Slinsi skewered him open from behind.

"That's my singer, stupid," she told the dying man, before yelling enthusiastically down at the two renegades fleeing like lunatics out of range. "Farewell, Singer!" Slinsi called down, though Erun was now too far gone to hear. "Anytime you want a rematch, I'll be waiting!" She blew him a kiss and then left the battlements to the milling, wasp-angry, guards.

Once they were out of sight, Torrig dragged his suffering friend away from the path and reaching a thorn brake, crouched down allowing Erun to sit holding his head up, slowing the blood that still coursed in sticky streams down his chin.

"Your nose is broken," grinned Torrig as though that were good news." But it'll mend straight enough...you'll keep your looks, I daresay. Besides a bent nose is more interesting and it goes with that red scar. When did you get that one? It's a beauty."

Erun said nothing. He felt cold and weak, sick to the bone, and with the searing pain in his face, was close to passing out. "Wait here, Singer," Torrig said, "I'll be back directly." Torrig slid out from the bushes and soon vanished into the rainy morning.

"Where you going..?" Erun yelled out after him, shaking his head and then wincing at the pain.

"I'm thinking we need horses," the Rodruthan's hoarse shout drifted back through the mist.

"Are you mad, those bastards be on us in seconds...?" There was no answer. Red Torrig had gone.

Erun clutched his head in his hands and wished he were anywhere else. He waited in miserable, wet silence. Long minutes passed—maybe an hour.

Nothing. At any moment Erun expected to hear shouts, or else the tramp of marching feet as the patrolling Treggarans discovered his hiding place. But nothing happened and time just dragged on and on. He now suspected that the mad Rodruthan had got himself killed, or else recaptured—and serve the crazy bastard right too. What should he do though? Go back and try to rescue the fool? Bugger Red Torrig—that would only get Erun killed too. He doubted that Slinsi would vouch for him now—she would more likely do the killing after he ran out on her. Fine woman, that one.

Despite his pain Erun Cade felt a fresh stirring in his groin.

Erun had to do something. He couldn't leave his new idiotic friend to the Treggarans. God's only knew what they would do to him now. Those bloody twins would be capable of anything. Erun muttered equal amounts of curses aimed at Torrig, the freezing rain, and the relentless stabbing pain in his nose. Then, (just when he had decided to make a move toward the castle) a clatter of hoofs and a hoarse shout told him that, somehow, impossibly, Torrig Red Hair had returned.

"Come on, Singer," Torrig laughed across at him, "time we vacated this hedgerow, methinks."

Erun jumped up and grinned with stunned relief when he saw the Rodruthan. Torrig was now leaning forward over the stolen saddle of a chestnut charger, while loosely leading a similar beast behind him, the reins trailing in the long frozen grasses. Torrig reined his beast in feet away from Erun and motioned the Barolan to mount the other horse.

"I'm not familiar with horses," Erun complained. In Barola thoroughbreds were the property of the Baron. Few commoners rode anything other than ponies or mules. Erun, to date had stayed well clear of both. A mule had bit him when he was a small boy and he hadn't trusted the beasts since. He remembered how accomplished a rider Lissane had been, and felt a stab of guilt when he thought about her. That was then...

"Time to learn," urged Torrig, enthusiastically. "Best hurry too, we've company."

Erun glanced back up the hill toward the castle that bulked gloomily close, its walls and the slopes of the slatey hills still shrouded by the morning mist and rain. Erun saw shapes and heard shouts as the first riders filed out onto the road.

Shi— not again!

Erun leaped up at the horse in a panic, his left foot wildly stretching for the stirrup, and his right arm yanking hard at the reins. Torrig glared at him as though he'd lost his wits.

"It's a horse, not a bloody woman—calm down, boy. Here, I found this in my travels." He tossed Erun a bundle, which the

Barolan was delighted to discover contained his bow and sack of arrows.

"How did you find these?" Erun asked his friend as the horse snorted and kicked beneath him as though aware it was carrying an idiot.

"No questions...time to ride!" came the answer. Erun—feeling a bit braver now that he had his bow back—straddled the saddle and earnestly tried to make sense of his arms and legs. He had just found the other stirrup with his questing right foot when Torrig, hooting, slapped the horse's rump, and the beast sprung forward, nearly pitching Erun from the saddle. Erun grit his teeth and somehow hung on.

I hate this...

The Treggarans roared as they spotted the two riders fleeing down the hill, and rejoining the road a hundred yards ahead. Erun clung to the reins like a wind-battered owl on a gatepost, clenched his knees hard, and prayed to every god he could remember that he wouldn't fall off.

The chase was on.

Miraculously Erun Cade remained in his saddle, as his horse sped down the track at breakneck speed. Ahead, Torrig's wild red hair streamed behind him, and his bare feet shunned the stirrups as he guided his own beast expertly by thigh and calf. This Rodruthan seemed to be very good at everything he did. It was most annoying. They rode thus for an hour, the Treggarans neither gaining or falling back, and the rain still cascading in curtains, blinding Erun from the way ahead.

"Their beasts will tire soon," yelled Torrig, turning in his saddle to grin back at him. "Weighed down by all that bloody armour. Can't stand the stuff myself. Restricts movement. You did alright back there for a stupid singer, boy," he added. "How's the nose holding out?"

"It hurts..." Erun dared a glance behind and saw that Torrig was right. The Treggarans were already dropping back. He thanked his collective deities, long forsaken; now feeling a flood of relief wash over him. They were going to make it after all.

Torrig called a halt when they crested a low rise, awarding wide views of the land thereabouts. Looking back they saw the enemy halt and sit their horses a half mile or so behind. "They'll send word via pigeon to the soldiers at the ford," Torrig told him. "We'd have a hard time getting through that way."

"What do you propose..?" Erun was at a total loss and, short of escaping from Dreekhall's fury, hadn't formulated any kind of plan.

"We'll make for Longships on the east coast in my country. It's not that far. Once there, we can commandeer a vessel; reach Druthan Crags in a week."

"Druthan Crags..?" Erun's face blanched hearing that name. Druthan Crags was the home of 'Mad King Brude' who was rumoured to have eaten various members of his household, and though he doubted this were true, Erun Cade had no wish to go anywhere near the place.

"Aye, Father will be glad to meet you, Singer." Erun let that one hang in the air.

Father? He's not Brude's...?

Erun glanced sidelong at his wild haired companion. "You're not *the* Torrig Red Hair are you?" Torrig grinned at him. That did it. Torrig Red Hair had as bad a reputation as his father, the self proclaimed 'King' Brude. Were Erun to spend time with such a one? Well, it couldn't end well. No, he would escape from the present danger, and then part companies with this mad Rodruthan as soon as was politic.

He liked Torrig, but then he'd liked Slinsi Garron too. But these northerners were clearly all deranged and Erun daren't trust anyone related to Mad Brude of Druthan Crags. Scaffa's island lay somewhere off the north coast of Red Torrig's country, so at least they were going in the right direction. That was something. He'd hang on to that.

"They're turning back," announced Torrig, twisting round in his saddle again. They reined in and Erun watched, as the distant riders turned their steeds and filed back along the road, their long ashen spears now sloped across their shoulders. "They know they'll never catch us now—with all that steel they're weighed down with," said Torrig. "We'll rest for a while, Singer...wait till nightfall, then make our way across the plain. I know this country well enough from the raiding seasons."

They dismounted, much to Erun's relief, and Torrig tied off the horses to a stump after tending to their needs. "Here, laddie," he said when he returned to find Erun sitting as one dazed by the rain. "Let me have a look at that nose."

Before Erun had time to object, Torrig's right hand shot out and gripped Erun's aching nose betwixt forefinger and thumb. He gave a sudden violent tug, and Erun yelped like a puppy as a sharp lancing pain brought tears to his eyes. "That's better," grinned the Rodruthan. "It's straight again now....well not quite so bent, any-how." But Erun never heard him. He'd already passed out.

***

When he woke it was dark and the rain had finally ceased. Erun Cade was cold, despondent, and soaked to the bone. His nose throbbed and the endless sogging had crept in beneath his cloak, rendering the garment useless and very heavy besides, and now adding to his catalogue of miseries.

Even his harp strings were sodden. Erun took the instrument out and wiped the damp off with his shirt sleeve as best he could. Erun also suspected that he had a head cold coming on, just to dampen his spirits further. He sneezed twice and then cursed as his nose throbbed as though struck by hammers.

Torrig, crouching close, tossed something his way and Erun recognised food. His stomach rumbled: he had forgotten about food and now he was starving.

"It's salt beef," Torrig told him. "I got it from the kitchens before I acquired our horses. It's good—though a bit hard on the teeth. Chew for a while and it will soften."

"How did you get back into the castle?" Erun munched at his dried beef stick, he felt more cheerful now that he was eating. "I mean... it must have been like entering a hornets' nest."

"It was easy enough," shrugged Torrig. "The stables were over the far side. I scaled the flank of the nearest hill until I could look down on the walls. I then jumped and slipped inside the castle. It was chaos in there...they'd all woke up with sore heads. That tosspot Rante was swearing at Slye, Slye was hitting someone with something hard, and Slinsi was hitting him...with a kettle I think—at least that's what it looked like."

Torrig picked his nose and examined the contents. "So, I saddled fast, and beat a way out the main gate, just before they managed to muster a pursuit. I found your bow in one of the passageways, Singer, with a guard fingering it. I slew the guard and pilfered it, and then I noticed that it had a foreign look. It *is* yours, I trust?" Erun nodded. "I thought so," munched Torrig. "It is well made...good yew—hard to come by. How did you acquire it?" he asked, his shrewd eyes reading Erun's blue-grey stare.

"A friend," responded Erun and then quickly changed the subject. "Didn't they try to stop you..?"

"Yep," acknowledged Torrig with a nod, "but I gutted another half dozen, and the rest soon lost heart." Erun closed his eyes and counted to ten. He wondered if all Rodruthans were as dislodged between the ears as his new companion. He *was* grateful though, and, despite copious misgivings, was growing to like this Torrig Red Hair of House Rodrutha.

An hour later they were back on the road, the lowering sky still heavy with cloud, and no moonlight paving their way. Despite that, Torrig steered a confident course through the gloom, guiding his beast over wild windblown heather, and through tangled breaks of gorse and brier. Erun was more relaxed in his saddle now, and his horse had forgiven him his earlier incompetence.

By midnight the two riders had left the hills flanking Dreekhall well behind them. They rested their steeds for a few hours, and took to shelter in a clutch of low trees when the rain started again. "Does it always rain in Treggara?" grumbled Erun, gazing out gloomily from their soggy hide.

"Mostly," replied Torrig, "Save when it's snowing or sleeting."

"What about your own country?

"The sun always shines in Rodrutha." Erun doubted that but

he kept his own counsel on the matter.

Morning found them underway again. Torrig had discovered another road, this one leading north east to the coast of his own country, which he told his companion was now quite close. "You'll like Longships," said Torrig with a grin. "We can stay in Helga's brothel; I daresay she'll have a spare wench there that you can poke, for a penny or two. She keeps a fine strong brew on the go as well."

Erun thought of Lissane and said nothing. He now felt rather ashamed about his exertions back in the castle, with Slinsi Garron. The thought of jostling with yet another woman felt like total betrayal, though his loins tingled a touch at the idea. But it had been a long time since he'd enjoyed any action in that department, until Slinsi launched herself on him.

Erun had once had a bit of a reputation back home. Poets usually did. Girls liked poets. Before Lissane Barola stole his heart, rendering him moongazy and stupid, the young Erun Cade had sowed many a wild oat, and had lain with a good few lasses in the rooky woods near his father's forge. But that was long dead history now. He had to move on. Lissane was gone, but part of him still hoped to see her again. *Stranger things have happened.* He turned his thoughts to other matters.

By mid morning the rain eased and then stopped altogether. Ahead showed a pale strip of blue, and a sudden breeze carried with it the salty promise of the ocean. Erun gazed about with searching eyes. The country here was flatter, and he could see for miles ahead through heath and moor, until, after scanning for several moments, his keen gaze glanced a ribbon of water ahead.

"Is that the sea?" Erun pointed to that distant blue glimmer.

"No, that's Creekywater on its way down to the brine," replied the Rodruthan. "It's a marshy stream, separates Treggara from my own country. Longships is on the far side, a few miles upstream from the sea."

Erun had a sinking feeling in his stomach. "How do we cross it?" he asked, thinking of crocodiles and pike. He'd never seen a crocodile but was certain that if they existed at all they would be found in abundance here.

"I was coming to that," responded Torrig with an expansive wave of the hand. "At low tide the way across is navigable to the careful and sure of foot. It's quite safe, Singer, as long as you steer clear of the quicksand and crocodiles," (Torrig winked at him annoyingly as though he had read Erun's thoughts like a map), "and don't let the salt leeches creep up your legs and drain your vitals." *Salt leeches*...Erun's groin tingled for all the wrong reasons.

"I can't wait..."

By afternoon they reached the southern banks of Creekywater. Ahead was a sea of reed and marsh, and humming, biting gnats. Beyond that a muddy strand of shallow, churning water. Torrig slid from his horse. "We had best lead the beasts behind us," he told Erun, as he started to venture toward the reeds. "Oh, and mind where you place your feet too, Singer." Erun dismounted and tenuously led the beast behind him; both his eyes fixed studiously on the watery ground.

It took over an hour to cross. Once Erun's horse's hind legs sank into quicksand, but the two of them managed to tug her free, and twice Erun spied what he thought were sea crocodiles, their reptile heads showing above the shallow water. Torrig informed him that they were baby krakens—as though that was something to be pleased about. Erun was heartily relieved when they reached the northern bank without further mishap.

They remounted in haste and Torrig, eager now, led the way up a narrow track that climbed up to a small ridge, before spilling out upon a wide expanse of featureless open country. Torrig held out both his hands wide on either side and shouted up at the sky. Erun thought he might be having a turn.

"Rodrutha!" Torrig yelled and his voice echoed across the land. "I'm back. It's me...Red Torrig. Torrig Red Hair. Torrig the truly wonderful! Have you missed me?" Torrig tossed the double headed axe high into the air and caught it deftly on descent. "Come on, Singer," he grinned wildly back at po-faced Erun. "Let's go see my fat Helga and her gals. She'll like you, Singer. My Helga's always had a thing about poets and such." Erun raised a brow and wondered what the next hours would bring. If Rodruthan women were anything like Slinsi Garron he must needs enter training.

Longships proved a ribbon of low thatched cottages lining the northern reedy bank of Creekywater. There were fishing craft listing on exposed mud strands, these awaiting the incoming tide, and various scruffy figures could be seen ambling about their tasks. Here was a red faced woman lifting water from a well, and there an old whitebeard mending nets in front of his cottage, a broad pipe clenched tight between his teeth. Thick smoke drifted up in coils from the haphazard roofs, and dogs lurked lazily in muddy alleys.

A well worn track led along the edge of Creekywater and this they followed, reaching the town just as evening darkened the sky.

Torrig halted his steed outside a long house with twin chimneys, and low heavy thatch from which issued a thick trail of smoke. It dwarfed the other houses Erun had seen so far, being two storeys in height, and constructed of rough brick rather than the white wattled plaster coating the other dwellings that clustered around.

Glancing in through the dirty windows, Erun could see a large low-beamed room with a bench at one side and a lit fire the other. Rickety stairs led up to the second storey.

"Wait here a moment." Torrig handed his reins to Erun, vaulted from his horse, hurdled the gate, and knocked loudly on the door with his knuckles three times. Seconds later it groaned ajar.

A woman stood there in a pale gown that did little to conceal her ample breasts and white, chubby thighs. Her hair was a pale orange as opposed to Torrig's flame red, but she was comely enough, thought Erun, watching from behind. She'd large smiling eyes, and a pert nose, dusted by freckles on either side.

Erun heard the woman laugh bawdily at something Torrig said, and he saw that they were both grinning over at him from the door. Erun felt his face flush red when she called him across. Her teeth were yellow with several missing, despite this she appeared a friendly soul.

"Torrig tells me you're a songsmith," she said, her voice husky and warm as heated mead. "And that you impressed the sons of Baron Garron and especially his favourite daughter." She laughed at his expression. "That's no small achievement, Singer. Slinsi Garron in particular takes a lot of pleasing. You must have something good between your legs. I'm Helga, by the way," she continued, with Torrig laughing at her side, "and this is my establishment. You'll not find a finer one along this coast."

Helga turned, hollered something obscene, and a pale boy with a shock of yellow hair emerged sleepily, and hastily took their stolen steeds off to the stable at the rear of the building. At a nod from Torrig, Erun entered the house, his eyes smarting at the cloying, smoky atmosphere.

"There's ale if you want it...and plenty," continued Helga, who seemed to have an endless capacity for talking, and not allowing Erun so much as a "thank you" or grunt of acknowledgment. "And I'll bring you some food along presently...you'll doubtless be famished, my lovely. All that jumping about at Dreekhall...my, my," her wink was both saucy and suggestive.

"Oh, if you want a girl to share your bed tonight, if you've still energy left, my sweet one, then Nel'll oblige. She likes young lads and she'll put that Treggaran slut to shame."

I doubt that...

Erun muttered thanks and took a seat near the fire while Torrig, still grinning, followed Helga into another room and within minutes he could here groaning and the creaking of a bed and "My...I've missed that" and, "It hasn't shrunk none since last I saw it." Laughter followed and then silence for a time. Erun rubbed his scar and tenderly fingered his nose. It seemed his fate to be surrounded by enthusiastic weirdoes.

Well at least they are friendly...too bloody friendly.

Erun, though, was happy to be forgotten for the moment. There was much to think on. He sipped his ale, (which was excellent and very strong) and watched the fire chase shadows through the low beamed room. His mind wandered and he felt sleep stealing close. He was about to drift off when Torrig remerged, tugging at his drawstrings and humming loudly. He'd gained a woollen shirt from somewhere, and now had a pitcher of mead cradled under his right arm.

"You alright there, Singer..?"

Erun nodded. "I'm just tired," he said. "It's been an eventful day." *I need to sleep...*

"It isn't over yet," laughed Torrig, leaning forward to fill Erun's mug with strong mead, which after the ale was not the best idea. Torrig held out a grubby hand, the fingers were scarred and covered with bands of copper and silver. He poked Erun in the ribs.

"I owe you for saving me back there, boy," he said and then hiccupped noisily. "You can count Torrig Red Hair your friend now...that's no small thing. I ain't got that many friends," he added, his expression now rather lugubrious.

Erun grinned at him.

That's not surprising really...

Erun succumbed to the mead which finally banished the pain in his head, and left him both stupid and happy. That night passed in drunken smog. Erun hadn't tried mead before and was soon befuddled. Torrig, now on his third pitcher, was joined by Helga and another girl, a dark haired, skinny type, who turned out to be the aforementioned Nel. Helga asked Erun why he was travelling alone in the north country, especially at winter.

"You're young for a songsmith," she told him, and his sodden eyes failed to notice the shrewdness of her glance. "You journey with an enigma, Torrig," Helga told her lover and he grunted in agreement. She prodded Erun some more and Torrig poured him yet more mead and, at last Erun Cade could bear it no longer. He blurted out everything, caring no longer, and telling them of his journey's destination, and of old Irulan and Lissane Barola, and the murder of his father, and his longing for revenge. Out it all came until he could say no more.

On hearing Scaffa's name all three Rodruthans paled, and Helga placed a warning hand on his shoulder. "No sane man goes near that island, sweetheart. It's bewitched." She urged him, "Stay here with us in Longships, or else fare off to the Crags...Torrig here will teach you how to fight proper, so that you can see to that scum as did for your father."

"Let him be, Helga. We'll speak of this more in the morning," said Torrig, his face looked uncommonly drawn and grim and his eyes were sharp, despite him having nearly drained Helga's barrels dry. The mention of Scaffa and her island had had a sobering effect on their erstwhile jocular conversation.

"I'm away to bed," Torrig grunted, "you coming, wench?" Helga nodded and took to her feet. She blew Erun a kiss, leaving him alone with the doe eyed, skinny, Nel.

"Cheer up, Singer, you can have a go for free," Nel told him. She slipped a warm, searching hand beneath Erun's trousers, and then sighed in appreciation when she found what she sought. It was no good, however. Erun Cade was sound asleep. Nel continued fumbling for a while, sighed again, and then she too drifted off.

***

The Chancellor stood hovering and fidgeting at the door, his jewel-covered hands sweaty, and his pale, powdered face tense. The Emperor was not to be disturbed, the head of his concubines had informed him with distaining eyes.

"But I have dire news he must hear," pleaded the Chancellor. "Xandoria is under new threat," he told her. "There is a rising in the west, far beyond Lamoza. Some reckless warlock has unleashed a horror—"

The jewel-studded door slammed hard in his face, and the muffled sound of the courtesan's brisk steps faded into distance. The Chancellor bit his lip. He would return tomorrow and the next day too. The Emperor *must* be informed: if his astrologers were right, then Xandoria was in direst peril.

A month went by. Another. Still he wasn't received, and still, the rumours came from the west. Spagos gone! Aketa and Siotta reduced to ash. The wilds of Ketaq ravaged by fires! Lamoza?

The Chancellor had also sent scouts west though Darl wasn't among them. The once bold adventurer had recently taken ship bound south to the Island States. That had surprised the Chancellor. He'd never taken his prime agent for a coward. The once vain courtier had returned to him a gibbering fool.

"The hills are ringed with Demon fire!" Darl had yelled at him until the Chancellor bid him retire and clean himself up. That said, something was clearly amiss. The Chancellor spoke with the three generals too, but they paid him no heed, being engrossed with their ongoing conflict with the Lamozan Rebels. And so two more months passed by. Scouts came back their news, never good, though none had had the courage to ride as far west as Darl had.

Week on week the Chancellor requested his interview with the Emperor and week on week he was turned down. But this Chancellor was a persistent man. He would try the Palace in Xenn again tomorrow. And the next day and then on until the Emperor chose to give him ear. For the Emperor needed to know and it was his place to tell him.

Meanwhile in the west, the storm clouds mustered.

Chapter 17

The Blow

The worry was a worm swelling deep inside her breast, growing bigger day by day, and draining colour from her once so sunny face. Bel hated Galanais. She detested the arrogant, stiff necked courtiers, the bitter squabbling slaves, and ever so slightly superior servants with their cold glances and mocking tones. Most of all she loathed the family her beloved Lissane had just wed into.

She missed Barola so much. Her life in the castle had had its problems, for certain; Bel had learnt to steer clear of the grim Baron and his wild unruly sons. But Eon Barola had never troubled her overmuch, and though Rosco had tried it on once, he had quickly lost interest when she'd mentioned Lissane's name.

Things had been simple back in Barola; Bel knew her place there and liked it well enough. She and Lissane had grown up together, and though she was but the serving- maid they had always been more like best friends, confiding in each other, and sharing day dreams and such.

Bel's warmth had done much to soften Lissane Barola's customary coolness. It had been Leanna, Liss's dear mother, who had cared for Belshareze, after the fire that had put an end to her poor parents and their humble home. Leanna had been so kind back then, treating Bel as though she were a second daughter and not some dead fisher's brat.

But those days were long gone, fallen leaves, lost and fading on a lonely winter track. Leanna Barola was dead, and if her daughter wasn't careful she would be too. And soon—most likely. And if her mistress died then so would Bel—of that there was no doubt. No doubt at all.

Their life in Galanais was both indolent and tense, the boredom and monotony allowed Bel's well-founded worries to fester and thrive. And the whisperers were everywhere. Throughout the citadel Bel heard subtle nuances and dark sneering jibes. She was witness to sniggled hints spoken by this servant or that slave, who soon grew quiet when she steered close.

Even the dour guards occasionally muttered and hinted at the rumours going round. Nasty, spiteful rumours, about her mistress and a certain southern lord. What if that evil bitch Sophistra got word? Or twisted Morwella—not to mention Varentin? Those terrifying thoughts sent an icy stab of pain deep inside her stomach. No more, Bel decided. It was well past time. Belshareze would speak to her mistress, before Liss's reckless behaviour destroyed them both.

But how to do it? How could she confront her oldest friend and confidante with the harsh reality before it was too late?

It had begun when that bastard Varentin had raped Lissane on the eve of their nuptial. Word had soon got out about that, and Lissane, proud as ever had said nothing—not even to Bel. But over the following weeks Belshareze noticed a subtle change in her mistress's behaviour. Lissane was becoming furtive, even secretive, her eyes avoiding Bel's and her answers (when given) both elusive and dismissive. Something was going on.

Then the day came when she caught them together, naked and entwined: Lissane Gallante and Estorien Sarfe. They had not seen her for the hour was late, and Bel had woken on a noise in the room next door. Dreamily she had wandered in; the gasp freezing on her lips.

How long had this been going on? Belshareze thought she

could answer that one herself. She (and others) had found it odd that Estorien Sarfe still lingered in Galanais so long after the nuptial feast. Surely he had duties back home. Everyone knew the situation between Sarfania and House Gallante. And although he was gone now, this Estorien had stayed for some considerable time, allowing the secret rumours to take root.

Now she knew the answer, Bel drew scant warmth from it. Oh, she could see the appeal, Estorien Sarfe was everything Varentin Gallante was not. He was handsome, kind and eloquent—not a clumsy dreamer, like that damned fool Erun Cade. Whatever had Lissane seen in that one? Belshareze had never understood. Though she'd liked Erun well enough Bel had considered him foolish and vain. But that was history now and so was Erun Cade. That stupid affair had ended badly and this would too, were she not to act—and act fast—on her mistress's account.

Were either Varentin or his foul mother made aware, the world would come crashing in on Lissane Barola and her lover. Estorien doubtless would flee back to Reveal—his father's hidden castle, deep in the swamps. Gods only knew what would happen to Lissane—and herself too for that matter. Nothing good... She had thought about having it out with Grale, but Belshareze hardly saw him these days, and anyway, he would soon be returning to Barola—lucky soul, him. No, it was down to Bel to save her mistress from herself.

Another thought lanced like a cold blade into her belly, and Bel paused to shudder, before renewing her ascent of the long spiral stairs to their chambers above.

What if Liss is with child? What if it's born with dark skin—and soft brown eyes? The game would be over then for sure. Sophistra would have the child quickly strangled and the mother too—lest the shame get out.

This last notion wasn't to be borne, Bel decided. Tonight she would speak with Lissane, come whatever. Harsh words would be needed to shake some sense into her only friend and idol. But Belshareze got no opportunity to speak with Lissane that night, nor the following. And when she finally did it was already much too late.

***

Late spring had arrived in Galanais. It was a time of revelry and jollity, with copious festivals to the gods. High days when Hal Gallante and his colourful court would honour the lower streets with their grace. It was a time of celebration within and without the lofty walls of that wealthy western city. The quays were busy with traders from Rakeel, Murkai and beyond. Farmers and merchants brought their wares daily from the fields and lands outside, and fishers paraded their catch—all fresh produce for the bustling markets of the city.

But for Lissane Gallante it was a difficult time. Almost two months had passed since she had last seen Estorien. Two dreary months of Galanian intrigue and spite, comprising petty squabbles with Varentin—who still mostly ignored her, cold shoulders with Sophistra, and smirky glances and half smiles from the mad girl-child, Morwella.

Such were Lissane's warm sun-drenched days spent in the Citadel at Galanais. For several wild, wonderful weeks her Sarfanian lover had filled her soul with secret rapture—she'd borne her nightly nuptial duties with Varentin stoically. Mercifully, he had soon become bored and left her to her own devices.

That had left the door wide open for Estorien Sarfe. They were most discreet of course. No one knew. Lissane would take to evening strolls, flitting through the palace in serene silence, returning to her bower where *he* was always waiting. There they would make sweet love: talk, laugh, scheme, and plan, vow... and then love again, until morning's promise drove him hence. They would dream, too. Estorien vowed to avenge her treatment by Varentin, and aid her escape from Galanais. Such bold dreams of freedom they had had during those wild heady weeks.

Lissane knew that their love was dangerous. It was a kind of madness, but they were both willing slaves to its pattern. Estorien vowed to take her home one day, though Lissane saw not how such a thing could ever happen. She frequently told him so in hushed whispers as they lay together, the moon watching them while casting its silvery hue on the western waters, far below.

But he was determined, this lover of hers, and he hated Varentin dangerously, knowing how the heir of Galania had treated his new bride, despite Lissane's continual insistence that it was not worthy of mention, and that she lived only for their secret moments alone in that deepest silent dark, when citadel and palace slept.

Lissane had become wary of Morwella though. That strange girl had a creeping habit—a lurking, peeping tendency. She could turn up anywhere (at any hour), accompanied only by her cats, to scold servants and slaves, or else goad the dozing hounds that frequented the palace avenues and halls after dark. The lovers had to be very careful lest Morwella spy them entering the bower together.

The girl had a crush on Estorien too. Lissane had seen how her odd black eyes followed him like a hunting hawk. Sophistra also was a worry to Lissane. The Chatelaine's questing eyes were often surveying her from a distance—though she seldom deigned to speak to Lissane, saving a brief patronising comment or cynical quip.

But then Estorien had left her at winter's end, returning to that southern province Lissane now so longed to see. Now she had to focus her every day thoughts on surviving this new family of hers until he returned, as he promised he would, later in the year.

Fortunately, both Hal Gallante and the Razeas Sarfe were trying to bridge their differences and quash their enmities. Hence Estorien's overlong long stay at Galanais (his reasons so given at court, anyway). Prince and baron were now seeking closer ties between their provinces, and Estorien made the perfect ambassador for his father, with his easy charm and eloquent tongue.

Lissane missed him horribly. She clung to the vain hope that one day they would elope. He had more than hinted at such so many times as they lay tangled beneath the sheets. Estorien would free her from this vipers' nest. Let House Gallante fight it out with her father and the other players. Lissane, worried by his violent passion, had made Estorien vow to her that he wouldn't do anything rash—for if she could find any fault with Estorien, it was his impetuous nature. He would steal her away in the night, were it down to him—and Shadowman take the consequences.

But Lissane was wary: she'd lost her first love to her family—of that she was now convinced, though she couldn't prove it. She wasn't about to lose Estorien. No, they would have to find another way. She kept her counsel well hidden—not even Bel could have an inkling, though her maid was acting queer of late. Belshareze was homesick—was all. She would have to adapt. That was life. You just get on with it. That or drown. It was simple really.

Lissane often thought about Erun Cade, and whether—impossible as it seemed—he was alive. They had been so young back then. So naïve. It was still less than a year ago, but events and changing situations had distanced Lissane's heart from that fiery dreamer who had so wanted to risk all for her.

What was it about her that thrived so amid danger? Poor Erun, too, had wanted to elope with her. He had never got the chance—thanks to her ghastly brothers. Lissane would not make that mistake again. Here in Whispering Galanais, (as she had come to call it) none spoke overly loud, nor were their words, when spoken, without hidden, malicious agenda.

During those months in Galanais, Lissane studied the fine arts of deception and guile, until she became as proficient as, or more so even than, those who surrounded her life every day.

She learnt which slaves she could trust, (very few) who would talk and who would not, and which guard would look the other way, and which one would report on her movements to Sophistra, or worse her husband.

She wrote her lover as much as she dare. Those sealed letters she sent secretly whenever she was down in the city. He came to her one clear spring night, unannounced with dark eyes—wild and hungry, and in deepest joy they had loved long into the night. Estorien had been on an urgent mission and had returned south the very next day.

The following weeks passed slowly, drifting on like the brown sluggish Gal that lapped idly at the northern edges of the city. Spring waxed to summer, sweaty, hot and heavy. Occasionally Varentin still did his duty by her before dismissing her forthwith, so that he could return to his preferred diversions. It was rare enough though, and she closed her mind to it when it happened, her young heart yearning for her lover's return.

She kept her teeth together. During that hot early summer, Lissane told herself that she was ready for everything. But that was a lie because when she failed to show on her regular moon, Lissane's newly ordered world caved in on her.

At first Lissane kept the news to herself, barely quelling the panic inside. She cursed herself for a damned fool. She should have prepared for such an outcome, should have taken moon-dark, or else some other potent unguent that would stop the seed from taking fruit. But she stupidly hadn't bothered...and right now this was the very last thing that Lissane wanted.

I am such a fool...

In court and citadel people stared and mouthed their silent nuances, as they always did. Chatelaine Sophistra's cold eyes kept probing hers, in that half-knowing, mocking way she had. Lissane retained her cool under that witchy gaze, her demeanour she held serene, though inside she churned more every day.

Whose would be the child? Was it Estorien's or *his?* If it was Varentin's she would happily drown it. But if the child were her lover's...? Lissane turned away from that thought. She had to find a way through—somehow. Then came the day when she could hide the news no longer, lest in the weeks ahead her body betray her. She went to the Chatelaine first.

Sophistra had retired early from court attendance to take in the afternoon delights of the water gardens, as was her usual solace at this time of year. Barring her maids and clucking attendants, none accompanied her. She was seated regally beneath the canopy of her small gold-hemmed pavilion. Her left hand wielded a fan in quick darting motions, and her right—the fingers ring-sparkly and long, tipped by perfect nails blood red in colour—twirled the stem of a crystal wine glass, from which she sipped in hostile silence. Her flinty eyes studied the gardens' doves as they circled and swooped low over the fountains, which chimed so cheerfully close by. Lissane, choosing her moment thoughtfully, approached the Chatelaine with heavy heart and fretful mind.

Sophistra watched her enter the gardens in predatory silence, that knowing half-smile lifting the right side of her upper lip. It was the closest she got to warmth.

"Come, sweet daughter, take a seat beside me," Sophistra motioned with a languid flop of pale bangled arm. Lissane, obeying in silence, took to the chair by her right. "We speak so little, child; it is kind of you to seek me out...I know that you are busy with learning our customs and such. I, however, have so few diversions these hot days, what with the Prince away up trading with those ghastly Treggarans your father so hates."

Sophistra motioned a retainer to pour Lissane a glass of honey wine and hand it over to her. Lissane received it with a strained smile and allowed her gaze to take in the tranquil beauty of this quiet place.

How do I approach this...?

"I am with child," Lissane said, after a long controlled sip at the cool clear liquid. "I would have spoken before but I wanted to be certain of it, and, now that I am, I thought it best to inform you first...mother."

"How sweet of you, my dearest." Sophistra's lips barely alighted on her glass, and her cool clever eyes revealed nothing as she watched the younger woman shift with evident discomfort. "But of course it's wonderful news, my daughter. But who is the father? Is it my own dear son—or Estorien Sarfe, I wonder?"

Lissane's jaw dropped in alarm. She tried to speak but could only manage a strangled gulp. Sophistra placed a heavily ringed hand on her arm. It felt like ice and made Lissane shiver inside. *I am such a damned fool—why am I so stupid?*

"Don't fret, my love," Sophistra crooned, "we all must have our diversions... and I know that my Varentin is a difficult child. But most wait a year or two before straying. You were overly hasty, I believe, and a touch naive. This *is* Galanais."

"I...love him," Lissane's words fell from her lips, betraying her heart and filling her with dread. "I didn't want to cause trouble.... we thought that we were being careful."

"Foolish child." Sophistra's dark eyes glinted like jet daggers: Lissane almost winced under that abrasive stare. "*Careful...* In Galanais everyone is careful. You, my sweet naïve child, were rather obvious. But then you hail from rustic stock."

"Who...?" Lissane's mind was racing. This woman was her enemy and now she had given her what she wanted. God's only knew what game this spider Sophistra would play next. *And now I am trapped in her web...*

"Morwella of course," smiled the Chatelaine. That smile said 'yes, you are caught, fool'. "Oh the poor child detests me so, but she still tells me her secrets for small rewards. Morwella is my master spy about the citadel. She'd seen the Sarfanian slip into your bower on numerous visits, as has your frumpy little maid. Even her slow servant-mind has worked it out."

Belshareze knows...she's said nothing to me...

"Morwella's just plain jealous—the poor twisted child." Sophistra lip curled a fraction higher. "You see, my daughter has had quite a crush on Estorien Sarfe of late. She hates you, dearest, and thought it hilarious to inform me of your 'covert' idiocy."

That little bitch...I should have known. "What will you do?" Lissane's violet orbs were defiant again. Her fury at Morwella had given her new strength to face this cold, most dangerous woman.

"I shall do nothing, my dear, providing you let this nonsense die a death, before my obtuse husband...or worse, spiteful son, get to hear of it." Sophistra sipped at her goblet and smiled at the doves. They cooed back at her as though party to her schemes. Away to the left, and perched on a cherry tree, a song thrush serenaded them both with piping perfection.

"It was a flight of fancy and folly...no more," said the Chatelaine. "You're a sheltered girl, Lissane. That father of yours is known for his dominating ways with his womenfolk. I remember what his poor wife put up with. Leanna Barola was a sweet thing back then, though I never knew her well—your mother, of course."

The Chatelaine tapped her glass with a manicured finger. "To meet a man like Estorien Sarfe: your own age and so comely ...well, most maidens would succumb to that charm in no time. We will say no more about it...providing House Gallante has a healthy heir, of course."

"But what if the baby is not your son's...?" Lissane asked. *She'll kill it. That much is obvious. Why even ask?*

"Best not dwell on the finer details, yet," Sophistra dismissed her query with a curt wave of her hand. "Varentin must have an heir. I am, however, well aware of his preferences, though he so endeavours to keep them secret and is a deal more discreet than you are at doing so—I might add."

Sophistra waved Lissane away with another brusque jerk of her hand as though now bored with her company. "We will announce the joyful news tomorrow at court. A celebration will follow. Farewell, child, for the nonce."

***

That afternoon Lissane banished the world from her room. For over an hour she wept in frustration and self-pity—the last a rare emotion for her. How could she have been such a fool? Now Estorien was lost to her forever—just like Erun Cade had been last autumn. She was trapped like a fossil in amber.

There was to be no escape from Varentin Gallante. Lissane gazed from her window, taking in the wide panorama; wondering whether she should jump, but once again she refused to take her mother's path. She had to get word out to Estorien.

But who could she trust? No one in Galanais, that much was woefully obvious to her now. Belshareze would help of course, but then poor Bel would be watched as much as she. That left Grale.

Lissane sent word for her old travelling companion who, despite the Baron's wishes, had insisted on staying behind in Galanais. His wife had died years before in a raid by Treggarans. Rumour was he'd found a woman down by the docks, though he'd said nothing of it to Lissane. An hour later Grale was at her door, his beardy face flushed and grimy from afternoon weapon-play. Lissane bade him inside and swiftly banished her two girl slaves, along with the frowning Bel, from the chamber.

"I am grateful that you remain here in Galanais," she told the old champion, bidding him be seated across from her favourite window perch. "You will have greatly displeased my father with your absence, Grale. That's a rash action even for a fighter as worthy as you. The Baron will be missing your sword arm, I imagine."

"Then he should not have sold his daughter to the highest bidder," replied her old friend with customary bluntness. "I lost faith in your father years ago, my lady. And his sons. I would stay here with you...I feel strongly that you need every friend you can find among these...people."

Lissane thanked him for that. "I'm glad you stayed," she said. "Although I heard you've other reasons besides the love of your charge."

Now Grale looked uncomfortable and shuffled his feet. "She's just a friend...a good gal, her old man was a sailor. He drowned a while back and she's taken no one since then. We both needed *company*...she's from Rakeel originally...you know—dark eyed dark haired. Sultry...temper like a wild cat. I like her..."

"I'm happy for you, Grale, truly I am," Lissane told him, and then placed a warm hand on his knee. "But I need a favour from you, my dear old friend. I've a confession. I'm afraid I've been very foolish, here in Galanais."

Then Lissane told her trusted confederate about her 'not so secret' trysts with Estorien Sarfe, and the dire outcome following her tense discussion with Sophistra Gallante, earlier this afternoon.

Grale looked older after hearing her words, and his heavy brow was creased with frown. "She's the real power here, that one," he said of Sophistra. "Her husband's a pompous prick and her son's an idiot...pardon my saying so—your husband. I know that you loathe him, and none could blame you for shunning his cold touch. It was rash though, girl...this affair...and very dangerous. But what's done is done. So. What would you have me do?"

"Get word out to Reveal in Sarfania without any here knowing," Lissane responded. "No small task, I realise...but Estorien must be told. It could be his son, Grale. I...I don't trust Sophistra. I mean, would they let the child live if it wasn't Varentin's? They would only have to look at the colour of its skin." Lissane's eyes were pleading pools of violet. "I'm scared, Grale, and I'm sorry to burden you with this...trouble."

"And what good could Estorien Sarfe's knowing possibly achieve?" countered Grale, awarding her a measured glance. "He's hot headed, is young Estorien—famous for it throughout Gol. He's liable to react hastily after receiving such grim words from his newest love. Were he to find out in due course he mightn't prove so impetuous...time changes everything. Estorien Sarfe was ever a lady's man. I am sorry, Liss," (he had always called her that when she was a child), "but my advice to you is let this charming Sarfanian go from your head. Don't give these Galanian bastards any more chances to hurt you. Chatelaine Sophistra has a hold over you now. She will play on that one day. Of that you may be certain."

"I love him, Grale...I'll not be parted from him," stressed Lissane, her pale fingers gripping his knees and squeezing tight. "Not...not like poor Erun Cade. No, Estorien Sarfe has to know the truth."

"Then I'll tell him myself," answered Grale, heaving his heavy body up from his repose. "I'll depart before dawn, although I'm given to say I've a very bad feeling about this," he added.

Lissane didn't reply and Grale turned and grim-faced made for the door, stopping for a moment before opening it. "House Sarfe will know within the week, Lissane. I'll acquire a fast horse. That much I promise. After that...?" He opened the door and shuffled outside without further word.

"Thank you, my old friend," Lissane whispered after him as Grale's slow measured footsteps faded below. Once again she was alone.

That night Lissane kept to her rooms. She deemed that by now Sophistra would have informed Varentin of her situation—giving her an excuse to avoid his attentions. He, now having performed his duty for House Gallante, would hopefully let her be. If challenged Lissane would say that she was unwell. But she heard nothing and for three nights saw no sign of her husband.

The following morning he approached her and placed a sweaty hand on her belly. "The child will be called Argones after my noble grandfather," he announced. "That's if you do your duty correctly and produce a male heir for House Gallante." She said nothing, just watched him leave with balanced loathing, imagining the jewelled hilt of his own dagger protruding from his back. *One day...*

Lissane spent the following days fretting and sweating as summer blazed, awaiting word from Grale on his return. Nothing. Another week passed and another. Why was it taking so long?

Lissane was becoming anxious and very restless. On a whim, she announced to Belshareze that she wanted to visit the city proper. Her maid advised against this, but under duress stoically organised the trip. They left the citadel with two guards filed either side of the palanquin and four slaves sweating underneath, their muscles coiling as they bore the carriage. Behind the curtains, the girls lounged idly and peeped at the sights. The palanquin was luxury itself and they had copious refreshments to ease their hours in the comparative coolness inside.

Curious, Lissane motioned that she wanted to see the poorer sector of the city, a district she hadn't happened upon before, for obvious reasons. Galanais was huge and teeming, and where its northern edge fringed the river lay the poorer quarter. This area stank of unmentionable filth and detritus. It sprawled for miles inside and outside the great walls.

Her guards were unhappy coming here and Bel was fretting too. Lissane ignored them. She ordered the four slaves to carry them down to the filthy, twisting alleys flanking the north shore of the River Gal. They obeyed, though were clearly unhappy too.

Their path led down toward the docks and tanneries. Here were mostly wattle and daub huts, and wooden shanty dwellings, looking to Lissane as if they would collapse at any moment. Scabby faced children ran amok and tired eyed women called after them. Dogs yelped and crapped on the already stinking dirt. Everywhere was misery and dejection.

This was the slavers' catchments area where their human produce was bought and sold along by the riverside. Here too, was the abode of every pickpocket; cut-throat and assassin who spent their days plying their trade in the upper city above.

They had reached a sharp corner when the slaves stopped

suddenly at a sharp word from the guards. Ahead and below, the dirty river churned and eddied its lazy path toward the sea. Lissane saw sailboats and ketches chopping into the brown currant, making for the docks upstream.

"What is down there?" Lissane demanded from Fassel her male slave, who she trusted as much as anyone. "Why have we stopped?"

"We cannot go further, milady, the Chatelaine forbids nobles from this vicinity. This sector of the city is very dangerous. She would be most angered were she to discover that you ventured hereabouts."

Good..."Well, she won't know, will she, if none present tell her." Lissane was sick of Sophistra's spidery influence over everyone here in Galanais. She was determined to defy the Chatelaine this once—be it childish and dangerous, Lissane didn't care. "We're going that way," she told them, leaving no further room for argument.

Fassel took a step toward her. "My lady, this is most unwise. I—"

"What's he doing there?" Lissane had seen a familiar figure stroll out of one of the squat, grubby buildings lining the river. It was the boy slave she'd seen that first awful time she went to her husband's room.

"Heh, you! Stop there!" Lissane yelled across to him. The boy looked up and about, then saw her face. He paled visibly. Before she realised what she was doing, Lissane had shoved Bel aside, and jumped free from her couch inside the palanquin to thud with both feet onto the grubby ground below. Her pulse racing, Lissane started running toward the boy, and he, alarmed by her shouts, fled back inside the building. Lissane's mind was full of questions. If that boy was here then Varentin can't be far away. But why?

Her guards followed noisily behind, though by now an inquisitive crowd had gathered and they must needs push their way through, amid cuffs and cusses.

Lissane heard Belshareze shout a warning from inside the palanquin, Bel was pleading with her to return. Lissane closed her ears, striding on, foolishly paying no mind to the sweltering mid-day heat, and the foolish recklessness of such action in her current state. She reached the shabby door where she'd had seen the young slave emerge from seconds earlier.

Lissane turned the handle and pushed inwards. The door creaked ajar, spilling afternoon light into what appeared a gloomy low-beamed warehouse. The small, grimy windows were covered with moth-eaten drapes, and wan candlelight flickered and guttered in the sudden draught.

There were three people inside as well as the youth she had followed. Two of the others were also slaves: one female, one male—both naked and perfumed.

The third was her husband.

Varentin was standing over the kneeling slave girl, his face covered by a mask fashioned in the form of a snarling bull, with lolling red tongue, and broad, curling horns at its apex. Aside the mask, he wore a long cloak of sable velvet. Beneath this he was naked, and the girl slave now attending him assiduously, her busy mouth working back and forth, taking in his length. The naked boy had bloody whip marks along his back and thighs: he and the other boy (Varentin's favourite—she now recalled) glanced over at the door in shock as Lissane barged in. The whipped boy gaped in horror when he saw the murderous glint in Lissane's eye.

Varentin groaned and shuddered as he released his seed into the girl slave's fleshy mouth. His eyes were closed.

The blow from the candle-holder cut hard into his head above his right eye and sent him spinning backwards. All three slaves screamed and fled from the room, disappearing behind a screen. Lissane, wild with rage, strode forward readying another swing with the candle-holder. She swung down—

Varentin rolled out of range. He leapt up, grabbing her arm and knocking the sconce out of her grasp. By now the blood was streaming down his face and he was yelling foul expletives at her. He hit her hard in the face, sending her sprawling among the dirty cushions and lice-ridden carpets, partially covering the floor. Lissane's head spun, she tried to rise but Varentin kicked her back down again.

"You bitch!" He kicked her again, harder, and Lissane doubled over in sudden sharp agonising pain, "you stupid fucking slut...I ought to kill you!" He loomed close until his hated face was only inches above hers. He struck her again and again with his fists. Lissane cried out in rage and agony. She wanted to tear his face off, claw at his eyes, but she couldn't move. She tried to cover her face and body from further blows, but he, exhausted now, had ceased his assault, and instead merely glared down at her for several moments, before storming out of the building and vanishing into the labyrinth of filthy street beyond.

Lissane glanced down at her thighs, showing clearly where her blue silk dress had torn. They were soaked with her own blood, and the agony in her belly contracted like a rusty spring opening and closing inside her. The room was spinning now as she threw up on the floor. Someone, Belshareze perhaps, cradled her head and spoke in her ear. She couldn't hear anything. Then the pain engulfed her like molten fire and Lissane swooned into blissful dark.

Belshareze, her face awash with tears, bade the guards gently carry Lissane's unconscious body back to the palanquin. The guards cleared the way as they hurried back to the citadel. Once they were back, the physicians drugged Lissane with milk of the poppy, to ease the pain, and she slept peacefully until the following morning. Of Varentin Gallante there was no sign.

***

Since his promise to give the demon Xandoria, Ozmandeus's strength had returned tenfold. And so had his confidence—yes the demon still burnt him when the mood was upon it. But Ozmandeus's protective mind spells warded him well. For a long time he was at ease. Free from pain and doubt. And free to let his minions wreak ruin on the wide lands ahead.

They'd left Gortez with a force comprising five thousand strong, the host having grown with Ozmandeus's reputation. Each new mercenary dreaming of gold and fortune despite rumours that there would be a price. They didn't care. Life was short, they said. Live for the now. Kill, rape and ruin—steer clear of the sorcerer and his creature, but take his gold and bugger tomorrow. And this they did.

Throughout the following months those huge estates owned by the notaries of Zorne were brought low by torch and fear. Cities tumbled, temples burned and that once cultured land fell into chaos. And this all achieved on Ozmandeus's reputation—the horror of Zorne City's last hours. Now Ozmandeus ruled by fear alone. The Renegade kept Ashmali locked away in the amulet but the rumour of his menace still travelled before him.

With Zorne's fertile valleys stripped and her people slain or enslaved, Ozmandeus turned east, crossing into Spagos and Ketaq. In Spagos he freed Ashmali for a brief time—careful now lest the demon turn on him again. And so Spagos perished too, the bright cities of Siotta and Aketa reduced to ash. After that Ozmandeus reined his demon in. He'd spent all last winter on his locking spells and this time he was successful. Ashmali withdrew inside the amulet to smoulder and brood.

Ozmandeus was triumphant. He now controlled the demon fully. Nothing and no one could stop him now. Not even the gods.

Ahead ranged the vast plains of Lamoza, the last country this side of the Gap. Beyond that Xandoria. An empire that boasted wealth far beyond the Magisters of Zorne. A land so vast even Ozmandeus couldn't imagine. Of course his army would be outnumbered, the Xandorian elite were rumoured half a million strong. They would laugh at this westerner despite his reputation. None of that mattered because as he had in Zorne and the other cities, the Renegade would free the demon before the walls of Xenn City. The emperor would roast and so would his empire. Mighty Xandoria would topple—the last domino. After that a phoenix would rise up. A new order in which he, the Firelord of Zorne, would rule supreme.

Chapter 18

The Price of Love

The dust settled in the following week. Lissane lost the child. Sophistra had the guards whipped bloody and Lissane's slaves killed out of hand. The terrified Bel she let live, if only for the reason that she was most precious to Lissane, and therefore could be manipulated later. Grale had returned by now. After hearing of the incident by the river, and visiting Lissane while she lay recovering in her bed, he sent further word via pigeon to Reveal. This time he had needed no prompting after seeing the state of Lissane.

Estorien Sarfe raged and seethed murder when he received word of Lissane's miscarriage. Despite his impetuous vengeful nature, her lover bided his time, waiting for the right moment to strike. Let them think he'd lost interest. Let them grow complacent. The time arrived four months later when Lissane (her body anyway—if not her mind) was recovered from both trauma and hurt.

Since that fateful day House Gallante had left her well alone. Varentin had vanished—though the rumour was he had quarrelled savagely with his mother, and now spent his time sulking like a petulant child alone in his quarters. Prince Gallante had returned from the north and, after hearing the news, had shown little compassion for Lissane, now evidently finding her presence an embarrassment best ignored.

Sophistra kept her distance, watching and waiting, scheming and contriving—expecting some treachery to show its face. Only Morwella remained her usual capricious self. The girl seemed to thrive in the tense, brittle atmosphere, and she was clearly delighted that she had been the architect for the rift now forming in House Gallante.

There were many nobles that sided with Lissane, for Varentin was not loved and neither was his mother. Sophistra had her eyes on them too, but they were Galanians and knew how to mask their emotions. And so the tension built as that long summer wore on.

At last autumn arrived, cooling nights and shortening days. One evening, just before dusk, Lissane took to strolling through the wide palace gardens. It was a clear enchanting night, and the cool brisk air reminded her of far off Barola. Lissane strolled past the large tingling fountain where she had passed those brittle moments with Sophistra, and walked on, through the olive grove and down to the wall at the southern side of the citadel.

A guard nodded politely as she passed him, and Lissane smiled in return. She was making friends in the citadel these days. The rulers of House Gallante might not like Lissane overmuch, but the servants, slaves, and soldiers had recently come to love her. For this sad, violet eyed lady from distant Barola was kind and genuine, which was a thing unheard of in the citadel before. She learned their names and listened when they spoke of their concerns. Lissane had never been one for making friends before, but she needed them now.

She passed beneath the sweeping canopy of a date palm: it was such a beautiful night. The long summer's haze had been replaced by a crisp clarity, and stars studded the firmament above. Lissane tried to count them as she walked on, then she froze when a figure blocked her way.

It was Estorien.

He'd worked it all out over time. He'd bribed the right guards and had fresh horses tethered and waiting outside the walls. It was easy. Lissane wept and laughed: she fell into his arms and Estorien gathered her in. For a brief few joyful moments they embraced, lost in each other's smiles. At last Estorien spoke. "Love, we've need of haste—we dare not tarry here." Lissane nodded and without further word her lover led her outside the walls to where the horses waited, tethered.

Once mounted, they'd trotted through the city streets without any thought or care of pursuit—few in the citadel deigned to look toward the city after dark, nor did the riders glance down at the few slack-jawed citizens stopping to watch them pass. Estorien had insisted Lissane don a long, deep hooded cloak to hide her features from the city's gate guards. And so with her thus disguised, they passed beneath the city walls without any challenge to their business, the guards assuming they were foreign nobles—which of course they were.

Grale met them outside the city, accompanying him was Belshareze whose pretty face looked both terrified and flushed with excitement. Both were stood with horses bridled and waiting, under the swaying shadow of a large willow tree. Lissane dismounted, and laughing, hugged them both for several minutes, the emotion building inside her. Her friends mounted up and Lissane reclaimed her saddle. After a brisk word from Estorien, the four let their horses take them down to where the road ribboned silver, as it left the walls behind and faded from view.

Night deepened. Only the moon witnessed their flight: Galanais was sleeping. Far behind a single light winked from the citadel, but all else was darkness and chilly air.

Lissane was free at last. She smiled as she felt the night air tingle her skin. She had escaped and was with her lover and dearest friends. She had never felt such joy.

But joy is a fleeting emotion. It seldom lasts. And the Shadowman is always watching—waiting to strike like a viper in the dark...

They led their steeds through a tangle of woodland, leading down to a hurrying stream; Lissane noticed the seven mile marker stone, glinting up at her from beneath its mossy coat. She smiled, feeling the thrill of this night's bold work race through her veins.

They were free! It was all that mattered. Let tomorrow deal with tomorrow. The four riders forded the stream and crested the far bank, which rose up muddy and steep. Beyond this rise the land opened out, awarding broad vistas for miles, the fields ahead lit by the wandering moon.

Suddenly Estorien reined up, his keen eyes scanning the way ahead. "What is it?" Lissane asked him, reining in alongside, her face pale beneath the moon and her words anxious. *Something's wrong...*

"Riders," responded her lover. "Coming this way—and fast."

"I see them," Grale pointed across, and Lissane saw the quick moving, dark shapes, of what appeared to be six cloaked horsemen hurrying their way. "Soldiers...probably up from the border," continued Grale. "It may be nothing to worry about."

But Estorien swore vehemently when his sharp eyes discerned the lead rider, whose black glinting armour was whipped by a sable cloak flapping up behind his racing steed. The other five riders wore helms emblazoned with House Gallante's silver ship on green, but the leader's helmet was unadorned and black as his cloak and armour.

"We had best cut fast across country," said Estorien, "I've no wish to encounter that rider on a night such as this. Come on!" Grale made to challenge that but saw the concern on Estorien's handsome face and quickly changed his mind.

"Who is he?" Lissane could see that the riders had spotted them and were now cutting a sharp angle toward them. She urged her beast to follow her lover's.

"Torlock," Estorien yelled in her ear, as Lissane clung hard to the reins of her mare, and dug her ankles in its flank to spur the beast on to speed. "His name is Torlock and he's a murdering bastard." Lissane recalled the brutal faced, black garbed rider that had accompanied Hal Gallante that time he'd returned from the north. Her heart sank. *Torlock...I fear that man...*

"The Galanian champion," she responded, remembering the way he had stared at her with those cruel mocking eyes. "A cold killer, methinks...”

“The same...” Estorien yelled across at her. They were racing like wild things now, but the Galanian soldiers were closing on them from scarce a quarter of a mile away. Estorien, on a sudden whim, steered his beast toward a dark clutch of oaks ahead and urged the others to follow. Once amongst those trees they could lose them in the darkness and break free the other side. The four riders cut fast for the woods, and Lissane, twisting in her saddle and looking back, saw in relief that Torlock’s patrol wouldn’t reach them before they made the trees. But then Bel’s mare threw a shoe, and slipping on a loose stone, bucked its rider from the saddle.

Belshareze landed badly and was clearly hurt. She stood after a struggle, and began limping toward them. Estorien, cursing, turned his horse about and cantered back down to help the weeping, girl. Estorien was only yards away and closing fast, his right hand reaching out for her, and her looking up at him—the terror showing on her face. But he was too late. Torlock got there first.

Those next seconds were lodged like poison daggers in Lissane’s memory. She watched helpless, as the black-clad rider cut across the now fleeing girl’s path. In Torlock’s right hand was an axe, while his left gripped a curved black sword. Lissane witnessed the axe arc then fall with gruesome accuracy, its broad blade glinting in the moonlight for a half second, before burying itself in the back of Bel’s skull with a sickly thud.

Lissane screamed as she saw the blood jet in the moonlight and her maid’s body crumple, twitch, and then lie still. There was no time for weeping. The enemy was upon them like a storm of swirling black.

Estorien had halted his horse when he saw the girl die. Now he urged the beast forward again and, grimfaced, slid his blade free of its scabbard, his dark vengeful eyes focused at Torlock’s kettle helm. But Grale crashed past him, his own longsword levelled at Torlock’s gorget.

“Fly..!” Grale shouted back at Lissane and her lover. Estorien hesitated for a moment longer, but Grale’s insistent yell spurred him into motion. “Take the girl, Estorien! I’ll keep these bastards busy. Go—damn you! Don't let me die in vain!"

Lissane felt sick to the bone. She recalled seeing Grale's sword meet Torlock's axe in a clang of sparks that sent the Galanian champion off balance. A second rider steered close and thrust his spear toward the Barolan fighter's midriff. Grale cut down hard, snapping the shaft of the weapon and following through with a lunge that tore out the rider's throat. Grale was yelling and hewing all about him.

Two more cloaked soldiers tumbled from their saddles, but the others closed in around Grale, their weapons hedging him whilst Torlock struck out with sword and axe. The clash of steel ceased, and Lissane saw no more. She and her lover had finally reached the trees and her moon-aided vision was now blocked by their ivy-clad trunks.

The shouting faded as they cut through the wood lengthwise, distancing themselves from the fight. Lissane heard another brief brave clash of steel and then... silence. Grale was dead.

It was dark—so dark, when they cleared the trees, and the moon now shrouded by a wrack of cloud. There was no sign of Torlock or his men. They rode on deep into the night, counting the long miles to the Sarfe River and Estorien's homeland. Lissane started in alarm when an owl hooted close by. Aside that, the only sound was the constant thud of their horse's hooves, and the thump of Lissane's heart, hammering like a dull drum deep inside her chest.

Lissane wept as she urged her steed to follow her lover's horse along the road that still showed pale in the gloom ahead. Lissane had escaped from Galanais with her lover, but she'd lost her only friends. Her selfish folly had killed them both. She had lost dear Erun Cade, back then. Now she had lost her darling Bel, and valiant loyal, Grale too—her old champion had given his life to save her. It was far too high a price to pay for love, thought Lissane. But it was too late now—the Shadowman had done his work. They rode south and Lissane wept until sunrise and warmth finally stilled her tears. They reached the border three days later.

***

Rakaro crouched low in his saddle, ignoring the icy wind that whipped hard as knives into his leathery, moustached face. Xandorians. A score at least, he'd best ride for camp, and fast. Toskai and the rest would need some warning; lest the raiders caught them unawares.

But it was too late. They'd seen him, and with their usual discipline, were already guiding their mounts in parallel perfection, up the hill to where he watched them. Rakaro shrugged with slight disappointment—down to him now

He casually slid his horn bow free of its saddle holster, and reaching down placed an arrow on the nock. He pulled back to the corner of his mouth. Rakaro waited as they thundered close, and then loosed, and the goose-fletched arrow took flight with deadly accuracy.

Rakaro reached for another, as the leader fell from his saddle with the shaft protruding from his throat. The next rider fell several seconds later, and then three more followed—the last one's foot caught in his stirrups, and his limp body crashed through the ice covered couch-grass as his horse cantered on.

But now they were upon him!

Rakaro calmly slung his bow aside and released his curved scimitar from its sealskin scabbard. He would take a few more before they finished him. Xandorians were good fighters usually, but these were foreigners and mercenaries by their look—big ugly black skinned brutes from the distant Island States, or else pale-eyed strawheads, from that strange gloomy country beyond Rakeel.

They had slowed their mounts now, biding their time, all were vengeful, angry and full of hate. They wanted him alive. The riders rode up the incline, quickly surrounding Rakaro with a ring of spears. Rakaro braced his fur clad body for that sudden rush of steel, he counted: one...two...three...then a loud whoop announced Toskai's welcome presence behind him.

Rakaro turned and grinned when he saw his brothers descend on the surprised patrol like a pack of snarling, starving wolves. "What kept you idle bastards?" Rakaro yelled as he joined his friends in the fray. "Must I do everything myself?"

The fight was over in seconds. Toskai swiftly hewed the heads off every mercenary with his razor-edged scimitar, whilst his men cut stakes and thrust them hard into the icy ground. On each one they mounted a head, the glazed eyes all facing south across the arid plains toward Xandoria proper

"Let them greet the next patrol!" Toskai was happy today, and not too drunk—which was unusual for him. "Teach those southerners not to venture through our lands without shatting themselves." Toskai's swarthy, battered face was all broken nose and criss-cross scars—much like Rakaro's for that matter (though Toskai still had all his teeth, whereas Rakaro had the front two missing.)

The Hillmen were a wild people, their lands vast and undulating. They were a nomadic folk, and though they called themselves 'Hillmen', they mostly ranged free across the vast windy plains north of Xandoria, sometimes faring right up to the frozen wastes, where the white bears wandered free.

They were a ferocious people: wiry, tough, and short of build—more at home on a horse than on two feet. They hated strangers and loved to fight. Mostly the family-based clans fought each other, but now that the Emperor was encroaching more and more on their lands they had united joyfully to defy him. This had been the third patrol they'd broken in a week, and the carrion birds were gathering in the hills below.

Toskai let his horse drift across to where Rakaro now sat his saddle in silence. "Greeting, brother." Toskai's lopsided smile revealed those brown teeth, and his voice was harsh as raven caw. "Were you asleep just now?" the leader enquired.

Rakaro shrugged, nonplussed. His eyes were small black chips, like Toskai's, they curved upward slightly on outer corners. His catalogue of scars he'd dyed bird's egg blue, where as Toskai's were yellow and red—the marks were a sign of virility and competence among Hillmen, awarding them a demonic look that terrified their enemies. You couldn't have too many scars if you were a Hillman.

"I was merely taking some air and ...thinking," responded Rakaro, spitting a gobbet of phlegm on the frozen grass below. "I thought perhaps I'd make for the Gap...see what these latest rumours are about."

"What rumours?" Toskai watched his men flay the hides from the corpses below, and then with casual efficiency, stake their skins out to dry in the east wind.

"You spend too much time in your tent with that fat slut, brother," said Rakaro, looking up suddenly as an eagle ranged high above, its shrill calls plaintive and remote. "*I* like to know what's going on in the world," he added.

Toskai pulled a face. "What care I for any of that nonsense? We're Hillmen, brother; we live for fighting, shagging, and swilling liquor. What else is there?"

"War," responded Rakaro, now scratching his ear. His greying, black mane lifted slightly in the keen breeze. Rakaro wore it free, unlike Toskai who sported a pigtail that reached down to the small of his back. "And fresh trouble on its way." Rakaro was maybe two or three years older than the other, but both were nearing forty winters—hard fighters and veterans of many a squabble.

"There are always wars, Rakaro." Toskai was losing interest now. He was looking down, watching his pony graze lazily on the rough terrain below. "They don't concern us usually."

"But this next one will," countered Rakaro. "I heard rumours whilst travelling south last week. Some trouble way beyond Lamoza. A new invasion, they say—from Zorne maybe. A sorcerer's involved. That's the story anyway."

"Sorcerer, pah...You listen to too many stories, brother," scoffed Toskai. "Besides, what goes on beyond the Gap don't concern us Hillmen—never has done. Xandoria will quash that rebellion in Lamoza in a few months, you'll see, and while they're over there, they will soon sort out any 'would be invader' from the far lands—sorcerer or not.

"The Emperor ain't accustomed to defeat; it's why he hates us so much." Toskai awarded the other rider a hard stare. "You worry too much, Rakaro," Toskai told his brother. "Thinking's for seers and philosophers: I try not to do it overmuch—it gives me toothache." Rakaro wasn't listening, his mind was far away.

Back at camp, the clan celebrated their latest victory with fermented yak milk and stewed goat meat. Rakaro didn't share in the revelries. Something still troubled him. Something was coming—something bad. He felt it in the wind and saw its warning in the starry skies above. *A terror is coming...*

That night, whilst his brothers snored alongside their women, Rakaro's dreams were full of screaming voices and crackling fires. He woke wild eyed—something *was* wrong, he felt certain of it. A new danger, or maybe an ancient one returned, but it would change their lives forever—of that he was sure. It fell to him to discover what he could. Rakaro had made his mind up.

He would ride west for the Gap tomorrow, he decided, and glean what he could from those dwelling thereabouts. Let the other fools tarry here. Rakaro needed to know what was coming before it was too late. He rode out before dawn while the others' snores still thundered through the camp.

Three weeks later Rakaro got word of the Demon. Fearful, he rode back full of his tale. But the others just laughed at him and left Rakaro to brood in gloom. Months past. They raided, drank and screwed. Rakaro alone watched the stars every night. It was the following spring, when the stranger came among them, that the nightmare became real.

Chapter 19

The Island

The ketch cut clean through wave and chop, her clinker strakes repelling the icy water that lashed and spumed in salty fountains. Erun's stomach churned and his head spun with the reckless, random motion. And his new found companion was only making matters worse.

Red Torrig was in his element at sea and, like all Rodruthans, was salt blooded. The craggy flame-haired northerner seemed to be enjoying Erun's evident discomfort, he kept grinning at him annoyingly from his place at the tiller, only ceasing when Erun scowled back in return.

They were three days out from Longships. Three days and nights of winter cold and storm tossed ocean, and Erun Cade now heartily wished that he'd never set foot on this creaking, lurching tub. It was all down to Torrig, of course. The indefatigable Rodruthan had insisted they take the sea trip, hugging the coast across and up to Northtown, where Torrig would part company with Erun, and continue on to his father's stronghold at Druthan Crags.

Or 'Prince' Torrig as Erun decided he should call his new comrade at arms—if only to annoy him. Nelys had told him Torrig was the fourth son of Brude and stood to inherit little—not that he cared overmuch. He'd tried to enquire further from Helga in the morning, questioning her during breakfast about her relationship with Torrig. She had just laughed at his tactless questions and blown him a kiss, confounding him more than ever. It wasn't important: he and Torrig would be parting company soon enough.

The two wayfarers departed later that very morning against both women's protestations, for Nel had taken quite a fancy to Erun—who was now caught like a hooked fish between his fading love for Lissane, and a constant swelling in his groin whenever he thought about Slinsi Garron—which he did rather a lot.

Another woman dribbling over him was the last thing Erun needed, and so he'd been glad to go. But that was then. Now he'd wished that he hadn't left so promptly. These northern folk (Erun decided on reflection) were a bad influence on him.

Torrig had not mentioned Scaffa since the morning of their departure, when both he and Helga had again tried to dissuade Erun from his proposed crossing to that distant island.

"It's a bad place is that one," Helga had warned him. "None that venture there ever return." When Erun asked her how many people she knew that *had* ventured there she grew silent, but Torrig cut in.

"Scaffa's got an evil name," he muttered, brooding into his morning brew and trying to focus his bloodshot eyes under the ruthlessly bright morning sun. "She's a witch-queen born of a demon...eats babies, so men do say."

"I've heard them say that about your father," added Nelys, receiving a murderous glance from Torrig. Erun winced, he'd heard that too.

"That's just Treggaran hogshite," Torrig growled, "besides, Father enjoys evil embellishments to his reputation—however false—it puts the wind up his enemies, and he's got no shortage of those." Torrig scratched his rump and belched before continuing. "Scaffa is twisted. They say she's immortal and her island's a place of darkness and shadow, inhabited by cannibals and weird beasts. The seas around the island are infested with krakens, and the cliffs hemming her shores rumoured unassailable. Beyond those lies her domain. No one with half a brain would venture close. Not even you, Singer."

"I made a promise," Erun had replied then. "Irulan warned there would be danger, but he said I would get by and that this Scaffa owed him."

"Well, I'll drop you off at Northtown then," Torrig had told him, wiping the froth from his whiskery mouth. "That's only a few miles from the island's nearest shore—though just how you plan to get across that benighted channel is beyond me. I'll not set foot on that haunted coast nor will any sane Rodruthan."

Erun recalled questioning at the time whether there were any 'sane Rodruthans'; nevertheless Torrig had given him cause for concern. Was Irulan sending him to his death and a horrid one at that? What purpose would that serve? Erun decided not to dwell on that thought and from then on kept his own counsel. Besides, these northerners had little else to do during the long winter nights other than make up witchy tales about their neighbours. The others, seeing his heart was set, had let the matter rest.

And so they had boarded the ketch, a small fishing craft comprising twin sails and half dozen oars. It was one of the many idle vessels cluttering the creek and was owned by Helga's cousin, Orme, and his boys. At that time Erun recalled he'd been quite enthusiastic, happy to be outward bound again. Until the swells picked up.

Erun had tossed a bag (freshly acquired from Nel) in the hold below, which contained his harp, knife, and some other stuff—mainly food. His bow and arrows he had kept handy—just in case one of those kraken things showed up. The Treggaran guard's stolen sword he still wore at his waist belt.

Torrig had told Erun that morning that he had his own fleet of raiding ships moored hard off Druthan Crags, and was itching to return to them. He'd lost two good ships in the failed raid that had culminated in his capture last month, and was still furious about it.

Most of his crew had escaped but Torrig—hot for vengeance after learning that one of his sisters was rumoured murdered by

Rante Garron's hand—had insisted on taking the fight as far as he could, (which had turned out to be the feasting hall at Dreekhall where Erun had encountered him.) It hadn't been one of Red Torrig's must illustrious raids. But he would be back. Rante Garron was a marked man.

The Rodruthans were indifferent fisherfolk at this time of year, preferring to sit indoors quaffing huge quantities of ale. But the wind had eased that morning, so they were bound, north by west, for crabbing, cod, and Druthan Crags market. Torrig had cadged a ride and insisted on this Barolan 'singer' friend joining them too.

"You can sing bawdy songs and play that harp," he grinned, "That should keep all the krakens and weather wizards at bay—it's hard to eat ships and crewmen whilst holding your ears from such unearthly din."

Erun hadn't responded to that. Three days into their voyage Erun Cade had scarce managed to eat, never mind play his harp and sing. The wind had freshened the minute they'd left the creek, and once on open water squally rain had joined in too, soaking crew and passengers to the skin.

At least the rain had stopped now. These northern countries seemed so dull and dreary after the warm winds and early springs of distant Barola Province. Here was only pitiless wind and lowering hurrying sky. The Rodruthan coast paraded their progress to port: a dreary continuation of sandy strands, remote skerries, and storm-tossed ragged firs. Even the beach's sands appeared grey and stony in hue, mirroring the slate grey of rushing wintry cloud above. He saw seals sometimes, and high above the terns swore and swooped. It was a miserable trip.

A day later they changed course. Erun saw that the coast had now broken off into a cluster of craggy skerries and weed strewn rocks, where gannets dived and gulls circled seeking fishy prey. Beyond these outcrops lay open sea for countless leagues until it eventually fused with ice and endless cold.

They had reached the north coast of Gol and now they would steer west toward Druthan Crags. Late that afternoon they raised tall cliffs on the northern skyline. Erun gazed out at what appeared a distant wall of rock, dark and foreboding, mantled by lowering sky and heavy rain-cloud. The sight made Erun shiver to his boots.

"Is that...?"

"Aye, it's *her* island," muttered Torrig. "We're nearing Northtown now. Look ahead...do you see those towers crowning that far headland?" Torrig tugged at Erun's sleeve, urging the Barolan to look far beyond the plunging prow of the vessel and brooding line of cliffs. Erun, shielding his eyes beneath the slatey glare, could just about make out what looked to be a ruin of some huge fastness thrust out like a giant's broken snaggled teeth from the headland.

"That's my home," Torrig told him, slapping him hard on the back. "That's the Crags, Singer...a place of roaring fires, farting dogs, and wanton women. We've also fine hunting thereabouts. Sure you don't want to come visit?"

Erun pulled a face, but Torrig ignored him and continued his reverie with dreamy, eager eyes. "The old man will like you, Singer; he always loved a good yarn. He'll ply you with gold rings, healthy wenches, and more ale than you can stomach. The old man's alright really, discounting the fact he's a blood-hungry, murderous lunatic—but then we all have our faults, eh Singer. Father's just a bit misunderstood, is all."

"Hmm...sure." Erun let that one go.

"I take after my mother," Torrig added when he saw the quizzical expression on his new friend's face. Erun chose not to respond to Torrig's banter, his mind was wandering everywhere and it was hard enough concentrating his thoughts without Torrig filling his ears with enthusiastic babble.

It was impossible to think clearly with queasy stomach and thumping head, and so he gave up and instead let his gaze return to the brooding line of towering cliffs occluding the northern skyline. Those stark bluffs appeared impenetrable, without seam or gap, forbidding to the eye and yet somehow weirdly compelling. Paradoxically, Erun felt drawn to those cliffs.

What awaits me there? Would he survive this next adventure? And why he was even attempting it? Maybe Torrig and the girls were right. Was he wise to follow the guidance of that strange old man? Irulan had been very convincing back in that cave. But now he was so close? Not for the first time, Erun questioned his judgment. But it was too late now. He couldn't turn back. That would only mark him as a failure again. So Erun determined he would survive. Learn all he could from this Scaffa so that he could return, claim his vengeance and let his father's shade rest in peace.

A shout turned Erun's head. Orme swung the tiller hard to starboard and his burly sons tugged at sheet and cloth. The ketch veered shoreward leaving Scaffa's Island to stern, cutting a course toward the mainland with seabirds crying as they followed, swooping and whirling, high above the frothing wake.

Steep hills now parted ahead, allowing view of a deep rocky bay, with cascading torrents and sides flanked by stubby woodland. Now visible at the southern end of the bay and hedged by battered firs, was the stone washed harbour and collection of smoke ribboned dwellings that was Northtown.

Larger than Longships and roughly square in shape, Northtown was hemmed on three sides by rocky hills that bastioned the sea. It comprised granite harbour walls, stonewashed low-roofed houses: inn, forge and mill, all of them weighed down by rain-heavy smoke.

Beyond these buildings, a winding road led out through a scrubby slit in the cliffs before disappearing from sight. Three ships were moored at dock, their black hulls bobbing in the constant breezy chop. There were several smaller craft scattered about, their lines creaking and groaning in the blow.

Orme steered the ketch alongside the nearest vessel. He tossed the bowline to a fisherman who had watched their approach. Torrig was the first to leap ashore and Erun Cade needed no excuse to follow. He grabbed his bag of bits: knife, harp, stale oat cakes; his bow with shafts, and almost fell onto the jetty.

Then grasping the hilt of the Treggaran sword so he wouldn't trip, Erun eagerly distanced himself from Orme's ketch and—with as much speed as he could muster with wobbly legs and giddy head—began cutting a rapid eager path behind the loping Torrig, who now arrowed enthusiastically toward the large inn that dominated the centre of the town.

When they reached the inn Torrig bade Erun wait outside. "They're rough hereabouts," the Rodruthan explained, "not sensitive like me." Erun said nothing. "I'll go have a word," added Torrig, "see if there's some bugger inside daft enough to ferry you across for an exorbitant price—you never know your luck. Wait here, Singer..."

"I've still got some money." Erun reached inside his cloak and produced a small bag that still contained most of the coins Irulan had given him on his departure, long weeks ago. He loosened the drawstring, tilted the bag, and emptied the clinking contents into Torrig's open palm.

"That's not even enough to get you out of the harbour," Torrig told him, shaking his fiery mane and tutting. "You can keep those shiny southern pennies, Singer." He shovelled the coins back into Erun's bag with his hand, ignoring the Barolan's protestations.

"I'll do some talking inside," Torrig told him, "maybe bang some heads together. But don't be too optimistic, Singer. That island is shunned hereabouts." Erun nodded glumly. He watched his friend vanish behind the shabby wind-bleached door that opened into the inn, leaving him abandoned, cold and fretting outside. Erun rubbed his scar and scowled at the door. He now had a bad feeling about this.

It was over an hour before Torrig's tattooed, grinning face, peered out at him from the doorway, beckoning Erun to join him inside. Erun, now frozen to the bone, didn't hesitate. "I've found someone—though he's not present at the moment," announced Torrig cheerfully, as Erun entered the alehouse behind him and gagged at the cloying stench inside. The stuffy atmosphere was laden with eye-stinging wood smoke, accompanied by the stale aromas of wet hound, crusty vomit, and often spilled ale. Erun also caught a whiff of fresh ale on his friend's breath, and wondered sourly just how much time Torrig had spent sourcing this *someone*, and how much quenching his bottomless thirst for ale. That was a given.

The inside of the inn wasn't encouraging, with its damp spitty fire and gloomy tallow lamps casting weird shadows on the flickering walls. The two windows showing were so encrusted with salt and grime that they awarded scant light from outside. The half dozen loiterers at tables were all rough looking (even by Rodruthan standards) with their hard tattooed faces and long reddish braids.

One or two glanced curiously over at Erun as he took a seat by the miserable fire and tried capturing what little warmth it had to offer. A mousy haired girl with a squint produced a bowl of suspect soup and some hard bread, alongside a flagon of watery looking ale. These offerings Erun accepted with a nod and thank you. At least his stomach had settled now and he was hungry. The girl ignored him.

"He'll be in this evening—so they tell me," Torrig informed Erun Cade between soggy, noisy bites, "So I'll have to leave you here, Singer. Don't worry...." Torrig grinned when he saw the alarm showing on Erun's face. "They'll leave you be...I told them you're a warlock with a magic harp. That you slew nine Treggarans and freed me from Dreekhall single-handed. So all you've got to do is sit here and wait till your man shows up."

"Is that all?"

"No. I've told the innkeep to send his tariff, together with the ferryman's price for the crossing, over to the Crags—least I could do. He's happy about that, Singer; the Crags always pay though not always promptly—though I didn't see any cause to mention that adage to him."

Erun was taken aback by Torrig's generosity. "I owe you, my friend." He felt suddenly at a loss for words now Torrig was leaving him. He had itched to be free of the Rodruthan during their sea voyage, but now that he was at the Island's gate, the thought of continuing on alone was not a cheerful one.

Torrig smiled. "You owe me nothing, Singer," he slapped Erun's back so hard he choked on his soup and spat bubbles on the table, "but I owe you my life, Erun Cade. You can count Red Torrig as a friend—and there's few as can do that. And," continued Torrig with a whisper, "should you, by some uncanny chance survive Scaffa's Island and glean from her what you need, then do come call on my family at the Crags. We're rather nice when you get to know us."

Erun, smiling between slurps, promised he would. Then Torrig thrust out a grubby hand which the Barolan clasped tightly with his own. "I must go now, Singer—Orme will be fretting else. I shall miss you. Stay alive!" Torrig took to his feet with a lithe twist, winked at the squinty girl—who gawped back—and then sauntered jauntily out of the inn, leaving Erun to his forlorn thoughts for the second time that day.

At least it was dry in here, which was an improvement. He had his knife and bow with him too, and some arrows—so that was good as well. And the sword Torrig had pilfered for him was still attached to his waist, which also was comforting, (but not overly comforting—since he hadn't yet learned how to use it.) It least it made him look efficient, less like some redundant wailing singer banished from the south.

Despite his loneliness and misgivings, Erun Cade felt better than he had for days. The motion nausea had departed and the food now strengthened him, as the struggling fire and weak ale warmed his soul and body. Time passed like judgment, Erun drifted from random thought to random thought, his mind freed to roam at will by the ale and warmth now infusing him.

He spoke to no one and they in turn let him be. It was evident that Red Torrig had a reputation in Northtown. Were that not the case, Erun suspected he'd be gutted with a fish knife by now and probably eaten as well. But Torrig was Brude's son and they were hardly going to upset Druthan Crags. It didn't make for happy company though.

Erun brooded away that afternoon, drinking too much and fretting about what lay ahead. It was almost dark when a grimy hand nudged his shoulder. Erun had been dozing and the shake jolted him alert and made him spill his ale. Erun looked up in alarm, saw a stranger leaning over him and breathing foully in his ear. An old man he was, swamped by an oversized dripping, dark woollen coat. Long greasy grey-black tangled hair stuck like wet seaweed to his pale bony features. One eye was blue, the other white as a gull's egg. This newcomer was both dismal and morose in appearance, his scarecrow presence did little to raise Erun's wan spirits. *He's like Irulan's ugly brother.*

"Can I be of assistance?" Erun crinkled his nose. This stranger had an unsavoury odour hanging about him as if he had spent too much time sleeping among farm stock. "What do you want, old man?"

The stranger's good eye pinned him in a most uncomfortable way that made Erun fidget and wish Torrig was still with him. He couldn't help but notice how the other Rodruthans, who until now had been relatively boisterous with their dicing, had grown silent in their cups, and now looked askance at the grim old stranger.

The old man was oblivious to their stares, his unsettling gaze was locked on Erun and wouldn't let go. He spoke then, his words croaking out in a way that set Erun's teeth on edge.

"You wanted to speak to me?"

"Did I? Can't say I remember putting forward that request." Erun gagged. This was an untidy creature leaning over him, Erun heartily wished the wretch would go prey on someone else instead. This place was cheerless enough without old laughing bones here.

"Well?"

"Could be, I could do you a service," croaked the stranger, his good eye boring into Erun's face like an ice blue dagger.

Erun turned his head away. "Such as?" Surely this wretched creature wasn't his ferryman. Please, no.

Soon as drown me as look at me, this one...

The old man barked something that might have been a laugh were it to belong to any other individual. "Don't play coy with me, laddie," he croaked. "I know where 'tis you want to get to...your red-haired friend agreed my price after a time discussing. If you want to continue you had best sup up and follow me now."

Thanks, Torrig...

"I...how do I know you're genuine?" Erun had no wish to board boat again this evening, particularly with this ungainly creature. He'd been hoping to meet the ferryman, (any other ferryman) discuss the voyage with more revolting Rodruthan ale (which he was now finding himself happily accustomed to) and sail out on the morrow, after a good sound sleep. "I mean...you don't look much like a sailor, stranger. How do I know you can be trusted?"

"You don't," responded the old man, "but if you still want to get to that dark shore then you had better stop gawping like a guppy and follow me without. I'm not one to tarry in idleness when there is a task waiting. Come on!"

Without further word the stranger straightened his shabby coat, scanned the dingy room with his good eye, and then made for the door, without so much as a glance behind to see whether Erun followed.

And of course Erun did. What else could he do? After half a second's bleak deliberation, Erun Cade gulped back his tankard and struggled to his feet, feeling oddly wobbly legged again—but this time from the weak-looking ale that had proved on reflection, quite strong and now had set his head to spinning again.

Outside a horned moon painted silver on the dark churning water of the harbour side. All was quiet, saving the habitual keening of the wind and the surging thud of wave on stone. Erun, thoroughly miserable again and still doubting his senses, grabbed his belongings, and followed the crow-like ferryman along the harbour wall path. Eventually the old man stopped beside a battered shabby skiff that looked well past its best days. Erun was horrified.

"Surely you don't intend to ferry me across in that bathtub," he complained. The old man ignored him. He untied the bobbing skiff and then with startling agility for one so decrepit, leapt on board and began readying the small craft for the voyage. Erun, questioning his sanity and cursing Irulan and Torrig with equal measure, gingerly placed a foot on deck, and then followed after with the other.

The craft lurched treacherously beneath his feet, and Erun hurried to seat his wet behind on a plank, his bundle and weapons to hand. The ferryman ignored him. Now safely aboard Erun took to crouching grumpily on his wet plank at the stern of the craft and eying his unsavoury pilot with deep misgivings.

The stranger still paid Erun no heed as he deftly prepared the craft for sail. Within minutes the battered looking vessel was ready for departure, with small sail ribbed and rudder in place. Once underway the triangular cloth soon tautened and bellied outwards, allowing the skiff to cut a swift channel out of the harbour and at an alarming speed too.

Erun clung to his plank and watched his pilot steer a confident course deep into the night. This ferryman wasn't one for talking, which suited Erun well—he being in no mood for conversation either.

Theirs was a joyous crossing. Erun was now-adrenaline fused with both dread and excitement. A small part of him felt like a bold adventurer from an ancient fable: a much larger section (centred on his bowels) felt like a sacrifice being led out to slaughter.

Erun steeled his nerves and focussed on the positive as Irulan had taught him. He set his mind to quash the icy dread seeping into his already shivering bones. He thought of his dead father and those murderous sons of the baron whom he vowed to kill one day. And then Lissane. Beautiful, proud Lissane—lost to him forever now.

Gone. Banished to the memory of that blissful summer a thousand years ago. And just what had he gained since then? A few disputable friends and a decidedly murky outlook. Not much, all things considered.

It seemed an age later when the skiff finally crunched on pebbly sand amidst total blackness. Erun thanked the pilot and jumped across onto the chiming shingle, soaking his legs to the crutch, and almost dropping his bow in the dark water, gasping at the cold, and cussing imaginatively as the black spray almost engulfed him.

The ferryman glanced back at him and Erun felt the keen barb of that icy cobalt glare. That last glance reminded him of someone else—someone familiar. Erun was about to shout something but the strange old man had already turned his craft away, leaving Erun shivering and stamping his feet. He watched the ferryman pole his craft out free from the surge and, before he could count to ten, both skiff and pilot had vanished into the night.

Once again Erun Cade was alone. He shrugged, shouldered

the bow and slung the bag across his back, beginning the long wet trudge towards the vague blackness of cliff ahead. And then what? Keep walking. Erun had no plan as such; just a vague notion that, when morning came (if it ever did in this cheerful place) he would somehow discover a way to scale said cliffs now flanking the darkness off to his right. It was quiet. Erun could hear the crashing surge of wave to his left and the eerie persistent sigh of wind—aside those, nothing.

Just silence. The watchful, waiting silence of a patient hunter scanning his prey. Erun felt cold eyes boring into his back and put it down to ale-filled imagination.

And it was so dark here; the moon had stayed behind at Northtown. Perhaps it too shunned this mournful shore.

Erun picked up his pace, walking briskly along the beach, the wind whipping his cloak and salt spray stinging his face. Hours it seemed before a pale line greyed the eastern horizon, lightening and widening out to a broad bar of steel, until at last grey daylight turned shadows into shapes.

Erun rested under a rock for a time, his eyes adjusting quickly to the growing light. He glanced about at the cheerless terrain—rocks and sea and sea and rocks. Not a lot else. The cliff to his right was a vast slab of dark stone, smooth and towering, its top lost in cloud. Erun was cold and hungry again now, and though tired, it was his discomfort that forced him on again. But he soon began to despair as the wall of rock to his right showed no fissure or fault for him to begin an ascent. Erun steeled himself. There had to be a way up. He would just have to keep walking until he found it.

But by afternoon Erun was exhausted. He now suspected he'd circumnavigated the entire shoreline. The island had appeared small from Orme's ketch—only four or five miles in length. Erun was convinced he had trudged at least twenty along this bloody beach. Eventually weariness ceased his limbs, if not his determination.

Momentarily defeated, Erun slunk behind a large rock, taking what shelter he could from the ceaseless batter of the freezing wind. He must have slept for a time. Fortunately Erun was awake when the cannibal women came to pay a hungry visit.

***

Inside his prison Ashmali waxed stronger than ever. Yes, the sorcerer contained him for now, but his jailer's hold was more fragile than he believed. Each soul he'd devoured had strengthened Ashmali. Soon he would be unstoppable. Soon he would break free from the amulet holding him. The runes were unravelling. His jailer would become his prisoner. Servant would be master.

The demon's hunger was satisfied for a time after the rending of Siotta. But that time had passed. He was hungry again. Now Ashmali raged inside his prison, his fiery essence burning through and scorching the sorcerer as he slept. This time Ozmandeus's ward spells stopped the alien heat from further penetration. The next time too.

But Ashmali was patient. He persisted, applying the pressure more and more each time. A week passed. Another. The army was now on the move again, heading south east toward Lamoza City. It was during that arduous long march across the Lamoza plains that Ashmali broke through again.

Maelchor witnessed it first-hand. The warlord had been riding alongside Ozmandeus discussing their plans after sacking Lamoza. Maelchor wasn't convinced by the sorcerer's argument that they needed to face down Xandoria. Bring the empire to heel. When would this all end and what would be left for the likes of him and his men? Even with the reckless demon fire Maelchor doubted they could defeat the might of Xandoria. A land more powerful by far than any they'd taken. And what if they did defeat Xandoria? What next?

The destructions of Aketa and Siotta had been horrific. Worse, there had been precious little spoil, the Renegade's fiery monster having reduced even the walls of those cities to ash. Maelchor now doubted Ozmandeus could control the creature for much longer. It wasn't a comforting thought. And during that march he was proved right.

***

He'd been arguing the case for a parley with Xandoria when the sorcerer yelled in pain and pitched from his horse. There Ozmandeus lay on the dusty ground writhing and screaming, his face and arms coaly red and his cloak blazing with sudden flames. The amulet throbbed on the sorcerer's chest, blackening his skin and burning deep into his flesh.

Still Ozmandeus screamed. Maelchor and his closest captains dismounted and ran across. They stopped in horror when they saw the face inside the sorcerer's face. Ozmandeus's eyes were not his own. Something moved behind them, some other life force. The demon! Then the sorcerer's eyes blazed white fire, causing Maelchor and his officers to turn and run.

Maelchor halted the march. They pitched camp by a struggling stream whilst the warlord and his captains decided what to do next. They waited. Ozmandeus recovered in time but was clearly shaken. He ordered the march continue and reluctantly his captains obeyed. The Renegade no longer rode horse with the captains but had slaves fashion a palanquin to carry him and keep him hidden from the blazing Lamoza sun. Even this early in the year the plains were hot. Maelchor stayed well away from it. The one exception was when he stuck his nose into report sightings of Lamozan scouts in the hills ahead. Ozmandeus had turned toward him, his face blistered and scabby and the skin on his arms red raw. Maelchor had imparted his message and departed at speed.

Chapter 20

The Village

When the shout came Erun leapt to his feet with eyes wide and heart thumping in his chest. There were three naked women running towards him. But for once this wasn't good news. The word 'women' didn't really describe them. They wore skins around their waists and their hair was very long. Two had spiked and bleached theirs into weird shapes, giving them a bestial appearance. One had a beard. Each savage carried a long spear plus a sling which, even now, the closest whirled over her head and a stone whacked onto the gravel a few feet from Erun's erstwhile resting place. Erun reached for his bow, then realised it was missing.

Shit! His arrows were missing too, and his sword! Stolen. But by whom and when?

Shit!

Too bad. Dithering and fretting would get him dead; Erun decided he had better get moving. And fast.

Erun ran. They whooped excitedly as they took chase, their thick sinewy legs bulging and their odd shaped breasts bouncing about. They moved quickly, Erun noted, and were closing on him fast.

Shit.

Something hard thudded into Erun's shoulder, knocking him from his feet. Instinctively he rolled, breaking his fall and willing out the crunching pain of the blow.

Another stone smacked against the rock at his side. Somehow Erun got his legs under him again and started to sprint, but he was winded and didn't get far. Within moments the madwomen had him cornered with broad headed spears held ready, and wild, deranged eyes hungry for the kill. The nearest stepped forward. Her grin showed filed teeth.

"Strip you!" she said.

"Finger you!" the second added. The one with the beard.

"Eat you!" This from the third.

"Piss off!" Erun let his arms drop down by his sides. He banished his fear and instead greeted the void as Irulan had taught him back in the woods. Erun slowed his breathing, let his body relax with arms still loose at his side, focussed on the enemy and waited for them to approach. During those seconds Erun had more than enough time to study his adversaries.

They were not overly attractive. Savage in appearance, their faces heavy set, with beetle brow and thick hair carpeting their skulls and faces, and almost occluding their hostile manic eyes. Their naked torsos and filthy necks were festooned with strings of beads and pebbles, and the teeth of gods only know what dreadful creatures. The one with the beard had painted her left breast green. Erun wondered if he should enquire why. Perhaps not.

Now Erun's sudden calm had slowed their approach. The women now seemed uncertain what to do. It was clear to him that these weren't the most intelligent of individuals—despite their ferocious appearance. Perhaps it was their diet, a small part of him wondered. Then with a predictable wailing the closest attacked, still showing those razor teeth whilst lunging her spear hard at Erun's midriff, and then grunting in surprise when its target was no longer there.

Erun's mind's eye had watched the spear's approach. Time slowed, his heartbeats were like the tolling of some distant bell. He spun on his heels, his right hand reaching out, gripping the ashen shaft behind the spear tip and pulling hard, while his left formed a blade and slid down the length of the weapon, chopping into the exposed throat of his attacker, and knocking her from her feet.

Erun now gripped the spear with both hands and waited for the other two cannibal women to pounce. A shadow loomed behind him. Instinctively Erun ducked as a second spear passed clean over his head. His left foot shot out with cobra speed, hooking behind the beardy woman's knee and tripping her.

Once again Erun rolled clear. The third beauty lunged at him screaming hatred, and Erun batted the spear away with his own stolen shaft. But it was to no avail, the other two had regained their feet and now all three women were closing in on him again.

Erun didn't hesitate. He took the first in the throat with a wild desperate lunge that gored open the cannibal-woman's neck and spewed her scarlet lifeblood onto the stony ground. She pitched forward, twitched for a time then lay still, while her companions looked on in stunned disbelief.

Erun saw their hesitation and seized his chance. He kicked sand and small stones up into the face of the nearest, and then turned and sped toward the wall of stone ahead, vainly seeking any kind of purchase on its surface.

It was then that he saw the ladder. How had he missed *that* earlier? He must have run right passed it when the madwomen were pursuing him. Erun doubted his senses as he cut a desperate path toward the ladder. The two remaining women were almost on him again, their heavy voices grunting with rage at the death of their sister.

Erun reached the ladder.

He stopped to quickly shove the spear shaft through his belt, allowing him to climb freely, and then leaped up, grabbing the rope rungs and heaving his body up behind him until his feet found purchase on the swinging, dancing rungs of rope.

Erun climbed like a madman, heaving and pulling at the swaying rope of the ladder. Up and up, cursing in sudden pain when a cast spear cut a deep slice along his leg. Erun didn't look down, just kept willing his aching body forward, rung by ropey rung.

Mercifully the cannibal women seemed unable to climb and they too appeared perplexed by the sudden appearance of the ladder. Erun doubted they knew what a ladder was. They were no more baffled by its appearance than Erun, though he was heartily grateful for its intervention.

His leg screamed at him. Erun could feel warm blood trickling down onto his feet and squelching with the seawater inside his sodden boots. He hoped that the wound wouldn't slow him too much. What if it was poisoned? It didn't hurt much—yet. But then that was probably just the adrenaline kicking in again.

Erun climbed. A stone thudded into rock a yard to the right of his head, and then another cracked beneath him, but then thankfully he was out of range. Erun took a necessary rest. Swinging round he stole a glance below where the madwomen could be seen glaring up at him, yelling fiercely, and shaking their spears. The bearded one grabbed her crutch and started ululating enthusiastically.

Love you too.

Erun pressed on upwards with what small vigour was left to him, the creaky ladder spinning wildly from right to left, as he forced his frozen, leaded body into frantic motion yet again, and all the time that spear weighing him down, and threatening to snare his legs.

Somehow he kept going. An hour passed. Another—still Erun climbed. How long could he keep this up? By now his battered body was screaming at him and his frozen limbs were weighty as lead. His leg was getting painful too. Erun couldn't hold out much longer. What if he slipped?

Must...keep...climbing.

Erun shut out the fear of falling, willing himself on, gripping the rungs and focussing on Lissane's lovely face and when that didn't work, Slinsi Garron's arse. Once he did slip, falling backwards and yelling in fear. But his legs and the spear got trapped in the ladder's rungs below, and after dangling stupidly for a minute in horrified panic, Erun was able to pull his exhausted body erect again. His leg was on fire now. Erun shut out the pain and climbed again. Up and up. On and on.

Then when the best part of that miserable day had gone, and with his cut leg feeling about to buckle beneath him, Erun Cade—exhausted and bloodied yet triumphant—gained the top of the ladder. He rolled clear onto the wide level grassland that covered its crown.

There Erun sprawled, panting and gasping as one delirious and drunk with joy. For many minutes he just lay there, too exhausted to move. Then, rested at last, Erun struggled to his feet and stole a glance about at this new vista surrounding him.

Ahead and to either side was a wide plateau of wind-blown grass fading pale-green and lush into the middle distance. Beyond that a wood showed dark and creepy, its bare branches forming a thorny crown around the conical head of a rocky knoll.

Erun tugged at his trousers, baring his flesh so that he could examine his wound. It wasn't that bad, he decided, and hopefully those primitive women weren't adept in the use of poison. Satisfied with his inspection, he rested a while longer and then took to his feet again.

Erun now made good progress using his stolen spear as a staff, and without any better notion in his head, cut a clear path toward the dark cluster of woods ringing that hill. These he soon reached, and climbing the steep slope beneath their wintry limbs, began his ascent of the knoll. Wind and rain tore at him again but by now Erun was oblivious to both. The knoll wasn't high but once reached the summit awarded a wide panorama of the countryside beyond.

It was then that Erun discovered there was something not quite right about this island and that Torrig's countrymen were wise to steer clear of its forlorn shores.

Here was enchantment for certain. Impossible, but there before his eyes. Erun Cade now looked down upon a land of golden summer. It was wonderful to see. Behind him the stark grey skies and winds still held court. But ahead...

Ahead were green open fields and chiming streams. Swallows soared through skies the colour of Lissane Barola's eyes, and doves cooed contentedly somewhere close. Erun saw fertile valleys down below him, where fruit-laden trees and ordered vineyards shimmered in the afternoon sunlight.

A mile beyond these, he spied the friendly coiling smoke of what could only be a village. If this was a dream it was a good one, and he was more than ready to take a chunk out of it. Erun felt the strength flow back into his weary limbs as he strode toward that summer, letting the sound and smells of its blessing enter his soul and warm his heart. He descended the knoll like a grinning child, drugged with joy and smiling, letting the welcoming warmth filter through his clothes and caress his tired, battered features. What strange country was this?

Within an hour Erun Cade had reached the village and stood looking on by a small wicker bridge that hurdled a clear bright stream; watching and smiling as the tranquil occupants went about their normal day. If they saw him standing there Erun couldn't tell, for they paid him no heed. They seemed content and at peace with their environment, and Erun was filled with a sudden desire to join with them and venture no further than this restful, happy place.

Eagerly, and with mind made up, Erun crossed the bridge and then stopped dead when he heard the eerie sound of a harp somewhere in the distance. It didn't sound like his harp but it *did* sound oddly familiar.

Where have I heard that uncanny melody before?

Erun felt a sudden icy stab of doubt grip him. His scar twitched on his face and he reached inside his cloak to wrap his fingers around his harp (he couldn't remember putting it there— but at least he still had it. Perhaps the thief on the beach wasn't fond of harp song.)

The strings tingled slightly at his touch as though the instrument was answering those distant chords. The harp-song was now everywhere around him. Beautiful yet disturbing. Could no one else hear it? Was it only playing for him? It was uncanny. Weird.

Erun felt another shiver telling him something wasn't right here. He ignored it, shouldered the spear, and continued his casual stroll into the village. The harp-song followed behind him but he closed his ears to it. As Erun approached them a few of the citizens gazed his way and smiled, though most seemed unaware of his presence.

Then he saw the girl.

She was tall. Her hair raven-black and glassy smooth, flowing down passed her shapely shoulders. She was walking away from him, her hips swaying as she shouldered a broad urn of water taken from the stream. As one entranced, Erun followed her. There was something hypnotic about those hips. He called out to the girl and she turned and smiled back at him.

It was Lissane Barola.

She was older than last he'd seen her, her hair greying at temples and her violet/blue eyes shaded by dark lines. But it was still Lissane. Beautiful Liss—the only girl he'd ever loved. Impossibly she was here. Erun, feeling like a lost stray dog, called out to her.

"Liss…do you not recognise me? Lissane!" Erun called again, desperate this time. "Lissane!"

But she cried out as though he'd struck her, and turned away, dropping the urn and at once began running full pelt as though she were a deer caught by sudden fear in an open field. *Liss, love…don't run from me!*

It was then that Erun heard the hollow clatter of hoof on stone, and the accompanying shouts of riders approaching at speed. Erun turned, watched in stunned horror, as the troop of armoured horsemen crashed into the village amid shouts. They were clearly brigands, their rude voices destroying that perfect summer day like a rogue wave obliterating a child's castle of sand.

They were almost upon him. The leader sported a horned helm that covered his features entirely; his armour too was the colour of scorched jet. No sun reflected from that cold steel. He hefted a huge mace, broad and weighty. This he brought down on the head of an old man who had been trying so desperately to flee.

The man's skull burst open like an overripe fruit, and blood and brains spilled free to mingle with the dust. The leader laughed and then signalled his men forward for the kill. All were garbed in dullest black, their faces hidden behind featureless helms of steel— though only the leader's bore horns.

As one, the marauders tore violent into the village, killing and destroying all in their path. Some carried blazing brands and these they hurled onto thatch roofs and withy fences which caught at once. Soon the entire village blazed. Erun, they ignored.

Then the leader spied the girl. She'd been running for the far gate that led north out of the town. He cantered after her, his mace making casual loops in the air. He was almost on her!

"No!" Erun yelled and ran to intercept the horseman, his spear gripped in hand. But he was too late to save her. Erun saw the mace rise and then fall, saw the girl's broken body crumple and lie motionless on the bloodied ground—a widening pool of crimson staining the dust.

"Bastard!" Erun yelled again. The horned rider hearing him at last, turned his horse upon this challenger. The leader laughed when he saw the hatred and fury in Erun's blue-grey eyes. Erun levelled his stolen spear and braced it into the earth as the metal clad horse bore down on him at speed. He'd impale the beast first then when the rider was unhorsed he'd finish him too. Cut the bastard to bits—so he would.

This rider was no fool. He swerved at the last moment and his mace swung low, knocking Erun's spear aside, and sending a violent shudder up his right arm, leaving it both numb and useless. Erun rolled on the ground in agony. The horned rider left him to it, returning to his bloody sport with the villagers. They were rounding up the people now with whips and black-shafted spears. Once they were hemmed together the killing began in earnest. There were none spared on that brutal afternoon.

Erun shut the dreadful screams from his ears. He painfully regained his feet, and then approached the broken body of the girl. He could feel the tears streaming down his face. The mace blow had smashed her shoulder bone and snapped her neck and her long hair was matted with crimson ooze. Erun reached down and gently turned her head so he could gaze upon her face.

Lissane..?

Erun screamed. The dead eyes glaring back at him were the eyes of a shrunken hag: ancient, cruel and mocking. Her mouth opened, revealing broken teeth, and Erun gagged at the stench of her foul breath. She spat red filth up at him, and Erun reeled away from her in repulsion and alarm.

His mind was racing and he felt sick with pain and horror. Erun heard urgent hooves behind him. He turned, saw the rider too late. Then the mace crashed nail hard into his chest and Erun's world exploded into scarlet agony. The pain engulfed him for a time, fading only when a cold dizzy greyness took over.

Erun knew that he was dying and the thought suddenly angered him. "I'm not done living. I haven't even started. I cannot die now!" Erun heard his voice cry out. It sounded miles away. *This cannot be!* The world spun a million turns. Erun was falling... down...down. An age passed and still he fell. Then Erun Cade heard someone laugh close by and the pain faded as the welcome void swallowed him up.

***

Throughout the teeming streets of Xenn City word was spreading fast concerning spiralling events far beyond the Lamozan Gap. Rumours abounded that an army now marched across the Lamoza Plains. A horde bent on conquest and aided by some flame- wielding sorcerer. The countries beyond had already fallen to his fire.

Nothing was clear. Some said a new Firelord had risen—the first in over a thousand years. Most argued it was a Lamozan stunt to put them off guard—that the crazy Lamozans were destroying their own cities to lure Xandoria across the Gap. Once the elite were through, the Lamozan rebels would ambush them and thus score feeble successes against the Empire. Those victories would be scarce more than a wasp stinging a tiger. But then Lamozans were reckless and random – capable of all kinds of nuisance. They were crafty too. It was the reason they still held out against their overlord the Emperor, against all odds.

There were a few zealots in Xenn who warned that the gods were angry and the Empire would be punished, but these were laughed down as fools and troublemakers. Most sensible folk in the city were of the opinion that whatever happened west of the

Gap was of no concern to them. There was always trouble out there in the bad lands. No need for civilised Xenn to worry. Let Lamoza deal with its own issues. They were all mad over there anyway. Why should Xandoria care? Let Lamoza City crumple and fall. No loss to Xenn. The Empire was strong. No invading army (even one aided by sorcery) could rival the might of Xandoria. So what if Zorne and those other distant lands had fallen? They were nothing more than bandit states.

And so the rumours came and went. In the main people lost interest, returning their attentions to the everyday hassles of city life. A few kept an open ear but no one really cared bar the zealots and doom-mongers. As for those—the Emperor ordered them whipped bloody through the streets out into the deserts beyond. Let those fools bark at the moon until hunger and heat drove them witless.

But there was one high-placed noble who watched and listened with growing dread. In his office the Chancellor now held urgent parley with the three generals in charge of Xandoria's vast army. It had taken considerable effort to persuade them to come.

Only last week the Emperor had deigned to see him. The Chancellor had had scarce five minutes to warn his ruler about the sorcerer Ozmandeus before he was laughed out of court. Mocked and ridiculed for even hinting there could be any danger to the Empire.

Undeterred he had changed tack: approached all three generals. Pleaded (even begged) them use their considerable influence in court and address the Emperor themselves. It hadn't been easy— no one liked disturbing the Emperor. Xandoria's current ruler was known for his capricious nature and short fuse.

The Chancellor had had to employ all his persuasive skills, pointing to the portents, the signs in the skies; the growing rumours, and the many refugees seen by their scouts up in the mountains, fleeing in droves from the west and making for the Lamozan Gap. War was coming. That much was certain. But it wasn't war that worried the Chancellor. It was the sorcerer Ozmandeus and the power he wielded.

At last the three generals had agreed to put his fears to the

Emperor. They too had their worries about this business, so they told him. Their assurance left the Chancellor with the small satisfaction that he had done all he could. It was down to others now.

But as that day grew long the Chancellor took to fretting again. He'd heard the stories about Siotta and Aketa. He was a learned man who in his younger days had travelled far. He'd visited Aketa once. An exotic and beautiful city hugging the coast of Spagos. Its walls (though not nearly as high or thick as Xenn's) had looked strong enough to withstand any siege for months.

But there had been no siege there. Rumour was both Aketa and Siotta held out for less than a day before the fires closed in. In his heart the Chancellor knew his people were putting their heads in the sand. Fools led by a bigger fool. Destruction was coming to Xenn. It was only a matter of time. Not in the form of an army but something much worse. The demon Ashmali.

Chapter 21

Queen of Death

"He has courage, this one. Perhaps we can use him after all." It was a woman's voice. Husky, deep and resonate. And frightening. Her words filled his giddy head.

I'm alive...

"Yes you are—for now," the voice whispered in his ear. "Whether you stay that way depends on much. Should I choose not to like you..."

Erun opened his eyes. He felt no pain now and gazing down at his body, was alarmed to discover that he lay spread out and pale naked on a slab of cold stone.

Sacrificial stone.

Erun saw the shadowy shapes of men gathered all around him, their faces concealed behind dark helmets. The horned leader he saw standing to his left. A grim sentinel, watching him silently through those narrow slits in his helm.

You murdering scum. Erun turned his face away.

A woman leaned over Erun now, and he guessed that she must be the leader of these cruel raiders. It was her voice he had heard. She was large in build and appeared uncommonly tall, for though she crouched over his prone body her handsome head was of a height with the men standing behind her.

The woman's face was ageless. The eyes ice blue, cold and merciless as polar skies. Her hair she wore long, ash pale in hue and tied in a single thick woven braid that trailed the length of her back. Her breasts were large and firm, the nipples hidden by the silver plate armour she wore covering her torso and upper thighs. Erun noted how her lips were fruit ripe and full. They parted slightly as he watched her in a manner that was both sensual and erotic. Erun couldn't take his eyes off her. She smiled, teasing him further. Despite his predicament Erun could think of nothing else except what it would be like to kiss those moist dangerous lips.

"I think there is something worth saving in this one," the giant woman said—speaking more to herself than those silent soldiers standing all around her. Her deep, sultry voice was having an alarming effect on Erun. He was shockingly aware of the blatant swelling between his legs. His face reddened in alarm and outrage. The woman laughed like a fishwife at his expression. "Might be that I have a use for *that* too one day." Erun closed his eyes. Being dead was preferable to this.

"But for now we have to discover where your fear resides, child. Time to show your mettle and prove your courage." The woman's eyes were now like ice pools, impenetrable and remote. Gone were mocking smile and teasing tones. Erun, watching in horror, saw that the giantess now held a stone dagger in her left hand, her cruel long fingers lovingly caressing the bone handle.

Where had that come from? Erun squirmed and struggled to free his shivering body from the slab. It was hopeless, he was held fast like a bug in tree glue—though no visible bonds constrained him.

She reached down then to caress him as a lover might. Erun shivered when he felt that ash hair touch his nakedness. Despite his terror he was still aroused. She kissed him then. Her mouth was like a hot wet sledgehammer. Erun couldn't breathe. Was she going to murder him or jump on him? Both probably.

Erun was giddy of her musky scent. It was almost overpowering (and that kiss), Erun felt his recently shrunken member leap to life again—but only for a moment—then the cold touch of razored stone cut deep into his face, just below his right eye.

Erun winced when he felt a hot bead of blood run down his chin and drip onto his white belly. He felt the glistening sheen of fear course down his legs. She was evil, this woman. Evil incarnate.

"Your riders butchered those people!" Erun spat the words up at her. "Why?" Erun gasped as the stone knife dug into his flesh again, this time slicing diagonally along his cheek, stinging his face like a thousand hornets.

"Maybe I'll pop an eye out," she said, casually rolling the knife around her deft long fingers. Her huge pale eyes were now akin to cat on prey—playful, capricious and cruel. "What think you, Cron?" The woman's eyes flicked like hurled knives across to the horned silent leader who was obviously her captain.

Cron said nothing—didn't even stir. The giant woman turned her gaze upon Erun again and smiled. "Cron here would have me blind you, geld you, and then gut you open, beautiful boy, before feeding your carcass to the hungry hounds without." She laughed out loud at his horrified expression. "But I deem we've better uses for you, young Erun Cade."

"You... How do you know my name?" Erun's growing curiosity was struggling for mastery with his fear. This giantess both fascinated and terrified him more than anyone he'd encountered—even Paolo Barola could learn from this bitch. There was something feral and raw about her, and yet she was alluring beyond any normal woman could be. Then it came to him. The name clanging like a gong inside his head.

Scaffa.

"You're the ruler of this island." It was a statement not a question. "You're the woman called Scaffa. It's you I've come to see."

"It is one name," she answered reflectively, and then began gently tracing her knife down his chest and resting it at his groin. "Though some call me the giantess and others 'Queen of Death'. Those fools have many names for me."

"That old bastard Irulan sent me." Erun gazed down, horribly aware of how close the stone knife was to his flaccid, shrinking sex. "He never told me that you were a murderess, savage bitch." It wasn't a sensible thing to say given the circumstance but it was too late now.

Her ice-eyes narrowed to feline slits and her mouth twitched with sudden annoyance. "I could so easily open up those old burns on your legs, fool—finish the work started by another."

She slid the edge of that cold sharp stone along his trembling thighs. Erun had almost forgotten about those old wounds. Irulan's healing salve had left little to show of the agony inflicted on him by Paolo Barola. The scars were pale and smooth now, just showing beneath the dried blood and bruising of his more recent scrapes.

Unlike the brand/scar on his forehead, which stuck out like a red badge for all to see—though even that he had become accustomed to of late.

The giantess Scaffa watched him like a hungry she-panther waiting to pounce. Slowly, she lowered the knife's point towards his groin again. Erun, gawping like a lamped rabbit and straining to keep his bladder closed, felt fresh beads of sweat slide down his cheeks.

Oh please...I'd so rather keep those...

She smiled evilly. "Or else I could work down here," she hinted, "one quick slice and—off!" Erun shuddered, imagining the sudden cold sharp sting of pain as his manhood was cut from him like freshly scythed barley.

But instead she laughed—a harsh sound blending dog's snarl with crow's mocking caw. Grinning, Scaffa withdrew the knife and shoved in into a loop on her belt. She stood then, and straightening her back now towered over her men. Erun could now see that the mail she wore glistened like moonlight in that gloomy place.

Scaffa's mile-long legs were sheaved by fur boots and skin tight trousers of the softest black leather. Her arms were bare except for the gold coils snaking along their length. Those arms were ivory white and looked very strong. A bit too muscular for Erun's taste. On her fingers too were many rings of gold, and around her neck Scaffa the giantess wore an amulet of deep blue stone the size of an eagle's egg. She was one big nasty scary woman—but in a way that excited Erun despite his predicament.

Scaffa gazed down upon him, no emotion now showing on her face. "What you saw was an illusion, Erun Cade—like your wounds. See....They are gone." Scaffa pointed to his legs. Erun looked down. No blood. Nothing. And then he realised that his cheek no longer burned from where she had sliced him, nor was there any lancing pain in his chest as there should have been. In his horror he'd forgotten about that mace blow. The graze in his leg was still there though—strangely that reassured him.

"I needed to test your mettle," Scaffa told him. "I don't trust Irulan—never have. I've known him a *very* long time. Far longer than you could imagine, child. He is wayward and fickle and not to be relied upon—never was. But I think that in you he has chosen well. Here, drink this..."

A cup had appeared in her left hand as if by magic. Scaffa now lowered it carefully to his lips. Erun, feeling suddenly very relieved and grateful, quaffed down the thick golden fluid like a man dying from thirst.

"Those wild women at the beach?" Erun asked her. "Were they illusions too? Oh, and who stole my weapons? Was that you as well?" *And if so how did you do it?*

"No they are real," replied Scaffa. "Those women guard the island. They live in caves along the shore and hunt and fish to stay alive. Occasionally they capture a hapless sailor to breed with then eat. Mostly they eat fish—but now and then each other.

"They're simple creatures, superstitious and spiteful but easily swayed. You did well down there for a novice fighter. And don't worry, you will have new weapons in good time. But this time you will be trained in their use."

"You saw me enter the island? How?"

"I have been watching you since you left the Treggaran castle with your red-haired friend who wouldn't accompany you here. Rodruthans aren't as daft as they look. I'd already received word from the hermit, and needed to see what new fool he was sending my way. There have been several of late. You wouldn't believe some of the clowns he's sent me in the past. But I cannot say I am disappointed this time. You have mettle, child, though clearly you've much to learn."

"How is that possible?" Erun found himself saying. It felt like someone was playing with his private regions and it wasn't him. Who were these people? Irulan? The ferryman? This scary gorgeous big mean woman? What did they really want from him?

It was all too much and had been a stressful couple of days. Erun yawned, feeling suddenly sleepy. It was the drink doing it. Some kind of mead—rich and strong. A nasty thought grabbed him then. Had Scaffa drugged him for some ghastly purpose, after all? He made to break free again. "And where are my clothes?" Erun demanded.

"Relax child," Scaffa's hypnotic gaze pinned him butterfly to board, and, aside from the shuffling silent shapes of Cron and his men, Erun Cade was aware of little else.

"This island is called Laras Lassladden," Scaffa informed him as he lay there. "It is my domain—has been for generations. It exists outside the confines of your own country's rigid dimensions. Time here moves at a different pace."

"You mean it's enchanted?" Erun said, "and that's why it's always summer."

Scaffa didn't respond to his question, but her eyes looked almost sad for a fleeting moment. She seemed to be recalling some ancient event and he could but wonder how old she really was.

Then her eyes were on him again—iron hard icy glints. This woman (if that was what she was) was not one to cross. "Enough questions," Scaffa told him. "You need to sleep, Erun Cade... while you can. The months ahead will be a trial for you."

Months...I'm going to be here for months?

Scaffa's next words tolled like a bell inside his skull. Erun felt his lids grow very heavy and his head loll backwards to rest on the stone. He closed his eyes but her heady words followed him into the misty realm of sleep.

"There will come a time, Erun Cade, when I need you to carry out three tasks. Three great quests that only you can achieve. For

such deeds you have been chosen. My weapon, you will become.
And... my message. After these tasks are successfully carried out
you will be freed from my charge, and with your newfound skills
will be ready to enact your revenge on those that have done you ill.
First though, we have to teach you how to fight."

***

During those turbulent years preceding the fall of Xandoria,
Erun Cade would come to convince himself that it had only been a
matter of months he'd stayed on Laras Lassladden under Scaffa's
strict tutelage, and not the three years it actually had been. Time
passed so much quicker on that island than on mainland Gol. But it
was three years: three, long years of hunger and hardship.

During that time the warrior giantess Scaffa and her silent
servants welded the youth that had been Erun Cade into the fighting
machine that would attend the Games at Torvosa the following year.

But that story is yet to tell. Those days on the island were
like quicksilver in his mind. But Erun Cade learned fast, mastering
every aspect of warfare. He gained confidence and competence by
ceaseless practice and repetition, learning how to handle all weapons: spear and bow, axe and mace—and especially the sword. This
last was his chosen weapon.

Erun mastered strategy and war-cunning also. For what use
is a sword without a cunning brain to guide it? He learned to cope
with the horrors and perils that the island turned against him, enduring hardships that would break other men, without complaint
or sufferance.

Laras Lassladden was an enigma to him. It was never the
same twice. Nor were the countless foes that Scaffa and her dark
lieutenant Cron sent against him. Erun Cade often fought hand
to hand with Cron and his men, gaining wounds—many proving
mortal (though the next day they were gone and he was healed and
ready to fight again.)

A day finally came when Scaffa approached him alone—the
first time in those three years. Erun was clad in black mail with
sword and axe hooked on his belt.

"Now you must journey overseas for a time," Scaffa told him, "and put to practice that which you have learnt on this island. The Emperor of Xandoria quarrels with his neighbour, a former vassal state, and mercenaries grow rich on the slaughter. Enlist in his army, Erun Cade. Fight for the Emperor against Lamoza.

"Kill quickly when you can and learn their subtle ways. Remember well what we have taught you. The day will come soon when you will need such knowledge if your land Barola is to survive. Ashmali is coming."

The following day Erun Cade left Laras Lassladden bound for Xandoria in the distant west. The ferryman was waiting for him with his accustomed silence. But his timely presence held no surprise for Erun Cade. He was well accustomed to enchantment and weirdness by now.

Of his journey to Xandoria there is little to report. Suffice to say that a few weeks later Erun arrived on the east coast of that other, far bigger continent. He fared west to Murkai, where he enlisted in the garrison as a mercenary.

During that next spring, whilst Lissane Barola loved and plotted with Estorien Sarfe in Galanais, Erun Cade earned coin as a freebooter across the sea. He fared well for a time. But it was on a raid north a few months later that everything would change.

***

The agony was a snarling beast inside Ozmandeus's head. The fires burnt his flesh hour on hour, searing through his veins and melting his eyes, until they ran like wax down his face. Everywhere at once. Pain and heat and the stink of his putrid crackling flesh.

The Demon's breath, he called it. Ozmandeus woke screaming as he had done last night and the night before, and indeed the many nights since he'd fallen from his horse on the march across the plains. He remained unharmed but a few scorch marks—the stench and agony imagined—his ward spells still just keeping the monster at bay.

Winter was over. Spagos had crumpled weeks ago and icy Ketaq was no more, the few terrified survivors having long ago fled across the West Lamoza River. As for Lamoza itself—the whole region was in a state of flux.

Poor savage independent Lamoza; caught up in its bloody, futile struggle against the Empire. And now this new army from the west was closing on Lamoza City day by day. A sorcerer's horde, rumour said—in its ranks shuffled ghouls and the undead. And a demon. A new Firelord come to trouble the world. Word spread quicker than the fear. Lamoza was done for. Down on the coast those who could were scrambling on board ships bound for the Island States and beyond, their purses eagerly emptied by the skippers of the brimming vessels. Soon the ships would be gone and those poor souls left caught betwixt steel and flame.

Because Ashmali was coming. Nothing could stop that certainty.

Ozmandeus dare not sleep most nights. There were deeper black rings now shadowing his eyes and his skin was pasty white. He was thin and wasted—drained by the raging force in the amulet, an apple worked by the worm. The Renegade told himself it would be worth it. He just had to hold out until the next city fell. But as time passed, and the burning spread like rage along his nerves, the Renegade came to doubt his wisdom.

A night came when he could take no more. The Demon, sensing his captor's weakness, erupted like magna inside his head. Ozmandeus woke screaming yet again. But this time, when he gazed down on his nakedness, Ozmandeus saw with horror that the sheets were on fire, and the amulet had melted deep into his chest!

A great fissure had now opened up, showing his rib cage and his beating heart. He screamed again. But it was too late. The Demon was inside him now and it drove the pain away. Ashmali spoke inside his head.

We are one now.

The voice was Ozmandeus's own but it hadn't been he that had spoken.

"I...am the master...you...will...serve." Ozmandeus summoned what will he had left to him.

No longer—we are united...fused into one being. You and I are now one and the same.

"No! I told you I would free you when the time came. I... promised. Just let me be...please."

It's too late for that now. We are one...

"Please!"

TOO LATE.

End of Book One

Book Two

Quickening And Fall

Quickening

Chapter 1

Torvosa

"The children! He's murdered the children!" Young Clarde's excited voice came from somewhere above. Duke Toreno briskly vacated his desk. *What's this?* The duke made it to the door in seconds, opening it just in time to witness his eldest son running full tilt down the stone stairs toward him.

"Whoa! What is it, boy? What nonsense is this?" Toreno had to step back lest Clarde crash into him in his urgent haste. "Stop! Talk to me!"

Clarde vaulted the last three steps and barely halted a yard from where his father stood with arms folded and frowning brow. For a moment the boy couldn't find his tongue. Then he blurted the words out. "He's killed them, Father! He's murdered them all."

"Who? Clarde, whatever are you talking about?"

"The king..."

"What?"

"Flaminius. He's killed his family, Father. The whole city's a-tremble with the news." Clarde's eyes were clouded by fear and disbelief. Toreno's eldest boy was not his energetic happy self today. He was usually so confident and at only fifteen captained his own troop of elite horse guards here in Torvosa. Usually Clarde's presentation was immaculate. He was handsome. Big, strong and wore his blue armour with comfortable pride. Not today. This morning Clarde's flaxen mop was dishevelled and his attire a shabby mess. Not that any of that mattered now.

"Gods protect us." Toreno slumped against the wall, feeling suddenly sick. He blamed himself entirely. Why hadn't he acted earlier? He'd seen the signs, knew the king was losing his mind.

"What of the queen?" Toreno demanded of his son.

"No one knows for sure but I suspect she's dead too. The king set light to the palace and fled. Nobody knows where."

***

It had been the barons who found Flaminius's body crumpled and broken at the foot of the walls. How they had cheered—those vicious wolves. Toreno and Clarde had ridden out in parley just in time to witness Baron Barola hewing the dead king's head from his corpse and thrusting it hard onto his young son Rosco's spear tip.

The king's body was now a mess of blood and mud and shit, having been trampled by the rebel leaders' horses. They all had a go: Barola, Garron, Brude and Galiant, the four leaders of the rebellion. For them this was a joyous hour.

It had been Barola that witnessed Clarde's troop issuing from the main gates. "Look who's coming!" Barola yelled as he sped his horse up the steep crest toward them, halting only twenty feet away. Baron Garron of Treggara joined him and then soon after the others.

Clarde's elite horse guards lined up alongside their captain. The horses snorted and stamped as their riders levelled their spears and glared behind their helmets. They were outnumbered but would sell their lives dearly should they have to.

But Barola hoisted his hand palm forward. "What now, Toreno?" Barola yelled. He'd untied his helmet and tossed it on the ground. His shaggy black hair glistened with sweat. "The day is ours, Toreno. Your mad king's reign is over!"

"He was your king too, Barola," Duke Toreno replied, urging his mount forward slowly whilst bidding his son's guard stand easy. Clarde made to question his sire but Toreno's sharp glance pursed the boy's lips. "I will handle this," the duke told his son. "Keep your temper." Reluctantly Clarde did as he was told. The boy watched as Duke Toreno halted his mare scarce yards in front of the enemy. Barola watched him with those cold black eyes whilst by his side Garron hawked and then spat down on the dirt below.

"What now indeed, Barola?" Toreno felt no fear that day. Only anger. Rage at these rebellious barons and seething fury with his king. Flaminius the weakling. Flaminius the mad. Last in a great line of rulers. Flaminius the Third who had neglected his people and let his kingdom fall into ruin, allowing the unruly barons to rise up against him. And now it was over. The king was dead and it was left to Toreno to pick up the pieces. Again. "Do we fight?" Toreno stared coldly across at the rebel nobles.

"Fucking right—I'm going to slice your head off, tosspot duke. And then feed it to my pike!" The shaven-headed Brude hoisted his war axe and hooted joyfully, the Rodruthan baron being in his element today. "Aye—let's cut 'em to pieces!" Garron yelled in Barola's ear but the younger baron shook his head.

"You're too hasty, you pair. The duke here isn't our enemy. Not now. Just a sad loyal old fool who was content to watch Gol collapse like a deck of cards. Tell me, did Flaminius fall from those walls, Toreno, or did you push him?"

The duke didn't respond but his eyes held Barola's in check.

The baron changed tack. "Besides," Barola said, "we have our honour to think about. Duke Toreno here knows I wouldn't allow our lads to butcher his boys outside his castle. Not the done thing that. And," Barola added grinning, "—it is your castle now, my lord."

"Toreno smiled his thinnest smile. "You are transparent, Barola. You know full well your army cannot take Torvosa whether you break truce, kill us or not. And as for that—my archers would pepper your rabble with holes before you could even release a fart. You are a brigand and a rogue, Barola. But we need no longer be enemies. The war dies with the king."

Baron Barola laughed then. A dog's laugh, short and sharp. "I weary of this farce. Go back behind your walls, sir duke. Let your fiery-eyed stripling son (who so hates me) stew in his posh armour and retire with you.

"The Rebellion is over and we have won. Tonight and for many nights to come we victors will make merry outside your walls—you're most welcome to join us. Or failing that, invite us in." Before Toreno could respond, Barola had turned his horse and cantered back down the hill. Garron hesitated for a minute then spat again and followed his ally.

Brude grunted and slammed his war axe back into its sheath. "Aye, duke—let us in so I can bugger your wife and shag your daughters!" Brude laughed. He turned his horse about with a snarl, the other barons and their captains soon following suit.

"Bastards!" Clarde hissed through his mouthpiece. "Bloody bastards—we could have killed those leaders, Father! All four of them!"

"And what, pray, would that achieve?"

"At least some bloody satisfaction." It was Clarde's turn to spit on the turf. "How could you let that savage yell at you like that? Say those things about Mother?"

"Words are worms. They can be venomous sometimes but they don't break walls. You, boy, have much to learn." Toreno heeled his mare and guided her back toward the castle gates. Clarde glared after his father. He swore, spat again and then urged his sweating troop follow him back through the gates.

That had all been fifteen years ago.

***

And how that time had flown. Now Toreno Dovess, Lord Duke of Torvosa City and Dovesi Province, watched from his high window in the Starlit Tower, his tired eyes observing the dust whip cloudlike behind the score of riders, now approaching at speed from the dew-glinted fields beyond the city.

Even at this distance the duke recognised the erect proud posture of his eldest son, Clarde. He strained his weary eyes to make sure, and when the sun glinted off his steel plate armour a sudden flash of azure left no doubt to the identity of the closest rider.

My son...back so soon?

Toreno frowned and chewed his greying moustache. This didn't bode well. On a whim he turned briskly to address the silent servant minding the door behind.

"Prepare food and wine, Armilian," Toreno said, his crisp patrician tones cutting through the quiet spring afternoon like scissors on vellum. "My son and his captains have returned to the city."

Armilian bowed before withdrawing from his master's study, his thin face lined with worry and watery eyes filled with doubt. Why would Clarde Dovess return in haste so soon from his venture north? Trouble was coming to Torvosa City. That much was certain.

Clarde Dovess reined in at the stables, and vaulted from his mare after tossing the reins in the face of a startled stable lad. The captain of guard awaited him at the door, eyes expectant and querulous beneath his highly polished helm. "My lord...we didn't expect you back so soon. Is something amiss?"

Clarde curled his upper lip and shouldered past his captain without breaking stride. "Most likely—I shouldn't wonder," he snapped. "Is my father present?"

"He's with his astrologer up in the west tower, my Lord," answered the captain, his long face worried. Clarde rolled his eyes but refrained from comment.

Head in the stars again, Father.

Annoyed and filled with impatience, Clarde Dovess distanced himself swiftly from the noise and bustle that accompanied his men's hasty dismounting and their conspiratory banter with the city guards. Clarde reached the north tower in minutes and began the long climb up. *Astrologers...* Clarde's soldier heart had little time for his father's obsession with lore and alchemy.

The only way to fend off the other barons was with strength and steel. Not stargazing. Bastards like Eon Barola and Volt Garron respected nothing else. Those two had pissed on the corpse of the dead king after the Rebellion and they'd do the same to Toreno Dovess, given half the chance.

Flaminius wasn't missed by anyone, but Clarde's father still commanded respect. At least in Dovesi if nowhere else. Duke Toreno was the last true noble left in Gol. The other provinces were bled dry by their leech rulers. Only Razeas Sarfe could be trusted, he and his son Estorien. Sarfania alone had stood by Dovesi during the Rebellion, capitulating only at the last minute and when there was no other choice, lest their people be starved and butchered by the hounds of the conquering barons.

Clarde knew that were it not for Estorien Sarfe and himself the Games held in the fields below annually would be dominated by such as Paolo Barola, the Garron brothers and Black Torlock.

The Games were a farce but at least they allowed the provinces' nobles to challenge each other without open warfare—though the likes of Barola were always jostling for advancement. The whole thing stank, in Clarde's opinion.

The sub-continent Gol was a festering pit of mediocrity these days. The barons bickered and bit each other's arses, while the Emperor overseas waxed in power and awaited his time. They would come soon—that's what Clarde believed. Poor, weak confused Gol would crumple like a winter leaf beneath the boot of mighty Xandoria.

And these Xandorians had tried to conquer Gol before—back in the days of the first king—glorious Kelperion. That great tactician and warrior had decimated their advance in a series of guerrilla ambushes that had finally broken their resolve. But should they try again? Best not dwell on that.

There were no Kelperions these days. No saviour would aid their final hour this time. Even the gods had forsaken Gol—and who could blame them? Priests were scarce, having been banned by the barons for secretly spreading the word of the kings. For all their faults the kings had at least been devout. The barons...well.

No, thought Clarde as he clattered noisily up the stairwell, if the Emperor attacked Gol's fate was sealed. And Clarde knew it was only a matter of time, he'd tried to warn his father but the duke just wouldn't listen. Toreno Dovess was stubborn by nature, he alone had remained stoically loyal to King Flaminius during the

Rebellion, and for longer than he should have, in his eldest son's opinion. Clarde loathed the barons but even back then as a green lad of fifteen summers he could see how things would turn out.

Everyone had known that the last king was moon-dog mad. He'd butchered his wife and children in that fit of raging despair. His madness had nearly destroyed Dovesi. Fortunately the barons hadn't wanted to push the fight any further—they'd been happy to gloat on their victory—back then.

But we could have taken the fight to them, thought Clarde, rousted them and then governed Gol with some kind of order. Instead his father had done nothing. Total folly and wasted opportunity, in Clarde's opinion.

Clarde didn't blame the barons for rising up against their king but he did blame them for all that had happened during the Rebellion and since. The murders, the double-crossings, and the brutal subjugation of the small-folk. If Toreno Dovess had been more proactive back then, the banal ambitions of Barola, Gallante and the others could have been contained. Instead they had festered like gangrenous wounds. Squabbling, fighting their petty wars year on year, draining the land and its people.

Clarde shook his head free of his helmet and shoved it under his sweaty arm. His father might be dazzled by altruism but he, Clarde Dovess, was a realist. Clarde was dismally aware that the dire news he now carried would spur on the very civil war they had sought so hard to keep at bay. And of course it had to concern Barola.

Always bloody Barola.

Not the Baron this time—but his thrice cursed daughter. Lissane Barola: newly wedded and rumoured fat with child. What had Estorien Sarfe been thinking of? Although a good friend to House Dovess, the heir to House Sarfe had always been a hothead. But this latest stunt had proved rash even for him. At last Clarde reached the level where his father held his studies. He didn't delay and made straight for the door.

***

Beneath the clear cold waters of the Lake of Clouds a figure stirs into fluid motion. For years she has chosen the shape and form of a young maiden, not dissimilar to those short-lived usurpers who long ago drove her people into the quiet recesses of this world.

But Aqueous knew this green world Ansu was always turning, cycle after cycle, and her master the great Lord of Oceans, was again claiming back what he had once owned. This almost-island that men called Gol would be Zansuat's domain once more. She and her kin would be free to roam again, as they once had in those halcyon days before the coming of the mortal invaders from the west.

Her people were few now. Fewer than few, and their cousins of Earth and Air scarcer still. Of the surviving Fire Elementals she knew nothing—though she suspected Ashmali still endured. He had always been the strongest of them, but had turned to evil at that earlier time. Alarmed by Ashmali's wrath, the gods had quenched his fires and had him entombed, last she'd heard.

Aqueous knew that Tertzei (her Earth sister) was now imprisoned inside the Jewel of Rakeel—trapped by sly sorcery, and Borz (her unruly Air cousin) held fast at the whim of the Aralais warlock now calling himself the Wizard of the Winds.

Aqueous would learn more if she could but she too was a prisoner of sorts. Although the wiliest of the surviving Water Elementals, Aqueous had been duped by sorcery, trapped within the deep confines of this lake for countless years, preying on whoever strayed close to ease her hunger, whilst eagerly awaiting the one destined to set her free. A mortal man chosen by fate to act as the fulcrum.

It would not be long now. Aqueous could feel his footsteps in the distance and, in the ripples high above, she would sometimes see his face. A young face and a handsome face—were it not for that scar...

Chapter 2

Mercenaries

"Too slow!" Rakaro lashed out with his right boot. Again the boy rolled free and this time he kicked Rakaro hard in the face.

"Yer little twat!" Rakaro laughed. "I'll have you yet!" The Hillman changed tact and shoulder-charged his opponent but to no avail, the shithead foreigner brought his knee up fast under Rakaro's chin and the older fighter saw stars. Rakaro threw a fist at his opponent's jaw, but that too was blocked and then next he knew Rakaro was flying through air and crashing into the dirt.

"That hurt." Rakaro rolled onto his feet and readied his fists for another bout whilst the skin and bones lad just stood there grinning at him.

"Shit, you're quick, laddie. And how did you learn all that flashy arm locking and high kicking stuff? It's damned sorcery," Rakaro grumbled.

Erun laughed at his friend. "You're too fat, Rakaro. And too slow!" The outlander stood with his arms folded, watching amused as Rakaro wiped the blood and snot from his nose.

"Yeah, well—we'll see about that." Rakaro's left boot shot out fast and hard toward Erun's groin. The younger man blocked that savage kick with a twist of his knee, locking Rakaro's leg with his own. Erun yanked his leg back and Rakaro pitched on top of him.

There the two fighters rolled and grappled in the blood and dust for several minutes before Rakaro broke free by biting a chunk out of Erun's left forearm. Next thing the Hillman had Erun Cade in a firm headlock, both arms pressing while his right knee rammed down on the boy's back.

"Submit?"

"Fuck you!"

Rakaro grinned and squeezed harder. "Submit, shit for brains."

"I said, fuck you." It was Erun's turn to see stars. He was feeling giddy now and beginning to lose consciousness.

"Submit, you fucking idiot, before you pass out on me." Erun knew Rakaro wouldn't let go his vice grip until Erun gave in. The boy had beaten him in the last four bouts. Hillmen weren't used to being beaten in hand to hand. Rakaro had been sulking for the last two days. Now, however he was grinning. "Submit?"

"Oh...alright—just this once," Erun's eyes were going in different directions. He had to admit he wasn't feeling that well. Then Rakaro released his hold and Erun staggered to his knees and spewed green and red gobbets on the ground. Meanwhile Rakaro clapped and grinned in delight, this proving a marvellous day.

"That was cheating," Erun Cade complained as he nursed his bruised neck. He was a mass of aches and pains but then so was Rakaro.

"No such thing," Rakaro said. "You were overconfident. I just had to wait my time."

"You're full of shit, Rakaro."

"I know—it's why I'm still alive."

And so things had gone for the last three weeks. There were no enemies present so between the two of them they'd passed their leisure time playing dice and wrestling. Usual mercenary stuff. For Erun Cade it was kind of fun. But then the day came when they saw the smoke. That was the first sign that things were going seriously wrong.

***

Rakaro glanced sideways at his new friend. The outlander sat his mare to the archer's left, fretting and squinting in the early summer heat. "It's just a smoke trail, boy," Rakaro told him. "Merchants or renegades—fleeing the chaos in Spagos or Ketaq, I would guess."

Rakaro fingered his drooping moustache with customary fastidiousness. "There are always folk hurrying east these days." Erun Cade said nothing, which was unusual for him. Rakaro was most often the taciturn one. But the outlander was intrigued and continued to watch in thoughtful silence as the dust trailed skyward.

They had crossed the Lamozan Gap two days past and this arid country seemed strange and remote to the foreigner. Even the far ranging Rakaro found it a cheerless region—stretching flat for miles upon miles until it became the Brown Desert, an impassable ocean of stone and sand.

Lamoza City was still many days ride away—so they had to be careful with their water and rations. "They'll pass to our north, I reckon," added Rakaro, "looks like more refugees from the carnage. Here..." The diminutive archer passed his prized Xandorian spyglass over to his young companion. He'd won it in a gamble last month, and after having discovering its use (Hillmen had no such intricacies) had grown very fond of the thing.

Erun grunted thanks and squinted into the tube. After a minute's searching he found it: a large trail of dust darkening the sky. Beneath that a seemingly endless snake of wagons was crossing the grasslands to their west.

"There must be hundreds out there," Erun exclaimed as he returned the spyglass. "Where are they making for, I wonder?"

Rakaro shoved his glass back in its pouch beneath his saddle seat. "They'll make for the Gap, and then the Emperor's finest will cut them to pieces. The Indulgent One doesn't tolerate refugees in his realm."

"Surely they must realise the risk they're taking," said Erun. "I mean, why make for enemy country instead of settling here in

Lamoza?" Rakaro snorted and awarded his comrade an old fashioned grin.

"Lamozans would kill their men, rape their women, and then sell the children to the slave masters in Xenn City. The two countries may be at war but that doesn't get in the way of a good bargain.

"That's monstrous," said Erun, shaking his head. He felt a surge of pity for the distant wagon riders. Their fates were already sealed, so it seemed.

Rakaro studied the face of his new friend with those shrewd, slanted nomad eyes. Young Erun Cade was a mystery to the archer. An enigma. The Hillman had known the outlander for over two months and still couldn't fathom him out entirely. Which was unusual—the sharp Rakaro was most times a quick judge of character.

This lad was something else. Erun Cade possessed a demon's skill with sword and knife, and a man could wish for no better companion. And yet he was like a child sometimes—so innocent, having no concept of the way of the world.

Perhaps everyone was like that in his Gol, thought Rakaro. If so then it was a wonder they had survived this long. Rakaro hadn't even heard of Gol before his young friend arrived so noisily in their camp. And what an arrival that had proved to be. He cast his mind back as his friend still watched the dust trail in silence.

Erun Cade had been one of a score of mercenaries hired by the Xandorian Century they had ambushed. These Xandorians were fresh out from Murkai Garrison, unlike the last three lots that had hailed from Xenn. They were good fighters and had fought with their usual stubborn, predictable courage. Outnumbered, they dismounted to form squares and lock shields together-but the Hillmen's questing arrows had found them all in less than an hour. It had been so easy.

The big mercenaries (mostly from the Island States) had tried to cut and run—as was expected. All save the stranger, Erun Cade. This insanely brave young idiot, from gods knew where, had remounted and charged them at full tilt, with long Xandorian lance held ready and shield tucked tight.

Rakaro smiled as he recalled that spring afternoon. It had

made for splendid viewing. Some of the riders drew lots on who would skewer the lad first. Certainly his courage had earned him more than a random arrow in the throat.

It had been Pashaci who won the bet, and sauntered down lazily on his pony to meet the fast approaching rider, his bola held ready and lean wiry frame at ease in the saddle. But Pashaci had died moments later. Then Tsuki had died and Sulimman too. The rider just kept coming, his large horse pounding the turf and beating a manic track up the rise, where Toskai and Rakaro watched on with the other clan leaders.

The other mercenaries were all shot full of arrows and dead by the time they reined in this madman, and already the bloody vultures were circling high overhead. They settled soon after and the feasting commenced.

It had taken six of their best 'rope men' to bring the lad down in the end—and two of those fellows wouldn't ride again. Rakaro grinned, recalling how the boy had fought like a cornered wildcat, but with a skill far greater than any they had encountered before— and especially for one so young. Steel was alive in this stranger's hands and his lithe body danced swiftly to its tune.

Toskai had wanted to butcher the boy at once, but some of the others suggested that they save him for later, when they were drunk and their wives had all been serviced. But there was something about the boy that convinced Rakaro that he should live. It wasn't just his courage. There was something remarkable about this outlander with the red scar on his forehead.

So that night (and totally against character) Rakaro had cut the young warrior free from his bonds before the others came for him and, aware of the risk he was taking, joined the boy in flight from the camp.

Rakaro knew that should Toskai see him again one of them would die. But Rakaro was ever pragmatic, by nature a loner—he'd only been back two weeks after his last foray through the Gap, gathering information and news. He'd grown bored of late with the Hillmen's ceaseless raids on the Empire's outlying towns, and the growing amount of soldiers now sent their way in revenge.

It could only end one way. Rakaro knew that, in time, the Xandorians would catch up with them all and the nomads would be finished—crucified along the high road, or else impaled on wooden stakes under the merciless sun. It was only the vastness of the sprawling Xandorian Plains that had kept the wild Hillmen alive for so long.

So with Rakaro now a traitor and his newfound friend a deserter—the Emperor didn't tolerate failure in battle, a soldier fought and died as was his duty. If he were victorious he became richer, but if he lost he died—simple as that. And foreign mercenaries weren't exempt from the Emperor's grace.

So the two riders had headed west through the Gap into Lamoza and enlisted in that country's rebel army. Within days they had been fighting Xandorians along the front in this skirmish and that raid. It wasn't long before wily archer and gifted swordsman made a name for themselves among their confederates.

But that too couldn't last. The war was going badly for Lamoza. The Empire was too strong to keep at bay. Rakaro knew that it was only a matter of time before Xandoria crushed the rebel force.

Erun had suggested that they return to his far country (he had unsettled business there—something about a girl and vengeance and stuff.) Rakaro hadn't pursued the matter after noting the haunted look in his young friend's eyes. Perhaps he still had business with the individual who had given him that curious red scar on his face. It was the only visible blemish the boy had, and Rakaro, who had several interesting scars on his own face, (all of them dyed brightly for maximum pathos) was fascinated by it. Erun Cade never spoke of his scar, however, and Rakaro let him be. This lad was touchy at times.

The wily Hillman advised they fare south instead. Rakaro had no great wish to return to the plains just yet—and there was no other way to reach this Gol place, save by ship—and that a voyage of several weeks. Rakaro had only seen the ocean twice and had no great desire to repeat the experience—let alone set sail. So much water, ugh. It made him shudder at the thought. He was a Plains warrior, not a duck.

So on Rakaro's suggestion, and for want of a better notion, they had turned south for Lamoza City, where Rakaro proposed a week of dicing and drinking while they decided on their next course of action. Erun Cade had agreed readily enough. That had been just yesterday.

"We had best be moving," said Rakaro as Erun still watched the wagons filing along the horizon. "Daylight's fading; we need to look for shelter lest one of those rain storms beckon." He urged his horse forward and began the descent of the rocky rise where they had been watching the column worming east for nearly an hour.

Erun nodded thoughtfully and spurred his own beast into motion. Since journeying to this vast continent he had seen many wonders, but nothing had impressed him as much as the sheer expanse of the lands through which he'd fared.

Xandoria alone must be three times the size of Gol, perhaps four. Barola Province was no bigger than some of their cities. Both Rakeel and Murkai were vast and sprawling, but the Emperor's own city Xenn was rumoured to spread for more than three hundred miles from wall to wall in all directions. So huge a city was beyond Erun's comprehension.

But it wasn't just the size of everything here. The people were so alien to him. Erun hadn't much liked the Xandorians, and didn't miss their dour dispassionate ways. These Lamozans were proving a cruel hard lot, and the residents of lands west rumoured worse still—or so Rakaro had told him.

Rakaro... Erun had been fortunate meeting him when he did—though why the taciturn nomad had pitched in with an enemy and abandoned his own people, Erun still couldn't fully comprehend. He liked his tough little companion, though; Rakaro had nut brown slanted eyes, skin like leather, and long smoke coloured hair which he tied back at the nape of his neck.

The 'Hillman' (stupid name for people that ranged the plains of northern Xandoria) was resilient and cunning and hard as nails. Rakaro spoke little, but when he did wry humour was never that far from his tones. His superb horsemanship was matched only by his skill with a bow. Erun had of late become more than proficient with horse and bow, but Rakaro was something else—his sheer dexterity and lightning speed were a phenomenon to behold.

Erun watched the leather-clad nomad steer his horse down the steep slope with a casual skill he couldn't begin to emulate—even with all his training. Rakaro was one with his saddle; he had an easy manner that could only be possessed by one who had ridden every day of his life. Rakaro was perhaps forty years old with missing front teeth, lean face and those dark clever eyes that could blaze with sudden fury when the killing lust was on him.

In a strange way Rakaro reminded Erun of Red Torrig—though the two couldn't look more different to the eye. He smiled at the thought of Rakaro and Torrig in a scrap—one to watch for certain. But who would come out on top? Erun couldn't pre-guess that match.

He felt a pang of homesickness when he thought of his red haired, foul mouthed friend. Erun closed his mind to what was occurring back home. Instead he focussed on Rakaro's back, as the Hillman hunched comfortably in his saddle several yards in front.

Rakaro was garbed like most of the wild nomadic peoples whom Erun Cade had found himself fighting since enlisting in the Xandorian Irregulars back in Murkai, three months past. Rakaro favoured a high backed saddle, housing three short spears, two horn bows, a collection of saddle knives, and the lethal lead-weighted rope that Erun had come to respect so much. The bolas, the plains people called it. Aside the bow it was the nomad's deadliest weapon. When cast by one with skill it could snare a fleeing enemy's legs, or else strangle him from afar and crack his windpipe. Needless to add Rakaro was expert with the bolas too.

Erun still found it hard to believe his enlisting at Murkai Garrison had only been three months ago. It seemed like year at least, so much had he learnt during his sojourn through Xandoria and beyond.

When Erun now looked back on his voyage from distant Laras Lassladden he recalled little. It was as though that part of his life were a dream still. Scaffa. His training—all a mystery.

The journey from Barola to her island seemed so distant now.

Something that had happened to another individual. A boy fresh and naïve, not the competent swordsman who now sat his horse. Erun's weird arrival at her island seemed so vague—he couldn't quite recall what had actually happened back then. Scaffa had drugged him somehow, he remembered that much. As for the following months (or years) on her island, they were just a hazy fog. And he had no sense of time. Had he lost time or had he gained it? Impossible to tell.

Sometimes Erun wondered if his random memories had taken place at all. Perhaps he wasn't even from Gol. Perchance there was no such place. Maybe he was just a roving freebooter—his mind all messed up with weird imaginings after taking a bad fall from his horse. Then he saw Lissane Barola's beautiful sad face, and Erun Cade's memory came rushing back in torrents of grief.

I still love you, Liss...part of me always will.

She would be married now, of course, and most likely heavy with child. How had he ever believed that it could work between them? What an innocent he had been back then. What a fool.

But that was ancient history. Erun Cade was a veteran now. A killer—and a lethal one at that. Erun hoped Lissane Barola fared well in her life, and that Varentin Gallante wasn't as bad as he'd heard. Erun would let her be. The fog of his memory came and went, screwed up by his time on that island.

But every time he scratched his forehead Erun saw Paolo Barola's smiling face as he worked that poker. During those brief lucid moments Erun recalled his business with the other Barolas. Paolo was marked, as were his brothers. It was only a matter of time.

Erun Cade had changed so much. A bold confident phoenix had clawed free from the ruined ashes of the blacksmith's stargazy son. That softheaded fool Lissane Barola had loved had perished back at the forge, along with his father. Erun Cade had a different identity now and one he liked. A new name given him by Rakaro, after the Hillman first witnessed him at battle.

Kell. It meant simply 'skill' in the guttural tongue of the nomadic peoples. Kell rhymes with hell. "And you are that, boy," Rakaro had told him. "You are hell to pay." Kell. Erun had liked its simplistic sound and had adopted its use since that day. They rode south through shimmering heat as summer waxed to full.

It was a week later that they first saw the fires.

***

Sujano Opashi the Third, Lord Emperor of Xandoria, Lamoza and Khandol, leaned back in his divan and smiled with deepest contentment. It was early spring in Xenn City—a time of year he loved. The skies above were blue and clear and the air full of summer's promise. Winter—it never lingered long in southern Xandoria—had now retreated. Doves were cooing close by, just for him, and his beloved cherry trees were unfolding their blossoms in profusions of soft pink and white—their sweet scent filling his afternoon. All was as should be.

Sujano Opashi patted the girl's coaly hair affectionately as she worked her sweet, wet mouth up and down the Imperial penis. This was the first time he had honoured her, she was new to the harem and very young. She was enthusiastic, however, and serving him well enough for one so inexperienced. Besides, the novelty of this new little virgin kept him keen—he was almost there.

The Emperor felt at peace today. All about him were his chosen slaves and concubines, most of them in various stages of undress, and some performing erotic acts for his casual perusal. He had music too, and colour, and chiming fountains, and clinking, spilling waterfalls that emptied noisy into wide basins of gold leaf and sapphire-studded silver.

There was all manner of rich food on the tables below, to-gether with fine Lamozan wines—taken by his soldiers in raids last summer. The Lamozans had dared to rebel against his rule, so the armies had gone in and put things right. Not that wars and such concerned the Lord Emperor—he never left Xenn. Why would he? Sujano Opashi had all he desired inside his Imperial palace and grounds. And now he had springtime also. Truly he was blessed by the gods.

Now Sujano Opashi's lazy, sardonic gaze roamed across his gardens, taking in the tall, leaning palms shifting so easy in the breeze; the magnolias and camellias, boldly winking out at him from shady corners—it all added to the perfection of the moment. The Water Gardens of Imperial Xenn were the Lord Emperor's particular pleasure at this time of year. Not too hot and not too sultry—just right.

Sujano Opashi watched in casual indolence, as two caged monkeys capered and cavorted inside their gilded prison—a beautiful crafted cage hanging from an arch in the far corner. Behind the Emperor, on raised marble plinths were stood two slave boys. They carried reed fans that worked welcome breeze into the still atmosphere. Looming silent and dark behind these two was Grode, his seasoned champion. Xandoria's prime fighter stood bare-chested with heavy curved sword to hand—a shaggy-haired giant and a wall of scar and muscle.

It was at that certain special moment that the three worried generals weaselled nervously into his private gardens. Sujano Opashi laughed at their evident discomfort at his 'recreations', and then sighed lovingly as his seed spilled urgent inside the girl's hard working mouth.

He let her clean his shrinking sex and replace his robe before turning his attention to the sweaty, unhappy men waiting below. This she did efficiently for a beginner, and quietly retired to the poolside with the others. There were all manner of girls lounging over there: dark ones, pale ones, some thin, a few on the plump side, even the odd boy—lest the lord Emperor require a change from the norm, as he sometimes did. One of the generals coughed politely. He awarded them his snake-eye stare.

"Well?" demanded Sujano Opashi with a petulant tilt of his lip. "What news bring you?" They were grubby uncomfortable creatures—these generals. They didn't like being here. And he didn't much like them being here either. It wasn't their place. Their kind belonged down at the barracks, or else drilling the parade grounds, or perhaps keeping order inside the stinking, turgid city without. But needs must... and besides, their discomfort was amusing for the moment.

They stood glum and hesitant, with plumed helmets thrust

hard under sweaty arms, and stiff po-faced expressions. The tall-est—Romul, the Emperor now recalled his name (their names were of little interest—he'd executed so many over the years, and his father before him. It didn't do to get to know them that well) took a step forward and bowed low before Sujano Opashi's gilded feet. "Untouchable One... Lamoza has fallen!" Romul blurted the words out into the afternoon.

"Well," the Emperor let another girl feed his mouth with a plump grape. Her skin was sleek and black as the fruit's. She was from the Island States and very beautiful. He felt a stir below again. "So?" Sujano Opashi mouthed the word whilst sliding a greasy hand inside the girl's silk gown, and fumbling for the moist shaved region between her legs. "That's good, isn't it? Now you can go and squash those turd-eating rebels up north."

"Untouchable One. Though our enemies are defeated there is a new threat to your Empire." This was the second general—a ro-tund squat ape of a man, whose rancid ugliness offended the Lord Emperor's person.

"Enlighten me," Sujano Opashi's heavy lids were half closed now. He was becoming bored. It wasn't good to linger too long when the Lord Emperor became bored. People had a habit of get-ting killed—or worse. Sujano Opashi jerked a manicured finger up inside the girl, making her jump nervously. He was getting irritated now—which was even more dangerous. These annoying buffoons were spoiling his moment. Sujano Opashi withdrew his sticky finger out and licked his lips slowly. "Go on," he motioned the gross one continue, "before I have your ugly hide stripped bare, and your fat stupid head impaled over the gates."

"An invasion...from Zorne, Untouchable One." Romul again—the other fellow seemed to have lost his voice for some reason. "A warlock they say, wielding fire and ruin on the west lands. He has openly vowed to destroy your Empire, Untouchable One. We must needs prepare."

Sujano Opashi the Third stood up abruptly, knocking over the table that held the grapes and wine, and angrily pushing the now cowering slaves aside. "How dare you fools bring these craven lies before us? Maggots!"

The lord Emperor minced down the broad stairs and spat savagely in Romul's face. The general didn't flinch—had he done so the Lord Emperor would have sliced open his throat with the curved gold knife he always wore at his belt.

"Slime..! You dare lie to us. We will have you cooked and boiled slowly in buttermilk before this day is out. Guards!"

From everywhere at once, a rush of armoured men carrying heavy pikes exploded into the gardens. Some of the girls screamed and the monkeys gibbered and larked about. "Seize these craven traitors and throw them in the oubliettes!" The soldiers obeyed at once, and noisily dragged the miserable generals outside, and far away from his Imperial Presence. Romul's turquoise plumed helmet clattered noisily on to the floor and rolled about at the lord Emperor's feet. Sujano Opashi glowered at it as though it were a coiling serpent about to strike up at him, then it settled and he forgot about it.

But everything was spoilt now...ruined by morons, and his moment gone. Bludgeoned aside by idiots and liars. Buttermilk was too good for those three, he'd order they heat up cow piss instead. Sujano Opashi fussed and fretted for a moment as quiet re-entered his gardens.

Needing to inflict hurt on something, the Lord Emperor minced across to the cackling monkeys and spitefully poked the nearest with a rod he kept handy for such a purpose. It hollered and spat at him, so he poked it again and harder this time. How dare they lie to him? There was no warlock (however powerful) that could threaten Imperial Xenn.

Just let them try...

Sujano Opashi was bored and peeved now with the Water Gardens. The fountains were a noise and the stupid musicians a sham—maybe he should have them flogged. The lord Emperor needed change from this now morose scene. He would retire to his other, more exotic diversions. Sujano Opashi motioned Grode escort his Imperial Magnificence back inside the Inner Palace.

On reflection, he decided to release the generals. It was a

nuisance but they were the only three he had left—so he had best spare them, really. One had to be realistic. Shame though—he'd love to have watched those three idiots boil for an hour or two. Now he would have to find some new diversion. But maybe they should boil up some cow piss, anyway—should he change his mind. He did that sometimes, without word or warning. Let the generals sweat down there for a time. Sujano Opashi would think on it as he took his scented bath that evening.

Chapter 3

The Duke's Dilemma

Toreno Dovess studied the sky-chart as he waited for his son
to arrive, his quick mind deeply troubled and his nerves on edge.
He loved Clarde—everyone did. But the boy was impetuous, like
his friend Estorien—though not that bad. Clarde, although nearing
thirty winters, still saw things with a child's simplicity—believing
that most solutions could be achieved through strength and bold-
ness. Clarde was honourable and honest, but the world he inhabited was twisted and deceitful.

Toreno knew that bluffs and counterbluffs and subtle nuances
were the real weapons of the ruler. That the sword alone would not
protect them from what was coming. Even he knew not what shape
this impending disaster would take—an invasion from Xandoria
perhaps? He doubted that, though Clarde believed it would be so.

From Toreno's constant consultations with Armilian and
his charts, and regular word from his reliable contact in Rakeel,
Toreno now suspected something more terminal than the clash
of enemy steel; something that involved the dark will of the gods
themselves. Perhaps they were vengeful; angry because the barons
had neglected them of late. Those remote divinities would have

small reason to show kindness for men. The kings had been devout—but these barons. And the gods were ever capricious, spiteful beings. The Weaver's children. His first born—what a disappointment they must be to Him.

Only the peasant folk had kept up with sacred tradition—mainly out of fear. Even here in Royal Torvosa, the temples and holy places were rarely frequented. Most of the old priests had been murdered by Volt Garron after the Rebellion. They say he caught one with his wife and used that incident as an excuse to start a slaughter in the temples. Few took the calling these days. So if the gods were angry it was hardly surprising.

There were stranger rumours: merchants and sailors from the Island States, or distant Lamoza muttered warnings that a powerful sorcerer had emerged in the far west. A Firelord like those in ancient times, controlling a captured demon that brought fiery ruin on his foes. Those stories were often muddled and confused by the time they reached Toreno's ears. One thing was certain. Those bringing the news had been scared by what they had seen—very scared.

And meanwhile the seas rose higher every year. Was it only Toreno who noticed such things? Year by year storms waxed stronger along the coast and more and more ships were lost to wave and wind. The Sea God was stirring in his watery depths.

Toreno knew that cold Zansuat, more than any other god—except the one they dare not name—harboured little love for mankind. This fertile subcontinent Gol had erupted from the Sea God's domain in millennia gone by, and since that primordial time he had wanted to reclaim it.

The stars now pointed to a conjunction—a quincunx charting final doom for Gol. It was just a question of when it would occur. Toreno had studied and charted and plotted for many years now, always seeking clarity, a way through the murk but had found no answer. Neither he nor Armilian—his servant and astrologer—held to hoping much these days. They had three years; Toreno had worked it out—perhaps four. No more...and maybe less. A loud rapping at the door shattered his thoughts to splinters.

Clarde. Abrupt as ever.

Clarde Dovess knocked the door and pushed it open without waiting for an answer. His father looked up from his various charts and maps strewed across his great oak table, and partially covering the flagged floor at his feet. Toreno looked older and frail, though it had scarce been two weeks since Clarde had left on his trip bound for Galanais. That trip had been cut short when they had encountered soldiers from that province in the mountains and had heard the news. News of great import. It had left Clarde little choice but to return to Torvosa and impart all he knew to his father. He waited by the door mustering patience (his father was never one to rush things.)

Duke Toreno's close-cropped hair and beard shone argent in the morning sun thats golden glow cast dancing dust motes in from the high arched window above. The Duke's tanned, thin face was lined with worry, and the rich blue velvet cloth he wore hung loose from his spent frame like redundant sailcloth.

Once Toreno Dovess had been a handsome man, but when Clarde's mother, Kaska, had died, bleak winter had entered his life. He mourned her still. Toreno's was a loving nature. Since then the Duke had taken to brooding and stewing over his charts. It rankled Clarde so. Day upon day, his father would be up here in his tower with the servant and astrologer, Armilian, his only companion. Were the city to burn down to ashen ruin all around him—would he notice? It was highly irresponsible, in Clarde's opinion.

And today Clarde was tired and irritable. He rubbed his beard and shuffled his feet as he waited for his father's full attention. He was also in bad need of a bath and a large flagon of wine, and then he would see his beloved children and his darling, Camille. But first to business...

Toreno reluctantly tore his rheumy gaze from the crinkled scroll that defined Gol's position in the world, with open sea to the east and part of that much larger continent flanking its west. He glanced over at Clarde; motioned his son to pour them both a glass of claret from his crystal decanter on the table.

Clarde obeyed, handed a glass to his father and then squeezed his bulky, still partially armoured frame, into a large leather chair. Toreno took a careful sip, wiped his lips daintily on his sleeve, and then awarded his son a quizzical look.

"Well, you had better tell me everything, I suppose." The Duke's voice was calm; it belied the worm he felt crawling inside his belly. He watched on as Clarde drained his glass urgently and then refilled it. Thirsty news, it would seem.

The boy looked shattered, thought Toreno as he studied his son. Even Clarde's usually immaculate azure plate-armour was spotted with grime and dust, and there were new dark rings under his eyes and his beard was already showing grey. Clarde might be only be thirty winters but looked closer to forty in his father's worried eyes.

Toreno's first born was a big man in every sense of the word. He was beloved by the people as their champion and protector. He had three daughters and two sons—his darlings they were—and Clarde had only ever loved one woman, his beloved Camille. His square, blunt face was freckly and honest: friendly and open mostly but florid and furious when roused. His hands were big and scarred from his many fights down in the arena outside the walls. Clarde now flexed them open and shut as he tried to find the words. Toreno waited. Finally they came out.

"Father, I..." *shit, there is no easy way to do this.* "Lissane Barola has fled Galanais with Estorien Sarfe (now her lover.) They now abide in Reveal with Estorien's family." Clarde drained his glass a second time before continuing. "Galanais is in uproar. That cretin Varentin's calling for their heads and Hal Gallante has sent his butcher, Black Torlock, south to bring her back. I fear civil war, father."

"Toreno rubbed his tired eyes. He hadn't expected this news but then it didn't really surprise him. Very little did these days. Young Estorien Sarfe had ever had an eager eye for a pretty girl, and was not one to let protocol get in the way of passion. But Lissane Barola...? The Duke felt a shudder pass through him at the mention of that name.

And yet he knew but little concerning her. He had met her

once or twice, when she was a child, but hadn't taken much notice. He regretted that now.

"This Barola girl?" Toreno pinned his son with a cold grey stare. "What do you know of her?"

"Word speaks well of her," replied Clarde, "oh, she's said to be headstrong like her father, but unlike him kind of nature and gentle of heart. Though proud—they do say. They also say she was happy to leave the baron and his sons though 'Prince' Varentin was hardly a catch worth having. That man's a mire of corruption, father. Small wonder the poor girl leapt into Estorien's arms. I'm sure he offered them willingly enough."

"I expect so." Toreno rubbed his tired grey eyes again and took to his feet.

Lissane Barola...why does that name send a shiver through me?

His son watched in dismal silence as Toreno paced to and fro, his eyes now troubled and twitching. "I am bothered by this, yes," he said eventually, "though I'm not that surprised, really."

Toreno took to staring out of one of the large slanted windows, surveying the fields and road far below. The sun would be setting soon—another day nearly over. How many had they left? He turned toward his son. "Little startles me in these dark times, Clarde. Hal Gallante will play this to his advantage, of course; he'll demand compensation—squeeze an extortionate sum from House Sarfe, I'd imagine. Razeas hasn't the monies to satisfy greedy Galanais. Gallante knows this—he'll expect us to intervene."

"What will you do, Father?"

"Get word out fast to Reveal," replied Toreno. "Demand the whole story and then ascertain the best way ahead. Razeas Sarfe *is* our friend and we have few enough of those at present. I expect we will have to dig deep into our coffers to assay House Gallante's wrath—especially that scheming bitch Sophistra. The Prince would most likes let the quarrel pass for enough coin coming his way.

"But the Chatelaine? No, Sophistra will press home the advantage—just you wait and see." Toreno turned to once more survey the wide panorama from his window, taking in the now darkening fields and crystal clear River Dove. To right and left dark mountain slopes loomed close, their flanks lined with firs.

Toreno smiled bleakly. "She'll be in her element now, will Sophistra." Clarde scratched his beard and wondered where this was going. His father had long harboured a deep detestation for Prince Gallante's conniving consort. There were reasons for that but Clarde chose tact.

"Black Torlock will make things worse," he said. "The Galanian soldiers I spoke with were loyal to Hal Gallante. They were most concerned about master Torlock. He's become quite powerful of late. They say he's the Chatelaine's favourite, and well is it known that Gallante and his consort haven't shared a bed for years. Not since the birth of that twisted girl child, Morwella."

Toreno winced at the mention of that name but his son pressed on without noticing. "They informed me that Galanais has two factions taking hold in secret places. Most remain loyal to Prince Gallante, but many others favour his wife—and that means Torlock. I don't like Torlock, father."

And I don't like Sophistra.

"Well," said Toreno after a pause where father and son exchanged heavy glances and sipped their wine. "House Gallante has always loved intrigue, and we can be sure that they will settle their internal differences now that they have a common agenda. This folly by your best friend could bring us to the brink of ruin, my son."

"Estorien isn't a fool." Despite his own misgivings Clarde found himself defending his closest friend. "That Barola girl must be something special for him to risk all, and so rashly. They say Varentin was beating her regularly."

Toreno pulled a face. "Well is it known what Hal Gallante's heir is like, and I pitied the girl when hearing of her betrothal, so I did. But that's life and small fry too. Estorien's been a damned fool in this, and don't bother defending him again, Clarde. You're a bad judge of character. Estorien is a charmer with his easy smile and glib tongue, but he's also a bloody nuisance. I hope his father holds him to account—not that that will make any difference, that one's as headstrong as you are."

Clarde raised a brow but chose not to challenge what he knew to be the truth. The Duke glanced his way again; his tired old face softened as if seeing his son for the first time that day.

"Go hence now. You look tired and hungry...leave me to dwell on these heavy matters." Clarde stayed put. "Go." Toreno motioned his son away with a brisk wave of his hand. Clarde nodded, took to his feet, taking care not to disturb the abundance of vellum and parchment covering the floor space.

"Give my love to Camille and my grandchildren," said Toreno as he made for the door. "I see them so little these days."

Whose fault is that, Father? Clarde quietly closed the door behind him and steered a weary course down toward the bath-houses below. A hot bath, more wine and then some time spent with his loved ones. It was what he needed and he couldn't wait. Tomorrow they could fret again, and assuredly would. Tonight Clarde Dovess would seek solace in the arms of his wife. He smiled, there were advantages in coming home before time. Camille and the children would be delighted to see him. The thought cheered him as he made his way to the bathhouse. But then Clarde Dovess was never one to mope that long.

After his son had departed, Toreno turned to his charts again. For hour after hour and long into the night he studied, but to no avail. A guard informed him at some point that urgent word had been sent across to Sarfania, by pigeon: he'd expect a reply from Raz in due course.

It was a small matter, really. Toreno would have been able to dismiss it were it not for two names that cast such disquiet in his heart. Lissane Barola and the girl child Morwella—a daughter of light and a child of darkness. Both were children of destiny, he was sure of it. And both would play a key part in this approaching struggle—though quite how and why, (particularly in Morwella's case)—he couldn't yet hazard a guess.

Lissane Barola was a pawn caught in the politics of ruthless players—at least she wasn't a threat in herself. But Morwella... there was something *wrong* about that girl. Something twisted.

She would make trouble whenever possible and soon too, Toreno now suspected.

Still, why should he fret so over Galanais? It wasn't his concern. But Toreno did fret, for such was his nature, and he knew that what happened in Galanais would influence the whole country. They were heading for meltdown. Toreno could see it coming but saw no way of averting it. He would not give up, he determined, but would increase his studies to maximum. There had to be a way through this. Somehow, he and Armilian had to crack the code and fend off this coming disaster. But how could mere mortals divert fate? It was depressing and he was so damned tired.

Heart full of foreboding, the Duke turned to the wine again. He wasn't a heavy drinker usually, but of late...well, he needed solace where he could get it. Outside and far below the gate bells tolled midnight. But what was that? A harp? Toreno shook his head, doubting his senses. They had no resident harper in Toreno's tower, though there were several down in the city.

And there it was again...somewhere below and quite close. A sad, melancholy sound—the chords plucked by a musician of great skill. It was both haunting and uncanny. Toreno felt an icy shiver creep along his spine. That was no earthly harp. He closed his ears, but the harp's chords drifted and pealed through the tower for several minutes, before eventually fading out into the night. Toreno heard it again the following night. He questioned the guards and retainers, but it seemed that no one else had heard it. From then on the Duke kept a lit candle by his bedside.

***

Reveal was unlike any other stronghold in Gol. The ancestral home of House Sarfe was hidden in the midst of a vast reedy lake, its immeasurable shoreline hedged by mangrove and marsh, and almost impossible to discern. Reveal was a timber structure built on tarred stilts. The only access being by boat—save one rickety bridge that awarded little chance for invaders. Its current master was sitting in his favourite rocker and watching in silence, as the fireflies flickered on and off away across the water. Razeas liked fireflies; they mirrored people, he often thought—burning brightly for a while then fading forever, lost to time and space.

Toreno's message had reached him this very afternoon, and he'd replied with accustomed promptness. They owed much to Dovesi already, and it balked Razeas that they had need of that province again. He had so wanted to rage at Estorien, but when he had seen the girl something had stopped him. She had a certain look...those big violet eyes and pale patrician countenance.

Oh she wasn't *that* comely—Stori had had prettier girls. But there was something special about this Barola girl, and against his own counsels, Razeas found himself forgiving his son almost at once. They were away at present, those troublesome lovers; Estorien was showing his stolen prize the wonders of the lake country. Razeas suspected that they wouldn't return before nightfall.

To be young again...ah, well.

He eased back on the rocker and pulled at his pipe—a calming habit he'd acquired from the merchants that had once so often frequented Galanais. Razeas smiled ruefully: that had been a different Galanais back then. He'd been young then, long before the cursed Rebellion had placed Hal Gallante and his cronies at the top of the pile.

At that time Galanais had been the busiest port shoring the shimmering sea—the jewel of the west coast. But those once teeming docks had since fallen into disrepair as that city's current ruler spent all on his gaudy palace and estates. Those docks were a grubby hive of cutthroats and footpads these days—or so Estorien told him. Razeas seldom travelled far now days, leaving such trips to his son. Which on reflection...

Razeas re-read the words he'd dictated earlier; Toreno would receive them by morning the next day. It had humbled him to accept the monies offered. Twenty thousand Regals was an extortionate amount—though he doubted it would appease grasping Gallante and his wretched son.

There would almost certainly be trouble at the Games later this year. That was a given. They would have to be on their guard for treachery when in Torvosa. Treachery was never far away in these turbulent times.

Razeas pulled at his pipe, and watched for a time as the fireflies dwindled and finally faded into evening mist. Inside the chamber his beloved Arabella was already asleep. She was a morning creature, but Raz liked to stay up late and smoke, and watch the silver moon cast its witchy light on the mirrored lake's surface below. *Life,* thought Razeas Sarfe, *is a reckless journey from dust to dust. But at least we get a chance to blaze like fireflies—if only for an instant. Let Stori and Lissane have their moment of happiness before the storm. For it is coming. Toreno Dovess is right about that much.*

***

If Reveal's strength was in its impossible access then Torvosa's was in its daunting walls and high sweeping parapets. Torvosa City dominated the valley surrounding it. The mountains rose higher and higher to north, east and west; but south of the walls were open fields leading down to Turftown, the arena, and the sparkling River Dove.

The castle main had been constructed in the latter days of the fifth king—Kelperion, after his celebrated victories against the Xandorian invaders. The walls of Torvosa were vast, spanning over six miles from east to west. They encased the valley and spanned the gap between the snowy heights behind. Those walls were forty feet thick and buttressed at every corner. They were believed unassailable—certainly none had attempted to do so. Those walls were what kept the barons at bay. Were Torvosa less strong, then Dovesi would have fallen to the greedy hands of Eon Barola or Hal Gallante. As it was the high walls and bold Clarde's reputation kept the wolves at bay. For now.

At every hundred paces a round tower stood proud from the wall, each one two hundred feet high, and linked by a walkway bridging the entire circumference of the walls. On every hour blue-cloaked guards could be seen pacing its length with spears slanted over shoulders.

Occasionally their azure armour would glint in the sunlight, making them sparkle like new toys in a giant child's nursery. The Royal City (some still called it) lacked the dizzy, gaudy splendour of Galanais. Nor could it be compared with the sheer size and exotic grandeur of Xenn in remote Xandoria—though few indeed from Gol's provinces had journeyed that far in recent times.

But Torvosa was a proud city. The ancient centre for an almost continent that had dared to cut away from the greater lands flanking the west coast. The towers of Torvosa—though austere grey and unadorned—were flawless and cunningly built. It was said that Kelperion the Defender had employed a million men in their construction—for he it was that banned slavery in Gol, a practice that held out for hundreds of years—until Hal Gallante reintroduced it to Galania in the months following the Rebellion.

During the reign of Terces the Steadfast the first Games was held in the fields below. But it was in his son, Castales the Warrior's, time that they evolved into the annual splendour that had continued unbroken to this day, barring the two years surrounding the Rebellion.

A town had grown up haphazard around the arena, three miles outside the city. It had no name as such although the common folk called it Turftown. It comprised a mish-mash of canvas and hide, permanent and yet shifting in colour and hue, as each merchant and trader came and went during the seasons.

At Games season (late summer) Turftown swelled and spilled into the green fields parading the river, sprawling untidy from mountain slope to mountain slope—the valley where sat Torvosa was a spoon shaped bowl scooped out from the foot of the mountains.

The whole region was a natural amphitheatre, the kings had chosen the site for their Royal City as much for its grand setting as its strategic value. From down by the river those stark walls, and the mountains looming behind them, dominated the northern skyline without compromise. The main road led up that way alongside the riverbank. Strangers visiting Torvosa for the first time would often stop and gape in awestruck wonder at the sight.

In the fifteen years since the Rebellion, Duke Toreno had

ruled Torvosa and Dovesi Province. Born into one of the noble families, the young Toreno had served the king and had for a time been placed high in Flaminius's affection. For the last king to rule Gol hadn't always been what he became. In those days Flaminius was golden. The king stood tall, with long flowing, sun-bright locks and clean cut limbs. Flaminius towered over his subjects, as his fathers had before him. Kelperion's line had always spawned tall sons.

The king's nature had been merry at that time—it was in later days his drinking habit got the better of him, and eventually paranoia took hold. Flaminius sank into decline, he saw treachery everywhere. In many cases he was right to do so, but eventually it led to his downfall, giving the plotting barons the ammunition they needed to topple him from his fragile throne. And then the madness had claimed Flaminius. He'd taken that axe to his children and wife, thus cutting off the seed of a thousand years.

But that was almost sixteen years ago. A time long past, when Toreno's hair didn't resemble the snow that still clung tenaciously to the higher slopes of the towering mountains behind. Toreno's sixty five years hung heavy on him these days. He worried incessantly—not for himself, his course was nearly run. But for Clarde and his other offspring, and their laughing, sunny children.

What would become of them in the dark days ahead? How would those sweet lovely children survive this impending storm? Toreno sighed, and wearily took to his feet; he expected to hear from Raz in the morning. No doubt the days ahead would prove troublesome.

He cast his aching eyes on the parchment once again, straining hard and long to see if there was something he had missed, and if by random chance such a miracle existed, whether he still had the strength to steer Gol's lost children clear of what was coming. For it would soon be upon them. That night Duke Toreno heard the eerie harp music again. He closed his ears and thought of times long past.

Chapter 4

Ashmali

They were huge towering, flickering tendrils of flame: impossibly high—smudging the horizon with crimson glow for mile upon mile to the south. Even from this far distance the two riders could feel the searing heat of that awful inferno.

Rakaro and Erun exchanged glances. *Shit.* This wasn't good news. "Looks like our planned week's debauchery's buggered," Rakaro muttered. Erun just gaped. They reined in, both deeply shocked by the sight. Erun heard harsh calls above and looking up, saw a cloud of birds winging north at speed. They were the lucky ones. They had escaped. He lowered his eyes and, slack-jawed, continued gaping at the furnace ahead. Meanwhile Rakaro fumbled for the glass at his side and steadied his jittery horse.

"It's Lamoza City," Rakaro said despondently after a minute's hard study with the glass. "The whole fucking place is on fire. It's totally crazy—a city made of stone. What could cause such a blaze?"

"Xandorians...?"

"Unlikely."

"Zorne..? That warlock you were talking about?"

"Let's go see." Rakaro spurred his beast into motion again.

He was edgy and had very bad feelings about this, remembering what he'd learnt earlier in the year. He turned and awarded Erun a sharp look. "Are you coming, friend Kell, or are you going to sit there gawping?"

"I'm coming." Erun hesitated a moment longer and then urged his steed forward to accompany his friend. "Though I have to say I don't think it's my best decision." Erun's horse was nervous too and he had to go carefully. The boy who had once been plain Erun Cade would have turned back at this point, but the proven swordsman Kell was curious. He wanted to see first-hand what had caused this vast inferno the ravens were fleeing so urgently.

It wasn't long before their curiosity was sated. Just half hour later they reined in again, the smoke now stinging their eyes so badly they had to douse their faces, and the horses with wet cloths soaked from their rapidly diminishing water supply. But they had come near enough to witness the abomination raging monstrous high over what had once been Lamoza City.

The entire sky appeared to be melting like so much candle wax. The whole horizon appeared a blazing crackling, amber crimson mix. The air was almost too hot to breathe. It choked their breath and felt like molten lead on their nostrils. The stench of flame and the reek of violent death was everywhere. The stifling atmosphere screamed outrage. This clearly wasn't your average bonfire. There was more at work here than just flames—however raging. Erun sniffed.

Stinks of sorcery.

As the riders watched in awe whilst trying to control their now panicking beasts, a great bastion of city wall exploded from sheer heat. Stone shot skyward in blazing jets, and then tumbled to ruinous rubble and dust. Beyond the broken walls, the only visible part of the city was an ash pile a hundred feet high. It was then that they first heard the screams and saw that a small rag-tag of people were running their way.

Rakaro saw them first them first, his left eyelid singed by his glass scope's rim. A few survivors, running like mad frantic fools, delirious with terror, pelting down the road toward the place where the two horror-struck companions barely sat on their bucking horses. Both men had to will themselves to wait. Both were terrified of what raged ahead. Hardened warriors or not, this was something else.

An impossible inferno, Erun couldn't fathom out how such a thing could exist. But his eyes were proof. It was though the fire itself was somehow sentient, feeding on its own voracity. That some malicious destructive loathing of all life controlled that furnace. An alien wanton evil rather than pure purging heat and random winds. Then Erun and Rakaro saw the flames congeal like lava jelly into something that (impossibly) resembled a face.

They couldn't move for terror, despite every nerve and muscle urging them to flee. The horses bickered and shied but also seemed numbed by dread. It were though a headman's axe was suspended above, waiting to descend on their necks and banish their souls to the Shadowman's castle. Rakaro dribbled as one rendered witless and muttered meaningless words in his horse's ears. Erun was on the verge of spewing. Both riders almost lost their saddles at that point. If they fell they'd be finished. The horses would be gone in seconds. Somehow the two clung on and with faces set grim and silent waited for the first desperate runners to arrive.

"Flee..!" It was a young soldier who addressed them, his long legs carrying him quicker than his struggling companions behind. But these too were approaching, puffing and wheezing and gibbering like mad things. They joined the soldier to collectively gape at the two strangers struggling with their wild eyed horses.

"Are you mad?" the soldier yelled up at Rakaro and his green looking friend. "The Demon is upon us! Flee, fools, lest you be scorched to ash!" He didn't wait for an answer, just tore on down the track, his strong legs pumping, and his desperate friends following wearily behind.

Rakaro made to call after them but Erun placed a warning hand on his shoulder. "Look," he said, his mouth dry as ash. Rakaro, turning slowly, felt his jaw drop further. The archer tried to speak but words wouldn't come. There was no way to describe such horror as they witnessed on that day. What words (or even thoughts) could serve to explain so horrendous a spectacle?

Suffice it to say that the two riders were rooted to their saddles, and their horses to the steaming earth below. Unable to move, they watched the nightmare tapestry unfold. The horror of those scorching minutes would stay with Erun Cade and Rakaro the Hillman to the end of their days. The pair witnessed the flames rearing and dancing—a host of biting serpents—up and up, flickering mile-long tongues of orange and yellow, and savage wicked red.

The sky now spilled fireballs on the fields in front of them. Erun felt his beard hairs singe and his eyes smarted and stung. He had to keep blinking or else he lose his vision—or worse become blinded. The sky darkened to a cauldron of bubbling lava threatening to spill over and eat up the smoking countryside surrounding the city.

As they watched the furnace congealed, almost solidified to recognisable matter. The face was there again now, manifesting before their eyes. It appeared almost human and yet both alien and weird—like the twisted, raging visage of a tortured god. It was the face of evil incarnate—there was no questioning that. Erun, petrified, saw blazing eyes filled with white-hot hate. They seemed to pull at his innards with invisible tongs. Erun could take no more: he spewed on his horse's saddle. Rakaro, beside him, was retching too.

Erun Cade willed his eyes to study the demon again. Its flickering visage now resembled an aging, bearded man fused with something else, something inexplicable and wrong in every sense. Time passed like judgment. The apparition loomed high over the smoking ruin of the city. For what seemed an age those damning eyes blazed mercilessly down on the two stricken riders.

The atmosphere was searing hot—far worse was the raw hatred emanating from that hideous gaze. The sky crackled and banged and spat gobbets of ash all around them. Erun's stomach heaved again. He was about to faint, fall from his horse. He held on—somehow.

Then mercifully, just as Erun was losing his will to hang on, the wind took hold in the scorched air above. The monster was now loosing shape and identity. Both riders watched stupefied as the face in the sky faded and then drifted back to honest smoke again. And following that, as if obeying some silent command, the fire snakes coiled back down to coaly circles of crimson and the ruddy clouds paled to ashen, pinkish grey. The Demon had departed and a mournful silence now surrounded them instead.

The strengthening wind now buffeted their faces, shaking the riders from the trance state they had fallen into.

"Look," croaked Rakaro, grabbing Erun's arm and shaking him. Amongst the city's ruin, and as the smoke cleared enough to let him, Erun now saw tiny figures crawling like ants among the piles of smoking stone. Even from this distance he could see that they were armed with spears and wore helm and armour.

"Zorne then..." Erun grunted.

Rakaro shrugged. "Those ain't normal soldiers. No mortal could withstand that furnace. An army of ghouls, I suspect. Time to go, don't you think?" Rakaro wiped the sweat from his brow. Both he and Erun Cade had seen enough. More than enough. It was past time they depart this blasted region lest the monster stir again, or else those zombie soldiers come their way.

The two glanced hard at each other and then nodded in agreement. They were alive, and though both badly shaken, were determined to stay that way for as long as they could. Time for departure. The horses needed scant encouragement.

They raced back along the road, soon passing the runners who cried out to them as they sped by. "Help us..." said one, "The world is ended," another. They rode past and didn't look back.

***

It was nightfall before they finally reined in, exhausted, and commenced making a rudimentary camp beneath a shock of thorns. Both were shattered by what they had seen. Neither man wanted to speak of it. They made no fire. Both would rather freeze than stare at flames again. So they just sat in morbid silence and watched the night's stars wink down on them.

Eventually Erun Cade broke the stony silence: "That thing?

Ashmali?" Somewhere he'd heard that name before. He couldn't remember when. "The Fire Demon you were told about? I..."

Rakaro didn't respond at first. When he did speak his words were weary and morose. "A Fire Elemental, yes," he said as if he knew what he was talking about—which he didn't, he now realised. "A Demon from past ages. My people say these lands were ruled by such *things* once, long before the coming of man... so the shamans in the Ice Hills say. They—"

"The wizard Ozmandeus has freed Ashmali." Erun now remembered the words spoken by Irulan in his cave. It seemed so long ago that he had heard them.

"What's that?" Rakaro gazed hard at his companion. "What know you about these things, boy?"

"Someone said that to me once," Erun told him. "A wise man—though at the time I took no heed and didn't believe him. But now I know, having seen *that*." Erun shuddered and pulled a face. His mind was made up now.

"I must go home," he told Rakaro. "Warn my people. If this Ashmali thing reaches Gol...? I have to do something, Rakaro. I can't just let it happen."

"We'll never get through the Gap alive," muttered Rakaro as he sipped at his flask. He still had a bit of the foul liquid left that he had won in a dice game with Toskai last winter. He kept it stowed for special occasions. This was one such. Rakaro tossed it across to Erun, who sniffed it suspiciously, then took a wary gulp.

"Yugh," Erun's mouth stung. "What is that, bloody acid?"

Rakaro grinned at him. "It's rare stuff, is that." The Hillman was slowly recovering from their ordeal and getting his wits back. His face still stung from the heat of the Demon's fire and he was dog tired. Rakaro was worried about his own people now. But should he warn them? To return to the Plains would only earn him a slow death at the hands of Toskai and his other brothers. Hillmen were not a forgiving lot.

"Over the mountains?" Erun suggested, reading his thoughts.

Rakaro shook his head. "Impassable: even in summer."

"The coast then..."

"I'll not go by ship," replied Rakaro, a stubborn look showing on his face.

"Well, you had best make a choice, friend nomad," said Erun. "Fry or drown. You never know, Rakaro, you might come to like the ocean—they say it's full of wonders."

"It's full of drowned sailors," responded Rakaro. He yawned, spat, and then rolled into his blanket. Moments later he was asleep and snoring. Erun gaped at the stars for a while longer, and then he too curled up to rest for the remainder of the night.

In the end they had no choice. Rakaro was right; crossing the Gap would be suicide. The coast was their only chance of escape from Lamoza. So the next morning, and only after replenishing their water in a struggling stream they had been fortunate to find, the two riders fared south east toward the distant mountains and Xandoria beyond. They crossed more arid terrain for several days until they joined the coast road that clung to the forested skirts of the mountains, passing to their south.

Close by was the ocean. Rakaro viewed it with distrust, and Erun laughed and teased him mercilessly, until the Hillman punched him in the ear. They followed the coast road for many miles until finally reaching a small port huddled beneath the shadow of the southernmost mountain. They dared fare no further. The frontier was scarce ten miles east of this place. There would be troops stationed at the border and they were outlaws now. So (despite Rakaro's misgivings) they scoured the inns for merchants and traders, and though having little luck initially, eventually got a ride on a Salt laden dhow.

They took grateful passage (well, Erun was grateful)—the merchant was making for Rakeel. That busy port was only a short distance from Gol's western shores. It would serve well enough.

The captain was called Gonnel—a black skinned barrel-chested, bull of a man. He and his sinewy, ebony crew hailed from the Island States in the far south. During their last voyage they had got word of the carnage in Lamoza.

"Far worse back west," Gonnel informed Erun and Rakaro when they joined him at the helm. "Zorne City's a goner. Spagos and Ketaq are history. And now Lamoza City too." The captain shook his head. "How can a man trade when everything's gone to rat shit and fumes? The whole fucking continent will be cinders within a year—mark my words, lads. Ozmandeus of Zorne was always a nasty customer—even for a warlock. Chip on each shoulder, that one. I had dealings with folk who dwelt near his castle—horrible place way up in the hills."

Erun had asked Gonnel what he knew about this Ozmandeus, and how the sorcerer had come to control such a terror. "Gods only know, boy," he'd responded. "But that Ozmandeus was ever a sly one. They kicked him out, you know."

"Who..?" Rakaro cut in mildly interested now. He wasn't comfortable with all this water so close to his feet, but at least he hadn't drowned yet—so that was good.

"The Order—you know, those wizards on that cursed island off Zorne's west coast." Erun and Rakaro looked blank. Gonnel didn't notice. "Ozmandeus got too powerful, even for them. So they banished him from the Citadel."

"Perhaps they'll put an end to him then," suggested Erun, feeling a vague glimmer of hope. Rakaro nodded enthusiastically. This would be the best outcome.

"Unlikely," laughed the captain. "They're all dead—cooked in their own bloody tower. The story reached us last winter—though no one at that time suspected he'd freed Ashmali from a cave on that other island. The volcano way out west. Know the one?" They didn't.

"I mean who'd be insane enough to do that?" Erun and the Hillman didn't respond and, both deep in thought, left the captain alone at the helm.

***

The voyage took almost two weeks. In the main Erun enjoyed the journey, though he was anxious to reach Gol's shore and warn Scaffa of the horror he and his friend had witnessed. He could think of no other tactic. Perhaps *she* would know how to stop Ozmandeus and his Demon should they threaten invasion. Having seen what he had, Erun now believed this Ashmali capable of anything. He had to do something and so he would make for her island again.

Rakaro moped beneath decks most of the time. When he did surface the Hillman walked as though the ship's timbers were unstable jelly and not good honest oak—much to the crew's and Erun Cade's amusement. He bore their looks with superior indifference and counted the hours until they reached shore.

That day arrived hot and bright. Erun was gazing out from the foredeck: he heard the crew holler that they'd raised the Gates of Rakeel. That afternoon saw them moored and disembarked. They paid Gonnel off with stolen coin and left the harbour behind.

After entering the bustling winding streets of Rakeel, Erun and Rakaro took stock. Although part of Xandoria, the city of Rakeel was heavily influenced by its trade with Galania which lay only a short sail across the Shimmering Sea. The people here were a mixed variable bunch, most caring little for the Emperor away in Xenn.

There were few soldiers evident (the main barracks were further west at Murkai and Tashkaan, as Erun was aware). Rakeel was more of a trading city where the wealthy came to gamble and whore. Rakaro, free at last from the rigours of the ocean, loved it at first glance.

"This is a place to grow rich in," he chuckled, gripping Erun Cade's hand as the younger man swung up into his saddle. "I will linger here for a while, friend Kell. Look after yourself, lad. Should you need my assistance then seek me out in the backstreets of Rakeel. I'm going to like it here."

"What about your people? Aren't you going to warn them about the Demon?"

"I'll send word," Rakaro replied. "I expect they'll head north to Khandol when they first hear the news. It won't be long before the whole bloody continent knows about Lamoza City. My people are tough—they will pull through. The high tundra surrounding Khandol is vast and desolate, it's where we nomads came from originally—before we were Hillmen. It's frigging chilly up there— that's why we left. Whale and walrus goulash gets a bit boring after a while. That's said, it's safer than most places, I reckon."

"What will you do when the Demon reaches Rakeel?" Erun asked him.

"Worry about it then, "responded Rakaro with a wry grin. "I don't think this Ozmandeus is in any great hurry, do you? And he'll want to take on the Emperor at Xenn City before he worries over Rakeel."

"I admire your optimism."

Rakaro showed his gap-tooth grin. "I've got time enough to make a few deals, and if Gonnel was right it took that warlock months to get to Lamoza City. Those lads on ship told me that the Demon drains his strength and this Ozzy fellow has to rest after each burning—and for weeks sometimes. They also said he raises the corpses the Demon's fried and enlists them into his ranks. An army of stiffs—imagine that."

"A cheerful thought," replied Erun with a curl of his lip. He grabbed the reins. "I'll take my leave then."

"Aye—look after yourself, shit for brains. I'll give you a good beating next time we meet. You've been fortunate so far."

Erun laughed. "So I have. Farewell, Rakaro." They gripped hands and smiled. "Take care in this wicked city—lest they corrupt you. Don't get a dose from those grubby whores. I've seen them eyeing you up. They can smell gold a mile off."

"I should be so lucky..."

***

In the following days Erun Cade (now calling himself Kell) rode east alone and at great speed. He avoided the treacherously marshy isthmus that sometimes joined Xandoria to Gol, and instead took brief sea passage from a northern village via skiff across to Rodrutha. Once there he stole a horse and rode east at speed.

Days later Erun spied the lofty cliffs of Scaffa's Island, and at Northtown sought out the old ferryman again—but to no avail. He asked around but no one appeared to remember the man. Unperturbed, Erun slipped along the quay after dark and 'borrowed' a sturdy craft. When finally he reached that bewitching shore, Scaffa stood on the beach waiting for him. "I have been expecting you," she said. For some reason he wasn't that surprised.

***

He is sleeping...

Ozmandeus opened his eyes slowly. He was tired: so terribly tired. But who save he could map the mind of a demon? Ashmali's fires were latent for now. The Demon had departed deep inside him after its furious feasting on Lamoza City. For days Ashmali had waxed to raging ruin, destroying all in range until nothing lived—no beast, no man, and no plant or tree.

Ozmandeus had been part of that burning. Though the demon raged at will, its violent untapped energy filled its host with ecstatic joy. And power. This was how the gods must feel! Every nerve and muscle in his body had been charged with electricity. Ozmandeus had stood tall as a mountain, whilst his inner demon's reckless rage fell all about in ruin and ash.

But that had been a week ago. Now Ozmandeus, the once so agile and strong, couldn't move a muscle and was left frail and wan—the worry beetle boring once more inside his mind.

Can I control him, yet? Can I stop him when I need to? I must...must. Must!

The truth was that he knew he couldn't. That sane fraction still surviving inside Ozmandeus's ravaged mind knew that he was doomed—that master had turned slave. But the greater part of him, the section now fused with the Demon, was still deluded. This stronger, insane Ozmandeus believed he still held the reins of power, and that in due course he would fully control his reckless demon side once again.

Xandoria. It would take Xandoria to quell the monster's lust for ruin. When that mighty Empire was brought to its knees the Demon would be so bloated...so sated and overfed, that he, Ozmandeus, would take control again. The problem was that he was so weak when Ashmali slept. A shadow of his former self or else just a hollow shell. Ozmandeus was unable to move, even his bodily functions he performed in his bed.

It was debilitating, but the mad voice inside his mind insisted that it were necessary for him to grow alongside the Demon. All would come right—the mad Ozmandeus promised his saner self—after the fall of Xandoria across the mountains. That was the key.

But that would not take place for some while yet. Ashmali too, was drained, and though each ecstatic fire-surge strengthened the demon's hold, the Elemental also needed long periods of rest. The demon would withdraw inside its host for many days, only to emerge much hungrier and even stronger than before. It had happened after the destruction of Spagos and Ketaq, and it would happen after Lamoza too. Only this time it would be worse.

And there were other issues playing on Ozmandeus's shattered mind. The mercenaries followed him now mainly by fear alone. The Renegade paid his captains well—and though hard men—they were ill at ease in his company and many of their hired swords had deserted, fleeing east or south overseas. There was trouble brewing in the ranks, those bootlegging soldiers liked not the fact that the undead filed silently by their sides. Burnt shrivelled corpses recently raised by his necromantic arts. His was an unholy force—but one that would conquer all in time.

But the Renegade couldn't rely on cadavers alone to file his ranks. Who would serve him when the war was over? Ozmandeus would need living servants as well as copious slaves to populate his new realms. The dead, like the demon, were a weapon of fear. All would flee before them, but once their purpose was served he would send them back to their shadowy guardian, whence he had summoned them last winter.

The Renegade now commanded a force comprising over ten thousand souls—some living, most dead. The Emperor in Xenn was rumoured to control three well disciplined armies—in total over a hundred thousand warriors, and each force led by an experienced general. But that was of no account—they would scatter like wind-blown splinters when Ashmali descended on them. Fear would unman them. The Demon Fire and living corpses would do the rest. That was the easy part—simplicity itself.

Next came the hard part. It would prove his greatest test,

but somehow he would achieve it. Ozmandeus would learn a way to control this Ashmali. There had to be a way of controlling the demon. He would find it. All he required were strength and time. Xandoria—he would start planning the invasion while he rested. Ozmandeus would choose his time, and somehow he would work the problem through. But for the time being he had to rest. It would all work out in due course. It had to because this was his destiny—he'd seen it in the stars. Patience was the key. Ozmandeus slept peacefully for a time but then the demon woke inside him.

Chapter 5

Fireflies and Gold

"I want her head, the bitch-cow!" Varentin was having a fit—
not for the first time recently. "I want her head cut off and shoved
on a greasy spike, so the whole fucking city can see the crows feasting on her deceitful eyes. I want -"

"Be silent!" Hal Gallante had heard enough. For over half
an hour his ranting son had battered his ears with vitriol. Lissane
this... Estorien that...The prince had borne most of it with brittle
patience as he troubled to find a way of turning these unfortunate
events to Galanian advantage.

But Hal Gallante's patience was not immeasurable. He had
his limits. His fuse had finally sparked after this last tantrum
performed by his son. Did the stupid boy honestly think he was
guiltless in this business? Varentin had kicked the girl bloody when
she'd caught him at play—little wonder she turned to another for
affection. And now here he was—the idle, spoilt heir to everything
Hal had built—slumped lazily on the couch, playing with some of
the gold retrieved by Torlock from the border yesterday.

What a coup that had proved—twenty thousand gold pieces
fresh from Torvosa's coffers. House Sarfe had no such monies, and

Razeas would be itching with embarrassment at having to borrow yet again from his only friend. Toreno was a soft-headed dolt. Clarde would have sent Sarfe packing—friend of Estorien or not. It was something of a joy to Hal Gallante, seeing his enemy squirm so.

The prince couldn't comprehend why his petulant son was creating such a fuss about it all. It wasn't as though Varentin had even liked the stupid girl. Good riddance, was Hal Gallante's opinion of the matter. He smirked, picturing how Eon Barola would have received the news that his only daughter was a harlot. No, thought Hal Gallante, the whole ridiculous episode had turned out for the best, and more importantly, House Gallante had emerged much richer from it. If only his son would shut up.

"Our dear son has been cuckolded, husband." The Chatelaine's voice was both reasonable and calm, and he detested every word she spoke. She always had to interfere. Sophistra's crisp tongue was sharper than a headman's axe—and yet soft as silk. Her serene tones severed his thoughts with ruthless precision—but then they always did.

Wife...how like you to take the boy's side....

"They must be made to pay with more than coin, my Prince. Or do you want House Gallante to become the laughing stock of Gol? That bitch needs punishing, Varentin is right—although I wouldn't advocate such crudeness as he suggests. That's only his hurt speaking. Do not you understand, beloved?"

Oh, I understand that you seek to undermine me every time, woman.

Hal Gallante turned his shrewd green-eyed gaze from the high window, where he had been monitoring the guards as they were put through their paces by Torlock's second—the fair haired Jerrel. The prince's gold flecked gaze narrowed dangerously as he saw the look his wife was giving him. "They will be made to pay, of course," he dismissed her words with a wave of his hand. "But in good time, Sophistra. There is much to gain for us in this."

"I want vengeance," sulked Varentin, annoyed that his parents seemed to have forgotten he was in the room. "I want it now!"

Varentin seized a fistful of gold and let it spill through his grubby fingers. He'd been eating olives and the grease of their oil smeared his clothing and face. "This mere gold is not enough," he told them.

"You shut up now, you worthless prick!" Hal's patience had left him with the arrival of his wife. He was furious now and snapped out at his son with sudden venom. In his younger days Hal Gallante's temper had been something all men avoided, but he had been so controlled of late. No longer—he had had enough.

Varentin cowed back from the onslaught as though his father had struck him. His look became indignant and he feigned disinterest, though his eyes were full of hate for his father. Varentin devoured another olive and flicked the stone at a slave stood minding the doors. The slave hardly blinked as it hit his nose—he was well used to this treatment and grateful that the missile was tiny on this occasion. It was not usually so.

But Hal Gallante hadn't finished. He was raging now, his handsome face almost purple. The prince stood up then, knocking his chair over and spilling his wine. He began pacing the floor in hurried, angry steps whilst his sulking son and cat-eyed wife watched him in wary silence. The slave looked uneasy in the corner. Things were getting dangerous now.

"Of what use are you to me, boy?" Hal Gallante demanded of his heir—voice raw with emotion. "You can't fight, can you? You've scant sense between those perfumed ears. All you're good for is tupping whores and getting serviced by slave boys—I know how low you have sunk. You're a coward and a craven, Varentin." The prince waved his hands to the ceiling and shook with rage. "Gods, how did I spawn such a creature as you?"

Varentin lurched to his feet on hearing this, spilling the bowl of olives across the polished marble floor, of this their private feasting hall, where none save family Gallante and trusted servants may enter.

"A pox on you, Father," snarled Varentin, "and a pox on your bloody honour too!" He kicked the olive bowl over again and then stormed out of the room, his long shirt swishing behind him, pausing only to slap the slave hard in the face with the back of his hand.

Within moments the heavy thud of Varentin's booted footsteps were echoing hollowly down the stairwell.

"I trust you feel purged now that is off your chest." Sophistra had watched her son's departure in studied silence, her thoughts calculating and cool. She let her dark eyes drift to the window.

Black Torlock stood out there in his customary midnight leather and lacquered steel, scarce twenty feet away, his features revealing nothing, though he must have heard the argument between prince and son. Sophistra subtly studied his lean, sinewy body and hawk-nosed face.

Torlock was a handsome brute in his way. The Champion of Galanais radiated an arrogant confidence that only ever accompanied those with total self belief. Black Torlock was a man the Chatelaine could rely on to get things done. The Champion caught her eye and his back straightened. Sophistra's upper lip tilted a touch and her flinty gaze raked along his muscular frame.

She let her eyes slide away almost reluctantly, then reached for a grape and, most delicately, placed the fruit between her pouty moist lips. Sophistra bit hard into the sweet flesh of the fruit and then carefully removed the stone with a precise finger. Her husband was choosing to ignore her. He looked pained and edgy and stood silent by the door. Prince Gallante had recovered from his earlier rage: he now feigned serenity, but Sophistra could see through that. She turned toward him now.

"That was unnecessary, husband." Sophistra's cool jet gaze duelled briefly with the Prince's icy green. She smiled slightly at the open hostility in his expression, and then reached for another grape from the platter to her left. "You have never given our son the love he deserved—hardly a wonder he turned out as he did." Sophistra munched her grape. This time she spat the stone on the floor, following her son's example. "You've more affection for your hounds, my Prince, than you have for Varentin."

And your wife for that matter...

"The boy's a weakling," riposted Gallante, waving a dismissive arm her way. "I should have had him strangled at birth. He is most to blame for this... nonsense." He exchanged a long hard look with his wife and then sighed in defeat. Sophistra always won these days. She sapped him dry—drained the marrow from his bones. "Oh, maybe I didn't mean all I said...it's just..."

"It's simply that you are in foul humour, my love," she responded, tossing her head back and spilling the long, glossy curls around her oval features. With a corner of her eye, Sophistra noticed how Torlock's dark gaze still followed her every movement from outside the window. She smiled slightly. *Impudent dog.* He was attractive—a touch, raffish and rough—but interesting still. She opened the window.

"Have you no business to attend, Captain?" Her words were crisp with sharp authority. She could see how they stung him. *Keep them keen but keep them edgy...*

"Chatelaine..?" Sophistra felt a wicked glow of warmth when she saw the ill disguised disappointment in Torlock's eyes.

Hal Gallante turned his troubled gaze to the window as if noticing his champion for the first time. "Leave us, Torlock," the prince said. "Attend your men outside. We have family matters to discuss, and you've soldiers to inspect."

Torlock saluted stiffly and strode out of the courtyard. She soon heard his rough voice growling at the soldiers across the way. But before he'd left, Torlock's stony gaze had met the Chatelaine's... lingered for the briefest defiant instant, and then he had gone. Sophistra smiled openly at the space he left behind him.

How insolent, but I might have need of you later...urgent need...

The Chatelaine reached for another grape and crunched this one hard between her perfect teeth, snapping the stone in two. A plan was evolving in her clever head, and when her husband next spoke she hardly heard him, letting his stiff awkward words roll over her, and nodding sagely from time to time—all the while her quick mind focussing on the scheme she was now constructing.

A ploy so wickedly perfect, Sophistra could scarce keep the smirk from her lips. She was so lost in thought that she didn't notice when her husband vacated the chamber. It was a fine summer's day outside. Hal would be out with his hounds this evening—before

it got too dark. She'd construct a reason to keep Torlock from going with him. The champion was ever loyal to his lord and always
accompanied him at hunts. But there were ways of turning a man
like that. Subtle, feminine wiles that could prove most diverting to
one of her multifarious tastes...

***

Leagues to the south, the Sarfanian summer waxed hot and
steaming. The sultry, humid climate of this swampy region was so
unlike her native Barola, and hotter by far than the breezy clear
sunshine that blessed Galanais. But Lissane loved it. Every moment...every breath she shared with Estorien Sarfe was purest joy.
She had never felt so happy.

She was tired though—exhausted. The two of them had stayed
out till dawn, making love on the dunes that paraded the coastline
a score of miles west of Reveal. She and her lover went there often
during that golden summer.

They would gallop at speed sometimes, racing their horses
through the frothy waves, or else simply walk and talk—but always laugh and love for hour upon hour. At twenty-six he was
seven years her senior but sometimes Estorien seemed so young
when compared to her brutal brothers, and the spoiled deranged
Varentin Gallante.

Estorien was nothing like Erun Cade, of course. The only
other man (or rather boy) that she had loved would have been no
contest, had she met Estorien earlier. She'd been so young back
them, though Lissane would always hold affection in her heart for
poor lost Erun. That was then. It was something that had happened
to a different girl, a lifetime ago and, dare she say it, for the first
time since those heady foolhardy days in distant Barola, Lissane
was delirious with joy.

It had though taken months to settle things after the furore
she and her lover had caused following their flight from Galanais.
Lissane had apologised to Razeas Sarfe and his kindly wife—the
dark skinned Arrabella. She had been relieved to discover that both
Estorien's parents were easily won over.

They neither blamed her or their son overmuch, and devout
Arrabella just put it down to the will of the gods. Razeas had had
some sharp words with Estorien shortly after their frantic arrival—
but nothing untoward. These were gentler folk by far than she was
used to. Lissane had presented herself as well she could. Razeas
had capitulated to (as he worded it) her bountiful charms. Arrabella
had hugged her and bade her welcome as a long lost daughter—for
she had only boys and one was away in the foreign.

There were of course dark moments when the ghost of memory stalked her dreams. Lissane missed Bel's laughing smile and
Grale's kind bluffness too. She felt a pang of guilt whenever she
thought about them—though that wasn't as frequent as it should
have been. They had died for her, after all. But that was over and
they were gone.

Lissane had to move on. That ghastliness was down to Torlock
not her. It was just the nature of things on this turbulent continent.
Her friends were lost to her forever, confined to memory, as was
Erun Cade, who Lissane now felt certain had been murdered by her
brothers that night.

She'd told Estorien of her suspicions and he had vowed to
have it out with the three, when chance occasioned. But that too
was the past. Just as sulking, brutal Varentin Gallante was the past.
Those days were winter leaves, brown and crumbling—soon to be
dust on some forgotten road. Nothing lasted for ever.

But Lissane rarely looked to the future nowadays either. She
and her sweetheart lived in the present and that was a wonderful
place to be. They seized every moment possible and during most of
that long summer life was good to them both.

Her time with Estorien was one joyous cocktail of exhilara-
tion followed by another. Always they'd have fun—they had so
much in common. Whether racing their lathered mares along the
sandy strands of the coast, or hawking further inland, or else maybe swimming naked—him dusky brown and her ivory white—in the
meres that peppered this humid watery province.

There had been one awkward moment, Lissane recalled. A
rider, travel worn and weary, had arrived at Reveal at dusk, his

saddle bags bulky and his manner ill at ease. The rider had informed them that he'd travelled alone and with care—lest he be
seen by any on the road. Then he had placed two large sacks on
Razeas's high table, and Lissane, watching on, had stifled a gasp.

Twenty thousand in gold glittered in those sacks. She'd never
seen so much coin as these now sparkling beneath the rush lights.
But Lissane's wonder had turned quickly to shame when the tired
courier curtly announced that the moneys came from Torvosa, and
were the price demanded from Hal Gallante for the treachery of his
son's beloved spouse.

The courier had had a dour look, like most Dovesians she had
encountered. His tough face betrayed little—but Lissane couldn't
help seeing a glint of accusation in his tired blue eyes when he
glanced her way. She had reddened at that point. Razeas Sarfe had
smoothed it over with his accustomed easy manner. The rider left
after a hot meal.

A month later Razeas and his son had ridden north and met
with Hal Gallante and his brutal champion at the border. That had
proved a cold encounter. The gold had been exchanged with few
words from either party, Estorien had told her on his return.

"They are all about money, those Galanians," he had said, ruf-
fling her hair and smiling as only he could. "They'll not trouble us
now they've got that gold." Lissane recalled how his glib words had
sent a cold shiver through her body that day. It was no premoni-
tion, she told herself. Just a sudden chill. But in this sweltering
heat? Lissane decided not to dwell on that thought overmuch.

But as that summer wore on, lazy and slow, with swallows
swooping and clear blue skies, Lissane heard nothing from either
Galania or Barola, which, although welcome, she deemed rather
odd. The only fresh news came across from Torvosa City via coded
word and pigeon—from Clarde Dovess, in fact. It seemed his
doom-laden father, Toreno, whom she had met briefly as a child,
although she couldn't remember much about that meeting, was up
to his star-gazing again. It was a morose habit of the old Dukes, so
Estorien informed her.

Apparently whilst locked up in his high tower with his astrologer, Duke Toreno had had a vision. Witnessed some unspeakable horror occurring in the remote vastness beyond Xandoria. The Duke had been quite shaken apparently and had warned of fresh perils in the years to come.

Clarde wasn't impressed, and it all seemed a bit vague to Lissane. She'd heard of Xandoria of course, and remembered some of the other lands from her childhood lessons. Spagos...Zorne, the Island States. They were uncountable miles away, though. Even Rakeel, the nearest Xandoria city, might as well be on the moon for all Lissane knew about it.

It was what happened in Gol that concerned her, and happily at present that wasn't much. But something troubled her about Clarde's letter to his friend. Lissane couldn't see any relevance in it for her or Estorien. Then she remembered Rani's warning in her bower on that very night Erun disappeared, and a cold shiver crawled along her spine. Lissane now determined to find out more.

Ashmali. She heard the name first from a half drowned sailor. His beached vessel had been torn up on the strand after a particularly violent storm. He was out of Xenn City where the Emperor ruled, and had ranted like a mad thing to Estorien on the beach. It made little sense and his accent didn't help either.

The gist was some Fire Demon had been unleashed by a wizard (from Zorne apparently) and had destroyed great swathes of the sprawling lands west of Xandoria. This Ashmali creature had brought ruin in millennia past (so the sailor informed them) and the wise had warned of his return one day when he would destroy the entire earth with ruinous flame.

She and her lover had felt sorry for the foreigner. He was obviously haunted by the horror of his near drowning, and the ordeals that he and his few surviving crew members had endured. But to fabricate such a tale? Why? Razeas had taken them in and they were currently occupying the servants' quarters at Reveal. Lissane steered well clear of them.

But the sailor, Quoll, had stubbornly stuck to his story after recovering from his trauma. Razeas was intrigued, though Estorien had little interest. Curious, his father sent word across to Torvosa

City by bird. Toreno's response had been both swift and discomforting. It read thus:

Razeas
This Ashmali is the creature I have dreamed of.
We must unite the barons before all is lost, my friend.
Is Gol to be caught between fire and water?
Zansuat's domain is rising on the hour- we must make
ready!
Forget our petty quarrels - we will speak more at the
Games.
Until then be vigilant - your friend.

Toreno

Razeas had shaken his head sadly after reading the note a second time. "Duke Toreno Dovess was ever a good man," he told his son and Lissane as they took their leisure beside him that evening. "But he changed when they butchered King's body outside those walls. Flaminius deserved his fate. He was a mad dog but his Duke never quite saw it that way. Toreno always blamed himself for the king's demise, quite wrongly I believe." Razeas sighed and gazed out across the lake where a heron watched them from under a dreamy moon. "Since the Rebellion he's spent an unhealthy amount of time with his astrology and such. It saddens me, my children."

"Clarde has no time for it," said Estorien, his tone indicating clearly that he shared his friend's opinion on this matter. He took a cool, long sip from his wineglass and then gripped Lissane's hand and smiled. "Never has done...says his father's got worse over the last year or so. Perhaps the old boy's getting senile."

Lissane said nothing; she recalled who had cut off Flaminius's head from his shoulders after they found his body outside the walls. Eon Barola—a young ambitious rebel leader from east across the mountains. He and his brutal cohorts had butchered the dead king like a pig. Her father's bloody past. Lissane was no longer part of that. If she ever saw Eon Barola again it would be too soon.

But in the following weeks they heard no more dire portents concerning demons and floods, much to Lissane's relief. It was now late summer and the annual Games were nearly upon them. Razeas had urged his son not to attend the festival this year, but Estorien would have none of it.

"I've never missed a contest, Father," he argued. "Besides, what would our enemies think were Liss and I to stay away?" Estorien's face was fuelled with passion, he slammed his fist on the table and spilled his wine. "They would deem us cowards and would be right to do so—shored up like frightened hares in the safe confines of Reveal Castle."

"You cannot trust Hal Gallante," Razeas countered. "Nor Barola—begging your pardon, Lissane, but your father is no great friend to this house."

"He's no friend to anyone," replied Lissane. "Least of all his daughter."

"But surely your father will try to apprehend you, were he to encounter you at the Games...and he's bound to hear of your attendance."

"Eon Barola shan't bother me again," responded Lissane with a certainty that surprised her. "And if he does I have Estorien Sarfe to keep him and his conniving sons at bay." She smiled at her lover, who grinned back fiercely and clasped her hand tight.

"You see, Father," laughed the heir to Sarfania Province. "Lissane's as strong willed and determined as I am."

"So be it then," replied Razeas gloomily after a minute's thoughtful silence. He turned away so they couldn't see the sudden tears welling in his eyes; luckily Arrabella had gone to bed, though she would have words on this subject in the morning. It wouldn't avail though, Razeas knew that now.

The three sat in silence for a time watching the fireflies glow, flicker and fade. Father and son sipped cool wine, whilst Lissane gazed dreamily as the moon broke free from a wrack of cloud, spilling silver on the lake and then vanishing somewhere out beyond the mangrove trees.

It was very quiet and still. Then a faint sound caused Lissane raise her head—jolting her free of her dream state. Faint music. Eerie notes drifting out across the lake.

I'm sleepy, is all, and my imagination's getting the better of me.

But she wasn't sleepy, not now, and there it was again. Closer this time. Lissane felt certain she heard the faint peal of harpsong, rising up in clear chords from the shadowy mangrove, far out over moon-clear water.

She strained to listen but the notes faded back out of earshot and sudden as it had come was gone again. *Must have been a bird.* But Lissane recalled when last she had heard such weird wonderful music and what had followed soon after, and then Lissane too felt a tear rimming at her eye. So the ghostly harper has returned.

Change is coming...

"I was ever too soft with my children," Razeas broke the silence with a rueful smile. "Kael will be upset that you're going to Torvosa." Estorien's youngest brother was only sixteen and was itching to usurp his eldest sibling's current status as Darling of the Games—the senior two brothers took turn at events most years. Carlo Sarfe was a good fighter but indifferent to glory. But not young Kael. The junior of the family had a ferocious nature and was more impetuous even than his eldest brother. However each combatant had to be seventeen or over, thus fiery Kael would have to wait until next year.

"But you will ride out in good number and not tarry on the road, yes?" Razeas was insisting.

"That we will, Father," Estorien promised and so the matter was settled.

Two weeks later and days before Lissane considered herself fully ready, they were on the high road faring east with their complement. Lissane gazed back only once. Reveal's wooden halls and surrounding waters and mangrove trees were swallowed by haze and dusk. She would never see then again.

Razeas Sarfe stayed up late again that night, his heart heavy with worry. Arrabella had just retired. She'd been upset at the children's departure, despite Estorien's insistence they would be fine.

She had only Kael to fuss over now that Carlo was abroad at sea.

Had Razeas been wrong to let them go? Estorien would have ignored his command in any case—so he'd had little choice. But Lissane Barola in that hornets' nest? Razeas was fond of the girl but a shadow clung to her and he worried for his son. Time would tell—he and Arrabella would just have to wait.

God's please be kind just this once...

All around him on the terrace the fireflies danced and flickered, burning so brightly and then gone forever...never to return. Razeas felt an icy shiver passing through him. He glanced out across the lake. It was probably his imagination, but he could have sworn that he saw an old man watching from the shoreline, his arms cradling a harp or some kind of instrument. Razeas didn't dwell on it; he rubbed his tired, worried eyes, and retired to his bed. The world seemed suddenly very empty and silent. *The calm before the storm*, he thought.

The quickening...

Chapter 6

Queen of Cats

Morwella missed the lovers' stupid antics. She missed Estorien especially—not the pale faced stick-insect that he'd run off with. She'd known about their goings on for ages: of course she had—and they thinking they were being so clever. But Morwella missed *nothing*. And should she miss something then one of her cats would tell her.

They were her only *real* friends—her cats: Paws, Claws, and Lady Slinks. All jet black in colour—the last one named after Slinsi Garron, who Morwella liked the sound of. She had new recruits too, three young tabbies and a cheeky black kitten called Smudge, because of the white spot on his nose. Morwella had named them all but the names were a secret—only she and the cats were in the know. She was their captain, their queen. Queen of Cats. Morwella liked the sound of that.

Not that anyone in the citadel was interest in anything *she* did. Her brother was too busy sulking since Lissane Flower-Face had fled. Her father, always off with his hounds a hunting. Mother, huh. The Chatelaine had other matters to attend these days, it seemed.

Morwella had seen how many times Bad Black Torlock entered her bower of late, and in the silent dark of night. She thought it so funny. Bad Torlock servicing mother, while father serviced his hounds in the kennels, and Varentin attended himself. They were all so wrapped up in their boring little games, far too busy to pay heed to Morwella or her cats. But that was how she liked it. That way she saw everything.

Morwella missed Estorien horribly. He was so handsome and he had smiled at her twice, and no one else had smiled at her even once. She loved him—had for ages. If it hadn't been for that stupid wallflower with her dark locks, big purple eyes and horrible long legs, Estorien might have run away with Morwella instead. They would have had to have taken the cats of course, but then Estorien would have kept them as his servants, far more useful than the fat, ugly slave girls that always shrieked so when she spiked them with her special stabber.

Morwella smiled, thinking of the day that she had filched the weapon from the ladies' sewing rooms below. A knitting needle, one whole foot in length—she'd filed the end to make it really sharp and nasty. She had drawn blood on several of the slave girl's bare legs upon occasion. It was so funny watching them yelp in terror and then run away crying.

They were all so scared of her—those pathetic things. Morwella proudly fingered her stabber now, poking it between cracks in the wall of her mother's closet (where she was hiding this time) and wriggling away at it, until a chunk of plaster split and crumbled to the floor.

Mother would be back soon. Back for her afternoon rest and escape from her hectic day—poor thing. Morwella giggled at the stupidity of her family. She poked at the wall again, harder this time, her face darkening to a sudden twisted scowl, when she again thought of her Estorien off with that Barolan Bitch-face.

She had spoilt everything, had Lady Longlegs. Everything! It should have been her...it *could* still be her if she used her noddle. Yes, thought Morwella as she gouged a vicious chunk off the wall with her needle. There simply had to be a way. It was just a matter of planning: she and the cats would work it through.

***

The knock came just when she'd expected it. Torlock was ever prompt, thought Sophistra, as she slipped silently from her gown and turned toward the door, sliding her pale naked legs out from under the covers. She stood awaiting her visitor, smiling silkily as she caught the lusty gleam in his eye when the trapped moonlight revealed her voluptuous curves.

She watched him disrobe, casting his hunting garments and heavy mail shirt on the floor in his haste; smiled again as she saw his manhood stiffen to greet her.

Torlock approached her then, his heart thudding and his cruel nasty eyes hungry as a wolf's. She slid to her knees, still smiling, and took in the length of him, working her wet mouth back and forth until she felt the sudden rush of his hot seed spilling into her throat. Sophistra laughed as he threw her back on the large bed and began sliding his hard callused fingers up between her open thighs. She sighed and closed her eyes when those fingers found what they sought and then hungrily probed inside her...

Later, when they were done, she'd informed him of her notion. Sophistra had to test him first of course. She needed more than sex to see where his loyalties lay. But ambitious men like Torlock were nothing if not predictable it seemed.

"My husband's health is not as it was," she announced after he'd entered her for the third time that night. "He neglects me...I am not a woman to be neglected."

"No, indeed..."

"Do not mock." The slap was playful but still caught him off guard.

This one needs to know his place...

"Chatelaine...I—"

"They say he loves his hounds more than his wife." She reached forward and placed a moist kiss on his rouged cheek, noticing with interest how his manhood rose slightly at her touch.

This one is hungry...

"Well? You know him better than any here at court. Tell me... is it true?"

"Chatelaine, it's not for me to comment on my Lord Prince's affairs...I—"

She cut across his words with sudden vitriol. "It's not for you to fuck his wife either! But you do."

"What do you want from me...?" Torlock looked uncomfortable. A look she hadn't observed in him before.

"Loyalty—among other things."

"That you have, and my love to boot."

"I don't want your love, Torlock." She stared at him her eyes flinty and hard. "Not that sort of love, anyway. Lust is more than sufficient. What I need aside that is the assurance that you can be trusted."

"But of course..." Torlock was looking irritated now.

"In a matter of highest discretion..?"

"I'm your man."

"That's good to know," Sophistra purred and traced her fingers up his thigh, "because with your help I intend to dispose of my husband." Torlock's eyes widened in shock and she laughed at the sudden worry creasing his heavyset features.

"Well? Do we become shy, sir?" The Chatelaine raised a questioning brow at his evident discomfort. "And I thought that you were ambitious, Torlock." She teased his now limp manhood with a probing finger and he pulled away slightly, his usually arrogant eyes clouded by doubt. "Perhaps I should find another candidate?"

"I'll do it." He blurted it out.

"Well, that's good, and I'll inform you of my other notion after..." She kissed him then long and hard, and Torlock (his doubts banished by fresh rising lust) grinned as she reached for his rising sex again. Sophistra pushed Torlock down on the bed and then straddled his muscular hide. She took him in amid moans. It was almost dawn before he left her sated and wet; alone with her dark thoughts.

***

"They are going to murder Father, Claws!" Morwella told her favourite cat with a conspiratory whisper, and he thrust his furry face against hers with purring approval. "It's so exciting. But maybe we should warn him?" Morwella scratched her chin and pondered her conundrum for a moment. "But then we'd never get to see how they did it. And...there might be lots of blood and guts and stuff, like when you opened that mouse yesterday. That was interesting. Only Father's much bigger than a mouse—he'd make a lot more mess. All that blood, Claws..." Morwella could hardly contain her excitement. "I wonder how they'll do it—will it be today do you think? Maybe we should ask Mother? No, silly idea that one—she'd murder us instead, and we can't have that, can we, Claws?" The black cat purred his agreement and rubbed her leg again.

That settles it, thought Morwella. They would watch and wait. There were lots of ways to kill people; it would be such fun guessing the one they would use. Throughout that following week she made herself busy with watching and listening discreetly from her various hideouts. She sent her cats out to listen but they returned with little to tell her. No matter. The waiting was exciting the suspense filling her every hour.

The dire deed, when done, proved an utter disappointment for Morwella. She'd heard nothing, received no warning from her cats that the murder was imminent. If it hadn't been for a wretched slave crashing down upon her, running and yammering down the stairwell like a mad thing, and then almost falling over her where she squatted with stabber and cats.

"What is it?" Morwella had yelled out furious at his fleeing back. "What have I missed now?"

"L...Prince Gallante your father...dead..." The slave had barely stopped to spill out the awful words and within half a heartbeat he was off again, vaulting madly down the stairs, as if the Shadowman himself was after him.

"What? I've missed it?" Morwella's shriek sent her cats running in all directions.

How dare they kill him without me being there!

Morwella gathered her dusty skirts together and, barefoot, ran back up the stairs to the private chambers, where her family had been feasting an hour before.

The sight that greeted her managed to dispel at least some of Morwella's chagrin. Her dead father's colour was a most peculiar yellowy-green. His mouth gaped open and his teeth were speckled with crimson spittle. It was fair to say he didn't look very well.

Morwella, gawping hard, saw that Father's be-ringed hands still clawed at the sequined cloth of the table—he must have pulled that down with him as he fell.

I'll have to report that back to Claws.

It was plain as her nose that father but recently voided his bowels. That stink was something Morwella hadn't prepared for and she pulled a face. Prince Gallante's eyes were wide and staring, and a look of horrified betrayal still haunted that lifeless gaze. Morwella fiddled her fingers as she watched on. It was fascinating really—were it not for the stinky pong. But then her mother saw her standing there with tongue out and quizzical expression.

"Morwella! By the gods, child—what are you doing there?"

"I came to see."

Sophistra made to swat her daughter but Morwella skipped out of reach. "She did for him!" Morwella pointed an accusing finger at her mother who screamed at the slaves to remove her child from the room.

"Mother did for Father—and I missed it." Morwella pointed again to where the Chatelaine stood, incensed and raving. "It was you. It was you! Stinky poo stinky POO!" Morwella screamed until a slave grabbed her from behind and, nervously following her mother's furious orders, removed the screaming mad girl from their chambers.

Damn that child...

Sophistra glared at the departing slave, who even now still struggled with the kicking, yelling, needle poking, messy mass of bones and wild dishevelled hair that was her only daughter. Eventually the slave made it to the door and dragged her outside.

With Morwella finally gone a frosty calm entered the chambers. Sophistra reached down to catch the faint odour still lingering close to her dead husband's now greying face.

It had taken Torlock a week to find the right poison. Oh, digitalis or monksbane would have done the job, of course. But that would leave them guessing at who had dared such an act—and most knew of her skill with poisons. Sophistra could not risk being implicated. Let the gossips gossip but no proof would they attain.

No, it had had to be marshreek (that some called swampfire)—the favoured tool of House Sarfe in recent years—acquired as it was from their marshy creeks. With the Sarfanians now the obvious suspects and her husband neatly out the way, the path was clear for Sophistra and her paramour to act on her second notion. This year's Games would prove an interesting one, Sophistra thought pleasantly. She vacated the room while the slaves dealt with her husband's reeking corpse. Swampfire. An apt name for a poison that burns the victim from inside. Not a pleasant to go. Sophistra smiled for a brief moment..

How the mighty fall...

***

They buried Prince Hal Gallante with full honours. Both Torlock and his second Jerrel presided over that grim day-long ceremony. Sophistra thought that Torlock looked particularly magnificent in his black lacquered armour and sable cloak, with its silver brooch and fur-lined trims. He caught her eye once and turned away. It was hard to suppress a smile but she managed it all the same.

Chatelaine Sophistra Gallante was no average player. Over her long years spent in the Citadel at Galanais, Sophistra had employed stealth and guile, finding so many subtle ways of getting rid of her rivals and those malcontents who saw through her schemes.

Hal had never suspected his wife's hand in all those murders, the fool. All those poor concubines that had sought the Prince's attention during his younger days—each one had met with a sorry fate.

No one had ever suspected Sophistra (or if they had she'd soon silenced them too.) For good reason the Chatelaine came to be feared by all, in both court and city. And for long years now Sophistra had influenced matters with her cunningly planned and patient kills. Hal Gallante had been oblivious to it all. He'd let her be mostly, content as he was in his own world. Their brittle relationship had nevertheless proved successful for many years.

But of late Hal Gallante's rigid attitude had come to vex her, and his outburst at Varentin the other week had left her mind made up. It irked her that the Prince would settle for recompense from coin alone after so blatant an insult to House Gallante. Her husband's response to the rebuff had been both weak and indifferent—neither were things Sophistra could tolerate in anyone, let alone a spouse.

It wasn't to be borne. So he had had to go—and a good job done. Prince Hal Gallante was for the worms now and not before time. She, Sophistra, would rule Galanais through her son, and Black Torlock would be their enforcer and protector. The three of them would return Galania Province to its former glory in good time. Under Hal Gallante the people had become complacent. The Chatelaine and her grim protector would soon alter that. Sophistra smiled secretly to herself as she watched them lower her husband's gilded coffin deep beneath the earth. One job done: now to the next. She must set in motion that other business she had told Torlock about. It was a business that would suit her paramour's skills very well.

***

"He's dead!" Eon Barola couldn't contain his mirth. "He's bloody well dead, I tell you! Poisoned at the feasting table! Can you imagine?" Paolo raised a questioning brow, whilst his brothers looked up from their supper and exchanged quizzical glances. Their father—who it must be said was in rare jocular mood this eve—tossed the parchment across to his sons for their perusal. He leaned forward still chuckling, and grabbed his goblet, downing the honeyed contents with a noisy gulp, and then waving his hand for the servant to refill.

Paolo, grinning broadly, read the missive out loud to his brothers. "It's from old Pug-face in Galanais," he laughed; the brothers had ever mocked Sophistra for her short height and slightly turned up nose. Their father, however, had always been wary of her. "Looks like someone's done for old Hal Gallante. Poisoned the poor fucker in his cups. Who'd have thought it?"

"Let me read it." Aldo made to snatch with his remaining hand, but Paolo pulled it out of reach. "*My dearest Eon*"—it's the Chatelaine's spider hand," he told them before continuing with a grin. "*My deepest sorrow is to inform you of the murder of my beloved Lord and Prince, at the hands of Sarfanian assassins. It is now apparent that one skilled with marshreek (their preferred poison) entered our kitchens and fixed a lethal brew, which so cruelly took the life from our beloved Prince...*"

"She hated him," belched Rosco, "beloved Prince—crap."

Paolo waved him quiet. "*I have disposed of all the kitchen staff and most of the household slaves*, she says, *though I deem the wretch culpable would have planned his exit well before his heinous actions. Lord Torlock though is proving very assiduous in his questioning of those possibly culpable.*"

"Lord Torlock? I'll bet he bloody is," cut in Aldo. "That one's almost as bad as you, Paolo...almost."

Paolo ignored him and continued relating the Chatelaine's eloquently scrolled words. "*We have contained the growing outrage in the city and will be looking to question the Sarfanian ambassador should we encounter him at the Games next month. I do hope that Galanais can count on Barola's full support in this, most sorrowful time. Yours, in deepest mourning - Sophistra Gallante.*"

Paolo let the parchment drop to the table with a flourish of his hands. He then leaned back, stretched out both arms and yawned loudly. "Looks like the Games'll prove entertaining this year, what with Liss's antics and now this."

The Baron's face darkened at the mention of his daughter. He sipped his mead and turned his florid features toward the door. Almost he saw Lissane standing there, watching him with those accusing violet eyes.

You killed Mother—didn't you...

"Estorien Sarfe's right in the shit—that much is certain," smirked Aldo. He hated Estorien, who had trounced him in contests at the Games on numerous occasions. "First goosing Lissane and now this murder."

"I'll not here that name in this hall!" Eon Barola slammed his goblet on the table, spilling mead across its surface and soaking his scarlet doublet. "I have no daughter," he told them as they watched his sudden outburst with wary sobering eyes. Only Paolo seemed relaxed—but then he always did.

"Are matters continuing as planned, father?" Paolo asked, changing tack after an uncomfortable pause. His brothers looked at him gormlessly without a notion of what he was meaning.

"They proceed, yes." The Baron had reined himself back from the brink. He could never forget how she had accused him that time...*so like her mother*. But Lissane was stronger than Leanna had been. She was a feisty one, his daughter, Eon would allow her that much. The Baron had drunk heavily since Lissane's departure last year. It showed on his face, the loose sagging jaw and the bags beneath his eyes—and those eyes more often bloodshot than not.

"And Treggara...?" Paolo enquired, enjoying the perplexed expressions on his brothers' faces.

"As planned," responded the Baron. "It all goes as we planned." He took to his feet then, slurping down the last gulp of mead and wiping his mouth on the servant's sleeve.

"I must respond to Sophistra Gallante, and promptly," Eon informed his boys. "Don't get too drunk. We're hunting tomorrow or had you forgotten that, Rosco?" The Baron left them to their idle sport and staggered aloft to his quarters. The girl would be waiting for him there, though Eon doubted he'd have the energy to pump her tonight. It *was* funny, though—old Gallante dead. He hadn't seen that one coming.

Sarfanians... Chatelaine, you were ever transparent in your cleverness. Despite his mirth Eon was wary. Galania in the hands of Sophistra and this Torlock was not a thought to be taken lightly. Things would change now. He would have to watch and wait.

The Games—it all hinged on the Games.

Eon managed a wry chuckle as he fumbled for the door lock. Inside was gloomy, and the girl looked pensive in the corner. "Relax," he told her, "I've more important matters concerning me tonight than you." She didn't respond—just watched him with those moon eyes as the shawl slipped from her shoulders, shedding candlelight on her nakedness.

Women...you all hate me, don't you?

Eon found his table in the murk, ordered the wench pour him a drink, and then with full goblet close by, took pen to parchment. He only managed a few words before his head hit the oak surface, knocking his goblet askew. Within seconds the Baron's throaty snores were echoing noisily down the stairwell.

The girl watched him in silence for a while and then took her leave. She would make for the kitchens for some supper. She had a lover in town, she would spend the night with him and then would return in the morning. They both knew what they were risking but the baron was mostly drunk these days. She would creep back into his bed shortly before dawn. Eon Barola would doubtless have need of her sometime that morning, though not early—that much was certain.

***

"She killed him! Mother killed him, Claws! And now she's denying it!" Morwella had recently promoted Claws to Chief Cat. Events meant she needed serious back up now that things had shifted down there in court. Mother was lording it up and Big Black Torlock was everywhere. Whisperers ruled Galanais these days—even more than before. Morwella must needs be on her guard.

"They'll come for us next, Claws. You must train the others!" Claws purred loudly in her ear. "I know—but we have to be ready. They could come any moment. You must place guards! Recruit more cats. We need an army, Claws!" Again her favourite purred but didn't look like he was going to act on her orders any time soon.

After the excitement (and disappointment) of seeing her father dead, Morwella's attitude had shifted abruptly. She now realised that her mother was the enemy. Chatelaine Sophistra would stop at nothing until her daughter was dead. Why? Because she was an evil twisted cow. Her mother knew Morwella was the only one left smart enough (and certainly brave enough) to thwart her wishes. It wouldn't prove long before Mother yelled out at Bad Torlock, "Off with that little bitch's head!" Torlock would happily swing that big axe of his and she would be splattered to nasty pieces.

"And we can't have that, can we, Claws?" Morwella winced at the thought. But she wasn't overly worried. She was Queen of Cats: she had her feline allies and confederates. Each one loyal and dedicated to the cause. That said, they needed to be careful from now on.

"Best not upset Mother again until we have enough troops. It might take a while. But we can storm the palace when they're all asleep, or fucking, or whatever horrid things they do up there in the dark of night." Claws buzzed agreement in her ear and Morwella grinned as the Great Plan took hold inside her head. It was simple. Patience and precision. Gain the upper hand in Galanais. Employ cat craftiness. Win the respect and love of all. And if not—KILL THEM! Then go rescue Estorien Sarfe from that floozie with the mile long legs. He would be so grateful to be free of the witch. And if he was good to her then Morwella would make him king. What a festival they'd have! The King and Queen of Cats.

***

The Chancellor looked up as Tall Romul, the general commanding the Third Imperial Army entered his office. Romul was sharper than the other two officers. More discreet—that said, the Chancellor couldn't trust him fully. Not yet. But Romul's patience was no longer than his fellow warlords. He was irritated at being summoned here at such short notice. When he spoke his tone and manner were both abrupt and dismissive.

"You have information for me, Chancellor." A statement not a question.

"Yes, General," the Chancellor motioned toward the gilded

chair at the far side of the carved mahogany desk where he managed his affairs of state. "Please be seated."

Romul pulled the chair back and perched warily, his hard grey soldier's eyes locked on the Chancellor's watery brown. The Chancellor wiped his nose with a silk handkerchief and sighed with resignation. None of this was easy for him.

"Tell me, General," he leaned forward his elbows on the desk, his tone now urgent and pressing. "What do you know about the creature, Ashmali?"

Romul rolled his eyes, he had suspected that this was why the Chancellor had summoned him. He needed an ally to help him convince the Emperor of this *threat* beyond the Gap. Everyone knew that he was obsessed with it.

"Only the same stories that fill the streets of every city in Xandoria," he replied. "It's just rumour, Chancellor—nothing substantial."

"You are wrong, General. Very wrong. This is no time for insouciance—I know what is coming in the months ahead. Chaos and death—mark my words." Romul raised an eyebrow; the Chancellor was well known and respected in Xenn for his accurate predictions and forewarnings of coming events, despite him being prone to fret. Romul was not usually sold by such philosophies. He was a fighting man and he needed plain hard facts.

"You may well doubt my words, General—the other generals, Dilon and Garryon did too. But I deem you a shrewder man than those two. Tall Romul, I thought, would at least give an ear to what I have to say."

"Very well," replied Romul. "You have both ears, Chancellor. Pray continue."

"Good—that's good, because we are going to have to move His Magnificence from the Imperial Palace, and re-establish his court in the old Palace over in Rakeel."

Romul laughed and shook his head; he hadn't time for this—idiocy. It was sheer paranoia. The Chancellor was a doom merchant was all. "The Emperor has never left his palace," he argued. "Nothing will alter that—"

"Xenn City will be burned to the ground in less than a year, General." The Chancellor's words cut like knives into the musty atmosphere of his office. His now steely expression brooked no argument and kept Romul on his seat.

"The Demon is coming, Romul," the Chancellor continued in a softer voice. "That is a certainty, not idle fabrication, my friend. It was prophesied years ago, that one day a warlock from Zorne would release Ashmali the Fire Demon from his prison where he was placed millennia past by the gods. And that once free the Demon's hunger for destruction would prove unstoppable. But," he added, "despite the portents, there yet might be a way to salvage most of Xandoria. If we sacrifice our Imperial City to the fire. And the fire *is* coming, Romul—it's not as if we have a choice."

"What do you propose then, Chancellor?" Romul wasn't won over yet but at least he was listening now.

"We strike at the enemy's heart before it's too late. Send an assassin into their camp to slay this Ozmandeus when his guard is down," the Chancellor replied. "Without his mortal conduit, this Ashmali creature will lose focus and fade—that's what my studies inform me. The demon's spirit needs matter to channel its fires."

"But how could an assassin—however skilled—hope to achieve such a bold deed?" Romul demanded. "I mean, if this Ozmandeus is everything they claim he is, then nobody could come close without getting fried."

"Timing," answered the Chancellor, his weary gaze straying to the window. "Timing is the key. You see, Romul, both the warlock and his Elemental have a flaw. After Ashmali destroys he must rest and his conduit too. Reports say Ozmandeus was too weak to move for weeks after the demon destroyed Lamoza City. Ashmali was quenched and latent also—hence the perfect time to strike."

"I could send a killer through the Gap," suggested Romul, "take this Ozmandeus out before his army even arrives at our doors."

"No," responded the Chancellor. "It would take too long—every day the Demon and his sorcerer gain strength. Soon Ashmali will hunger again and well is it known how this Ozmandeus lusts for the Empire's wealth. The enemy won't tarry in Lamoza for much longer now. Once through the Gap they'll make straight for Xenn. Strike at the heart of the realm. We cannot alter that fact. Xenn City is doomed, General."

Romul hated the fact that he was being won over by the Chancellor's words despite his determination not to be. "But should we choose to sacrifice Xenn City to the Demon's fires and regroup," the Chancellor urged. "We could then watch and wait. Infiltrate their camp and hit hard when they least expect it—when Ashmali's flames are exhausted."

"It would take high courage and perfect timing. But yes, I believe it might work, Chancellor."

"Just so... I am glad you understand." The Chancellor rubbed his eyes. "Have you an agent that could achieve so daunting a task?"

"Karali will do it—if it comes to that. He is the finest assassin east of the mountains. A killer, subtle and skilful."

"He will need to be—and more," replied the Chancellor. "And be assured, General, it *will* come to it. We cannot save Xenn, but we might perchance save Xandoria—it is all we can hold to, regrettable, I know. You are leaving so soon? I've not offered refreshments."

Romul had briskly taken to his feet with mind made up. Despite the radical suggestions he was now converted. He had been in denial, he realised that now. No one wanted to believe this threat was for real—that everything they cherished would soon be gone forever. But Romul too had heard the prophecies concerning Ashmali's return. He knew in his heart that the Chancellor spoke sooth.

"Methinks I'd best not tarry," Romul told the older man. "The armies have all returned from Lamoza by now, but I'll send fresh scouts through the Gap to glean the latest. I'll prime Karali too. That just leaves the Emperor."

"Leave him to me," responded the Chancellor.

"Gladly," replied Romul, and with a curt nod vacated the room.

The Chancellor watched the door shut as Romul departed from his office leaving him in silence. *A good man, that.* But that was the easy part. Now he had to convince the Emperor and get past those bloody courtiers. But he had a notion. *They do say that the gardens in Rakeel are most divine at this time of year.* He sighed once more, straightened the parchments on his desk, and then took to his feet. No reason to delay. He made for the palace at once. This time the Chancellor wouldn't take no for an answer.

Chapter 7

Journeyman

The castle was the weirdest structure he'd ever seen. From a distance it appeared as some bizarre quirk of nature that had tumbled from the sky in times long past. An alien rock, bizarre and surreal, perhaps tossed down by some reckless god in ages gone by. Or else a fallen star come from the outer fringes of the gods only know where. Whatever it was, this huge chaotic pile of stone didn't look natural and didn't belong with the land and seascape surrounding it. There was no evidence of any kind of order, no sign of habitation. Surely this couldn't be what she had meant. But as Erun Cade approached warily along the sand strewn road, the Castle of Winds began to reveal its secrets.

There were no windows visible. He could see no arrow slits, murder holes, or even parapets and crenulations in view. The only light came from a small round hole at the very top of the highest tower. Tower was a loose term. More like a jagged spike; it thrust out from the main rock at an impossible angle and spiralled upward like frozen lightning.

It didn't make any sense. A maze of grey granite tinted with rose-pink quartz, the castle (if that was what it was) squatted upon sea-washed bedrock, towering over the surrounding ocean like a bloated legless spider. Unravelling within its mass was a twisting contortion of random wall and tangled roofs, almost impossible to discern. To Erun Cade, the Castle of Winds appeared totally alien—fashioned by a mad god in millennia gone by.

But then no sane mortal ventured near this place. Somewhere high up in that jungle of spiralling peaks dwelt the castle's lone occupant—if one were to discount the creature, Borz (the reason why he had been sent here.) Just why he had so readily agreed back then, Erun Cade now had no notion. Scaffa's ways were ever beguiling. There was something impossible about that big woman—he just couldn't refuse her when she pinned him with those scary eyes. And so here he was, and wishing he was anywhere else.

Best get on with it.

Mind full of misgivings, Erun walked on, hand on sword hilt and eyes squinting in the sun. It was already very hot and he was sweating profusely. He stopped for a minute, wiped his brow so he could better survey the way ahead, and once satisfied continued on.

The cobbled road leading down to the castle gates was washed by waves on either side, but this wasn't a causeway like the one leading to Castle Barola. This craggy horn was the southernmost tip of Sarfania Province. It ran barren and bleak for many miles—a crooked dagger of reed and marsh; treacherous and remote, until finally narrowing like a spear tip into this rocky sea-soaked track. Hovering in the haze beyond was the bizarre tangle of coloured rock called the Castle of Winds.

Weirdest of all was the sound emanating from that leviathan of stone. It came from somewhere deep within the castle's heart, and reached Erun's ears, setting his teeth on edge—even at that distance. A horrible sound, high in pitch—as though a puppy's cries had been crossed with the mournful sighing of a forgotten kettle. What caused such a din, Erun couldn't begin to guess. But it certainly wasn't encouraging.

He was still a good few miles distant but aware that any watching from that high place would mark his approach before too long. It was time to apply subterfuge. Part of the plan. Her plan—

not his. Erun was still questioning why he was here.

Erun stopped again and fumbled in his bag, his keen eyes never leaving those chaotic walls. Erun gulped as he vainly tried to take in the monstrosity dominating the horizon. He now questioned his sanity, journeying to this awful place. But then Scaffa could be very persuasive when the mood was on her. And at the time, and after a fresh dose of Laras Lassladden's magic, he'd been quite enthused. But not now he could see the nature of the place he'd soon have to enter.

Erun unravelled the long cloak she'd given him before his departure. It was a shabby affair—all tears and tatters. He draped it over his shoulders despite the ghastly humidity.

"There is sorcery sewn within these folds," Scaffa had informed him back on the island. "It will conceal you from the Aralais." This *Aralais* apparently was a very odd creature. A mad deranged wizard—immortal and torn by bitterness concerning some ancient event, hence not the perfect host. The Wizard of the Winds, most called him in this vicinity, and kept a safe distance from his home. The only dwellings Erun had seen were fishers' hovels and that was three days past.

Ships feared him most, apparently. This Aralais fellow (Erun had no real notion who the Aralais were but obviously they must have been unpleasant) had long held sway over the weather in this region (which was tricky enough without his meddling) Out of pure malice, this warlock character was known to have often lured vessels to their ruin on his rocky cliffs surrounding his castle. Why? Erun didn't care as he wasn't in a ship.

The Wind Elemental this Aralais had captured and now controlled would batter them for days, forcing the traders and galleys and skiffs shoreward to their grief, perhaps for no other reason than perverse pleasure at the terror and woe he caused. Some sailors occasionally survived the wreckage, but once ashore were soon enmeshed in the weirdness of the castle and never seen again.

Erun pulled the deep hood down over his head as much to dull the awful noise as anything. It was much louder now—almost a child's scream. It battered his senses and he had to steel his nerves before taking the next shaky step forward.

The road zigzagged across to the castle like the twisted broken spine of some long dead sea monster. A difficult path to negotiate and dangerously narrow, it crooked twenty feet above the crashing white spume of wave and sea.

The road was scarce two feet wide in places, with no rail and treacherous under foot. Weed coated the slippery cobbles of its surface, and in places there were wide gaps where the sea surged through below in eager eddies and whirls. These Erun had to jump, and somehow keep his balance on landing—not easy with a sword strapped across your back, a harp and flapping bag tied to your belt; not to mention the worn mail shirt and long wet manky cloak. Despite all this clutter and his gloomy thoughts weighing him down, Erun Cade made fair progress.

Erun could see the gate now—if that were the right word for such an entrance. It was more akin to a yawning, grotesque mouth. The stones encircling it were painted garish red—like the lips of some cheap Lamozan whore. Within showed no teeth. Only gloom. It wasn't remotely enticing.

Closer now, the high whistle stinging his ears like angry bees, Erun Cade could see that there were steps of some sort leading up from the road to that gaping, horrible mouth. They were cut into the rock face and looked worn and dangerous. Erun pulled the cloak tighter across his chest and fingered the long hilt of his sword. The creature he'd come for existed somewhere inside that awful place.

Borz. A wind spirit or 'Elemental' as Irulan had called them back in that cave a million years ago. Somehow (Erun had no notion as to how) he was to steal this *thing* from the mad bad Aralais wizard within. It had seemed highly plausible back there on Laras Lassladden.

But that had been three long weeks ago. Today Erun's task looked ridiculously impossible. But he had sworn to carry it out— idiot that he was. Erun had promised *her* this Borz creature—quite why he couldn't remember. But then that was *so* Laras Lassladden. The upshot was, he had best get to it.

Almost an hour later he reached the bottom step.

Erun scanned the way up with a miserable forlorn expression. Those 'steps' looked all but impassable to anything that didn't have suckers on its feet. Somehow he would manage—or else plunge to his ruin on the black shiny rock below.

Erun felt suddenly very weary, worn down by heavy garb and the thought of his impending climb and daunting task ahead. A short rest was needed, then he'd have his strength back.

Erun unfastened the longsword from his back and leaned back against the wet rock, letting the surge and sigh of wave and breeze calm his fraying nerves. Erun yawned and scratched his old scar, which was now itching in the sticky heat.

He covered his ears from the awful racket above and closed his eyes for a short time, summoning calm—a knack he'd learned from Rakaro during those months spent overseas. As he rested his aching bones, Erun cast his mind back over the last three weeks, starting with his panicked return to Laras Lassladden.

***

Scaffa's bewitching Island had appeared different again on his return from Xandoria. This time there were no dark cliffs in view. Instead Erun was greeted by wide sweeping bays, and lazy palms fanned welcome shade over hot sandy paths.

Scaffa had been waiting for him, her long supple curves displayed wondrously in a green-gold, mermaid tight dress. Her pale yellow locks were braided back in thick cords, and her big eyes heavily kohled in aquamarine. Erun recalled how his loins had stirred at the sight of her near naked body (she always had this effect on him—he'd never been one for large woman before.) Those tanned sinewy legs, the sweet (and copious) curve of breast and hip—all enticing but forbidden. She was such a tease.

As before, Scaffa both terrified and aroused him: a giantess true, but a beautiful, wickedly sensual one, whether dressed in her customary armour or (much more so) as on that sultry day garbed in feminine wear.

As Erun dozed on his perch, he remembered how he had

spilled out the woeful news concerning Ashmali and the horrific ruin of Lamoza City. He'd voiced his fears that this Ozmandeus nutter and his pet demon would one day cross the isthmus, bringing similar ruin to Gol.

Scaffa, serene as summer skies, had not responded to his words. Instead she'd bid him follow her up a sandy track that threaded lazy between the palms, and then led up to a cool, hidden cave in a wall of rock. Once within its gloomy confines Scaffa had spoken to Erun of his task.

The first of three he would have to undergo.

"I can see that your months abroad have served their purpose," she told him, her voice a husky whisper in the dark. "Now it's time to put your new skills to use, my little protégé. Follow me." She had then led him deeper into the cavern until they reached a wide, mirror-smooth pool, its silent still waters lit by burning rushes that flickered and cast dancing shadows far out across the water.

Erun remembered how entranced he'd felt as he had watched that tranquil water. "Where is this uncanny place?" he had asked her back then.

"It is nowhere you could mark on a map," Scaffa answered. "A place between worlds—just another aspect of my island realm. Laras Lassladden shifts through space and time. I had thought you'd realised that, bright boy that you are." She'd then lifted a burning rush from its bracket on a wall of rock, and urged him follow her down to the coppery coloured water below. "Three important tasks do I have for you, young Erun Cade," Scaffa informed him as she ran her long cool fingers through the crystalline surface of the water.

"I have cast aside that name," Erun had told her then. He'd been trying to impress and no longer liked being called young. "I am called Kell now—a warrior's name given me by a friend. It means—"

"Yes, I know what it means." Scaffa curled her lip in the closest thing to a girlish grin he'd ever seen from her. "You will need all the *skill* that you can muster to survive the weeks ahead—warrior."

She rose smoothly and loomed over him—her eyes now like silver moons probing deep inside him.

"Look over here." Scaffa held the torch aloft so that it spilled flickering light on an adjacent wall. There were artefacts on the wall. Various objects of strange shapes and colours, many difficult to define.

"What are those?" Erun had enquired. There were all manner of curios bolted to that wall, varying from outlandish garments, to weapons—and even a golden lyre of weird eldritch beauty. Erun's harp-deft fingers had twitched when he'd seen that beautiful instrument. It had been a while since last he'd played Irulan's gift, what with all his hurried travels and such.

"A few concern you," Scaffa had told him. "Most do not." She'd then reached for a shabby looking cloak (the one he sweated under now) and unfastened it from its wall hanger. "This should prove useful, methinks," Scaffa had said whilst Erun had pulled a face and grumbled. That battered cloak was the very least impressive article in that fine collection. Scaffa had ignored him. "While clad in this cloak you are invisible to mortal eyes—and more importantly—protected from sorcery."

"Sorcery..?" He'd seen more than enough sorcery back in Lamoza.

She'd turned to face him at that point. Her eyes had narrowed when they met his, and Erun remembered how he had recoiled from that fathomless gaze that had darkened to polished slate. Fear, dread and arousal: she played his emotions like Erun played his harp. "Irulan has told you of the Elementals—the beings that dwelt in Gol and beyond, long before the noisome coming of mankind drove them far away."

"He did," Erun had nodded. It was at that moment that he should have stopped her, but then that hadn't occurred to him at the time. "Ashmali the Fire Demon is one such creature, is it not?"

"He is by far the greatest of those still living," Scaffa had responded then. "There are few left now, and only three linger in this region of Ansu—against their wish. It is these other three Elementals that concern us," she had said.

"To stop Ashmali we will need the combined power of all the other elements: wind, earth, and water. Or as you will come to know them: Borz, Tertzei, and Aqueous."

"And these creatures I am to find and bring back to Laras Lassladden?" It hadn't even seemed difficult he now recalled morosely. *Damn you, Scaffa.*

"Indeed so," she had replied. "But that finding and bringing back here could prove rather challenging. I trust that you are up to the tasks?"

"Of course," he'd answered like the idiot he was, and Scaffa had smiled at his confidence back there in the cave. Erun wasn't even slightly confident now, sitting and melting on this wet slippery rock with that horrendous shrieking still assaulting his ears.

"There will be a reward should you return with all three Elementals safely contained," Scaffa had added, and her wicked eyes had hinted as to what manner of award that would be. Erun recalled miserably how his loins had stirred again. The only reward that seemed likely at the moment was an abrupt and most likely unpleasant demise.

"Tertzei and Aqueous will concern you later," she'd said. "First Borz—air. You must steal him from under the nose of his master."

"His master—another sorcerer..?"

"Not like Ozmandeus of Zorne—so don't fret." (Erun hadn't back then but he was making up for it now.) "But yes, an enchanter of sorts. An Aralais Wizard from far across the ocean." She'd then reached across to where an old rusty sword rested on a frame on the shadowy wall.

"This is Callanak, an ancient glaive forged by the Aralais race millennia ago. It will be effective against Borz's captor should you be unlucky and encounter him. I would advise stealth, however—in an out quickly, that's best. "

"It looks a bit battered," Erun had said, surveying the old weapon with a disapproving eye.

"Looks mean little when sorcery is involved," she'd dismissed his protestations. "This blade was fashioned with Earth-Magic on a distant continent. It's forged from a kind of crystal—much harder than steel. And a lot sharper too."

Erun had watched then, as Scaffa ran a long finger down the length of the blade and, at her touch, the rust powdered and fell away to dust. The sword now glittered in the rush light impressively. Blade, hilt and crossguard were of a bluish smoky texture, the sword was nearly five feet long from tip to heavy pommel.

"This sword was once owned by Torro—an Aralais king in an age long gone by. No steel blade will sever the witchy bonds that constrict Borz. But Callanak will. Here... take it." Erun had reached across and grabbed the leather-bound hilt with both hands. He had groaned as he felt how heavy it was.

"It's somewhat weighty," Erun had complained.

Scaffa had nodded. "They were mighty, those Golden Aralais, before the long war with their dark cousins wore them down. But that tale is for another time."

"And where do I find this Borz creature?" Erun had asked while strapping the heavy sword to his back with the broad, black steel-studded leather harness, and scabbard that accompanied the weapon.

"Trapped within the maze that is the Castle of Winds, in distant Sarfania," she had answered. "You will journey by boat and horse over land and sea, speaking not a word of your quest to any on the way.

"A hundred miles south of Reveal—where reside Baron Sarfe and his family—that humid swampy country funnels into a long, narrowing finger of rock. The Aralais's influence can be felt even at this distance, so you will need to be wary. You must continue on foot for the last stretch. No beast will bear you far down that road without becoming dangerously twitchy. Should you return here with Borz tied safe within his bag I will be waiting with details concerning your second venture."

"What of my vengeance?" Erun had demanded then. "I've still a score to settle with House Barola."

"In good time..."

Erun recalled how Scaffa had faded from view after saying

that; just dissolved before his eyes, as had the cave and pool of water below. How she achieved that was something he couldn't grasp—particularly now, sitting on this rock. But then nothing was normal for Erun Cade any more.

He blamed it on Irulan. Ever since he'd met that sly old mock hermit his life had turned cartwheels. And who were these bloody people? And why choose him for their antics? But then nothing was simple anymore. Everything had got jumbled up—and here he was. Erun remembered how Laras Lassladden too had, like a mirage, slipped away. Banished by cracking thunder and blinding light. He recalled falling through space for long, weird moments... spinning, down and down.

When, after an age, the falling stopped, Erun had opened his eyes to discover himself at sea—sick and giddy and soaked through, sprawled akimbo like a landed squid on the creaking timber deck of a lurching ship, somewhere far out across the ocean. His only companion a dour old mariner stubbornly manning the tiller, his features hooded and cloaked—almost invisible.

But Erun had glimpsed just enough of the pilot's grim visage to recognise the old ferryman who had borne him to Laras Lassladden from Northtown. Another player in this game.

Erun, despite his grumblings, was becoming accustomed to the mysteries concerning Scaffa and her world. Since returning from Xandoria he had reluctantly come to accept that he was part of that mystery too. Besides, back then, with belly heaving and dancing head, it didn't do to dwell on such stuff. But he was dwelling on it now.

He recalled how some time later (Erun had no notion as how long he'd been on board—too long, was all he knew) the creaky tub had beached on the reedy marsh that heralded the Sarfanian coast.

Armed with the huge sword, Callanak—he'd left his other weapons behind, as they would have been too much to carry, and anyway, Scaffa had told him that they would prove useless and just be an encumbrance to him. (He had brought his harp, though, to keep him sane on the trek ahead.)

Erun remembered leaping ashore and clambering across the

reedy dunes. He'd looked back once, watched for a moment as pilot and craft were swallowed by the heavy mist that clung to that reedy shoreline. Mist and fog: fog and mist.

Like everything in my life.

Erun's eyes opened: all around him was sea and surge. He must have dozed off for a while. He stretched and yawned and again cast his mind back to his voyage south through Sarfania Province. That dreary road had cut through swamp and fen for mile upon mile, with mournful birds his only companions.

Each day the leaden sun would torment him, darkening to cruellest crimson at evening, and flooding the horizon before finally sinking far beyond this desolate land. And each day passing proved hotter and stickier than the last. The slow, tortuous miles dragging on, and his horse (a healthy palfrey bought with Xandorian coin from a villager near the coast) lathering nosily beneath him.

Erun Cade had wondered how any human could stand living in this sticky climate. Not to mention the flies that had constantly swarmed and buzzed about his head from dawn to dusk. At least he was free of those now. After leaving that village with his new horse and saddlery, Erun had encountered no one. Except on that afternoon when he came upon the riders.

Erun had reached a clearing and saw them at the other end. He'd reined in, eyes wary. Two riders: they sat their horses in silence, their faces shaded beneath the arms of a large willow—perhaps thirty feet away. A man and a woman, both richly dressed.

The man had the hawk-nosed look of a warrior. He sat his horse with confident ease and waited for Erun to approach. His skin was the colour of polished mahogany and his eyes, nut brown and razor sharp. The warrior appeared of an age with Erun, though he could have been a year or two older.

The woman was veiled: her face hidden, but her small be-ringed hands were pale in striking comparison with the man's. She gripped the reins tightly and stared across at Erun. Her stiff manner and poise bespoke unease and a guarded anger—obviously some stuck-up noble's daughter, Erun recalled thinking at the time.

Her escort had urged his horse forward after whispering

something in her ear. She had nodded curtly and watched on in uncomfortable silence, as her beau briskly urged his mount across to where Erun Cade waited with cool dispassion.

The nobleman had reined in a few yards short, his dark eyes locked on Erun's blue grey. "Stranger;" the voice was rich and confident and stank of aristocracy. Erun had felt his fingers itching for the sword strapped across his back. He hadn't moved though, and gave nothing away. "What business have you here?" The man's look had been far from friendly.

Erun recalled how he'd straightened in his saddle, spoiling for a fight. "My business is my own," he'd answered curtly. "Leave me be... friend."

His challenger had then slid a curved sword out from its silk scabbard with one smooth fluid motion. He was bloody quick—Erun had noted that. He hadn't risen to the bait, though. *Keep the bastard guessing.*

"You are trespassing here," the noble had pressed. "These lands belong to Reveal Castle, the home of Baron Sarfe. Methinks, you're here to spy on us...friend." He'd then flicked the blade casually toward Erun's face with cold provocation. "Did Black Torlock send you—I wonder? Or was it Sophistra Bitch-face herself? Well...?" He'd let the blade hover in front of Erun's face. But the Barolan hadn't flinched and that evidently vexed him "Answer, stranger, my patience wains."

"I know of no Black Torlock," Erun had responded, his gaze now icy and measuring his accuser's, whilst watching the rhythmic movement of the sword tip, ready for any sudden shift. "And I am no spy, either—just a traveller faring south."

"South...?" The rider hadn't swallowed that. "None sane venture that way," he'd said.

"And yet that is my destination." Erun had wondered if he was going to have to kill this nobleman. He'd hoped not, what with his leman watching on and screaming at him. "I'll soon be gone from your country," he had told the warrior. "Let me pass."

The other had shaken his head slowly. "I wonder at your words, stranger," he'd said. Erun had noticed how the woman was looking on intently, "you're clearly not Galanian," his accuser had seemed puzzled about something. "Were that so, then I'd have gutted you here and now. Pray tell me, where is your home, far wanderer? What brings you to my country?"

"I have no home," Erun had responded "But I have important business and my destination lies south. I'll not tarry here longer."

The rider had smiled then as one would at a simple child. He'd turned back to the silent woman who still glared behind her veil. "He's riding south!" the Sarfanian had called across to her and she'd shaken her head as if disbelieving. "You are a fool, traveller, or else mad," the rider had turned on his saddle to address Erun again. "None of sound mind fare far in that direction."

"And yet that is my way," Erun had answered.

The rider had thought for a minute and then shrugged as he made his decision. "Well, carry on then, friend," he had said. "But take heed, you are riding to your death. That said, you have my leave to pass—and should any other question your passage, tell them that Estorien Sarfe has given you permission to cross through these lands. I can see that you are no Galanian spy...and oddly I trust you. Though I've no notion why. But there is something... familiar about you. What name go you by?"

"Some call me Kell."

"A strange name for a strange man. No matter." The noble had raised his palm then. "Farewell then, Sir Kell, and good luck—you will need it. I doubt we'll meet a second time."

Erun had returned the gesture and left them behind without further ado. That had proven a strange encounter. He'd heard of Estorien Sarfe, a great champion of the Torvosan Games in recent years apparently. He seemed far too honourable and likeable to be a baron's son—despite his initial hostility towards Erun. Perhaps things were different in Sarfania. It would have been a shame to have killed him back there.

Erun again wondered who the woman had been; there had been something alluring about her he couldn't grasp. Estorien had said he'd looked familiar. Erun had no idea why but then the mystery woman had seemed familiar to him. She had looked so beguiling beneath that veil. That long lissom body had caught his eye too, as she sat her horse with stiff unease. Just another mystery. Nothing new there. Erun hadn't dwelt on the matter. Doubtless she had been some grand lady. A Sarfanian beauty. That Estorien Sarfe was a lucky fellow.

An hour later Erun had forgotten the encounter in the woods, focussing instead on guiding his palfrey round the copious sticky mires and tangles of mangrove that everywhere hemmed that muddy, fly-cursed road.

The day arrived when his horse started shying and kicking up a fuss.

I must be getting close.

Erun had slipped from the saddle, patted the beast's sweating back and freed him from his bridle. Within moments the relieved palfrey's hoof beats thudded into fading distance back whence they came. That had been a low point—seeing the horse canter off. He'd continued on foot. That had been a week ago.

His lids closed and Erun felt his mind drifting. He dozed awhile longer.

Chapter 8

Borz

When the shrieking wail suddenly ceased Erun Cade opened his eyes. *Shit. How long have I been asleep?* It seemed so deathly quiet now after that awful din. The sea frothed all around him; its warm briny touch had dampened his boots where he had been dozing just above its reach.

Tide's rising fast—I'd best get moving.

Erun slapped his face to wake himself up. He pulled the cloak tighter around his frame, and then clasped it at the front with its wooden toggle buttons. The thing was a sack of shit but never mind. *As long as it does the job.* The cumbersome sword he re-slung across his back alongside his bag—supplied for Borz's capture.

Here we go. Erun reached the first step. It was more like a cut in the rock face, six inches in depth and just wider than his foot. A hand hold showed above.

He started climbing...reaching up...stepping and trying not to slip. That climb must have taken over an hour, and Erun was panting when at last he heaved his bruised body onto the rocky plinth that stretched across to the castle's ghastly mouth.

Erun, while getting his breath back, scanned the area for any sign of life. He saw nothing but wasn't reassured. This place gave him the creeps. It felt *wrong*, the atmosphere both menacing and tense. As if he was expected. There was no wind, not even a sea breeze to ease the stifling heat, and the only sound came from the sea itself, now far beneath him and spilling like cream on the dark rock below.

Erun rose from a stiff crouch, checked that cloak and hood covered his entirety, and then silently slid the heavy blade free of its scabbard. Hidden by his cloak, and with both sweaty palms locked around the hilt of his weapon, Erun Cade strode toward that yawning mouth, his heart thudding and his buzzing head full of trepidation. Erun shivered when he stepped beneath that mouth, despite the humid warmth.

Ahead were only gloom and silence and still that watchful menace. Erun took a step forward.

"You must ignore shapes and sounds," Scaffa had told him back in the comfort of that cave. "Keep heading for the middle of the castle; avoid stairs leading off to the right. Climb those that head left, they will lead up to the tower where Borz is contained."

"How do you know all this?" Erun had asked her but he'd received no answer. Instead she had told him about the bag (or rune-sack, to quote its technical name) he was to use to trap the Elemental. "This is bound with spell-runes," Scaffa told him, "and once tied he'll not escape unless you permit it."

"How do I catch him?" Erun had asked and Scaffa had smiled in return.

"That," she had replied, "is the interesting bit." When she informed him just how, Erun's eyes had widened in disbelief, and now that that uncomfortable moment was looming he again heartily wished he were anywhere else.

Too late...

The walls lining the castle interior looked almost organic, their surfaces ribbed and veined and the colours (even in that gloom) were garish and surreal. Erun felt queasy as he walked. It was though he was inside the stomach of some alien creature—and perhaps he was.

Discipline...Stay your mind. Keep going and don't stop.
Erun stoically kept his mind closed to the endless questions assaulting it. Instead he concentrated hard on moving forward with wary steps, until he reached the first stairs that led left. These spiralled up with sickening circles. There was no rail, and the treads shuddered and quivered beneath Erun as his steel-shod feet sank into them, leaving a soft moan after he raised his heels again. He steeled his nerves once more.

I am not enjoying this. Erun continued up and up, finally reaching another mouth-like door at the top. This one led deeper into the castle gloom. He willed his body forward. Eventually it became so dark that Erun began to suspect he'd had been swallowed alive.

Keep going, don't stop. More stairs led off right—these Erun avoided. Strange murmurings echoed around him, and every second he had the feeling of being watched by some evil.

Erun stopped. A long shadow now stained the wall to his left. Where had that come from? Erun moved on, forcing his knees to bend. He noticed with alarm that the shadow moved with him, and stopped when he stopped. But it wasn't his shadow. It was much too large, and besides, its long fingers were clawed and curved. Erun was sure those claws were getting nearer.

He turned. Nothing... Then something whispered in his ear. Erun muttered an obscenity. He walked on, stubbornly ignoring both voice and shadow, though every nerve in his body urged him to run.

Erun now made briskly for the next flight of stairs leading off left. Three more dizzy flights and three more shadowy passageways brought him at last to that final lofty place. A door barred his way—the first real door he'd encountered. Erun Cade spoke the words Scaffa had bid him recite. The lock shattered to powder and he stole nervously within. Borz the Elemental was waiting...

***

Erun's first impression was one of dazzling blinding white light. His eyes stung at the sudden glare as the door opened into a whirring, dizzy explosion of brightness. Erun pulled his hood down hard and low. He took a tentative step into the light and then another. Erun continued forward, straining his eyes and urging them adjust from the gloom they had become accustomed to.

Then, after he had groped blindly for five minutes (and despite that room's blurring shifting motion) Erun's eyes made out something ahead. It was no more than a twisting whirl of light, flickering across to him from the far end of the chamber. But Erun recognised it for what it was.

Borz...

He strode toward the whirring source of light, sword in right hand and rune-sack in left. *Let's get this over with...*

It was vaguely triangular in shape: a spinning contortion of shrieking light. Drawing near at last, Erun Cade recognised the wailing voice that had heralded his approach to the castle. His eyes struggled to lock onto it as the Elemental's shape shifted constantly.

He staggered nearer, determined, his left arm held out before his face, the sack shielding his aching eyes from that glare, and his right palm squeezing hard on the hilt of the heavy sword. As Erun loomed close to the shimmering whirl it slowed just enough for him to discern its shape.

Borz was vaguely human in appearance—in as much as it had limbs and a torso. The thing's legs and arms were so entwined Erun couldn't hazard a guess at which bit belonged to what. The Elemental's naked skin gleamed silvery in hue, but it was the quicksilver of shifting metals, and it was from here that the light radiated out.

Borz's face (if he had one) was hidden by a tangled shock of spiky hair—bluish in colour like freshly polished steel. Erun could just see—now that his eyes had fully adjusted—that the being's bare feet were held fast by cords that appeared as writhing serpents.

The Elemental writhed and bucked as though in torment and, as Erun approached, he could see now that Borz was held down by sorcery—an evanescent substance that floated several feet above the plinth where he was held fast. Erun froze. Then Borz began wailing again and, as he screamed this time, his shape twisted and whirred into a vortex of spinning motion.

The sound was so awful at this close proximity that it drained all the colour from Erun Cade's face, and almost sent him scampering back for the door—now lost somewhere behind him. Somehow Erun quelled the panic threatening to unman him. He took a slow, long breath, and addressed the Elemental with the words he had prepared.

"Greeting, Borz, child of Air." Erun's voice sounded muffled and faint—almost a whisper. "I come from Scaffa, who you know and will free you for a price."

This was what she had told him to say and it worked, for Borz had ceased writhing and was suddenly quiet. The head turned toward him then, and Erun felt the full force of that weird, alien face searching for him—the cloak keeping his exact location hidden.

Borz's features were triangular, with upswept ears and narrow chin. His ageless face was dominated by huge yellow eyes and gaping toothless mouth. That mouth yawned wider and a force of air hit Erun, lifting his body and hurling him back for several yards, before dropping him like discarded offal on the hard floor.

Borz shrieked again. Erun rolled on impact, kept his sword free of his crashing limbs, and then angrily struggled to his feet again. Cloak wrapped tight about his shoulders, Erun tried again.

Now you've pissed me off.

Borz's yellow eyes were scanning for him everywhere, his round ugly mouth stretching huge as it shot forth gusts of lethal wind across the chamber. Erun dodged and danced through that chaotic tumult until he was again within reach of the Elemental. And sensing Erun's approach, Borz wailed again, this time it was all that Erun could manage to cover his ears from the agonising ululation, and wait miserably in frozen silence for Borz to shut up. Mercifully it did.

"Who dares intrude upon us?" The voice when it came was like a thousand hissing serpents. Erun had heard nothing like it before.

"I am called Kell the Warrior," he answered, as though that would impress such an oddity as this Borz. But it was worth a try.

"I am come here to free you from your confinement—for a price." Erun shook the rune-sack so that it opened out.

"Thou art mortal—small love have our kind for yours. Why should I not tear you asunder with my breath, intruder? Why should I trust you?" Borz's eyes had narrowed to amber slits of hatred. They flicked across the room as they tried to pin the exact location where this bold impostor stood.

Erun, with sword and sack ready, took a slow step slow forward. He locked his gaze on the whirring fusion of light that enclosed the serpent cords writhing at the spirit's feet. "Scaffa sent me," he said again. "The Queen of Death wishes you no harm, Borz. All she requires is that you help us stave off your reckless brother, Ashmali. After that you will be freed—I promise."

On the mention of his brother's name Borz's eyes narrowed to slits. *"Why would I aid you against our own kin? Ashmali I do not love, but why should I care if he rends the world, I have no love for it anymore..."* Borz's whiny voice trailed off then as a new sound entered the white giddy atmosphere of the chamber. It was the heavy sound of footfalls approaching from behind. Borz's eyes widened then and his mouth betrayed what might have been a malicious smile, were it from human lips. *"He approaches...you are trapped, foolish mortal. He will steal your soul away and suck the essence from your bones. Look... HE IS COMING!"*

The footfalls were louder now, heavy and slow. Erun, on the verge of panic, turned wide-eyed with sword ready. It was the shadow of a tall man that he saw—nothing else. There was no substance—just creeping shadow and thud of heavy tread. The shadow manifested, stealing shape from the light in the chamber. Erun, watching in horror, could see the dust motes rise up from the movement of those invisible feet.

The Aralais!

What followed then made no sense. Even much later when he had the time to think about it, Erun couldn't comprehend what actually had transpired in that baroque castle. Suffice it to say that he sliced Callanak wide—cut the bonds from the Elemental's feet, and those serpents curled and died as the sword sliced through.

Erun then hurled the open rune-sack over Borz's head and yanked down tight until the Elemental's screaming, shifting shape vanished within. Erun yelled the spellbinding words taught him by his giantess mentor. Borz writhed and kicked in fury but the runes held fast. Within seconds of Erun wording the enchantment the stitching had completely knitted, and now contained Borz trapped inside.

Phew...

But then the shadow loomed over him, its long claw-like fingers reaching out. Erun didn't hesitate as fresh adrenaline rushed through his veins. He swung the blade hard around in a wide searching arc, and then shuddered as the old steel bit deep into the sickly thud of warm flesh.

Got you!

A deep voice groaned close to his right shoulder and Erun gagged at the reek of fetid breath smothering his face. He tugged the sword free and swung hard again—another moan.

Erun hacked and cut, again and again, until something heavy thudded to the floor. The shadow had disappeared. Instead Erun gazed down at the headless handless corpse of what had been a tall, elegant looking man. Erun gaped at the corpse for a moment— there was blood everywhere.

The Aralais's dead face was noble. He'd expected a monster, not those clean patrician features and high clear brow. His dead eyes glared up at Erun like raging sapphire disks. Those eyes narrowed, and Erun realised in horror that the Wizard of the Winds was still alive. Erun felt the vengeful menace of that gaze working upon him now, his knees trembled and he struggled to hold his heavy sword whilst almost dropping Borz's sack. *Time to leave.* But his legs wouldn't work.

Then one of the severed hands jerked twice, bunched, and hopped horribly. Erun looked at it mournfully. This wasn't good news. The-long nailed fingers were now spidering towards him. Clicketty click. Tapperty tap. Scrape hop scrape.

This is not happening.

The hand shot up—clutched Erun's leg hard and squeezed.

Fuck! Erun gasped in pain as that grip tightened like corded wire. Horrified, he noticed that the torso of the wizard was coming back to life as well—that just left the head gaping at him over there. Erun shuddered, somehow he wrenched free from that iron grip. He kicked the clawing hand aside and then turned; rammed his blade point first into the Aralais's head, right between his eyes.

The scream was horrible and seemed to last forever—and that made worse by Borz's accompanying wailing inside the rune-sack.

Erun ran: heedless of anything but a wild manic desire to win free of the Aralais's castle. Somehow he willed his exhausted limbs to carry him, and barely controlling the terror that now threatened to engulf him, Erun fled the chamber with Borz in tow. All the while the sack tugged and bucked in his left palm as its virulent occupant tried to win free. He ran, closing his ears to the dreadful noise of the dying Aralais and the disgruntled, wailing, Borz.

Erun Cade could never quite recall how he eventually won free from the Castle of Winds. That harrowing, headlong flight might have taken an hour or a month—he couldn't tell. But at last (and just as his legs were about to buckle beneath him) Erun gained the passage leading out beneath that yawning mouth, and rushed to embrace the most welcome blues of summer sky and sea.

Erun slipped and tumbled down the foot holds—Callanak across his back and the sack tied to his belt. Incredibly he made the road without breaking any bones, and, after the briefest pause to get some strength back, Erun began jogging back along the broken spine, his aching legs carrying him away from the castle and its dying lone inhabitant.

Erun stopped only once, when the sound of thunder hitting rocks behind turned his head. A mile behind him now, the tumbled mass of confusion that had recently been the Castle of Winds had just fallen in on itself. Erun saw it implode and collapse to powder and dust, and then watched as its haphazard walls crumbled and fell, and were swallowed up by the churning ocean at its feet.

As Erun watched in stunned silence he witnessed the last dying groans of the Aralais wizard as his castle sunk from view. Then were only bubbles and eddying wave and spume. The Castle of Winds was no more. Erun Cade turned away at that point. He tore the cloak free, and now less encumbered, hastened back along the track.

Some days later Erun took passage on a ship bound north for Galanais and, from there on up to Treggara. Once there Erun stole a horse from a farmer and rode like a mad thing for Northtown and the Island where, once again, Scaffa was waiting for him with news of his next task. It wasn't encouraging and he got no thanks either.

**

The lone rider watched from his hide as the horde spilled like lice falling from a rotting log through the Lamozan Gap, contaminating the grasslands of the Xandorian plain below. Ankai knew they should have listened to Rakaro. His uncle had warned of this last winter, but the others (especially Toskai) had laughed him off.

And then Rakaro had disappeared after freeing that pale-eyed prisoner—the one that had put up such a fight. And now the invaders had arrived east of the mountains, and in such numbers too.

Ankai shielded his dark eyes from the noonday sun as the horde continued to spew infection into the green below. He was hidden in the woods flanking the foothills, scarce two miles north, and had a commanding view of the wide lands beyond.

Ankai sat his fidgety pony: he watched for an hour. Two. Still they came. It was an army of ten thousand at least. All clad in black and dun and silent as gravestones as they marched. Only the van rode horses, and these grim captains held aloft streaming gonfalons of sable and red—the colours of Zorne and the emblems of the sorcerer, Ozmandeus.

Ankai had heard of this Ozmandeus—everyone had. And of the horrors he had perpetrated in the west lands—these were legendary now. They said he had control of fire itself, or a demon, or maybe both—nobody really knew. Certainly the rumours of Lamozan ruin had sent a wave of fear throughout the Xandorian plains. It was these stories—mostly carried on the lips of fleeing merchants and refugees—that had persuaded Ankai to go see for himself.

And here he was, and it wasn't a pretty scene unravelling

down there on the plain. Ankai now saw that the leaders had turned south and were hugging the mountains, just below the timber line. They were making for Xenn City—that much was obvious. At least that meant that Ankai's people would be safe for the time being. Let the Emperor deal with the invaders if he can, the Hillmen would steer well clear and watch and wait the outcome. That outcome was already a foregone conclusion in Ankai's opinion. Relieved, Ankai motioned his pony out from their hide. He must away and inform the others. But then something stopped him, and beneath him the pony trembled in sudden fear. Ankai fingered his bow and sweated. He now had the nasty sensation of biting ants crawling all along his spine.

Ankai turned in his saddle, and gazing back noticed that a single rider had now ridden free of the van. This rider sat on his horse only a mile below where Ankai sweated beneath the shade of tall pines. He had the weirdest feeling that this rider—cloaked and hooded in midnight cloth—was staring straight at him and could read his mind.

Ankai shuddered, feeling the baleful power of that gaze. The air around him had become very hot, he noticed. There was something wrong here. Ankai knew somehow that the sudden scorching heat was radiating across from that rider—impossible yet true.

Then he gasped in alarm as a lofty pine, some twenty feet away, blazed into raging flame right before his eyes. Sorcery—this stank of sorcery! A second blast made Ankai lurch in his saddle and he saw another tree explode into a fireball. Then a third caught, its tinder limbs crackling bright and yellow—and on and on.

In seconds the whole copse was ablaze, the rich, sickly stench of resin clung to his nostrils, threatening to choke him. Ankai didn't hesitate a moment longer. It was past time to go. Within minutes rider and pony had won free of the blazing forest and had vanished north; the dust kicking up behind the pony's drumming hoofs.

Much later, Ankai dared to look back. The whole forest was a furnace and the sable army had vanished beyond the veil of smoke. That night he spoke of what he'd seen and wished that Rakaro was with him.

Chapter 9

The Quarrel

Jerrel had been dreading this interview. There was something about the Chatelaine that left him cold inside. He was a fighting man used to soldiers and their bluff coarse ways. Not for him the intricate and often lethal nuances of courtroom life.

So he'd always steered clear out of choice. Left that side to Black Torlock, his mentor and senior, whose jaded character was much more suited to deal with those palace whispers—colder and sharper by far than daggers.

Until now. Now it was different and Jerrel could no longer watch on, he was involved and wasn't sure how that left him.

Jerrel's military world had changed with Prince Gallante's murder. Black Torlock—now styled Lord Protector—had approached his second last week. Just a month had passed since Hal Gallante's nefarious demise. Jerrel had had his suspicious but dare not voice them. You had to be wary around Torlock too. The Protector had his own quarters in the palace now, close by Sophistra's. It was so he could 'protect' her from insurgents, or so Torlock claimed—fooling no one.

But what did that matter? Torlock was the real power in

Galanais now, the former champion was the queen's darling and though Varentin ruled in name, none were deluded about the real power over palace, citadel and city.

And Jerrel stood to gain by this new shift of power. Hal Gallante's rule had stiffened to starch; there had been no flexibility under the prince. But Sophistra and Torlock had different ideas. The Chatelaine was adamant that Galania—under her son's "blessed" guidance—reclaim its former position as the greatest of the six provinces. All Jerrel had to do was keep his lips together and do as he was told. That was a soldier's lot, after all, and should prove easy. But it didn't and wouldn't—that much he knew.

The problem was that Jerrel hated all three of them: the spoiled, decadent youth, the spiteful conniving mother, and their cruel ambitious guardian. All three were the Shadowman's children.

Sophistra and Varentin were loathed and feared by all—as was sensible. But Black Torlock had been noble once—though always ambitious and ruthlessly efficient. For years Jerrel had idolised his tough, resourceful captain, but as time wore on the young and loyal lieutenant had witnessed more and more of Torlock's brutal actions. Both with common folk and slaves, and down on the border, his cruel dispatches of Sarfanian prisoners whenever the fighting broke out.

But Jerrel was a practical man and this was a high honour they were bestowing upon him today. So he would accept gracefully and Galania would do well by him. But that didn't make it easy being here. Jerrel shuffled his feet and sweated as the snake stare of the Chatelaine coldly measured his resolve. She spoke first, but then he had expected that.

"Captain Jerrel, we commend you. You are now promoted for your loyalty and competence." The words, though silky, were barbed with latent menace. Jerrel bowed slightly and shifted his feet again. *How long will this last...?*

"He is suitable, Chatelaine, that I can assure you." Torlock's heavy tanned face was dominated by those brooding, malevolent eyes. He was dressed in polished leather, with velvet cloak and gold trimming at cuff and sleeve. A gauntleted hand rested idle on his sword hilt.

Black Torlock oozed power and confidence this morning, Jerrel only wished he could tap into some of it. "Jerrel has never let us down these half score years." *Has it been that long..?* "He is proficient with both blade and bow and is tough and resilient. I vouch for him." Torlock awarded Jerrel a wolf smile at those last words. "I know Captain Jerrel won't let us down at the Games, next month."

"I want you to gut Estorien Sarfe," a peeved indolent voice reached them from the other end of the room. Jerrel turned, saw the languid silk-garbed body of his new ruler sprawled prone across a lounger, wetting his lips on a cool glass of claret, despite the earliness of the hour. "Gut him open like this," Varentin made a vulgar motion with his right hand and Jerrel turned away.

"I doubt Sarfe will attend, beloved," responded the mother. "Those foolish lovers would be wise to keep a low profile at present, methinks. But then..." She winked knowingly at Torlock whose black gaze revealed nothing in return. "Estorien Sarfe is prone to rashness."

"But that need not concern you, Captain Jerrel." He raised his head as the Chatelaine's shrewd eyes pinned him again. "You are proclaimed Champion of Galania. Your sword shall represent our Prince Varentin at this year's Games in Dovesi. For obvious reasons you'll be aware that both our new Prince and Lord Protector are unable to attend. We are still in mourning, after all."

I hadn't noticed...

Jerrel inclined his head and muttered thanks. She continued as though he were invisible. "You will journey on the morrow, Captain, allowing time for the trip across the mountains, and to settle in Torvosa in preparation for the month's events. Torlock here has comprised a list of the party to accompany you. Galania's finest, or so he informs us."

Torlock nodded. "I do hope so," she continued. "Disappointment is not an emotion I entertain readily and shall hold you accountable, Captain."

"Oh, and Jerrel," her eyes tore into him and he suddenly pitied Hal Gallante, married to this spider all these years.

He's better off dead.

"You will report back to us any who fail during the contests. New Galania has no place for failure. I am sure that the Lord Protector has more to say to you later. But for now you are dismissed." She waved an imperious arm and Varentin belched agreement. "You may leave us, champion," he added, aping his mother's tones.

Jerrel saluted stiffly: he stepped backwards three paces, found the door entrance, and then turned swiftly before vacating the room. Once outside in the breezy corridor Jerrel breathed a sigh of relief. He quickly made his way down toward the armoury and stables beyond the palace, where no doubt Torlock would apprehend him soon enough.

As he strode through the early morning sunshine, its light tinting the palace walls to warm ochre, Jerrel couldn't quite quell a shiver. What was the matter with him today? He was Champion of Galania and should be delighted. Something was wrong though. He had a flickering image of Lissane Barola (a girl he'd only met the once and that briefly) watching him with accusing eyes. He shivered and hurried on.

New Galania...Am I wise to be part of this? What choice did he have?

The following morning Jerrel departed for Torvosa with the twenty horsemen Torlock had selected for him. All were proven warriors and many were his friends of old. Jerrel felt better this morning—away from the eyes of the citadel. He was in charge of his destiny now.

As he rode out beneath the south gate, Jerrel grinned. He was twenty-six years old and Champion of Galanais. He would marry a nobleman's daughter and buy some good land by the sea. Jerrel's future was made—he had only to keep his head. First, though, he would win renown at the Games.

Jerrel motioned his men follow him as he spurred his mount down the road, dreaming as he rode of the forthcoming challenge.

Whatever lay ahead, Jerrel was ready for it. But then had he known what the future held he would never had left.

***

Turftown. The name, uncouth as it was, did rather fit this place, with its maze of coloured tents and canopies, its scents and smells of every spice and choice viand. Lissane loved it every inch. And to be here with Estorien too.

Above and beyond the canvas city, the high white walls of Torvosa glistened as a row of giant square pearls, three miles distant. They had been entertained by the Lord Toreno last night, and the evening had passed with a great pyrotechnic display that had left Lissane gasping at the screeching, whirling rockets of silver, red and gold. She had never imagined such a sight before.

There had been one awkward moment when her father had arrived with the noisy Barolans. Eon had not spoken to her, however, and only Paolo cared to glance her way. His mocking, cat-green eyes had locked with Estorien's steady nut brown. He'd smirked and then, sporting a mock bow, had rejoined his brothers as they wended their way to the wine tents at Turftown's vibrant centre. That had been early this morning and Lissane had already forgotten about it.

She felt safe with Estorien, as well she might. After all he had bested all her brothers at earlier Games—even Paolo. Her lover had unhorsed Clarde Dovess (the current champion), three times over recent years and none other could boast of such prowess.

Estorien was also well known and loved among the commoners and traders that thronged amongst the haphazard mish-mash of colourful stalls and markets stands.

Everywhere they went people called out to Estorien and he smiled warmly in return, always seeming to remember the name of this fletcher, or that farrier. A gypsy girl offered to read his palm but he shooed her away, saying he already had everything he desired, and therefore cared not to hear his fortune.

She had grinned and blown him a kiss. Estorien had the common touch and Lissane loved him all the more for it. She caught the gypsy's canny gaze for a second, but failed to capture the sadness beneath those heavily kohled ebony orbs.

An hour ago she'd witnessed the Galanians arrive amid plume and bustle. To Lissane's vast relief neither Varentin nor Torlock were among them, although that really wasn't surprising. Galanais, so she'd heard, was in a state of flux after the sudden assassination last month of Prince Hal Gallante.

Lissane couldn't quite dispel the notion that his own wife had done for the old prince. But that didn't concern her and she wouldn't waste any further thoughts in that area, either. Galanais was past tense, and good riddance too. The new champion of her husband's province had saluted her outside the castle gates earlier. A man named Jerrel—honourable if rather dense, or so Estorien told her. She half recalled meeting the fair-haired Jerrel but couldn't be sure.

Lissane forgot Galanais and instead laughed, witnessing a rotund fire-eater belch a huge flame skyward. The wind caught it and next thing the adjacent jeweller's tent was alight, and panicked shouts resounded from within. The jeweller's heavies attacked the remorseful fire-breather with sticks, but he blew out at them and singed their eyebrows, causing great amusement amongst the gathering crowd.

A dog running passed stopped briefly to cock his leg, filling a drunken woman's abandoned bag with a steaming deposit. She kicked out at the rangy hound and swore extensively.

Estorien, deeming it time to move on, steered his laughing lady through the throng toward the High Pavilion where they were to take their honoured seats to the right of Duke Toreno himself. The first event was only an hour away and Lissane, who had only attended the Games but once, and that as a child in the coarse company of her brothers and father, could scarce contain her excitement.

There were troubadours and clowns gallivanting down there. She saw looning jesters, hopping and skipping, and re-enacting mock battles amid hoots from the crowd. But the real cheers announced the arrival of the first combatants. These were naked

wrestlers: huge gnarly men (and women)—there various append-
ages swinging freely in the breeze, causing some of the coarser
present to call out in bawdy jests, pointing lewdly at their bare
heaving buttocks, and making obscene suggestions as they locked
arms and struggled beneath the late summer sun. Lissane giggled
at so much naked flesh, saw Estorien raise an eyebrow at her and
then covered her mouth. This wasn't the place to be girly.

Next came barefooted spearmen from Xandoria across the
sea, displaying their skills at thrusting and casting their weapons.
An archery tourney followed and then a riding contest. Finally, as
evening cooled grass to glistening dew, the six provinces' premier
warriors strode out to challenge each other with bold shouts and
display their finesse. Tomorrow was their day.

Lissane, engrossed by the spectacle, saw her brothers among
them, swaggering and flexing their sword arms—evidently drunk
already. Rosco's face was almost scarlet as he brandished a huge
double headed axe, and Aldo (now fully recovered) showed his skill
with short sword and buckler—the latter strapped to his handless
arm.

Paolo looked resplendent in emerald lace and leather, his slim
rapier dancing forth like an adder's tongue, dispatching countless
invisible foes.

She saw big Clarde Dovess—resplendent in sparkling blue
armour—defend himself against a dozen of his guardsmen in mock
battle. The current Champion of the Games fought with limitless
skill for well over an hour, though Estorien, returning to her after
his own brave show of arms and whispering in her ear, said Clarde
lacked the grace of some of the other combatants.

Strangest to behold were the Treggarans. Barola's enemies—
they kept a healthy distance from Eon's terrace, she noted. On
the field now were three of Volt Garron's offspring: two men and
a woman. The men were huge and shaggy haired—one blond, the
other dark. Their bodies (the parts not covered in sweaty fur) were
crisscrossed with faded tattoos and scars. They were savage-look-
ing brutes and wielded their axes with arrogant precision.

But it was the girl warrior that fascinated Lissane. Slinsi

Garron was known to all present. Long-legged, loose limbed, and comely—in a feral, hungry-eyed way. Slinsi Garron was the darling of House Treggara. She was a prolific killer, though. Estorien said that Slinsi took no quarter and that her brothers (though very good) were no match for the wildcat beside them.

In Barola they called her a witch, but as Lissane watched Slinsi juggle her twin swords and toss her many knives at the wicker target with spellbinding speed, she couldn't help but admire her, and almost wanted to be her—this wonderfully violent woman who matched any man with sword and knife. Lissane would root for Slinsi Garron tomorrow, she decided. Hopefully she would skewer one of her brothers. It would irk her father to hear her cheering Treggara, and that was reason enough.

After that day's exciting events Lissane took to strolling down by the river with her lover, arm in arm. Behind them, subdued music and laughter wafted down from the now dusky Turftown. Beyond that the walls of Torvosa City flanked lofty and grey—in turn dwarfed by the snow-clad peaks rearing like filed teeth beyond. Happy and enthralled, Lissane slept soundly that night. The following week it would become fine wine to her memory. Because in this life, all things change.

***

The crossbowman watched the lovers stroll along the riverbank. It was almost dark now and he needed to get back. He could still hear the last of the revellers up at Turftown and half wished he was up there too—as he had been on numerous occasions. But he was playing a different game now. A dangerous game.

This hunter knew that there was a time to watch and a time to strike. That time was close—but not yet. Not here amidst all this bustle and merriment. Satisfied, he buckled up his cloak—its colour as dark as his eyes—and then shouldering his heavy crossbow, the stalker crept back into the thickening shadow of woodland beyond...

***

"I tell you, I'm going to spit that prick Estorien if I get near him," boasted Aldo.

"He isn't entering this year, you idiot," replied Paolo, draining his wineglass, and then grinning lewdly at the servant girl he'd abducted for the night. Rosco just belched neat ale and said nothing. "Well if he does, I'll have him," persisted Aldo, who had become even more belligerent since the loss of his right hand. He had got round the loss well on the whole, but still resented the fact that his brothers were more skilled than he was.

Eon hadn't been listening; instead he'd been watching the fight between Slinsi Garron and Red Torrig (the new king of Rodrutha). Brude apparently had drowned himself in ale six months ago. The fight was proving a great entertainment. These two clearly had scant love for each other, but try as he might the red-haired young king couldn't get passed the guard of that Treggaran witch.

He was good though, this Torrig Red Hair. Eon had never heard of him before but then Brude's women spat brats when other maids farted. He grinned when Slinsi produced a knife as if by magic at the end, and tossed it at Torrig who caught it deftly and hurled it back, and she in turn knocked it aside with a flick of her wrist. Good stuff!

Red Torrig leapt close and then punched her to the floor, but she tripped him and he fell on top off her. The next minutes were full of laughter, as the watching crowd delighted in the scenes of King Torrig Red Hair and Slinsi Garron's tussle. She was half naked by the time the arbitrator called a halt and he, bitten and scratched bloody. They parted, Torrig awarded her a mock bow and for her part, Slinsi Garron spat in his eye.

Eon laughed and turned his attention to his wineglass. He loved the Games—always had. It wasn't just the atmosphere, the wenching and drinking and gambling. Something always seemed to happen at the Games.

Something unexpected. This year was to prove no disappointment. The baron still couldn't bring himself to look at Lissane, despite the fact that the stupid girl spent her entire time moongaping at that oily Sarfanian. Lissane hated her own family now, and Eon was surprised how much that upset him.

Sure, he'd known Varentin Gallante was an indulged bastard—but that was the world. But for the girl to have done this thing, and acted it out with such blatant insouciance, was risible. Leanna would never have behaved so. But Leanna Barola was long dead. Her sad life obliterated by Eon's brutal neglect, or so his daughter would have it. His big-eyed little girl was now the talking point of Gol. She and her lover were on everyone's lips. Lissane Barola this...Estorien Sarfe that. And to come here parading like king and queen. It was barely tolerable. Not only that. It was beyond stupid.

The Baron's face darkened as he watched her now. She was seated across the arena, over at the southern end. Lissane was all silly smiles and happiness today; she'd never been like that back in Barola. Eon signalled an attendant for more wine and then turned his attention back to the event. It was bear-baiting this time, a particular favourite of Eon's. He leaned back and groped the thigh of the plump Dovesian servant-girl at his side.

Behind him, his noisy boys still quarrelled and bickered as they cheated at dice. Eon watched Lissane leave with her lover. The girl had always hated bear-baiting, strange that he should spawn such a stuck-up, rigid creature.

*Bugger it all...*Eon Barola drained his glass and allowed the attendant replenish it. Eon felt a stirring: he grinned at his leman and slid a greasy hand up between her thighs. She moaned as he worked his finger back and forth, all the time watching the hounds snap and snarl as they surrounded the roaring bear. He would get drunk tonight, Eon decided. But then he did every night.

***

The final contest during that joyous week was between current champion, Clarde Dovess, and Slinsi Garron. Slinsi had been awarded victory over that tattooed savage, Torrig, on points—mainly because he had been drunk and therefore shouldn't have entered.

The wild Rodruthan didn't seem that bothered. He had leered at her earlier and Lissane couldn't recall such a hideous individual,

and a king besides. All those tattoos and earrings. Not to mention
the scars on his face. It almost beggared belief, she had vowed there
and then never to journey to Rodrutha. They were all evidently
mad up there.

Clarde Dovess had retained his title by bludgeoning his spitting, kicking, and viciously clawing combatant unconscious with
his padded leather fists. It had proved a bit of an anti-climax to
Lissane, who had so wanted Slinsi to win, and she had scowled seeing her father laugh over at the Barolan side as they carried the
sprawled girl off like so much useless baggage.

She'd do for you, Father—so would I if I had half the chance...

And so that glorious week ended at last. Another Games over.
Another summer gone. Estorien, mindful of the road ahead and
how the Games were always chaotic for those leaving late, suggested they make ready their departure.

Lissane, though disappointed, couldn't complain. The week
had been wonderful and although they had only attended the last
part of the Games she would never forget it. Besides, Estorien had
told her the first three weeks were mainly for the merchants and
traders to do business, most of the barons and nobles only attended
the contests at the end. Such had proved the case this year.

An hour later they were on the sunlit road that ribboned
southwest toward the sea and distant Sarfania Province. Ahead
showed a line of low green hills they would have to pass before
entering the flat marshy country beyond. Estorien had chosen a
different route back to show her more of the south lands. Despite
that, Lissane was looking forward to seeing Reveal again, she had
not lived there long but it now felt more a home than Castle Barola
ever had.

Just before dark they reached the hills and after cresting
them, led their weary mounts down into a darkly wooded vale. Mist
hung low above the dusky road and all was still and silent. From
somewhere near an owl called out. That sudden haunting sound
made Lissane shiver.

It was then that she saw the rider. He was dressed all in black,
cloaked and booted, his face hidden beneath a deep hood. Beside

her Estorien tensed, and his hand slid down to rest on his sword hilt.

The rider eased his steed toward them. There was something familiar about him. Suddenly Lissane remembered the lone stranger they had encountered south of Reveal that afternoon. The one bound for the Horn. Kell the adventurer. Could this be him? If so then why was he dogging their passage again?

She felt suddenly worried. "Estorien...I—"

"Don't worry, my sweet," he grinned at her, "I've no fear of common footpads, and Toreno's people keep these hills clear of brigands." He urged his horse forward, his hand on sword hilt.

But then Lissane saw the crossbow.

She screamed a warning as the rider levelled his weapon at her lover. *No!* She heard the click and snap as the crossbow string released its missile.

No, please gods, no! Estorien had his sword half out of his scabbard when the black quarrel pierced his shoulder, spinning him round and then pitching him from the horse. The horse bucked and kicked out at its rider. Estorien rolled clear and struggled to his feet, blood welling dark over his cloak and tunic, his eyes full of agony and outrage.

Lissane screamed again as a second bolt tore into her lover's stomach. Estorien slumped to his knees. His mouth sprayed crimson as he tried to warn her to flee. But it was too late. There were other riders now—at least a dozen or more—and they were encircling her, their faces hooded and their arms wielding hempen ropes and whips.

They closed in on Lissane as though she were a wayward faun, trapping her flailing arms and dragging her from the horse. Lissane heard Estorien groan as the leading horseman dismounted and kicked her lover hard in his face. Estorien sprawled to the floor and a familiar gravelly voice called over to the hooded men surrounding her.

"Bring the whore; Varentin will decide what we do with her in good time. I'll deal with this bastard."

Lissane saw a sword slice through the twilight air: she heard a meaty whack and then something crumpled and rolled close. Lissane Barola's last sight before they gagged her was of her lover's dead eyes staring at her in surprise, as his head came to rest a few feet from where she knelt captive. She screamed again.

Black Torlock grinned wolfishly as he threw the hood back to reveal his brutal features. He grabbed Lissane beneath her chin, forcing her head back hard. She spat at him and he rewarded her with a hard cuff that sent her sprawling to the damp earth. He kicked her then, in the stomach, and the world went black.

"Tie that bitch to her saddle and let's get moving fast. We can catch Jerrel and the others before they reach the mountain roads. We best not tarry. Come on!"

Lissane's last thoughts were of what a wonderful week it had been. Foolish girl, she should have known that happiness was not permitted for such as she.

The gods must hate me so...

When Lissane awoke it was to pain and darkness, and the inevitability of what awaited her at Galanais. She closed her eyes and willed her lids to hold back tears. Somewhere close by came the mournful peeling of a melancholy harp.

Chapter 10

Fugitives and Thieves

It was early autumn but Rakeel stank worse than he remembered. It teemed too: soldiers, sailors, whores, traders, beggars and merchants, and countless pitiful refugees from the horror in the west. Everywhere he ventured was bustle and mayhem. And the noise...

Erun drew his cloak over his shoulders to conceal his features and muscled his way into a grubby alley where dark, surly faces peered at him out of the gloom. He moved on, hand on sword hilt, scanning every corner. Twilight beckoned and still he hadn't found his quarry.

Rakaro had to be here somewhere; he had it on three accounts now how the crafty Hillman had launched a prosperous career by procuring artefacts and monies from wealthy folk. In other words his old friend had become a thief, and apparently quite a successful one—hence the reason why Erun was seeking his aid in this—task two. With the archer's new (and old) skills alongside, Erun just might pull off what he was planning. Just, might—tenuous words both. It was absurd; who did Scaffa think he was, a human fly?

"You must venture overseas again, Erun Cade, and steal the

Jewel of Rakeel from the Emperor's Palace." As simple as that. Why was he complaining? Never mind that palace and grounds were surrounded by unassailable walls, and these patrolled by crossbow wielding hawk-eyed guards. The only way through was by the great iron gates that opened on the barbican with its murder holes and huge portcullis, where the Xandorian elite were stationed—two hundred highly trained spearmen, each sworn to death to protect the Emperor's person, and vast wealth too.

And just Erun's luck, the Emperor had only arrived here from Xenn last month—hence the double guards. It was hardly an assignment for a virgin thief to cut his teeth on. The Jewel of Rakeel was legendary, even Erun had heard of it way back in Barola. A huge ruby, carved in the shape of a coiling serpent, with jaws gaping and fangs sliver sharp, and with glittering eyes of some unknown metal that apparently glowed in the dark. The Jewel was said to contain the captured essence of the Earth Elemental, Tertzei—the objective of this madcap mission.

Apparently the Emperor had just rediscovered the bloody thing. The word on the street was that he never let the prized jewel out of his sight; even sleeping with it, some people told him when he discreetly enquired. Erun wondered at his sanity in accepting this quest. Once again he'd been beguiled by Scaffa's subtle persuasions, and, in Laras Lassladden, as usual, everything appeared possible—plausible even.

Whenever he returned to that cursed island it appeared different. This last time he'd found *her* waiting at the shore of a vast lake, its waters chiming glass and its shores hazy and indefinable with distance. *She'd* been dressed in the flowing hues of autumn. That season had reached the world outside, and Laras Lassladden for once was in tune.

Scaffa had produced a scarf, a wondrous thing of pale blue silk. It shimmered and felt soft as he ran it through his fingers.

"Speak the words and this scarf will aid your access into the palace at Rakeel. The Emperor resides there now, having left Xenn under the advice of his generals, and because of the trouble in the west. He now covets the jewel so you will have to be careful," she had told him. *Careful—an interesting word to describe a task only a complete lunatic would happily undergo.* Or maybe just an idiot like him.

"Take Borz, but only free his winds if you must, for he will try to escape and your binding runes must hold him. Remember, every time an Elemental is used they become stronger, and in time, can overpower their custodian. Only a powerful sorcerer like Ozmandeus can master such potency indefinitely and even then... time tolls."

"This Tertzei," he'd enquired. "What do I need to know?"

"Each Elemental is unique and Tertzei is no exception. However, because she is held fast within the ruby prison, and placed there by cunning spell-craft millennia ago, you need not fear her escape. Your challenge will be getting in and out of the palace with your head staying on your shoulders." Scaffa had smiled at his quizzical brow, "I've every confidence that you will succeed, Erun Cade," she'd told him. "Bring the Jewel to me, my bold venturer, and your reward will be closer. Farewell for now."

And that had been that. Simple. Erun had watched mournfully as giantess and lake blurred and then vanished from his vision. He should have been used to the enchantment by now but it still made his stomach churn. He'd blinked and again discovered his wet buttocks cramping the rear of the grizzled ferryman's craft, and Old Happy himself steering him back to the shore at Northtown.

From there Erun had taken a fast horse to the boggy isthmus in west Treggara. Thence on he'd crossed into East Khandol—a cold, desolate, empty region once frequented by Rakaro's people and perhaps soon to be inhabited by them again—lucky souls. He'd cleared East Khandol as quick as was possible and entered Xandoria guised as a mercenary again. Once across the border, Erun made prompt for Rakeel, arriving this very morning and getting to work fast on seeking out his friend.

Erun had had little confidence of Rakaro remaining in the city but had been relieved to hear from several traders that the Hillman lived close by. One bleak glance at the palace had told him that he could never achieve this lunacy alone, and Rakaro was just mad enough to enjoy this sort of venture. So Erun had searched alley after alley and street after street. Rakaro lived somewhere in this grubby vicinity. He had a woman now—a gypsy and talented cutpurse herself—a boy had told him for a coin.

It was getting dark: a hot stifling night beckoned despite the lateness of the year. Not that far across the sea, the brutal Torlock was even now entering the gates at Galanais, his weeping trophy tied to saddle, battered and shattered but yet still defiant.

Erun entered a cobbled street. A shadow crossed his path. He saw the knife and leapt aside as the steel whooshed passed his arm. Erun grabbed the assailant's arm and twisted his wrist, freeing the weapon. He then rammed his elbow up hard into his attacker's face, snapping his nose.

A sound to his right, Erun spun round just in time to block a sword thrust from the brigand's companion with his other arm; knocking the sword away, his palm whacking the flat of the blade.

Erun then lunged at the second footpad, striking him under the chin with the palm of his hand. The man dropped like a felled tree. Erun heard a loud click. He turned again; a third cutthroat had entered the street and was now grinning at him down the sights of a loaded crossbow.

Shit..

Erun took a slow breath and waited but the bolt never reached him. Instead the shot went wide and the quarrel skidded into a wall, and clattered amid sparks off along the alley. The crossbowman was kneeling in evident pain, and Erun could just make out the glint of steel from the cast knife that now protruded from his back. He thrashed a bit then slumped and lay still. *Must have pissed off his mates.* Fortunate, that. Timing is everything.

A noise to Erun's left. He turned slowly; the first knifeman had regained his feet and was frothing at the mouth, his eyes wide with hatred. Erun kicked him hard between the legs and, as he lurched forward, grabbed the back of his greasy hair, and then brought his knee up sharp into the man's face. Bones crunched and he crumpled to lie alongside his associates.

One dead and two buggered—best get moving...

Someone laughed then and Erun turned to see that a figure blocked his way—the knife thrower evidently, his features occluded by a long shabby cloak. Then the stranger laughed at him again.

"I heard rumour you were looking for me," said Rakaro, and still grinning, cast back his hood before striding forward to embrace his former comrade. "Well met, master Kell," Rakaro slapped his back. "I see that you still retain your talent for attracting trouble."

"I'm glad that you turned up just then—that crossbow bolt would have taken some swift evading."

"I would have hated plucking it out of your arse, boy." They clasped hands and then Rakaro led his friend through several rat-runs and dingy corners, until they reached a dark building, shadowed by a huge fig tree and walled with red, crumbling brick. An expensive looking gate led into spacious gardens, and beyond that the dark shape of a large house loomed out of the night.

"Is this your new establishment?" asked, Erun impressed by the affluent surroundings, a complete contrast from the other buildings they had weaved passed on their hurried journey here. "Thieving in Rakeel must pay well."

"Oh, we get by." Rakaro led him toward the bright red-painted oak door. "It used to belong to a wealthy merchant, but he got stabbed a month ago—so we two took to squatting hereabouts."

"Didn't the soldiers pay you a visit, or else the city watch?"

"They've other matters to attend to," Rakaro told him. "Rakeel is poised on a knife's edge these days, and anything goes. So if a fellow can look after himself he just takes what he wants, and I rather fancied retiring in one of these old houses. It beats a tent and a farting herdswoman's fat rump keeping you warm at night. And besides, Lissi likes it."

Lissi waited for them indoors, her dark gypsy eyes shrewdly weighed up her lover's companion as he followed him inside.

"Stew's on," she said, her voice sultry in the evening gloom. "Take a seat, Master Kell." She laughed at his surprised expression. "We've been expecting you since this morning," she informed him, "there's been word of some noisy, blundering outlander, stomping about looking for my own dear trouble here."

Erun sat down by the fire and Lissi put spark to kindling, for the night air had cooled noticeably. Rakaro lounged idly back in a deep divan and stretched his tired neck. "Well?" he asked after a moment's reflection. "How can I help?"

***

"You're mutton-headed fools, the pair of you," Lissi had said after hearing Erun's insane proposal, and worse, Rakaro's enthused endorsement of it. "You'll most likes be crow-feed on the morrow, with your thick stupid heads, spiked and bloody above the city gates—and so serve you right, you daft twats." Erun winced, he now suspected this Lissi might have moved here from Rodrutha. Why was it that most the women he met had tongues sharper than his sword?

"Well, to my mind you daft pair deserve each other. You might as well both clear off and get to it." She turned away then, hiding the tear that now glistened on her cheek.

Lissi's heart had missed a beat when the tall, scar-faced stranger had entered the house. That branded face was so familiar. Not from Rakaro's elaborate stories, but from her own troubled dreams. Her gypsy's intuition left her no doubt that this 'Kell' was the one the old folk had talked of when she was a girl. The pale-eyed harbinger from foreign shores, whose sudden appearance pre-empted the end. The demon was coming—everyone knew—and now the Shadowman's messenger had arrived too.

Lissi packed her things that night; she wouldn't be waiting for Rakaro. Instead Lissi would return to her people in the mountains near Khandol and wait for the outcome, however dire. Outside night deepened and the city slept. The only sounds came from skulking beasts, and once briefly the muffled cry of some poor victim being strangled down a nearby alley. By morning she had gone.

***

Erun and Rakaro spent most of that night studying every detail of the walls and the only visible gates of the palace. They decided on the former: it would be suicide to go near that barbican.

But how to scale and where?

After a long, careful walk they reached the rear of the palace, where its sandstone yellow walls hugged the shoreline, looming high and majestic over the harbour. Here there were fewer guards but the walls were higher—over one hundred and fifty foot—with vast buttresses thrust out at regular intervals like bear's claws, scraping at the incoming tide. Interesting challenge. They scratched their heads and watched for a time in measured silence before reaching the same decision.

This was not going to be easy.

But what the heck.

Erun caught Rakaro's eye and the archer winked. "Why not," he whispered, "there is still plenty of night left, and as long as we don't tarry we can be gone before dawn. Besides, that water's getting close, I'd rather not drown."

Erun nodded, the tide was creeping up fast behind them, and if they were to act then they had better get on with it. "My own thoughts exactly," he said and unravelled his shabby cloak.

"What is that?" Rakaro pulled a face.

"It's a cloak of concealment."

"It looks a bit decrepit."

"It's enchanted and will enable our ascent unseen."

"What—like something out of a story?"

"Yes, only this isn't something out of a story."

"Right..."

Rakaro huddled close so that the threadbare garment worked its magic over him as well. He saw the odd shaped sack swinging from Erun's belt but let that one go. This boy had acquired a deal of clutter since last they'd met. Aside from that mysterious sack hung the wooden harp, his sword (a bloody great thing) and a sturdy knife.

Rakaro had his horn bow and quiver, now containing forty shafts. He also carried twelve throwing knives on a holster lashed tight around his middle—pilfered from the fair last week.

They exchanged nods. *Time to go...*

Stealing silent along the beach, they reached the foot of the walls and crouched behind the shelter of the closest buttress. Close behind the sea surged and sighed. Erun slid the scarf he'd been loaned from his pocket and Rakaro raised another questioning brow.

"What do you propose do with that flimsy thing?" he whispered.

"Watch and learn," replied Erun in hushed conspiratory tones. "Every thief should have one of these. It is stronger than rope and easier to store."

"That's impressive," responded Rakaro, "but how are you going to get it over those crenulations?"

"I hadn't got to that bit yet," admitted Erun, po-faced.

"Don't worry," Rakaro winked at him. "I've a notion."

Moments later the Hillman had vanished beneath Erun's cloak, and had commenced his agile scaling of the walls. Painfully slowly, Rakaro climbed with the aid of his stolen knives. He would reach up, thrust a knife between the cracks in the soft sandstone, and then heave his wiry body up. Then he would reach down and retrieve the knife he'd been stepping on, and so forth. Again and again.

This process involved the use of six knives and took almost half an hour. And all the time Erun Cade waited below with wet, squelching feet. He saw nothing, save once only, when Rakaro's left foot missed the knife, slipped out of the cloak's protection and then waggled about in mid air, high above—a bizarre sight that proved to be, and not for the sober. Fortunately no guards were visible.

During that long frustrating wait the only sounds in Erun's ears were the night breeze, the approaching waves and, (much quieter), the scrape of knife being thrust in and then pulled out again, and each time the sound coming from slightly higher up.

Erun was getting more agitated by the minute; he felt both abandoned and forlorn and cursed Scaffa yet again. Then, when the sea was lapping below his knees, Erun heard a whoosh. Glancing up he was rewarded by his own invisible cloak hitting him hard in the face and knocking him over.

Soaked and grumbling, Erun checked his equipment: the

sack containing Borz, the harp, his weapons—all present though wet through. Now for his turn. Erun then swiftly untied the cloak from the scarf, donned the first and began scaling the walls with the second. After many panting, heaving minutes, Erun Cade joined Rakaro on the battlements above.

"You look a bit damp," whispered the archer. Erun ignored that. Instead he took silent stock of their situation. Over to the right, a bored sentry shifted his feet and gazed empty eyed into the gloom. To their left were two silhouettes—more guards. These were further away though, and their gaze rested on the city lights beyond.

Rakaro motioned Erun to stay put a moment. Erun nodded and watched his accomplice steal catlike toward the nearest guard. The soldier turned too late. Rakaro's knife hilt bludgeoned into his temple and he crumpled silent to the stone floor of the parapet. Erun joined him, and then sharing the cloak again, and both silent as the night sky above, they crept along the walkway, pausing only to render the other two sentries silent.

At last they found a narrow stairwell that turnpiked down to the inner wall below. Erun stowed his cloak. Space was at a premium now and they would rely on speed henceforth.

They hurried down the winding stair. Below were ornate gardens, with ferns and leafy shrubs that clung to the inside of the walls allowing immediate cover. Once safely beneath that dense canopy, the two interlopers paused to survey their way ahead.

A quick glance around revealed no movement. Erun, taking the lead, fumbled and groped through the midnight foliage, making for the distant gleaming stone of the palace ahead.

The gardens circled the entire palace. Here were fountains, and there statuettes whose dead silent eyes followed their progress through the verdant maze of growth and cut lawn. They stopped a third time when they spied the ornate jade-studded gates that opened into the palace proper. There were several guards lounging in the shadow, most carried spears but there were one or two crossbowmen among them.

Rakaro scowled. "Mayhap there's a postern round the back,"

he suggested to his friend. Erun shook his head as he shuggled the cloak free of its bag again. He cast it over his shoulders and bade Rakaro huddle close once more.

"This should serve us well here," Erun said, "but keep your arms, in old friend; they might get spooked should they chance glance a redundant limb. It certainly freaked me when I saw your leg dangling halfway up that wall."

Rakaro pulled a face. "It didn't do wonders for my nervous system, either," he admitted. The guards saw and heard nothing as the two cloak-wrapped infiltrators slipped past in tense silence. Moments later they were inside the palace and dared breathe again.

Were they not so rushed, Erun would have taken time to gawp at the splendour of the Xandorian Emperor's summer residence. A palace that until now the ruler hadn't even seen, let alone frequented, Rakaro had told him.

Everywhere Erun glanced was wealth beyond his imagination. He saw urns of gold and silver, great glinting gems that studded huge tapestries—like so many stars blanketing the sconce-lit walls of the palace. Marble statues lined the wide, smooth passages that led arrow-straight toward the central dome. Somewhere beyond that dome they would find the Emperor's quarters—and the Jewel too. Rakaro had mentioned that the palace at Rakeel was as nothing compared to his main residence in Xenn City. Erun found that difficult to believe.

They kept close and friendly beneath his cloak. There were a few guards wondering about in the palace too, though most appeared bleary-eyed and sleepy—doubtless looking forward to the end of their watch. Scaffa had informed Erun that the Emperor's private rooms were at the far end of the palace.

Here a large wing—reserved for Imperial pleasure and cultural indolence—led off for several yards from the main dome. Erun and Rakaro now headed that way, stopping in their tracks when they spied the massive lone guard manning the doors to the Emperor's rooms. He didn't look sleepy in the least. Erun now had that nasty feeling that from this point on things were going to get shambolic. And for once he wasn't wrong.

***

Bodies everywhere. Flyblown and rotting, the limbs hewed and hacked; eyes pecked out by crow and raven, and the gagging stench of ruined flesh.

All that remained of the Xandorian Third.

That fine elite body of infantrymen that had so stoically marched out from Xenn City, to stop the advance of the chaotic horde spilling down from the Gap.

But the necromancer from Zorne and his army of corpses had fallen on those brave fighters as scythes on ripe barley. A slaughter: it was over in a single day. Fifty thousand souls sent screaming down to the Shadowman and nothing but miles of open countryside left between the invaders and Xenn City.

Romul read the hastily scrawled parchment with a shaking hand. What to do? At least the Emperor was now safely ensconced in Rakeel. But how to stop this approaching storm? Karali—the assassin was their only hope. Strike while they are weak—yes.

This Ozmandeus hadn't even needed his fires to destroy the Third—doubtless he was saving the demon for Xenn. The Chancellor was right all along. So be it then. Let Ashmali's flames eat Xenn City as they had Lamoza, and then, when demon and sorcerer are sated, let Karali strike with cobra's swiftness.

It was a reckless gambit, but it was all that Romul had for the moment. But should Karali fail—what then? Xandoria was finished—it would take months, even years perhaps but the outcome was inevitable. Romul was now glad that he'd opened those secret talks with the greedy barons in Gol. That smaller continent might just prove their final hope. Gol was weak—and if the barons let him in? A subtle invasion with more following on. *Let the monster ruin his country if he must*, Romul mused. There might just be another way. But first Karali—he would send for him today.

Chapter 11

Tertzei

"He's a big lardy lad," muttered Rakaro. "All that muscle and bulk can slow you up though." He freed a knife from his belt but Erun grabbed his arm.

"Only if we have to," he whispered. Rakaro nodded agreement but still gripped the knife as insurance. The guard was massively built with huge sinewy arms and powerful legs, bulging out from the gaps in his gold plated armour. His dark eyes were stone hard and wary, and his right hand rested lightly on the hilt of a huge jewel-encrusted tulwar.

A golden helmet enclosed his head and half his face, and a broad headed spear rested idle on the wall beside him. His brawny arms were folded as he stared like thunder into the gloom.

Rakaro, after a grunt from Erun, slipped out from the cloak and hid behind a huge urn. The guard's eyes flickered toward the urn and then relaxed. Erun chose his moment well. Approaching at speed and barely making a sound, he deftly slipped the scarf around the champion's bull-like neck, shoved a knee hard up into his back and then tugged. The guard choked, and though caught off balance, thrashed so violently he almost threw Erun from his grip.

But Rakaro was on him then. The Hillman struck out at an exposed side of the giant's knee with a cunningly aimed kick. The champion toppled with Erun Cade falling on top of him and the scarf biting deeper into his neck, choking him further. For what seemed an age Erun gripped the scarf with grim determination and hung on tight while the brute thrashed and writhed.

Die—you fat bastard!

Then, just when Erun's exhausted arms were cramping badly, and only after Rakaro had stamped three times on the back of the big guard's head, their enemy finally lay still with Erun (half visible) sprawled and panting on top of him.

Rakaro awarded him a resigned look. "Are you planning on staying there all night?" Erun swore in reply and regained his feet. He opened the cloak so that Rakaro could share it again. It was just as well they were invisible because they would look so utterly ridiculous should someone see them.

Erun feathered a gap in the door with his left foot. He glanced into the gloom. Nothing. They entered with stealth, carefully checked, but the rooms in this section were all empty, it seemed. So Erun stowed the cloak again and they began in earnest the search for the jewel.

That search took the best part of an hour. The Emperor's private wing seemed to go on forever. Erun was beginning to sweat and curse when Rakaro whispered over to him from a side passage that led out from another chamber.

"In here...I think we're on to something."

This room was smaller than the others, though still very large by Erun's modest standards. Once within they were aware of an odd rosy glow that stained the walls and furnishings like freshly spilled blood. Erun's heart missed a beat.

Ahead was a bed, four-posted and wide. Erun, stepping closer, froze when he spied three figures apparently asleep beneath those sumptuous covers. The middle sleeper was a fleshy faced, balding man in his middle years currently snoring like a summer storm. His scabby right arm was entangled around the second sleeper—a boy half the other's age, with long oiled hair the colour of winter

straw and heavily kohled eyelids. The third occupant of the bed
was a woman, her skin the colour of polished mahogany and her
large breasts spilling out of the covers.

Erun gawped and Rakaro almost crashed into his back. At the
foot of the massive bed stood a table carved out of solid marble, its
surface polished and veined with the rock's strata. Upon this heavy
table, perched on a golden trivet, was a huge ruby resembling a
rearing flat headed serpent about to strike. Though no larger than
a man's fist, the Jewel resonated energy and pulsed red light across
the room. Evidently this was the source of the rose-pink glow that
filtered into every corner of the sleeping chamber.

The Jewel of Rakeel. They had found it at last.

Erun's first impression was one of immense power radiating across to him from that pulsating Jewel. He had been exposed
to that feeling twice before now, although this was different—as
Borz's dizzy, whirling screams, had been different to the horror of
Ashmali's wanton destruction.

Tertzei's cold red stare was both hypnotic and implacable.
She radiated power and silent hatred from deep inside her prison.
He could see the faint tiny shape of a naked woman staring at him
from inside the Jewel. The cruel throb of that ruby stare stung
Erun's eyes, and yet he couldn't turn away.

Behind him, Rakaro was muttering expletives, his voice
unusually edgy. Erun could feel Borz coming alive in his sack at
his waist as the Wind Elemental sensed the closeness of his sister. Tertzei responded to her brother's muffled shouts. The Jewel
blazed crimson in fury and both Erun and Rakaro gasped at the
stab of painful light.

Erun dared delay no longer. He spoke the words, breaking
her spell and then reached out to grasp the ruby with both hands.
The Jewel was hot: it burnt his hand painfully, but Erun hurriedly
wrapped it in a cloth he'd torn from a table, close by.

The other thing that surprised him was the weight. It was
though he was lifting an anvil from his dead father's forge—not a
fist-sized ruby. Erun knew that this was Tertzei's raw earth power
that still rooted her to the marble plinth.

Erun didn't hesitate; he strode up, bag in hand, and lifted the Jewel free of its plinth. He spoke Scaffa's words again and again. Then at last the weight lessened; he was able to thrust the hot ruby inside the sack containing Borz.

Phew...

Bound by runes, Tertzei was now his prisoner. Erun shuddered at the frustrated energy emanating from that sack as the Elementals came together. Let them do their worst, Scaffa's runes would keep them in place. Now all that remained was to vacate the palace. And promptly. He turned to Rakaro, who still stood gawping behind him.

"You ready to go, Hillman?"

"I thought you'd never ask." They turned, made for the door. Mercifully the bedfellows were still, all three of them, sound asleep.

But then Borz did his special thing. And it all went horribly wrong.

***

The Wind Elemental was obviously overwrought by the sudden appearance of his sister. He couldn't contain himself, and now a horrid wailing shriek spilled out from Erun's rune-sack. Erun winced and Rakaro was already reaching for a knife.

"The whole fucking palace will hear that din," complained the archer. Erun just gaped at him.

And Rakaro was right. The sleepers awoke amid the racket, the boy started yelling, and the girl screamed enthusiastically. The balding man just gaped at the intruders, with bug-eyes bulging, and the boy (yells now finished) swiftly hid, terrified, beneath the covers.

Then came the best bit. The monstrous guardsman (fully recovered) rounded the corner and fell upon them like a building.

"I thought you had killed this bastard," cursed Rakaro, as the giant guard collided into his gaping friend like a battering ram striking a gate. Rakaro hurled his knife but the giant battered it aside with a contemptuous shake of his wrist, his other hand bludgeoning into Erun's shoulder, knocking him hard against the wall.

It was all happening so fast: the girl was screaming and screaming, and the middle-aged man (obviously the Emperor—judging by his arrogant manner and expensive nightgown), was jumping about and waving his arms like a windmill in a gale.

The terrified boy was still buried deep beneath the covers, and Borz (bless him) was whining like a gelded hog. Rakaro reached for another knife, but Big Ugly shook his tulwar free from its scabbard and batted the missile aside. He turned the curved blade toward Rakaro, but then Erun crashed into his broad back, allowing the archer dive out of the way of its lethal sweep.

Erun had Callanak out now. He lunged at the giant guardsman, but the other parried with ease; re-launched his tulwar at the Barolan with appalling savagery. Scaffa's training served Erun well. Somehow he kept the brute at bay. But the man was a skilled killer and Erun was tiring fast, and he didn't have the room to swing Callanak as he'd like to, there were too many damn furnishings to trap the long blade. He retreated towards a wall, fended and blocked—tried to get a cut in but this troll-man was far too quick.

"Rakaro—wake up, for fuck's sake. I've need of back up!"

Rakaro—forgotten by the big lad—tried yet another knife, but this too was disdainfully knocked aside. Then Big Lardy lashed out at Rakaro with a savage kick that sent him sprawling and thudding into the wall. He crumpled and lay still.

The Xandorian monster now closed in on Erun for the kill, his eyes two chips of flinty hate, and his ugly mouth leering like a hungry bear intent on squashing an irritating bug. Behind him the portly Emperor was yelling encouragement and stomping about in his silk nightgown.

Erun slumped in defeat and exhaustion. The giant warrior grinned at him. He took a step forward, and then swung hard and fast with the gleaming tulwar.

That mighty blow cut through air alone. Erun had leaped aside with blinding speed. The ruse had worked well, Erun stabbed out and up with practised precision. Callanak's razor tip found its target in a tiny gap between the champion's armour, where his shoulder joined his neck. Erun sliced hard and deep, sawing his blade into the giant's tree-thick neck.

Callanak bit deep. The guard's life-blood gushed out and upwards, spraying the walls and drapes. Then—like a falling tree—the giant warrior crumpled, shuddered and lay still; his half severed head askew, the dead eyes staring balefully up at his master, whose own orbs were now wide with excitement at the sight of so much blood.

Mouth drooling and eyes hungry, the young Emperor took a step toward Erun's exposed back, a dagger now showing in his right sweaty fist. But Callanak was still hungry, and, as if acting on its own volition, Erun's sword arm swept backwards with deadly accuracy.

There followed a sickly thud and muffled scream from the boy on the bed. Spinning on his heels like a dancer, Erun came about, saw the Emperor's head totter free of his corpulent body, spewing crimson gore as it rolled across the rug-rich floor.

"I think perhaps you shouldn't have done that," said Rakaro. His eyes were slightly crossed and he was nursing an egg-like lump on the side of his head. All was suddenly very quiet in the chamber. Even Borz had shut up.

"Whoops," said Erun looking around at the mess. A room filled with blood. Two corpses, a naked woman—her face now silent in shock, and a sobbing, trembling shape buried beneath the covers of that very expensive bed.

Time we weren't here.

They scattered like rats fleeing an incoming flood. On through the Emperor's quarters and wing, into the main palace, sprinting at full pelt like mad things toward an exit (any exit). Then suddenly soldiers were everywhere, spilling out like so many angry ants, from every orifice the palace contained.

Rakaro's knives took the first three; Callanak felled the next. They reached the jade gates leading out to the gardens beyond, Rakaro's bowstring sang and another soldier sprawled and wriggled in the soil.

Once amid the fronds and flora they crisscrossed toward the shadow of the wall. Somewhere off to his right Erun heard harsh shouts, as a gaggle of spearmen filed out from the barbican and sped furious toward the palace main. The walls above now bristled like a porcupine's back with the glinting spears of the vengeful guards.

They had no chance that way—not even with the cloak. There was but one choice. They made straight for the barbican amid wild shouts.

Miraculously, Erun's dancing sword and Rakaro's lethal shafts won them through. For all was chaos now and the guards still sleepy and unsure what was going on. After leaving half dozen corpses behind them they accessed the gates. Erun stopped to skewer a couple more guards with Callanak, whilst Rakaro cranked open the iron-ribbed doors. Then, free at last, they vanished into the shadowy streets.

***

Outside the city woke to mayhem. Trumpets blared, filling the night and voices cursed, while waking dogs howled until they were kicked to silence.

Amidst this confusion, the two thieves coolly threaded their way toward Rakaro's stolen home. There was no sign of Lissi, and Rakaro was in no mood to tarry.

"I'll track her down later," he said, "We had best not linger here."

Dawn beckoned by the time they reached the docks. Soldiers were everywhere, but they had no notion of who they were seeking. Erun was able to jump aboard an abandoned boat and set about getting it ready for departure.

"I'll not journey with you this time," Rakaro yelled across at him.

"Well—you can't stay here," Erun replied as he freed the craft from the mooring poles, and tossed the coiled line into the hold. He grabbed an oar—steadied the boat. "Are you coming—or what?" Erun demanded.

"Nope," replied Rakaro shaking his head. "I'll take my chances in the streets, friend Kell. I will find that troublesome gypsy of mine and then make fast for the hills of home." Erun tried to persuade his friend as he readied the sails, but to no avail. Seconds later he watched Rakaro trot coolly along the quay before vanishing into the predawn grey. *Go carefully, my friend.*

Erun had scant time for reflection. The soldiers were spilling onto the quayside. He took to oar in each hand and dipped their blades in the water. Once free of the harbour's arm, Erun spoke the words that freed Borz from his sack. Tertzei stayed within while Borz worked his magic—useful for once.

The Wind Elemental's breath filled the sailcloth to bursting point, and, as if propelled by some powerful engine, the small craft cut arrow-swift out across the water.

Two weeks later Erun Cade arrived back at Laras Lassladden, with two out of three tasks achieved. As expected, Scaffa was waiting for him with news of the third.

***

How had it come to this? What kind of fool had he been, following and believing in this madman? Greed and avarice had fuelled his veins back then, but where had they got him? Nowhere. The captain was but a shadow of his former self—such horrors had he witnessed. It was enough. He could take no more. He had to go.

Maelchor squinted up at the three charred corpses dangling from the cages Ozmandeus had ordered them left to rot in. Three brave men—all old friends of his. They had dared challenge the necromancer's wisdom and had paid the highest price.

Of the several thousand freebooters that had so eagerly rallied to the Renegade's cause back in Zorne, few were now left. Most had deserted to far flung places after Lamoza. Many had been killed, and more still executed by the mad sorcerer.

Ozmandeus no longer needed Maelchor's fighters. He had his corpse army now; the stench of it lingered all around the camp. That ghoulish horde festered and moaned just outside the walls of Xenn City, a legion of enslaved souls—the butchered victims of his master's brutal conquest.

And when would it end? Maelchor had witnessed firsthand

the burning that had levelled Lamoza. There was no plunder from that ruin—only ashes. That apocalyptic destruction had shaken him badly. What purpose did it serve?

Lamoza had been the turning point. Back in Zorne he'd believed in the Renegade. But no longer: it was though the demon had possessed Ozmandeus and now dwelt inside him. The once articulate sorcerer had changed beyond reckoning. Ozmandeus was a tormented, feverish maniac now, desiring only destruction and fire. It made no sense.

And tomorrow they would level Xenn. Once again Ashmali would wax horrible over the city and its people roast on his breath. It was insane, and he, Maelchor, would no longer be a party to it. So at nightfall he would gather his basics: his horse, sword, axe and kit bag, and just enough coin, and then he would flee the camp.

Maelchor, the once so proud and much feared mercenary captain, would become a craven deserter—everything he despised. So be it—Maelchor no longer cared. Survival was all that mattered. He'd range south for the coast and then take passage to the Island States, leaving this country to the necromancer and his demon.

The following morning Maelchor felt the heat of Ashmali's flames scorching his back as he fled towards the foothills, at last joining the road wending south to the coast. He didn't look back. Instead Maelchor urged his beast to gallop on through the hill-clad forests flanking the mountains, to sanctuary, safety and escape.

Chapter 12

The Needle

Another year wanes. Seasons shift, every day passing with the promise of death just that little bit nearer. But Eon Barola had no fear of death. What he *did* fear was a life without achievement, bereft of glory. A life dull and ordinary as the peasants', leading to a passing, un-mourned and soon forgotten, as wormy-earth takes hold of body, and soul fades to oblivion.

Not for him.

Eon was nothing if not ambitious, and there were things needing to be done, not for him but for Barola and the greater good—or so he deemed it. His people feared and loathed the baron and his sons, but Eon cared little for that. What did they know? The little people, whose only challenge was to survive from dawn to dusk in a world so mediocre, it appalled him to dwell on it. They were his minions; at least they had their freedom, unlike many in Galania.

The Baron stood watching the autumn sun slide slowly beneath the hills of his beloved province, flooding the sky with crimson. The reflective mood had been upon him all day, which was hardly surprising considering the events of recent months.

Three things concerned him now: the Emperor's assassination in Xandoria and its implications for Gol, Treggara—their costly hostilities with the Garrons, and what to do about his daughter. The first two were situations Eon could turn to Barola's advantage—of that he was sure. But Lissane? Whatever was he to think about a daughter who had failed him so utterly?

Just like her mother...

Word had arrived that week from Toreno in Dovess, informing him of the Xandorian Emperor's murder and the bold theft of the Jewel of Rakeel. Whoever the villains were they were highly efficient, the Xandorians were renowned for their loyalty to their emperor and competence at guarding him. No assassin had managed to get within a mile of their ruler before.

And the Jewel of Rakeel lifted too—small wonder his contact in Rakeel was wobbling. Their Emperor was gone, and rumours abounded that new and violent factions were already at odds in that huge country. Were these to overspill into Gol it could prove dire for the barons—Rakeel was not so far from Galanais.

There were other factors, weird stories concerning distant Zorne and a demon wreaking ruin. Eon had dismissed these as folklore—there were always wars and troubles out there. But something radical was going on overseas. The patterns were shifting again, so the wise woman in the woods had told him.

Eon Barola had always had a keen nose for sniffing change in the wind. It had helped him instigate the Rebellion, knowing just when to topple Flaminius's brittle hold on the realm. Eon now sensed another such time drew nigh. He would send word to his contact in Rakeel—add his condolences and commiserations. Paolo would make the trip across to see how matters lay. There would be many leaderless soldiers over there now. Their service could be bought easily now that their Emperor had fallen.

And Eon needed additional forces to achieve his planned coup. Paolo was subtle enough to know what was required. First though, he needed funds and they were short coming. Next summer would change that. This time next year House Barola would be wealthy, well able to buy enough mercenaries to take hold of matters in Gol. And where better to hire freebooters than Xandoria just now?

He also needed Treggara to cease in its endless petty raids across the river. The torching of villages, the rapes and wanton murders had gone on for years—on both sides of the border—and for little gain. Volt Garron and his spawn traded insults with Barola every Games. And for what purpose?

It was time to end that rift. Eon would propose a truce. Find something that would entice House Garron to forget its grievances with Barola. Mad King Brude had died (drowned in his own soup apparently) and a new feisty ruler held power in the Crags. Under Red Torrig, Rodrutha had renewed its attacks on the Treggarans; hence Volt Garron was stretched and should be easy to sway. Eon knew the very thing that could tempt his neighbour alongside, (and with Gallante dead, House Barola stood to gain little from Galania now.) That province had its own problems, many of which concerned his daughter.

Just what madness had possessed her to run off with that foolish Sarfanian? Eon had tried to warn Lissane of her blatant folly at the Games, but he hadn't found the words, and instead only succeeded in insulting her. He had felt bad about that afterwards. She was too proud, that girl. The fact that she hated him was irrelevant. A baron needed to be strong, and his daughter should be obedient and useful. Instead Lissane had proved a wilful liability and had failed to see the connotations of her selfish, reckless actions.

The Sarfanians were soft, without Toreno's support that province would be nothing but swamp and bugs. Eon hadn't been surprised to hear of Lissane's recapture and her lover's death at the hands of Gallante's henchman, Torlock.

One I need to watch.

Galanians were vengeful creatures and Eon had suspected they'd act at some point. But Estorien Sarfe had been popular; his butchery during the annual truce of the Games had rocked the fragile stability of Gol. Hal Gallante, though vain, had been a subtle man. He would have found a quieter way, but he was dead and rotting.

This Varentin was a different creature than his father had been. Varentin kept his brains in his groin. He was the puppet of his conniving mother and her ambitious lover.

Sophistra was dangerous, Eon allowed, but she overestimated her own cunning, and Black Torlock's growing power in Galanais was turning the people against them both.

Trouble loomed in the west. Word had reached the Baron from traders and sailors taking shelter from storms in his bay. Galanais was in turmoil, and Torlock's recent actions had caused a rift amongst the ranks of the Galanian Household Guard. Adding to that, Varentin's wanton excesses were driving the people toward incitement.

Meltdown was approaching.

He had received word from Sophistra after the Games, stating that his daughter had not been harmed by her abductors, though her son had 'quite understandably' found it difficult to forgive the girl. She, (Sophistra) had smoothed the troubled waters, and now assured Eon that the silly girl (though chastised) was now forgiven, and had quietly and contently rejoined House Gallante.

Lying bitch.

What was increasingly apparent to Eon was that the 'silly girl' was fighting back, and that now, Lissane had new friends in that province. A serendipitous split was cracking open Galanais. Could it be that Lissane might be of use to him after all?

Eon would watch and wait he decided. A winter's planning and contemplation approached. There was much to put in motion next spring. Things would reach boiling point at next year's Games. That would be the time to act. During the peace itself. Preparation was the key factor. House Barola stood to gain everything if Eon held his nerve during these next few months.

It was a challenge but Eon Barola liked a challenge. It kept him young, like the girl that warmed his bed each night. Kept death at bay. Eon rubbed his greying beard with a greasy hand. The sky had darkened toward dusk, and already tiny stars studded the silent heavens above. Far below black waves assaulted his walls with rhythmic murmur and thud. It was getting chilly so he went inside, deeming it past time for a flagon of red. Then he would write Volt Garron and set things in motion.

The quickening had arrived.

***

Jerrel had never wanted this to happen. Had never believed he'd turn against his captain, the man he'd almost worshiped in his younger days. But events changed a man's perceptions and, for a while now, Jerrel had become increasingly at odds with Torlock's actions.

Of late, the 'Protector of Galanais' had held the city in a brutal headlock, imposing curfew on the people. Arresting many of the noble families, accusing them of Gallante's murder. It was obvious Torlock acted on the Chatelaine's wishes, using her husband's death as an excuse to eliminate any who might come to challenge their rule.

It was also evident that Torlock revelled in his new task, and now wielded a power that terrified the inhabitants of citadel and city. Jerrel had been unaware of most of this before his hasty departure for the Games. At that time he still held some respect for Torlock.

But that respect had vanished after the despicable murder of Estorien Sarfe. A nobleman who, though a foe to Galania, had always been courteous and honourable, and had for so long held the respect of all combatants at the Games. Jerrel had dreamed of crossing swords with Sarfania's champion one day. That would never happen now, thanks to Torlock and Sophistra. The thought of such a worthy fighter butchered and left for carrion in woods outside Torvosa had appalled Jerrel.

He recalled the moment Torlock had caught up with them in the mountains, the girl Lissane slung prone across his saddle, as though she were a deer trussed and bleeding. He'd caught her eye then and knew at that very moment that he loved her. That he, Jerrel, too was trapped as Estorien Sarfe had been, by those huge violet eyes and that austere beauty. He had railed at Torlock then, insisting the captain free the girl to ride as befitted her estate—

something he wouldn't have dreamed of doing, even a month ago. Torlock had laughed at him as though he were a foolish boy. Since that day Jerrel had loathed his leader.

The months passed. Summer fled from field and wood. Leaves fell and days shortened, and visions of Lissane Barola's lovely sad face filled his every moment. If she knew how he felt, she gave little sign. Remote and aloof, she responded to his attentions with insouciance, though she thanked him for the many kindnesses he'd offered to ease that cruel journey back to Galanais.

Jerrel persisted. But it was as though something inside Lissane Barola had broken. Her eyes were glazed and her soul seemed far away.

At least Varentin let her be, after stiff words from his mother. Besides, Galania's new 'prince' was more inclined to seek out other entertainment in the city, and after an initial outburst at his betrothed, had left her to her moping—or so he'd put it.

With Torlock now ruling openly alongside Sophistra (they didn't even bother to pretend that Varentin was anything more than a puppet) Jerrel's former captain was more at court and less at the barracks. It gave Jerrel the time that he needed. He took it upon himself to find out where the soldiers' loyalties lay. Many still idolised Torlock and these he steered clear of. But there were others (and not few in number) that were discontented with the way things were going in Galania.

Many were suspicious of the Chatelaine, believing—rightly, in Jerrel's opinion—that she had worked her evil on Torlock and that she was also responsible for Hal Gallante's poisoning.

Jerrel listened and watched as autumn faded to winter. When occasion allowed he voiced his opinions to those malcontents, subtly inciting rebellion against Torlock and the Chatelaine. Their numbers grew in time. Jerrel shared his thoughts with Lissane who now tolerated his friendship—if only as a buffer against Sophistra and Torlock, although they mostly ignored her too.

It had been Lissane who gave Jerrel the idea about the slaves. She had always despised Galania's use of slavery, and, although Jerrel had no problem with it, he could see their potential as freedom fighters. Once freed and trained these slaves would prove invaluable against House Sophistra (as many citizens had started to call it).

So what Jerrel had started amongst the rank and file of his soldiers, he now continued down in the streets of Galanais. Whisperers whispered, inciting insurrection and promising military aid should the people revolt. Watch and wait—the whisperers said. The time will come soon.

But a day came after midwinter when Torlock got wind of his actions. Jerrel was forced to flee Galanais, taking what men he could and making for the snow-clad mountains. Five hundred went with him, mostly the younger, less experienced of the soldiers, and these joined by many of the poorer citizens, and the few slaves who were able to escape.

Before fleeing the city, Jerrel had sought out Lissane and persuaded her to join him in flight. It was during that tense, hurried conversation that the mad-girl Morwella had rushed in upon them, her arms and dress splattered with blood, and her large eyes wide with terror.

Jerrel's stricken gaze had settled on the long dripping spike the poor child gripped between her dirty fingers. A knitting needle, almost two foot in length and covered in blood. Morwella's words, when they eventually came out, rocked the room and left Jerrel's head spinning with shock.

***

For Lissane, life had ended with her lover's death. She felt nothing. The only thing that stopped her from slashing her wrists open was the thought that one day she would kill them: Torlock, Sophistra, and Varentin—all three. She'd gore them bloody with a long cold knife.

In one glorious joyful day she would avenge Estorien's death. Then she would be free to take her own. She'd lost Erun Cade all those years ago and now Estorien Sarfe was taken from her too. Her brothers were out of reach and Erun's shade still roamed unavenged. She would not let that happen to Estorien. Lissane's soul

lived in the shadows now, in the dark places where the damned
wandered lost and the Shadowman held court. They had left her
be, her enemies at court. Only the mad-child Morwella still plagued
her upon occasion, though she too had desisted of late, receiving
no joy from the Barolan. Then a day came when Morwella changed
tack.

***

"I hate Torlock too," the girl had whispered in her ear one
afternoon, before running off down a corridor—a whirl of wild hair,
bare grubby feet and harsh giggly laughter. Lissane had paid her no
heed at the time.

Jerrel, the new Champion of Galanais, visited her often,
showing a kindness that was lost on Lissane. His sandy hair and
pale blue eyes irritated her but at least she was polite to his attentions. Jerrel had obviously fallen for her but that was of small
concern. She hated him only a little less than the others. He *was*
Galanian, and all Galanians—apart from the slaves and the poor
folk—were now her enemies.

But Jerrel persisted stubbornly and she grew weary of conflict. A time came during winter that Lissane finally withdrew her
hostilities toward Jerrel. Though she gave him little room for hoping; her heart, she told him, had died with Estorien Sarfe. Jerrel
settled for friendship—for the moment.

It had been that day Jerrel chose to impart to her his dream
of striking out at Black Torlock and the Chatelaine. That hushed
conversation had installed new fire into Lissane's withered heart.
Together they had schemed and plotted away that winter. Both
were discreet, yet Torlock eventually heard.

But Lissane was well prepared. She too had spies in the palace now. Many of the servants and slaves confided in her, knowing
she was empathic to their concerns. The palace guards were fond of
her too, and so when Jerrel came for her Lissane was ready. She'd
gathered clothes and riding gear for a winter's journey.

Torlock was rousing the army to deal with the rebels now
fleeing the city, and both Sophistra and Varentin were elsewhere.

So they had time to wait for darkness. Once night arrived the two would flee palace and city, joining Jerrel's force at the prearranged place. Jerrel had been shrewd enough to plan well ahead, knowing that Torlock would find out one day. They'd make for Torvosa. Once there a combined force of Sarfanians, Dovesians, and rebel Galanians would descend on Torlock's army. House Sophistra would crumble and her lover's spirit be allowed to rest at last. They had it all to play for and Lissane was more than ready.

The two plotters had waited in watchful silence that night until it was certain their departure wouldn't be witnessed. They were on the point of leaving when the girl child, Morwella rushed so noisily in on them, her thin arms and straggly hair dripping with blood, and her wild eyes lost to any kind of reason.

Together they witnessed her horrible story.

***

"Morwella!"

Mother's voice—calling me.

She hid. She didn't want to speak to Mother.

Hate Mother. She lets Him fuck her and He murdered Estorien. My Estorien...

He had to die, and since the Barolan girl was so pathetic in her moping misery it would fall to Morwella to do the deed. Well, she and her cats were up to the task and they would get it done. If only she could get at *Him* with her stabber or else get her cats to claw his ugly fat face.

"Morwella!"

Sophistra's voice was louder now—angry. "Where are you, child? Come out from your skulking...I wish to talk with you."

Go away...hate you!

Footsteps heralded her mother's approach.

"So...you're in there, child. No, don't run, I can see your feet. Come out, Morwella. Game's up...I've a treat, should you wish it."

Morwella slipped stabber into its hiding place in the fold of her shabby dress. Moon eyes resentful, she stepped out from the corner where she'd been hiding for most of that day. "Good," the

Chatelaine presented an elegant powdered hand, and Morwella sulkily offered hers up in return.

"What treats?" Morwella demanded as her mother dragged her out of the library where she had been accustomed to lurk of late.

"You must grow up now, dearest," Sophistra said instead, "I know you're still grieving Father's loss, but we will apprehend his murderers soon enough. My Lord Protector has already hung a score of suspects. Justice will be done, my love. Do not fear."

"Justice!" Morwella shrieked out the word. "What justice? *You* poisoned father, you fat lying cow! And Bad Black Torlock murdered Estorien. That's all He does, isn't it your paramour? Butchers people and fucks you silly! I've heard you honking like a heated sow when he shoves his cock deep inside you, Mother. The whole Palace knows what a slut you are. And a fucking liar too!"

Silence.

Sophistra's eyes smouldered like coals. Words failed to leave her lips. Instead her free hand lashed out, smacking Morwella hard across the girl's face, sending her sprawling across the polished floor. "I'll beat you senseless, you sick little cunt. Get up, you little bitch. Get up! Now!"

Morwella slunk away, suddenly scared by the black fury in her mother's eyes. She shuffled backwards, reclaiming her feet and made to run. But Sophistra was quicker, moving sideways and blocking the doorway ahead. "No you don't, little madam," Sophistra took a step forward. "You are going to pay for those foul words, child."

Morwella hissed at her then and took another skip backwards.

"Well, deny it's true and I'll say I'm sorry," the girl spat up at her mother, who now loomed over her like a thundercloud.

"Oh, I'll not deny it," Sophistra's voice had softened to silk. A cruel smile now curled a corner of her lip. "You loved Estorien Sarfe, didn't you? Silly little bitch." The Chatelaine laughed at the hurt and hatred now showing in her daughter's eyes. She took a step closer.

"I saw you mooning after him before the coward ran off with

your brother's wife. Well listen good, silly one." The Chatelaine leaned so close that her musky breath nearly choked Morwella.

"Torlock killed Estorien, yes, but acting on my orders, Morwella. MY ORDERS! Someone had to show leadership. That Sarfanian prick had mocked us with his actions. Were we to do nothing in return? Your father was weak, child...I had to kill him. Had to take hold of the situation. We had our honour at stake. The other provinces were laughing at us. I—"

Sophistra's voice trailed off in sudden horror. Her dark eyes fell on the iron spike now protruding oddly from her belly. Her mouth formed a question. But then the pain came and she screamed instead. Sophistra doubled over and sunk to her knees. Morwella, laughing now, stabbed her again and again and again. Her mother screamed and screamed, as Morwella's knitting needle stung her time after time, its slender point red and slippery with blood.

So much blood.

Crimson pooled around Sophistra's shuddering body and soaked the marble, gold traced floor of the upper hallway. And still Morwella stabbed her, kneeling over her now prostrate body, and jabbing the spike deep into her soft plump flesh, rendering the Chatelaine a gored obscenity of the handsome woman she had been. Her mother's dead eyes gaped up at her and Morwella giggled as she stabbed down, yet again.

Voices announced the arrival of guards. Morwella had just enough presence of mind to flee before they were on her. But where to go? There were no hiding places for her now. They would murder her cats, she knew, but Morwella couldn't help that. Poor Claws! As she ran through the empty rooms of the darkening palace Morwella thought of the one person who might help her. The one individual who shared her cause...

***

"And so I avenged him! Your beloved," Morwella told Lissane Barola and the stunned Captain Jerrel amid gasps and sobs. "Can I come with you?" she asked, suddenly looking down at the blood soaking her torn satin dress and pale blemished skin, and dropping in bold droplets from the long needle she still clung to. "I don't want Black Torlock to hurt me." Lissane exchanged wild glances with Jerrel, who nodded. Mad or bad, Morwella was one of them now. And she'd done them a great service so they couldn't let the girl die here.

So they had fled deep into the night, those three: the disillusioned soldier, the cold vengeful lady, and the crazy-eyed girl-child. Three refugees to the dark. As they ran Lissane couldn't help thinking of that earlier time when she had fled this palace with her lover. How ironic was this life, she thought as they wended their way out of the city, spurring the mounts Jerrel had bade a soldier make ready and wait for them to arrive, and then riding hard for the rime-studded fields ahead.

There was no pursuit. Even now, Torlock knelt over the butchered body of his consort, and Varentin Gallante, watching on, shrieked vengeance and struck out murderously at anything that moved.

***

By midnight they joined the rebel army on its way up to the mountains. Thanks to Morwella they'd struck the first blow.

Weeks later as spring's promise greened the valleys, and soft gentle rain drenched horse and rider, Jerrel's force arrived safely in Torvosa amid turmoil and consternation.

Both Duke Toreno and Baron Sarfe counselled the pair against acting too early.

"We'll wait for the Games next year," big Clarde Dovess told her after supper. Toreno's first born had been a good friend to Estorien and, although hot for vengeance, he was prudent enough to know the right time to act upon it.

"Let the insurrection grow momentum in Galanais," Clarde told her. "More will desert. Torlock will attend the Games next year; he'll have to, if only to keep face and show he has no fear—Varentin too. While they're away the city will reach bursting point, you'll see." Clarde smiled, "Protector and prince will be caught between hammer and anvil."

Jerrel, though disappointed agreed with this logic. Lissane didn't but had to capitulate. She wished the Games were tomorrow. She took Morwella under her wing, since everyone else steered well clear of the mad child.

***

Across the shimmering sea Ozmandeus's demon fell on Xenn City, rendering its jade towers to ashy dust, whilst on Laras Lassladden, Erun Cade departed for his final task.

Chapter 13

The Final task

With both Borz and Tertzei upon his person and two out of three tasks completed successfully, Erun Cade had a right to feel pleased with himself. But when Scaffa met him at the shore of a midnight murmuring sea, his well-earned joy was washed clean from him.

"The hardest task still remains," she told him. The giantess was clad in steel plate; her long pale hair pleated, and coiled high on her head. In her left hand she held a golden harp. A thing of rare beauty, uncannily wrought.

"Aqueous is second only to Ashmali in might," Scaffa told him. "But her strength is in beguilement rather than rage. She is most devious and will deceive you while her guardian devours your flesh. You must stay awake at all times; Aqueous is artful and will try to get inside your head."

"How do I overcome such a creature?" Erun had asked her his eyes still on the harp. He hadn't played much since leaving Rakeel, and his fingers itched. Besides, this harp was beautiful unlike the battered wooden one he'd got from the hermit—fond of that though he was.

Scaffa read his thoughts as though they were written on his face. "The harp is yours, Erun Cade, and Callanak too, should you achieve this final task for me. You'll need to take the harp with you—it has stronger resonance than your own, and Aqueous's one weakness is a love of music."

"What am I supposed to do—just sing to her?" Erun found that notion so ridiculous it almost amused him. "Wouldn't Callanak's steel prove more useful?"

Scaffa's cold eyes settled on his own and he felt suddenly sober again. "Fool, what good is a sword against water?" she snapped, suddenly annoyed. "You must match cunning with cunning, Erun Cade. Use the harp to lure her to the surface of the lake while her guardian sleeps. Once she has risen you must keep her occupied—somehow."

"With the harp..?"

"That and...other things. Use your imagination." responded Scaffa, a wicked smile now tracing her lips. "Water Spirits have certain appetites and require a lot of sating when roused."

Erun didn't know how to respond to that and decided not to pursue the matter. Instead he enquired about the guardian. Scaffa's answer wasn't reassuring. "A nicor—a water creature," she told him. "They're scaly and sinuous to behold. Not dissimilar to those krakens that haunt the Rodruthan coast, although smaller and more secretive—inhabiting lakes and meres instead of open sea."

"Where will I encounter this Aqueous and her monster?"

And how am I supposed to kill the nicor...Do I sing to that too?

"At the Lake of Clouds," she answered, and then reading his thoughts added, "Use your intuition, or else seek aid from another."

"And where is this Lake of Clouds?"

"It lies north of the mountains in upland Treggara," Scaffa replied. She bid him follow her then to a place where the lake shimmered and glistened in the dark. Erun's eyes rested on objects lying beside the water: a hauberk suit of chain mail, a long hafted axe, and a helmet with face mask and neck plates. All were cunningly wrought, fashioned from some strange metal and coloured the black of winter night.

"These you may claim on your return," Scaffa told him, "and something else besides—should you wish it....Go now. The ferryman is waiting."

And so he had left her for the fourth time, and yet again the dour grizzled ferryman carried him from the island without a word spoken. As always Erun felt as though he journeyed through a dream. Whenever he approached Laras Lassladden everything changed—not just the shifting physicality of Scaffa's domain, but his perception of it and the way his mind worked too. Everything appeared achievable while on that island, but once he left it all the doubts came rushing in again. It just wasn't fair. Part of him wondered if he would ever be free of the giantess and her enchantments.

The cold grey skies of Rodrutha brought him swiftly back to earth. The boat had gone and instead he sat a horse. It was hard approaching winter in the northlands, and his thoughts on the task ahead were not encouraging. Somehow he had succeeded in tasks one and two: both Borz and Tertzei were with Scaffa now. But with those quests at least Erun had had a plan of sorts. This time he hadn't even a notion.

It came to him as he cantered down the shabby streets of Northtown toward the woods and cliffs ahead. The ferryman had supplied the horse—he hadn't asked; he'd learnt not to question that grim boatman.

Seek out the aid of another, she said...

And I know just the person.

Erun guided his mount up the steep incline slicing through the hills above Northtown, turning once only to gaze down at village and grey angry ocean beyond. Scaffa's cliffs reared black and bleak, scarce more than a smudge darkening the horizon.

The road south wound through forest and moor until reaching the uplands of Treggara. But Erun chose another route, steering his beast along the high coast road that paralleled the clifftops awarding stunning views of the ocean beyond, where seabirds swooped and dived. Now and then the black bobbing dots of seals could be seen far below. He rode thus for a time until the path steered north along tall bluffs.

A mile ahead reared a dark promontory of rock. Forlorn and forbidding. A great fastness of stone resembling a castle hewed from solid rock, its outer walls broken off into sharp, jagged crags that strode out defiantly into the ocean, their weed-bearded knees washed with the frothing white spume of wintry water.

Erun spurred his horse along the track until the headland dominated the skyline in front. His keen eyes made out the faint lines of walls jutting out from the cliffs ahead. Druthan Crags: home of Torrig Red Hair—his old friend, and someone hopefully just insane enough to help him. Rakaro might be nuts but Torrig was in a class of his own. Hence perfect for this next job.

The gate leading to the fortress wasn't inviting. A horse's skull adorned the top of a long pole; its hollow gaze watched his approach with disdain. Beyond that, gibbets paraded the road; the rotting occupants left their stink with him as Erun urged his steed trot toward the gates ahead.

These reared strong and stark, and beyond them a courtyard lead toward the castle main. A shape moved. It became a guard, bleary-eyed and bulky beneath his fur and iron. He levelled a spear and grunted a challenge as Erun dismounted and led his steed toward the gate.

"Hoi, stop there! Who the fuck—?"

The Rodruthan charm was lost on Erun. He batted the levelled spear aside with a forearm and grabbed the man's steel collar. It was the only language Rodruthans understood—Torrig had taught him that much. The guard spat at him but Erun tightened his grip on his neck and growled in his ear.

"I seek Prince Torrig son of Brude," Erun said before adding, "I'm a friend to his Highness and would expect more courtesy at his gates." He let go then, and the guard coughed and grunted for a minute before regaining his dour station.

"Prince Torrig? No such geezer. You mean King Torrig of Rodrutha."

Erun was surprised and his face showed it.

"I didn't know."

The guard grinned evilly, believing he had the advantage again. "The old king drowned in his soup a while back," he informed Erun, as if only a moron wouldn't know that. "A scuffle followed as the children crawled over each other to get the crown. Then our new king came back from his wanders, banged a few heads together and took the crown for himself."

Erun winced.

King Torrig...he'll be worse than ever now.

The guard wound the creaking portcullis up just enough for Erun to lead his horse underneath. Beyond this the stone courtyard was dark and damp, and at its far end were rusty steel doors hewn into the bedrock. "Wait here, stranger," said the guard, "I'll go and see if my lord is awake."

"Awake..? It's almost noon."

"Aye, well, *they* were feasting last night," the guard grumbled, and then left him to the cold stone of the empty courtyard. For an hour Erun waited in the chilly gloom, his mood darkening and his patience thinning fast. Perhaps this had been a mistake? Torrig had been good to him but then Erun had rescued him from the Garrons. Perhaps now that he was king he no longer cared for his old companion. Why should he? Erun was on the point of leading the horse back under the yawning portcullis when the far door creaked open and a familiar coarse voice yelled across to him.

"Singer..! By the holy farts of Talcan it's good to see you!" Red Torrig's grinning tattooed freckled face banished Erun's doubts in an instance. His old friend was garbed in rich woollen cloak and gaudy tunic of scarlet and yellow, with tight fitting leather trousers, tucked neatly into long calfskin boots.

A huge golden brooch clasped the cloak in place, fashioned in the shape of a horned helmet crossed by two spears—Rodrutha's emblem. At Torrig's waist were heavy sword and axe, both supported by a silver-studded belt of leather, six inches in girth. The young king grinned like a wolf, strode toward him and then slammed a tattooed fist into Erun's shoulder.

"By the gods you've changed, Singer." Torrig's clear blue eyes studied his friend and his smile widened. "You're leaner, harder. You stand different and have the look of a fighting man about you now. Quite impressive for a soppy singer. What happened on that bloody island? Did she beat you with hot spoons or something?"

"Worse."

King Torrig shouted something obscene and the surly guard appeared and, still grumbling, led the horse away to be stabled and fed. "Norris has got the right hump today," Torrig explained. "He caught Cedric Three Fingers poking Hilda, his missus, behind the coal shed. Norris doesn't much like his missus but he had no notion of sharing her with Cedric. Bit of a scrap yesterday." Erun nodded sympathetically despite this being too much information.

"Come we'll drink some ale and you can tell me everything," said Torrig "If you want a wench I've several lively lasses." Erun declined politely.

I've come for aid," he said, "not fornication. I didn't know you were king now. I've been away. Perhaps I shouldn't have come..?"

"Don't be stupid, Singer. I owe you, and Rodruthans always repay their debts, king or no. Besides you're a friend. There is only so much wenching and drinking a king can do this time of year before monotony takes hold.

"An adventure might well prove welcome. So, how can I help? Start at the beginning. Scaffa's island—what's it like? I thought that I'd lost you for ever that day, boy. I was saddened for a time, back then."

At Torrig's word Erun followed him deep inside the castle. Druthan Crags was vast and airy (and freezing cold), its halls being carved out of solid rock. There were echoes everywhere, and most of the lofty draughty rooms they crossed were empty and silent. There was hardly any furniture, Erun noted, though all manner of weaponry adorned the dreary walls.

They passed through several draughty halls, the fires blazing at hearth but doing little to dispel the damp chill. They reached a passage that led out into the open air. Erun's eyes gaped. A wooden bridge of flimsy construction lurched across a yawning gap, reaching over to the nearest crag—where Torrig's private quarters were, so he learned. They hastened across the rickety bridge, Erun's stomach heaved when he saw the spray and wash of white water far below. He gripped tight on the rope handrails and was pleased to reach the other side. Torrig told him later that the best way to cross was when drunk, it helped with the rhythm—or so he said. Erun wasn't convinced.

Torrig's rooms were spacious and airy—though no warmer than anywhere else. Fully glazed salt-stained windows awarded panoramic views of coastline to east and west, whilst ahead a second stack reared tall from the ocean, and a second swaying bridge led out across to it. Erun was relieved to hear that the outer stack served only as a lookout tower, where the Rodruthan kings went to spy on traders and merchantmen who dared trespass the northern waters. Once he spotted them the lookout would launch birds and light beacon fires; soon after the ships at Northtown and Longships would put to sea and the hunt would be on. Druthan Crags was a place of terror for seafarers.

And so for the greater part of that entire day, Erun drained tankard after tankard of heady ale and painstakingly recounted his various adventures since they'd parted company the year before. Torrig's eyes widened as Erun recounted his journeys across Xandoria and told of his quests for Borz and Tertzei.

"So you killed their Emperor." Torrig had been particularly impressed by that bit. He liked the sound of Rakaro too. And he always could do with more good archers. "You're some character, Singer," Torrig slurped when Erun finally finished his tale. "But, this quest of ours is the hardest one, yes?"

Erun nodded and told his friend all that Scaffa had told him about Aqueous and her guardian—which wasn't much, to be fair.

"A nicor...they're nasty beasties" frowned Torrig when Erun ceased his words. "Fuck it, though—sounds like fun. When should we leave?"

Fun. Yes I was right to come here.

"The sooner the better, methinks."

"First light then," said Torrig, and then yelled a maid for more ale. Erun became very drunk that night. There was a girl at some point, though the morning after he couldn't quite recall what had happened—much to Torrig's amusement and his own embarrassment.

The king had woken him at first light amid grins. Torrig—horribly bright-eyed and sober—had been wide awake and dressed, despite their lateness to bed. Erun's head felt like a swollen water melon at bursting point. Even the cold grey northern light was far too bright for his bloodshot squinting eyes.

They rode south, Torrig had given him a thick woollen cloak to keep off the chill and he'd been glad of it that morning. The king looked splendid in his richly hued furs and polished iron ring mail. He carried a longbow with a full quiver alongside his sword and axe, and his manner was annoyingly cheerful, with ceaseless bantering about his time as king and his bold plans for Rodrutha Province.

Torrig still craved vengeance for the wrongs done his kin by Treggarans but was willing to wait for the right time. Now he was a king he had to employ patience—a rare challenge for Rodruthans, that.

The journey south took over a week and the weather worsened all the time. They crossed the border in a snowstorm, and Erun was reminded of that earlier time when he had happened upon Dreekhall and its fierce occupants. His mind had a fleeting image of Slinsi Garron naked in front of the fire, her snake eyes winking at him as she lowered her thick lips onto his rampant sex. He swiftly changed his train of thought. That had been a close call back then.

At last they reached the foothills heralding the start of the large mountain range that dominated central Gol and acted as a border between Treggara, Galania, Dovesi and far off Barola. They skirted the hills until they reached a valley that opened upon a wide lake, its still tranquil shores coated with snow, and its clear water mirroring the sweeping clouds above. They approached with care, eyes wary and bone-cold fingers brushing bowstring and sword.

It was a tranquil scene despite the cold wind that penetrated clothing and howled mournfully at their ears. The lake was alluring; it promised peace. A deep contentment and rest from the multifarious worries of the world. They had only to reach it and they would be in peace. Torrig sighed theatrically and spurred his mount forward. Erun, reminded of Laras Lassladden, caught his arm and his friend reined in.

"Be careful," he warned, "there is enchantment here, and this Aqueous is rumoured to be a subtle creature."

Torrig nodded, though he didn't normally do subtle. "It's beautiful though," he added under his breath. "Strange...I know this country well enough from our many raids, and yet I've never heard any speak of this place, let alone seen it."

Erun thought of Scaffa and her games and his mouth tightened. "Come on," he said. "Let's get this done and be away."

They had the bones of a plan. Whether it worked or not was anybody's guess. Torrig would remain mounted. The king's job was too cement both eyes on the lake watching out for the nicor and, should it appear, keeping the bloody thing occupied. It wasn't a task that Erun envied but his friend was more than up for it.

While Torrig sat his horse and waited, he, Erun, would dismount and file down to the shore. Once there he would unwrap the golden harp Scaffa had given him and commence playing. After that..? Erun didn't dwell on that bit.

The water chimed softly as he approached with caution. From somewhere behind, Torrig's horse snorted and her rider steadied the nervous beast. It was so quiet. Even the chilling wind had ceased and, just yards ahead, the lake shimmered and beckoned him close.

Erun exposed the harp, hidden until now on the same loop that had carried Borz's sack. His fingers sought the strings and reaching them plucked a single chord. The harp-note sang out clear and bold, its tone venturing far out across the lake before returning to him in an echo.

He plucked again and waited for the echo—a beautiful sound and a golden sound, both evocative and haunting. Erun played on, his agile fingers dancing on the strings. The tune was one he didn't know but seemed to come from somewhere deep within him. For an hour he played, his breath steaming and his fingers weaving magic over the taut strings. The music filled him—all else slipped away. Torrig, forgotten and bored, still watched the lake from a wary distance.

***

It was then that she appeared. Aqueous. Her pale face surfacing above the water, and her cold eyes watching him from far out across the lake. Long time she watched the stranger play on the shore, her huge aquamarine eyes resting on his long smooth fingers as they curled around his instrument. It had been so very long since Aqueous had encountered such innocence and beauty.

Her nakedness stirred to wanton life beneath her, and her small cleft tongue slithered hungrily out from the gap between her pouting wet lips. The music had called her up from her deep lair in the cave at the lake's forgotten bottom. Curious and eager was she now. It had been time immemorial since Aqueous had heard such lovely music, and she so liked music.

At last her hunger tempted her nearer. Aqueous kicked and dived, and ripples followed her lissom form as she sped silent and swift toward harper and shore. Her head broke surface again with a soft *plunk,* and the water chimed as it spilled from her long pale silver-blue tresses. She was close now but still he hadn't seen her.

Who was he? *Could he be the one?*

Aqueous trod water for a time watching and listening...and yearning. She saw the other man sitting his horse a distance off, but paid him no heed. Her eyes and ears were only for the harper and his beautiful song. Slowly and purposefully, Aqueous began to swim to the shore, her hungry quicksilver gaze never leaving her prey. She spoke the words in her fishy tongue and her guardian stirred in its cavern far below.

I have need of you now.

***

A cold day. He leans against the tent wall feeling sick and giddy. The burnt shrivelled corpse of the assassin still smoulders at his feet. Karali. A lethal killer and Xandoria's best. No longer—he laughs—instead just another blackened corpse. The fool had stalked his tent while he rested after the carnage of Xenn's demolition.

But then how would Karali know that Ozmandeus didn't sleep anymore? The Demon was growing inside him like a tumour, eating him slowly—inch by fiery inch. The small seed of sanity the Renegade still retained knew that he had lost. That Ashmali was the victor. And that Ashmali was growing stronger inside him every hour. He was a hollow shell and the time was drawing nigh when he would crack, allowing the monster to break through. The Demon was barely diminished after his recent venting over Xenn. Unlike Lamoza, his fires were unquenched and he still hungered for more. Ozmandeus was Ashmali's slave: the demon controlled his body and almost ruled his mind.

Soon he would die—he knew that now. He had gambled and lost. Ozmandeus allowed his fire-rimmed gaze to drop to Karali's corpse. Another soul for Ashmali's army and another slave to the demon. Xenn was no more and soon Xandoria would be ashen ruin. What then? But he knew the answer: more and more and more. All shall be ruined as Ashmali reaches climax, and he, the instigator, cast aside like just another pawn in the game. How the gods must be laughing at him. But they had better not laugh for long. Else Ashmali hear them and eat them too.

Chapter 14

Aqueous

King Torrig was feeling restless and abandoned. Erun Cade had been playing for over an hour and nothing had happened. Boring. He hadn't come here to be bored. Occasionally the harp music filtered up to him and he was amazed by the richness and beauty of the sound—he'd never been one for music before unless it was some bawdy wench-tossing jig. But this..?

Erun Cade was a mystery to Torrig, and the king of Rodrutha was no fool. Hidden beneath his coarse banter was a shrewd cunning mind. Erun's tale had alarmed him. Things were astir in the world and the gods, as ever, were playing them for fools.

Erun was caught in their web now that he was Queen Scaffa's pawn. That Queen of Death would have her pound of flesh. Torrig worried for his friend who had altered so remarkably since last he'd seen him.

The Erun Cade he'd met in Dreekhall had seemed a naïve, gentle—if angry, vengeful boy. This new Erun Cade had the look of a hardened veteran. A warrior grown up with war. Little mercy showed in those grey-blue eyes. And his friend looked so much older though so little time had passed. It didn't make any sense.

Torrig suspected sorcery. The Island's witch had worked upon him. But what game was Scaffa playing?

He didn't like this place anymore, Torrig decided. It was too quiet: too still. There was bewitchment here for sure. Torrig, who feared no mortal foe or challenge, had a terror of sorcery and magic. Inherent in all Rodruthans—a legacy of long dark winters—when toothless grandmothers terrified little children with tales of fire demons and foul creeping ghoulies in bogs. Cheerful memories those. But when Erun had mentioned Ashmali's name Torrig had felt an unmanly stab of fear in his loins and had struggled to hide it.

Ashmali.

Ancient lore had long foretold a time when the gods would forsake Gol, and a ruin of fire would come from overseas and destroy all. And this water spirit—what part would she play? What use Scaffa planned for such beings Torrig couldn't begin to guess, but that didn't concern him.

What did concern him was that his friend was caught like a hooked trout in a game played out between beings possessing extremely dodgy morals—and damned elusive motives.

Torrig would keep an eye on Erun Cade, he decided. That's what friends were for, wasn't it? He'd invite him back to the Crags when this bizarre trip was over—try and steer him away from the Witch Queen and her island domain. But that wouldn't be easy.

What's that?

Torrig stiffened in his saddle, suddenly alert. His horse's head shot back in nervous alarm and a cloud of steaming breath vented out from her nostrils.

"Easy girl, I don't like this either." The king's eyes scanned the waters for any sign. Then he saw it. Movement far out at the centre of the lake. Something was approaching the shore—and swiftly. It was too far off to make out for certain but looked to be a woman's naked shape, kicking fast and hard toward the place where Erun still played by the lonely shore.

Torrig made to call out in warning to his friend but there came a shuffling, scraping noise behind him. He turned in his saddle and, too late, saw the scaly sinuous tree-thick limb, jab across at him like a questing serpent and knock him over. Torrig swore as the blow knocked him clean off his saddle.

Shit, shit and more shit!

Torrig's body sailed through air, he was dimly aware of the horse's agonised scream as the monster tore upon her.

Poor thing. Torrig heard Erun shout something inaudible then the ground rushed up at him and he rolled on impact. Bruised and aching but mercifully unbroken, Torrig leapt to his feet. Bow in hand and arrow on the nock, he slowly peered out from the rock now, most conveniently, hiding him.

A monstrosity had risen from the water's surface. It was thing of remarkable ugliness that stank of a thousand rotten fish, with countless writhing tendrils spreading out from a central dome-like skull and single horrid lidless eye. A cruel beak-mouth closed with a snap over the broken body of his horse and all the while the claws on the end of the creature's tentacles searched the shore for Torrig's whereabouts. Torrig had been in worse predicaments but he couldn't recall quite when. And that smell...

Torrig loosed the arrow: it took the nicor just above its eye. The monster roared, its horrid noise filling the valley and echoing through the hills like a chain of nightmares. Torrig swore and fired again but the shot went wide. He nocked another, swore, drew back taut, and swore again. Too late, the honking acre of ghastliness was already upon him...

***

The music flowed out from Erun's soul. He was witness to nothing. Clouds scurried overhead, the lake's surface mirrored their passage and the cold nip of wind blued his fingers, yet still they worked their magic. If it hadn't been for the horse's screams she would have been upon him with her nets, and all would fall to ruin. As it was, Erun Cade had just time enough to roll aside as Aqueous cast the nets his way.

She smiled then, revealing finely filed teeth, "You're a clever boy." Aqueous drank in his tanned face, his determined look and the way his bony man's fingers clutched hard at the harp strings.

"I meant not to harm you, my young love, only to ensure that you didn't flee. You mortals are so fragile."

Erun watched her body rise dripping and naked from the water. Behind him a sudden twang, thud and roar, announced that Torrig's first arrow had landed. Erun dare not turn. Instead, he kept his cool grey-blue gaze on the Water Elemental now approaching him. Aqueous tossed the nets she had carried aside and smiled again as his eyes took in her nakedness.

"Do you like what you see?" Aqueous's lips promised a million things and Erun dared not consider any of them. Instead he hurriedly fumbled for the sack Scaffa had given him, now tied to the back of his belt. Erun waited, watched her slow, sensual approach, his gaze taking in the huge scary aquamarine eyes, the lithe sinewy body, with its small pert breasts and the triangle of wet fur glistening like quicksilver between her legs. Erun felt his sex swelling, and she, sensing that, smiled again.

"Come," her voice was sultry and beguiling and her tones both reasonable and calm. All was serene and quiet. The sounds of Torrig's continuing struggles seemed unimportant and far away. Then Aqueous reached toward him with a pale webby hand, and he gasped as her wet cold fingers traced a line up his thighs until they came to rest on his bulging manhood.

"Love me," she said, her huge eyes working their magic upon him until all else was nearly forgotten. Erun reached for her then and Aqueous laughed as she slithered and spilled into his arms. He kissed her neck and hair, marvelling at the fishy taste, which though different, was strangely attractive.

He kissed her mouth then, and shuddered as her cool hands unfastened his belt and slid beneath his smallclothes. His tongue found her nipples and worked lower until she groaned with ecstasy. He took her then. Hard and fast, her joyous wailing screams filled the valley accompanying the guardian's awful grunts and Torrig's desperate expletives.

It all made for an unholy racket. When they were done Erun rolled free but she crawled after him. "That was just the beginning." Aqueous reached for him again but Erun pulled away. The

Elemental's eyes darkened to angry wells at his rejection of her, and her mouth widened to show again those pointed razor teeth.

"Dare you shun me, mortal creature?"

Aqueous spell broke then. A gong went off in Erun's head but at least he was himself again. Torrig's battle continued somewhere close, somehow his friend still lived and the roars of the vengeful nicor were still trying to alter that.

He needs my help.

Aqueous reached for Erun again, her anger temporarily quelled by fresh rising lust. "My sweet love, come...don't fear me. I will show you my kingdom—you'll be my consort and play to me in the depths forever." She reached for Erun hungrily but he proved far the quicker. With a striking cobra's speed Erun retrieved the sack from its abandoned place by his redundant trousers, and pulled it down hard over Aqueous's head, his hoarse shouts wording the binding-runes Scaffa had taught him.

Aqueous screamed horribly. She lashed out at him blindly with her dagger-like nails, scoring long cuts down the length of his body. Erun, stubborn faced, completed the rune-spell and fastened the sack at her neck.

"You are mine now," he told her, "You serve me, Elemental. So call off your monster!" As he spoke the sack expanded in size until it covered Aqueous's nakedness down to her feet, closing rapidly over them, the invisible cords sealing the gap. Then Water Spirit slumped in defeat and completed the sealing runes as the sack swallowed the last of her body. Erun leaned across and yelled as close to her ear as he could (without knowing precisely where that appendage was.) "I SAID CALL OFF THE BLOODY NICOR!" Aqueous, sobbing, obliged. Sulkily she spoke the words and suddenly everything fell very quiet.

***

Torrig clung to life like a drowning beetle in a flood. He'd severed three of the monster's tentacles with his axe, but now the haft was broken and he had only his sword—and that badly blunted too. Every inch of his painted body screamed at him in pain, and there were deep cuts on his face and hands where the nicor's steel claws had sliced open his flesh. He only hoped the wounds contained no poison. Even were that not so, Torrig was weakening fast. He couldn't hold out for much longer, and he'd hardly damaged the monster beyond his lucky first arrow.

And what the fuck was that singer doing with that fishy slapper down there?

No time to think. Torrig dived low as another mile long tentacle shot toward him, passing just inches over his head. He sliced his sword up in a wild, frantic cut, but the thing was so blunt it just bounced off the tentacle and sent a jolt of pain up his arm.

Shit, shit and shit again.

Torrig rolled to his feet, painfully rubbing his arm. A shadow loomed to his right. Slowly, Torrig turned and then looking up, saw that the monster had crawled from the water and now bulked over him like a thousand ton stinking jelly.

It wasn't pretty. Torrig waited for those steel jaws to cut him in two: he was trapped—his sword abandoned and useless. Not the best way for the King of Rodrutha to end his days. He closed his eyes and wrinkled his nose at the stench of the creature now drooling over him. He waited.

Come on, fucker—do your worst.

Nothing. Torrig dared open one eye. Gone. Not even a sucker remaining. Vanished. The creature had disappeared and, even better, had taken its stink with it. Now instead he was rewarded by the gormless grinning face of Erun Cade.

"About time you showed up, Singer," Torrig said, clasping his hand and somehow staying on his feet.

"You're still alive." Erun's grin widened as he stated the obvious. Torrig rolled his eyes and muttered something obscene.

"I think so but I may be wrong." Torrig pulled a loose tooth from his mouth and tossed it on the ground. "Tell me it was worth it. Did you bag the fishy bitch?"

Erun pointed to the sealed bag left redundant on a rock behind him.

"She's in there," he nodded.

"She's a bit small." The sack was no larger than the wine sacks carried by Torrig's maids.

"I shrank her with spells Scaffa taught me. Aqueous can't harm us now."

"I worry about you, Singer," said Torrig, "You're becoming too much of a sorcerer for my liking."

"Tricks of the trade," replied Erun, shouldering the sack (the contents now whining dismally) and heading up toward the hills behind. "Are you coming? I've no wish to linger here longer."

Torrig swore again. "What happened to that obscenity I was fighting? The bloody thing was hell-bent on making me its lunch."

"I made her send it back to its lair down at the lake bed. Now are you coming?"

"I suppose so." Torrig gave the lake a last suspicious glance, checked his body was still intact (mercifully it was) then picked up his battered sword and broken axe, and whistling followed his friend out of the valley. He pulled a face at the dismal racket exuding from inside the rune-sack.

"Is she going to do that the whole way back?"

"I expect so, she's related to Borz."

"Then remind me to shove some cheese in my ears."

"Will do."

They recovered the surviving horse, shared saddle, and by nightfall of the following day reached Rodrutha.

***

King Torrig and Erun Cade parted company a week later where the road split above Northtown. Erun vowed to seek out his friend after he had attended business with Scaffa. His tasks were achieved and he was now free to pursue his overdue revenge against the Baron and his sons. Though that memory was distant, the brand on his forehead tingled as a sudden reminder of a task undone.

Time for retribution. And Lissane's violet eyes he hadn't forgotten. Erun would avenge his father. Rosco and Aldo could live. Even the Baron he'd spare, for Lissane's sake. His memory of her deserved that much.

But Paulo Barola had to die. It was long past time.

Before they said farewell, Torrig proposed that Erun join his Rodruthans at the Games in Torvosa next summer and Erun agreed, liking the idea.

Once my vengeance is achieved.

Erun now desired to make a name for himself here in Gol, and where better to warn the barons of the horror erupting across the sea?

"I'll see you there," Erun promised his friend.

They clasped hands then and bade each other cheery farewell. Erun watched the king ride west and disappear. Then, as evening beckoned, Erun Cade took to strolling down into the rain-washed streets of Northtown with Aqueous in tow. The ferryman was waiting for him in the harbour.

For the final time Erun Cade left the mainland bound for Laras Lassladden. On this last occasion he felt neither fear nor trepidation. Now Scaffa owed him. Erun smiled as the cliffs of her island reared close. He would claim his prize and then leave. Erun Cade the boy was dead; he was Kell the warrior now, lean and deadly: none would stop him. Erun vaulted from the craft and strode ashore. This time lanterns lit the way into a grove of oaks. A woman waited in the shadow. She turned toward him slowly and smiled.

It was Lissane Barola.

***

The wind cried cold and ice rimed the fields that glittered so steely-blue, reflecting back the moon's lonely path. High above his head the sky danced in vivid purples and greens and a distant booming filled his ears. Rakaro had ridden so many miles in search of his people, but at last he had found them. Way up here beyond Khandol on the very edge of the world where frozen seas merged with bleak stony shore.

Ahead tents studded the flatness. The yellow flicker of tallow lanterns cast wan light over tiny figures moving to and fro. The Hillmen, his kinfolk. Rakaro approached warily, expecting no great welcome here. He dismounted from his pony and led her in between the tangled mish-mash of tent and corral.

Beasts stirred and the odd individual looked up as Rakaro shuffled by, seeing a dark hooded figure—perhaps a hunter back from the ice fields beyond. No one seemed to care.

Then a young warrior stepped laughing out of a tent, unlaced his hide trousers and pissed a steaming hole into the ice. He was singing very badly and was evidently drunk. Rakaro smiled, he had always liked Ankai.

The younger man glanced his way: his eyes sobering quickly when he saw Rakaro standing there. Ankai reached for his nearest knife but Rakaro just laughed at him.

"I'd finish that piss, Ankai, before you get too excited and slice off your organ." Rakaro stepped closer out of the gloom and Ankai gasped when he recognised Toskai's former right hand man.

"Rakaro, you've some gall coming here. If Toskai finds you creeping about he'll have you tied to a wheel and left for the bears. The bears are always hungry up here."

"I know—I've seen them stomping about." Rakaro cut to the chase. "Ankai, I need your help...I know of a place where our folk can settle. A warm fertile country—I've a friend there."

"You'll find none willing to roam south," responded Ankai, looking dubious. "I saw the demon army entering the Gap," he added and shuddered at the memory. "Xandoria is finished, Rakaro."

"My destination is east over sea—not south," answered Rakaro. "A land called Gol, rich with grazing pastures, so I'm told. Besides, there's no future up here for our people, grubbing blindly at mealworms and swapping glum tales with the seals."

"This is about survival, Rakaro, and our people once lived up here and were content enough."

"That was then."

"We can learn to re-adjust—besides we're nomads, remember. I don't think.." Ankai stopped speaking. A man had just ventured out of a nearby tent and now stood staring moodily across at them. It was Toskai, but then Rakaro had expected that.

"That you, Ankai?" Toskai's face was partially hidden by the night. "Who's that with you?"

"Greeting, Toskai, friend and brother," said Rakaro.

"You." Toskai's arm was a blur. Rakaro dived low as the knife arced toward him, a silver sliver in the dark. He rolled and lashed out with a leg, but Toskai was already upon him—a second knife now gripped in left hand, the right one's fingers jabbing viciously out at Rakaro's eyes.

Rakaro dodged and wriggled. He caught Toskai's knife-wielding wrist and twisted sharply, unbalancing his attacker and deflecting the blade. Somehow, Rakaro got his knee up under and rammed it hard into Toskai's belly, but otter-lithe, the other Hillman rolled free—not before biting a chunk off Rakaro's right earlobe.

By now there was shouting and hoots as several folk gathered close to see. Among them were sleepy-eyed women and animated, yelling youngsters, together with a few drunk bravados who shouted insults at the two brawlers tussling and grunting beneath the lamplight.

Rakaro's ear bled profusely in the cold. He ignored it. They rolled and spat in the freezing night, punching and biting meaty chunks off each other. Neither was winning, but then Rakaro got a fist around Toskai's balls. He squeezed hard, twisting the loose cloth of Toskai's trousers. Toskai spat in his eye and swore but had to let go. Rakaro, arms now free, rammed an elbow up into Toskai's face, breaking his nose and sending him sprawling in the frozen mud.

He stood up then and wiped the blood from his face. Toskai glared at him from the mud. "Enough, Toskai. There's no time for this. Hear me out—"

"Fuck you." Toskai leapt to his feet with another knife in hand, but Rakaro launched a savage kick between his legs and Toskai slunk groaning to the earth again. But only for a minute. Toskai snarled; he rolled, spun the knife between his fingers and made to throw, but Rakaro kicked him again—this time hard in the face. That did it. Toskai slunk prone and didn't stir. There were a few sighs and appreciative grunts. Aside that quiet.

Job done.

"Well," said Rakaro after a long pause while he got his breath back, "I have returned and I have much news and a proposal for you all. But first I would eat—I'm starving."

That night Rakaro managed to persuade his people to begin a long arduous faring across northern Khandol and beyond. He promised them a new life in another country. A land free from horror and ruin. A promised land. That night Rakaro didn't sleep, so that when Toskai came for him he was ready, and Toskai's bright blood spilled and congealed on the bearskin rugs below his cot. It was a shame, they had long been friends. But that was history, dead and gone like the fire in Toskai's eyes. What mattered now was the future. That future was in Gol.

Later that year their exodus began.

Chapter 15

Departures

Winter. Skeins of geese cut wedges through slate grey skies, their plaintive calls reaching him as he watched from the deserted parapet. It was cold this morning, very cold. Below, the sea-lashed causeway was coated with rime, and far beyond the distant hills gleamed white with fresh snowfall. And the skies promised more. The hardest winter in years...but what would follow? A spring of opportunity followed by a golden summer, allowing a chance for him to activate his plans.

Eon Barola smiled at that thought and well he might, for those plans were reaching fruition. The Baron ignored the biting wind that reached his bones despite the heavy wool cloak and thick garments he wore. He leaned out and watched as the departing geese were swallowed by dark eastern skyline.

Next summer would see it done. Eon reached down, retrieved the parchment that had arrived last night from far off Xandoria. Paolo had written him from Rakeel, his words full of pride and excitement. He had been right to trust in Paolo, the boy had a negotiator's talent as well as a torturer's soul.

The money had changed hands and the deal was done. He

had only to wait, and then strike hard when they least expected it. Hard and fast. Eon fingered his goatee and let his thoughts take him where they would.

He had done well. Treggara, he'd neutered with a promise of wealth, Galania was in turmoil, thanks to his daughter's latest actions. That girl was proving an asset to him at last, though inadvertently. Rodrutha caused him little concern, neither did Sarfania. That left Dovesi...

A time of change was coming: soon Gol would become great again. Strong as it once was before the kings' blood thinned and their rule decayed from within. It was time for these lands to be led by a warrior again, as they should be. And who better for that task than the original instigator of the Rebellion? Who else was worthy or strong enough now Hal Gallante was dead? It had to be Eon Barola.

Eon crunched the parchment between his strong fingers and grabbed the wine sack from its resting place on the wall. He took a long satisfying pull, belched, and then wiped his newly greying beard with his expensive ermine sleeve. The cold was getting to him at last. It was time to retire. Tomorrow, he and his boys would hunt deer and wolf through those snow-clad hills. But this day he would rest with his thoughts.

The Baron took a last searching glance at the stark skyline and then retired below. In his chamber more wine waited and firelight crackled with welcome warmth. And then later, the girl...

***

The world had ceased from turning. Dusk hung in silence all around. The lanterns cast no flicker. No sound entered that hallowed glade. All was still...silent.

She came to him then with arms out wide, her naked body white beneath the crescent horned moon. They loved: again and again—fiercely... gently.

Erun kissed those sweet nipples and traced long questing fingers down the goosebumps covering her thighs. She laughed as he took her once more. Was this a dream? He didn't think so—not this time. They must have slept for a time with limbs entwined. He woke alone and cold.

Lissane...?

She is gone; instead he hears laughter all around him.

What's this? And then he is falling, down, down, through racing heady skies.

"Lissane..!" Erun calls her name, but his love has gone—left him again. He weeps and the laughter mocks those salty tears. Still he falls...

Time shifts: the shadows depart. He now stands on a cold plateau of land; a bitter wind batters his face, freezing the tears on his cheek. He hears footfalls behind him and turns...

***

"Did you enjoy my gift, Erun Cade?" Scaffa's laughter was husky and her quicksilver eyes smiled at his nakedness. The sky shimmered. He'd been duped—yet again.

"But...Lissane? She was here..." Erun's mind spun, he tried to shut out the jabbing thoughts now assaulting his senses as harsh reality stole upon him. "It was you, Scaffa, in the glade back there. You deceived me!" Erun felt suddenly foolish and very angry, "made me believe it was Lissane returned to me, beyond all hoping."

"You should be honoured," Scaffa told him as the wind tossed the platinum braids of her hair. "Few mortal men have lain with a Goddess, Erun Cade. But you have earned my affection...and, so..." as Erun watched in wonderment, Scaffa's giantess form shifted like windblown smoke. Gone was the warrior queen. A stranger gazed down upon him now. Impossibly tall: green gold eyes surrounded a perfect face. Too perfect to be human, the long red-gold hair fell to her knees, covering her nakedness. Her skin had a bluish tinge. Around her essence the air fused and crackled with power. Erun lost his tongue.

Who are you..? He felt her thought penetrating his mind as she replied without speaking.

I am Elanion of the Woods, by some called Laniol. Know that your love has freed me from my prison, child of man. A curfew placed by my husband long ago for a crime I never committed. There is no more need of Scaffa, and with Tertzei's help Laras Lassladden can once again shift free through the many dimensions.

The green gold eyes of the goddess looked upon him with sudden kindness.

Irulan chose well, though he will not be pleased by this outcome. Leave now. At the seashore Scaffa will bid you a last farewell.

Elanion's astral body faded then, passing over him like departing morning mist. Once again he was alone. Utterly alone. Erun gazed down at his body, noticing without much surprise that he was still clad in his travelling fare.

This has all been a dream. When will I waken? Will I ever be free from her?

Erun Cade reached the shore some time later under the canopy of another star-studded night. The cliffs had vanished. Instead a long sandy track led to high dunes. Beyond these the mournful surge of breakers filled the night. Scaffa awaited him at the shoreline; her big blue-silver eyes glistened—but with sorrow or starlight?

"The time of parting is now upon us, Erun Cade," she told him softly. "We shall not meet again in this life. But one thing more remains. Come." She beckoned him follow her along the shore.

"Here," Scaffa said as they reached a flat rock that barred their way and parted the black waves sucking and surging around it. There were objects that glittered on the rock's barnacled surface, and though they were partially occluded by weed, Erun recognised the black ring mail shirt and helm. Accompanying them was the axe and Callanak, freshly honed and polished. Aside these were the cloak she'd given him, the golden harp, and the battered sack still containing the Elementals.

"Tertzei, I have retained," Scaffa told him, "for she is of mine own kin. Borz and Aqueous, you may take with you. The time will come soon enough when you will need them both."

"This time spent...has it all been a dream?" Erun asked her.

"On Laras Lassladden there is no such meaning." Scaffa's voice seemed far away now and her body swallowed by shadow. He could barely make her out in the dark. "Go now, beloved of Elanion. Your mortal love you will see again soon.

"Journey south when you reach the shore. It is now high summer in Gol. At the Games in Torvosa things shall reach a head. You have three weeks to get there. Lissane Barola will be there, and others too. It will fall on you alone to warn the barons of Ashmali. For the demon is coming, Erun Cade, that's as certain as night follows day."

"High summer?" Erun was struggling to take it all in. "How is that possible? It was still icy winter two days past?"

"I told you before, mortal, time moves differently here— sometimes quicker and sometimes more slowly. Laras Lassladden is not of your dimension."

Erun scratched his head. "One more thing," he called out to the fading shadow of the giantess. "Why was I chosen? I mean what's special—"

"Your sons shall father kings of men in a distant country," her voice was barely a whisper now, "and the seed that you have planted in me shall bring forth the greatest warrior born to Ansu, although his fate will not entwine with your own—nor shall you ever know him. Just as Lissane Barola's blood stems from the Sea God's own, yours comes from my husband's warlike kin. You are of good stock, Erun Cade."

"Your husband...who is he?" Erun's mind was wandering; he could no longer see Scaffa. Her reply reached him as a distant whisper over waves.

"Irulan, of course—haven't you guessed? The hermit guise is one of his favourites. Another is the dark rider that sails the skies on moonlit nights. The Huntsman, some call him, I believe. Farewell, most recently beloved. Farewell!"

Then, as though the dream were still upon him, Erun Cade lifted the mail shirt and donned it, marvelling at how well it fit him and how light it was upon his body. Callanak he lifted high above his head, starlight shone along the runes etched into its surface.

Strange that he hadn't noticed those before. Although the symbols meant nothing to him Erun found that he could read them.

Callanak: Sword of Light.

Then with heart heavy and shouldering his gifts and burdens, Erun Cade waded out into the dark chilling water as the skiff loomed like a ghost ship out of the night. The ferryman glowered at him as he leapt on board, his single baleful eye reflecting the moon's pale gaze. Erun turned away, and the ferryman in silence guided the craft from Scaffa's shore.

Erun watched from the stern until the night engulfed Scaffa's Island. It had seemed less than a day since he'd been in Northtown last. But now summer's blessing filled the air and, as morning greeted him, Erun vaulted ashore. The ferryman's single eye watched him go. On strange impulse, Erun turned. He smiled across at the old man.

"Yet another guise, Irulan?" The ferryman said nothing but turned and poled his craft softly from the jetty. Strange it was how boat and pilot vanished in the sunshine.

***

When Erun Cade crested the cliffs above Northtown, he turned just once to look out to sea. Erun gasped at what he saw (or rather what he didn't.) The horizon was clear and flat where sky fused with sun-kissed ocean. Erun saw no island, as should have been. Scaffa's domain had vanished from the morning. Perhaps it had never been there.

Erun rubbed his tired eyes and turned away. Weary now; and tired of mystery, he began the long trudge along the cliff tops toward distant Druthan Crags. He hoped that Torrig hadn't left yet. The Torvosan Games were fast approaching. After that?

***

Spring had finally reached the mountains after the longest winter in years. But for Lissane it was still midwinter. She hated Torvosa now. Hated their kind words and platitudes. Everywhere Lissane went she recalled the time spent here last summer. That blissful happiest time with Estorien Sarfe. Cut so brutally short by her husband's henchman. There was no joy for Lissane in Torvosa now. There never would be. Since their arrival here long months ago, when they had staggered—a rag-tag gathering of renegade soldiers and camp followers; weary, blistered and hungry—down from the high passes, Lissane had said little of their plight.

Both Duke Toreno and his son let her be. They were good men but she knew how awkward they must feel around her. The child Morwella clung to her like a second shadow. The girl was wretched: skinny as a rag doll, torn and battered by children that had long disowned it. Morwella spoke little and only to Lissane.

Woman and girl made for a forlorn sight as they wandered feral-eyed and lost along the high walls of Torvosa City. Folk avoided them mostly. Even Jerrel had learned to stay clear of late, realising that Lissane's heart was not for such as he to obtain.

Instead the young captain spent his time fretting and plotting a return to Galanais, with fire and sword through palace and town. He would spare the common folk but Galanais would be purged from the stench of House Sophistra's stain.

But Clarde Dovess and his father eventually steered Jerrel away from this course of action, bidding him wait until the Games this summer, when he could formally challenge Torlock and his master for right of rule. Though Jerrel knew himself no match for Torlock, Clarde had vowed death for the killer of his friend Estorien Sarfe.

"He was murdered like a dog not far from these gates," the big champion had growled. "Therefore it falls to me to avenge the Sarfanian. You, Galanian, can gut that bastard Varentin. But honourably mind, and at the Games. With those two dead Galanais will be free for the taking, Captain Jerrel."

"What if they don't attend the Games?" For Jerrel the thought of waiting until late summer was intolerable. "I mean, wouldn't it be foolhardy of Varentin and his henchman to leave Galania? They know how hated they are here."

"Torlock is arrogant enough not to care," responded Clarde with a grim smile. "The bastard knows that we would never break the truce. He might have no honour but Torvosa does and so Torlock will be safe...for a time.

"And they dare not lose face. If they avoided the Games it would show that they are afraid of us. And there would no longer be any doubt of their culpability. Varentin might well be afraid to come, but he's only a puppet now so won't have a choice. As for Torlock?" Clarde smiled grimly. "That one will enjoy the confrontation. They will come, Jerrel, do not fret. And when they do they will die."

But Jerrel had fretted and for months now, so Clarde Dovess had learned to let him be also.

Lissane paid no mind to Jerrel, he might as well have been invisible. She didn't want to think about the Games as they loomed ever closer. Her father would be there and her filthy brothers.

All her enemies would be there. The only two people she had ever loved were dead and gone from her. Erun was an old memory but Estorien's dying gaze haunted her dreams every night. There was only one reason to live now. Let the men plot and fret and Shadowman take the lot of them. Lissane would wait for that precise moment then claim her revenge—whether at the Games or later when chance opportuned.

Lissane gazed down at Morwella who smiled adoringly back at her. The child's huge eyes were lopsided pools of night and she still carried the awful needle that had spilled her mother's life blood. Morwella was mad, clearly. Despite that, Lissane had found herself warming to the child. And Morwella in her turn had come to love Lissane as a sister in sufferance. Tarnished coins. They made for an unlikely pair.

As spring warmed to summer, little changed. Razeas Sarfe arrived. He sought Lissane in her chambers one morning. That was a frosty encounter. She knew that Razeas partially blamed her for his son's death, though he'd never say it. The elder Sarfe was polite. Kind even. But she'd been glad when he'd departed.

Since that time he too had avoided her. Months passed like a lit fuse creeping slowly toward the inevitability that was the Torvosan Games. Summer sweltered and waxed. Before she was ready that time of festival and challenge was upon them. Lissane determined to have no part in it. She hid herself away for as long as she could. But when the Rodruthans arrived amid uproar and colour she just had to go see.

And that was the day when everything changed.

Chapter 16

The Stranger

Since the rebels had fled like the rats that they were, Black Torlock's iron fist had battered Galanais into sullen submission. There were torchings, beatings, and executions on the hour. While Varentin still wailed the loss of his mother, Torlock combed city and citadel for any sniff of insurrection. If in doubt he killed them anyway: nobles, commoners, slaves, husbands and wives, children—even dogs, until the streets of Galanais ran red with blood, and the stench of the charnel houses reached the fields outside the walls.

Torlock had appointed a new lieutenant, a man as black of heart as he was; Cort was efficient and loyal, a boon after the disappointment of Jerrel. Cort could be trusted and would govern the city in Torlock's fashion, whilst Varentin and he journeyed to Torvosa. Torlock smiled when he recalled the fuss Sophistra's spoilt firstborn had made when he had proposed their attendance at the Games.

"But they hate us!" Varentin had shrieked at him from his puke-stained divan, where he spent most his days masturbating and filling his face with sweets and fruit. Since his mother's murder,

Varentin had slunk into a well of depravity. His eyes were blood-shot sunken pools, his mouth a down turned twisted scowl, and his clothes—more often than not soiled with his own urine and worse.

The boy was becoming as mad as his sister—a curse Hal Gallante's family had suffered for several generations. The cost of their pride, some said. None of this concerned Torlock, who now had complete control of Galanais and the wealthy province beyond. Sophistra's death had been timely indeed. He missed fucking her, but there were many others when the need was on him. Besides, power was his real hunger. Varentin Gallante was his puppet now and when the time came...

"They can do nothing under the law of the truce," he'd told the protesting 'prince'. Garbed in his accustomed black, Torlock had waited in measured silence for Varentin's shouting to cease. "We leave next month, my Prince," he'd said eventually. "You're coming if I have to chain you to the saddle."

He'd ducked then as a missile flew over his head and crashed into the wall. Anger had blazed across Torlock's face as he watched the shards of the plate explode. He'd taken a brisk step forward and struck Varentin hard across his chubby face with the back of a gauntleted hand, knocking him from the divan to lie sprawled and dishevelled on the marble floor. Varentin had gaped up at him in terror as Torlock had stood over him—all muscle and frowns.

"Clean yourself up, my Prince," he had snapped. "You look like a sack of shit; I want you looking your best for the barons next month." Torlock had left him then and strode sharply back to the barracks, where Cort waited with more traitors attending the queue at the gallows scaffold. Torlock had watched them kick and dance as the ropes hoisted them slowly skyward.

He was looking forward to the Games now. At Torvosa he would kill the traitor Jerrel and stake his claim before all as the new legal ruler of Galanais. They had no proof that it was he that had killed Estorien Sarfe, (though they doubtless suspected, and that bitch from Barola would have told them,) and anyway, when they saw the state of Varentin they could only comply with his wishes—like it or not.

Torlock's dark eyes scanned the summer sky where ravens circled high above. A few had settled on yesterday's traitors, feasting on their eyes and clawing at their purple faces. Torlock's stony gaze returned to the current victims. He watched the last one's kicks weaken and finally stop. Torlock grinned briefly and then turned away. Let them hate and fear him. Power was the key. Below and beyond the city burned in places with the fires set by his men.

***

They had spent two nights at the Crags: fighting, drinking, and wenching in good Rodruthan fashion, although Erun Cade received little pleasure from it, restless as he was to get going. Scaffa/Elanion's words and hints seemed no more than a dream to Erun now, and Lissane Barola a distant memory of a boy now dead.

But the heavy thought of his revenge against House Barola filled his waking days. Enough time had passed. The brand burned on his face like an accusation, reminding Erun that his father's shade could not rest until his killer was brought to justice.

Torrig, finally sated, announced their departure amid wild promises of returning glory for House Rodrutha. Torrig hadn't done as well as he had wanted at last year's Games, (particularly where Slinsi Garron was concerned). As a new king he needed to prove himself to all.

And so outside the gates of the Crags, King Torrig Red-Hair declared with passion that he would return with the title of Champion of the Games. The crowd had roared their approval while Erun Cade watched on in sober silence, restless in his saddle.

They rode south at speed. Forty warriors, crossing through Treggara and eastern Galania without event, and then toiling over the high mountain passes and, three weeks later, dropping down on Torvosa City three days into the Games.

Within half an hour Torrig's boys were set to brawling with some Treggaran rabble. Bloodshed (except in legal arbitrated combat) was banned during the truce of the Games, but fighting and brawling seldom ceased. Erun left them to it, and instead followed his nose to the stalls where piping meats and viands tempted his nostrils and made his stomach grumble.

Turftown was full to bursting, its teeming crowds reminded Erun of Rakeel, what with the colour and spectacle and noise all around. Indeed there were many Xandorians here, doubtless fleeing the wrath of Ashmali. Torrig had put his name down for every contest he could while Erun took to strolling through the fair. His eyes briefly locked on Rosco Barola, who stood at an ale tent belching and farting. The big redhead looked straight at him before turning away.

You don't remember me, Rosco...You will soon.

Erun felt the brand itch on his cheek again. Revenge was close now: it burnt like fire in his veins. But first he would seek out Lissane. Erun wanted to gaze on her lovely face again. Just once, then he'd let her be. Erun had only recently heard of her elopement with the Sarfanian and of Estorien's murder last year. His thoughts had been scattered by that. He recalled his encounter with Estorien Sarfe on his journey for Borz.

The woman with him... was it possible?—could she have been?

Erun felt a sudden stab of resentment. Lissane Barola had promised herself to him forever. But that was long ago. Erun Cade was gone—dead and buried. He was Kell now. Man of skill. A warrior proven and ready to unleash himself on his foes.

He would find her though—just to see those violet eyes one last time. Lissane must be here somewhere, or else up there in the castle mass beyond. Erun walked on, heart heavy and fingers twitching at the hilt of Callanak strapped at his waist. He'd left the sack containing the Elementals in Torrig's tent alongside his armour, axe and golden harp, (the wooden one he had forsaken during his travels along the way. Erun wasn't worried, and he doubted he'd see Irulan again.) Thieves were not tolerated at the Games, the punishment being instant death. Besides, none dare enter where the Rodruthans loitered and diced so noisily in the southern sunshine.

***

Lissane was seated next to Morwella and big Clarde Dovess, who wasn't fighting today. Morwella was enjoying the colourful spectacle of the Games. For the first time in months Lissane saw the child relax. It warmed her heart a little.

Then she witnessed her father taking his seat in the Barolan corner, near opposite and scarce a hundred yards away. Her expression darkened. If he saw her the Baron gave no sign. Lissane, watching her father for a while, noticed something strange.

It was the man seated beside him—a Treggaran by his dress. On closer inspection she saw that it was Baron Garron himself, the much hated Volt, laughing and joking with her father. What chance connivance had occurred to bring two such vehement foes together? Lissane couldn't begin to guess. It stank, Lissane knew that much.

What are you about, Father?

Volt Garron was a bloody brigand, and Eon Barola had spent the last ten years trying to kill him, and now suddenly they were friends. And good friends too, by the way they were laughing. It didn't make sense.

A voice whispered something obscene in her ear. She turned sharply and looked straight into the grinning face of her despicable husband. Before Lissane could respond Varentin had shuffled passed and mingled into the throng, for the briefest moment he'd brushed her hair with a languid finger. That oily touch felt like poison slime. It made her shiver all over.

If I had a knife...

That hot afternoon's events started with a troop of musicians and acrobats awhirl, and then came the challenges and following fights. Anyone with a score (whether commoner or noble) could settle it here in honourable combat. These early days were always reserved for smaller frays and petty minor squabbles. Lissane watched with glazed eyes while Morwella giggled and hooted beside her.

Last year's Games had seemed splendour of magic and colour.

This year all appeared jaded and grey. She saw a tall hooded man watching her from his perch at the stalls. Doubtless some would-be assassin in Torlock or Varentin's pay.

She didn't care and stared back hard at the fellow. He turned away then, vanishing behind a crowd of disgusting Rodruthans that now tumbled into the stalls amid coarse laughter and spilled ale.

Lissane sighed, two weeks of this, somehow she'd get through it. She would have to keep her cool though and not act so jumpy; it wouldn't do to see cutthroats in every corner. If she stayed close by Clarde she would be alright. It wasn't that she was afraid of dying, no, not that, but Lissane needed her vengeance first.

She received a glass of deep red from a passing attendant and nodded curt thanks. Lissane sipped slowly and let the smooth rich taste sooth her nerves. Eventually she relaxed and, for a time, even enjoyed the events of that hot afternoon. Tonight there would be feasting away up at the castle. Her father would be there, and Varentin.

One step at a time...

***

His face stung as though she'd slapped it. Their eyes had met for the briefest instant and he had seen the loathing in that glance. But why would Lissane hate him? Erun cursed himself for a fool. She hadn't recognised him, was all. Hardly surprising with the hood down over his face and the snake-red brand marring his once comely features.

It had hurt though, that look. Brought back so many memories of better times—how many years ago? Erun's journeys to and from Scaffa's isle, and the confusing time spent there, had left him uncertain, but seeing his only love again brought the past hurtling back. Almost, Erun felt the red hot poker hissing as it seared open his thighs. But the pain of Lissane's cold glance was worse by far.

I always loved you, Lissane Barola, but it seems you have forgotten me.

Erun left the stalls where he been spending that afternoon

with Torrig's louts. The King was away up in the castle being entertained by Lord Toreno and his lady wife. Torrig returned at sundown. He'd been invited to attend the banquet that evening but had neglected the offer, preferring to stay in Turftown where, as he said, the taverns were rougher and the wenches more grateful.

Besides, there would be feasts and banquets aplenty these weeks, culminating in the celebration supper at the end of the Games, where all nobles were to attend. But that was a while away yet.

That night Erun took to the taverns also. He wasn't an avid drinker like Torrig's gang, but the various inns cluttering Turftown were as good a place as any to gather information. In one, Erun learned about the newfound friendship between Eon Barola and Volt Garron. He found that hard to believe. Paolo, apparently, wasn't attending the Games until the second week, having business elsewhere. But Erun could wait.

The big news was what was happening over in Galania Province. It was a region Erun knew little about. He'd crossed through it several times on his travels, and of course knew that Lissane had dwelt there, though not of late.

The murders of Hal Gallante, and later his wife by her own daughter, had rocked Gol. (That scrawny, bug-eyed gargoyle had been seated next to Lissane in the Dovesian corner this very afternoon). Morwella—people shuddered when that name was spoken. To Erun she was just a child, pale and ugly—of little interest.

Galania was known as the proudest and wealthiest of the six provinces, but now it poised on the brink of civil war. Or revolution. And all of this brought about by Lissane Barola, or so he had heard. Liss had certainly kept herself busy these last years, he owned.

But Erun determined not to be bitter. The girl had believed him dead, after all. What choice had she had? Her brutal father had thrown her at the feet of Varentin Gallante, who by all accounts was as mad and bad as his little sister. Small wonder she ran off with that Estorien Sarfe. Erun still couldn't quite forgive her though, not here, amongst all this pomp.

Erun enquired of an innkeep about the big fights that were

held in the final week. These were the legendary conflicts between the contesting provinces. The arena had six entrances whence the champions of each region would issue, amid roars of approval or derision. The stadium surrounding it contained many seats and was shaped like a hexagon. Each ruler and his nobles had a side (or hex)—though often they shared with others, to exchange gossip and bargain between fights.

Erun was surprised to hear that Slinsi Garron was one of the favourites this year. The wild Treggaran beauty was renowned for her skill with spear and knife. Slinsi was cat quick and lithe. She was also a man-eater. That night he hadn't forgotten, though at the time he remembered having little choice in the matter. Perhaps he'd play a different game with her during these contests.

But when to enter and under what guise? Torrig had said that he could fight as a Rodruthan—an honour bestowed on few. But Erun had declined politely. Kell the Avenger, he told his friend, would stand alone and pick his moment well.

The other favourites this year were Paolo Barola, (when he showed up) and Black Torlock, the stone-faced brute accompanying Varentin Gallante. Erun had heard a lot about Black Torlock; he was reputed a ruthless killer, and had once been Hal Gallante's champion.

Rumour was this Torlock had done for Estorien Sarfe last summer, just after the Games and thus a year ago. Nothing had been proved but Erun didn't doubt it were true. He'd seen Torlock up close this very afternoon as the big man barged passed him.

Clad in black, Torlock moved with blithe confidence. He was tall, heavyset in body, with dark murderous eyes. His stare, when it locked briefly on Erun, was iron hard. It said 'stand before me and you die, scum'. An arrogant bastard, that one. Erun disliked him at first glance.

There were others contending, though wildcards mostly. Kael Sarfe was an outsider, he was still very young (just seventeen) but wanted to make a name for himself by avenging his brother. The other Sarfe brother, Carlo, was still lost overseas—had been for years. Torrig, too, was an outside bet. That left Clarde Dovess, the Garron twins, and the other Barola boys—though Aldo wasn't reckoned up to much these days. Erun managed a grim smile when he thought of his dead father's axe cutting off that bastard's hand. *At least you hurt one of them, Father.*

Erun relaxed, he supped with Torrig's 'boys', and even occasionally joined in with their bawdy songs, though his heart was elsewhere. That night he got to bed late and strummed a few lonely chords on his harp. His fingers itched though and the music wasn't in him, so he slept instead. The following days proved much the same. Torrig won all his contests: swimming in the river below, wrestling and boxing, and stave fighting too. Pleased with himself, the young king stayed drunk all that week. Erun waited...

***

The feasting was the worst of it. Both the glib snide comments from her two present brothers and glaring animosity from Varentin at the other table were hard to bear, though endure them she did in stony silence. Varentin looked awful, his skin was blotched and pasty and his long hair greasy and lank.

Lissane allowed herself a small smile as she watched him quaff and gurgle at his wine-cup like a hog at trough. Torlock glanced her way and winked at her. Were Lissane's eyes daggers she would have gored him there and then. Instead she turned away and feigned indifference.

Her father accosted her after the meal. He was drunk as usual and had some doe-eyed, stupid looking serving girl hanging on his arm. The girl was half her father's age and giggling. Lissane wanted to slap her face.

"It's good to see you again, daughter," Eon Barola said. His florid face had aged these last years. The drink was taking its toll.

I hope you drown in the stuff one day...

"Father..." She made to walk past but he blocked her way.

"We should not be enemies, Lissane." The Baron's eyes showed an uncertainty she hadn't seen before. "I was sorry to hear of your lover's death—a treacherous act. He was a valiant boy."

"Don't contaminate his name on your vile lips, Father,"

Lissane snapped, and the Baron recoiled as though she were a spitting cobra. The girl beside him blanched.

"I want nothing to do with you. Not now. Not ever. So stand aside and let me pass." She forced passage through and the Baron scowled as she showed him her back.

"Suit yourself, you pompous bitch." Eon yanked the girl's arm and half dragged her over to the long tables where the servants attended the wine. The mad-child Morwella grinned up at him, and then followed his daughter's haughty steps out of the feasting hall.

Eon shuddered when he saw that girl. Hal's twisted brat. There was something unclean about her. Perhaps she had poisoned Lissane with her madness too. Lissane made no sense to her father. But Eon soon forgot about his daughter. The hour was late and he was angry with lust, so he took the girl to his chambers and filled her with his urgent seed.

***

At last the final days arrived. Tension filled the air and the bets were on for the winner. Slinsi Garron was expected to win, although some believed Clarde Dovess could still pull it off, though he wasn't the fighter he had been—forty summers took their toll on a contestant.

Lissane watched the fighters emerge resplendent from their provinces' gates. In this final challenge each champion would fight in a melee until only the winner remained on his (or her) feet.

First out was King Torrig Red-Hair, the tattooed Rodruthan, sporting twin short swords strapped across his back, and brandishing an evil looking spear in either fist. The northerner carried no shield, deeming it unworthy of the Games.

Red Torrig's long hair was starched and waxed into garish orange spikes. Beyond savage, he was the strangest looking warrior Lissane had ever seen—and to think he now called himself king. Barbarian, or just plain chancer, would be more apt.

The Rodruthan sported a steel shirt, but his legs were bare and colourful tattoos spidered up their sinewy length. He wore large gold hoops in his ears and prowled around like a cornered lynx.

Next came the Barola brothers, amid boos and hoots from the Rodruthans whose hex was next to theirs. Paolo had arrived late last night, this was the first time Lissane had seen him at these Games. She watched the three strut arrogantly into the arena as King Torrig Red-Hair (ignoring them completely) limbered up in the Rodruthan hex. Rosco bulked and sweated in sable armour like a randy bull. He carried a mace and a double headed axe. A round wooden shield was slung over his back with the Barolan Hawk showing crimson on jet.

Aldo had had his shield strapped to his maimed arm whilst his remaining hand gripped a curved sword. Her middle brother was garbed in Barolan scarlet, with matching greaves and clanking plate of finest enamelled steel.

Paolo stole the show though—as was to be expected. Her hated youngest brother beamed at the hisses and insults thrown his way. Only the Treggarans let him be—strangely. Paolo revelled at every shout and jeer. He juggled twin swords back and forth, now and then tossing one high over his head and catching it blade first between his fingers. Lissane hoped that one would slip passed his guard and gut him, but it never did. He'd always been good—the little shit.

Today, Paolo wore a knee-length steel shirt of finest Xandorian design, its cost almost priceless. This too, was scarlet in hue; each link cunningly fashioned into the shape of a hawk. He wore a kettle helm also resembling a hawk, with wings opening out in flight. Like Torrig Red-Hair, Paolo Barola shunned a shield.

Then in stark contrast, Torlock strode into the arena. The butcher of Galanais (as some were calling him now) was garbed in his accustomed black and showing no adornment or design. He wore plain black-linked ring mail, with steel-studded trousers of coarse boiled black hide. His shield was oval and heavy, and at his waist hung a long sword. Black Torlock's right fist was wrapped around the metal haft of a spiked mace—this too gleamed with polished jet.

Then came the host, Clarde Dovess, clad in sapphire iron, and carrying shield and longsword with jewel hilted poniard at his hip. His helm gleamed azure in the sun, its blue resembling summer seas. He looked magnificent, Lissane thought. The crowd roared and cheered at their hero and Clarde saluted them. He then turned and nodded to his father, who in acknowledgment clapped approval from the Dovesian hex.

Then she saw Kael enter from the Sarfanian gate. Lissane almost wept when she saw how close he now resembled her dead lover. Kael was shorter and slighter of build than Estorien had been, but he'd grown taller since last she'd seen him. He looked proud and dangerous in his Sarfanian gold trimmed armour. But up against Torlock and Paolo? Lissane worried for him. Kael hefted a long spear and a small buckler. At his waist was a curved scimitar which glistened beneath the sweltering sun.

Last out were the Treggarans: Cruel Rante and Slye the Albino, looking every bit the sulking brutal twins they were, with heavy fur covering their armour despite the heat, and their long shaggy hair tangling loose down their backs. The twins hulked and scowled about in green steel shirts, both carried heavy double-headed axes, with long swords strapped to their waists. Neither wore a helmet. Slye's ghostly pale complexion and shocking white hair sent a shiver up her spine.

Then Slinsi Garron prowled into the arena and the crowd exploded with uproar. She wore armour of sorts, though it did little to hide her curvaceous, supple body. Slinsi sported long, steel shod boots of black lacquered leather. Thrust into these were tight fitting steel-studded trousers, and a sleeveless jerkin of circular steel links, each the size of an apple and differing in colour.

Her arms were bare as was her freckled cleavage, this last revelation had been the reason for the sudden surge of enthusiasm, particularly from the drunks clinging to the stalls at the back of the arena.

Slinsi loved the attention. Her prowling and posturing were easily a match for Paolo's, but the crowd loved her whereas they hated him—all bar the Rodruthans who now spat and swore obscenities which Slinsi returned with flamboyant imagination.

Lissane thought that Slinsi looked wonderful—even better

than she had last year. The Treggaran beauty smiled like a she-panther as she whirled the sling she carried over her head, launching a stone high above the arena walls.

Slinsi had a bag full at her waist, and across her shoulders she'd strapped a thick belt containing seven throwing knives that hung from it in loops. These she juggled from time to time in her left hand instead of the sling. Her right hand gripped the ash shaft of her broad headed, three barbed spear—the weapon for which Slinsi was best known and feared.

At last the yelling and clapping subsided and the tension grew as the crowd quietened, waiting for the first clash of arms. The Champions made ready then, each claiming their place in that dusty dry arena.

Lord Toreno raised his hand, was about to bring it down but then something stopped him. A stranger had entered the arena from the Rodruthan gate. An impostor, tall and lean. Clad in dull black armour, a longsword hanging from a belt at his waist, and an axe slung across his back. The stranger's arms were folded in nonchalant ease. He wore a black helm with a mask of linked chain which concealed his features from the watching and whispering crowd. Lissane's eyes widened: this was unprecedented. Toreno spoke then, his words were stern.

"You arrive late, stranger." It was an accusation not a statement. "And you trespass. What cause or right have you in this place at this time? Name thyself and swiftly!" Toreno was furious. Protocol had been broken. But the newcomer appeared unfazed by the furore he was causing. Lissane strained her neck to see better who this stranger was. He spoke then.

"I am Kell," the stranger said, "and I come from distant Laras Lassladden with a message for you all." The voice was muffled behind the mask and yet there was something familiar. All sound had ceased in the arena. 'Who is this?' was written on everyone's lips.

Then Lissane heard the faint notes of a harp drifting in from somewhere outside. She felt a cold sensation crawling up her spine.

It cannot be...

Then the stranger turned and stared straight into her eyes.

Chapter 17

Treachery and Cold Steel

Lissane gasped. She felt her body give way beneath her, fortunately no one noticed and the chair took her fall. She couldn't see his face but she didn't need to. Lissane knew him instantly. Oh he'd changed clearly, but still that jaunty stance, that spare frame and cocky bearing.

Erun...is it really you? How can that be possible?

The stranger turned away. He now approached the Dovesian hex where Duke Toreno still scowled down upon him. He spoke a second time, and now Lissane had no doubt as to who was currently addressing the lord of Torvosa with such confidence.

"To some here I am a friend. But to others..." the mask turned to where Paolo watched curiously from the Barolan hex.

"By what right do you come here, stranger?" said Toreno, leaning forward with arms gripping the rail. "Only known combatants and worthy champions may enter this arena on this day. Do not you know this?"

"That doesn't apply to me, my lord. I am a messenger from those gods your people have long forsaken." Lissane blanched, it was a ridiculously arrogant reply.

"I need not your blessing, Lord Toreno, nor any other worthy here." The stranger reached up then and with his left hand, freed the helmet strap and tossed the mask aside. Lissane gasped when she saw the ugly scar marring his forehead like a scarlet serpent. The work of her brothers, she just knew it. "I bring warning of a terror approaching Gol from overseas."

"What nonsense is this?" That dark voice belonged to Torlock who now called across to the soldiers manning the gates. "Fill this fool full of arrows before he talks any more shite." The soldiers hesitated and looked to Toreno for guidance, but their lord shrugged them back and bade Torlock be silent.

"What peril is this...and *who* are you really?" Toreno pressed, he could feel his authority slipping away. There was something about this stranger.

"He's the by-blow of a certain blacksmith," said Paolo Barola in a soft voice that somehow everyone heard. "He would be dead were it not for an incompetent and deceitful servant. No matter, I'll dispose of the wretch now."

Paolo too a step forward. The stranger watched him with calm, measured eyes. There was such loathing in that gaze, Lissane felt a shiver. She watched her first love slide the longsword free of its scabbard and was almost blinded by the glare of its uncanny steel. Not steel, surely? It looked like glass and sparkled so.

Erun Cade, what have you become?

"Well, you've a talent for survival, peasant," Paolo's eyes were dangerous chips of emerald, "I'll award you that much. But how came you by these comely objects, *boy*?" That last word oozed contempt. Paolo waved a sword point at the stranger's armour and dazzling sword.

"Steal them from some sleeping warrior, did you?" He took another step forward. Erun Cade just watched him. Lissane covered her eyes.

I cannot stand this.

"I've come for you," said Erun Cade. He re-sheathed the big sword, unslung the axe from his back and gripped it with both black-gloved hands. "I'd not stain Callanak with your blood, Paolo, but this axe shall serve you well enough. My father's ghost is watching on. He has waited long enough for this moment."

"Well then," responded Paolo, "best we get to it, boy." Paolo grinned like a lynx and made his swords dance.

"Enough!"

Toreno's shout stopped Paolo's feline advance. The other combatants were forgotten now, like the hushed crowd they were just motionless statues watching on in awestruck silence. Even the lecherous drunks had sobered up. Everyone was captivated except King Torrig, who for some reason just looked bored.

"I suspect you to be an impostor and an arrogant knave to boot," continued Toreno. "But I will hear you out, stranger, for we are civilised here—most of us, at least."

Lissane saw Red Torrig wink at the Duke after hearing that.

"Speak wisely," continued Toreno, "lest I heed Lord Torlock's words and bid my guards fill you with arrows."

Lissane horrified, saw Erun Cade turn his back on her brother, her heart quailed when she saw the fury contorting Paolo's features at that disdain.

Erun, he'll...

A shout from outside shattered the silence surrounding the stadium. Lissane turned, saw a guard stagger into the arena, his face bloody and his sword red in his hand.

"The castle—my lord..!" he struggled for breath, "...Torvosa... is under attack!" It was only then that Lissane noted that both her father and Baron Garron were missing from their seats. But she had no time for thought as more guards sped into the arena, shouting and waving their weapons in the air.

"Xandorians!" yelled one wild-eyed soldier. "Xandorian mercenaries are ransacking the city!"

"What's this? ...I—?" Duke Toreno's words were cut short as the knife dug deep into his throat and slid across until scarlet gushed, drenching seat and cloth. Toreno slumped. The assassin threw back his hood, and in horror Lissane witnessed the cloaked figure of her father leaping over the lord of Dovess's prone body and yelling across the arena.

"It is time!" Eon Barola roared.

What followed was both chaotic and confusing. Lissane was pushed hard from behind, her head struck the rail, she heard shouts, screams, the clash of steel on steel, then her vision blurred and her world went black.

A hand gripped her then and someone spoke, but Lissane had already lost consciousness. Meanwhile, a mile away inside the walls, Torvosa burned. Eon Barola and Volt Garron laughed as they slew and slew. Their trap was sprung. The long wait was over and at last the bloodletting had begun.

***

Romul read the parchment sent by Horgreb with great satisfaction. It read thus:

Lord General.

Your volunteers have arrived at Torvosa with the Barolan as arranged.
We await word from our allies as when to strike.
All is prepared and made ready for the next stage.
I will send further word when the city falls.

Captain Horgreb.

Romul smiled as he folded the parchment and stowed it away. Horgreb had done well. The captain of his elite had always been competent. That was why Romul had sent him. Several months ago, when the Barolan envoy had first sought him out, Romul had been suspicious.

That young foreigner had had a dangerous look to him and Romul had disliked him intently. But after hearing this Paolo's proposition the canny general had altered his opinion. The Barolans and Treggarans of Gol, the boy had told him, needed a thousand mercenaries from Xandoria to aid their proposed coup at Torvosa City.

The leaders, (Volt Garron and Eon Barola) sought to dislodge the current ruler, (Toreno Dovess) and set themselves up in his stead. But they needed more men. And who better to call on than the Xandorian Elite?

That Barolan boy had a silk tongue and had spoken well. Romul still didn't like him but despite that he had obliged cordially. He had had his reasons, of course. Romul would give these foreigners what they wanted and then take it off them when the time was right. Simplicity itself.

Romul, emulating the boy's enthusiasm, had neglected to tell him that these thousand elite were just the start—a bridgehead. More would follow and then more still. And so the flood gates open.

In time these chosen thousand would turn against their employers and be aided by the rest of Romul's force—arriving at Galanais via ships now moored at Murkai. Then the invasion could commence in earnest. Romul smiled, it would take time and planning but things were underway.

The green-eyed Barolan had played right into his hands. This clever boy was just another fool.

Xandoria was finished. The empire no more. The demon was getting nearer all the time. They had a few months if they were lucky, but no longer. Soon Murkai and even Rakeel would be ash, but by then Romul's main army would be under sail.

Gol—that strange little country he knew so little about—lay across the Shimmering Sea. A short voyage, leading to a land safe from Ashmali's flames, and ripe for their taking. There was no time to waste; Romul would send word, via bird, to the docks tomorrow.

They would need more ships—the sooner constructed the quicker his invasion proper could take place. Rumour was Ashmali's army still loitered idle in the west. The demon—well sated from Xenn's ruin—seemed in no hurry. Romul prayed aloud that that remain so, at least until he was ready to set things in motion.

A week later he received further word from Gol.

***

It had actually been very easy. Both Clarde and Toreno had been so accommodating with the lies he had told them concerning

Paolo's absence, and the reason for his and Treggara's extra troops stationed close by.

It started last winter. Volt Garron had been suspicious at first as Eon knew he would be, but greed had eventually won him over. The promise of plundered Dovesian gold was all Eon had needed to win his former enemy to his cause.

The monies he'd bled from his people these last years had paid for the mercenaries, via Paolo. The trouble besetting Xandoria's west had made it easy for Paolo to recruit a large force. General Romul had sent a thousand of his best—all hardened veterans from the wars with Lamoza.

Paolo paid the fee up front but promised more when the deed was done—if swiftly and successfully. With that arranged, they could sit back and enjoy the Games where all players would be present and unsuspecting. Then, at the appointed hour the trap had been sprung.

Eon Barola hadn't wasted time. In the confusion following Toreno's murder he had cut down a dozen guards and then slipped through the arena, hooded and concealed, and aided as much by the chaos as by his shabby attire.

All about him was mayhem. Everywhere people were fighting and no one seemed clear who the enemy was. Galanians battled against Sarfanians, Rodruthans fought Treggarans. As he left, Eon saw Slinsi Garron cut down three of Torrig's men with her barbed spear.

Eon smiled. The Dovesians {those that hadn't fled to the burning city) had crowded stupidly around the murdered body of their lord like so many sacrificial sheep, while Barolan and Treggaran warriors cut them down from behind. Eon grinned and left them to it. He had business in the castle above. Torvosa: the throne of Kings would soon be his. But before that happened he need finish the task at hand...

***

Jerrel carried the prone Lissane free of the carnage. Once away from the madness and murder of the arena, he placed her down on the grass and swabbed her bruised brow with a damp cloth he'd torn from his shirt and doused in a nearby stream. She stirred and moaned and then opened her eyes.

"Estorien...Erun...?"

"It's Jerrel..."

Jerrel...Lissane's head pounded and she felt sick but at least the world had stopped spinning. She could still hear fighting somewhere off in the distance.

"Where are we?"

"Safe for the moment," he replied, looking around to make sure no one was about. "I carried you out of Turftown," he told her, "it was easy in the chaos."

"My father murdered Lord Toreno," Lissane said as much to herself as to Jerrel.

"I saw it done..."

"My family is cursed. I am cursed. Everything I do...go near."

"It is not your fault...you are not your father, Lissane." Jerrel reached down to stroke her face and brush the dark locks free of her eyes. "Let us depart this place...go anywhere. I love you, Lissane."

But Lissane hardly heard him. "My place is with Erun Cade now," she told him.

"Erun who..?"

"I lost him once before, Jerrel, I'll not lose him a second time." Lissane pushed him aside with sudden urgency and staggered to her feet. "I *must* find Erun Cade."

Jerrel's expression was half pain, half confusion. "I'll come with you," he offered.

"As you wish," she responded, "but my way lies back to the arena—to the fighting."

Within minutes Lissane's strides were taking her back through Turftown, her ears closed to Jerrel's protestations.

When Lissane reached the gates to the arena she nearly gagged, seeing the corpses sprawled everywhere, hacked and bloody. Someone tugged her arm then, and Lissane looking down; saw Morwella grinning up at her.

"So much blood" Morwella's dark eyes were wild with excitement. She gripped her needle—the same one she'd murdered her own mother with. Lissane noticed it was stained with fresh blood; she shuddered and Morwella licked her lips.

Revolted, Lissane shook herself free of the girl and, steeling her nerves, waded out into the carnage as though she walked through someone else's nightmare. Sad-faced Jerrel and the grinning child followed behind. Jerrel's eyes were dulled with failure, but Morwella's flinty jets shone with savage glee. The girl was in her element today.

It was then that Lissane saw him again. Tall and bloodied, Erun Cade stood with glittering sword in hand and corpses sprawled all around him. He turned toward her then, slowly, as though sensing her approach and, for the second time that day their eyes met through the murdering crowd. Lissane could take it no more; she waded forward, oblivious to the fighting and heedless of the risk. Inside her head a bell tolled doom and somewhere close amidst the sounds of battle she'd heard the doleful notes of a solitary harp.

Chapter 18

The Raven Season

Cut and hack! Lunge and stab and hew. Kill! The raven season had come. He was Kell of Laras Lassladden and killing was what he did best. Today it felt easy as drawing breath. After so long a wait the time for his vengeance had finally come.

Barolans, Galanians and Treggarans—it mattered not now Callanak was unleashed and the blood-rage was upon him. The great sword clove through steel as other blades sliced flesh. He was invincible. Nothing could stand in his way. Cut and hew. Slice and slay!

In his rage, Erun had tried to win across to Paolo Barola, but the Baron's youngest son had fled with his father back to the city, leaving his soldiers to deal with the mess left behind. Aldo and Rosco too were nowhere to be seen. That had fuelled Erun's anger further, seeing those bastards run from the fight. It mattered not though. Kell the Avenger would find them—even if he had to butcher every soldier between here and the castle gates.

A shadow blocked his way: Callanak bit and the shadow was gone. A spear sought his throat, but Erun turned the thrust aside with contemptuous ease and stoved in the assailant's face with hilt of his heavy blade. A shield rammed hard into his back: Erun spun on his toes, cutting the legs from under the Treggaran as though they were made of lard. Erun turned again—cat-like and lithe. He stopped. Saw that a man now barred his way, the other fighters having stepped back to allow this newcomer room.

Erun's grey-blue stare clashed with the coaly glare of a merciless killer. A big man, like him garbed in plain black steel and heavy helm, hiding all save those dangerous, murdering eyes. Confident and arrogant he appeared. At ease with the carnage unfolding.

Erun grinned at him; he swung the axe still gripped in his left hand.

The other's black mace battered it aside in a blaze of sparks, whilst his curved sword danced low under Callanak's arc, stabbing fast toward Erun's groin. Erun leapt out of reach, but stumbled over the bodies of his previous victims. He cursed: this bastard was good. Erun rolled aside, the spiked mace missing his head by inches.

Torlock smiled as the impostor rolled free of his mace and regained his feet with athletic grace. "You fight well, stranger. But your life is over, I am Torlock of Galanais." Torlock stepped forward again, his curved sword-point flicking toward Erun's eyes whilst his mace awaited its chance to cleave his skull.

The one that butchered Estorien Sarfe.

Erun spat a gobbet of blood in his opponent's helmeted face.

This I do for you, Lissane.

Erun dodged another lunge and snarled back a challenge. Then he leapt at his foe, axe swinging in low, and Callanak blazing toward Torlock's sword. Steel clashed with crystal-steel; Callanak's adamant edge biting deep into that hard metal as though it were tin. Torlock swore and hewed again.

Erun turned Torlock's thrust aside with a flick of his right wrist, knocking the Galanian off balance. He waded in then with axe swinging for Torlock's neck.

He missed. Torlock dived close, ramming an armoured shoulder hard into Erun's stomach making him grunt in pain, and Erun was forced back again.

Torlock's mace struck Erun's axe in midswing with a clunk, the power of that blow sheared clean through the axe's haft. Erun tossed the useless handle aside as the axe-head fell to the floor.

Torlock smiled, and sensing he'd won, took a wary step forward with both weapons primed. Erun waited, both fists now gripping Callanak's hilt and feet braced parallel.

Then Torlock was on him. That assault (though cobra quick) wasn't quick enough.

The Galanian lunged fast at Erun's throat, the sword gripped tight in his left hand, while his right fist brought the mace down hard to dent the younger man's helm.

But the mace missed its target and the sword stabbed thin air. Instead, Torlock gaped incredulous at the widening hole in his belly as Callanak cut through steel shirt, leather, and flesh.

Torlock gasped. He slunk to his knees, his bloody, trembling fingers, failing to stop his entrails from escaping like so many unravelling worms from his belly. Torlock sobbed. He folded over, still clutching his belly, trying in vain to hold his guts in. Erun stepped over his body.

"Please," Torlock begged looking up at his victor. "Finish it... have you no honour?" Torlock pleaded and wept but to no avail. Erun Cade left him to his fate.

"Please...have mercy!"

Not for the likes of you.

The last thing Black Torlock saw was the raven that settled to peck out his eyes. He screamed while the black bird feasted. Even then there was no mercy. It took Torlock hours to die.

***

Varentin Gallante had distanced himself from the melee as quick as was possible. Most of his people were with Torlock but the prince had no desire to be caught in the madness. Find a corner—any corner - and await an outcome. Any outcome. Then, if needs be, sue for peace from the victor. It was as good a plan as he could muster for now.

The fighting and slaughter both excited and terrified Varentin.

There were men screaming and dying everywhere; there was no order, just mayhem and carnage and so much blood.

"The world has gone mad," Varentin muttered as he stumbled through the chaos. He saw his baby sister in the thick of it, stabbing out at legs with that nasty spike of hers, and grinning like the twisted gargoyle she was.

"Sister," he giggled, "what has become of us?" Then he saw the tall woman beside her and Varentin's heart turned black. "It's all your doing, you fucking bitch."

Varentin's sulky eyes watched as Lissane approached a fighter clad in black steel. At first he thought it was Torlock, but then he saw the slaughtered mangled body of his mentor and protector lying close by.

Varentin gulped at that sight. He couldn't comprehend that the indestructible Torlock was dead. But dead he was or else dying, if Varentin was to trust his bloodshot eyes.

Something hardened within him then.

It's down to me now.

A wormy, bitter hatred rose like bile inside his belly. It chased away Varentin's fear, filling him with but one desire.

Lissane Barola's death.

No one noticed Varentin Gallante in that crowd. Stooping, he gained a knife—long and sharp. She was scarce yards away, locked in embrace with Torlock's killer. Varentin smiled: his hand felt greasy where he gripped the knife's bone handle. His hungry gaze focussed on the spot between her slim shoulder blades.

Lissane wore only pale, blood-splattered silk. His strides took him there: one, two, three and four! Varentin lunged hard and eager, the steel glinting murderous beneath that golden afternoon sun.

***

She came to him like a dream of his past. The hatred, the war lust and rage: all were gone. Chased away by those violet eyes.

I never stopped loving you.

Erun tossed aside his helmet and gulped in air as she fell into his arms, her eager lips seeking his again and again, and her joyful tears streaking her face. If the fighting continued, neither Erun nor Lissane were aware of it.

They kissed and stared and stared and kissed. Blood stained her silk gown, and his black mail was wet with gore and flies buzzed noisily all around. But these two were oblivious to it all.

It was Morwella's laugh that saved them.

Her giggly shriek, seeing her brother stealing upon them with knife held high, caused Erun Cade to look up, and just in time see the glint of steel slicing toward Lissane's back. He twisted: blocked the dagger's path and its blade scraped against Erun's steel shirt, the violence of that thrust making him buckle forward in pain and lose his balance.

Varentin's wrist snapped like a dry twig following that impact. He screamed, but that yelp was cut suddenly short.

Lissane knelt and retrieved the dagger. Slowly, carefully, she rose to her feet. Varentin turned toward her, sobbing, and Lissane Barola buried the blade to its hilt in her husband's chest, twisting the steel nastily, and yanking it free again.

Varentin gasped; he staggered to his knees, clutching his gaping chest and weeping at the agony erupting through his body, his eyes agog at the blood welling out between his fingers.

Lissane's mouth tightened. She got behind him, rammed a knee hard into the small of Varentin back, then pulling her husband's head back by his long greasy hair, Lissane sliced the dagger along his exposed throat. She watched cold and calm: saw Varentin shudder, gurgle and void his bowels. She smiled then—the ghost of a grin—and turned away.

Estorien, my darling—avenged at last.

Morwella stooped over the body of her dead brother and grinned down at him. "There's only me left now," she told the oozing fly-clustered corpse. "I'm Princess Morwella now, and you're just a sack of rotting shit, brother mine." She looked up then. "Why has the fighting stopped?" Morwella asked.

And she was right, the fighting had stopped. Jerrel's tired eyes took stock. The Rodruthans held the arena; their young king had joined with the black-clad stranger, who (and he couldn't come to terms with this) was yet another of Lissane's lovers.

There were some of Jerrel's people around—their badges showing that they opposed Torlock. Both his former captain and Varentin were dead—another shock, that one, especially seeing Lissane do for her husband in such a savage way.

He saw a party of Sarfanians led by the fiery Kael who, he learned later, had almost single-handled put paid to half of Torlock's finest fighters in his zeal to avenge his brother's murder.

The Barolans had vanished to a man and the surviving Treggarans also, though Slinsi's body lay hacked and bloody near the gates, her head nowhere to be seen. Jerrel felt shattered, exhausted and confused. The world was not as had been this morning. Everything had changed. Gone was his ambition like a soaring hawk shot from the skies by fate's determined archer.

His dreams and hopes now shattered by seeing her reunited with another lover, someone Jerrel had never even heard about. A stranger and a killer incarnate. It all left him dazed and morose. Jerrel made to walk away but Lissane turned, seemed to notice him for the first time that day.

Lissane motioned Jerrel stay put. "This is a friend," she told Erun Cade. They had been talking together while Varentin's life-blood stained the soil. Both at ease in the setting. "Jerrel is the nobleman that kept me sane after Torlock dragged me back to Galanais. He is a friend to us." Erun nodded across to the sandy haired Galanian, and Jerrel inclined his head stiffly in return.

"Greeting, warrior," Erun smiled, "As you see, Lissane and I were *friends* once."

"I know..." *Now.* Jerrel looked around searching for something appropriate to say. Eventually he found it. "Hadn't we better see how things stand up in the city?"

Erun shrugged, "the city has most likes fallen by now and the castle too." He turned to Lissane. "Your father and Garron have long planned this. I now suspect those Xandorians were brought here by Paolo—it would explain his absence from the early Games."

Lissane hung her head: "my house is a scourge on Gol," she

said. "I can only apologise." The king, Torrig, had just appeared and now awarded her a ghastly smile.

"You are blameless, my lady," he said. This Torrig's words were genuine and kind and Lissane wondered why she had thought him such a savage. "Well," Torrig added to those now gathered around—already their little party was swelling beneath the Rodruthan king's banner

"We are now at war: I for one will not kowtow to Eon Barola—begging your pardon, lady."

Lissane shook her head in disgust. "He is no father of mine," she told them. "Both Eon Barola and his sons are my enemies now. I saw what father did to Duke Toreno. They are lost to me—the Barolas."

But it wasn't just that. They had hurt her Erun Cade, sending him on a journey into darkness of which she yearned to learn more, and worst of all, they had killed her mother. Not with knives, but there were other ways to murder a soul as kind as Leanna's had been. "House Dovess was ever a friend to Estorien Sarfe and myself," she told them. "I shall not rest until the murdering Baron is made to pay for his crimes."

"That might be some while," responded Erun Cade. "Come, Lissane, my King and friends. Let us gather what fighting men we have and go see how things stand at Torvosa Castle."

So they left the arena with its stench and flies and corpses, and ventured—a rag tag force of mixed fighters—out to where summer evening's quiet settled on the fields around the castle. The only sounds were the plunging river below and the dull thud of wing and harsh caw, as crow and raven lifted from nearby trees, to wing low, settle and feast in greedy clusters on those dead and dying left behind.

Near the arena main gates Erun paused for a moment, his face pale with shock. Slinsi Garron's dead eyes gazed up at him in the fading light. Her honey hair was tussled and almost she was smiling at him. Slinsi's body was nowhere to be seen. He turned away. *You were a fine woman.*

***

An hour later and accompanied by a scratchy force of several hundred loyalists, Erun Cade, King Torrig Red-Hair; Jerrel, Kael Sarfe, and Lissane Barola approached Torvosa City. The main fires within had died down now but the sky was dark with smoke. Rooks wheeled and cawed high above the battlements. It was a sight that horrified Lissane. Toreno was dead and she now suspected Clarde and his captains too. Clarde had hastened back to the castle at the start of the fight, obviously fearing the worst for his kin. They would all be dead now. Butchered or else trapped in that blaze. That was Lissane's bleak assumption.

For though Torvosa's walls stood clean and silent, beyond them some flames still crackled as the inner castle smouldered. Were she able see inside, Lissane would discover just how much damage the fires had caused. The King's old palace was a blackened shell. The stables, barracks and armoury were missing their roofs, and the houses and taverns closest to the palace had been reduced to piles of wanton ash and rubble. Gone was the ancient splendour of the kings. And now gone too was the noble house that had offered her sanctuary and always been her friend. And she had never even thanked them.

Instead Xandorians manned the gates now. Strange looking soldiers with long nasty spears. As she looked up Lissane noticed them watching from the walls as well. How could her father have allowed such as these to destroy and then occupy the greatest stronghold in Gol? Worse than betrayal, that. It was a new low even for him. And there he was now. Her father. Waiting with arms folded outside the gates.

Chapter 19

Fate's Children

The Xandorian Elite had fought with the tenacity of soldier ants. Led by one Horgreb, and directed by Paolo and himself, the foreign mercenaries had soon reduced the castle's surviving occupants to a pitiful remnant of defiant women and weeping children. Eon had these rounded up. The surviving nobles (including Raneas Sarfe and his spouse Arabella) were despatched swiftly in the Hall of Kings, where years ago Flaminius had gone berserk and butchered his wife and children. That left Clarde Dovess who still held out, walled up inside the keep with a diminished force of diehards. They wouldn't last long. Eon's guards had piled dry logs against the keep's oak doors. It would take a while but once inside the fire would flush them out, or else more probably they would choose the flame over surrender. The Dovesians were ever a proud lot. More fool them.

Rosco and Aldo were leading the crew setting torch and hammer to those heavy doors. They would either smoke or batter Clarde out—it mattered not as long as he joined the pile of corpses in the square. That or perished inside the keep. By evening the fighting stopped, Rosco reported back to him that the hall inside the main keep had collapsed, and all within were surely crushed beneath.

So much for Clarde Dovess.

And so it was done. He, Eon, Baron of House Barola, was now ruler of Gol, with Volt Garron his lieutenant, as was agreed. Eon smiled at the power he felt rushing through his veins as he took his seat in the vacant throne.

There would doubtless be a few rebels to mop up. Aldo had informed him that most of the fighters down in the arena were dead. Gone to the crows, that flower of nobility, replaced by a new order, as was fitting. This was Barola's time and he had worked hard toward this goal.

Two things marred his joy. The first was Lissane. The girl would oppose him at every turn—Eon knew that now. She hated him so much and he couldn't blame her for that. But though unfortunate, it was the way of things. Lissane, like her mother before, had never had a solid grasp on reality.

The other irritant was Erun Cade. The sudden appearance of that boy, so long assumed dead, had shocked Eon to the core. How that dreamy youth had become such a fighter was beyond his ken. But his untimely reappearance sent a shiver through Eon's bones. Nothing was happenstance. Everything occurred for a reason. Were the gods mocking him? 'I come from the gods,' Erun Cade had said. Eon had long forsaken those gods; perhaps it was time now to renew his vows. But enough of these misgivings. This was his day. They would celebrate late into the night.

The Baron was draining his third tankard when an excitable Rosco announced that Lissane and this Erun Cade and that scruffy Rodruthan 'king', were leading a small army toward the castle. Eon hurled his tankard across the room.

Damn that girl!

He bade archers line the walls and ventured without, impatiently awaiting the group's arrival beneath the darkening shadow of the main gates. That meeting proved frosty and short. Eon urged his daughter join in his victory and was rewarded by her spittle on his cheek.

"We are at war now, Father," she hissed at him. "Or should I say—murderer and usurper of Gol." She spat again: this time in his eye. "When next we meet it will be at your funeral, Father."

He had raged at her then, nearly hit her, and ordered her friends filled with arrows, but something in Erun Cade's eyes had stopped him signalling the archers to shoot down on her companions. Instead Eon Barola had turned his back on them and re-entered his city with a face as black as midnight thunder.

Damn that bitch.

Several minutes later the Baron yelled down to them from the battlements above, his voice hoarse and commanding.

"I will wear you down, Lissane, never fear," Eon Barola shouted. "Your paltry army I shall pursue as rats and crush like winter leaves beneath my feet. Go wherever you wish, daughter, but do not doubt I shall smoke you out—you and these fools you align with. The next time we speak will be with steel!"

This last address was for Erun Cade standing beside her. Eon left them then and returned to his cups, moody and dour. But before he retired from the wall a challenging voice reached him from below.

Eon turned, and stone-faced gazed back down from the battlements, saw that his daughter and her pathetic army had retreated just out of arrow range. Now a lone armoured warrior stood looking up at the castle wall. Erun Cade—the stone in his boot. Now back from the dead.

"Baron Barola!" Erun Cade's voice carried easily. "This war is folly. Gol cannot afford it. Ashmali is coming—it is foretold. The only chance we have is by uniting against the demon...this I heard from the gods themselves."

Eon turned to a nearby archer. "Shoot that noisy bastard," he said. But when he gazed back down Erun Cade had gone. Vanished from sight altogether, although Lissane and her followers were still clearly visible in the middle distance. The archer muttered something inaudible. Eon blanched and turned away from the walls.

What sorcery is this? Gods, I need a drink...

That night Eon Barola dreamed of flames and ruin. Everything he had built was reduced to ashes, and amidst it all strode Erun

Cade, whilst the sound of Lissane's mocking laughter echoed through the walls.

Is this your vengeance, Leanna?

By dawn he was at his cups again.

That night as they camped in a wood some miles north of Torvosa City, Lissane came to him. Erun awaited her in silence. Since their initial joy there had been awkwardness between them. Their paths had been very different and both bore scars, and though hers were hidden they were the deepest.

"I cannot love you as I once did." Lissane's eyes were filled with the moon and her pale face perfect in the night.

"I know—you loved Estorien Sarfe. I...understand."

"I believed you dead, Erun," she answered him. "You had my heart once long ago, but we were children back then. Estorien will always be my darling. I'm sorry Erun, I really am, but I cannot lie."

"Nor should you," Erun relied quietly. "I too have loved another," he lied. "But that was then. I still love you, Lissane Barola—I always did."

"I don't deserve it,"

"I would have you for my wife,"

She didn't respond.

"I know things have moved on, Liss," he pressed, "but our time left should be as good as we can make it."

"It should." She smiled for the first time that night. It made her look younger, Erun thought, less drawn. Almost he saw that wild-eyed girl again. Almost. He stroked her face.

"Will you take me as your husband?"

"I shall..." She kissed him then, twice on the lips and he gathered her in. That night they made love as they had down on the beach all that time ago, but in the morning Lissane was a stranger to him again. Jerrel had watched their passion from afar—he hadn't wanted to but had felt compelled nonetheless. A moth to her flame—such was her draw, this Barolan beauty.

Wherever you go you break men's hearts, Lissane Barola. Most surely have you broken mine.

***

A small gathering of renegades sleeping in a hollow below. Hardly an army. Irulan scratches his ear, while his wife watches from beneath the leafy glades of the forest.

"It has gone as we planned," he says.

She shakes her head, "Ashmali has consumed the sorcerer's mind, rending him insane, Ozmandeus is burning within, husband. The demon rules him now and will not stop until all is oblivion. Remember the trouble this Ashmali caused us before. He is a product of Old Night, after all. We should have done for him when we had the chance."

"That was then—we were naive, sister. Besides, our boy has learned so much," counters Oroonin the One Eyed Huntsman. "And he has both Borz and Aqueous to aid him."

"This petty war of theirs plays right into our brother's hands," responded Elanion. "Ashmali was ever the Shadowman's creature, husband." She glances across at him. "And our little brother now stirs in his watery domain—he'll not tolerate the return of the demon—fire was ever his enemy. You know how short-fused Zansuat is when roused."

"He'll not act unless goaded directly by Ashmali's flames—or some other stupidity."

"And there is no shortage of that where mankind is involved," scoffed Elanion—her all-seeing gaze strayed toward the crashing ocean, miles away.

"The seas rise as they sense their master's return," she added in a whisper that spoke of leaves stirred by a sudden breeze, "Gol is lost, brother and husband mine. But the greater part of Ansu shall remain. But alas—the candle gutters for this sorry land. Zansuat will claim back his former domain rather than let Ashmali ruin it. So it is either fire or water. Poor Gol." She shakes her head. "There is little time left for your hero, husband."

"There is time yet," replies Irulan, dismissing her words with a brush of his hand. "Those two are fate's children. Brave Kell and proud Lissane shall spawn a line of kings strong endure to the final war. It is the gift I bestow them, my wife."

"And yet I fear for her..."

The hermit turns then but Scaffa has already left him. He chuckles before taking his leave. He still loves her in his way—his only sister and long time spouse. He would win her over yet he determined. She'd been frigid toward him for millennia now, holed up in that cursed island of hers, blaming it all on him—just because he'd sent her there after that last major row.

Elanion was free now, however—thanks to Tertzei, her creature. That was part of the deal—and he *had* needed her help. Let Elanion doubt him for another thousand years—it didn't matter. In time Oroonin would prove her wrong.

Yes, in good time he would prove them all wrong. For that final war was coming and when it did Erun Cade and Lissane Barola's descendants would carry the banners of Oroonin's army.

Irulan's single silver eye pierces the heavens above—his domain. A third and conclusive war was now brewing between Darkness and Light. Law and Chaos. The last conflict between his noble siblings and their outcast elder brother, Old Night, who men here call the Shadowman.

Irulan had yet to pick his side in that fight. He was a fickle spirit and there was yet much to play for. He turns his immortal gaze toward the west, sees the flames rising higher and higher, closer and closer. The demon is coming.

Irulan merges: becomes an eagle, soars close—but not so close that the flames singe his flight. Oroonin smiles as he swoops high overhead. He feels the Elemental's fiery essence swelling like magma inside the mortal sorcerer's brittle shell. Ozmandeus was finished but Ashmali had only just begun.

***

Fire was everywhere, it consumed his world. When he slept dreams raked his slumber with blazing, burning rage. Waking, the pain would sear inside his head until he cried out, begging like a child for it to stop.

But it never stopped.

Ozmandeus knew in his rare sane moments that Ashmali

was devouring him from within, like a starving, swelling parasite. Day by day, hour by hour, and moment by agonizing moment, the demon grew larger inside him. He was but a shell. This could only end one way—and soon.

Yet, despite all, he'd achieved everything he desired. The entire continent from Zorne to Khandol was his to rule. To what avail? And what price for such efforts? His new dominion was a desert of ruin and ash, his only subjects soulless, defeated shadows. Undead slave and shuffling corpses. They had been too thorough by far in their conquest, Ozmandeus and his demon.

Ashmali's hunger had wrought destruction so total few living things remained. Trees were shrivelled charcoal-black, rivers drained to steam, and myriad fleeing creatures scorched to blackened meat.

Mankind too had fled (those that could) overseas to the City States, or else east to Gol. One by one those great old cities of Xandoria had tumbled into piles of ash. All that history and beauty—gone forever. All those stories lost to time.

What a waste. And for what—his personal glory? His vengeance? He no longer knew. Ozmandeus had been used as a tool by his demon, just as he had used others during his ascent to power. It was fitting in a way.

The last city to crumble had been Rakeel by the Shimmering Sea. Just days ago it had raged like a furnace at the whim of the demon's breath. There was nothing left of Xandoria now. Nothing but ash and hot blazing wind.

Ozmandeus was so very weary, so pathetically weak, but the demon inside him was waxing to full. Ashmali never rested these days. The demon had grown so strong feeding on the life-force of all he destroyed. Soon his tormentor would emerge as pupating larvae from his temporary prison inside Ozmandeus's soul. Ashmali had shattered the amulet that once held him at bay, soon he would do the same to his host. Then at last he would be free to scourge and burn for all eternity.

Ozmandeus had lost and would soon pay the ultimate price— a victim of his own success. How the gods must be laughing at the presumption of this arrogant and foolish man. The self pity was a hot knife twisting in his soul. But Ozmandeus had one last act to enable before the demon finished with him. One last desperate gambit. He could still be useful to his master—if only for a short while. It would prolong his suffering but it would also prolong his life.

Gol—there lay Ozmandeus's fleeting salvation. *I shall give you Gol, demon, and then you shall let me be to die in peace and be rid of your pains.* That tiny, insular continent would be the last to fall beneath Ashmali's purifying flame. Its shores were close by now. Of course that would only postpone his death, but the larger insane part of him didn't care—that part was already half Ashmali and just wanted to burn.

Ozmandeus had had no choice. Driven on by the demon's lust and his own febrile mind, he'd gathered his horde for that final conquest. An army of fiends, lashed on (like him) by the rage of Ashmali's insatiable hunger. All were slave to the demon now.

And so that fateful day arrived. The army of ghosts paraded the shores, and the Renegade signalled his dark host forward with a gauntleted hand. Even that movement charred the aging skin, peeling old blisters from his brittle, parched flesh. Ozmandeus hardly noticed, instead he felt the demon surge inside him.

Then, like a storm of angry blowflies, Ashmali's terrible army swarmed across the mile wide isthmus reaching Gol's western shores. And Gol's people were taken unawares. And so we reach the final days. The fall of Gol. What follows is the only surviving account of that disaster.

Fall

Chapter 20

Garron Fields

Garron Fields at dawn. Winter skies brooded over rime-spar-kled grass, and a mist clung to trees whose silent, bare branches watched over the valley below like impartial judges awaiting the battle's commencement.

Lissane Barola watched as dawn light slowly revealed the secrets of that icy northern combe. It wasn't long before she made out the nearest tents of her father's army. A force more than three times the size of their own.

And so it had come to this—the final battle.

But Lissane was ready today. Garbed in trousers of dun leath-er and glimmering hauberk of finest steel link, and covering these, an otter-skin cloak stitched with midnight blue wool, fastened at collar by a golden broach of Galanian craft, which glinted faintly in the morning light.

Lissane hadn't slept last night—no one had. But she wasn't tired, and saw no reason to remain idle within her blanket while the men rose early to prepare for this deciding fight. Behind her, Anyetta (a slave she'd freed after returning to Galanais) calmed the twins as they grew restless with the cold onset of dawn. They had the souls of warriors those boys, but she would they were grown men and not mewling babes. Thanek and Wynna—her sons by Erun Cade. They were the future. Nothing else mattered.

Eighteen brutal months had passed since the treachery at Torvosa. A year and a half of bloody campaigns, guerrilla skirmishes, and then that final bitter siege. Lissane had lost friends to plague and famine, as well as hired Xandorian steel. Nothing had gone as planned. When they had entered Galanais last autumn the people had greeted them with cheers. Lissane their emancipator had returned. That had been a joyful time, but brief—so very brief.

During that winter, Erun, Jerrel, and King Torrig Red-Hair had led bold raids against her father, driving him out like a wounded bear from Torvosa City, and he in turn had furiously sought to crush them. And so it dragged on until spring. Then came more Xandorians, and with his army now big enough, Eon Barola marched west, setting iron siege to Galanais.

Stalemate followed. That summer it rained as never before. Disease entered city and camps without. Everyone suffered. Soldiers, camp-followers, citizens and defenders: they died in their hundreds—maybe thousands. Eon Barola built siege towers. He had trebuchets and scorpions too—all the best equipment, but still the city defied him. Summer waxed full and the dying continued on both sides of the walls. Amidst that continuing horror, Lissane presented Erun Cade with two healthy sons—a moment's blissful joy in that bitter, brutal summer.

Three times Eon Barola called a truce. The baron had become disillusioned as things had not gone as he'd wished. Erun Cade would have accepted—he sensed Ashmali's sudden approach and worried that they wasted time. But Lissane was unmoved. She had become haughty and proud, blaming all their woes on her father and siblings.

Then that dire day arrived when they spied the fleet approaching. Xandorian galleys, their garish sails filling the horizon and their broad hulls bobbing up and down, like so many floating bugs.

It was then that they realised they had lost.

But as those ships drew close and sailors furled sails before taking to oar, a great shudder shook the walls of Galanais, heralding the first earthquake in a hundred years. Buildings trembled, shivered and then collapsed, the screaming and dying lost beneath. The earth shook, again and again, pitching soldiers from the walls like so many ants. That day huge chunks of both city and citadel crumbled and fell.

But the Xandorian fleet was destroyed utterly when a monstrous wave devoured it—the gaudy ships reduced to splinters by that mighty wash. All drowned in that deluge including the warlord, Romul.

Eon Barola also had his problems. The Baron's camps were beset by lightning and flash-floods. Beset, he ordered a hasty withdrawal to the foothills seeking shelter from the ruin. Then Erun Cade, his wife and friends, after seeing their enemy retreat, gathered all those they could and vacated the city in great haste, as it crashed to dust and ruin all about them.

They too fled to the hills, those battered survivors, camping several miles north of the enemy. Once safe, they had witnessed the final destruction of Galanais City. Erun, watching with a chubby son on each knee, saw the sea rise up impossibly high, swallowing the city whole as it had the Xandorian fleet. Never had they known such watery violence as happened on that day. But worse was still to come.

Then had followed weeks of skirmish. Attack and counter attack. Neither force gaining the advantage, but just stinging each other—and everyone weary and drained. Barola had the numbers still, but Erun Cade's cunning battle-craft kept them several steps ahead of the Baron. But then as autumn fell to winter the weather worsened again. It was relentless that winter. Storms battered them incessantly: icy rain and sleet pounded their everyday. All along the coast waves surged higher claiming yet more land.

They endured: marched east. Crossed to Treggara in a last desperate ploy. The Baron followed on, weary and battered, desiring now only a swift conclusion. Then at bleak Garron Fields, Eon Barola finally caught up with his daughter.

Six battles they had fought since Torvosa. *One for each province*, Lissane thought, although they hadn't been battles in the true sense, but rather guerrilla raid and run.

She knew today would be different—the decider.

Her army was weakened by hunger and fatigue, their garments torn and frayed, and their numbers greatly depleted. Disease, blight, and the terrible winter had all taken their toll. Their army, unlike Barola's, had not been bolstered by foreign swords.

There was some good tidings. Volt Garron and her father had fallen out (their scouts discovered,) the Treggarans having since returned to Dreekhall. It made little difference though. They were still outnumbered.

There had been that rare sunny day, when a wild-haired horseman had galloped into their camp amid shouts. Lissane had feared yet another raid, but this rider turned out to be one Rakaro (an old friend of Erun's), and accompanying him were two hundred nomads on shaggy little ponies. But Rakaro's words on entrance were not encouraging:

"The demon has destroyed Rakeel," he had told them, "I fear it will turn this way next."

They had very little time left, Rakaro said, and Erun raged to her that they wasted the hours they had in foolhardy conflict. But what else could they do? An endgame must be reached.

Twice that winter they had held bitter parley, Lissane and her father—the others watching on. Neither would give. Eon's jaw was set with determination, though his eyes were sad; and nothing would soothe Lissane Barola's loathing of the Baron.

And so it came to this final battle in a winter held valley, just three score miles from Garron's stronghold at Dreekhall. This stark location had been a masterstroke of her husband. During the conflict the warlord Kell had proved himself a peerless tactician. Working from their hidden base deep in the foothills of Galania they had lashed out at Eon Barola's forces, time and again before fleeing into the night. And this last wild gambit had been Erun's idea.

One final forced march through winter's worst to steal upon

Volt Garron, while he and his sons wintered at home. They would take Dreekhall at night, (both Erun and Torrig knew how to get in) and then range out from that stronghold with renewed vigour at her father and his allies.

But Barola's spies were everywhere. Their movement had been witnessed, so when they ranged free of the mountains in eastern Treggara they found the enemy waiting for them. But her husband had not been fazed. His eyes blazed with the determination of the warrior born. There was little of Erun Cade remaining in this grim, lean-faced warlord. But that was just as well, Lissane too had changed. Weakness was not to be borne. Lissane was a mother now and, at twenty-seven winters, a woman past her prime. Though still beautiful she was gaunt, and her proud violet eyes were seldom free of determined loathing.

She was an iron rod, her father too—both of them rigid and unyielding. One of them would give today. Lissane vowed it wouldn't be her.

I will break you, Father, as you broke my mother.

Lissane felt a cold wetness settle on her cheek and looking up, she saw the fresh fall of snow settle on their tents. Dawn was struggling beneath lowering snow clouds. The sky (what showed) was pinky-grey, the atmosphere tense and silent. A cold wind shivered along her spine. Lissane tugged at her cloak and ignored the chill; instead she let her bitterness fuel her frozen veins. Snow and fog and chilling damp. Treggara was a forlorn country in winter.

Movement caught her eye in the valley below. Lissane, watching, saw an owl glide on silent wings betwixt dark sentinels of larch and pine, before settling on a branch just yards beyond their staked defences. The owl watched her keenly from its perch. It became a woman, and like the snow drifted slowly to the ground.

The owl-woman beckoned to her with a pale arm, and Lissane thought that she recognised Rani the Sea God's daughter, she that had visited her dreams that night so long ago. But this was another. The woman's witchy gaze held her own and, compelled by the power of those uncanny eyes, Lissane pulled her heavy hood over her damp head and quietly made her way down through the waking camp, ignoring and ignored by those now making ready with saddlery and weapons. She walked as though she were in a dream and perhaps she was.

The woman was cloaked in shadow; her face shrouded by the murk, but those green-gold eyes never blinked as Lissane approached her. Somewhere close by, she noted the faint peel of harpsong and smiled.

The phantom harper—so you have returned.

"Greeting, daughter," the owl-woman's voice was both rich and deep like summer night's breeze through warm southern woods. It soothed Lissane's soul—softened her sharp edges. "You have done well, Lissane Barola," the woman told her.

"You are not Rani."

"No indeed," responded the woman, "though young Rani is of my kin, being a daughter of my youngest brother." She smiled then like sunlight on still water, radiance and warmth exuded from this strange lady, piercing the mist and shedding gold on that grey northern morning.

"My name is of little import in this place," the woman said. "I mean you no ill, child...but came to...." Her gold-green gaze looked sad for a moment and she seemed lost in distant thought. She sighed then, as if struggling for the right words.

Lissane spoke instead: "This battle? Will we survive it—me and mine? I think of my sons mostly."

The woman turned her hypnotic gaze upon Lissane. "Perhaps..." she answered and then shook her head, and Lissane was suddenly aware of copper locks cascading down the woman's back. She was so beautiful, this stranger.

"This war of yours is pride and folly, Lissane," the owl-woman told her. "You cannot bring your erstwhile lover or your mother back. Look to the future of your sons—yes. What's past is gone forever, girl. Estorien, Leanna; Belshareze and Grale, they've all crossed the final river. There they wait in the halls where even I cannot enter.

"Vengeance is forlorn, Lissane, and the real threat to Gol approaches now from across the sea. This fight today will change nothing, daughter. Gol—this entire continent of yours—is in direst peril."

"So my husband tells me." Lissane pulled a face. She didn't like being challenged, even by this strange woman, though she sensed she was in the presence of someone gifted with powerful foresight.

"Ashmali," she said, trying to resist the hypnotic draw of those wonderful eyes, "Erun has spoken of him often of late—he is obsessed, I fear, with this thing, and his friend Rakaro too," said Lissane. "Is the creature truly so terrible a threat?"

"That and more," replied the woman. She leaned forward, placing a pale hand on Lissane's shoulder, and Lissane caught a scent of honeyed wine and wild rose. "Now listen," the owl-woman said, "this must you do to save those that can be saved. Heed these words and remember what Rani told you that night when you thought you were dreaming. You will need to gather ships worthy of a voyage far over ocean. Doom approaches this land; fire and water—I would have you and yours survive, Lissane."

"Where will I need these ships and where to sail—the Great Continent is ash, they say? I know of no other sanctuary, except perhaps the Island States."

"A voyage east—not west, and many days sailing. There are realms that you know nothing about. Ansu harbours many folk beside yourselves, child."

"Ansu? I'm not familiar with that name."

"This green world. It was given to the gods by the Maker when I was young. Since that ancient time it has fallen into decay and rust. The seed of evil has grown. But that doesn't concern you now. What concerns you is survival.

"Ashmali has returned and my brother, the Sea God, will not tolerate his presence in this, His former land. Fire and water have little love for each other, and this 'demon' was ever a creature of Old Night, who you mortal folk call the Shadowman. He who is the enemy of all worlds, not just this one."

Lissane stood as one frozen in time. The woman's words were like living creatures, they had a life of their own. All seemed quiet and still. Then a soft breeze lifted Lissane's hair and she felt an inner calm soothing her cares and easing her frets. The woman watched her, her copper hair burnished with sunlight. About her head brightly coloured butterflies danced and fluttered. But as Lissane gazed into those gold-green eyes she found them lost in some ancient sorrow.

"Lissane, daughter, I would help you and yours but my direct involvement is forbidden. Mighty Zansuat too is your friend: you have His blood on your mother's side. Leanna Barola was a direct descendant of one Miriel who once dwelt with the Sea God for a time. Hers is a sad tale and my brother still mourns her for He loved her back then as He has loved no other. Not before nor ever since."

"What became of this Miriel?" Lissane heard herself ask.

"She was lost in a terrible storm. A tumult caused by Zansuat himself who wrongly suspected she had another lover. Too late Zansuat realised His folly. To this day my brother searches the wide oceans with His nets, trawling and scooping, looking for the mortal maid that so long ago stole His heart.

"But the Sea God has small love for most mankind since they've shunned Him of late, and I fear that Ashmali's imminent arrival on these shores shall wake Him from his restless slumbers. Already He frets at the shores. Once roused He is terrible. That earthquake was but a harbinger."

"Where will I find these ships? How—"

"I must leave you—the sun has risen and day is come." It was true, Lissane saw now that the snow had abated and a pale wintry sun had steered free of pinkish cloud, spilling yellow light on the valley below. Men fretted and stamped their feet at either end of the valley. They were edgy and awaited orders. Horses snorted and jittered alongside. It was almost time.

"Will I meet with you again?" Lissane called out as the woman turned away.

"Not in this life..."

Her voice trailed off like distant smoke and suddenly she was gone. Gone too was the warmth, the butterflies and bright calming sunlight. Instead cold and damp reclaimed the valley. Lissane's gaze wandered to the trees.

Nearby a large owl stared down at her from the bare branch of a rime-cloaked larch. Those gold-green eyes locked on hers for a second. They say the Mistress of the Trees sometimes takes the form of an owl.

I know who you are.

Lissane was almost struck dumb by the power of that stare, she blinked and the bird vanished, disappearing into the partial mist below. Heavy hearted, Lissane watched for a time then returned to the camp where her husband and his cohorts now consulted over a cold meagre breakfast.

Chapter 21

The Last Battle

They were all there, clad in their steel hauberks and woollen cloaks, their various weapons close at their sides: The warlord Kell, young Kael of Sarfania; fair-haired Jerrel, wild King Torrig, and Rakaro the squint-eyed archer. All wore determined expressions. They knew they had little chance of winning this fight.

Then Lissane strolled upon them, her face set and determined. Erun looked up and smiled, but his eyes were dark with worry.

"Liss, what ails you? You are pale as a ghost. Did you dream our ruin in the night?"

"I had a visitation," Lissane nodded thanks as a soldier spooned some gruel into a wooden bowl and handed it her way. "And a warning..."

"From whom?" Erun studied her face, trying to read her thoughts.

"Laniol of the Forests. It was Her—the goddess. Mistress of the Trees. I realise that now. She said that She wanted to help us."

"No way," muttered Torrig with a shudder. The Rodruthans alone of the people of Gol still feared the gods' intervention in everyday life. The mention of Laniol scared him more than a hundred screaming foes.

Lissane ignored him. "We need ships," she told them, "and as many as can be found and made seaworthy for a long arduous voyage." They all looked at her in silence. Torrig's mouth was open. "I was warned to prepare for this long ago but had forgotten. I am sorry. There is little time left to us," she urged them. "Gol is on the brink of some calamity. If we are to survive what's coming we will need those ships."

"And just what is coming?" Jerrel enquired.

Lissane's gaze fell on Rakaro seated next to Erun. "You were right as was my husband. There is little time left. This Ashmali creature is coming to Gol and his enemy the Sea God awaits him. The outcome of such an encounter? Well, you can guess the rest."

Rakaro's faced blanched after hearing this, "I fear we are finished," he said.

"Not so," Erun awarded his friend a tired smile. "I still retain both Borz and Aqueous, they'll protect us from Ashmali—somehow. Once we've won this field we can prepare for Ashmali's arrival. We will survive, my friends, I have—"

"—not without ships," cut in Lissane.

"And I have ships aplenty." King Torrig wiped a blob of gruel from his mouth and yawned. "There's a dozen at least lying idle in Longships creek, over-wintering away from the wild weather back at the Crags." He grinned at them and seemed fully recovered from his earlier shock. "I could have them crewed and fitted in no time. We'd be under sail just days from now," Torrig promised.

Erun exchanged a brisk glance with his wife and she nodded. "Do so," he said to the young king, "please."

"Consider it done. But where should I make for?" Torrig enquired before devouring another spoon full of porridge and belching enthusiastically.

"Barola Bay," answered Lissane.

Erun laughed. "Yes, that is only fitting. Let the fleet await us outside your father's walls."

And so it was settled. King Torrig and his men departed

within the hour. Erun watched them leave wistfully; those hardy fighters would be sorely missed today.

They waited. The sun shone briefly before more cloud occluded the glare, then the clouds passed overhead and the sun held the valley again. Men coughed and yawned and shivered, whilst horses snorted steam.

Still they waited. Across the valley the Baron's forces were lining up—a host of Xandorian spearmen topped up with Barolan veterans. Few were mounted on either side, the horses had fared badly during the winter, and many had served as meat for the hungry fighters.

Erun's soldiers lined up behind the sharpened stakes they'd erected and awaited his word. Erun wanted to see what Eon Barola planned before acting out any manoeuvres. The Baron had the advantage so it made sense to let him come to them.

Then at last, just as the final strands of mist fled Garron Fields, the brazen sound of horns filled the valley announcing the enemy was finally on the move.

Down they came from the far side, shouting and yelling, their armour and helmets glistening in the pale morning sun, and their spears countless as those cladding a porcupine's back.

Lissane retired to her tent. She would not engage in this struggle as she had in many others, as she had her sons to watch over now. "What of your kin—shall I spare them?" Erun had called out as she retired.

"No, kill them—every one," she had answered before adding, "If you don't then I will."

***

Eon Barola had never wanted it to end this way. He had envisioned a swift campaign following his victory at Torvosa. The rebels would be squashed and his wayward daughter reined in. He would show clemency to most, although Kell the warlord he would execute for his haughty words outside the city gates.

Erun Cade—the bastard had cost them dear these months. How was it that an idle useless dreamer had proved time and again such a resourceful and resilient foe? Eon just couldn't get to grips with it.

After finally securing the lands surrounding Torvosa, Eon, bolstered by more Xandorians, had made haste to Galanais where his daughter was rumoured to have freed every slave and tasked her captains to train those who could do so to fight. Volt Garron was left with the simple task of breaking Sarfania—not difficult with Razeas dead and the remaining noble, Kael, holed up with the rebels. Swiftly accomplishing that, Garron had joined them as they set siege to Galanais.

That proved an unhappy time. During the stalemate of that wet violent summer, the Barolans and Treggarans quarrelled and bickered. Fights broke out often and not infrequently resulting in death. Then weeks after the chaos that followed the earthquake and destruction of Galanais, Volt Garron had dared accuse him of incompetence and, after a heated row, had led his troops away across the mountains.

"And good bloody riddance!" Eon had yelled as they had ridden out that cold morning a month past.

Since then the war had trudged on, neither side gaining the upper hand. Even Paolo had become bored with it all. As for Eon, he spent as much time gulping ale or wine as he could. But that too was taking its toll.

But the rebels were weakening fast. This 'Kell' was a rat running out of places to hide. The boy's army was depleted to a rag-tag bunch of desperados, while Eon still had reinforcements arriving—though not so many now, and these mostly hired killers and thugs from Khandol.

What madness had driven so many warriors across from the Great Continent was certainly cause for alarm, but Eon Barola gave scant heed to the ravings of some of the new arrivals. His practical soldier's sense allowed no room for their talk of demons and necromancy. Whatever was happening across the sea could bloody well stay there. And if not, then he would deal with, whatever it was, when he had won this most irritating war.

And that time had come at last. Today he and his allies would crush Lissane and her lover's desperate little army. Lissane would be chastised, of course, and perhaps imprisoned. Her sons (Cade's brats) put to the sword at once, and all the surviving rebels gutted open and then staked out across the valley for crow feed. Eighteen months of frustration had left scant pity in Eon Barola's heart.

It had been sly old Grudge that informed him of this Kell's latest ploy. The servant had lived in terror of Paolo punishing him after his deceit concerning young Erun Cade—the very same bastard they were fighting now. Eon knew Grudge to be both competent and cunning and so he had forbade Paolo from working on the servant, although his youngest son had so wanted to. Relieved and his loyalty reinforced by terror, Grudge had proved by far the best spy in the conflict.

"They mean to take Dreekhall at night,"

Grudge had told him and he had smiled. And so, when Kell and Lissane's rebels cleared the forest fringing the foothills of western Treggara they had found him waiting for them at the far side of a steep valley.

Eon smiled at the irony. Garron Fields, one of the preferred hunting areas of House Garron—and there was old Volt and his boys holed up and sulking in their nest, while he, Barola took victory alone. Maybe he should march to Dreekhall when this battle was finished. He could put that lot to the sword as well. He would give that matter some thought tomorrow.

As for now...

Eon Barola grinned like a meat-hungry wolf as Rosco (clad in rusty steel) thrust a horn of ale in his right hand. Yes, Eon thought, here at Garron Fields they would break the rebel force—it would be over in hours, this fight.

He gulped his ale and tossed the horn aside. Then Eon Barola leapt upon his saddle and yelled for the horns to announce the attack. His sons were at his side as the Baron spurred his beast forward at speed.

"Barola and beyond!" Eon yelled the battle cry. Helmets were slammed down over the rider's faces and behind them the spearmen ran apace, their weapons pointing up to the far ridge where the enemy waited. Hoofs thundered. Steel-shod feet muddied wet ground where the ice had melted. They reached the bottom of the valley; the sun glinted off to their right—no advantage for either side. Then a buzzing whoosh announced the first arrows coming their way.

Eon ducked as that volley stung horse and rider, causing the odd one to fall, and behind him he heard men cry out as they were hit. He grinned, revelling in the moment, and urged his steed into gallop leaving the Xandorians far behind. He, Eon Barola, had been born for days such as these. To his left Paolo whooped, the boy was in his element too. They would crush the foe easily today, and then he would silence House Garron with knives at midnight.

At last! After months of frustration he was free to let rip on his enemies. Eon laughed out loud as the battle rage surged into his veins. He was forty-four years old and within a month he would be the undisputed ruler of Gol.

The land raced beneath him as they gained the ridge, the faces of the enemy looming close. More arrows stung men at his either side but none dared settle on Eon Barola and his sons.

Behind, the Xandorians had reached the valley floor, in minutes they would join him. Eon reined in briefly when he saw the sharpened stakes raised against them; he noticed the swiftly dug trench that would slow their attack, and the hoof-crippling caltrops clustered within.

None of it fazed him. The Baron spurred his horse forward again, his sword swinging out, hewing the top off a stake. Seconds later his sons and the other riders followed suit. Their horses took the ditch at full gallop, avoiding the spikes, and battering resistance aside; as one they raced into the enemy camp.

Then the real killing began.

***

Erun and Jerrel yelled at their men to hold but it was useless. The enemy kept coming, swarming like enraged ants across the valley. Barola's horse had broken through their stakes and cleared the ditch easily, but they had been forced back and made to wait for their foot to arrive.

Since then they had repelled four charges from the Baron and a constant push by the advancing spearmen. But Erun's fighters had the high ground and were making good use of it. Already the field was bloody with enemy dead. But still they came, and Erun's much smaller force had shrunk to scarce three hundred, as arrow and spear lunge took its toll. Yet still they held—somehow. He could hear Eon Barola's enraged frustration as he cajoled his soldiers into fresh attack. The Baron was foaming at the mouth, kicking out and slashing at any who dared stray near, a bloody sword gripped in either steel-gauntleted hand.

Slowly and inevitably they had to give ground as the stakes were knocked aside, and the Xandorians surged through the blood-soaked mud to hack at the defenders. The camp was soon encircled, the Xandorians sheer numbers pressing down on those that still guarded the camp's rear, whilst the Baron and his sons slashed at tents and urged their beasts this way and that, seeking to slay all in their way.

But Kael and Rakaro were there, and Jerrel too. And then Erun Cade sought out the Baron and his sons, hacking and cleaving a way through Xandorians, across to the main camp where Paolo and Rosco were delivering bloody death on all who faced them.

Erun felt the warrior's rage surging along his veins: cut, hack and slice! Kill and kill! He lunged, sliced, parried and hacked. No blade or spear tip checked his progress. He was Kell the Avenger again and his enemies fell beneath his advance like scythed barley at summer's end.

He saw the baron. Eon was about to ride him down. Erun snatched a spear from a Xandorian mercenary, and dispatched the man with a backhanded swipe of his sword. He tossed the spear at the Baron's horse as the beast reared up. The shaft tangled between forelegs, the horse fell, pitching its rider in the mud.

Erun leapt forward with Callanak held ready, but then a heavy blow knocked him sideways as Rosco Barola rammed an armoured shoulder hard into Erun's back.

He fell and rolled on impact, Callanak now gripped in both

hands. Rosco's double headed axe splattered the mud an inch from his left ear. Erun lunged up, hard and fast, as Rosco leaned forward to tug at his axe and free it from the mud. The crystal-steel sword sliced open a shallow gap between Rosco's helmet and mail. Rosco cursed as he bled and jumped back, clutching at his throat in alarm.

Erun Cade rolled to his feet, Callanak balanced and poised to finish this eldest son, but then a foot tripped him from behind and he slipped over a Xandorian's corpse. Mud splattered into his face, marring his vision. Erun heard someone laugh at him.

On instinct he rolled again, wiped his eyes on his sleeve and then looking up, saw Paolo Barola grinning at him with slim rapier in either hand. Paolo's helmet was abandoned and his horse dead but he was having a terrific day. Eon Barola's brightest son grinned down at Erun who now crouched with sword held ready.

Paolo's long hair was matted with blood and sticking to his pale features. Those cat-eyes widened with sadistic anticipation. Paolo took a slow theatrical step forward, relishing the moment. And, as he watched his enemy, the warrior Kell felt his strength desert him to be replaced by fear. He was Erun Cade the youth again, and Paolo the torturer was set to finish the task he'd started way back at the forge. Paolo saw the fear in Erun's eyes and his grin widened.

"Time to die, peasant."

Erun spat and struggled; he tried to rise but Rosco's steel-shod foot slammed hard into his neck and he choked for breath. Panic replaced the fear then rage tore upon him again. *Bastards!* Erun remembered his twin boys back in the camp, he thought of Lissane close by, a knife in her hand to protect them.

I'll not die like this!

Desperate, Erun swung Callanak at Rosco's steel-shod boot but missed, cutting through air instead. Now Rosco loomed over him all sweat and dribble. The axe came down. Erun closed his eyes.

Forgive me, Lissane, I have failed you and our sons.

Nothing. Then Erun heard a muffled scream and a thud, and looking up saw no boot pressing down on him. Turning slowly, warily, Erun saw that both Paolo and his father had forgotten him and were watching some new occurrence at the northern edge of the valley. Whilst to his right Rosco Barola rolled in the filth, a grey-fletched arrow protruding for his gut. Erun rolled to his feet. It was his turn to smile now.

"Goodbye, Rosco."

The big Barolan tore at his helmet, freeing the strap and tossing it aside as he gulped for air. Where had that shaft come from? They had killed all the archers. Rosco sweated and swore as the agonising pain of the poisoned shaft shot up through his veins. A shadow clouded his vision. Rosco looked up and his jaw dropped.

Please help me...it burns!

Erun let the double-headed axe fall at speed, splitting Rosco's skull open like a ripe melon, and splattering blood and brains up his legs.

I'd not stain Callanak with such as you. He slung the axe away, and then waded over to where the fighting now continued outside the stockade.

One down, father...two to go.

***

It was some time later when Erun Cade discovered what had happened. He'd been pressed in on all sides, the dead and dying trampled and gored at his feet. Then that pressure had suddenly abated and Erun, unbelieving, saw that his enemies were on the run, making fast for the woods at the other end of the valley.

Blue-armoured horsemen were everywhere, pursuing Barolans and Xandorians, riding them down, or else gutting them from behind with lance and spear.

A horse thundered close. Erun wiped fresh blood from his face so that he could see better. The rider grinned down at him. A big man cloaked in blue fir and shining sapphire steel. Erun recognised Clarde Dovess, Champion of Torvosa. Impossibly, he had survived that treacherous day at the Games, and now rained urgent death on those who had murdered his family and kin.

Clarde's men, it turned out, had been fighting in the mountains all that time. Both Barola and Garron had assumed they were part of Kell and Lissane's rebel force. They had killed silently at night and faded like shadows before any retribution was possible.

Clarde had followed the creepy Grudge, as Eon's spymaster stole upon the rebels' camp to get word of their intentions. Clarde had got the truth out of the wretch with red hot steel held close to his face.

Seeing the way the man was, Clarde had then promised him a sizeable sum to go warn the Baron to meet with the rebel force at Garron Fields. A place Clarde Dovess knew well from past hunts with House Treggara—perfect for the ambush they had planned.

But first he had made this Grudge call on Dreekhall after dark. When the guards had let him in (they all knew him as the Baron's man) Clarde's men had sneaked behind, done for the guards and filtered into the castle. They caught Volt and his sons and warriors snoring amid spilt beer and filth. They slit their throats like so many sheep. So much for House Garron. A cruel end to a cruel family. Only Slinsi's name would be remembered with honour.

Clarde had wanted to intervene earlier in the battle, but they were only a hundred horsemen and had to wait for the critical point when Eon Barola would be most vulnerable. That had come when the Baron's army surrounded their enemy's camp.

Clarde's riders had sped up the valley like blazing blue comets, taking the Xandorian mercenaries unawares from behind. Their number, though small, was amplified by surprise and speed of their mounted attack, and then Erun's few remaining archers, led by the quick-thinking Rakaro, had peppered the backs of the fleeing foe.

Within half an hour of Clarde's appearance Eon Barola's army was broken and on the run, and his allies from Xandoria cut down, or else rounded up like stray cattle. The surviving Xandorians, (not many) sued for peace and were spared the sword. These now swore fealty to the warlord Kell and his ally, Clarde Dovess. Shattered yet triumphant, the victorious army salvaged what they could of their camp. That evening Erun Cade was reunited with Lissane and his sons; together they watched the sun set like a blood orange behind the shoulder of the mountains.

"The day is won," Erun had told her, although she already knew, having witnessed all at first hand, a knife gripped ready should the enemy reach her—and they very nearly had. But Erun and Lissane's joy was short lived. Rakaro, who had been mopping up the last Xandorians and scourging the woods, crashed in on them white-face and eyes wild with dread.

"The northern hills are ringed with fire!" the archer told them, his hand shaking as he clutched his bow. "The sky glows and flickers all along the horizon!"

Minutes later Erun Cade, Lissane, Clarde and several others accompanied Rakaro up through wintry woods, eventually cresting a high ridge. From this height they could clearly see the open country where Treggara met the Rodruthan border. Lissane felt her heart plummet as leaden stone. The northern skyline was red with fire.

"I warned of this," said her husband grimly. "Ashmali...the demon. He has come at last." Erun shook his head. It seemed that they were out of time. He was so tired, and Lissane and his friends looked battered and torn in that ruddy afterglow. "You had best pray to Elanion that Torrig reached those ships on time," he said, "I fear Rodrutha is lost. As for us—we march on the hour." No one challenged that.

***

That night they broke camp and started the long gruelling trek south to Barola Bay. Each day they marched and at night rested without much sleep, instead watching the distant flames lining the northern skyline—that bit closer every day.

Word reached them that Lissane's father and surviving sons were bolted up in Castle Barola like rats in a barrel. Erun had informed Lissane of Rosco's demise. She hadn't responded, except to clutch his arm tightly once and then turn away.

Days passed. Weeks. The fear of what followed behind drove their bodies far beyond normal endurance. But at last that haggard little army crossed the swollen Stonewash and entered Barola Province. Only a few miles behind them the Treggaran heights blazed with Ashmali's ruin.

Chapter 22

The Causeway

She watches as the ocean rises up all along her shores. It is time to depart. Zansuat awakens now the demon has arrived in his domain. She calls on Her creature—Tertzei. On Her command they fuse and meld into one being. Lightning splits the sky above; its jagged spears lancing the ground by her feet. Her lightning this time—called down by Her powers. She speaks the words, and the thunderous echoes of Her immortal voice boom all around.

At Elanion/Tertzei's command, Zansuat's angry seas fall back and the island, (once rid of his violent wash,) rises up higher and higher. Then follows a sound of scraping and groaning; a violent wrenching and jolting shudder, as the island root shears clear of the bedrock cementing it. Goddess/Elemental: She chants incantation with both Her voices.

The island spins on its axis: faster and faster, whirling up into cold blue distant void. Laras Lassladden is no longer Her prison. Island and Goddess: both now free to sail between worlds as they had in eons gone by. She shudders and spews Tertzei's essence free of her mouth, setting her daughter loose.

As Tertzei tumbles, light glows from her ruby skin allowing

her to streak like a comet, eventually landing in a lost far corner of the world. Of what becomes of her there no story can tell. The island sails through space and sky. From afar Elanion/Laniol looks down, both curious and eager to capture the final outcome.

She hasn't long to wait.

***

King Torrig Red-Hair wept tears of pure fury as he looked back at the withered hills of his country. Beloved Rodrutha was no more. Heath and moor, forest and crag: all scorched to blackened ash and burning still. He feared his people were lost too, (all save those few with him now) charred and shrivelled by the horror of the demon. The Crags would be gone by now. And Northtown too. Almost all his kingdom reduced to ash. The omens had been right after all.

Torrig had reached Longships scarce ahead of the flames. He found its terrified occupants already hard at work manning sail and oar—luckily all tarring and caulking had been completed early. In past years Rodruthans had left such chores to late winter, preferring to keep the darkest days for drinking and dicing.

But as soon as he'd gained the throne, King Torrig had swiftly put paid to that indolence, insisting his sailors had all tasks completed to a high standard before the heavy drinking started.

And thank the gods he'd moved the fleet to Longships!

His father had never bothered sailing far from the Crags at summer's end, but then King Brude never really liked his ships. Torrig, a passionate sailor unlike Brude, had not been idle during his brief reign and had constructed more ships since his father's death.

On a whim, he'd ordered his wrights deepen keels and fashion clinker hulls for longer treks. *You never know what's round the corner. Best to be prepared.* The young king had convinced himself he was planning a raid against Treggara next year, but something inside him knew that that wasn't true. An instinct maybe, or else some hidden warning system tolling bells deep within. Whichever—Torrig thanked the gods for that as well.

They filed out of Creekywater and set to sea during winter's worst. Thirty ships. All fine sleek vessels, hewed from oak and elm; planked and decked with skilled precision. The brightly painted sails emblazoned with sea eagle, osprey; kraken, or else black double-headed war-axe—the symbols of his people. On any other day King Torrig Red-Hair would have felt so proud. Instead he felt like weeping tears of ragged rage.

They tacked south, hugging the Treggaran shore. Night and day a dull red glow flickered off to west. Doubtless the fires flanking their voyage as they blazed huge and hungry all across Treggara. Torrig thought of Dreekhall and Garron's vile brood reduced to hissing charcoal, but even that cold comfort failed to raise a smile on his lips.

Still, they were faring well enough; a week's voyage from here and they'd raise the bluffs heralding Barola Bay.

Torrig had never seen those cliffs—never sailed that far south. He prayed again to Talcan the Sky-god—his current favourite, (Torrig had never been very devout, but he'd prayed more in the last ten days than his entire earlier life) that he would find his friends still living, and that they all could make safely their escape.

And as for after that and to where they would fare? He would worry about that later. Doubtless the wide oceans hold many secrets. Torrig prayed one more time that he'd get to explore some of them. Adventure. He always hungered for it. This time the dinner plate contained a bit more than he was used to. *No matter*, thought Torrig. That was life (and death), so bring it on. He stole a quick glance at the ruddy glow flickering over the Treggaran hills, swore twice, and then retired below for some strong ale.

Dusk found them farther down the coast.

***

Barola Bay at sunrise. Pink sky and scurrying cloud open on a fine winter's morn. Cocks crow noisy and beasts stir in byre and stable. Hounds bark and waking soldiers cough, and down below, the sea's roving wash crashes into the stone causeway with booming, rhythmic thuds. The camp was already stirring. Everyone up and about, with breakfast now underway, and tense chatter and whispering accompanying the clatter of plate, trencher; bowl and spoon.

Clarde Dovess talked with Jerrel and the other captains as they spooned broth into their mouths. But Erun Cade took no part in these social mutterings. He remained in his tent, his mind troubled and his hands rubbing tired red-rimmed eyes. He hadn't slept last night or the night before. Things weighed so heavy on him now.

Lissane steered close and awarded Erun a probing glance. Her husband looked exhausted. But they were all of them shattered. Their forced march had worn them down, add to this the horror of what followed and the urgency of their plight. It was all too much.

The battle's legacy and raging destruction behind them weighed heavy on the survivors. But most still retained a grim determination. They would survive...somehow. But Erun Cade looked lost. It was so unlike him, he who'd been so strong during their fraught time spent since Galanais's fall. Whilst Lissane and others had fretted, Erun had always been positive and confident of their chances. But not this morning. Today Kell the warlord looked a defeated man. She didn't like that look. It suited her husband ill.

Quietly Lissane knelt beside him. For a moment she watched Erun stare blankly into the flapping canvas of their tent's opening, his blue-grey gaze haunted and racked by self-doubt. This would not do.

"The boys are awake," she whispered softly in his ear, "You should speak with them, my love."

"I've scant time for baby talk, Lissane," his eyes flicked across the tent wall, met hers and then faded. "The twins will have to wait."

Her face darkened with annoyance. Lissane had no tolerance of weakness—least of all in her husband: "I'd not call those two babies now," she replied hotly. "You've hardly acknowledged their presence these last few days, and Wynna cries at your grim face. You know how sensitive that boy is."

"I have more pressing worries than Wynna," Erun argued. He

turned to her then, and, as if waking from a troubled sleep, sighed and rubbed his eyes again. "I'm sorry, Liss," Erun said, "I'll fuss them after breakfast. I promise. It's just…"

"The demon closes on us by the hour and you are uncertain of our wisest course," she answered for him and Erun nodded miserably in return.

"If only I knew how to use the other Elementals against Ashmali," Erun said. "Scaffa told me nothing; she only hinted at how they would save us from his ruin."

"Then we have to hold to hoping—when the time comes it will be made clear." Lissane gripped his scarred forearm with a pale hand. "Don't give up now. We need you to be strong, my love." Lissane forced a smile. "Courage shall see us through, you will see…and then when Torrig arrives—"

"We desert Gol. Flee the death and ruin, yes I know," he laughed bitterly. "And then we set sail into the gods only know what. Lissane, I cannot believe this is happening to us. What have we done to anger the gods so?"

Erun shook his head thinking off Scaffa/Laniol and Irulan/Oroonin and what games they played at man's expense.

I thought you believed in me, your chosen one…If you do, then guide me now, for I know not where to turn.

"The kings were ever ardent in their worship," Lissane answered. "But since the Rebellion men like Hal Gallante and my father scorned the gods, and even dared deny their existence. The gods have come to loathe us, I fear. Save perhaps Laniol, for she is kind.

"And I was warned of Zansuat's anger long ago—this demon's coming will have stirred him up. That is why the seas are so rough this winter." Lissane gripped his hand and squeezed hard. "I think this Ashmali is a creature of Old Night, Erun. The Shadowman himself, and thus a servant of the Sea God's greatest foe."

"Well that's as maybe," responded Erun. "It is not the Sea God who worries me at present—and yes, I've heard the history whilst on Laras Lassladden. I do remember that bit."

"Irulan was your friend. Scaffa too. You should have more faith, Erun Cade."

"But I don't trust either of them, Lissane. Not even Scaffa or Laniol or whatever form she takes. She's as bad as Irulan. They all play us as pawns, my wife. I believe them capricious and malicious, and fear they tamper with our lives out of boredom alone."

"Can you hear me, hermit? Giantess?" Erun glared at the roof of his tent. "Didn't think you were listening, well, Shadowman take you both."

"Enough! Your mood wearies my bones. Who are we to question the high gods?"

Erun shrugged his shoulders. "We have two, perhaps three days maximum before this demon and his corpse army descend on us. I saw what happened to Lamoza, Liss—I know what is coming and it scares me beyond words. But far worse than that, I have not the slightest notion what to do about it."

"Have some breakfast—you'll feel better." Lissane shouted for her maid who followed seconds later with steaming broth. "Eat that then go out," she told him, "greet the morning sun—it's a fine day out there already. Play with our boys—they'll love you for it—and then share a joke or two with your warriors. We're all afraid—not just you."

"There is that other matter..."

Lissane pulled a face. "You know how I feel about that...let them rot behind those walls, Erun. I care not for any of them."

"And yet they are still your kin—your blood."

"They are dead to me." Lissane's eyes were cold knives. She turned, made for the flapping opening and left him to it. Erun watched her go as he spooned down his broth.

Outside, Lissane Barola embraced her tots fondly, and together the three gazed down at the sea-locked castle below. It seemed so close—her boys' inheritance, were the world a fairer place. If she could have, Lissane would have torn apart that hated castle with her own bare hands.

Your course is run, Father. You have lost.

***

The sun highlighted grey on his temples as the Baron watched from the Keep. Draped in warm scarlet, his hard eyes scanning along the hastily erected camp now surrounding his town. It was chilly, but the sun's weak glow and the wine he'd consumed since dawn warmed his aging bones. For the first time in his energetic life, Eon Barola felt his years. He was weary. Defeat and flight had taken heavy toll, his confidence had been knocked his pride toppled.

How had it come to this unhappy pass? He had never envisioned this. This wasn't the outcome he'd worked so hard toward with all his immaculate scheming and careful, patient plotting.

And all for what? A once treasured daughter sworn his mortal enemy, and a world he'd dreamed of ruling, soon to be lost to flame and ruin. It was his fault, he knew that now. Eon and the other barons should never have forsaken the gods. Gods bear grudges and have long memories. But in their arrogant youth the proud victors of the Rebellion had poured scorn on the sanctimonious devotions of their former masters. Eon Barola and his cohorts had forgotten the gods. What was now apparent was that those divinities had not forgotten them.

A pox on all of them.

Eon drained his flask and feeling giddy, leaned hard against the rail topping the parapet. He hawked loudly; spat a bloody gobbet of thick mucus down on the surging spume below. He wasn't feeling well today—he was feeling old. Frail and defeated—everything he'd fought so hard for—lost. His bloody daughter. This was all her fault. That and her husband, Garret's get.

If only Lissane had been more like Leanna.

None of this made any sense to Eon Barola. His boys had failed him too. Paolo should have skinned that creature Grudge, after learning of his deceit, and not listened to his father and spared him. Eon's judgement had gone so awry of late. Grudge had betrayed them a second time. Traitor. The word stank.

Oily as ever, the servant had slipped away again before Garron Fields. Eon knew Grudge must had turned coats and led Clarde Dovess down upon them—though why he would do that beggared belief. Another bloody mystery. Flaying would be too good for that contemptible creature.

With tired eyes Eon watched the sun climb and the clouds race high overhead. That sight would once have stirred him, today it left him indifferent. Later Paolo joined him and Aldo too, the latter bringing yet more wine despite the cellars running low.

Paolo, alone of the three, remained in good cheer. His mood was jovial despite everything that had happened, and would continue happening until the end—which looked to be close now judging by those fires on the horizon.

But what cared Paolo if the world were to end? Life was just a game—all of it one vast cosmic joke to Paolo Barola. Eon envied his youngest pup today. Nothing fazed Paolo. Not even the certainty of death's swift approaching.

"We should hold parley with our beloved sister and the farrier's get." Paolo motioned lazily toward the camp with his wine cup, spilling its ruby content on the ice-glazed flagstones at his feet.

"For what purpose?" Eon awarded his youngest a bloodshot glance.

"For pure theatre, Father," responded Paolo, waving his cup about and grinning. "We must act out this final dramatic scene for the gods—must we not?" Aldo belched back a bitter laugh, but Eon scratched his greying beard and rubbed his rheumy eyes.

"Mayhap you are right; I would see Lissane again before the end," the Baron said.

"Well that's settled then," responded Paolo. "We'll call a truce and arrange to meet them outside the barbican at lowest tide. It should prove a diverting interlude. I'll send a man across immediately."

Half hour later the three watched as Paolo's envoy navigated the shallows (the water had not yet withdrawn from the causeway although the tide was ebbing fast) carefully on his steed, to arrive soaked to the thighs at Barola Town.

From their high tower the three Barolans watched Paolo's messenger urge his mount up toward the camp, saw the soldiers jumping up with long spears to bar his way. A figure of authority approached their rider; judging by his size and the wind-tossed blue cloak he wore, it was Clarde Dovess.

Five minutes of talk passed and then their rider was cantering back through the town. Eon watched the horseman gain the causeway, then drained the last of the wine and followed his two surviving sons down the stairwell, to the castle grounds below where they would hear what Paolo's man had to tell them.

**

"We've nothing to discuss," Lissane told him. "Let them rot, I said."

But Erun shook his head; "Liss, it's only right we should hear them out before the end. I've scant love for them but I'm sick of all this pointless killing. I swore to avenge my father, but now in the midst of all this carnage every life seems precious. Even theirs."

"You are too soft, husband."

"I just tired, Lissane. Worn thin. Paolo, I hate. Aldo and your father, I could forgive in time, and certainly the tiny force they retain—our countrymen. And what of the small-folk still serving the Baron? Are we to abandon them also?"

"Well, I still say no," countered Lissane, but later when they discussed it through with the others she was overruled. Both Clarde Dovess and Jerrel were of a mind with her husband, as was young Kael. Rakaro alone sided with Lissane, but then Hillmen didn't go much on forgiving. Lissane capitulated reluctantly. But she warned them little good would come of this encounter.

She was proved right.

**

Just two hours later and at lowest tide, a small party of riders cantered along the causeway toward the distant castle. Erun Cade trotted ahead, unadorned kettle helm masking his features and long woollen cloak trailing behind him.

Lissane rode a pace behind her husband; the green-gold Galanian cloak billowing behind her and covering her horse's flanks. Her long black hair she'd tied back in a single braid.

Behind them rode Clarde Dovess and Kael of House Sarfe, both magnificent in their customary saffron and blue. Jerrel brought up the rear like a grey ghost. He rode stony-faced in plain fighting garb and kept glancing behind. Rakaro remained in camp, guarding the sack containing the Elementals and looking after Lissane's boys.

The five riders reined up just a short distance from the barbican gates. There they waited while below the waves lashed and gurgled as the tide turned. Cold wind battered their faces. Still they waited.

Then the gates creaked into groaning motion, widening out, spilling light on the inner barbican and those mounted within. The portcullis was raised high, and then the Baron, his two remaining sons and three steel-clad retainers trotted out, stopping a short distance from the cool-eyed party awaiting them.

None bore weapons as was the custom with truces—none save Paolo who kept a wound crossbow hidden beneath the folds of his cloak, and Kael, who'd slipped a small dagger up his sleeve following a hunch. Kael, unlike Estorien his brother, was not of a trusting disposition.

Eon Barola raised a gloved hand and urged his beast forward, stopping just a short distance from his daughter and her husband. The Baron spoke then, his voice sounding hollow beneath the heavy helm he wore.

"You have done well, Cade," Baron Barola said. Erun didn't respond. He sat his horse watching his enemies with flinty, wary eyes. Lissane, angry, urged her mount alongside her husband and glared across at her hated father.

"Greeting, beloved daughter mine." Eon slid the heavy helmet from his head so that he could show her his face. That face looked flushed and weary despite the determined fire in his eyes. "You appear well—if somewhat pale of face and gaunt of frame. But it does me good to see you, daughter."

"For me the opposite applies, Father. Against my counsel has this meeting taken place," Lissane told him. "Time is short, however. My comrades urge we bury our differences here at this final hour. Ships are coming soon that will carry us far from the demon's ruin."

"Ships?" Eon gazed out at the silvery horizon where a skein of geese winged south with mournful, plaintive cries. *Lucky birds. How I envy them now.*

"There won't be any ships, daughter," he said, "and were they to appear I doubt they'll save your little force. But I agree we should cast aside our differences and together await the end as friends." His eyes softened for a moment then.

"I would have you forgive me, Lissane—I realise I ask a great deal." Lissane refused to give—her eyes were amethysts, unblinking, hard and cold. Eon turned, signalled his sons approach. "Come, boys..." Aldo saluted but Paolo's cat-eyes gleamed with sudden anger beneath his ornate hawk's head helm.

"What folly is this, Father?" hissed the younger Barola. "I'll not get cosy with such as these." As he rode up, Paolo fumbled at the hidden bow behind his back, and then shrugged his cloak aside to allow a free shot.

Kael, watching wary from the right, saw that subtle motion too late. His hidden knife darted free from his blurring palm only seconds after Paolo Barola's bolt sped home. Erun Cade hadn't seen the shaft coming. But Lissane had. The second she'd seen her brother's cloak unpinned she'd urged her horse across, blocking her husband's mount.

The crossbow levelled and the quarrel sprang free, piercing Lissane's shoulder and spinning her body round as though she were a whirling top. She screamed when that shaft bit into her body, her horse reared and Lissane's cries were cut short as she was pitched from the saddle. She hit the weed-strewn stone like a discarded doll—torn dress and pale arms akimbo, those long legs grazed and bloodied by her fall.

Kael's thrown knife narrowly missed Paolo's head, burying itself instead in Eon Barola's left bicep. The Baron roared like a cornered bear when he saw his daughter tumble, but if he was aware of the dagger now sticking in his arm he didn't show it.

Erun Cade, mouth gaping in disbelief, had watched in disbelief as his love fell so violently from her horse. Stunned seconds passed: the world stopped turning. Clouds froze in the skies above;

the sea held its breath and the wild-wind held back its bitter fingers. Somewhere near a drum-beat sounded, louder and faster—the sound of his heartbeat gaining momentum.

Erun blinked back tears of fury. He felt the red rage filling him as though it were Ashmali's breath. He mouthed a word but no sound came, so instead Erun urged his stead forward, on to where Paolo sat his horse in glum silence, his handsome face forlornly gazing down at the motionless body of his sister. That expression might have been regret or sorrow, had it come from any other man.

"Lissane. Sister, I...didn't mean to do that." Paolo shivered, and glanced wild-eyed at the approaching Erun Cade. He managed a grin of purest loathing, his composure regained; and then Paolo Barola steered his horse around and slapped the rump of his father's beast, urging it follow.

He turned back just before reaching the barbican walls; saw Erun Cade watching in silence at the causeway's end. "We'll meet again soon," Paolo yelled back. Erun Cade didn't respond—just stared, his eyes colder than the granite of the castle walls. They retired inside, the Baron, his sons and their three retainers. Within minutes they'd vanished inside the barbican, the portcullis was lowered noisily and the gates creaked shut.

***

He still couldn't speak. The rage and fear was a living beast: it tore at Erun, threatening to unman him. He wanted to batter down those castle walls and pull out Paolo's black heart with his raw, bloodied fingers. But not while Lissane lay prone and wan on the cold cobbles of this weed-strewn causeway. She needed warmth and healing attention fast—why was he hesitating? His friends were now rushing to assist his fallen wife. Clarde was stooping alongside.

Erun, shaking motion into his numb limbs, slipped from his saddle; crouched low at her side. Clarde stepped back, allowing room, and gazed down at his friends with worried eyes. Erun listened. Lissane's breathing was shallow and her violet eyes appeared glazed and remote.

"Liss...Lissane..." Erun whispered as he hugged her close and the tears now streamed all along his cheeks. She couldn't hear him, her face had gone deathly pale. Erun's eyes strayed to the cruel jutting iron of Paolo's quarrel that had marked her.

That shaft was meant for me yet you took it instead. Why? I am nothing without you.

"That will have to come out and soonest," Clarde Dovess yelled in Erun's ear, as the others loomed close. Erun didn't respond so Clarde grabbed his shoulder and shook it hard. "Wake up, man, we cannot tarry here!"

The spell broke then and violent noise rushed through Erun Cade's head. He gazed about—wild-eyed and stricken. The sea was rising fast now, soaking the causeway at his feet. Erun didn't notice that cold salty caress as it seeped into his boots. Nor did he respond to his friends calling his name, urging him move. He was a man broken and lost—stranded and abandoned by all that he held dear.

But while Erun Cade knelt there as one frozen in time, Clarde Dovess and Jerrel had not wasted a minute. Moments later, sprinting soldiers led by a shouting Jerrel and carrying a hastily fashioned stretcher, were racing along the causeway. They reached her as the waves closed all around and bore the unconscious Lissane Barola back to the camp where men skilled with healing, now hurriedly readied a fire and sharpened knives for the black quarrel's swift and clean removal. Erun remounted and followed that train in a dream, guiding his steed along the causeway as the tide tugged at its flanks and dark water rose high all around—his mind numb and his eyes devoid of any emotion.

***

Occasionally Lissane moaned. Now and then she fluttered her lashes. Aside that, nothing. Erun watched unblinking from the corner of the tent, He witnessed his wife drift in and out of consciousness as they slowly, and so very carefully, worked the barbed bolt deeper into her shoulder, until the point cleared her back and fresh blood stained the rushes below.

They pushed and wiggled; prised and eased. Carefully, tenderly as they could, working the bolt's steely length out through Lissane's back. Outside, forgotten evening closed in and the flickering shadows surrounded the tent like probing, witches' fingers.

Then at last, as the first owl announced night, the black shaft was pulled free of Lissane's flesh. She screamed as the steel cleared her skin then sunk back into dreamy oblivion. Her surgeon made to hurl the bolt in the fire, but Clarde Dovess stopped him and bid him toss the shaft his way. Clarde caught the missile, sniffed suspiciously at the quarrel's point and then shuddered in revulsion.

"What is it?" Erun Cade glanced up at his friend with terrified eyes.

"Poison," responded Clarde. "The quarrel has been dipped in poison. I fear we will lose her."

"No!" Erun screamed the word, his eyes tortured and his mouth contorted as one struck by sudden mind-numbing pain. "That cannot happen! Liss! *Liss*?" But she couldn't hear him now, her gaze was so very far away.

Erun called to her, coaxed her; jested and joked in her ear—trying anything he could. Occasionally the sharp, sudden pain brought her back to him for fleeting seconds, but mostly Lissane wandered through feverish dreams.

It was quiet and still for a time. The wind had eased and night deepened outside—a black stone plummeting into blacker water. Erun sat by her side—the others had left them alone—his big rough hands (so gently) clutched her cold pale fingers. Erun's cheeks were stained wet with fresh tears.

The twins he'd put to cot amid weeping wails – Erun had no room for their grief alongside his own. Rakaro had seen to the boys—they liked Rakaro, he always made them giggle, though not tonight. He was a good man—a small part of Erun's mind acknowledged that much. Erun, gazing silently and long into those flickering violet eyes, could see in the rush-light she was slipping away—fading deeper and further with every shallow breath.

"I always loved you, Liss," Erun told her. "From that first sweet moment I set eyes on you at the market—years ago. You were always my darling—there was nobody else. You, Lissane, are the only one I have ever loved. Who could compare? Not even Laniol herself could work such sorcery on me. What lives we have lived, you and I."

She smiled then, and for the briefest joyful moment Erun thought she would return to him. But her smile faded like dawn-mist on bright summer's morn. Her last words, when she forced them out amid coughing, were terse with agony.

"Erun...our bairns. You must save them from the flames," Lissane said. "Promise me."

"I will," he vowed, smoothing her sweat-frozen brow and weeping fresh tears. "But first I will save you, my only love." But it was too late, she'd already left him. Those violet gemstones had faded to smoky glass.

Lissane Barola was dead.

Chapter 23

The Broken Harp

He sat in silence for the longest time. Gazing at her stiffening body as though she were a statue cast from bronze or stone. Night deepened outside. The camp was silent. The calm before the final storm.

Rakaro and Kael had watched over Erun Cade for an hour after Lissane's death, but as night wore on, they'd deemed it best to let him grieve alone. Some time before dawn, Erun Cade reached for the harp Scaffa had given him. He stared long and hard at the fine gilded detail—the curved shape and intricate workmanship.

He played. At first slowly then with more and more passion. Notes fled that tent like stinging bees, their anger filling the night outside. Erun played thus for over an hour, his face lost to shadow. Finally plucked a solitary chord and sent it peeling out into the night. The note lingered for long moments then faded into nothing. The music too had died. Erun knew that from that day on he would never play again.

He stood up like a man waking from drunken slumber. Gripping the golden harp tightly, Erun tore the strings apart with his strong fingers, causing them bleed on the gold. Next Erun seized the harp with both bloodied hands, and with a savage wrench pulled the instrument almost in two. Finally, and with a bestial snarl, Erun Cade hurled the twisted, broken harp into the dying embers of the fire. Silence. Then far away the faint haunting echo of harp strings crept back into the night. Erun heard them for just a moment then they were gone.

A noise outside. Erun turned, heard a rustle of movement behind him. The man Grudge shivered beneath the folds of the tent entrance. The lost echo of harp-song rose up in Erun's head like a hissing snake. He laughed and retrieved a hot knife from the brazier where the physicians had left their tools hours ago.

The killing can start with you, turncoat.

Erun folded his bleeding fingers around the hilt of the knife. He smiled: took a slow step forward.

"I know a way into the castle," said Grudge eyeing the blade warily. "A postern...I could show you, take you there." Erun Cade's eyes narrowed to killing slits but he let the fool continue. "The postern," Grudge was sweating. He looked like a trapped weasel beneath that guttering rush-lamp, "It's from there that the brothers slipped out unannounced the night they killed your father."

And you, slime, were part of that.

"I still retain the key," Grudge told him—the wretch was trying to smile. "It was my task to look after it and I always have—"

The hot steel cut the last words from Grudge's mouth as its sharp edge opened his throat. Erun stepped over the shuddering, gore-soaked body. He wiped the knife clean on Grudge's soiled jerkin, and then re-stowed it beside the fire.

Erun turned and, gazing back awarded Lissane a final mournful stare, before parting the tent flap and hastening outside to where dawn pinked sky far out over ocean.

He left three corpses behind in that tent: beloved Lissane, vile Grudge and the boy who'd once been Erun Cade. He was Kell the Avenger and there was one task yet to do before the Demon's flames arrived.

Erun dressed quickly in black leather but left his armour, helmet, the rune-sack containing Borz and Aqueous, and his sword Callanak behind in the tent. He required stealth for this next job—stealth and skill. Then in the semi-light, Erun slipped silent through the camp—a vengeful ghost clad in midnight black.

Rakaro alone saw his friend guide the small skiff free from its town-mooring, and glide out around to the rear of the castle until lost from sight. Frowning with worry, he left the boys' tent where he had spent the long hours watching over them. Rakaro wandered over, glanced inside Lissane's tent.

Rakaro's dark eyes widened when he saw the pool of fresh warm blood and the surprised horror on the face of the dead man lying there. Grudge's neck yawned open from ear to ear; his head almost severed by the violence of the blow that had taken his life.

Rakaro closed the tent flap and returned to his own. He told a guard to watch over the sleeping twins, and then grabbed his bow and some shafts and trotted down toward the waking town.

***

The skiff eased alongside the wave-tossed dock. Erun leapt across to the slippery weed-strewn steps that led up to the heavy iron-ribbed oak door that was the secret postern—known only to the Baron and his staff and hidden from the shore. It was still quite dark. Morning was taking its time, but then that suited Erun well.

He rammed Grudge's heavy key home and turned it, and then hearing the latch's loud clunk, shoved his shoulder hard into the door's timber. It creaked inward noisily, opening into a dark, narrow anteroom revealing more shadowy steps ahead. These Erun took three at a time, he'd tied rags to his boots' soles so his approach wouldn't be heard.

At the top of those stairs Erun encountered the first guard.

And so the killing began.

He was armed only with the long knife that Lissane had favoured during the war with her father. It seemed fitting somehow. And, as Erun stole and stalked from stable to tavern; from privy to barrack bed, that knife hungrily took the lives of all it found.

There were not that many. Baron Barola's was a depleted force now. That said, Erun soon lost count of those he butchered—

counting seemed irrelevant, all that mattered was the killing. The swift clean taking of life—what he did best these days.

What few servants and maids he saw, Erun spared. They would run off in terror, or else hide from this black-clad butcher in the gloom. Most the soldiers were still asleep; Erun cut their throats swiftly as they snored—harvestime for the slaughterer. As for those awake, few knew what was upon them before that cold steel sliced along their necks, or else punctured their hearts in the murk.

He found Aldo Barola on the privy; the middle brother's red face was straining with effort as he battled with his bowels. Aldo saw a shadow loom across him and looked up.

"Who the fuck are you?"

"The Shadowman," came the muffled reply. "Come to take your miserable life, Barola." Aldo's reluctant loins opened freely as the steel of Lissane's knife tore into his gaping mouth and severed his tongue. Erun stepped back, swiped a clean slice, slitting open Aldo's belly and leaving him to thrash, wallow and yammer in his own filth.

Two more...

Erun reached the inner guardhouse. Three soldiers rushed at him and three soldiers died. He left their stiffening corpses behind and made urgently for the High Keep. Erun found Paolo Barola hard at play with his father's wench. The younger Barola, on hearing Erun's rushed approach, hissed and sat up—green eyes on fire.

The girl stifled back a scream. Paolo kicked her from the bed and reached for his rapier, left close by. He laughed, seeing his would-be assassin was armed only with a knife.

"Think that you can pierce me with that, peasant?" Paolo slid out from the covers: stood before Erun, naked and slick, his sex rising slightly at the thought of blood spilled.

"It will suffice for such as you." Erun's blue-grey glare held Paolo's cat-green slits. That hatred fused to almost affection—they were like two lovers poised on the brink.

It was Paolo who moved first. Cat swift he pounced at his foe, the rapier whipping up fast and hard at Erun's face, making the taller man leap aside.

Erun laughed. He blocked that murderous lunge almost casually with his knife's short blade. The knife turned the rapier thrust askew, sending its length past his head. Erun grabbed Paolo's wrist with his left hand and then rammed his right elbow up under Paolo's jaw, knocking him off balance.

Paolo wrenched his sword-arm free and back-swung his rapier viciously toward Erun's head again. Erun ducked beneath that slicing steel. He kicked out, his steel-shod boot thudding hard into his enemy's exposed balls.

Paolo gasped. He groaned, sobbed and slunk to his knees before vomiting noisily on the flagstones. But Paolo wasn't done yet. Still gripping his rapier, he stabbed up—vicious and lightning fast—as Erun ventured close.

But Erun, anticipating such a move, kicked the sword from Paolo's grasp and then brought his foot down hard on Barola's wrist, snapping the bone like a brittle twig.

Paolo screamed as red agony lanced up his arm. He tried to reach for the rapier with his good hand but Erun Cade's boot stamped on that wrist too, and Paolo yelled again.

"Finish it, you whoreson!" Paolo coughed blood and then vomited again.

But Erun had no need of haste. Not today. He knelt down beside Paolo and smiling, retrieved a small vial containing some dark liquid. Erun had kept this hidden until now, reserved for such a purpose.

He tore off a slice of Paolo's expensive silk, poured the steaming contents of the vial on the cloth, soaking it, and then with meticulous care lest it cut him, he commenced wiping the length of Lissane's knife with the stuff. Erun smiled at the horror now registering on Paolo's face. Still grinning, he scored a shallow cut along Barola's naked belly.

"You should recognise the smell, Barola," Erun Cade informed him. "It's the same filthy crap you used on your sister yesterday. Oh, and I took the liberty to add some Sarfanian Swampfire to prolong the agony—just for you. It should take several hours—maybe longer."

"Shadowman take you, Cade..." Paolo's mouth filled with blood. He could no

longer speak though he tried making sounds until the choking stopped him. Blood also now seeped from his eyes and nose. He lay shivering and sweating for a moment. Then the pain came rushing at him.

And there Erun left him, screaming and retching. He could see that Paolo's skin was already blotching crimson with the poison's savage taint.

"That'll be the Swampfire—nasty shit so I'm told. Goodbye, Paolo."

Now it's your father's turn.

Erun vacated Paolo's chamber, leaving the younger Barola to his screaming and retching. Outside in the castle grounds cold grey morning was at last taking hold. Of the Baron's girl there was no sign. Not that Erun cared a jot—he had already forgotten that she existed. He made swiftly for the dull blunt figure that was the Keep. He entered; climbed up—Kell the Hunter closing on his final prey.

Erun found Baron Barola waiting for him behind his oak table, his heavy gloved fist gripping a tumbler of mulled red.

"I knew that you would come," Eon Barola told him with a wry smile as Erun quietly shut the door behind him. "How does it feel to be the bane of House Barola, Erun Cade?"

Instead of replying, Erun reached across the table, poured a large amount of wine into a redundant goblet and then took a sip. The baron watched him—a hawk studying its prey.

Erun shrugged. "You are your own nemesis, Baron—you always were," Erun told Eon Barola after gulping back a long swig. "This is excellent wine," he added.

"Only the best for such an occasion," responded the Baron, "though with your lowly breeding I wonder you know the difference, Cade."

Erun shrugged. "My father always said that you kept the best wine up here in the Keep's crown," he smiled. "Best not let the filthy peasants near it, heh? Lowly grape can suffice for them, or small beer. Lowly everything for the low-born stock—wasn't that your creed since you came to rule? So my father told me, Baron. He also told me how he looked up to you once, before the Rebellion, even admired you, so he did."

"Oh, and he would know, of course," the Baron chuckled, "poor Garret, butchered bloody by my lovely boys."

"Your lovely boys are greying flesh now, Baron," responded Erun, taking another slow sip at his wine. "They are all dead save Paolo who will join them eventually—crow feed, the three of them, and at my own hand too."

"Then I shall kill you and put an end to this charade." Then with a speed that belied his age, Eon Barola kicked the table hard into Erun Cade's legs, knocking him backwards. Dagger gripped tight in gloved hand, the Baron leapt at the younger man and raised his weapon high for the kill.

But the Baron, though quick, was not near quick enough. His descending knife cut clean through air. Erun was now behind him, Lissane's poisoned blade already moving in. Eon grunted as Lissane's dagger pierced his back between the shoulder blades, knocking him forward with the violence of a hammer blow.

Eon Barola laughed bitterly once and then slunk to the floor— his scarlet lifeblood pooling all about him. The room spun crazily as Eon Barola's vision blurred.

"Shadowman take you, Cade, and Shadowman wash your soul with night-soil." The Baron coughed blood on his expensive carpet. He spewed when he felt the poison kicking in. Eon wiped his mouth on his sleeve. He reached across for the goblet he'd knocked askew. It was still partially full.

Just one last sip...

But Eon Barola lacked the strength to lift the heavy goblet, and anyway it was much too late, for the darkness had already closed in on him. At least he was spared the kiss of the swampfire. He fell: lay prone on the cold stone, his body twitching briefly before stilling as death took hold. Eon Barola's last fading thoughts were of his daughter's eyes. Those gorgeous violet eyes so unlike her mother's.

I bet you're laughing now, Leanna...

And so fared House Barola at the hands of Erun Cade.

Erun stepped over the Baron's corpse, left Eon Barola lying in his own blood, with his daughter's sharp knife buried to the hilt in the broad gap between his shoulder blades. Erun drained the last of the Baron's excellent wine on his way out, and then tossed the goblet into the dying fire.

You can rest now, Father, and you too, my love—soon now will I join you.

Erun Cade left the Baron's chamber behind and quickly made his way down the spiralling stairwell of the Keep. He passed a door, partially open; it spilled light into an airy spacious room. Looking in, Erun saw a high window seat awarding wide views of ocean and sky, below and beyond.

Lissane's bower. She had often spoken of it and how she used to sit here—thinking and dreaming away her lonely hours. Erun felt the tears well up again. He was so very tired now. With his vengeance now achieved the light had gone out in his eyes.

Erun cast his battered body upon Lissane's bed. There he slept for a time consumed by sudden exhaustion. He dreamed of nothing.

***

When Erun awoke it was long passed noon and a storm raged violent outside. The sea lashed above the hidden causeway, white-horses cantered haughty and the shore was strewn with foam. High above, Erun heard the Baron's hawk banner straining ragged in the blow. And away to the north the hills were ringed with Ashmali's fire.

It was almost time. Erun strode back to the postern, ignoring the shrieking gulls that had settled to feast on the flesh of the recently slain. The few he'd left living were already gone.

The skiff was gone too: taken by storm-tossed waves. But Erun didn't care. He sat there alone and waited for the final confrontation. Fire versus water—it wouldn't take long. Rakaro had loan of Aqueous and Borz and the archer was his friend. He would care for the boys should their father not return.

Erun was happy to let Zansuat's angry waves take him far

away from this wretched life. And happily the Sea God would have granted his wish. But the other gods weren't done with Erun yet. So when Scaffa's silent ferryman poled alongside the dock Erun showed no surprise, but vaulted on board and let the canny craft steer him shoreward through wild wave and heady spume.

So you still have need of me then?

At Barola Town, Clarde Dovess greeted him with the joyous news that King Torrig had arrived in Barola Bay. Even now the ships were battling with storm and gale as they made for the quays. But Erun feared it was too late.

Ashmali's fires had reached the fields just outside the town. Smoke occluded the northern hills and they could hear the demon's voice, a relentless roaring carried close on the wind.

Erun forced motion into his stiffened limbs. He hugged his squalling boys and bid Anyetta take them to the dock. Then Erun retrieved the sack that contained Borz and Aqueous from Rakaro, and followed the shouting, milling exodus, down to the creaking jetties where the van of Torrig's small fleet were now hurriedly making fast.

But the sea level was rising swiftly as the storm raced urgent overhead. Palms tossed crazy all along the shore; in town, roofs ripped and then lifted to come crashing down. Dogs howled and whined, and the people (those left living) ran headlong and desperate for the ships.

Ahead reared the ocean. Iron grey and furious—announcing Zansuat the Sea God was stirring from his deepest slumber. Waking to fury and vengeful wrath. Had it come to this? Were the remnant of Gol's stricken people to be trapped like bugs between raging fire and towering water?

Most reached the ships as Ashmali's fires destroyed the camp. Erun was one of the last—his boys were yelling encouragement at him from the deck of the nearest. But Erun didn't board. Instead he turned and walked slowly back toward the flame. Now a wall of fire rearing and spitting, occluding the sky. Erun held Callanak in his right fist whilst his left hoisted the sack containing Borz and Aqueous.

And so it had come to the final confrontation.

Chapter 24

Demon's Ruin

He is slow to anger and His patience immeasurably long. But that patience is over now, and His anger roused beyond the ken of mere mortal man. He has seen His daughters die. Miriel's descendants: blood of His blood. First Leanna and now Lissane.

Rani has told Him of this and also of the demon's return as was prophesied millennia past. Fire His enemy and the servant of His eldest brother—the one foolish mortals called the Shadowman. That same entity He once knew as Cul-Saan the Firstborn, now branded Old Night.

And now Old Night's ancient servant Ashmali has returned. Zansuat's elder siblings should have destroyed the demon when they had the chance. Instead they'd done nothing as was usual. Oroonin wrapped up in His games and riddles. Too clever by half, that one. Laniol lost in Her dreams and philandering. Fools—the pair of them. Just like the rest of His kin. It was down to Zansuat to put things right and claim back what was once His.

He stirs in the deep. Begins the long ascent from His dreamy mansions to the world of man above. The greedy seas heave wild at His bidding. On Zansuat's command they rise to quell the fires eager to reclaim what was once their Master's.

Gol. A land taken from Zansuat by His trickster siblings. Given to their new playthings. First the Elementals then mankind. Both races had forsaken their right to rule this land; the Elementals He could forgive. But mankind must be punished.

And so the Sea God rises, thrusts His vast bulk up from deepest depth, His god-eyes gazing toward the lightened surface, piercing the murk of His domain and focusing on the burning land above. Gol. Now blazing bright under Ashmali's wanton ruin. Zansuat's fury grows as He nears the surface; He beckons the seas rise up and claim back what had once been theirs and His. The time has come. Let the purity of wave and brine wash clean the ash of demon's ruin. The Sea God rises.

And so begins the final hour.

***

Stop! Demon—your work is overdone. There is nothing left. Is it all for ruin?

The small corner of his mind still retaining a measure of sanity challenged his tormentor. But Ashmali mocked him with barbed burning words.

Soon I shall take your soul, wretched mortal. You were my conduit—nothing more. What care I for your petty desires? I live to burn.

Part of Ozmandeus still lived—the body had long blackened to charcoal, scorched—as was his reasoning and memory also. But a small corner of his soul still held out against the monster.

The demon still channelled through that part of him, and still the remnant remaining Ozmandeus felt that alien joy surging through his molten veins. He knew the demon's mind—knew how Ashmali liked to play.

Ashmali was eating him from within. Slowly and cruelly. He was the Shadowman's creature, after all. The great destroyer doing his dark master's bidding and taking back the Shadowman's demesne.

Ozmandeus had shared the ecstasy of the demon as the

flames claimed so many souls. He'd revelled in their terror, and his host of dead souls had swollen to a million strong. Nothing could withstand their onslaught. Until now. For now there was no more land to burn and no more souls to claim.

Ahead was sea (*our enemy*) and all around. Ozmandeus felt his mind shrinking as the demon waxed a thousand foot high. Ashmali was angry now, recognising his ultimate foe and rising to the challenge. He surged and he spewed, and the thing that had once been Ozmandeus of Zorne screamed as the fire tore through his veins.

BURN!

Far behind, the mountains blazed and proud Torvosa's walls yawned and splintered to broken teeth. Galanais was gone and Druthan Crags also, whilst Reveal and the Castle of Winds had succumbed beneath Zansuat's rising waves. All that remained was Barola—this tiny stretch of country.

Behind the sky glowed dun and orange, and hot ash choked the thick air. With Ashmali's eyes (his own had melted weeks ago) Ozmandeus saw tiny ships in the bay. Pathetic things and a wild storm tossing their fragile hulls—mankind's remnant daring to flee.

Then Ashmali surged with purest joy—the purity of flame. Ozmandeus screamed as that reckless surge of heat tore out the last atom of his sanity and willpower, and combusted his withered mind from within.

And so the instigator died at last. But the Elemental that had once been his tool waxed huge toward completion. The army of souls he'd forgotten, and they too were wiped clean by this last purging fire.

Ashmali was free at last! Demon's ruin would prevail. Then his amber gaze fell on the specks of fleeing mortals making for the rocking ships below, and his flames sprang forth—each licking tendril hungry for the last remaining mortal.

And so Ashmali's flames fell upon Barola Town.

A solitary man refused to flee. He alone hadn't boarded a ship. This one stood tiny and defiant, blocking the path that led down to the jetties, in one gloved hand he held a shimmering blade that mirrored Ashmali's flames, whilst the other he clutched a sack. The man's strong voice was chanting ancient words of power. Words that Ashmali had heard before.

WHO IS THIS THAT DARES DEFY US?

The demon stopped then. Ashmali was curious and his anger abated for a moment. He felt the presence of his kinfolk struggling inside that sack. Borz? Aqueous? What has become of you?

No matter—I will burn you all. Hesitation banished, Ashmali's fires rose like towers of licking flame. They encircled the lone chanter, and the demon Ashmali—now taking on the form of the exhumed sorcerer who had freed him—blazed down upon him. But Ashmali's hungry amber gaze was checked a second time, seeing no fear in that mortal's eyes. *HOW DARE YOU CHALLENGE US? BURN AND DIE!*

The flame belched out, withering the ground where the impostor stood.

***

The last of Torrig's vessels lined the quayside, the sailors aiding all those they could to clamber on board, as the sea tossed and spewed foam, and monstrous white caps lashed out frothy spears.

Jerrel and Kael had led the common folk through the town before the flames took hold, and Clarde gathered up those caught behind. But the flames were almost upon them. Scarce half mile distant and rearing hundreds of feet into the blackened sky above.

The demon's face showed in that blaze. Almost human, it resembled a strong man with short beard and heavy brow with eyes of amber fire. That orange gaze brought terror on all who struggled and sped pell-mell for the ships.

But just when the fire looked to take them all, the burning ceased its progress. The flames now surrounded the ruined town, licking and flicking, but not yet advancing to finish them down on the wharf. Those who dared stared back in wonderment, questioning what was occurring.

It was Rakaro that saw his friend Erun Cade standing there alone. Defying the furnace with his sack held high. Speaking words that checked the Demon's passage. Rakaro vaulted from the rail, hit the jetty running and raced back up the hill. Erun Cade was oblivious to his approach. He stood as one dreaming; chanting the dirge Scaffa had taught him so long ago.

Erun felt Aqueous and Borz stirring like angry snakes within the sack that imprisoned them. Both were eager to embrace their powerful brother. "Not yet," Erun hissed at them. "You must block his advance," he said, "and let my people make good their escape. I still have tasks for you pair. Once done then I will free you both to join with him—if that is still your wish."

It is...IT IS... came the answer from the sack.

Rakaro locked a strong arm behind Erun Cade's shoulder and spun him around.

"We are departing in case you hadn't noticed. Torrig's boys are readying oars and that stormy sea is threatening to undo us. But I'd sooner drown than fry, methinks. Come on!"

Erun didn't hear his friend as the roaring deafened him; he could feel the iron hot will of the demon grinding down on him. But he felt the power of Scaffa's words taking hold, and Ashmali's advance was checked again—at least for a moment.

Erun, briefly freed from the demon's malice, turned and noticed his friend for the first time. He nodded briskly and then sped behind Rakaro, who'd started sprinting back down to the one remaining jetty (the storm having torn all the others away).

As he ran, Erun heard the angry voices of Aqueous and Borz railing against him as they battled to be free to join their brother.

"Soon—I have promised. First you both must aid our flight."

Torrig, wielding a chain of expletives, helped the pair on board. He severed the lines with an axe, freeing their ship (the last) to lurch free of its mooring. Ahead the other vessels were already lost in the storm. Torrig yelled to his men to reef the sails. He set two men on the tiller, but it was hopeless; the waves rose higher and higher, crashing down on them. No ship could take such a beating for long.

And then He surfaced from the deep.

***

It was Morwella who spotted Him first from where she watched keenly and excitedly at the prow. The girl had waxed sullen since Lissane's passing, but the certainty of horrible death had urged her join in that reckless flight.

She'd mixed with the crowd, clambering on board the very last ship, her eyes meeting Red Torrig's for the briefest instant; "you—still alive then," was all he had said. She'd made for the prow and squatted down like a wet imp.

There Morwella sat giggling and raving at the tumult—such random chaos well suited her peculiar nature. Morwella watched the waves rise up and break high over her head, her sorrow long forgotten in the fury of that morning.

And then she saw Him. A giant framed by waves. Far out to sea and yet approaching at impossible speed. Striding toward them—a nightmare stroller from the depths. As the giant strode a great funnel of water rose up surrounding him and occluding his features. The waterspout tilted and swayed, coning up and up, the waves whirling higher and higher. Faster and faster.

Morwella cried out in terror, and those who heard hurriedly joined her at the bowsprit. Torrig stood there and Erun Cade too—his boys were with him.

The surrounding waves drew back with surging sighs and the sea calmed to still. Then the waterspout spewed open, revealing the giant to all on board. He bore the shape of a tall man, with huge torso and sinewy limbs and a glowering, hideous face. Dark waves lapped angry about his upper thighs and the huge swinging column of his flaccid organ. Green hair thick as forest covered his massive chest. As they watched he towered above them.

The Sea God had come. Zansuat the Terrible emerging out from his watery kingdom as the seers had long foretold. The spout rose up again behind him, higher than before—a spinning column of screaming dancing water. Again it spewed open—exploding into spray and brine. The water flew in all directions then froze in the sky high over their heads. There it hung: a million tons of brine awaiting its master's command.

The giant god reared above the fleeing ships, a mile high column of blue-green flesh—heaving, bulking and looming angrily over them, rendering those watching from the decks too terrified to scream.

Behind and momentarily forgotten, Ashmali's flames licked up the last timbers of Barola town. Only the castle remained—a stone lump dwarfed by the waves pulling at its walls. Soon it would crumble and slip beneath the brine. Lost for all time. But when Ashmali's fire met the water the demon paused, again uncertain, feeling the power of one even greater than he.

Erun braced his legs and fumbled with his sack, forcing the struggling Borz back down as Aqueous leapt free with a gleeful yell. His words held her yet though she struggled hard. *You cannot hold me for long, my treacherous lover!*

But Erun spoke the words, over and over, at last managing to enforce his will upon the Water Elemental. To his right he heard someone tumble and lie prone as the Sea God turned his monstrous visage upon them.

Zansuat's face (almost hidden behind that tangled mess of weed and barnacle clinging to his dishevelled hair) was a face so ancient and ravished it was almost impossible to comprehend. The god's straggly hair covered some of His nakedness. The skin showed weed-green and slimy: His unkempt beard tangled from shelved brow, wart-covered nose and dreamy, terrible storm-clad eyes, to fall in coiling tumbles all about His feet.

Zansuat's upper chest and shoulders was huge with muscle and corded vein. There were wet things clinging to His nipples— leeches, fishes or crabs. Erun couldn't begin to guess at their identity.

Then Zansuat's mouth gaped wide, revealing a cavern showing snaggle-teeth, and unleashing down on them a foul aroma of stale fish. His mouth opened wider. He spoke in a voice that jarred their ears, and obeying His word the seas unfroze and crashed down hard upon them. All seemed lost. In seconds they would be crushed to pulp by the weight of that deluge.

But just then several things happened at once.

As Zansuat's full fury descended upon them like a watery avalanche, Erun's incantation stopped that final blow. Zansuat paused. The water above slowed its descent. Time hovered. A jolt. Torrig's ship lurched hard to larboard, tossing many aside to vanish quickly in the cold dark water.

Then Aqueous, shrieking with joy on hearing her patron, broke free of Erun's bag, and weaved—an oily lithe water-ghost—for the prow to leap out into the water. A small figure caught her arm and gripped it hard. The madness in Morwella's eyes checked Aqueous's advance for a moment.

"Take me with you," the girl grinned at Aqueous, "let my soul join with Lissane's beneath the waves."

"Morwella, stop!"

Erun, rushing up behind leapt to grab the girl, but both child and Elemental leapt out into the spume and were swallowed swiftly by the ocean. Erun leaned over the rail, his head spinning as the ship lurched to larboard again. He saw nothing, but then somehow Morwella's distant squeaky voice reached him impossibly from so far beneath the waves. *"We have fused together, Aqueous and me...we are one being now, Erun Cade. One soul. Don't fret, we will sooth our Father's wrath. Make good your escape—and remember me..."*

"What can I do for you, Morwella?" Erun yelled down at the water, hoping the child would hear him. "I...we all owe you now."

"Name a country after me when you find your new home... for find it you will, Erun Cade. Farewell."

The voice trailed off as the wind strengthened again. Morwella was gone and Aqueous too. But girl and Element held true. The Sea God paused again as though puzzled. Silently He folded His great arms, allowing them passage, His waves abating just enough for Torrig's helmsmen to steer a course free of Barola bay, and out into the wider ocean.

Ahead were other ships. Erun counted six, the rest having succumbed to the storm. The giant watched them pass in mournful silence. Then, as they cleared the headland and steered wide from the bay, Zansuat called on His waves again to rise up, even higher than before. He now turned His terrible gaze toward the smoke-stained shoreline where still Ashmali waited—a fire within the fires.

There at last they met—leviathan and demon, coming together in a gargantuan clash of destruction and rage. From the stern of Torrig's ship they watched; saw the bright flames flicker forth, witnessed the sky lowering to smoky dark. The demon's final fury blazed and raged—violence incarnate. But Zansuat's monstrous waves fell down upon him, a billion tons of water, quenching his wrath and dousing his eruptions until the Elemental Ashmali was no more.

And then Zansuat sang. His full fury now unleashed as He quenched the last of the demon's fires. In His song Zansuat called upon His waters to rise up higher still and swallow the ruined lands that had once been the sub-continent of Gol.

And Gol was lost beneath the waves.

***

"We will be drowned by that!" Torrig yelled into the wind. Behind a wave reared a hundred feet high. A wayward wall of water racing helter skelter toward them from the maelstrom now engulfing Gol. "Row, you idle bastards," hollered Torrig. But it was useless—he knew it: they would be carried under—all of them. They had minutes, perhaps only seconds before that mile high ridge of water was upon them.

"Borz!"

Torrig, turning, saw Erun Cade free the Wind Elemental from his sack. Torrig's eyes widened when he saw the spinning fury of Borz's earthly essence leap free and hiss, and whirl high above their heads.

For the last time Erun mouthed the runes, spoke the spell binding the creature to his will, and stopping Borz from vanishing into the ether. "Yours is the final task, Borz," Erun Cade said, calling up to the whirling shimmering mad thing in the sky. The wave was closer now—they had just seconds left.

"Do this one last thing and you are free—what say you, Borz? Will you comply?"

"Speak and it shall be done if it lies within my power." The Elemental was spinning now, faster and faster, a whirling dervish of light. But time was running out. The tidal wave was almost upon them.

"Unleash your winds, Borz! Take us far from this place!" Erun yelled up at the dizzily-spinning Elemental. And, as the wave-cliff crashed down upon them, Borz unleashed his wind. That sudden uncanny blow propelled Torrig's craft into the air to crash down on the water just yards ahead of the deluge.

Borz's breath bellied the ship's sails, she lurched ahead easily catching the others, and they too were carried along by the violence of Borz's gust. To stern, the mile-high wave shrank behind them, eventually fading from view. Now all around was sea and air. Beyond hope they had survived the maelstrom caused by the fall of Gol, Borz's wind having carried them so many miles out to sea at impossible speed. Those still on deck blinked and looked around. Water everywhere. No sign of land.

Torrig smiled at Erun as the latter hugged his boys tight. Impossibly, they had survived.

"That was interesting," Torrig said. "But now what do we do?"

"We sail east," replied Erun and led his wide-eyed boys below the hatch.

"Of course we do. East. That way isn't it? Sorry I bloody well asked." Torrig gave his vessel one last critical eye and then, satisfied all was intact, followed his friend below deck. Time to crack open a keg or two.

***

Elanion/Laniol saw all. Watching while Her island spun through time and space. She was free to roam the universe again—thanks to Tertzei and Erun Cade. Oroonin had lost—this game at least, though there would be other matches.

It was a strange relationship She had with Her husband. Oh they loved each other in a bickering boisterous sort of way. And neither could stand losing. Both were always right. Just the way of things really. When you are immortal you have to be diverse. Things get boring else, and there are never enough games to keep One occupied. So you make new games. And the games recently played out in Gol had kept the goddess and her husband well entertained for a brief time. Scaffa the horny giantess and Irulan the pretend hermit were quite the capricious pair.

Elanion would return to Ansu at some other time, inhabit the forests again as She had at that earlier age. Let her siblings war and scheme and lust for the Weaver's blessing. And let Oroonin mope and scheme His rematch. Laniol didn't care. She (gazing down again) saw Erun Cade hugging his twin boys as morning spilled golden light on a vast silver ocean. *You did well, my brief lover and champion. Farewell!*

***

And so it came to pass as had long been forewarned by those men of wisdom. The waves rose up in final judgement, the Sea God's reclamation achieved. Gol was no more. Gone was fair Dovesi with her mountains and rivers. Lost too was green Galania—those glittering towers of Galanais never to be seen again.

Swallowed up were wild Rodrutha and bleak Treggara, those fierce warrior nations. Sunk was warm Sarfania, where beloved Estorien had lived for a time. And drowned was fair Barola, where a baron had schemed while his daughter and her foolhardy lover dreamed of better days. Gone was Gol forever. Only its memory remained.

But our story continues—if only for a short while.

***

Days passed like the mournful tolling of a monotonous drum. Borz's wind had carried them far indeed from Gol's departed shores. But they had food aplenty plus fresh fish and stored water and ale ballasted down below—Torrig had done well. Erun, a chubby son clutched in either arm, watched silently at the stern. He smiled at his boys and ruffled their dark locks—so like their mother's.

Thanek and Wynna: they would grow into fine men as the years stretched their legs. He had lost his love and the spark had gone out of his life, but Erun would live for his sons now. That and her memory. He would obey Lissane's final wish and ensure the boys' survival—somehow.

A night came when Erun Cade sat alone at the tiller. He often liked to steer by starlight and let his thoughts take him where they will. Torrig and the watch had let him be, trusting him to keep them afloat. Erun glanced up. A shadow loomed over him, and he nodded wryly as the ferryman took his seat alongside. The old man's features blurred and shifted. He became Irulan the hermit, watching Erun with his single beady eye.

"You have done well, boyo," Irulan told him then.

"How so—when all that I lived for is now lost?"

"Not so," Irulan shook his head. He sighed and looked up, allowing his single eye to scan the starry firmament above. "You have your sons. Both will survive this trip and help their father find a new realm. Via one of them, you, Erun Cade, will start a dynasty that will last into the distant future. No small achievement for a craphead poet. You have done well."

"I know who you really are." Erun's hard blue-grey gaze locked into the pretend hermit's mercurial quicksilver wink, and the latter laughed at the blatant animosity in that look. "You're old Oroonin the Meddler aren't you?"

"It is one of my names—I have many such. Lots of guises."

"This whole business, my healing and coaching by you, and your sending me up to Scaffa to polish my skills, all some weird game to amuse you and your wife—the Goddess Elanion who we call Laniol. Lissane and Estorien Sarfe; my friends, even the Baron and his sons, were all of them just pawns in your cosmic meddling. As am I."

Irulan's gaze chilled to northern ice; he pinned Erun with that single chilly eye.

"You have a limited vision, boy," he snapped. "And a small and unimaginative brain. But then you mortals aren't big on thinking. This world (universe) is a complicated place. All of us are at the whim of the Weaver's Dance, wily old Oroonin included. Father holds all the keys—even Old Night found out the hard way, but that one never learns.

"Yes, us old ones play games. You would too, were you in our shoes. And sometimes your little folk are involved. There's no malice in it. It's just old fashioned fun. And anyway you lot have souls and can escape. We the firstborn were not that blessed. You have no idea how monotonous it is living for all eternity and trying to outsmart my wife. You've met her so you know what I'm up against."

Erun could think of nothing to add to that last statement.

"Most of what I have done has been for the advancement of your race—who incidentally I helped create. (I like humans on the whole, though they can be so obtuse.) And for small thanks—I might add. Were it not for my many interventions Gol would have fallen long ago. But old wet grumpy always wanted it back. Our younger brother is the worst sulk in the galaxy. T'was only a matter of time before Zansuat threw a strop. Besides, you should be grateful that you were chosen, boyo, and that your name will live on for countless generations."

"What care I for that?" Erun turned away from the god's piercing eye. Oroonin didn't faze him, who had now seen so much. Erun let his faraway gaze scan the starlit horizon—focus on the place where Gol must now lie deep beneath the ocean.

He felt a salty tear trace a line from the corner of his right eye down to his newly bristling beard.

Lissane, wait there for me yet awhile.

He recalled when first his eyes had danced with hers. The tears beaded and rolled down his cheeks. Embarrassed, Erun turned back to award Irulan a damning stare. But there was no one there. He was alone with sea and starry-night, free to return to his roaming thoughts.

"You could have saved her," Erun's voice, though quiet, carried far out across the waves.

"Why would I? Why should I? All things pass in the end."

Irulan's voice trailed off and was soon lost to wind and wave.

Erun Cade was alone. When Torrig's man relieved him he retired to his cabin where the twins slept peacefully. But it was nearly dawn when sleep stole slyly upon him. But then in his dream Lissane came laughing and smiling into his open arms.

The sound of rain on deck woke him. A new day. Erun Cade rubbed his brand (now a faded old scar) and made across to the prow, where the bobbing silhouettes of Torrig's other ships paraded in the middle distance, a half mile or so to starboard.

***

Many weeks later they raised the cliffs of an unknown country. They shored on pebbled sand, found fresh water and beasts to hunt, and yelled and danced and sang for joy as they feasted long into the night. All save Erun Cade their leader—who they now called Kell. His heart still walked with Lissane Barola through the laden vineyards of her father's rich estate.

Finis

Legacy

And so the legend concludes. But further word reaches us from an appendage compiled by one Galed of Wynais, a devoted servant to Queen Ariane, direct descendent of King Wynna, Kell's son who came to rule his second kingdom—Thanek ruling the first after his father's passing. Galed, a learned scribe, was tasked with the chore of translating and compiling all nine Legends of Ansu, (Gol being the first) so the High King's citizens could read of those mighty days gone by. This task Galed achieved assiduously as was expected. His words follow:

...To our beloved Overlord and august champion.

History states that when Kell, our ancestor and first High King, landed on the shores of these, our beloved Four Kingdoms, he happened upon the final battle between the Aralais and Urgolais peoples, and saved the former from annihilation, sending the cruel Urgolais back to the darkness whence they had come.

This is I believe unlikely.

Kell's refugees would have comprised of few warriors and it is not known how many ships survived that long harrowing voyage—and there were only seven at the start. Suffice it to say the survivors of Gol's ruin gave what aid they could in that cataclysmic battle, and were rewarded with these fertile coastal regions by the grateful Aralais. It is hard to be certain, however.

We can ascertain this much. Kell became the first High King of Kelthaine, Kelwyn, Raleen and Morwella—more than a thousand years ago. With the Tekara—that gift of the Aralais in the form of a sacred crown wrought of solid crystal—Kell's wise rule proved long, and his son Wynna's longer still. Of the fate of his twin brother, Thanik—saving that his name lives on in Kelthaine—little is known.

Kael ruled in the south and his people—the dark-eyed Raleenians (named after his daughter)—always retained that olive Sarfanian skin, so different to Kell's pale-eyed descendants. Morwella got her wish. The girl's name was awarded to the northernmost Duchy, though there are few Morwellans now living that know the true origin of their country's name- (that sad lost girl-child of House Gallante.)

It has been my honour and challenge, (and indeed long study), to glean what knowledge I can from that distant, bloody time. If there are gaps in the account—specifically Kell's time spent with Scaffa on Laras Lassladden, and his faring as a mercenary with Rakaro in the Great Continent—then that is because the precise detail on those occurrences have been lost to us. One can only surmise.

Of Torrig, Rakaro, and Clarde Dovess, there is no further mention after the flight from Barola, though Jerrel is said to have become the first Duke of Morwella—our beloved Shallan his only living descendant. How long he ruled there is uncertain, however.

Of the fate of the Great Continent—nothing is known. Perhaps those lands too were consumed by Sensuata or mayhap they still remain parts of Xandoria and Zorne with scattered peoples. Not everyone was lost to Ashmali's flame. But we can only guess...

Of the Elementals no further word can I find—my own hunch is that they were cousins of the Faen, the faery folk who have always served Elanion. Ashmali, alone was evil—tainted by the stain of Old Night who they called the Shadowman.

The gods are our own gods though their names differ in our time. All else is as written above from sources I have found among the many vaults and histories of our venerable libraries. Thus I have compiled over these many years, what facts I can, and have welded and fused these facts and rumours into a tale of conflict, desire, ambition and corruption. I do hope that you enjoyed it, my Liege, and can feel pride that your noble blood continues the line started long ago by the reckless dreamer Erun Cade, and the proud, beautiful Lissane Barola—who he so loved.

As ever my deepest affections and best wishes to the queen and yourself

Your servant and friend - Galed of Wynais.

Glossary

Gods Aliens and Entities

Oroonin: the trickster. Sometimes called the Huntsman
Elanion: mistress of the trees. Also called Laniol
Zansuat: the sea god. Once Gol was his domain
Talcan: the sky god
Ashmali: a fire Elemental
Aqueous: a water Elemental
Tertzei: an earth Elemental
Borz: an air Elemental
The wizard of the Winds: an Aralais sorcerer
Scaffa: a giantess. Known as the Queen of Death
The Ferryman: her silent servant
Cron: her torturer
The Mystery Harper: no one knows.
The Nicor: Aqueous's guardian

Mortals

Barola Province

Eon Barola: baron and lord of Barola Province
Leanna Barola: his late wife
Rosco Barola: their eldest son
Aldo Barola: their middle son
Paolo Barola: the youngest son

Lissane Barola: the daughter
Belshareze: her maid sometimes called Bel
Grale: Barola's champion
Garret Cade: a smith
Erun Cade: his son
Irulan: not really a hermit

Galania Province

Prince Hal Gallante: ruler of Galania Province
The Chatelaine Sophistra: his spouse
Varentin: their son
Morwella: their daughter, Queen of Cats
Torlock: Galania's champion
Jerrel: his lieutenant

Dovesi Province

King Flaminius: late ruler of Dovesi province and
entire continent. Died in the Rebellion
Duke Toreno Dovess: current ruler of Dovesi province
Clarde Dovess: his son. Champion of Dovesi
Armilian: Toreno's astrologer

Sarfania Province

Razeas Sarfe: ruler of Sarfania province
Arrabella: his spouse
Estorien: their eldest son. Champion of Sarfania
Carlo their middle son. Missing at sea
Kael the youngest son

Treggara Province

Volt Garron: ruler of Treggara province
Rante and Slye: his twin sons and champions of
Treggara
Slinsi Garron: their feisty sister
Dorgan: Captain of Guard

Rodrutha Province

King Brude: ruler of Rodrutha Province
Torrig Red Hair: one of his many sons
Helga: a madam
Nel: one of her girls

The Great Continent

Ozmandeus: a sorcerer. Known as the Renegade
Maelchor: a mercenary captain
Rakaro: a Hillman
Toskai: a Hillman
Ankai: a Hillman
Lissi: a gypsy
The Emperor: ruler of Xandoria and Lamoza
The Chancellor: one of his chief advisors
Romul: one of his generals
Karali: an assassin
The Magister: ruler of Zorne

Printed in Great Britain
by Amazon

22188803R00320